Praise for

STEPHEN KING

and the #1 *New York Times* bestseller

DESPERATION

"A return for Stephen King to his old stomping grounds: supernatural horror and multicharacter plots that entertain with a vengeance. . . . Sure to keep you turning pages well past midnight."

—*Denver Post*

"*Desperation* is pure King, a rollicking good tale skillfully told of repugnance and godliness doing high-screech battle."

—*San Francisco Chronicle*

"No one is as deft with the carnage, or has as much fun with it . . . King is the Winslow Homer of blood."

—*The New Yorker*

"Heaps and heaps of surefire thrills."

—*Time*

"Our best novelist of horror and our most serious anatomist of 'horror' since Edgar Allan Poe. A tour de force . . . vastly entertaining. He is a quintessentially American writer."

—*Atlanta Journal-Constitution*

STEPHEN KING

Desperation

A NOVEL

G

GALLERY BOOKS

New York London Toronto Sydney New Delhi

G

Gallery Books
An Imprint of Simon & Schuster, Inc.
1230 Avenue of the Americas
New York, NY 10020

First Gallery Books trade paperback edition February 2018

GALLERY BOOKS and colophon are registered trademarks of Simon & Schuster, Inc.

For information about special discounts for bulk purchases, please contact Simon & Schuster Special Sales at 1-866-506-1949 or business@simonandschuster.com.

The Simon & Schuster Speakers Bureau can bring authors to your live event. For more information or to book an event, contact the Simon & Schuster Speakers Bureau at 1-866-248-3049 or visit our website at www.simonspeakers.com.

Manufactured in the United States of America

10   9   8   7   6   5

ISBN 978-1-5011-9223-4
ISBN 978-1-5011-4116-4 (ebook)

For Carter Withey

ACKNOWLEDGMENTS

They're in order to four people in particular: Rich Hasler, of the Magma Mining Corporation; William Winston, Episcopalian minister; Chuck Verrill, my long-time (and long-suffering, he might add) editor; Tabitha King, my wife and keenest critic. Now you know the rest of the drill, Constant Reader, so let's say it together, shall we? For what's right, thank them; for what's wrong, blame me.

—S.K.

**The landscape of his poetry
was still the desert . . .**

Salman Rushdie
The Satanic Verses

PART I

HIGHWAY 50:
IN THE HOUSE OF THE WOLF,
THE HOUSE OF THE
SCORPION

CHAPTER 1

1

"Oh! Oh, Jesus! Gross!"

"What, Mary, what?"

"Didn't you see it?"

"See what?"

She looked at him, and in the harsh desert sunlight he saw that a lot of the color had gone out of her face, leaving just the marks of sunburn on her cheeks and across her brow, where not even a strong sunblock cream would entirely protect her. She was very fair and burned easily.

"On that sign. That speed-limit sign."

"What about it?"

"There was a dead cat on it, Peter! Nailed there or glued there or some damned thing." He hit the brake pedal. She grabbed his shoulder at once. "Don't you even *think* about going back."

"But—"

"But what? Did you want to take a picture of it? No way, José. If I have to look at that again, I'll throw up."

"Was it a white cat?" He could see the back of a sign in the rearview mirror—the speed-limit sign she was talking about, presumably—but that was all. And when they'd passed it, he had been looking off in the other direction, at some birds flying toward the nearest wedge of mountains. Strictly attending to the highway was not something one had to do every second out here; Nevada called its stretch of U.S. 50 "The Loneliest Highway in America," and in Peter Jackson's opinion, it lived up to its billing. Of course he was a New York boy, and he supposed he might be suffering a cumulative case of the creeps. Desert agoraphobia, Ballroom Syndrome, something like that.

"No, it was a tiger-stripe," she said. "What difference does it make?"

"I thought maybe Satanists in the desert," he said. "This place is supposed to be filled with weirdos, isn't that what Marielle said?"

"'Intense' was the word she used," Mary said. "'Central Nevada's full of intense people.' Quote-unquote. Gary said pretty much the same. But since we haven't seen *anybody* since we crossed the California state line—"

"Well, in Fallon—"

"Pit-stops don't count," she said. "Although even there, the people . . ." She gave him a funny, helpless look that he didn't see often in her face these days, although it had been common enough in the months following her miscarriage. "Why are they *here*, Pete? I mean, I can understand Vegas and Reno . . . even Winnemucca and Wendover . . ."

"The people who come from Utah to gamble there call Wendover Bend Over," Peter said, grinning. "Gary told me that."

She ignored him. "But the rest of the state . . . the people who *are* here, why do they come and why do they stay? I know I was born and raised in New York, so probably I can't understand, but—"

"You're *sure* that wasn't a white cat? Or a black one?" He glanced back into the rearview, but at just under seventy miles an hour, the speed-limit sign had already faded into a mottled background of sand, mesquite, and dull brown foothills. There was finally another vehicle behind them, though; he could see a hot sunstar reflection pricking off its windshield. Maybe a mile back. Maybe two.

"No, tiger-stripe, I told you. Answer my question. Who are the central Nevada taxpayers, and what's in it for them?"

He shrugged. "There *aren't* many taxpayers out here. Fallon's the biggest town on Highway 50, and that's mostly farming. It says in the guidebook that they dammed their lake and made irrigation possible. Cantaloupes is what they grow, mostly. And I think there's a military base nearby. Fallon was a Pony Express stop, did you know that?"

"I'd leave," she said. "Just pick up my cantaloupes and go."

He touched her left breast briefly with his right hand. "That's a nice set of cantaloupes, ma'am."

"Thanks. Not just Fallon, either. Any state where you can't see a house or even a tree, in any direction, and they nail cats to speed-limit signs, I'd leave."

"Well, it's a zone-of-perception thing," he said, speaking carefully. Sometimes he couldn't tell when Mary was serious and when she was just gassing, and this was one of those times. "As someone who was raised in an urban environment, a place like the Great Basin is just outside your zone, that's all. Mine too, for that matter. The sky alone is enough to freak me out. Ever since we left this morning, I've felt it up there, pressing down on me."

"Me, too. There's too goddam much of it."

"Are you sorry we came this way?" He glanced up into the rearview and saw the vehicle behind them was closer now. Not a truck, which was just about all they'd seen since leaving Fallon (and all headed the other way, west), but a car. Really burning up the road, too.

She thought about it, then shook her head. "No. It was good to see Gary and Marielle, and Lake Tahoe—"

"Beautiful, wasn't it?"

"Incredible. Even this . . ." Mary looked out the window.

"It's not without beauty, I'm not saying that. And I suppose I'll remember it the rest of my life. But it's . . ."

". . . creepy," he finished for her. "If you're from New York, at least."

"Damned right," she said. "Urban Zone of Perception. And even if we'd taken I-80, it's all desert."

"Yep. Tumbling tumbleweeds." He looked into the mirror again, the lenses of the glasses he wore for driving glinting in the sun. The oncomer was a police-car, doing at least ninety. He squeezed over toward the shoulder until the righthand wheels began to rumble on the hardpan and spume up dust.

"Pete? What are you doing?"

Another look into the mirror. Big chrome grille, coming up fast and reflecting such a savage oblong of sun that he had to squint . . . but he thought the car was white, which meant it wasn't the State Police.

"Making myself small," Peter said. "Wee sleekit cowrin beastie. There's a cop behind us and he's in a hurry. Maybe he's got a line on—"

The police-car blasted by, making the Acura which belonged to Peter's sister rock in its backwash. It was indeed white, and dusty from the doorhandles down. There was a decal on the side, but the car was gone before Pete caught more than a glimpse of it. DES-something. Destry, maybe. That was a good name for a Nevada town out here in the big lonely.

"—on the guy who nailed the cat to the speed-limit sign," Peter finished.

"Why's he going so fast with his flashers off?"

"Who's there to run them for out here?"

"Well," she said, giving him that odd-funny look again, "there's us."

He opened his mouth to reply, then closed it again. She was right. The cop must have been seeing them for at least as long as they'd been seeing him, maybe longer, so why *hadn't* he flipped on his lights and flashers, just to be safe? Of course Peter had known enough to get over on his own, give the cop as much of the road as he possibly could, but still—

The police car's taillights suddenly came on. Peter hit his own brake without even thinking of it, although he had already slowed to sixty and the cruiser was far enough ahead so there was no chance of a collision. Then the cruiser swerved over into the westbound lane.

"What's he doing?" Mary asked.

"I don't know, exactly."

But of course he knew: he was slowing down. From his cut-em-off-at-the-pass eighty-five or ninety he had dropped to fifty. Frowning, not wanting to catch up and not knowing why, Peter slowed even more himself. The speedometer of Deirdre's car dropped down toward forty.

"Peter?" Mary sounded alarmed. "Peter, I don't like this."

"It's all right," he said, but was it? He stared at the cop-car, now tooling slowly up the westbound lane to his left, and wondered. He tried to get a look at the person behind the wheel and couldn't. The cruiser's rear window was caked with desert dust.

Its taillights, also caked with dust, flickered briefly as the car slowed even more. Now it was doing barely thirty. A tumbleweed bounced into the road, and the cruiser's radial tires crushed it under. It came out the back looking to Peter Jackson like a nestle of broken fingers. All at once he was frightened, very close to terror, in fact, and he hadn't the slightest idea why.

Because Nevada's full of intense people, Marielle said so and Gary agreed, and this is how intense people act. In a word, weird.

Of course that was bullshit, this really wasn't weird, not *very* weird, anyhow, although—

The cop-car taillights flickered some more. Peter pressed his own brake in response, not even thinking about what he was doing for a second, then looking at the speedometer and seeing he was down to twenty-five.

"What does he want, Pete?"

By now, that was pretty obvious.

"To be behind us again."

"Why?"

"I don't know."

"Why didn't he just pull over on the shoulder and let us go past, if that's what he wants?"

"I don't know that, either."

"What are you going to—"

"Go by, of course." And then, for no reason at all, he added: "After all, *we* didn't nail the goddam cat to the speed-limit sign."

He pushed down on the accelerator and immediately began to catch up with the dusty cruiser, which was now floating along at no more than twenty.

Mary grabbed the shoulder of his blue workshirt hard enough for him to feel the pressure of her short fingernails. "No, don't."

"Mare, there's not a lot else I *can* do."

And the conversation was already obsolete, because he was going by even as he spoke. Deirdre's Acura drew alongside the dusty white Caprice, then passed it. Peter looked through two pieces of glass and saw very little. A big shape, a man-shape, that was about all. Plus the sense that the driver of the police-car was looking back at him. Peter glanced down at the decal on the passenger door. Now he had time to read it: DESPERATION POLICE DEPARTMENT in gold letters below the town seal, which appeared to be a miner and a horseman shaking hands.

Desperation, he thought. *Even better than Destry.* Much *better.*

As soon as he was past, the white car swung back into the eastbound lane, speeding up to stay on the Acura's bumper.

They travelled that way for thirty or forty seconds (to Peter it felt considerably longer). Then the blue flashers on the Caprice's roof came on. Peter felt a sinking in his stomach, but it wasn't surprise. Not at all.

2

Mary still had hold of him, and now, as Peter swung onto the shoulder, she began digging in again.

"What are you doing? Peter, what are you *doing*?"

"Stopping. He's got his flashers on and he's pulling me over."

"I don't like it," she said, looking nervously around. There was nothing to look at but desert, foothills, and leagues of blue sky. "What were we doing?"

"Speeding seems logical." He was looking in the outside mirror. Above the words CAUTION OBJECTS MAY BE CLOSER THAN THEY APPEAR, he saw the dusty white driver's door of the cop-car swing open. A khaki leg swung out. It was prodigious. As the man it belonged to followed it out, swung the door of his cruiser closed, and settled his Smokey Bear hat on his head (he wouldn't have been wearing it in the car, Peter supposed; not enough clearance), Mary turned around to look. Her mouth dropped ajar.

"Holy God, he's the size of a football player!"

"At least," Peter said. Doing a rough mental calculation that used the roof of the car as a steering-point—about five feet—he guessed that the cop approaching Deirdre's Acura had to be at least six-five. And over two hundred and fifty pounds. Probably over three hundred.

Mary let go of him and scooted over against her door as far as she could, away from the approaching giant. On one hip the cop wore a gun as big as the rest of him, but his hands were empty—no clipboard, no citation-book. Peter didn't like that. He didn't know what it meant, but he didn't like it. In his entire career as a driver, which had included four speeding tickets as a teenager and one OUI (after the faculty Christmas party three years ago), he had never been approached by an empty-handed cop, and he most definitely didn't like it. His heartbeat, already faster than normal, sped up a little more. His heart wasn't pounding, at least not yet, but he sensed it *could* pound. That it could pound very easily.

You're being stupid, you know that, don't you? he asked himself. *It's speeding, that's all, simple speeding. The posted limit is a joke and everyone knows it's a joke, but this guy's undoubtedly got a certain quota to meet. And when it comes to speeding tickets, out-of-staters are always best. You know that. So . . . what's that old Van Halen album title?* Eat Em and Smile?

The cop stopped beside Peter's window, the buckle of his Sam Browne belt on a level with Peter's eyes. He did not bend but raised one fist (to Peter it looked the size of a Daisy canned ham) and made cranking gestures.

Peter took off his round rimless glasses, tucked them into his pocket, and rolled his window down. He was very aware of Mary's quick breathing from the passenger bucket. She sounded as if she had been jumping rope, or perhaps making love.

The cop did a slow, smooth, deep kneebend, bringing his huge and noncommittal face into the Jacksons' field of vision. A band of shadow, cast by the stiff brim of his trooper-style hat, lay across his brow. His skin was an uncomfortable-looking pink, and Peter guessed that, for all his size, this man got along with the sun no better than Mary did. His eyes were bright gray, direct but with no emotion in them. None that Peter could read, anyway. He could smell something, though. He thought maybe Old Spice.

The cop gave him only a brief glance, then his gaze was moving around the Acura's cabin, checking Mary first (American Wife, Caucasian, pretty face, good figure, low mileage, no visible scars), then looking at the cameras and bags and road-litter in the back seat. Not much road-litter yet; they'd only left Oregon three days before, and that included the day and a half they'd spent with Gary and Marielle Soderson, listening to old records and talking about old times.

The cop's eyes lingered on the pulled-out ashtray. Peter guessed he was looking for roaches, sniffing for the lingering aroma of pot or hash, and felt relieved. He hadn't smoked a joint in nearly fifteen years, had never tried coke, and had pretty much quit drinking after the Christmas party OUI. Smelling a little cannabis at the occasional rock show was as close to a drug experience as he ever came these days, and Mary had never bothered with the stuff at all—she sometimes referred to herself as a "drug virgin." There was nothing in the pulled-out ashtray but a couple of balled-up Juicy Fruit wrappers, and no discarded beer-cans or wine bottles in the back seat.

"Officer, I know I was going a little fast—"

"Had the hammer down, did you?" the cop asked pleasantly. "Gosh, now! Sir, could I see your driver's license and your registration?"

"Sure." Peter took his wallet out of his back pocket. "The car's not mine, though. It's my sister's. We're driving it back to New York for her. From Oregon. She was at Reed. Reed College, in Portland?"

He was babbling, he knew it, but wasn't sure he could stop it. It was weird how cops could get you running off at the mouth like this, as if you had a dismembered body or a kidnapped child in the trunk. He remembered doing the same thing when the cop had pulled him over on the Long Island

Expressway after the Christmas party, just talking and talking, yattata-yattata-yattata, while all the time the cop said nothing, only went methodically on with his own business, checking first his paperwork and then the contents of his little blue plastic Breathalyzer kit.

"Mare? Would you get the registration out of the glove compartment? It's in a little plastic envelope, along with Dee's insurance papers."

At first she didn't move. He could see her out of the corner of his eye, just sitting still, as he opened his wallet and began hunting for his driver's license. It should have been right there, in one of the windowed compartments in the front of the billfold, big as life, but it wasn't.

"Mare?" he asked again, a little impatient now, and a little frightened all over again. What if he'd lost his goddam driver's license somewhere? Dropped it on the floor at Gary's, maybe, while he'd been transferring his crap (you always seemed to carry so much *more* crap in your pockets while you were travelling) from one pair of jeans to the next? He hadn't, of course, but wouldn't it just be *typical* if—

"Little help, Mare? Get the damned registration? *Please*?"

"Oh. Sure, okay."

She bent forward like some old, rusty piece of machinery goosed into life by a sudden jolt of electricity, and opened the glove compartment. She began to root through it, lifting some stuff out (a half-finished bag of Smartfood, a Bonnie Raitt tape that had suffered a miscarriage in Deirdre's dashboard player, a map of California) so she could get at the stuff behind it. Peter could see small beads of perspiration at her left temple. Feathers of her short black hair were damp with it, although the air-conditioning vent on that side was blowing cool air directly into her face.

"I don't—" she started, and then, with unmistakable relief: "Oh, here it is."

At the same moment Peter looked in the compartment where he kept business cards and saw his license. He couldn't remember putting it in there—why in the name of God would he have?—but there it was. In the photograph he looked not like an assistant professor of English at NYU but an unemployed petty laborer (and possible serial killer). Yet it was him, recognizably *him*, and he felt his spirits lift. They had their papers, God was in his heaven, all was right with the world.

Besides, he thought, handing the cop his license, *this isn't Albania, you know. It may not be in our zone of perception, but it's definitely not Albania.*

"Peter?"

He turned, took the envelope she was holding out, and gave her a wink. She tried to smile an acknowledgment, but it didn't work very well. Outside, a gust of wind threw sand against the side of the car. Tiny grains of it stung Peter's face and he slitted his eyes against it. Suddenly he wanted to be at least two thousand miles from Nevada, in any direction.

He took Deirdre's registration and held it out to the cop, but the cop was still looking at his license.

"I see you're an organ donor," the cop said, without looking up. "Do you really think that's wise?"

Peter was nonplussed. "Well, I . . ."

"Is that the vehicle registration, sir?" the cop asked crisply. He was now looking at the canary-yellow sheet of paper.

"Yes."

"Hand it to me, please."

Peter handed it out the window. Now the cop, still squatting Indian-fashion in the sunlight, had Peter's driver's license in one hand and Deirdre's registration in the other. He looked back and forth between them for what seemed a very long time. Peter felt light pressure on his thigh and jumped a little before realizing it was Mary's hand. He took it and felt her fingers wrap around his at once.

"Your sister?" the cop said finally. He looked up at them with his bright gray eyes.

"Yes—"

"Her name is Finney. Yours is Jackson."

"Deirdre was married for a year, between high school and college," Mary said. Her voice was firm, pleasant, unafraid. Peter would have believed it completely if not for the clutch of her fingers. "She kept her husband's name. That's all it is."

"A year, hmmm? Between high school and college. Married. *Tak!*"

His head remained down over the documents. Peter could see the peak of his Smokey Bear hat ticking back and forth as he fell to examining them again.

Peter's sense of relief was slipping away.

"Between high school and college," the cop repeated, head down, big face hidden, and in his head Peter heard him say: *I see you're an organ donor. Do you really think that's wise? Tak!*

The cop looked up. "Would you step out of the car, please, Mr. Jackson?"

Mary's fingers bore down, her nails biting into the back of Peter's hand, but the burning sensation was far away. Suddenly his balls and the pit of his stomach were crawling with dismay, and he felt like a child again, a confused child who only knows for sure that he has done something bad.

"What—" he began.

The cop from the Desperation cruiser stood. It was like watching a freight elevator go up. The head disappeared, then the open-collared shirt with its gleaming badge, then the diagonal strap of the Sam Browne belt. Then Peter was looking at the heavy beltbuckle again, the gun, and the khaki fold of cloth over the man's fly.

This time what came from above the top of the window wasn't a question. "Get out of the car, Mr. Jackson."

3

Peter pulled the handle and the cop stood back so he could swing the door open. The cop's head was cut off by the roof of the Acura. Mary squeezed Peter's hand more violently than ever and Peter turned back to look at her. The sunburned places on her cheeks and brow were even clearer now, because her face had gone almost ashy. Her eyes were very wide.

Don't get out of the car, she mouthed.

I have to, he mouthed back, and swung a leg out onto the asphalt of U.S. 50. For a moment Mary clung to him, her hand entwined in his, and then Peter pulled loose and got the rest of the way out, standing on legs that felt queerly distant. The cop was looking down at him. *Six-seven,* Peter thought. *Got to be.* And he suddenly saw a quick sequence of events, like a filmclip run at super speed: the huge cop drawing his gun and pulling the trigger, spraying Peter Jackson's educated brains across the roof of the Acura in a slimy fan, then yanking Mary out of the car, driving her face-first into the lid of the closed trunk, bending her over, then raping her right out here beside the highway in the searing desert sunshine, his Smokey Bear hat still planted squarely on his head, screaming *You want a donated organ, lady? Here you go! Here you go!* as he rocked and thrust.

"What's this about, Officer?" Peter asked, his mouth and throat suddenly dry. "I think I have a right to know."

"Step around to the rear of the car, Mr. Jackson."

The cop turned and walked toward the back of the Acura without bothering to see if Peter was going to obey. Peter *did* obey, walking on legs that still felt as if they were relaying their sensory input by some form of telecommunications.

The cop stopped beside the trunk. When Peter joined him, he pointed with one big finger. Peter followed it and saw there was no license plate on the back of Deirdre's car—just a marginally cleaner rectangle where it had been.

"Ah, *shit*!" Peter said, and his irritation and dismay were real enough, but so was the relief beneath them. All this had had a point after all. Thank God. He turned toward the front of the car and wasn't exactly surprised to see the driver's door was now closed. Mary had closed it. He had been so far into this . . . event . . . occurrence . . . this whatever it was . . . that he hadn't even heard the thump.

"Mare! Hey, Mare!"

She poked her sunburned, strained face out of his window and looked back at him.

"Our damned license plate fell off!" he called, almost laughing.

"What?"

"No, it didn't," the Desperation cop said. He squatted again—that calm, slow, lithe movement—and reached beneath the bumper. He fumbled there, on the other side of the place where the plate went, for a moment or two, his gray eyes gazing off toward the horizon. Pete was invaded by an eerie sense of familiarity: he and his wife had been pulled over by the Marlboro Man.

"Ah!" the cop said. He stood up again. The hand he had been investigating with was clenched into a loose fist. He held it out to Peter and opened it. Lying on his palm (and looking very small in that vast pinkness) was a road-dirty piece of screw. It was bright in only one place, where it had been sheared off.

Peter looked at it, then up at the cop. "I don't get it."

"Did you stop in Fallon?"

"No—"

There was a creak as Mary's door opened, a clunk as she shut it behind her, then the scuff of her sneakers on the sandy shoulder as she walked toward the back of the car.

"Sure we did," she said. She looked at the fragment of metal in the big hand (Deirdre's registration and Peter's driver's license were still in the cop's other one), then up at the cop's face. She didn't seem scared now—not *as* scared, anyway—and Peter was glad. He was already calling himself nine kinds of paranoid idiot, but you had to admit that this particular close encounter of the cop kind had had its

(do you really think that's wise)

peculiar aspects.

"Pit-stop, Peter, don't you remember? We didn't need gas, you said we could do that in Ely, but we got sodas so we wouldn't feel guilty about asking to use the restrooms." She looked at the cop and tried on a smile. She had to crane back to see his face. To Peter she looked like a little girl trying to coax a smile out of Daddy after Daddy had gotten home from a bad day at the office. "The restrooms were very clean."

He nodded. "Was that Fill More Fast or Berk's Conoco you stopped at?"

She glanced uncertainly at Peter. He turned his hands up at shoulder level. "I don't remember," he said. "Hell, I barely remember stopping."

The cop tossed the useless chunk of screw back over his shoulder and into the desert, where it would lie undisturbed for a million years, unless it caught some inquisitive bird's eye. "But I bet you remember the kids hanging around outside. Older kids, mostly. One or two maybe too old to actually be kids at all. The younger ones with skateboards or on Rollerblades."

Peter nodded. He thought of Mary asking him why the people were here—why they came and why they stayed.

"That was the Fill More Fast." Peter looked to see if the cop was wearing a nametag on one of his shirt pockets, but he wasn't. So for now, at least, he'd have to stay just the cop. The one who looked like the Marlboro Man in the magazine ads. "Alfie Berk won't have em around anymore. Kicked em the hell out. They're a dastardly bunch."

Mary cocked her head at that, and for a moment Peter could see the ghost of a smile at the corners of her mouth.

"Are they a gang?" Peter asked. He still didn't see where this was going.

"Close as you'd get in a place as small as Fallon," the cop said. He raised Peter's license to his face, looked at it, looked at Peter, lowered it again. But he did not offer to give it back. "Dropouts, for the most part. And one of their hobbies is kifing out-of-state license plates. It's like a dare thing. I imagine they got yours while you were in buying your cold drinks or using the facilities."

"You know this and they still do it?" Mary asked.

"Fallon's not my town. I rarely go there. Their ways are not my ways."

"What should we do about the missing plate?" Peter asked. "I mean, this is a mess. The car's registered in Oregon, but my sister has gone back to New York to live. She hated Reed—"

"Did she?" the cop asked. "Gosh, now!"

Peter could feel Mary's eyes shift to him, probably wanting him to share her moment of amusement, but that didn't seem like a good idea to him. Not at all.

"She said going to school there was like trying to go to school in the middle of a Grateful Dead concert," he said. "Anyway, she flew back to New York. My wife and I thought it would be fun to go out and get the car for her, bring it back to New York. Deirdre packed a bunch of her stuff in the trunk . . . clothes, mostly . . ."

He was babbling again, and he made himself stop.

"So what do I do? We can't very well drive all the way across the country with no license plate on the back of the car, can we?"

The cop walked toward the front of the Acura, moving very deliberately. He still had Peter's license and Deirdre's canary-yellow registration slip in one hand. His Sam Browne belt creaked. When he reached the front of the car he put his hands behind his back and stood frowning down at something. To Peter he looked like an interested patron in an art gallery. Dastardly, he'd said. A dastardly bunch. Peter didn't think he had ever actually heard that word used in conversation.

The cop walked back toward them. Mary moved next to Peter, but her fright seemed gone. She was looking at the big man with interest, that was all.

"The front plate's okay," the cop said. "Put that one on the back. You won't have any problem getting to New York on that basis."

"Oh," Peter said. "Okay. Good idea."

"Do you have a wrench and screwdriver? I think all my tools're back sitting on a bench in the town garage." The cop grinned. It lit his whole face, informed his eyes, turned him into a different man. "Oh. These're yours." He held out the license and registration.

"There's a little toolkit in the trunk, I think," Mary said. She sounded giddy, and that was how Peter felt. Pure relief, he supposed. "I saw it while I was putting in my makeup case. Between the spare tire and the side."

"Officer, I want to thank you," Peter said.

The big cop nodded. He wasn't looking at Peter, though; his gray eyes were apparently fixed on the mountains off to his left. "Just doing my job."

Peter walked to the driver's door of the car, wondering why he and Mary had been so afraid in the first place.

That's nonsense, he told himself as he pulled the keys out of the ignition switch. They were on a smile-face keychain, which was pretty much par for the course—Deirdre's course, anyway. Mr. Smiley-Smile (her name for him) was his sister's trademark. She put happy yellow ones on the flaps of most of her letters, the occasional green one with a downturned mouth and a blah tongue stuck out if she happened to be having a bad day. *I wasn't afraid, not really. Neither was Mary.*

Boink, a lie. He *had* been afraid, and Mary . . . well, Mary had been damned close to terrified.

Okay, maybe we were a little freaked, he thought, picking out the trunk key as he walked to the back of the car again. *So sue us.* The sight of Mary standing next to the big cop was like some sort of optical illusion; the top of her head barely came up to the bottom of his ribcage.

Peter opened the trunk. On the left, neatly packed (and covered with Hefty bags to keep the road dust off them), were Deirdre's clothes. In the center, Mary's makeup case and their two suitcases—his n hers—were wedged in between the green bundles and the spare tire. Although "tire" was much too grand a word for it, Peter thought. It was one of those blow-up doughnuts, good for a run to the nearest service station. If you were lucky.

He looked between the doughnut and the trunk's sidewall. There was nothing there.

"Mare, I don't see—"

"There." She pointed. "That gray thing? That's it. It's worked its way in back of the spare, that's all."

He could have snaked his arm into the gap, but it seemed easier just to lift the uninflated rubber doughnut out of the way. He was leaning it against the back bumper when he heard Mary's sudden intake of breath. It sounded as if she had been pinched or poked.

"Oh hey," the big cop said mildly. "What's this?"

Mary and the cop were looking into the trunk. The cop looked interested and slightly bemused. Mary's eyes were bulging, horrified. Her lips were trembling. Peter turned, looking into the trunk again, following their gaze. There was something in the spare-tire well. It had been under the doughnut. For a moment he either didn't know what it was or didn't *want* to know what it was, and then that crawling sensation started in his lower belly again. This time there was also a sense of his sphincter's not loosening but *dropping,* as if the muscles which ordinarily held it up where it belonged had dozed off. He became aware that he was squeezing his buttocks together, but even that was far away, in another time zone. He felt an all-too-brief certainty that this was a dream, *had* to be.

The big cop gave him a look, those bright gray eyes still peculiarly empty, then reached into the spare-tire well and brought out a Baggie, a big one, a gallon-size, and stuffed full of greenish-brown herbal matter. The flap had been sealed with strapping tape. Plastered on the front was a round yellow sticker. Mr. Smiley-Smile. The perfect emblem for potheads like his sister, whose adventures in life could have been titled *Through Darkest America with Bong and Roach-Clip.* She had gotten pregnant while stoned, had undoubtedly decided to marry Roger Finney while stoned, and Peter knew for a fact that she had left Reed (carrying a one-point-forget-it grade average) because there was too much dope floating around and she just couldn't say no to it. She'd been up front about that part, at least, and he had actually looked through the Acura for stashes—it would be stuff she'd forgotten about rather than stuff she'd actually hidden, most likely—before they left Portland. He'd looked under the Hefty bags her clothes were stored in, and Mary had thumbed through the clothes themselves (neither admitting out loud what they were looking for, both knowing), but neither of them had thought to look under the doughnut.

The goddam doughnut.

The cop squeezed the Baggie with one oversized thumb as if it were a tomato. He reached into his pocket and produced a Swiss Army knife. He plucked out the smallest blade.

"Officer," Peter said in a weak voice. "Officer, I don't know how that—"

"Shhh," the big cop said, and cut a tiny slit in the Baggie.

Peter felt Mary's hand tugging at his sleeve. He took her hand, this time folding his fingers over hers. All at once he could see Deirdre's pale, pretty face floating just behind his eyes. Her blond hair, which still fell to her shoulders in natural Stevie Nicks ringlets. Her eyes, which were always a bit confused.

You stupid little bitch, he thought. *You ought to be very grateful that you're not where I can get my hands on you right now.*

"Officer—" Mary tried.

The cop raised his hand to her, palm out, then put the tiny slit in the Baggie against his nose and sniffed. His eyes drifted closed. After a moment he opened them again and lowered the Baggie. He held out his other hand, palm up. "Give me your keys, sir," he said.

"Officer, I can explain this—"

"Give me your keys."

"If you just—"

"Are you deaf? Give me your keys."

He only raised his voice a little, but it was enough to start Mary crying. Feeling like someone who is having an out-of-body experience, Peter dropped Deirdre's car-keys into the cop's waiting hand and then put his arm around his wife's shaking shoulders.

"'Fraid you folks are going to have to come with me," the cop said. His eyes went from Peter to Mary and then back to Peter again. When they did, Peter realized what it was about them that bothered him. They were bright, like the minutes before sunrise on a foggy morning, but they were also dead, somehow.

"Please," Mary said, her voice wet. "It's a mistake. His sister—"

"Get in the car," the cop said, indicating his cruiser. The flashers were still pulsing on the roof, bright even in the bright desert daylight. "Right now, please, Mr. and Mrs. Jackson."

4

The rear seat was extremely cramped (of course it would be, Peter thought distractedly, a man that big would have the front seat back as far as it would go). There were stacks of paper in the footwell behind the driver's seat (the back of that seat was actually warped from the cop's weight) and more on the back deck. Peter picked one up—it had a dried, puckered coffee-ring on it—and saw it was a DARE flyer. At the top was a picture of a kid sitting in a doorway. There was a dazed, vacant expression on his face (he looked the way Peter felt right now, in fact), and the coffee-ring circled his head like a halo. USERS ARE LOSERS, the folder said.

There was mesh between the front of the car and the back, and no handles or window-cranks on the doors. Peter had begun to feel like a character in a movie (the one which came most persistently to mind was *Midnight Express*), and these details only added to that sensation. His best judgement was that he had talked too much about too many things already, and it would be well for him and Mary to stay quiet, at least until they got to wherever Officer Friendly meant to take them. It was probably good advice, but it was hard advice to follow. Peter found himself with a powerful urge to tell Officer Friendly that a terrible mistake had been made here—he was an assistant professor of English, his specialty was postwar American fiction, he had recently published a scholarly article called "James Dickey and the New Southern Reality" (a piece which had generated a great deal of controversy in certain ivied academic bowers), and, furthermore, that he hadn't smoked dope in years. He wanted to tell the cop that he might be a little bit overeducated by central Nevada standards, but was still, basically, one of the good guys.

He looked at Mary. Her eyes were full of tears, and he was

suddenly ashamed of the way he had been thinking—all me, me, me and I, I, I. His wife was in this with him; he'd do well to remember that. "Pete, I'm so scared," she said in a whisper that was almost a moan.

He leaned forward and kissed her cheek. The skin was as cool as clay beneath his lips. "It'll be all right. We'll straighten this out."

"Word of honor?"

"Word of honor."

After putting them into the back seat of the cruiser, the cop had returned to the Acura. He had been looking into the trunk for at least two minutes now. Not searching it, not even moving anything around, just staring in with his hands clasped behind his back, as if mesmerized. Now he jerked like a man waking suddenly from a nap, slammed the Acura's trunk shut and walked back to the Caprice. It canted to the left when he got in, and from the springs beneath there came a tired but somehow resigned groan. The back seat bulged a little further, and Peter grimaced at the sudden pressure on his knees.

Mary should have taken this side, he thought, but it was too late now. Too late for a lot of things, actually.

The cruiser's engine was running. The cop dropped the transmission into gear and pulled back onto the road. Mary turned to watch the Acura drop behind them. When she faced front again, Peter saw that the tears which had been standing in her eyes had spilled down her cheeks.

"Please listen to me," she said, speaking to the cropped blond hair on the back of that enormous skull. The cop had laid his Smokey Bear hat aside again, and to Peter the top of his head looked to be no more than a quarter of an inch from the Caprice's roof. "*Please,* okay? Try to understand. *That isn't our car.* You *have* to understand that much at least, I know you do, because you saw the registration. It's my sister-in-law's. She's a pothead. Half her brain-cells—"

"Mare—" Peter laid a hand on her arm. She shook it off.

"No! I'm not going to spend the rest of the day answering questions in some dipshit police station, maybe in a jail cell, because your sister's selfish and forgetful and . . . and . . . all fucked up!"

Peter sat back—his knees were still being pinched pretty severely but he thought he could live with it—and looked out the dust-coated side window. They were a mile or two east of the Acura now, and he could see something up ahead, pulled over on the shoulder of the westbound lane. Some sort of vehicle. Big. A truck, maybe.

Mary had switched her gaze from the back of the cop's head to the rearview mirror, trying to make eye contact with him. "Half of Deirdre's brain-cells are fried and the other half are on permanent vacation in the Emerald City. The technical term is 'burnout,' and I'm sure you've seen people like her, Officer, even out here. What you found under the spare tire probably is dope, you're probably right about that, but not *our* dope! Can't you see that?"

The thing up ahead, off the road with its tinted windshield pointed in the direction of Fallon and Carson City and Lake Tahoe, wasn't a truck after all; it was an RV. Not one of the real dinosaurs, but still pretty big. Cream-colored, with a dark green stripe running along the side. The words FOUR HAPPY WANDERERS were printed in the same dark green on the RV's blunt nose. The vehicle was road-dusty and canted over in an awkward, unnatural way.

As they neared it, Peter saw an odd thing: all the tires in his view appeared to be flat. He thought maybe the double set of back tires on the passenger side was flat, too, although he only caught the briefest glimpse of them. That many flat shoes would account for the land-cruiser's funny, canted look, but how did you *get* that many flat shoes all at once? Nails in the road? A strew of glass?

He looked at Mary, but Mary was still looking passionately up into the rearview mirror. "If we'd put that bag of dope under the tire," she was saying, "if it was ours, then why in God's name would Peter have taken the spare out so you could see it? I mean, he could have reached around the spare and gotten the toolkit, it would have been a little awkward but there was room."

They went past the RV. The side door was closed but unlatched. The steps were down. There was a doll lying in the dirt at the foot of them. The dress it was wearing fluttered in the wind.

Peter's eyes closed. He didn't know for sure if he had closed them or if they had closed on their own. Didn't much care. All he knew was that Officer Friendly had blown by the disabled RV as if he hadn't even seen it . . . or as if he already knew all about it.

Words from an old song, floating in his head: *Somethin happenin here . . . what it is ain't exactly clear . . .*

"Do we impress you as stupid people?" Mary was asking as the disabled RV began to dwindle behind them—to dwindle as Deirdre's Acura had done. "Or stoned? Do you think we're—"

"Shut up," the cop said. He spoke softly, but there was no way to miss the venom in his voice.

Mary had been sitting forward with her fingers curled into the mesh between the front and back seats. Now her hands dropped away from it, and she turned her shocked face toward Peter. She was a faculty wife, she was a poet who had published in over twenty magazines since her first tentative submissions eight years ago, she went to a women's discussion group twice a week, she had been seriously considering piercing her nose. Peter wondered when the last time was she had been told to shut up. He wondered if *anyone* had ever told her to shut up.

"What?" she asked, perhaps trying to sound aggressive, even

threatening, and only sounding bewildered. "What did you tell me?"

"I'm arresting you and your husband on a charge of possession of marijuana with intent to sell," the cop said. His voice was uninflected, robotic. Now staring forward, Peter saw there was a little plastic bear stuck to the dashboard, beside the compass and next to what was probably an LED readout for the radar speed-gun. The bear was small, the size of a gumball machine prize. His neck was on a spring, and his empty painted eyes stared back at Peter.

This is a nightmare, he thought, knowing it wasn't. *It's got to be a nightmare. I know it feels real, but it's got to be.*

"You can't be serious," Mary said, but her voice was tiny and shocked. The voice of someone who knew better. Her eyes were filling up with tears again. "Surely you can't be."

"You have the right to remain silent," the big cop said in his robot's voice. "If you do not choose to remain silent, anything you say may be used against you in a court of law. You have the right to an attorney. I'm going to kill you. If you cannot afford an attorney, one will be provided for you. Do you understand your rights as I have explained them to you?"

She was looking at Peter, her eyes huge and horrified, asking him without speaking if he had heard what the cop had mixed in with the rest of it, that robotic voice never varying. Peter nodded. He had heard, all right. He put a hand into his crotch, sure he would feel dampness there, but he hadn't wet himself. Not yet, anyway. He put an arm around Mary and could feel her trembling. He kept thinking of the RV back there. Door ajar, dollbaby lying face-down in the dirt, too many flat tires. And then there was the dead cat Mary had seen nailed to the speed-limit sign.

"Do you understand your rights?"

Act normally. I don't think he has the slightest idea what he said, so act normally.

But what was normal when you were in the back seat of a police-cruiser driven by a man who was clearly as mad as a hatter, a man who had just said he was going to kill you?

"Do you understand your rights?" the robot voice asked him.

Peter opened his mouth. Nothing came out but a croak.

The cop turned his head then. His face, pinkish with sun when he had stopped them, had gone pale. His eyes were very large, seeming to bulge out of his face like marbles. He had bitten his lip, like a man trying to suppress some monstrous rage, and blood ran down his chin in a thin stream.

"Do you understand your rights?" the cop screamed at them, head turned, bulleting blind down the deserted two-lane at better than seventy miles an hour. *"Do you understand your fucking rights or not? Do you or not? Do you or not? Do you or not? Answer me, you smart New York Jew!"*

"I do!" Peter cried. "We both do, just watch the road, for Christ's sake watch where you're going!"

The cop continued staring back at them through the mesh, face pale, blood dripping down from his lower lip. The Caprice, which had begun to veer to the left, almost all the way across the westbound lane, now slid back the other way.

"Don't worry about *me*," the cop said. His voice was mild again. "Gosh, no. I've got eyes in the back of my head. In fact, I've got eyes just about everywhere. You'd do well to remember that."

He turned back suddenly, facing front again, and dropped the cruiser's speed to an easygoing fifty-five. The seat settled back against Peter's knees with painful weight, pinning him.

He took Mary's hands in both of his own. She pressed her face against his chest, and he could feel the sobs she was trying to suppress. They shook through her like wind. He looked over her shoulder, through the mesh. On the dashboard, the bear's head nodded and bobbed on its spring.

"I see holes like eyes," the cop said. "My mind is full of them." He said nothing else until they got to town.

5

The next ten minutes were very slow ones for Peter Jackson. The cop's weight against his pinned knees seemed to increase with each circuit of his wristwatch's second hand, and his lower legs were soon numb. His feet were dead asleep, and he wasn't sure that he would be able to walk on them if this ride ever ended. His bladder throbbed. His head ached. He understood that he and Mary were in the worst trouble of their lives, but he was unable to comprehend this in any real and meaningful way. Every time he neared comprehension, there was a short circuit in his head. They were on their way back to New York. They were expected. Someone was watering their plants. This couldn't be happening, absolutely could not.

Mary nudged him and pointed out her window. Here was a sign, reading simply DESPERATION. Under the word was an arrow pointing to the right.

The cop slowed, but not much, before making the right. The car started to tip and Peter saw Mary drawing in breath. She was going to scream. He put a hand over her mouth to stop her and whispered in her ear, "He's got it, I'm pretty sure he does, we're not going to roll." But he *wasn't* sure until he felt the cruiser's rear end first slide, then catch hold. A moment later they were racing south along narrow patched blacktop with no centerline.

A mile or so farther on, they passed a sign which read DESPERATION'S CHURCH & CIVIC ORGANIZATIONS WELCOME YOU! The words CHURCH & CIVIC ORGANIZATIONS were readable, although they had been coated with yellow spray-paint. Above them, in the same paint, the words DEAD DOGS had been added in ragged caps. The churches and civic organizations were listed beneath, but Peter didn't bother to read them. A German Shepherd had been hanged from the sign. Its rear paws tick-tocked back and forth an inch or two above a patch of ground that was dark and muddy with its blood.

Mary's hands were clamped on his like a vise. He welcomed their pressure. He leaned toward her again, into the sweet smell of her perfume and the sour smell of her terrified sweat, leaned toward her until his lips were pressed against the cup of her ear. "Don't say a word, don't make a sound," he murmured. "Nod your head if you understand me."

She nodded against his lips, and Peter straightened up again.

They passed a trailer park behind a stake fence. Most of the trailers were small and looked as if they had seen better days—around the time *Cheers* first went on the air, perhaps. Dispirited-looking laundry flapped between a few of them in the hot desert wind. In front of one was a sign which read:

> I'M A GUN-TOTTIN' SNAPPLE-DRINKIN'
> BIBLE-READIN' CLINTON-BASHIN' SON OF A BITCH!
> NEVER MIND THE DOG, BEWARE OF THE *OWNER*!

Mounted on an old Airstream which stood near the road was a large black satellite dish. On the side of it was another sign, white-painted metal down which streaks of rust had run like ancient bloody tears:

> THIS TELACOMMUNICATIONS
> PROPERTY RATTLESNAKE TRAILER PARK
> NO TRESSPASSING! POLICE PATROLED!

Beyond the Rattlesnake Trailer Park was a long Quonset hut with rusty, corrugated sides and roof. The sign out front read

DESPERATION MINING CORP. To one side was a cracked asphalt parking lot with a dozen cars and pickups in it. A moment later they passed the Desert Rose Cafe.

Then they were in the town proper. Desperation, Nevada, consisted of two streets that crossed at right angles (a blinker-light, currently flashing yellow on all four sides, hung over the intersection) and two blocks of business buildings. Most seemed to have false fronts. There was an Owl's Club casino and cafe, a grocery, a laundrymat, a bar with a sign in the window reading ENJOY OUR SLOTSPITALITY, hardware and feed stores, a movie theater called The American West, a few others. None of the businesses looked as if they were booming, and the theater had the air of a place that has been closed a long time. A single crooked *R* hung from its dirty, bashed-in marquee.

Going the other way, east and west, were some frame houses and more trailers. Nothing seemed to be in motion except for the cruiser and one tumbleweed, which moved down Main in large, lazy lopes.

I'd get off the streets, too, if I saw this guy coming, Peter thought. *You're goddamned tooting I would.*

Beyond the town was an enormous curving bulwark with an improved dirt road at least four lanes wide running up to the top in a pair of wide switchbacks. The rest of this curved rampart, which had to be at least three hundred feet high, was crisscrossed by deep runoff trenches. To Peter they looked like wrinkles in old skin. At the foot of the crater (he assumed it was a crater, the result of some sort of mining operation), trucks that looked like toys compared to the soaring, wrinkled wall behind them were clustered together by a long, corrugated building with a conveyor belt running out of each end.

Their host spoke up for the first time since telling them his mind was full of holes, or whatever it was he'd said.

"Rattlesnake Number Two. Sometimes known as the China Pit." He sounded like a tourguide who still enjoys his job.

"Old Number Two was opened in 1951, and from '62 or so right through the seventies, it was the biggest open-pit copper mine in the United States, maybe in the world. Then it played out. They opened it up again year before last. They got some new technology that makes even the tailings valuable. Science, huh? Gosh!"

But there was nothing moving up there now, not that Peter could see, although it was a weekday. Just the huddle of trucks by what was probably some kind of sorting-mill, and another truck—this one a pickup—parked off to the side of the gravel highway leading to the summit. The conveyors at the ends of the long metal building were stopped.

The cop drove through the center of town, and as they passed beneath the blinker, Mary squeezed Peter's hands twice in rapid succession. He followed her gaze and saw three bikes in the middle of the street which crossed Main. They were about a block and a half down and had been set on their seats in a row, with their wheels sticking up. The wheels were turning like windmill blades in the gusty air.

She turned to look at him, her wet eyes wider than ever. Peter squeezed her hands again and made a "Shhh" sound.

The cop signalled a left turn—pretty funny, under the circumstances—and swung into a small, recently paved parking lot bordered on three sides by brick walls. Bright white lines were spray-painted on the smooth and crackless asphalt. On the wall at the rear of the lot was a sign which read: MUNICIPAL EMPLOYEES AND MUNICIPAL BUSINESS ONLY PLEASE RESPECT THIS PARKING LOT.

Only in Nevada would someone ask you to respect a parking lot, Peter thought. *In New York the sign would probably read UNAUTHORIZED VEHICLES WILL BE STOLEN AND THEIR OWNERS EATEN.*

There were four or five cars in the lot. One, a rusty old Ford Estate Wagon, was marked FIRE CHIEF. There was another police-car, in better shape than the Fire Chief's car but not as new as the one their captor was driving. There was a single handicapped space in the lot. Officer Friendly parked in it. He turned off the engine and then just sat there for a moment or two, head lowered, fingers tapping restlessly at the steering wheel, humming under his breath. To Peter it sounded like "Last Train to Clarksville."

"Don't kill us," Mary said suddenly in a trembling, teary voice. "We'll do whatever you want, just please don't kill us."

"Shut your quacking Jew mouth," the cop replied. He didn't raise his head, and he went on tapping at the wheel with the tips of his sausage-sized fingers.

"We're *not* Jews," Peter heard himself saying. His voice sounded not afraid but querulous, angry. "We're . . . well, Presbyterians, I guess. What's this Jew thing?"

Mary looked at her husband, horrified, then back through the mesh to see how the cop was taking it. At first he did nothing, only sat with his head down and his fingers tapping. Then he grabbed his hat and got out of the car. Peter bent down a little so he could watch the cop settle the hat on his head. The cop's shadow was still squat, but it was no longer puddled around his feet. Peter glanced at his watch and saw it was a few minutes shy of two-thirty. Less than an hour ago, the biggest question he and his wife had had was what their accommodations for the night would be like. His only worry had been his strong suspicion that he was out of Rolaids.

The cop bent and opened the left rear door. "Please get out of the vehicle, folks," he said.

They slid out, Peter first. They stood in the hot light, looking uncertainly up at the man in the khaki uniform and the Sam Browne belt and the peaked trooper-style hat.

"We're going to walk around to the front of the Municipal Building," the cop said. "That'll be a left as you reach the sidewalk. And you look like Jews to me. The both of you. You have those big noses which connote the Jewish aspect."

"Officer—" Mary began.

"No," he said. "Walk. Make your left. Don't try my patience."

They walked. Their footfalls on the fresh black tar seemed very loud. Peter kept thinking of the little plastic bear on the dashboard of the cruiser. Its jiggling head and painted eyes. Who had given it to the cop? A favorite niece? A daughter? Officer Friendly wasn't wearing a wedding ring, Peter had noticed that while watching the man's fingers tap against the steering wheel, but that didn't mean he had never been married. And the idea that a woman married to this man might at some point seek a divorce did not strike Peter as in the least bit odd.

From somewhere above him came a monotonous *reek-reek-reek* sound. He looked down the street and saw a weathervane turning rapidly on the roof of the bar, Bud's Suds. It was a leprechaun with a pot of gold under one arm and a knowing grin on his spinning face. It was the weathervane making the sound.

"To your *left,* Dumbo," the cop said, sounding not impatient but resigned. "Do you know which way is your left? Don't they teach hayfoot and strawfoot to you New York Homo Presbyterians?"

Peter turned left. He and Mary were still walking hip to hip, still holding hands. They came to a set of three stone steps leading up to modern tinted-glass double doors. The building itself was much less modern. A white-painted sign hung on faded brick proclaimed it to be the DESPERATION MUNICIPAL BUILDING. Below, on the doors, were listed the offices and services to be found within: Mayor, School Committee, Fire, Police, Sanitation, Welfare Services, Department of Mines and Assay. At the bottom of the righthand door was printed: MSHA FRIDAYS AT 1 PM AND BY APPOINTMENT.

The cop stopped at the foot of the steps and looked at the Jacksons curiously. Although it was brutally hot out here, probably somewhere in the upper nineties, he did not appear to be sweating at all. From behind them, monotonous in the silence, came the *reek-reek-reek* of the weathervane.

"You're Peter," he said.

"Yes, Peter Jackson." He wet his lips.

The cop shifted his eyes. "And you're Mary."

"That's right."

"So where's Paul?" the cop asked, looking at them pleasantly while the rusty leprechaun squeaked and spun on the roof of the bar behind them.

"What?" Peter asked. "I don't understand."

"How can you sing 'Five Hundred Miles' or 'Leavin' on a Jet Plane' without *Paul*?" the cop asked, and opened the right-hand door. Machine-cooled air puffed out. Peter felt it on his face and had time to register how nice it was, nice and cool; then Mary screamed. Her eyes had adjusted to the gloom inside the building faster than his own, but he saw it a moment later. There was a girl of about six sprawled at the foot of the stairs, half-propped against the last four risers. One hand was thrown back over her head. It lay palm-up on the stairs. Her straw-colored hair had been tied in a couple of tails. Her eyes were wide open and her head was unnaturally cocked to one side. There was no question in Peter's mind about whom the dolly lying at the foot of the RV's steps had belonged to. FOUR HAPPY WANDERERS, it had said on the front of the RV, but that was clearly out of date in these modern times. There was no question in his mind about that, either.

"Gosh!" the cop said genially. "Forgot all about her! But you can never remember everything, can you? No matter how hard you try!"

Mary screamed again, her fingers folded down against her palms and her hands against her mouth, and tried to bolt back down the steps.

"No you don't, what a bad idea," the cop said. He caught

her by the shoulder and shoved her through the door, which he was holding open. She reeled across the small lobby, revolving her arms in a frantic effort to keep her balance, not wanting to fall on top of the dead child in the jeans and the *MotoKops 2200* shirt.

Peter started in toward his wife and the cop caught him with both hands, now using his butt to keep the righthand door open. He slung an arm around Peter's shoulders. His face looked open and friendly. Most of all, *best* of all, it looked *sane*—as if his good angels had won out, at least for now. Peter felt an instant's hope, and at first did not associate the thing pressing into his stomach with the cop's monster handgun. He thought of his father, who would sometimes poke him with the tip of his finger while giving him advice—using the finger to sort of tamp his aphorisms home—things like *No one ever gets pregnant if one of you keeps your pants on, Petie.*

He didn't realize it was the gun, not the cop's oversized sausage of a finger, until Mary shrieked: *"No! Oh, no!"*

"Don't—" Peter began.

"I don't care if you're a Jew or a Hindu," the cop said, hugging Peter against him. He squeezed Peter's shoulder chummily with his left hand as he cocked the .45 with his right. "In Desperation we don't care about those things much."

He pulled the trigger at least three times. There might have been more, but three reports were all Peter Jackson heard. They were muffled by his stomach, but still very loud. An incredible heat shot up through his chest and down through his legs at the same time, and he heard something wet drop on his shoes. He heard Mary, still screaming, but the sound seemed to come from far, far away.

Now I'll wake up in my bed, Peter thought as his knees buckled and the world began to draw away, as bright as afternoon sunlight on the chrome side of a receding railroad car. *Now I'll—*

That was all. His last thought as the darkness swallowed him forever really wasn't a thought at all, but an image: the bear on the dashboard next to the cop's compass. Head jiggling. Painted eyes staring. The eyes turned into holes, the dark rushed out of them, and then he was gone.

CHAPTER 2

1

Ralph Carver was somewhere deep in the black and didn't want to come up. He sensed physical pain waiting—a hangover, perhaps, and a really spectacular one if he could feel his head aching even in his sleep—but not just that. Something else. Something to do with

(*Kirsten*)

this morning. Something to do with

(*Kirsten*)

their vacation. He had gotten drunk, he supposed, pulled a real horror show, Ellie was undoubtedly pissed at him, but even that didn't seem enough to account for how horrible he felt . . .

Screaming. Someone was screaming. But distant.

Ralph tried to burrow even deeper into the black, but now hands seized his shoulder and began shaking him. Every shake sent a monstrous bolt of pain through his poor hungover head.

"Ralph! Ralph, wake up! You have to wake up!"

Ellie shaking him. Was he late for work? How could he be late for work? They were on vacation.

Then, shockingly loud, penetrating the blackness like the beam of a powerful light, gunshots. Three of them, then a pause, then a fourth.

His eyes flew open and he bolted into a sitting position, no idea for a moment where he was or what was happening, only knowing that his head hurt horribly and felt the size of a float in the Macy's Thanksgiving Day Parade. Something sticky that felt like jam or maple syrup all down the side of his face. Ellen looking at him, one eye wide and frantic, the other nearly lost in a puffy complication of blue-black flesh.

Screaming. Somewhere. A woman. From below them. Maybe—

He tried to get on his feet but his knees wouldn't lock. He fell forward off the bed he was sitting on (except it wasn't a bed, it was a cot) and landed on his hands and knees. A fresh bolt of pain passed through his head, and for a moment he thought his skull would split open like an eggshell. Then he was looking down at his hands through clotted clumps of hair. Both hands were streaked with blood, the left considerably redder than the right. As he looked at them, sudden memory

(Kirsten oh Jesus Ellie catch her)

burst in his head like a poison firework and he screamed himself, screamed down at his bloodstained hands, screamed as what he had been trying to burrow away from dropped into his mind like a stone into a pond. Kirsten had fallen down the stairs—

No. *Pushed.*

The crazy bastard who had brought them here had pushed his seven-year-old daughter down the stairs. Ellie had reached for her and the crazy bastard had punched his wife in the eye and knocked her down. But Ellie had fallen *on* the stairs and Kirsten had plunged *down* them, her eyes wide open, full of shocked surprise, Ralph didn't think she'd known what was happening, and if he could hold onto anything he would hold onto that, that it had all happened too fast for her to have any real idea, and then she had hit, she had cartwheeled, feet fly-ing first upward and then backward, and there had been this *sound,* this awful sound like a branch breaking under a weight of ice, and suddenly everything about her had changed, he had seen the change even before she came to a stop at the foot of the stairs, as if that were no little girl down there but a stuffed dummy, headpiece full of straw.

Don't think it, don't think it, don't you dare *think it.*

Except he had to. The way she had landed . . . the way she had lain at the foot of the stairs with her head on one side . . .

Fresh blood was pattering down on his left hand, he saw. Apparently something was wrong with that side of his head. What had happened? Had the cop hit him, too, maybe with the butt of the monster sidearm he had been wearing? Maybe, but that part was mostly gone. He could remember the gruesome somersault she had done, and the way she had slid down the rest of the stairs, and how she had come to rest with her head cocked that way, and that was all. Christ, wasn't it enough?

"Ralph?" Ellie was tugging at him and panting harshly. "Ralph, get up! *Please* get up!"

"Dad! Daddy, come on!" That was David, from farther away. "He okay, Mom? He's bleeding again, isn't he?"

"No . . . no, he—"

"Yes he is, I can see it from here. Daddy, are you okay?"

"Yes," he said. He got one foot planted beneath him, groped for the bunk, and tottered upright. His left eye was bleary with blood. The lid felt as if it had been dipped in plaster of Paris. He wiped it with the heel of his hand, wincing as fresh pain stung him—the area above his left eye felt like freshly tenderized meat. He tried to turn around, toward the sound of his son's voice, and staggered. It was like being on a boat. His balance was shot, and even when he stopped turning it felt to something in his head like he was still doing it, reeling and rocking, going round and round. Ellie grabbed him, supported him, helped him forward.

"She's dead, isn't she?" Ralph asked. His choked voice came

out of a throat plated with dead blood. He couldn't believe what he heard that voice saying, but he supposed that in time he would. That was the worst of it. In time he would. "Kirsten's dead."

"I think so, yes." Ellie staggered this time. "Grab the bars, Ralph, can you? You're going to knock me over."

They were in a jail cell. In front of him, just out of reach, was the barred door. The bars were painted white, and in some places the paint had dried and hardened in thick runnels. Ralph lunged forward a step and grabbed them. He was looking out at a desk, sitting in the middle of a square of floor like the single bit of stage dressing in a minimalist play. There were papers on it, and a double-barrelled shotgun, and a strew of fat green shotgun shells. The old-fashioned wooden desk chair in the kneehole was on casters, and there was a faded blue pillow on the seat. Overhead was a light fixture encased in a mesh bowl. The dead flies inside the fixture made huge, grotesque shadows.

There were jail cells on three sides of this room. The one in the middle, probably the drunk-tank, was large and empty. Ralph and Ellie Carver were in a smaller one. A second small cell to their right was empty. Across from them were two other closet-sized cells. In one of them was their eleven-year-old son, David, and a man with white hair. Ralph could see nothing else of this man, because he was sitting on the bunk with his head lowered onto his hands. When the woman screamed from below them again, David turned in that direction, where an open door gave on a flight of stairs

(Kirsten, Kirsten falling, the snapping sound of her neck breaking)

going down to street level, but the white-haired man did not shift his position in the slightest.

Ellie came to stand beside him and slipped an arm around his waist. Ralph risked letting go of the bars with one of his hands so he could take one of hers.

Now there were thuds on the stairs, coming closer, and scuffling sounds. Someone was being brought up to join them, but she wasn't coming easily.

"We have to help him!" she was screaming. *"We have to help Peter! We—"*

Her words broke off as she was thrown into the room. She crossed it with weird, balletic grace, stuttering on her toes, white sneakers like ballet slippers, hands held out, hair streaming behind her, jeans, a faded blue shirt. She collided with the desk, upper thighs smacking the edge hard enough to move it backward toward the chair, and then, from the other side of the room, David was shrieking at her like a bird, standing at the bars, jumping up and down on the balls of his feet, shrieking in a savage, panicky voice Ralph had never heard before, never even suspected.

"The shotgun, lady!" David screamed. *"Get the shotgun, shoot him, shoot him, lady, shoot him!"*

The white-haired man finally looked up. His face was old and dark with desert tan; the deep bags beneath his watery ginhead eyes gave him a bloodhound look.

"Get it!" the old man rasped. *"For Christ's sake, woman!"*

The woman in the jeans and the workshirt looked toward the sound of the boy's voice, then back over her shoulder toward the stairs and the clump of heavy approaching footfalls.

"Do it!" Ellie chimed in from beside Ralph. *"He killed our daughter, he'll kill all of us, do it!"*

The woman in the jeans and workshirt grabbed for the gun.

2

Until Nevada, things had been fine.

They had started out as four happy wanderers from Ohio, destination Lake Tahoe. There Ellie Carver and the kids would swim and hike and sightsee for ten days and Ralph Carver would gamble—slowly, pleasurably, and with tremendous concentration. This would be their fourth visit to Nevada, their second to Tahoe, and Ralph would continue to follow his ironclad gambling rule: he would quit when he had either (a) lost a thousand dollars, or (b) won ten thousand. In their three previous trips, he had reached neither of these markers. Once he had gone back to Columbus with five hundred dollars of his stake intact, once with two hundred, and last year he had driven them back with over three thousand dollars in the inner lefthand pocket of his lucky safari jacket. On that trip they had stayed at Hiltons and Sheratons instead of in the RV at camping areas, and the elder Carvers had gotten themselves laid every damned night. Ralph considered that pretty phenomenal for people pushing forty.

"You're probably tired of casinos," he'd said in February, when they started talking about this vacation. "Maybe California this time? Mexico?"

"Sure, we can all get dysentery," Ellie had replied. "Look at the Pacific between sprints to the casa de poo-poo, or whatever they call it down there."

"What about Texas? We could take the kids to see the Alamo."

"Too hot, too historic. Tahoe will be cool, even in July. The kids love it. I do, too. And as long as you don't come asking for any of *my* money when yours is gone—"

"You know I'd never do that," he had said, sounding shocked. *Feeling* a little shocked, actually. The two of them sitting in the kitchen of their suburban home in Wentworth, not far from Columbus, sitting next to the bronze Frigidaire with the magnetic stick-on daisies scattered across it, travel-folders on the counter in front of them, neither aware that the gambling had already started and the first loss would be their daughter. "You know what I told you—"

" 'Once the addict-behavior starts, the gambling stops,' " she had repeated. "I know, I remember, I believe. You like Tahoe, I like Tahoe, the kids like Tahoe, Tahoe is fine."

So he had made the reservations, and today—if it still *was* today—they had been on U.S. 50, the so-called loneliest highway in America, headed west across Nevada toward the High Sierra. Kirsten had been playing with Melissa Sweetheart, her favorite doll, Ellie had been napping, and David had been sitting beside Ralph, looking out the window with his chin propped on his hand. Earlier he had been reading the Bible his new pal the Rev had given him (Ralph hoped to God that Martin wasn't queer—the man was married, which was good, but still, you could never damn tell), but now he'd marked his place and tucked the Bible away in the console storage bin. Ralph thought again of asking the kid what he was thinking about, what all the Bible stuff was about, but you might as well ask a post what it was thinking. David (he could abide Davey but hated to be called Dave) was a strange kid that way, not like either parent. Not much like his sister, either, for that matter. This sudden interest in religion—what Ellen called "David's God-trip"—was only one of his oddities. It would probably pass, and in the meantime, David did not quote verses at him on the subject of gambling, cursing, or avoiding the razor on weekends, and that was good enough for Ralph. He loved the kid, after all, and love stretched to cover a multitude of oddities. He had an idea that was one of the things love was for.

Ralph had been opening his mouth to ask David if he wanted to play Twenty Questions—there had been nothing much to look at since leaving Ely that morning and he was bored out of his mind—when he felt the Wayfarer's steering suddenly go mushy in his hands and heard the highway-drone of the tires suddenly become a flapping sound.

"Dad?" David asked. He sounded concerned but not panicked. That was good. "Everything okay?"

"Hold on," he had said, and began pumping the brakes. "This could be a little rough."

Now, standing at the bars and watching the dazed woman who might be their only hope of surviving this nightmare, he thought: *I really had no idea of what rough was, did I?*

It hurt his head to scream, but he screamed anyway, unaware of how much he sounded like his own son: *"Shoot him, lady, shoot him!"*

3

What Mary Jackson recalled, what caused her to reach for the shotgun even though she had never actually held a gun—rifle or pistol—in her entire life, was the memory of the big cop mixing the words *I'm going to kill you* into the Miranda warning.

And he meant it. Oh God yes.

She swung around with the gun. The big blond cop was standing in the doorway, looking at her with his bright gray empty eyes.

"Shoot him, lady, shoot him!" a man screamed. He was in the cell to Mary's right, standing next to a woman with an eye so black that the bruise had sent tendrils down her cheek, like ink injected beneath the skin. The man looked even worse; the left side of his face appeared to be covered with caked, half-dried blood.

The cop ran at her, his boots rattling on the hardwood floor. Mary stepped back, away from him and toward the big empty cell at the rear of the room, pulling back both of the shotgun's hammers with the side of her thumb as she retreated. Then she raised it to her shoulder. She had no intention of warning him. He had just killed her husband in cold blood, and she had no intention of warning him.

4

Ralph had pumped the brakes and held the wheel with his elbows locked, letting it work back and forth a little in his hands but not too much. He could feel the RV trying to yaw. The secret to handling a high-speed blowout in an RV, he'd been told, was to *let* it yaw—a little, anyway. Although—bad news, folks—this didn't feel like just one blowout.

He glanced up into the rearview at Kirsten, who had stopped playing with Melissa Sweetheart and was now holding the doll against her chest. Kirstie knew something was going on, just not what.

"Kirsten, sit down!" he called. "Belt in!"

Except by then it was over. He wrestled the Wayfarer off the road, killed the engine, and wiped sweat from his forehead with the back of his hand. All in all he didn't think he'd done badly. Hadn't even toppled the vase of desert flowers standing on the table in back. Ellie and Kirstie had picked them behind the motel in Ely this morning, while he and David were first loading up and then checking out.

"Good driving, Dad," David said in a matter-of-fact voice.

Ellie was sitting up now, looking around blearily. "Bathroom break?" she asked. "Why're we tilted this way, Ralph?"

"We had a—"

He broke off, looking into the outside mirror. A police-car was rushing toward them from behind, blue lights flashing. It came to a screaming stop about a hundred yards back, and the biggest cop Ralph had ever seen in his life almost *bounded* out. Ralph saw that the cop had his gun drawn, and felt adrenaline light up his nerves.

The cop stared right and left, his gun held up to shoulder height with the muzzle pointing at the cloudless morning sky. Then he actually turned in a circle. When he was facing the RV again, he looked directly into the outside rearview, seeming to meet Ralph's eyes. The cop raised both hands over his head, brought them down violently, then raised and brought them down again. The pantomime was impossible to misinterpret— *Stay inside, stay where you are.*

"Ellie, lock the back doors." Ralph banged down the button beside him as he spoke. David, who was watching him, did the same thing on his side of the car without having to be asked.

"What?" She looked at him uncertainly. "What's going on?"

"I don't know, but there's a cop back there and he looks excited." *Back where I had the flat,* he thought, then amended that. *The flats.*

The cop bent and picked something up off the surface of the road. It was a meshy strip with little twinkles of light bouncing off it the way light bounces off the sequins on a woman's evening dress. He carried it back to his car, dragging one end along the shoulder, his gun still in his other hand, still held up at a kind of port arms. He seemed to be trying to look in all directions at once.

Ellie locked the aft door and the main cabin door, then came forward again. "*What* in the samhill is going *on?*"

"I told you, I don't know. But that doesn't look, you know, real encouraging." He pointed into the mirror outside the driver's window.

Ellie bent, planting her hands just above her knees and watching with Ralph as the cop dumped the meshy thing into the passenger seat, then backed around to the driver's side with his gun now held up in both hands. Later it would occur to Ralph just how carefully crafted this little silent movie had been.

Kirstie came up behind her mother and began to bop Melissa Sweetheart softly against her mother's stuck-out bottom. "Butt, butt, butt, butt," she sang. "We love a great big motherbutt."

"Don't, Kirstie."

Ordinarily Kirstie would have needed two or three requests to cease and desist, but something in her mother's voice this time caused her to stop at once. She looked at her brother, who was staring as intently into his mirror as the grownups were into Daddy's. She went over to him and tried to get in his lap. David set her back on her feet gently but firmly. "Not now, Pie."

"But what *is* it? What's the big deal?"

"Nothing, no big deal," David said, never taking his eyes off the mirror.

The cop got into his cruiser and drove up the road to the Wayfarer. He got out again, his gun still out but now held along his leg with the muzzle pointed at the road. He looked right and left again, then walked over to Ralph's window. The driver's position in the Wayfarer was much higher than a car's seat would have been, but the cop was so tall—six-seven, at least—that he was still able to look down on Ralph as he sat behind the wheel in his captain's chair.

The cop made a cranking gesture with his empty hand. Ralph rolled his window halfway down. "What's the trouble, Officer?"

"How many are you?" the cop asked.

"What's wr—"

"Sir, how many are you?"

"Four," Ralph said, beginning to feel really frightened now. "My wife, my two kids, me. We have a couple of flats—"

"No, sir, *all* your tires are flat. You ran over a piece of highway carpet."

"I don't—"

"It's a strip of mesh embedded with hundreds of short nails," the cop said. "We use it to stop speeders whenever we can—it beats the hell out of hot pursuit."

"What was a thing like that doing in the road?" Ellie asked indignantly.

The cop said, "I'm going to open the rear door of my car, the one closest to your RV. When you see that, I want you to exit your vehicle and get into the back of mine. And quickly."

He craned his neck, saw Kirsten—she was now holding onto her mother's leg and peering cautiously around it—and gave her a smile. "Hi, girly-o."

Kirstie smiled back at him.

The cop shifted his eyes briefly to David. He nodded, and David nodded back noncommittally. "Who's out there, sir?" David asked.

"A bad guy," the cop said. "That's all you need to know for now, son. A very bad guy. *Tak!*"

"Officer—" Ralph began.

"Sir, with all due respect, I feel like a clay pigeon in a shooting gallery. There's a dangerous man out here, he's good with a rifle, and that piece of highway carpet suggests he's nearby. Further discussion of the situation must wait until our position has been improved, do you understand?"

Tak? Ralph wondered. Was that the bad guy's name? "Yes, but—"

"You first, sir. Carry your little girl. The boy next. Your wife last. You'll have to cram, but you can all fit into the car."

Ralph unbelted and stood up. "Where are we going?" he asked.

"Desperation. Mining town. Eight miles or so from here."

Ralph nodded, rolled up his window, then picked up Kirsten. She looked at him with troubled eyes that were not far from tears.

"Daddy, is it Mr. Big Boogeyman?" she asked. Mr. Big Boogeyman was a monster she had brought home from school one day. Ralph didn't know which of the kids had described this shadowy closet-dweller to his gentle seven-year-old daughter, but he thought if he could have found him (he simply assumed it was a boy, it seemed to him that the care and feeding of the monsters in the schoolyards of America always fell to the boys), he would have cheerfully strangled the bugger. It had taken two months to get Kirstie more or less soothed down about Mr. Big Boogeyman. Now this.

"No, not Mr. Big Boogeyman," Ralph said. "Probably just a postal worker having a bad day."

"Daddy, *you* work for the post office," she said as he carried her back toward the door in the middle of the Wayfarer's cabin.

"Yup," he said, aware that Ellie had put David in front of her and was walking with her hands on his shoulders. "It's sort of a joke, see?"

"Like a knock-knock without the knocking?"

"Yup," he said again. He looked out the window in the RV's cabin door and saw the cop had opened the back door of the police cruiser. He also saw that when he opened the Wayfarer's door, it would overlap the car door, making a protective wall. That was good.

Sure. Unless the desert rat this guy's looking for is in back of us. Christ Almighty, why couldn't we have gone to Atlantic City?

"Dad?" That was David, his intelligent but slightly peculiar son who had started going to church last fall, after the thing that had happened to his friend Brian. Not Sunday school, not Thursday Night Youth Group, just church. And Sunday afternoons at the parsonage, talking with his new friend, the Rev. Who, by the way, was going to die slowly if he had been sharing anything with David but his thoughts. According to David it was all talk, and after the thing with Brian, Ralph supposed the kid *needed* someone to talk to. He only wished David had felt able to bring his questions to his mother and father instead of to some holy joe outsider who was married but still might—

"*Dad*? Is it all right?"

"Yes. Fine." He didn't know if it was or not, didn't really

know what they were dealing with here, but that was what you said to your kids, wasn't it? Yes, fine, all right. He thought that if he were on a plane with David and the engines quit, he'd put his arm around the boy and tell him everything was fine all the way down.

He opened the door, and it banged against the inside of the cruiser door.

"Quick, come on, let's see some hustle," the cop said, looking nervously around.

Ralph went down the steps with Kirstie sitting in the crook of his left arm. As he stepped down, she dropped her doll.

"Melissa!" she cried. "I dropped Melissa Sweetheart, get her, Daddy!"

"No, get in the car, get in the car!" the cop shouted. "I'll get the doll!"

Ralph slid in, putting his hand on the top of Kirstie's head and helping her duck. David followed him, then Ellie. The back seat of the car was filled with papers, and the front seat had been warped into a bell-shape by the oversized cop's weight. The moment Ellie pulled her right leg in, the cop slammed the door shut and went racing around the back of the cruiser.

"'Lissa!" Kirstie cried in tones of real agony. "He forgot 'Lissa!"

Ellie reached for the doorhandle, meaning to lean out and get Melissa Sweetheart—surely no psycho with a rifle could pick her off in the time it would take to grab up a little girl's doll—then looked back at Ralph. "Where're the handles?" she asked.

The driver's-side door of the cruiser opened, and the cop dropped into it like a bomb. The seat crunched back against Ralph's knees and he winced, glad that Kirstie's legs were hanging down between his. Not that Kirstie was still. She wriggled and twisted on his lap, hands held out to her mother.

"My doll, Mummy, my *doll*! Melissa!"

"Officer—" Ellie began.

"No time," the cop said. "Can't. *Tak*!" He U-turned across the road and headed east in a spew of dust. The rear end of the car fishtailed briefly. As it steadied again, it occurred to Ralph how fast this had happened—not ten minutes ago they'd been in their RV, headed down the road. He'd been about to ask David to play Twenty Questions, not because he really wanted to but because he had been bored.

He sure wasn't bored now.

"Melissa *Sweeeeeeetheart*!" Kirstie screamed, and then began to weep.

"Take it easy, Pie," David said. It was his pet name for his baby sister. Like so many other things about David, neither of his parents knew what it meant or where it had come from. Ellie thought it was short for sweetie-pie, but when she had asked him one night, David had just shrugged and grinned his appealing, slanted little grin. "Nah, she's just a pie," he had said. "Just a pie, that's all."

"But 'Lissa's in the dirty old *dirt*," Kirstie said, looking at her brother with swimming eyes.

"We'll come back and get her and clean her all up," David said.

"Promise?"

"Uh-huh. I'll even help you wash her hair."

"With Prell?"

"Uh-huh." He put a quick kiss on her cheek.

"What if the bad man comes?" Kirstie asked. "The bad man like Mr. Big Boogeyman? What if he dollnaps Melissa Sweetheart?"

David covered his mouth with his hand to hide the ghost of a grin. "He won't." The boy glanced up into the rearview mirror, trying to make eye contact with the cop. "Will he?"

"No," the cop said. "The man we're looking for is not a doll-napper." There was no facetiousness Ralph could detect in his voice; he sounded like Joe Friday. Just the facts, ma'am.

He slowed briefly as they passed a sign which read DES-PERATION, then accelerated as he turned right. Ralph hung on, praying that the guy knew what he was doing, that he wouldn't roll them. The car seemed to lift slightly, then settled back. They were now heading south. On the horizon, a huge bulwark of earth, its tan side cut with cracks and zigzag trenches like black scars, loomed against the sky.

"What *is* he, then?" Ellie asked. "What *is* this guy? And how did he get hold of the stuff you use to stop speeders? The watchamacallit?"

"Highway carpet, Mom," David said. He ran a finger up and down the metal mesh between the front and back seats, his face intent and thoughtful and troubled. Not even a ghost of a smile there now.

"Same way he got the guns he's toting and the car he's driving," the man behind the wheel said. Now they were passing the Rattlesnake Trailer Park, now the headquarters of the Desperation Mining Corporation. Up ahead was a huddle of business buildings. A blinker-light flashed yellow under a hundred thousand miles of blue-denim sky. "He's a cop. And I'll tell you one thing, Carvers: when you've got a nutty cop on your hands, you've got a situation."

"How do you know our name?" David asked. "You didn't ask to see my dad's driver's license, so how do you know our name?"

"Saw it when your dad opened the door," the cop said, looking up into the rearview mirror. "Little plaque over the table. GOD BLESS OUR ROAMING HOME. THE CARVERS. Cute."

Something about this bothered Ralph, but for now he paid no attention. His fright had grown into a sense of foreboding so strong and yet so diffuse that he felt a little as if he'd eaten something laced with poison. He thought that if he held his hand up it would be steady, but that didn't change the fact that he had become more scared, not less, since the cop had sped them away from their disabled roaming home with such spooky ease. It apparently wasn't the kind of fear that made your hands shake (*it's a* dry *fright,* he thought with a tiny and not very characteristic twinkle of humor), but it was real enough, for all that.

"A cop," Ralph mused, thinking of a movie he'd rented from the video store down the street one Saturday night not too long ago. *Maniac Cop,* it had been called. The line of ad-copy above the title had read: YOU HAVE THE RIGHT TO REMAIN SILENT. PERMANENTLY. Funny how stupid stuff like that sometimes stuck with you. Except it didn't seem very funny right now.

"A cop, right," *their* cop replied. He sounded as if he might be smiling.

Oh, really? Ralph asked himself. *And just how does a smile* sound?

He was aware that Ellie was looking at him with a kind of strained curiosity, but this didn't seem like a good time to return her glance. He didn't know what they might read in each other's eyes, and wasn't sure he wanted to find out.

The cop *had* been smiling, though. He was somehow sure of it.

Why would he be? What's funny about a maniac cop on the loose, or six flat tires, or a family of four crammed into a hot police-car with no handles on the back doors, or my daughter's favorite doll lying face-down in the dirt eight miles back? What could possibly be funny about any of those things?

He didn't know. But the cop *had* sounded as if he were smiling.

"A state trooper, did you say?" Ralph asked as they drove beneath the blinker.

"Look, Mummy!" Kirsten said brightly, Melissa Sweetheart

at least temporarily forgotten. "Bikes! Bikes in the street, and standing on their heads! See down there? Isn't that funny?"

"Yes, honey, I see them," Ellie said. She didn't sound as if she found the upside-down bikes in the street anywhere near as hilarious as her daughter did.

"Trooper? No, I didn't say that." The big man behind the wheel still sounded as if he were smiling. "Not a state trooper, a town cop."

"Really," Ralph said. "Wow. How many cops do you have in a little place like this, Officer?"

"Well, there *were* two others," the cop said, the smile in his voice more obvious than ever, "but I killed them."

He turned his head to look back through the mesh, and he wasn't smiling after all. He was *grinning*. His teeth were so big they looked more like tools than bones. They showed all the way to the back of his mouth. Above and below them were what seemed like acres of pink gum.

"Now I'm the only law west of the Pecos."

Ralph stared at him, mouth gaping. The cop grinned back, driving with his head turned, pulling up neatly in front of the Desperation Municipal Building without ever looking once at where he was going.

"Carvers," he said, speaking solemnly through his grin, "welcome to Desperation."

5

An hour later the cop ran at the woman in the jeans and the workshirt, his cowboy boots rattling on the hardwood floor, his hands outstretched, but his grin was gone and Ralph felt savage triumph leap up his throat, like something ugly on a spring. The cop was coming hard, but the woman in the jeans had managed—probably due more to luck than to any conscious decision on her part—to keep the desk between them, and that was going to make the difference. Ralph saw her pull back the hammers of the shotgun which had been lying on the desk, saw her raise it to her shoulder as her back struck the bars of the room's largest cell, saw her curl her finger around the double triggers.

The big cop was going like hell, but it wasn't going to do him any good.

Shoot him, lady, Ralph thought. *Not to save us but because he killed my daughter. Blow his motherfucking head off.*

The instant before Mary pulled the triggers, the cop fell to his knees on the other side of the desk, his head dropping like the head of a man who has knelt to pray. The double roar of the shotgun was terrific in the closed holding area. Flame licked out of the barrels. Ralph heard his wife scream—in triumph, he thought. If so, it was premature. The cop's Smokey Bear hat flew off his head, but the loads went high. Shot hit the back wall of the room and thudded into the plastered stairwell outside the open door with a sound like wind-driven sleet hitting a windowpane. There was a bulletin-board to the right of the doorway, and Ralph saw round black holes spatter across the papers tacked up there. The cop's hat was a shredded ruin held together only by a thin leather hatband. It had been buckshot in the gun, not bird. If it had hit the cop in the midsection, it would have torn him apart. Knowing that made Ralph feel even worse.

The big cop threw his weight against the desk and shoved it across the room toward the cell Ralph had decided was the drunk-tank—toward the cell and the woman pressed against the cell's bars. The chair was penned in the kneehole. It swivelled back and forth, casters squalling. The woman tried to get the gun down between her and the chair before the chair could hit her, but she didn't move fast enough. The chairback crashed into her hips and pelvis and stomach, driving her backward into the bars. She howled in pain and surprise.

The big cop spread his arms like Samson preparing to pull down the temple and grasped the sides of the desk. Although his ears were still ringing from the shotgun blast, Ralph heard the seams under the arms of the maniac cop's khaki uniform shirt give way. The cop pulled the desk back. "Drop it!" he yelled. "Drop the gun, Mary!"

The woman shoved the chair away from her, raised the shotgun, and pulled back the double hammers again. She was sobbing with pain and effort. Out of the corner of his eye, Ralph saw Ellie put her hands over her ears as the dark-haired woman curled her finger around the triggers, but this time there was only a dry click when the hammers fell. Ralph felt disappointment as bitter as gall crowd his throat. He had known just looking at it that the shotgun wasn't a pump or an auto, and still he had somehow thought it would fire, had absolutely *expected* it to fire, as if God himself would reload the chambers and perform a Winchester miracle.

The cop shoved the desk forward a second time. If not for the chair, Ralph saw, she would have been safe in the kneehole. But the chair *was* there, and it slammed into her midsection again, doubling her forward and drawing a harsh retching noise from her.

"Drop it Mary, *drop it!*" the cop yelled.

But she wouldn't. As the cop pulled the desk back again (*Why doesn't he just charge her?* Ralph thought. *Doesn't he know the damned gun is empty?*), shells spilling off the top and rolling everywhere, she reversed it so she could grip the twin barrels. Then she leaned forward and brought the stock down over the top of the desk like a club. The cop tried to drop his right shoulder, but the burled walnut stock of the gun caught him on the collarbone just the same. He grunted. Ralph had no idea if it was a grunt of surprise, pain, or simple exasperation, but the sound drew a scream of approval from across the room, where David was still standing with his hands wrapped around the bars of the cell he was in. His face was pale and sweaty, his eyes blazing. The old man with the white hair had joined him.

The cop pulled the desk back once more—the blow to his shoulder did not noticeably impair his ability to do this—and slammed it forward again, hitting the woman with the chair and driving her into the bars. She uttered another harsh cry.

"Put it down!" the cop yelled. It was a funny kind of yell, and for a moment Ralph found himself hoping that the bastard was hurt after all. Then he realized the cop was laughing. "Put it down or I'll beat you to a pulp, I really will!"

The dark-haired woman—Mary—raised the gun again, but this time with no conviction. One side of her shirt had pulled out of her jeans, and Ralph could see bright red marks on the white skin of her waist and belly. He knew that, were she to take the shirt off, he would see the chairback's silhouette tattooed all the way up to the cups of her bra.

She held the gun in the air for a moment, the inlaid stock wavering, then threw it aside. It clattered across to the cell where David and the white-haired man were. David looked down at it.

"Don't touch it, son," the white-haired man said. "It's empty, just leave it alone."

The cop glanced at David and the white-haired man. Then, smiling brilliantly, he looked at the woman with her back to the drunk-tank bars. He pulled the desk away from her, went around it, and kicked at the chair. It voyaged across the hardwood on its squeaky casters and thumped to a stop against the empty cell next to Ralph and Ellie. The cop put an arm around the dark-haired woman's shoulders. He looked at her almost tenderly. She responded with the blackest glance Ralph had ever seen in his life.

"Can you walk?" the cop asked her. "Is anything broken?"

"What difference does it make?" She spat at him. "Kill me if you're going to, get it over with."

"Kill you? *Kill* you?" He looked stunned, the expression of a man who has never killed anything bigger than a wasp in his whole life. "I'm not going to *kill* you, Mare!" He hugged her to him briefly, then looked around at Ralph and Ellie, David and the white-haired man. "Gosh, no!" he said. "Not when things are just getting interesting."

CHAPTER 3

1

The man who had once been on the cover of *People* and *Time* and *Premiere* (when he married the actress with all the emeralds), and the front page of *The New York Times* (when he won the National Book Award for his novel *Delight*), and in the center-spread of *Inside View* (when he was arrested for beating up his third wife, the one before the actress with the emeralds), had to take a piss.

He pulled his motorcycle over to the westbound edge of Highway 50, working methodically down through the gears with a stiff left foot, and finally rolling to a stop on the edge of the tar. Good thing there was so little traffic out here, because you couldn't park your scoot off the road in the Great Basin even if you *had* once fucked America's most famous actress (although she had admittedly been a little long in the tooth by then) and been spoken of in connection with the Nobel Prize for Literature. If you tried it, your bike was apt to first heel over on her kickstand and then fall flat on her roadbars. The shoulder looked hard, but that was mostly attitude—not much different from the attitudes of certain people he could name, including the one he needed a mirror to get a good look at. And try picking up a seven-hundred-pound Harley-Davidson once you'd dumped it, especially when you were fifty-six and out of shape. Just try.

I don't think so, he thought, looking at the red-and-cream Harley Softail, a street bike at which any purist would have turned up his nose, listening to the engine tick-tock in the silence. The only other sounds were the hot wind and the minute sound of sand spacking against his leather jacket—twelve hundred dollars at Barneys in New York. A jacket meant to be photographed by a fag from *Interview* magazine if ever there had been one. *I think we'll skip that part entirely, shall we?*

"Fine by me," he said. He took off his helmet and put it on the Harley's seat. Then he rubbed a slow hand down his face, which was as hot as the wind and at least twice as sunburned. He thought he had never felt quite so tired or so out of his element in his whole life.

2

The literary lion walked stiffly into the desert, his long gray hair brushing against the shoulders of his motorcycle jacket, the scrubby mesquite and paintbrush ticking against his leather chaps (also from Barneys). He looked around carefully but saw nothing coming in either direction. There was something parked off the road a mile or two farther west—a truck or maybe a motor home—but even if there were people in it, he doubted that they could watch the great man take a leak without binoculars. And if they *were* watching, so what? It was a trick most people knew, after all.

He unzipped his fly—John Edward Marinville, the man *Harper's* had once called "the writer Norman Mailer always wanted to be," the man Shelby Foote had once called "the only living American writer of John Steinbeck's stature"—and hauled out his original fountain pen. He had to piss like a racehorse but for almost a minute nothing happened; he just stood there with his dry dick in his hand.

Then, at last, urine arced out and turned the tough and dusty leaves of the mesquite a darker, shiny green.

"Praise Jesus, thank you, Lord!" he bellowed in his rolling, trembling Jimmy Swaggart voice. It was a great success at cocktail parties; Tom Wolfe had once laughed so hard when he was doing the evangelist voice that Johnny thought the man was going to have a stroke. *"Water in the desert, that's a big ten-four! Hello Julia!"* He sometimes thought it was this version of "hallelujah," not his insatiable appetite for booze, drugs, and younger women, that had caused the famous actress to push him into the pool during a drunken press conference at the Bel-Air hotel . . . and then to take her emeralds elsewhere.

That incident hadn't marked the beginning of his decline, but it had marked the point where the decline had become impossible to ignore—he wasn't just having a bad day or a bad year anymore, he was sort of having a bad *life.* The picture of him climbing out of the pool in his sopping white suit, a big drunk's grin on his face, had appeared in *Esquire's* Dubious Achievements issue, and after that had commenced his more-or-less regular appearances in *Spy* magazine. *Spy* was the place, he'd come to believe, where once-legitimate reputations went to die.

At least this afternoon, as he stood facing north and pissing with his shadow stretched out long to his right, these thoughts didn't hurt as much as they sometimes did. As they *always* did in New York, where everything hurt these days. The desert had a way of making Shakespeare's "bubble reputation" seem not only fragile but irrelevant. When you had become a kind of literary Elvis Presley—aging, overweight, and still at the party long after you should have gone home—that wasn't such a bad thing.

He spread his legs even wider, bent slightly at the waist, and let go of his penis so he could massage his lower back. He had been told that doing this helped sustain the flow a little longer, and he had an idea that it did, but he knew he would still have to take a leak again long before he got to Austin, which was the next little Nevada shitsplat on the long road to California. His prostate clearly wasn't what it used to be. When he thought about it these days (which was often), he pictured a bloated, crenellated thing that looked like a radiation-baked giant brain in a fifties drive-in horror movie. He should have it checked, he knew that, and not as an isolated event but as part of a complete soup-to-nuts physical. Of course he should, but hey, it wasn't as if he were *pissing blood* or anything, and besides—

Well, all right. He was scared, that was the besides. There was a lot more to what was wrong with him than just the way his literary reputation had gone slipping through his fingers during the last five years, and quitting the pills and booze hadn't improved things as he'd hoped. In some ways, quitting had made things worse. The trouble with sobriety, Johnny had found, was that you *remembered* all the things you had to be scared of. He was afraid that a doctor might find more than a prostate roughly the size of The Brain from Planet Arous when he stuck his finger up into the literary lion's nether regions; he was afraid that the doctor might find a prostate that was as black as a decayed pumpkin and as cancerous as . . . as Frank Zappa's had been. And even if cancer wasn't lurking there, it might be lurking somewhere else.

The lung, why not? He'd smoked two packs of Camels every day for twenty years, then three packs of Camel Lights for another ten, as if smoking Camel Lights was going to fix everything somehow, spruce up his bronchial tubes, polish his trachea, refurbish his poor sludgecaked alveoli. Well, bullshit. He'd been off the cigarettes for ten years now, the light as well as the heavy, but he still wheezed like an old carthorse until at least noon, and sometimes woke himself up coughing in the middle of the night.

Or the stomach! Yeah, why not there? Soft, pink, trusting, the perfect place for disaster to strike. He had been raised in a family of ravenous meat-eaters where medium-rare meant the cook had breathed hard on the steak and the concept of well-done was unknown; he loved hot sauces and hot peppers; he did not believe in fruits and salads unless one was badly constipated; he'd eaten like that his whole fucking life, *still* ate like that, and would probably *go on* eating like that until they slammed him into a hospital bed and started feeding him all the right things through a plastic tube.

The brain? Possible. *Quite* possible. A tumor, or maybe (here was an *especially* cheerful thought) an unseasonably early case of Alzheimer's.

The pancreas? Well, that one was fast, at least. Express service, no waiting.

Heart attack? Cirrhosis? Stroke?

How likely they all sounded! How logical!

In many interviews he had identified himself as a man outraged by death, but that was pretty much the same old big-balls crap he'd been selling throughout his career. He was *terrified* of death, that was the truth, and as a result of spending his life honing his imagination, he could see it coming from at least four dozen different directions . . . and late at night when he couldn't sleep, he was apt to see it coming from four dozen different directions *at once.* Refusing to see the doctor, to have a checkup and let them peek under the hood, would not cause any of those diseases to pause in their approach or their feeding upon him—if, indeed, the feeding had already begun—but if he stayed away from the doctors and their devilish machines, *he wouldn't have to know.* You didn't have to deal with the monster under the bed or lurking in the corner if you never actually turned on the bedroom lights, that was the thing. And what no doctor in the world seemed to know was that, for men like Johnny Marinville, fearing was sometimes better than finding. Especially when you'd put out the welcome mat for every disease going.

Including AIDS, he thought, continuing to stare out at the desert. He had tried to be careful—and he didn't get laid as much as he used to, anyway, that was the painful truth—and he knew that for the last eight or ten months he *had* been careful, because the blackouts had stopped with the drinking. But in the year before he'd quit, there had been four or five occasions when he had simply awakened next to some anonymous jane. On each of these occasions he had gotten up and gone immediately into the bathroom to check the toilet. Once there had been a used condom floating in there, so that was probably okay. On the other occasions, zilch. Of course he or his friend (his *gal-pal,* in tabloid-ese) might have flushed it down in the night, but you couldn't know for sure, could you? Not when you'd progressed to the blackout stage. And AIDS—

"That shit gets in there and *waits,*" he said, then winced as a particularly vicious gust of wind drove a fine sheet of alkali dust against his cheek, his neck, and his hanging organ. This latter had quit doing anything useful at least a full minute ago.

Johnny shook it briskly, then slipped it back into his underpants. "Brethern," he told the distant, shimmering mountains in his earnest revival preacher's voice, "we are told in the Book of Ephesians, chapter three, verse nine, that it matters not how much you jump and dance; the last two drops go in your pants. So it is written and so it is—"

He was turning around, zipping his fly, talking mostly to keep the megrims away (they had been gathering like vultures just lately, those megrims), and now he stopped doing everything at once.

There was a police-cruiser parked behind his motorcycle, its blue flashers turning lazily in the hot desert daylight.

3

It was his first wife who provided Johnny Marinville with what might be his last chance.

Oh, not his last chance to publish his work; shit, no. He would be able to go on doing that as long as he remained capable of (a) putting words on paper and (b) sending them off to his agent. Once you'd been accepted as a bona fide literary lion, *someone* would be glad to go on publishing your words even after they had degenerated into self-parody or outright drivel. Johnny sometimes thought that the most terrible thing about the American literary establishment was how they let you swing in the wind, slowly strangling, while they all stood around at their asshole cocktail parties, congratulating themselves on how kind they were being to poor old what's-his-name.

No, what Terry gave him wasn't his last chance to publish, but maybe his last to write something really worthwhile, something that would get him noticed again in a positive way. Something that might also sell like crazy . . . and he could use the money, there was no doubt about that.

Best of all, he didn't think Terry had the slightest idea of what she had said, which meant he wouldn't have to share any of the proceeds with her, if proceeds there were. He wouldn't even have to mention her on the Acknowledgments page, if he didn't want to, but he supposed he probably would. Sobering up had been a terrifying experience in many ways, but it *did* help a person remember his responsibilities.

He had married Terry when he was twenty-five and she was twenty-one, a junior at Vassar. She had never finished college. They had been married for almost twenty years and during that time she had borne him three children, all grown now. One of them, Bronwyn, still talked to him. The other two . . .

well, if they ever got tired of cutting off their noses to spite their faces, he would be around. He was not by nature a vindictive man.

Terry seemed to know that. After five years during which their only communication had been through lawyers, they had begun a cautious dialogue, sometimes by letter, more often by telephone. These communications had been tentative at first, both of them afraid of mines still buried in the ruined city of their affections, but over the years they had become more regular. Terry regarded her famous ex with a kind of stoic, amused interest that he found distressing, somehow—it was not, in his opinion, the sort of attitude an ex-wife was supposed to have for a man who had gone on to become one of the most discussed writers of his generation. But she also spoke to him with a straightforward kindness that he found soothing, like a cool hand on a hot brow.

They had been in contact more since he'd quit drinking (but still always by phone or by letter; both of them seemed to know, even without discussing it, that meeting face to face would put too much pressure on the fragile bond they had forged), but in some ways these sober conversations had been even more dangerous . . . not acrimonious, but always with that possibility. She wanted him to go back to Alcoholics Anonymous, told him bluntly that if he didn't, he'd eventually start drinking again. And the drugs would follow, she said, as surely as dark comes after twilight.

Johnny told her he had no intention of spending the rest of his life sitting in church basements with a bunch of drunks, all of them talking about how wonderful it was to have a power greater than one's self . . . before getting back into their old cars and driving home to their mostly spouseless houses to feed their cats. "People in AA are generally too fundamentally broken to see that they've turned their lives over to an empty concept and a failed ideal," he said. "Take it from me, I've been there. Or take it from John Cheever, if you like. He wrote particularly well about that."

"John Cheever isn't writing much these days," Terry replied. "I think you know why, too."

Terry could be irritating, no doubt about that.

It was three months ago that she had given him the great idea, tossing it off in a casual conversation that had rambled through what the kids were up to, what she was up to, and, of course, what he was up to. What he had been up to in the early part of this year was agonizing over the first two hundred pages of a historical novel about Jay Gould. He had finally seen it for what it was—warmed-over Gore Vidal—and trashed it. *Baked* it, actually. In a fit of pique he had resolved to keep entirely to himself, he had tossed his computer-storage discs for the novel into the microwave and given them ten minutes on high. The stench had been unbelievable, a thing that had come roaring out of the kitchen with quills on it, and he'd actually had to replace the microwave.

Then he'd found himself telling Terry the whole thing. When he finished, he sat in his office chair with the phone pressed to his ear and his eyes closed, waiting for her to tell him not to bother with resuming the AA meetings, that what he needed was a good shrink, and in a hurry.

Instead she said he should have put the discs in a casserole dish and used the convection oven. He knew she was joking— and that she thought at least part of the joke was on him—but her acceptance of the way he was and how he behaved still felt like a cool hand on a fevered brow. It wasn't approval he got from her, but approval wasn't what he wanted.

"Of course you never *were* much good in the kitchen," she said, and her matter-of-fact tone made him laugh out loud. "So what are you going to do now, Johnny? Any idea?"

"Not the slightest."

"You ought to write some nonfiction. Get away from the whole idea of the novel for awhile."

"That's dumb, Terry. I can't write nonfiction, and you know it."

"I know nothing of the kind," she'd said, speaking in a sharp don't-be-a-fool tone he got from no one else these days, least of all from his agent. The more Johnny flopped and flailed around, the more gruesomely obsequious Bill Harris became, it seemed. "During the first two years we were married, you must have written at least a dozen essays. Published them, too. For good money. *Life, Harper's,* even a couple in *The New Yorker.* Easy for you to forget; you weren't the one who did the shopping and paid the bills. I *loved* the puppies."

"Oh. The so-called American Heart Essays. Right. I didn't forget em, Terry, I blocked em out. Rent-payers after the last of the Guggenheim dough was gone; that's basically what they were. They've never even been collected."

"You wouldn't *allow* them to be collected," she retorted. "They didn't fit your golden idea of immortality."

Johnny greeted this with silence. Sometimes he hated her memory. She'd never been able to write worth a shit herself, the stuff she'd been turning in to her Honors writing seminar the year he met her had been just horrible, and since then she'd never published anything more complex than a letter to the editor, but she was a champ at data-storage. He had to give her that.

"You there, Johnny?"

"I'm here."

"I always know when I'm telling you stuff you don't like," she said brightly, "because it's the only time you ever shut up. You get all broody."

"Well, I'm here," he repeated heavily, and fell silent again, hoping she would change the subject. She didn't, of course.

"You did three or four of those essays because someone asked for them, I don't remember who—"

A miracle, he had thought. *She doesn't remember who.*

"—and I'm sure you would have stopped there, except by then you were getting queries from other editors. It didn't surprise me a bit. Those essays were *good.*"

He was silent this time, not to indicate disinterest or disapproval but because he was thinking back, trying to remember if they *had* been any good. Terry couldn't be trusted a hundred per cent when it came to such questions, but you couldn't throw her conclusions out of court without a hearing, either. As a fiction-writer she'd been of the "I saw a bird at sunrise and my heart leaped up" school, but as a critic she had been tough as nails and capable of insights which were spooky, almost like telepathy. One of the things that had attracted him to her (although he supposed the fact that she had the best breasts in America back in those days had helped matters along) was the dichotomy between what she wanted to do—write fiction—and what she was *able* to do, which was to write criticism that could cut like a diamond chip.

As for the so-called American Heart Essays, the only one he could remember clearly after all these years was "Death on the Second Shift." It had been about a father and son working together in a Pittsburgh steel-mill. The father had had a heart-attack and died in his son's arms on the third day of Johnny Marinville's four-day research junket. He had meant to focus on an entirely different aspect of millwork, but had changed course at once, and without a second thought. The result had been a wretchedly sentimental piece—the fact that every word was true hadn't changed that in the slightest—but it had also been a tremendously *popular* piece. The man who'd edited it for *Life* dropped him a note six weeks later and said it had generated the fourth-largest volume of letters in the magazine's history.

Other stuff started to come back to him—titles, mostly, things like "Feeding the Flames" and "A Kiss on Lake Saranac." Terrible titles, but . . . *fourth-largest volume of letters.*

Hmmmm.

Where might those old essays be? In the Marinville Collection at Fordham? Possible. Hell, they might even be in the attic of the cottage in Connecticut. He wouldn't mind a look at them. Maybe they could be updated . . . or . . . or . . .

Something began to nibble at the back of his mind.

"Do you still have your scoot, Johnny?"

"Huh?" He barely heard her.

"Your scoot. Your ride. Your *motorcycle.*"

"Sure," he said. "It's stored at that garage out in Westport we used to use. You know the one."

"Gibby's?"

"Yeah, Gibby's. Someone different owns it now, but it used to be Gibby's Garage, yeah." He had been blind-sided by a brilliantly textured memory: he and Terry, fully clothed and petting like mad behind Gibby's Garage one afternoon in . . . well, a long time ago, leave it at that. Terry had been wearing a pair of tight blue shorts. He doubted if her mother would have approved of them, God, no, but he himself had thought those discount-store specials made her look like the Queen of the Western World. Her ass was only good, but her *legs* . . . man, those legs had gone not just up to her chin but all the way out to Arcturus and beyond. How had they gotten out there in the first place, among the cast-off tires and rusty engine parts, standing hip-deep in sunflowers and feeling each other up? He couldn't remember, but he remembered the rich curve of her breast in his hand, and how she'd gripped the belt-loops of his jeans when he cried out against her neck, hauling him closer so he could come tight and hard against her taut belly.

He dropped a hand into his lap and wasn't exactly surprised at what he found there. Say, folks, Frampton comes alive.

". . . new bunch, or maybe even a book."

He settled his hand firmly back on the arm of his chair. "Huh? What?"

"Are you going deaf as well as senile?"

"No. I was remembering one time with you behind Gibby's. Making out."

"Oh. In the sunflowers, right?"

"Right."

There was a long pause when she might have been considering some further comment on that interlude. Johnny was almost hoping for one. Instead, she went back to her previous scripture.

"I said maybe you ought to drive across country on your bike before you get too old to work the footgears, or start drinking again and splash yourself all over the Black Hills."

"Are you out of your mind? I haven't been on that thing in three years, and I have no intention of getting back on, Terry. My eyesight sucks—"

"So get a stronger pair of glasses—"

"—and my reflexes are shot. John Cheever may or may not have died of alcoholism, but John Gardner *definitely* went out on a motorcycle. Had an argument with a tree. He lost. It happened on a road in Pennsylvania. One I've driven myself."

Terry wasn't listening. She was one of the few people in the world who felt perfectly comfortable ignoring him and letting her own thoughts carry her away. He supposed that was another reason he'd divorced her. He didn't like being ignored, especially by a woman.

"You could cross the country on your motorcycle and collect material for a new bunch of essays," she was saying. She sounded both excited and amused. "If you front-loaded the best of the early bunch—as Part One, you know—you'd have a pretty good-sized book. *American Heart, 1966–1996,* essays by John Edward Marinville." She giggled. "Who knows? You might even get another good notice from Shelby Foote. That's the one you always liked the best, wasn't it?" She paused for his reply, and when it didn't come, she asked him if he was there, first lightly, then with a little concern.

"Yes," he said. "I'm here." He was suddenly glad he was sitting down. "Listen, Terry, I have to go. I've got an appointment."

"New lady-friend?"

"Podiatrist," he said, thinking Foote, thinking foot. That name was like the final number in a bank-vault combination. Click, and the door swings open.

"Well, take care of yourself," she said. "And honest to God, Johnny, think about getting back to AA. I mean, what can it hurt?"

"Nothing, I suppose," he said, thinking about Shelby Foote, who had once called John Edward Marinville the only living American writer of John Steinbeck's stature, and Terry was right—of all the praisenuggets he'd ever gotten, that was the one he liked the best.

"Right, nothing." She paused. "Johnny, *are* you all right? Cause you sound like you're hardly there."

"Fine. Say hello to the kids for me."

"I always do. They usually respond with what my ma used to call potty-words, but I always do. Bye."

He hung up without looking at the telephone, and when it fell off the edge of the desk and onto the floor, he still didn't look around. John Steinbeck had crossed the country with his dog in a makeshift camper. Johnny had a barely used 1340-cc Harley-Davidson Softail stored out in Connecticut. Not *American Heart*. She was wrong about that, and not just because it was the name of a Jeff Bridges movie from a few years back. Not *American Heart* but—

"*Travels with Harley,*" he murmured.

It was a ridiculous title, a *laughable* title, like a *Mad* magazine parody . . . but was it any worse than an essay titled "Death on the Second Shift" or "Feeding the Flames"? He thought not . . . and he felt the title would work, would rise above its punny origins. He had always trusted his intuitions, and he hadn't had one as strong as this in years. He could cross the country on his red-and-cream Softail, from the Atlantic where it touched Connecticut to the Pacific where it touched California. A book of essays that might cause the critics to entirely rethink their image of him, a book of essays that might even get him back on the bestseller lists, if . . . *if* . . .

"If it was bighearted," he said. His heart was thumping hard in his chest, but for once the feel of that didn't scare him. "Bighearted like *Blue Highways*. Bighearted like . . . well, like Steinbeck."

Sitting there in his office chair with the telephone burring harshly at his feet, what Johnny Marinville had seen was nothing less than redemption. A way out.

He had scooped the telephone up and called his agent, his fingers flying over the buttons.

"Bill," he said, "it's Johnny. I was just sitting here, thinking about some essays I wrote when I was a kid, and I had a fantastic idea. It's going to sound crazy at first, but hear me out . . ."

4

As Johnny made his way up the sandy slope to the highway, trying not to pant too much, he saw that the guy standing behind his Harley and writing down the plate number was the biggest damned chunk of cop he had ever seen—six-six at least, and at least two hundred and seventy pounds on the hoof.

"Afternoon, Officer," Johnny said. He looked down at himself and saw a tiny dark spot on the crotch of his Levi's. *No matter how much you jump and dance,* he thought.

"Sir, are you aware that parking a vehicle on a state road is against the law?" the cop asked without looking up.

"No, but I hardly think—"

—*it can be much of a problem on a road as deserted as U.S. 50* was how he meant to finish, and in the haughty "How dare you question my judgement?" tone that he had been using on underlings and service people for years, but then he saw something that changed his mind. There was blood on the right cuff and sleeve of the cop's shirt, quite a lot of it, drying now to a maroon glaze. He had probably finished moving some large piece of roadkill off the highway not very long ago—likely a deer or an elk hit by a speeding semi. That would explain both the blood and the bad temper. The shirt looked like a dead loss; that much blood would never come out.

"Sir?" the cop asked sharply. He had finished writing down the plate number now but went on looking at the bike, his blond eyebrows drawn together, his mouth scrimped flat. It was as if he didn't want to look at the bike's owner, as if he knew that would only make him feel lousier than he did already. "You were saying?"

"Nothing, Officer," Johnny said. He spoke in a neutral tone, not humble but not haughty, either. He didn't want to cross this big lug when he was clearly having a bad day.

Still without looking up, his notepad strangled in one hand and his gaze fixed severely on the Harley's taillight, the cop said: "It's also against the law to relieve yourself within sight of a state road. Did you know *that*?"

"No, I'm sorry," Johnny said. He felt a wild urge to laugh bubbling around in his chest and suppressed it.

"Well, it is. Now, I'm going to let you go . . ." He looked up for the first time, looked at Johnny, and his eyes widened. ". . . go with a warning this time, but . . ."

He trailed off, eyes now as wide as a kid's when the circus parade comes thumping down the street in a swirl of clowns and trombones. Johnny knew the look, although he had never expected to see it out here in the Nevada desert, and on the face of a gigantic Scandahoovian cop who looked as if his reading tastes might run the gamut from *Playboy*'s Party Jokes to *Guns and Ammo* magazine.

A fan, he thought. *I'm out here in the big nowhere between Ely and Austin, and I've found a by-God fan.*

He couldn't wait to tell Steve Ames about this when they met up in Austin tonight. Hell, he might call him on the cellular later on this afternoon . . . if the cellulars worked out here, that was. Now that he thought about it, he supposed they didn't. The battery in his was up, he'd had it on the charger all last night, but he hadn't actually talked to Steve on the damned thing since leaving Salt Lake City. In truth he wasn't all that crazy about the cellulars. He didn't think they actually *did* cause cancer, that was probably just more tabloid scare-stuff, but . . .

"Holy shit," the cop muttered. His right hand, the one below the bloodstained cuff and sleeve, went up to his right cheek. For one bizarre moment he looked to Johnny like a pro football lineman doing a Jack Benny riff. "Ho-lee *shit.*"

"What's the trouble, Officer?" Johnny asked. He was, with some difficulty, suppressing a smile. One thing hadn't changed over the years: he loved to be recognized. God, how he loved it.

"You're . . . JohnEdwardMarinville!" the cop gasped, running it all together, as if he really had only one name, like Pelé or Cantinflas. The cop was now starting to grin himself, and Johnny thought, *Oh Mr. Policeman, what big teeth you have.* "I mean, you *are*, aren't you? You wrote *Delight*! And, oh shit, *Song of the Hammer*! I'm standing *right next* to the guy who wrote *Song of the Hammer*!" And then he did something which Johnny found genuinely endearing: reached out and touched the sleeve of his motorcycle jacket, as if to prove that the man wearing it was actually real. "Ho-lee *shit!*"

"Well, yes, I'm Johnny Marinville," he said, speaking in the modest tones he reserved for these occasions (and these occasions only, as a rule). "Although I have to tell you that I've never been recognized by someone who's just watched me take a leak by the side of the road."

"Oh, forget *that*," the cop said, and seized Johnny's hand. For just a moment before the cop's fingers closed over his, Johnny saw that the man's hand was also smeared with half-dried blood; both lifeline and loveline stood out a dark, liverish red. Johnny tried to keep his smile in place as they shook, and thought he did pretty well, but he was aware that the corners of his mouth seemed to have gained weight. *It's getting on me,* he thought. *And there won't be anyplace to wash it off before Austin.*

"Man," the cop was saying, "you are one of my favorite writers! I mean, gosh, *Song of the Hammer* . . . I know the critics didn't like it, but what do they know?"

"Not much," Johnny said. He wished the cop would let go of his hand, but the cop was apparently one of those people who shook for punctuation and emphasis as well as greeting. Johnny could feel the latent strength in the cop's grip; if the big guy squeezed down, his favorite writer would be keyboarding his new book lefthanded, at least for the first month or two.

"Not much, damned straight! *Song of the Hammer*'s the best book about Vietnam I ever read. Forget Tim O'Brien, Robert Stone—"

"Well, thank you, thanks very much."

The cop finally loosened his grip and Johnny retrieved his hand. He wanted to look down at it, see how much blood was on it, but this clearly wasn't the time. The cop was sticking his abused notepad into his back pocket again and staring at Johnny in a wide-eyed, intense way that was actually a little disturbing. It was as if he feared Johnny would disappear like a mirage if he so much as blinked.

"What are you doing out here, Mr. Marinville? Gosh! I thought you lived back East!"

"Well, I do, but—"

"And this is no kind of transportation for a . . . a . . . well, I've got to say it: for a *national resource.* Why, do you realize what the ratio of drivers-to-accidents on motorcycles is? Computed on a road-hours basis? I can tell you that because I'm a wolf and we get a circular every month from the National Safety Council. It's one accident per four hundred and sixty drivers per day. That sounds good, I know, until you consider the ratio of drivers-to-accidents on passenger vehicles. That's one in *twenty-seven thousand* per day. That's some big difference. It makes you think, doesn't it?"

"Yes." Thinking, *Did he say something about being a wolf, did I hear that?* "Those statistics are pretty . . . pretty . . ." *Pretty what? Come on, Marinville, get it together. If you can spend an hour with a hostile bitch from* Ms. *magazine and still not take a drink, surely you can deal with this guy. He's only trying to show his concern for you, after all.* "They're pretty impressive," he finished.

"So what *are* you doing out here? And on such an unsafe mode of transportation?"

"Gathering material." Johnny found his eyes dropping to the cop's blood-stiffened right sleeve and forcibly dragged them back up to his sunburned face. He doubted if many of the people on this guy's beat gave him a hard time; he looked like he could eat nails and spit razor-wire, even though he really didn't have the right skin for this climate.

"For a new novel?" The cop was excited. Johnny looked briefly at the man's chest, hunting for a name-tag, but there was none.

"Well, a new book, anyway. Can I ask you something, Officer?"

"Sure, yeah, but I ought to be asking *you* the questions, I got about a gajillion of em. I never thought . . . out in the middle of nowhere and I meet . . . ho-lee *shit!*"

Johnny grinned. It was hotter than hell out here and he wanted to get moving before Steve was on his ass—he hated looking into the rearview and seeing that big yellow truck back there, it broke the mood, somehow—but it was hard not to be moved by the man's artless enthusiasm, especially when it was directed at a subject which Johnny himself regarded with respect, wonder, and yes, awe.

"Well, since you're obviously familiar with my work, what would you think of a book of essays about life in contemporary America?"

"By you?"

"By me. A kind of loose travelogue called"—he took a deep breath—"*Travels with Harley*"?

He was prepared for the cop to look puzzled, or to guffaw the way people did at the punchline of a joke. The cop did neither. He simply looked back down at the tail-light of Johnny's bike, one hand rubbing his chin (it was the chin of a Bernie Wrightson comic-book hero, square and cleft), brow furrowed, considering carefully. Johnny took the opportunity to peek surreptitiously at his own hand. There was blood on it, all right, quite a lot. Mostly on the back and smeared across the fingernails. Uck.

Then the cop looked up and stunned him by saying exactly what Johnny himself had been thinking over the last two days of monotonous desert driving. "It *could* work," he said, "but the cover ought to be a photo of you on your drag, here. A *serious* picture, so folks'd know you weren't trying to make fun of John Steinbeck . . . or your own self, for that matter."

"That's *it*!" Johnny cried, barely restraining himself from clapping the big cop on the back. "That's the great danger, that people should go in thinking it's some kind of . . . of weird *joke*. The cover should convey seriousness of purpose . . . maybe even a certain *grimness* . . . what would you think of just the bike? A photo of the bike, maybe sepia-toned? Sitting in the middle of some country highway . . . or even out here in the desert, on the centerline of Highway 50 . . . shadow stretching off to the side . . ." The absurdity of having this discussion out here, with a towering cop who had been about to issue him a warning for pissing on the tumbleweeds, wasn't lost on him, but it didn't cut into his excitement, either.

And once again the cop told him exactly what he wanted to hear.

"No! Good gosh, no. It's got to be you."

"Actually, I think so, too," Johnny said. "Sitting on the bike . . . maybe with the kickstand down and my feet up on the pegs . . . casual, you know . . . casual, but . . ."

". . . but *real*," the cop said. He looked up at Johnny, his gray eyes forbidding, then back down at the bike again. "Casual but *real*. No smile. Don't you *dare* smile, Mr. Marinville."

"No smile," Johnny agreed, thinking, *This guy is a genius.*

"And a little distant," the cop said. "Looking off. Like you were thinking of all the miles you'd been—"

"Yeah, and all the miles I've still got to go." Johnny looked up at the horizon to get a feel for that look—the old warrior gazing west, a Cormac McCarthy kind of deal—and again saw the vehicle parked off the road a mile or two up. His long-range vision was still pretty good, and the sunglare had shifted enough for him to be almost sure it was an RV. "Literal and metaphorical miles."

"Yep, both kinds," this amazing cop said. "*Travels with Harley.* I like it. It's ballsy. And of course, I'd read *anything* you wrote, Mr. Marinville. Novels, essays, poems . . . hell, your laundry list."

"Thanks," Johnny said, touched. "I appreciate that. You'll probably never know how much. The last year or so has been difficult for me. A lot of doubt. Questioning my own identity, and my purpose."

"I know a little about those things myself," the cop said.

"You might not think so, guy like me, but I do. Why, if you knew the day I've put in already . . . Mr. Marinville, could I possibly have your autograph?"

"Of course, it would be a pleasure," Johnny said, and took his own pad out of his back pocket. He opened it and paged past notes, directions, route numbers, fragments of map in blurred soft pencil (these latter had been drawn by Steve Ames, who had quickly realized that his famous client, although still able to ride his cycle with a fair degree of safety, ended up lost and fuming in even small cities without help). At last he found a blank page. "What's your name, Offi—"

He was interrupted by a long, trembling howl that chilled his blood . . . not just because it was clearly the sound of a wild animal but because it was *close.* The notepad dropped from his hand and he turned on his heels so quickly that he staggered. Standing just off the south edge of the road, not fifty yards away, was a mangy canine with thin legs and scanty, starved-looking sides. Its gray pelt was tangled with burdocks and there was an ugly red sore on its foreleg, but Johnny barely noticed these things. What fascinated him was the creature's muzzle, which seemed to be grinning, and its yellow eyes, which looked both stupid and cunning.

"My God," he murmured. "What's that? Is it a—"

"Coyote," the cop said, pronouncing it *ki-yote.* "Some people out here call em desert wolves."

That's what he said, Johnny thought. *Something about seeing a coyote, a desert wolf. You just misunderstood.* This idea relieved him even though a part of his mind didn't believe it at all.

The cop took a step toward the coyote, then another. He paused, then took a third. The coyote stood its ground but began to shiver all over. Urine squirted from under its chewed-looking flank. A gust of wind turned the paltry stream into a scatter of droplets.

When the cop took a fourth step toward it, the coyote raised its scuffed muzzle and howled again, a long, ululating sound that made Johnny's arms ripple with goose-flesh and his balls pull up.

"Hey, don't get it going," he said to the cop. "That's *très* creepy."

The cop ignored him. He was looking at the coyote, which was now looking intently back at him with its yellow gaze. *"Tak,"* the cop said. *"Tak ah lah."*

The wolf went on staring at him, as if it understood this Indian-sounding gibberish, and the goosebumps on Johnny's arms stayed up. The wind gusted again, blowing his dropped notepad over onto the shoulder of the road, where it came to rest against a jutting chunk of rock. Johnny didn't notice. His pad and the autograph he'd intended to give the cop were, for the moment, the furthest things from his mind.

This goes in the book, he thought. *Everything else I've seen is still up for grabs, but this goes in. Rock solid. Rock goddam solid.*

"Tak," the cop said again, and clapped his hands together sharply, once. The coyote turned and loped away, running on those scrawny legs with a speed Johnny never would have expected. The big man in the khaki uniform watched until the coyote's gray pelt had merged into the general dirty gray of the desert. It didn't take long.

"Gosh, aren't they ugly?" the cop said. "And just lately they're thicker'n ticks on a blanket. You don't see em in the morning or early afternoon, when it's hottest, but late afternoon . . . evening . . . toward dark . . ." He shook his head as if to say *There you go.*

"What did you *say* to it?" Johnny asked. "That was *amazing.* Was it Indian? Some Indian dialect?"

The big cop laughed. "Don't know any Indian dialect," he said. "Hell, don't know any *Indians.* That was just baby-talk, like oogie-woogie, snookie-wookums."

"But it was *listening* to you!"

"No, it was *looking* at me," the cop said, and gave Johnny a rather forbidding frown, as if he were daring the other man to contradict him. "I stole its eyes, that's all. The holes of its eyes. I suppose most of that animal-tamer stuff is for the birds, but when it comes to slinkers like desert wolves . . . well, if you steal their eyes, it doesn't matter what you say. They're usually not dangerous unless they're rabid, anyway. You just don't want them to smell fear on you. Or blood."

Johnny glanced at the big cop's right sleeve again and wondered if the blood on it was what had drawn the coyote.

"And you don't ever, *ever* want to face them when they're in a pack. Especially a pack with a strong leader. They're fearless then. They'll go after an elk and run it until its heart bursts. Sometimes just for the fun of it." He paused. "Or a man."

"Really," Johnny said. "That's . . ." He couldn't say *très creepy,* he'd already used that one. ". . . fascinating."

"It is, isn't it?" the big cop said, and smiled. "Desert lore. Scripture in the wasteland. The resonance of lonely places."

Johnny stared at him, jaw dropping slightly. All at once his friend the policeman sounded like Paul Bowles on a bad-karma day.

He's trying to impress you, that's all—it's cocktail chatter without the cocktail party. You've seen and heard it all a thousand times before.

Maybe. But he still could have done without it in this context. Somewhere off in the distance another howl rose, trembling the air like an auditory heat-haze. It wasn't the coyote which had just run off, Johnny was sure of that. This howl had come from farther away, perhaps in answer to the first.

"Oh hey, time out!" the cop exclaimed. "You better stow that, Mr. Marinville!"

"Huh?" For one exceedingly strange moment he had the idea the cop was talking about his thoughts, as if he practiced telepathy as well as elliptical pretentiousness, but the big man had turned back to the motorcycle again, and was pointing at the lefthand saddlebag. Johnny saw that one sleeve of his new poncho—bright orange for safety in bad weather—was hanging out of it like a tongue.

How come I didn't see that when I stopped to take a leak? he wondered. *How could I have missed it?* And there was something else. He'd stopped for gas in Pretty Nice, and after he'd topped the Harley's tanks, he'd unbuckled that saddlebag to get his Nevada map. He had checked the mileage from there to Austin, then refolded the map and put it back. Then he had rebuckled the saddlebag. He was sure he had, but it was certainly unbuckled now.

He had been an intuitive man all his life; it was intuition, not planning, that had been responsible for his best work as a writer. The drinking and the drugs had dulled those intuitions but not destroyed them, and they had come back—not all the way, at least not yet, but some—since he'd gotten straight. Now, looking at the poncho dangling out of the unbuckled saddlebag, Johnny felt alarm bells start going off in his head.

The cop did it.

That was completely senseless, but intuition told him it was true just the same. The cop had unbuckled the saddlebag and pulled his orange poncho partway out of it while Johnny had been north of the road with his back turned, taking a piss. And for most of their conversation, the cop had deliberately stood so Johnny couldn't see the hanging poncho. The guy wasn't as starry-eyed about meeting his favorite author as he had seemed. Maybe not starry-eyed at all. And he had an agenda here.

What agenda? Would you mind telling me that? What *agenda?*

Johnny didn't know, but he didn't like it. He didn't like that weird Yoda shit with the coyote much, either.

"Well?" the cop asked. He was smiling, and here was another thing not to like. It wasn't a goony I'm-just-a-fan-in-love smile anymore, if it ever had been; there was something cold about it. Maybe contemptuous.

"Well, what?"

"Are you going to take care of it or not? *Tak!*"

His heart jumped. "*Tak*, what does that mean?"

"I didn't say *tak*, you did. *You* said *tak*."

The cop crossed his arms and stood smiling at him.

I want out of here, Johnny thought.

Yes, that was pretty much the bottom line, wasn't it? And if that meant following orders, so be it. This little interlude, which had started off being funny in a nice way had suddenly gotten funny in a way that wasn't so nice . . . as if a cloud had gone over the sun and a previously pleasant day had darkened, grown sinister.

Suppose he means to hurt me? He's pretty clearly a beer or two short of a sixpack.

Well, he answered himself, *suppose he does? What are you going to do about it? Complain to the local ki-yotes?*

His overtrained imagination served up an extremely ugly image: the cop digging a hole in the desert, while in the shade of his cruiser lay the body of a man who had once won the National Book Award and fucked America's most famous actress. He negated the image while it was little more than a sketch, not so much out of fear as by virtue of an odd protective arrogance. Men like him weren't murdered, after all. They sometimes took their own lives, but they weren't murdered, especially by psychotic fans. That was pulp-fiction bullshit.

There was John Lennon, of course, but—

He moved to his saddlebag, catching a whiff of the cop as he went by. For one moment Johnny had a brilliant but unfocused memory of his drunken, abusive, crazily funny father, who had always seemed to smell exactly as this cop did now: Old Spice on top, sweat underneath the aftershave, plain old black-eyed meanness under everything, like the dirt floor in an old cellar.

Both of the saddlebag's buckles were undone. Johnny raised the fringed top, aware that he could still smell sweat and Old Spice. The cop was standing right at his shoulder. Johnny reached for the hanging arm of the poncho, then stopped as he saw what was lying on top of his pile of Triple-A maps. Part of him was shocked, but most of him wasn't even surprised. He looked at the cop. The cop was looking into the saddlebag.

"Oh, Johnny," he said regretfully. "This is disappointing. This is *très* disappointing."

He reached in and picked up the gallon-sized Baggie lying on the pile of maps. Johnny didn't have to sniff to know that the stuff inside wasn't Cherry Blend. Stuck on the front of the Baggie, like someone's idea of a joke, was a round yellow smile sticker.

"That's not mine," Johnny Marinville said. His voice sounded tired and distant, like the message on a very old phone answering machine. "That's not mine and you know it's not, don't you? Because you put it there."

"Oh yeah, blame the cops," the big man said, "just like in your pinko-liberal books, right? Man, I smelled the dope the second you got close to me. You *reek* of it! *Tak!*"

"Look—" Johnny began.

"Get in the car, pinko! Get in the car, fag!" The voice indignant, the gray eyes full of laughter.

It's a joke, Johnny thought. *Some kind of crazy practical joke.*

Then, from somewhere off to the southwest, more howls rose—a tangle of them, this time—and when the cop's eyes rolled in that direction and he grinned, Johnny felt a scream rising in his throat and had to press his lips together to keep it in. There was no joke in the big cop's expression as he looked toward that sound; it was the look of a man who is totally insane. And Jesus, he was so fucking *big.*

"My children of the desert!" the cop said. "The *can toi*! What music they make!"

He laughed, looked down at the Baggie of dope in his big hand, shook his head, and laughed even harder. Johnny stood watching him, his assurance that men like him were never murdered suddenly gone.

"*Travels with Harley,*" the cop said. "Do you know what a stupid name for a book that is? What a stupid *concept* it is? And to plunder the literary legacy of *John Steinbeck* . . . a writer whose shoes you aren't fit to lick . . . that makes me *mad.*"

And before Johnny knew what was happening, a huge silver flare of pain went off in his head. He was aware of staggering backward with his hands clapped over his face and hot blood gushing through his fingers, of flailing his arms, of thinking *I'm all right, I'm not going to fall over, I'm all right,* and then he was lying on his side in the road, screaming up at the blue socket of the sky. The nose under his fingers no longer felt on straight; it seemed to be lying against his left cheek. He had a deviated septum from all the coke he had done in the eighties, and he remembered his doctor telling him he ought to get that fixed before he ran into a sign or a swinging door or something and it just exploded. Well, it hadn't been a door or a sign, and it hadn't exactly exploded, but it had certainly undergone a swift and radical change. He thought these things in what seemed to be perfectly coherent fashion even while his mouth went on screaming.

"In fact, it makes me *furious,*" the cop said, and kicked him high up on the left thigh. The pain came in a sheet that sank in like acid and turned the big muscles in his leg to stone. Johnny rolled back and forth, now clutching his leg instead of his nose, scraping his cheek against the asphalt of Highway 50, screaming, gasping, pulling sand down his throat and coughing it harshly back out when he tried to scream again.

"The truth is it makes me *sick with rage,*" the cop said, and kicked Johnny's ass, high up toward the small of his back. Now the pain was too enormous to be borne; surely he would pass out. But he didn't. He only writhed and crawdaddied on the broken white line, screaming and bleeding from his broken nose and coughing out sand while in the distance coyotes howled at the thickening shadows stretching out from the distant mountains.

"Get up," the cop said. "On your feet, Lord Jim."

"I can't," Johnny Marinville sobbed, pulling his legs up to his chest and crossing his arms over his belly, this defensive posture dimly remembered from the '68 Democratic convention in Chicago, and from even before that, from a lecture he had attended in Philadelphia, prior to the first Freedom Rides down into Mississippi. He had meant to go along on one of those—not only was it a great cause, it was the stuff of which great fiction was made—but in the end, something else had come up. Probably his cock, at the sight of a raised skirt.

"On your feet, you piece of shit. You're in *my* house now, the house of the wolf and the scorpion, and you better not forget it."

"I can't, you broke my leg, Jesus Christ you hurt me so *bad*—"

"Your leg's not broken and you don't know what being hurt is yet. Now get up."

"I can't. I really—"

The gunshot was deafening, the ricochet of the slug off the road a monstrous wasp-whine, and Johnny was on his feet even before he was a hundred per cent sure he wasn't dead. He stood with one foot in the eastbound lane and one in the westbound, drunk-swaying back and forth. The lower half of his face was covered with blood. Sand had stuck in it, making little curls and commas on his lips and cheeks and chin.

"Hey bigshot, you wet your pants," the cop said.

Johnny looked down and saw he had. *No matter how much you jump and dance,* he thought. His left thigh throbbed like an infected tooth. His ass was still mostly numb—it felt like a frozen slab of meat. He supposed he should be grateful, all things considered. If the cop had kicked him a little higher that second time, he might have paralyzed him.

"You're a sorry excuse for a writer, and you're a sorry excuse for a man," the cop said. He was holding a huge revolver in one hand. He looked down at the Baggie of pot, which he still held in the other, and shook his head disgustedly. "I know that not just by what you say, but by the mouth you say it out of. In fact, if I looked at your loose-lipped and self-indulgent mouth for too long at a stretch, I'd kill you right here. I wouldn't be able to help myself."

Coyotes howled in the distance, *wh-wh-WHOOOO,* like something that belonged in the soundtrack of an old John Wayne movie.

"You did enough," Johnny said in a foggy, stuffy voice.

"Not yet," the cop said, and smiled. "But the nose is a start. It actually improves your looks. Not much, but a little." He opened the back door of his cruiser. As he did, Johnny wondered how long this little comedy had taken. He had absolutely no idea, but not one car or truck had passed while it was going on. Not one. "Get in, bigshot."

"Where are you taking me?"

"Where do you *think* I'd take a self-indulgent pinko-pothead asshole like you? To the old *calabozo.* Now get in the car."

Johnny got in the car. As he did, he touched the right breast pocket of his motorcycle jacket.

The cellular phone was in there.

5

He couldn't sit on his bottom, it hurt too much, so he leaned over on his right thigh, one hand cupped loosely over his throbbing nose. It felt like something alive and malevolent, something that was sinking deep, poisonous stingers into his flesh, but for the time being he was able to ignore it. *Let the cellular work,* he prayed, speaking to a God he had made fun of for most of his creative life, most recently in a story called "Heaven-Sent Weather," which had been published in *Harper's* magazine to generally favorable comment. *Please let the damned phone work, God, and please let Steve have his ears on.* Then, realizing all of that was getting the cart quite a bit ahead of the horse, he added a third request: *Please give me a chance to use the phone in the first place, okay?*

As if in answer to this part of his prayer, the big cop passed the driver's door of his cruiser without even looking at it and walked to Johnny's motorcycle. He put Johnny's helmet on his own head, then swung one leg over the seat—he was very tall, so it was actually more of a step than a swing—and a moment later the Harley's engine exploded into life. The cop stood astride the seat, unbuckled helmet straps hanging, seeming to dwarf the Harley with his own less lovely bulk. He twisted the throttle four or five times, gunning the motor as if he liked the sound. Then he rocked the Harley upright, kicked back the center-stand, and toed the gearshift down into first. Moving cautiously to start with, reminding Johnny a little of himself when he had taken the bike out of storage and ridden it in traffic for the first time in three years, the cop descended the side of the road. He used the hand-brake and paddled along with his feet, watching intently for hazards and obstacles. Once he was on the desert floor he accelerated, changing rapidly up through the gears and weaving around clumps of sagebrush.

Run into a gopher-hole, you sadistic fuck, Johnny thought, sniffing gingerly through his plugged and throbbing nose. *Hit something hard. Crash and burn.*

"Don't waste your time on him," he mumbled, and used his thumb to pop the snap over the right breast pocket of his motorcycle jacket. He took out the Motorola cellular phone (the cellulars had been Bill Harris's idea, maybe the only good idea his agent had had in the last four years) and flipped it open. He stared down at the display, breath held, now praying for an *S* and two bars. *Come on, God, please,* he thought, sweat trickling down his cheeks, blood still leaking out of his swollen, leaning nose. *Got to be an* S *and two bars, anything less and I might as well use this thing for a suppository.*

The phone beeped. What came up in the window on the left side of the display was an *S,* which stood for "service," and one bar.

Just one.

"No, please," he moaned. "Please, don't do this to me, just one more, one more *please!*"

He shook the phone in frustration . . . and saw he had neglected to pull up the antenna. He did, and a second bar appeared above the first. It flickered, went out, then reappeared, still flickery but *there.*

"Yes!" Johnny whispered. "*Yesss!*" He jerked his head up and stared out the window. His sweat-circled eyes peered through a tangle of long gray hair—there was blood in it now—like the eyes of some hunted animal peering out of its hole. The cop had brought the Softail to a stop about three hundred yards out in the scree. He stepped off and then stepped away, letting the bike fall over. The engine died. Even in this situation, Johnny felt a twinge of outrage. The Harley had brought him all the way across the country without a single missed stroke of its sweet American engine, and it hurt to see it treated with such absent disdain.

"You crazy shit," he whispered. He snuffled back half-congealed blood, spat a jellied wad of it onto the cruiser's paper-littered floor, and looked down at the telephone again. On the row of buttons at the bottom, second from the right, was one which read NAME/MENU. Steve had programmed this function for him just before they had set out. Johnny punched the button, and his agent's first name appeared in the window: BILL.

Pushed it again and TERRY appeared. Pushed it again and JACK appeared—Jack Appleton, his editor at FS&G. Dear God, why had he put all these people ahead of Steve Ames? Steve was his *lifeline.*

Down on the desert floor three hundred yards away, the insane cop had taken off the helmet and was kicking sand over Johnny's '86 Harley drag. At this distance he looked like a kid pulling a tantrum. That was fine. If he intended to cover the whole thing, Johnny would have plenty of time to make his call . . . if the phone cooperated, that was. The ROAM light was flashing, and that was a good sign, but the second transmission-bar was still flickering.

"Come on, come on," Johnny said to the cellular phone in his shaking, blood-grimy hands. "*Please,* sweetheart, okay? *Please.*" He punched the NAME/MENU button again and STEVE appeared. He dropped his thumb onto the SEND button and squeezed it. Then he held the phone to his ear, bending over even farther to the right and peering out of the bottom of the window as he did so. The cop was still kicking sand over the Harley's engine-block.

The phone began to ring in Johnny's ear, but he knew he wasn't home free yet. He had tapped into the Roamer network, that was all. He was still a step away from Steve Ames. A long step.

"Come on, come on, come on . . ." A drop of sweat ran into his eye. He used a knuckle to wipe it away.

The phone stopped ringing. There was a click. "Welcome to the Western Roaming Network!" a cheery robot voice said. "Your call is being routed! Thank you for your patience and have a nice day!"

"Never mind the seventies shit, just hurry the fuck up," Johnny whispered.

Silence from the phone. In the desert, the cop stepped back from the bike, looking at it as if trying to decide if he had done enough in the way of camouflage. In the dirty, paper-choked back seat of the cruiser, Johnny Marinville began to cry. He couldn't help it. In a bizarre way it was like wetting his pants again, only upside down. "No," he whispered. "No, not yet, you're not done yet, not with the wind blowing like it is, you better do a little more, please do a little more."

The cop stood there looking down at the bike, his shadow now seeming to stretch out across half a mile of desert, and Johnny peered at him through the bottom of the window with his clotted hair in his eyes and the phone mashed against his right ear. He let out a long, shaky sigh of relief as the cop stepped forward and began to kick sand again, this time spraying it over the Harley's handlebars.

In his ear the telephone began to ring, and this time the sound was scratchy and distant. If the signal was going through—and the quality of this ring seemed to indicate that it was—another Motorola telephone, this one on the dashboard of a Ryder truck somewhere between fifty and two hundred and fifty miles east of John Edward Marinville's current position, was now ringing.

Down in the desert, the cop went on kicking and kicking, burying the handlebars of Johnny's scoot.

Two rings . . . three rings . . . four . . .

He had one more, two at the most, before another robot voice came on the line and told him that the customer he was calling was either out of range or had left the vehicle. Johnny, still crying, closed his eyes. In the throbbing, red-tinged darkness behind his lids he saw the Ryder truck parked in front of a roadside gas station/general store just west of the Utah–Nevada state line. Steve was inside, buying a pack of his damned cigars and goofing with the counter girl, while outside, on the Ryder's dashboard, the cellular phone—Steve's half of the com-link Johnny's agent had insisted upon—rang in the empty cab.

Five rings . . .

And then, distant, almost lost in static but sounding like the voice of an angel bent down from heaven all the same, he heard Steve's flat West Texas drawl: "Hello . . . you . . . boss?"

An eastbound semi blew by outside, rocking the cruiser in its backwash. Johnny barely noticed, and made no attempt to flag the driver. He probably wouldn't have done so even if his attention hadn't been focused on the telephone and Steve's tenuous voice. The rig was doing seventy at least. What the hell was the driver going to see in the two-tenths of a second it would take him to pass the parked cruiser, especially through the thick dust matted on the windows?

He drew in breath through his nose and hawked back blood, ignoring the pain, wanting to clear his voice as much as he could.

"Steve! Steve, I'm in trouble. I'm in *bad* trouble!"

There was a heavy crackle of static in his ear and he was sure he'd lost Steve, but when it cleared he heard: ". . . up, boss? Say again!"

"Steve, it's Johnny! *Do you hear me?*"

". . . hear you . . . What's . . ." Another crackle. It almost completely buried the next word, but Johnny thought it might have been "trouble." *I hear you, what's the trouble?*

God, let that not just be wishful thinking. Please God.

The cop had stopped kicking sand again. He stepped away for another critical look at his handiwork, then turned and began to plod back toward the road, head down, hatbrim shading his face, hands plunged deep into his pockets. And then, with a sense of mounting horror, Johnny realized he had no idea what to tell Steve. All his attention had been focused on making the call, ramming it through by sheer willpower, if that was what it took.

Now what?

He had no clear idea of where he was, only that—

"I'm west of Ely on Highway 50," he said. More sweat ran

into his eyes, stinging. "I'm not sure how far west—forty miles at least, probably more. There's an RV pulled off the road a little farther up from me. There's a cop . . . not a state cop, a townie, I think, but I don't know which town . . . I didn't see it on the door . . . I don't even know his name . . ." He was talking faster and faster as the cop got closer and closer; soon he would be babbling.

Take it easy, he's still a hundred yards away, you've got plenty of time. For the love of God, just do what comes naturally—do what they pay you for, do what you've been doing all your life. Communicate, for Christ's sake!

But he had never had to do it *for* his life. To make money, to be known in the right circles, to occasionally raise his voice in the roar of the brave old lion, yes, all those things, but never for his literal *life*. And if the cop looked up out of his head-down plod and saw him . . . he was crouched down but the phone's antenna was sticking up, of course, it *had* to be sticking up . . .

"He took my bike, Steve. He took my bike and drove it out into the desert. He covered it up with sand, but the way the wind's blowing . . . it's out in the desert a mile or so east of the RV I told you about and north of the road. You might see it, if the sun's still up."

He swallowed.

"Call the cops—the *state* cops. Tell them I've been grabbed by a cop who's blond and huge—I mean, this guy's a fucking *giant*. Have you got that?"

Nothing from the phone but windy silence with an occasional burst of static knifing through it.

"Steve! Steve, are you there?"

No. He wasn't.

There was only one transmission-bar showing in the phone's display window now, and no one was there. He had lost the connection, and he'd been concentrating so hard on what he was saying that he had no idea when it had happened, or how much Steve might have heard.

Johnny, are you sure you got through to him at all?

That was Terry's voice, a voice he sometimes loved and sometimes hated. Now he hated it. Hated it worse than any voice he had ever heard in his life, it seemed. Hated it even worse for the sympathy he heard in it.

Are you sure you didn't just imagine the whole thing?

"No, he was there, he was there, sonofabitch was there," Johnny said. He heard the pleading quality in his own voice and hated that, too. "He *was,* you bitch. For a few seconds, at least."

Now the cop was only fifty yards away. Johnny shoved the antenna down with the heel of his left hand, flipped the mouthpiece closed, and tried to drop the phone back into his right pocket. The flap was closed. The phone fell into his lap, then bounced to the floor. He felt around frantically for it, at first finding nothing but crumpled papers—DARE anti-drug handouts, for the most part—and hamburger wrappers coated with ancient grease. His fingers closed on something narrow, not what he wanted, but even the brief glance he gave it before tossing it away chilled him. It was a little girl's plastic barrette.

Never mind it, you've got no time to think about what a kid might've been doing in the back of his car. Find your damn phone, he must almost be here—

Yes. Almost. He could hear the crunch-scuffle of the big cop's boots even over the wind, which had now grown strong enough to rock the cruiser on its springs when it gusted.

Johnny's hand found a nest of styrofoam coffee cups, and, amid them, his phone. He seized it, dropped it in his jacket pocket, and pushed the snap closed. When he sat up again, the cop was coming around the front of the car, bent over at the waist so he could peer through the windshield. His face was more sunburned than ever, almost blistered in places. In fact, his lower lip actually *was* blistered, Johnny saw, and there was another blistery spot at his right temple.

Good. That doesn't cross my eyes in the slightest.

The cop opened the driver's-side door, leaned in, and stared through the mesh between the front seat and the back. His nostrils flared as he sniffed. To Johnny, each one of them looked roughly the size of a bowling alley.

"Did you puke in the back of my cruiser, Lord Jim? Because if you did, the first thing you're gonna get when we hit town is a big old spoon."

"No," Johnny said. He could feel fresh blood trickling down his throat and his voice was fogging up again. "I dry-heaved, but I didn't puke." He was actually relieved by what the cop had said. *The first thing you're gonna get when we hit town* indicated that he didn't intend to drag him out of the car, blow his brains out, and bury him next to his scoot.

Unless he's trying to lull me. Soothe me down, make it easier for him to do . . . well, to do whatever.

"You scared?" the cop inquired, still leaning in and looking through the mesh. "Tell me the truth, Lord Jimmy, I'll know a lie. *Tak*!"

"Of course I'm scared." "Course" came out "gorse," as if he had a bad cold.

"Good." He dropped behind the wheel, took off the hat, looked at it. "Doesn't fit," he said. "Folk-singing bitch ruined the one that did. Never sang 'Leavin' on a Fucking Jet Plane,' either."

"Too bad," Johnny said, not having the slightest idea what the cop was talking about.

"Lips which lie are best kept silent," the cop said, tossing the hat that wasn't his over into the passenger seat. It landed on a tangle of meshy stuff that appeared studded with spikes. The seat, bowed into a tired curve by the cop's weight, settled against Johnny's left knee, squeezing it.

"Sit up!" Johnny yelled. *"You're crushing my leg! Sit up and let me pull it out! Jesus, you're killing me!"*

The cop made no reply and the pressure on Johnny's already outraged left leg increased. He seized it in both hands and tore it free of the sagging seat-back with an indrawn hiss of effort that pulled blood down his throat and started him dry-heaving for real.

"Bastard!" Johnny yelled, the word popping out in a red-misted coughing spasm before he could pull it back. The cop seemed not to notice that, either. He sat with his head lowered and his fingers tapping lightly on the wheel. His breath was wheezing in his throat, and for a moment Johnny wondered if the man was mocking him. He didn't think so. *I hope it's asthma,* he thought. *And I hope you choke on it.*

"Listen," he said, allowing none of that sentiment to enter his voice, "I need something for my dose . . . *nose.* It's killing me. Even an aspirin. Do you have an aspirin?"

The cop said nothing. Went on tapping the wheel with his head down, that was all.

Johnny opened his mouth to say something else, then closed it again. He was in terrible pain, all right, the worst he could remember, even worse than the gallstone he had passed in '89, but he still didn't want to die. And something in the cop's posture, as if he were very far away in his own head, deciding something important, suggested that death might be close.

So he kept silent and waited.

Time spun out. The shadows of the mountains grew a bit thicker and moved a bit closer, but the coyotes had fallen silent. The cop sat with his head lowered and his fingers tapping the sides of the wheel, seeming to meditate, not looking up when another semi went by headed east and a car passed them going west, swinging out to give the parked police-cruiser with the ticking roof-flashers a wide berth.

Then he picked up something which had been lying beside

him on the front seat: an old-fashioned shotgun with a double-trigger setup. The cop looked at it fixedly. "I guess that woman wasn't really a folk-singer," he said, "but she tried her best to kill me, no doubt about that. With this."

Johnny said nothing, only waited. His heart was beating slowly but very hard in his chest.

"You have never written a truly spiritual novel," the cop told him. He spoke slowly, enunciating each word with care. "It is your great unrecognized failing, and it is at the center of your petulant, self-indulgent behavior. You have no interest in your spiritual nature. You mock the God who created you, and by doing so you mortify your own *pneuma* and glorify the mud which is your *sarx*. Do you understand me?"

Johnny opened his mouth, then closed it again. To speak or not to speak, that was the question.

The cop solved the dilemma for him. Without looking up from the wheel, without so much as a glance into the rearview mirror, he placed the double barrels of the shotgun on his right shoulder and pointed them back through the wire mesh. Johnny moved instinctively, sliding to the left, trying to get away from those huge dark holes.

And although the cop still did not look up, the muzzles of the gun tracked him as precisely as a radar-controlled servo-motor.

He might have a mirror in his lap, Johnny thought, and then: *But what good would that do? He wouldn't see anything but the roof of the fucking car. What in the hell is going on here?*

"Answer me," the cop said. His voice was dark and brooding. His head was still bent. The hand not holding the shotgun continued to tap at the wheel, and another gust of wind hammered the cruiser, driving sand and alkali dust against the window in a fine spray. "Answer me *now.* I won't wait. I don't *have* to wait. There's always another one coming along. So . . . do you understand what I just told you?"

"Yes," Johnny said in a trembling voice. "*Pneuma* is the old Gnostic word for spirit. *Sarx* is the body. You said, correct me if I'm wrong—" *Just not with the shotgun, please don't correct me with the shotgun.* "—that I've ignored my spirit in favor of my body. And you could be right. You could very well be."

He moved to the right again. The shotgun muzzles tracked his movements precisely, although he could swear that the springs of the back seat made no sound beneath him and the cop could not see him unless he was using a television monitor or something.

"Don't toady to me," the cop said wearily. "That will only make your fate worse."

"I . . ." He licked his lips. "I'm sorry. I didn't mean to—"

"*Sarx* is not the body; *soma* is the body. *Sarx* is the *flesh* of the body. The body is made of flesh—as the word was reputedly made flesh by the birth of Jesus Christ—but the body is more than the flesh that makes it. The sum is greater than the parts. Is that so hard for an intellectual such as yourself to understand?"

The shotgun barrel, moving and moving. Tracking like an autogyro.

"I . . . I never . . ."

"Thought of it that way? Oh please. Even a spiritual *naïf* like you must understand that a chicken dinner is not a chicken. *Pneuma* . . . *soma* . . . *and s-s-s*—"

His voice had thickened and now he was hitching in breath, trying to talk as a person does only when trying to finish his thought before the sneeze arrives. He abruptly dropped the shotgun onto the seat again, gasped in a deep breath (the abused seat creaked backward, almost pinning Johnny's left knee again), and let fly. What came out of his mouth and nose was not mucus but blood and red filmy stuff that looked like nylon mesh. This stuff—raw tissue from the big cop's throat and sinuses—hit the windshield, the steering wheel, the dashboard. The smell was awful, the smell of rotted meat.

Johnny clapped his hands to his face and screamed. There was no way not to scream. He could feel his eyeballs pulsing in their sockets, could feel adrenaline roar into his system as the shock-reaction set in.

"Gosh, there's nothing worse than a summer cold, is there?" the cop asked in his dark, musing voice. He cleared his throat and spat a clot the size of a crabapple onto the face of the dashboard. It hung where it was for a moment, then oozed down the front of the police-radio like an unspeakable snail, leaving a trail of blood behind. It hung briefly from the bottom of the radio, then dropped to the floormat with a plop.

Johnny closed his eyes behind his hands and moaned.

"*That* was *sarx*," the cop said, and started the engine. "You might want to keep it in mind. I'd say 'for your next book,' but I don't think there's going to *be* a next book, do you, Mr. Marinville?"

Johnny didn't answer, only kept his hands over his face and his eyes closed. It occurred to him that quite possibly none of this was happening, that he was in a nuthouse some-place, having the world's ugliest hallucination. But his better, deeper mind knew that wasn't true. The *stench* of what the man had sneezed out—

He's dying, he's got to be dying, that's infection and internal bleeding, he's sick, his mental illness is only one symptom of something else, some radiation thing, or maybe rabies, or . . . or . . .

The cop hauled the Caprice cruiser around in a U, pointing it east. Johnny kept his hands over his face a little longer, trying to get himself under control, then lowered them and opened his eyes. What he saw out the right-hand window made his jaw drop.

Coyotes sat along the roadside at fifty-foot intervals like an honor guard—silent, yellow-eyed, tongues lolling. They appeared to be grinning.

He turned and looked out the other window, and here were

more of them, sitting in the dust, in the blazing sun of late afternoon, watching the police-cruiser go by. *Is that a symptom, too?* he asked himself. *What you're seeing out there, is that a symptom, too? If so, how come I can see it?*

He looked out the cruiser's back window. The coyotes were peeling away as soon as they passed, he saw, loping off into the desert.

"You'll learn, Lord Jim," the cop said, and Johnny turned back toward him. He saw gray eyes staring from the rearview mirror. One was filmed with blood. "Before your time is up, I think you'll understand a great deal more than you do now."

Ahead was a sign by the side of the road, an arrow pointing the way toward some little town or other. The cop put on his turnblinker, although there was no one to see it.

"I'm taking you to the classroom," the big cop said. "School will be in shortly."

He made the right turn, the cruiser lifting onto two wheels and then settling back. It headed south, toward the cracked bulwark of the open-pit mine and the town huddled at its base.

CHAPTER 4

1

Steve Ames was breaking one of the Five Commandments—the last one on the list, as a matter of fact.

The Five Commandments had been given to him a month ago, not by God but by Bill Harris. They had been sitting in Jack Appleton's office. Appleton had been Johnny Marinville's editor for the last ten years. He was present for the handing down of the commandments but did not participate in this part of the conversation until near the end—only sat back in his desk chair with his exquisitely manicured fingers spread on the lapels of his suitcoat. The great man himself had left fifteen minutes before, head up and studly gray hair flying out behind him, saying he had promised to join someone at an art gallery down in SoHo.

"All these commandments are thou shalt nots, and I don't expect you to have any trouble remembering them," Harris had said. He was a tubby little guy, and there probably wasn't much harm in him, but everything he said came out sounding like the decree of a weak king. "Are you listening?"

"Listening," Steve had agreed.

"First, thou shalt not drink with him. He's been on the wagon for awhile—five years, he claims—but he's stopped going to Alcoholics Anonymous, and that's not a good sign. Also, for Johnny the wagon's always had a nonstick surface, even *with*

AA. But he doesn't like to drink alone, so if he asks you to join him for a few after a hard day on the old Harley, you say no. If he starts bullying you, telling you it's part of your job, you still say no."

"Not a problem," Steve had said.

Harris ignored this. He had his speech, and he intended to stick to it.

"Second, thou shalt not score drugs for him. Not so much as a single joint.

"Third, thou shalt not score women for him . . . and he's apt to ask you, particularly if some good-looking babes show up at the receptions I'm setting up for him along the way. As with the booze and the drugs, if he scores on his own, that's one thing. But don't help him."

Steve had thought of telling Harris that he wasn't a pimp, that Harris must have confused him with his own father, and decided that would be fairly imprudent. He opted for silence instead.

"Fourth, thou shalt not cover up for him. If he starts boozing or drugging—particularly if you have reason to think he's doing coke again—get in touch with me at once. Do you understand? *At once.*"

"I understand," Steve replied, and he had, but that didn't mean he would necessarily comply. He had decided he wanted this gig in spite of the problems it presented—in part *because* of the problems it presented; life without problems was a fairly uninteresting proposition—but that didn't mean he was going to sell his soul to keep it, especially not to a suit with a big gut and the voice of an overgrown kid who has spent too much of his adult life trying to get some payback for real or imagined slights he had suffered in the elementary-school playground. And although John Marinville was a bit of an asshole, Steve didn't hold that against him. Harris, though . . . Harris was in a whole other league.

Appleton had leaned forward at this point, making his lone

contribution to the discussion before Marinville's agent could get to the final commandment.

"What's your impression of Johnny?" he asked Steve. "He's fifty-six years old, you know, and he's put a lot of hard mileage on the original equipment. Especially in the eighties. He wound up in the emergency room three different times, twice in Connecticut and once down here. The first two were drug ODs. I'm not telling tales out of school, because all that's been reported—exhaustively—in the press. The last one may have been a suicide attempt, and that *is* a tale out of school. I'd ask you to keep it to yourself."

Steve had nodded.

"So what do you think?" Appleton asked. "Can he really drive almost half a ton of motorcycle cross-country from Connecticut to California, and do twenty or so readings and receptions along the way? I want to know what you think, Mr. Ames, because I'm frankly doubtful."

He had expected Harris to come busting in then, touting the legendary strength and iron balls of his client—Steve knew suits, he knew agents, and Harris was both—but Harris was silent, just looking at him. Maybe he wasn't so stupid after all, Steve thought. Maybe he even cared a little for this particular client.

"You guys know him a lot better than I do," he said. "Hell, I only met him for the first time two weeks ago and I've *never* read one of his books."

Harris's face said that last didn't surprise him at all.

"Precisely why I'm asking you," Appleton replied. "We *have* known him for a long time. Me since 1985, when he used to party with the Beautiful People at 54, Bill since 1965. He's the literary world's Jerry Garcia."

"That's unfair," Harris said stiffly.

Appleton shrugged. "New eyes see clear, my grandmother used to say. So tell me, Mr. Ames, do you think he can do it?"

Steve had seen the question was serious, maybe even vital, and thought it over for almost a full minute. The two other men sat and let him.

"Well," he had said at last, "I don't know if he can just eat the cheese and stay away from the wine at the receptions, but make it across to California on the bike? Yeah, probably. He looks fairly strong. A lot better than Jerry Garcia did near the end, I'll tell you that. I've worked with a lot of rockers half his age who don't look as good."

Appleton had looked dubious.

"Mostly, though, it's a look he gets on his face. He *wants* to do this. He wants to get out on the road, kick some ass, take down some names. And . . ." Steve had found himself thinking of his favorite movie, one he watched on tape every year or so: *Hombre*, with Paul Newman and Richard Boone. He had smiled a little. "And he looks like a man who's still got a lot of hard bark left on him."

"Ah." Appleton had looked downright mystified at that. Steve hadn't been much surprised. If Appleton had ever come equipped with hard bark, Steve thought it had probably all rubbed off by the time he was a sophomore at Exeter or Choate or wherever he'd gone to wear his blazers and rep ties.

Harris had cleared his throat. "If we've got that out of the way, the final commandment—"

Appleton groaned. Harris went on looking at Steve, pretending not to hear.

"The fifth and final commandment," he had repeated. "Thou shalt not pick up hitchhikers in thy truck. Neither male nor female shalt thou pick them up, but especially not female."

Which was probably why Steve Ames never hesitated when he saw the girl standing beside the road just outside Ely—the skinny girl with her nose bent and her hair dyed two different colors. He just pulled over and stopped.

2

She opened the door but didn't get into the cab at first, just looked up at him from across the map-littered seat with wide blue eyes. "Are you a nice person?" she asked.

Steve thought this over, then nodded. "Yeah, I guess so," he said. "I like a cigar two or three times a day, but I never kicked a dog that wasn't bigger'n me, and I send money home to my momma once every six weeks."

"You're not going to try to slap the make on me, or anything?"

"Nope," Steve said, amused. He liked the way her wide blue eyes remained fixed on his face. She looked like a little kid studying the funnypages. "I'm fairly well under control in that regard."

"And you're not like a crazy serial killer, or anything?"

"No, but Jesus Christ, do you think I'd tell you if I was?"

"I'd prob'ly see it in your eyes," the skinny girl with the tu-tone hair told him, and although she sounded grave enough, she was smiling a little. "I got a psychic streak. It ain't wide, but it's there, buddy. It's really really there."

A refrigerator truck roared past, the guy laying on his horn all the way by, even though Steve had squeezed over until the stubby Ryder was mostly on the shoulder, and the road itself was empty in both directions. No big surprise about that, though. In Steve's experience, some guys simply couldn't keep their hands off their horns or their dicks. They were always honking one or the other.

"Enough with the questionnaire, lady. Do you want a ride or not? I've got to roll my wheels." In truth, he was a lot closer to the boss than the boss would maybe approve of. Marinville liked the idea of being on his own in America, Mr. Free Bird, have pen will travel, and Steve thought that was just how he'd write his book. That was fine, too—great, totally cool. But he, Steven Andrew Ames of Lubbock, also had a job to do; his was to make sure Marinville didn't have to write the book on a Ouija board instead of his word processor. His view on how to accomplish that end was simplicity itself: stay close and let no situation get out of hand unless it absolutely couldn't be helped. He was seventy miles back instead of a hundred and fifty, but what the boss didn't know wouldn't hurt him.

"You'll do, I guess," she said, hopped up into the cab, and slammed the door shut.

"Well, thank you, cookie," he said. "I'm touched by your trust." He checked the rearview mirror, saw nothing but the ass end of Ely, and got back out on the road again.

"Don't call me that," she said. "It's sexist."

"*Cookie* is sexist? Oh please."

In a prim little no-nonsense voice she said: "Don't call me cookie and I won't call you cake."

He burst out laughing. She probably wouldn't like it, but he couldn't help it. That was the way laughing was, sort of like farting, sometimes you could hold it in but a lot of times you couldn't.

He glanced at her and saw that she was laughing a little too—and slipping her backpack off—so maybe that was all right. He put her at about five-six and skinny as a rail—a hundred pounds max, and probably more like ninety-five. She was wearing a tank-top with torn-off sleeves. It gave an awfully generous view of her breasts for a girl worried about meeting Ted Bundy in a Ryder van. Not that she had a lot to worry about up there; Steve guessed she could still shop in the training-bra section at Wal-Mart, if she wanted to. On the front of the shirt, a black guy with dreadlocks grinned from the middle of a blue-green psychedelic sunburst. Bent around his head like a halo were the words NOT GONNA GIVE IT UP!

"You must like Peter Tosh," she said. "It *can't* be my tits."

"I worked with Peter Tosh once," he replied.

"No way!"

"Way," he said. He glanced in the rearview and saw that Ely was already gone. It was spooky, how fast that happened out here. He supposed that if he were a young female hitchhiker, he might ask a question or two himself before hopping willy-nilly into someone's car or truck. It might not help, but it sure couldn't hurt. Because once you were out in the desert, anything could happen to you.

"When did you work with Peter Tosh?"

"1980 or '81," he said. "I can't remember which. Madison Square Garden, then in Forest Hills. Dylan played the encore with him at Forest Hills. 'Blowin in the Wind,' if you can believe that."

She was looking at him with frank amazement, unmixed— so far as he could tell—with doubt. "Whoa, cool! What were you, a roadie?"

"Then, yeah. Later on I was a guitar tech. Now, I'm . . ." Yes, that was a good start, but just what *was* he now? Not a guitar tech, that was for sure. Sort of demoted to roadie again. Also part-time shrink. Also sort of like Mary Poppins, only with long brown hippie hair that was starting to show some gray along the center part. "Now I'm into something else. What's your name?"

"Cynthia Smith," she said, and held out a hand.

He shook it. Her hand was long, feather-light inside of his, and incredibly fine-boned. It was a little like shaking hands with a bird. "I'm Steve Ames."

"From Texas."

"Yeah, Lubbock. Guess you heard the accent before, huh?"

"Once or twice." Her gamine grin lit up her whole face. "You can take the boy out of Texas, but—"

He joined her for the rest of it and they grinned at each

other, already friends—the way people can become friends, for a little while, when they happen to meet on American back roads that go through the lonely places.

3

Cynthia Smith was clearly a flake, but Steve was a veteran flake himself, you couldn't spend most of your adult life in the music business without succumbing to flakedom, and it didn't bother him. She told him she had every reason to be careful of guys; one had nearly torn off her left ear and another had broken her nose not so long ago. "And the one who did the ear was a guy I *liked*," she added. "I'm sensitive about the ear. The nose, I think the nose has character, but I'm sensitive about the ear, God knows why."

He glanced across at her ear. "Well, it's a little flat on top, I guess, but so what? If you're *really* sensitive about it, you could grow your hair out and cover it up, you know."

"Not happening," she said firmly, and fluffed her hair, leaning briefly to the right so she could get a look at herself in the mirror mounted on her side of the cab. The half on Steve's side was green; the other half was orange. "My friend Gert says I look like Little Orphan Annie from hell. That's too cool to change."

"Not gonna give them curls up, huh?"

She smiled, patted the front of her shirt, and lapsed into a passable Jamaican imitation. "I go my own way—just like Peter, mon!"

Cynthia Smith's way had been to leave home and her parents' more or less constant disapproval at the age of seventeen. She had spent a little time on the East Coast ("I left when I realized I was gettin to be a mercy-fuck," she said matter-of-factly), and then had drifted back as far as the Midwest, where she had gotten "sort of clean" and met a good-looking guy at an AA meeting. The good-looking guy had claimed to be *entirely* clean, but he had lied. Oh boy, had he lied. Cynthia had moved in with him just the same, a mistake ("I've never been what you'd call bright about men," she told Steve in that same matter-of-fact voice). The good-looking guy had come home one night fucked up on crystal meth and had apparently decided he wanted Cynthia's left ear as a bookmark. She had gone to a shelter, gotten a little more than sort of clean, even worked as a counsellor for awhile after the woman in charge had been murdered and it looked as if the place might close. "The guy who murdered Anna is the same guy who broke my nose," she said. "He was bad. Richie—the guy who wanted my ear for a bookmark—he only had a bad *temper.* Norman was *bad.* As in crazy."

"They catch him?"

Cynthia solemnly shook her head. "Anyway, we couldn't let D & S go under just because one guy went crazy when his wife left him, so we all pitched in to save it. We did, too."

"D & S?"

"Stands for Daughters and Sisters. I got a lot of my confidence back while I was there." She was looking out the window at the passing desert and rubbing the ball of her thumb pensively along the bent bridge of her nose. "In a way, even the guy who did this helped me with that."

"Norman."

"Yep, Norman Daniels, that was his name. At least me and Gert—she's my pal, the one who says I look like Orphan Annie—stood up to him, you know?"

"Uh-huh."

"So last month I finally wrote home to my folks. I put my return address on the letter, too. I thought when they wrote back, if they ever did, they'd be righteously pissed—my dad, especially. He used to be a minister. He's retired now, but . . ."

"You can take the boy out of the hellfire, but you can't take the hellfire out of the boy," Steve said.

She smiled. "Well, that's sorta what I expected, but the letter I got back was pretty great. I called them. We talked. My dad cried." She said this with a touch of wonder. "I mean, he *cried*. Can you believe that?"

"Hey, I toured for eight months with Black Sabbath," Steve said. "I can believe anything. So you're going home, huh? Return of the Prodigal Cookie?" She gave him a look. He gave her a grin. "Sorry."

"Yeah, sure you are. Anyway, that's close."

"Where's home?"

"Bakersfield. Which reminds me, how far are *you* going?"

"San Francisco. But—"

She grinned. "Are you kidding? That's so cool!"

"But I can't promise to take you that far. In fact, I can't absolutely *promise* to take you any farther than Austin—the one in Nevada, you know, not the one in Texas."

"I know where Austin is, I've got a map," she said, and now she was giving him a stupid-big-brother look that he liked even better than her wide-eyed Miss Prim gaze. She was a cutie, all right . . . and wouldn't she just love it if he told her that?

"I'll take you as far as I can, but this gig is a little weird. I mean, all gigs are *kind* of weird, show-business is weird by nature, and this *is* showbiz . . . I guess, anyway . . . but . . . I mean . . ."

He stopped. What *did* he mean, exactly? His span of employment as a writer's roadie (an ill-fitting title, you didn't have to be a writer yourself to know that, but the only one he could think of) was almost over, and he still didn't know what to think of it, or of Johnny Marinville himself. All he knew for sure was that the great man hadn't asked Steve to score him any dope or women, and that he'd never answered Steve's knock on his hotel-room door with whiskey on his breath. For now that was enough. He could think about how he was going to describe it on his résumé later.

"What *is* the gig?" she asked. "I mean, this doesn't look big enough to be a band truck. Are you touring with a folkie this time? Gordon Lightfoot, someone like that?"

Steve grinned. "My guy *is* sort of a folkie, I guess, only he plays his mouth instead of a guitar or a harmonica. He—"

That was when the cellular phone on the dashboard gave out its strident, oddly nasal cry: *Hmeep! Hmeep!* Steve grabbed it off the dashboard but didn't open it right away. He looked at the girl instead. "Don't say a word," he told her as the phone *hmeep*-ed in his hand a third time. "You might get me trouble if you do. 'Kay?"

Hmeep! Hmeep!

She nodded. Steve flipped the phone's mouthpiece open and then pushed SEND on the keypad, which was how you accepted an incoming call. The first thing he was aware of when he put the phone to his ear was how heavy the static was—he was amazed the call had gone through at all.

"Hello, that you, boss?"

There was a deeper, smoother roar behind the static—the sound of a truck going by, Steve thought—and then Marinville's voice. Steve could hear panic even through the static, and it kicked his heart into a higher gear. He had heard people talking in that tone before (it happened at least once on every rock tour, it seemed), and he recognized it at once. At Johnny Marinville's end of the line, shit of some variety had hit the fan.

"Steve! Steve, I'm . . . ouble . . . *bad* . . ."

He stared out at the road, running straight-arrow into the desert, and felt little seeds of sweat starting to form on his brow. He thought of the boss's tubby little agent with his thou shalt nots and his bullying voice, then swept all that away. The last person he needed cluttering up his head right now was Bill Harris.

"Were you in an accident? Is that it? What's up, boss? Say again!"

Crackle, zit, crackle.

"Johnny . . . *ear me?*"

"Yes, I hear you!" Shouting into the phone now, knowing it was totally useless but doing it anyway. Aware, out of the corner of his eye, that the girl was looking at him with mounting concern. "What's happened to you?"

No answer for so long he was positive this time he had lost Marinville. He was taking the phone away from his ear when the boss's voice came through again, impossibly far off, like a voice coming in from another galaxy: "west . . . Ely . . . iffy."

No, not iffy, Steve thought, *not iffy but fifty.* "*I'm west of Ely, on Highway 50.*" *Maybe, anyway. Maybe that's what he's saying. Accident. Got to be. He drove his scoot off the road and he's sitting out there with a bust leg and blood maybe pouring down his face and when I get back to New York his guys are going to crucify me, if for no other reason than that they can't crucify* him—

". . . ot sure how far . . . least, probably more . . . RV pulled off the road . . . ittle farther up . . ."

The heaviest blast of static yet, then something about cops. State cops and town cops.

"What's—" the girl in the passenger seat began.

"*Shh!* Not now!"

From the phone: ". . . my bike . . . into the desert . . . wind . . . mile or so east of the RV . . ."

And that was all. Steve yelled Johnny's name into the phone half a dozen times, but only silence came back. The connection had been broken. He used the NAME/MENU button to bring up J.M. in the display window, then pushed SEND. A recorded voice welcomed him to the Western Roaming Network, there was a pause, and then another recording told him that his call could not be completed at this time. The voice began to list all the reasons why this might be so. Steve pushed END and flipped the phone closed. "God *damn* it!"

"It's bad, isn't it?" Cynthia asked. Her eyes were very wide again, but there was nothing cute about them now. "I can see it in your face."

"Maybe," he said, then shook his head, impatient with himself. "*Probably.* That was my boss. He's up the line somewhere. Seventy miles'd be my best guess, but it might be as much as a hundred. He's riding a Harley. He—"

"Big red-and-cream bike?" she asked, suddenly excited. "Does he have long gray hair, sort of like Jerry Garcia's?"

He nodded.

"I saw him this morning, way far east of here," she said. "He filled up at this little gas station-cafeteria place in Pretty Nice. You know that town, Pretty Nice?"

He nodded.

"I was eating breakfast and saw him out the window. I thought he looked familiar. Like I'd seen him on *Oprah* or maybe *Ricki Lake.*"

"He's a writer." Steve looked at the speedometer, saw he had the panel truck up to seventy, and decided he could let it out just a little more. The needle crept up toward seventy-five. Outside the windows, the desert ran backward a little faster. "He's crossing the country, getting material for a book. He's done some speaking, too, but mostly he just goes places and talks to people and makes notes. Anyway, he's had an accident. At least I *think* that's what's happened."

"The connection was fucked, wasn't it?"

"Uh-huh."

"Do you want to pull over? Let me out? Because it's no problem, if that's what you want."

He thought it over carefully—now that the initial shock was receding, his mind seemed to be ticking away coldly and precisely, as it always had before in situations like this. No, he decided, he didn't want her out, not at all. He had a situation on his hands, one that had to be dealt with right away, but that didn't mean the future could be forgotten. Appleton might be okay even if Johnny Marinville had highsided his Harley and fucked himself up bigtime, he had looked like the sort of man who could (blazers and rep ties notwithstanding) accept the idea that sometimes things went wrong. Bill Harris, however, had struck Steve as a man who believed in playing Pin the Blame on the Donkey when things went wrong . . . and jamming that pin as far up the donkey's ass as it would go.

As the potential donkey, Steve decided what he would really like was a witness—one who had never set eyes on him before today.

"No, I'd like you to ride along. But I have to be straight with you—I don't know what we're going to find. There could be blood."

"I can deal with blood," she said.

4

She made no comment about how fast he was going, but when the rental truck hit eighty-five and the frame began to shake, she fastened her shoulder-harness. Steve squeezed the gas-pedal a little harder, and when the truck got up around ninety, the vibration eased. He kept both hands curled around the wheel, though; the wind was kicking up, and at these speeds a good hard gust could swerve you onto the shoulder. Then, if your tires sank in, you were in *real* trouble. Flipping-over trouble. The boss would have been even more vulnerable to windshear on his bike, Steve reflected. Maybe that was what had happened.

By now he had told Cynthia the basic facts of his employ:

he made reservations, checked routes, vetted sound-systems at the places where the boss was scheduled to speak, stayed out of the way so as not to conflict with the picture the boss was painting—Johnny Marinville, the thinking man's lone wolf, a politically correct Sam Peckinpah hero, a writer who hadn't forgotten how to hang tough and lay cool.

The panel-truck, Steve told her, was empty except for some extra gear and a long wooden ramp, which Johnny could ride up if the weather got too foul to cycle in. Since this was midsummer, that wasn't very likely, but there was another reason for the ramp as well, and for the tiedowns Steve had installed on the floor of the van before setting out. This one was unspoken by either of them, but both had known it was there from the day they had set out from Westport, Connecticut. Johnny Marinville might wake up one morning and simply find himself unwilling to keep riding the Harley.

Or incapable of it.

"I've heard of him," Cynthia said, "but I never read anything by him. I like Dean Koontz and Danielle Steel, mostly. I just read for pleasure. Nice bike, though. And the guy had great hair. Rock-and-roll hair, you know?"

Steve nodded. He knew. Marinville did, too.

"You really worried about him or just worried about what might happen to you?"

He likely would have resented the question if someone else had asked it, but he sensed no implied criticism in Cynthia's tone. Only curiosity. "I'm worried about both," he said.

She nodded. "How far have we come?"

He glanced down at the odometer. "Forty-five miles since I lost him off the phone."

"But you don't know exactly where he was calling from."

"No."

"You think he just fucked himself up, or someone else, too?"

He looked over at her, surprised. That the boss might've

fucked someone else up was *exactly* what he was afraid of, but he never would have said so out loud if she hadn't raised the possibility first.

"Somebody else might be involved," he replied reluctantly. "He said something about state cops and town cops. It might've been 'Don't call the state cops, call the town cops.' I couldn't tell for sure."

She pointed to his cellular, which was back on the dashboard.

"No way," he said. "I'm not calling *any* cops until I see what kind of mess he's gotten himself into."

"And I promise that won't be in my statement, if you promise not to call me cookie anymore."

He smiled a little, although he didn't feel much like smiling. "Probably that's a good idea. You *could* always say—"

"—that your phone wouldn't work anymore," she finished. "Everybody knows how finicky those things are."

"You're okay, Cynthia."

"You're not so bad yourself."

At just under ninety, the miles melted away like spring snowfall. When they were sixty miles west of the point where Steve had lost contact, he began slowing the truck a couple of miles an hour for each mile travelled. No police-cars had passed them in either direction, and he supposed that was good. He said so, and Cynthia shook her head doubtfully.

"It's *weird,* is what it is. If there's been an accident where your boss or maybe someone else got hurt, wouldn't you think a few cop-cars would've gone past us by now? Or an ambulance?"

"Well, if they came from the other way, west—"

"According to my map, the next town that way is Austin, and that's *much* farther ahead of us than Ely is behind us. Anything official—anything with *sirens* is what I mean—should be heading east to west. Catching up with us. Get it?"

"I guess so, yeah."

"So where are they?"

"I don't know."

"Me either."

"Well, keep looking for . . . well shit, who knows? *Anything out of the ordinary.*"

"I am. Slow down a little more."

He glanced at his watch and saw it was quarter to six. The shadows had drawn long across the desert, but the day was still bright and hot. If Marinville was out there, they would see him.

You bet we will, he thought. *He's going to be sitting at the edge of the road, probably with his head busted and half his pants torn off from when he spilled and rolled. And likely making notes on how it felt. Thank God he wears his helmet, at least. If he didn't—*

"I see something! Up there!" The girl's voice was excited but controlled. She was shading her eyes from the westering sun with her left hand and pointing with her right. "See? Could that . . . aw, shit no. That's *way* too big to be a motorcycle. Looks like a motor home."

"I think this is where he called from, though. *Somewhere* around here, anyway."

"What makes you think so?"

"He said there was an RV off the road a little farther up—I heard that part quite clearly. He said he was about a mile east of it, and that's about where we are now, so—"

"Yeah, don't say it. I'm looking, I'm looking."

He slowed the Ryder truck to thirty, then, as they approached the RV, to walking pace. Cynthia had unrolled the passenger window and was halfway out of it, her tank-top riding up to reveal the small of her back (*the* small *small of her back,* Steve thought) and the ridge of her spine.

"Anything?" he asked her. "At all?"

"Nope. I saw glint, but it was way out on the desert floor—a lot farther than he'da gone if he'd cracked up. Or if the wind pushed him off the road, you know?"

"Probably the sun reflecting off the mica in the rocks."

"Uh-huh, could have been."

"Don't fall out that window, girl."

"I'm fine," she said, then winced her eyes shut as the wind, which was becoming steadily more grumpy, threw grit in her face.

"If this is the RV he was talking about, we're already past where he called from."

She nodded. "Yeah, but keep going. If there's somebody home in there, they might have saw him."

He snorted. "'Might have saw him.' Did you learn that reading Dean Koontz and Danielle Steel?"

She pulled in long enough to give him a haughty look . . . but he thought he saw hurt beneath it. "Sorry," he said. "I was only teasing."

"Oh?" she said coolly. "Tell me something, Mr. Big Texas Roadie—have *you* read anything your boss has written?"

"Well, he gave me a copy of *Harper's* with a story of his in it. 'Heaven-Sent Weather,' it was called. I read that, sure did. Ever' word."

"Did you *understand* ever' word?"

"Uh, no. Look, what I said was snotty. I *do* apologize. Sincerely."

"Okay," she said, but her tone suggested that he was going to be on probation, at least for awhile.

He opened his mouth to say something that might be funny if he was lucky, something that would get her to smile (she had a nice one), and then he got a really good look at the RV. "Oh hey, what's this?" he asked, speaking more to himself than to the girl.

"What's what?" She turned her head to look out through the windshield as Steve coasted the Ryder truck to a stop on the shoulder, just behind the RV. It was one of the middle-sized ones, bigger than Lassie but smaller than the Godzillas he'd been seeing ever since Colorado.

"Guy must have run over some nails in the road, or something," Steve said. "Tires look like they're *all* flat."

"Yeah. So how come yours aren't?"

By the time it occurred to him that the people in the RV might have been public-spirited enough to pick up the nails, the girl with the punky tu-tone hair was out of the cab and walking up to the RV, hallooing.

Well, she knows a good exit-line when she gets one off, give her that, he thought, and got out on his side. Wind struck him in the face hard enough to rock him back on his heels. And it was hot, like air blown over the top of an incinerator.

"Steve?" Her voice was different. The prickly pertness, which he thought might have been the girl's way of flirting, was gone. "Come over here. I don't like this."

She was standing by the side door of the RV. It was un-latched, banging back and forth in the wind a little even though this was the lee side, and the steps were down. It wasn't the door or the steps she was looking at, though. At the foot of the stairs, half-buried in sand that the wind had blown beneath the RV, was a doll with blond hair and a bright blue dress. It lay face-down and abandoned. Steve didn't care for the look of this much, either. Dolls with no little girls around to mind them were sort of creepy under any conditions, that was *his* opinion, at least, and to come upon one abandoned by the roadside, half-buried in blowing sand—

He opened the unlatched door and poked his head into the RV. It was brutally hot, at least a hundred and ten degrees. "Hello? Anybody?"

But he knew better. If they'd been here, the people who owned this RV, they would have been running the engine for the air conditioning.

"Don't bother." Cynthia had picked up the doll and was brushing sand from its hair and the folds of its dress. "This is no dimestore dolly. Not huge bucks, but expensive. And someone cared about her. Look." She pulled out the skirt with her fingers so he could see where a small, neat patch had been sewn over a rip. It matched the dress almost exactly in color. "If the girl who owned this doll was around, it wouldn't have been out lying in the dirt, I practically guarantee you that. The question is, why didn't she take it with her when she and her folks left? Or at least put it back inside?" She opened the door, hesitated, went up one of the two steps, hesitated again, looked back at him. "Come on."

"I can't. I have to find the boss."

"In a minute, okay? I don't want to go in here by myself. It's like the *Andrea Doria,* or something."

"You mean the *Mary Celeste.* The *Andrea Doria* sank."

"Okay, smarty-britches, whatever. Come on, it won't take long. Besides . . ." She hesitated.

"Besides, it might have something to do with my boss? Is that what you're thinking?"

Cynthia nodded. "It's not that big a reach. I mean, they're both gone, aren't they?"

He didn't want to accept that, though—it felt like a complication he didn't deserve. She saw some of that on his face (maybe even all of it; she sure wasn't dumb) and tossed up her hands. "Oh shit, I'll look around myself."

She went inside, still holding the doll. Steve looked thoughtfully after her for a moment, then followed. Cynthia glanced back at him, nodded, then put the doll down in one of the captain's chairs. She fanned her tank-top at her neck. "Hot," she said. "I mean *boogery.*"

She walked into the RV's cabin. Steve went the other way, into the driver's area, ducking his head so as not to bump it. On the dashboard in front of the passenger seat were three packs of baseball cards, neatly sorted into teams—Cleveland Indians, Cincinnati Reds, Pittsburgh Pirates. He thumbed through them and saw that about half were signed, and maybe half of the signed ones were personalized. Across the bottom of Albert Belle's card was this: "To David—Keep sluggin'! Albert Belle." And another, from the Pittsburgh pile: "See the ball before you swing, Dave—Your friend, Andy Van Slyke."

"There was a boy, too," Cynthia called. "Unless the girl was into G.I. Joe and Judge Dredd and the MotoKops as well as dollies in blue dresses. One of the side-carriers back here is full of comic books."

"Yeah, there's a boy," Steve said, putting Albert Belle and Andy Van Slyke back into their respective decks. *He just brought the ones that were really important to him,* he thought, smiling a little. *The ones he absolutely could not bear to leave home.* "His name is David."

Startled: "How in the hell do you know that?"

"Learned it all watching *X-Files.*" He picked up a gas credit-card receipt from the wad of papers jammed into the dashboard map-receptacle, and smoothed it out. The name on it was Ralph Carver, the address somewhere in Ohio. The carbon had blurred across the town name, but it might have been Wentworth.

"I don't suppose you know anything else about him, do you?" she asked. "Last name? Where he came from?"

"David Carver," he said, the smile widening into a grin. "Dad's Ralph Carver. They hail from Wentworth, Ohio. Nice town. Next door to Columbus. I was in Columbus with South-side Johnny in '86."

She came forward, the doll curled against one mosquito-bump breast. Outside the wind gusted again, throwing sand against the RV. It sounded like hard rain. "You're making that up!"

"No'm," he said, and held out the gas receipt. "Here's the

Carver part. David I got from the kid's baseball cards. He's got some high-priced ink, tell you that."

She picked the cards up, looked at them, then put them back and turned slowly all the way around, her face solemn and shiny with sweat. He was sweating himself, and plenty. He could feel it running down his body like a light, sticky oil. "Where did they *go?*"

"Nearest town, to get help," he said. "Probably someone gave them a lift. Do you remember from your map what's around here?"

"No. There is a town, I think, but I don't recall the name. But if that's what they did, why didn't they lock up their place when they left? I mean, all their shit is here." She waved one hand toward the cabin. "Know what's back there by the studio couch?"

"Nope."

"The wife's jewelry caddy. A ceramic frog. You put your rings and earrings in the frog's mouth."

"*That* sounds tasteful." He wanted to get out of here, and not just because it was so nasty-hot or because he had to track down the boss. He wanted to get out because the RV *was* like the fucking *Mary Celeste.* It was too easy to imagine vampires hidden away in the closets, vampires in Bermuda shorts and tee-shirts saying things like I SURVIVED HIGHWAY 50, THE LONE-LIEST HIGHWAY IN AMERICA!

"It's actually cute," she said, "but that's not the point. There's two sets of earrings and a finger-ring in it. Not *real* expensive, but not junk, either. The ring's a tourmaline, I think. So why didn't they—"

She saw something in the map-holder, something that had been revealed when he stirred the crammed-in papers, and plucked out a dollar-sign moneyclip that looked like real silver. There were bills folded into it. She fanned them quickly with the tip of a finger, then tossed the moneyclip back into the map-holder as if it were hot.

"How much?" he asked.

"Forty or so," she said. "The clip itself's probably worth three or four times that much. Tell you what, pilgrim—this smells bad."

Another gust of wind splashed sand against the northern side of the RV, this one hard enough to rock it a little on its flat tires. The two of them looked at each other out of their sweat-shiny faces. Steve met the doll's blank blue gaze. *What happened, here, honey? What did you see?*

He turned for the door.

"Time for the cops?" Cynthia asked.

"Soon. First I want to walk a mile of backtrail, see if I can spot any sign of my boss."

"In this wind? Man, that's really dumb!"

He looked at her for a moment, not saying anything, then pushed past her and went down the steps.

She caught up with him at the foot of them. "Hey, let's call it even, okay? You made fun of my grammar, I made fun of your whatever."

"Intuition."

"Intuition, is that what you call it? Well, fine. Call it even? Say yeah. Please. I'm too spooked to want to piss in the catbox."

He smiled at her, a little touched by the anxiety on her face. "Okay, yeah," he said. "Even as even can be."

"You want me to drive the truck back? I can do a mile by the odometer, give you a finishing line to shoot for."

"Can you turn it around without—" A semi with KLEENEX SOFTENS THE BLOW written on the side blasted past at seventy, headed east. Cynthia flinched back from it, shielding her eyes from flying sand with one Kate Moss arm. Steve put his own arm around her scant shoulders, steadying her for a moment or two. "—without getting stuck?" he finished.

She gave him an annoyed look and stepped out from under his arm. "Course."

"Well . . . mile and a half, okay? Just to be on the safe side."

"Okay." She started toward the Ryder truck, then turned back to him. "I just remembered the name of the little town that's close to here," she said, and pointed east. "It's up that way, south of the highway. Cute name. You're gonna love it, Lubbock."

"What?"

"Desperation." She grinned and climbed up into the cab of the truck.

5

He walked slowly east along the shoulder of the westbound lane, raising his hand in a wave but not looking up as the Ryder truck, with Cynthia behind the wheel, rumbled slowly past. "I don't have the slightest *idea* what you're looking for!" she called down to him.

She was gone before he had any chance to reply, which was just as well; he didn't have any idea, either. Tracks? A ridiculous idea, given the wind. Blood? Bits of chrome or taillight glass? He supposed that was actually the most likely. He only knew two things for sure: that his instincts had not just asked him to do this but *demanded* it, and that he couldn't get the doll's glazey blue stare out of his mind. Some little girl's favorite doll . . . only the little girl had left Alice Blue Gown lying face-down in the dirt by the side of the road. Mom had left her jewelry, Dad had left his moneyclip, and son David had left his autographed baseball cards.

Why?

Up ahead, Cynthia swung wide, then turned the bright yellow truck so it was facing back west again. She did this with an economy Steve wasn't sure he could have matched himself, needing to back and fill just a single time. She got out, started walking toward him at a good clip, hardly looking down at all, and he had time, even then, to be moderately pissed that she should have found what his instinct had sent him out here to look for. "Hey!" she said. She bent over, picked something up, and shook sand off it.

He jogged to where she was standing. "What? What is it?"

"Little notebook," she said, and held it out. "I guess he was here, all right. *J. Marinville,* printed right on the front. See?"

He took the small wirebound notepad with the bent cover and paged through it quickly. Directions, maps Steve had drawn himself, and jotted notes in the boss's top-heavy scrawl, most of them about the scheduled receptions. Under the heading *St. Louis,* Marinville had scribbled, *Patricia Franklin. Redhead, big boobs. Don't* CALL HER PAT OR PATTY*! Name of org. is* FRIENDS OF OPEN LIBES. *Bill sez P.F. also active in animal-rights stuff. Veggie.* On the last page which had been used, a single word had been scrawled in an even more flamboyant version of the boss's handwriting:

$$For$$

That was all. As if he had started to write an autograph for someone and then never finished.

He looked up at Cynthia and saw her cross her arms beneath her scant bosom and begin rubbing the points of her elbows. "Bruh," she said. "It's impossible to be cold out here, but I am just the same. This keeps getting spookier and spookier."

"How come this didn't just fly away in the breeze?"

"Pure luck. It blew against a big rock and then sand covered the bottom half. Like with the doll. If he'd dropped it six inches to the right or left, it'd prob'ly be halfway to Mexico by now."

"What makes you think he dropped it?"

"Don't *you?*" she asked.

He opened his mouth to say he really didn't think anything, at least not yet, and then forgot all about it. He was seeing a glint out in the desert, probably the same one Cynthia had seen while they were coming up on the RV, only they weren't moving now, so the glint was staying steady. And it wasn't just mica chips embedded in rock, he would bet on that. For the first time he was really, painfully afraid. He was running out into the desert, running toward the glint, before he was even aware he meant to do it.

"Hey, don't go so fast!" She sounded startled. "Wait up!"

"No, stay there!" he called back.

He sprinted the first hundred yards, keeping that star-point of sun directly in front of him (except now the star-point had begun to spread to take on a shape he found dreadfully familiar), and then a wave of dizziness hit and stopped him. He bent over with his hands grasping his legs just above the knees, convinced that every cigar he had smoked in the last eighteen years had come back to haunt him.

When the vertigo passed a little and the padded-jackhammer sound of his heartbeat began to diminish in his ears, he heard a distinct but somehow ladylike puffing from behind him. He turned and saw Cynthia approaching at a jog, sweating hard but otherwise fine and dandy. Her gaudy curls had flattened a little, that was all.

"You stick . . . like a booger on . . . the end of a finger," he panted as she pulled up beside him.

"I think that's the sweetest thing a guy ever said to me. Put it in your fucking haiku book, why don't you? And don't have a heart attack. How old are you, anyway?"

He straightened up with an effort. "Too old to be interested in *your* giblets, Chicken Little, and I'm fine. Thanks for your concern." On the highway a car blipped by without slowing. They both looked. Out here, each passing car was a noticed event.

"Well, can I suggest we walk the rest of the way? Whatever that thing is, it's not going anywhere."

"I know what it is," he said, and trotted the last twenty yards. He knelt before it like a primitive tribesman before an effigy. The boss's Harley had been hurriedly and indifferently buried. The wind had already freed one handlebar and part of another.

The girl's shadow fell over him and he looked up at her, wanting to say something that would make her believe he wasn't completely freaked out by this, but nothing came. He wasn't sure she would have heard him, anyway. Her eyes were wide and scared, riveted on the bike. She fell to her knees beside him, held out her hands as if measuring, then dug a little distance to the right of the handlebars. The first thing she found was the boss's helmet. She pulled it free, poured the sand out of it, and set it aside. Then she brushed delicately beneath where it had been. Steve watched her. He wasn't sure his legs would support him if he wanted to get up. He kept thinking of the stories you saw in the paper from time to time, stories about bodies being discovered in gravel pits and pulled out of the ever-popular shallow grave.

Along the scooped declivity she had made, he now saw painted metal bright against the gray-brown sand. The colors were red and cream. And letters. HARL.

"That's it," she said. Her words were indistinct, because she was rubbing one hand compulsively back and forth across her mouth. "That's the one I saw, all right."

Steve grabbed the handlebars and tugged. Nothing. He wasn't surprised; it was a pretty feeble tug. He suddenly realized something that was interesting, in a horrible sort of way. It wasn't just the boss he was worried about anymore. Nosir. His concerns had widened, it seemed. And he had this feeling, this weird feeling, as if—

"Steve, my nice new friend," Cynthia said in a little voice, looking up at him from the little bit of fuel nacelle she had uncovered, "you're probably going to think this is *primo* stupid, the sort of thing dumb broads are always saying in lousy movies, but I feel like we're being watched."

"I don't think you're being stupid," he said, and scooped a little more sand away from the nacelle. No blood. Thank God for that. Which wasn't to say that there wasn't blood on the damned thing somewhere. Or a body buried beneath it. "I feel that way, too."

"Can we get out of here?" she asked—almost pleaded. She wiped sweat off her brow with one arm. "Please?"

He stood up and they started back. When she stuck her hand out, he was glad to take it.

"God, the feeling's strong," she said. "Is it strong for you?"

"Yeah. I don't think it means anything but being really scared, but yeah—it's strong. Like—"

A howl rose in the distance, wavering. Cynthia's grip on his hand tightened enough for Steve to be grateful that she bit her nails.

"What's that?" she whimpered. "Oh my God, what is it?"

"Coyote," he said. "Just like in the Western movies. They won't hurt us. Let up a little, Cynthia, you're killin me."

She started to, then clamped down again when a second howl came, wrapping itself lazily around the first like a good barbershop tenor doing harmony.

"They're nowhere close," he said, now having to work in order to keep himself from pulling his hand out of hers. She was a lot stronger than she looked, and she was hurting. "Really, kiddo, they're probably in the next county—relax."

She eased up on his hand, but when she turned her shiny face to him, it was almost pitifully frightened. "Okay, they're nowhere close, they're probably in the next county, they're probably phonin it in from across the California state line, in fact, but I don't like things that bite. I'm *scared* of things that bite. Can we get back to your truck?"

"Yes."

She walked with her hip brushing his, but when the next howl came, she didn't squeeze his hand quite so hard—that one clearly was at some distance, and it wasn't immediately repeated. They reached the truck. Cynthia got in on the passenger side, giving him one quick, nervous smile over her shoulder as she hauled herself up. Steve walked around the truck's hood, realizing as he went that the sensation of being watched had slipped away. He was still scared, but now it was primarily for the boss again—if John Edward Marinville was dead, the headlines would be worldwide, and Steven Ames would undoubtedly be part of the story. Not a good part. Steven Ames would be the fail-safe that failed, the safety net that hadn't been there when Big Daddy finally fell off the trapeze.

"That feeling of being watched . . . probably it was the coyotes," she said. "You think?"

"Maybe."

"What now?" Cynthia asked.

He took a deep breath and reached for the cellular phone. "Time for the cops," he said, and dialled 911.

What he heard in his ear was what he had pretty much expected: one of those cell-net recorded voices telling him it was sorry, but his call could not be completed at this time. The boss had gotten through—briefly, anyway—but that had been a fluke. Steve snapped the mouthpiece closed with a savage flick of his wrist, threw the phone back onto the dash, and started the Ryder's engine. He was dismayed to see that the desert floor had taken on a distinctly purplish cast. Shit. They'd spent more time in the deserted RV and kneeling in front of the boss's half-buried scoot than he had thought.

"No, huh?" She was looking at him sympathetically.

"No. Let's find this town you mentioned. What was it?"

"Desperation. It's east of here."

He dropped the gearshift lever into Drive. "Navigate for me, will you?"

"Sure," she said, and then touched his arm. "We'll get help. Even in a town that small, there's got to be at least *one* cop."

He drove up to the abandoned RV before turning east again, and saw the door was still flapping. Neither of them had thought to latch it. He stopped the truck, ran the transmission up into Park, and opened his own door.

Cynthia grabbed his shoulder before he could swing more than one leg out. "Hey, where you going?" Not panicked, but not exactly serene, either.

"Easy, girl. Just give me a sec."

He got out and latched the door of the RV, which was some-thing called a Wayfarer, according to the chrome on its flank. Then he came back to the idling Ryder truck.

"What are you, one of those type-A guys?" she asked.

"Not usually. I just didn't like that thing bangin in the breeze." He paused, one foot on the running board, looking up at her, thinking. Then he shrugged. "It was like looking at a shutter on a haunted house."

"Okay," she said, and then more howls rose in the distance— maybe south of them, maybe east, with the wind it was hard to tell, but this time it sounded like at least half a dozen voices. This time it sounded like a pack. Steve got up in the cab and slammed the door.

"Come on," he said, pulling the transmission lever down into Drive again. "Let's turn this rig around and find us some law."

CHAPTER 5

1

David Carver saw it while the woman in the blue shirt and faded jeans was finally giving up, huddling back against the bars of the drunk-tank and holding her forearms protectively against her breasts as the cop pulled the desk away so he could get at her.

Don't touch it, the white-haired man had said when the woman threw the shotgun down and it came clattering across the hardwood floor to bang off the bars of David's cell. *Don't touch it, it's empty, just leave it alone!*

He had done what the man said, but he had seen something else on the floor when he looked down at the shotgun: one of the shells that had fallen off the desk. It was lying on its side against the far lefthand vertical bar of his cell. Fat green shotgun shell, maybe one of a dozen that had gone rolling every whichway when the crazy cop had started battering the woman, Mary, with the desk and the chair in order to make her drop the gun.

The old guy was right, it would make no sense to go grabbing for the shotgun. Even if he could also get the shell, it would make no sense to do that. The cop was big—tall as a pro basketball player, broad as a pro football player—and the cop was also fast. He'd be on David, who had never held a real gun in his life, before David could even figure out what hole the shell went in. But if he should get a chance to pick up the shell . . . maybe . . . well, who knew?

"Can you walk?" the cop was asking the woman named Mary. His tone was grotesquely solicitous. "Is anything broken?"

"What difference does it make?" Her voice was trembling, but David thought it was rage making that tremble, not fear. "Kill me if you're going to, get it over with."

David glanced at the old guy who was in the cell with him, wanting to see if the old guy had also noticed the shell. So far as David could tell, he hadn't, although he had finally gotten off the bunk and come to the cell bars.

Instead of yelling at the woman who had tried her very best to blow his head off, or maybe hurting her for it, the cop gave her a brief one-armed hug. A pal's hug. In a way, David found this seemingly sincere little gesture of affection more unsettling than all the violence which had gone before it. "I'm not going to *kill* you, Mare!"

The cop looked around, as if to ask the remaining three Carvers and the white-haired guy if they could believe this crazy lady. His bright gray eyes met David's blue ones, and the boy took an unplanned step back from the bars. He felt suddenly weak with horror. And *vulnerable.* How he could feel more vulnerable than he already was he didn't know, but he did.

The cop's eyes were empty—so empty that it was almost as if he were unconscious with them open. This made David think of his friend Brian, and his one memorable visit to Brian's hospital room last November. But it wasn't the same, because at the same time the cop's eyes were empty, they *weren't.* There was something there, yes, *something*, and David didn't know what it was, or how it could be both something and nothing. He only knew he had never seen anything like it.

The cop looked back at the woman called Mary with an expression of exaggerated astonishment. "Gosh, no!" he said.

"Not when things are just getting interesting." He reached into his right front pocket, brought out a ring of keys, and selected one that hardly looked like a key at all—it was square, with a black strip embedded in the center of the metal. To David it looked a little like a hotel key-card. He poked this into the lock of the big cell and opened it. "Hop in, Mare," he said. "Snug as a bug in a rug, that's what you'll be."

She ignored him, looking instead at David's parents. They were standing together at the bars of the little cell directly across from the one David was sharing with white-haired Mr. Silent. "This man—this *maniac*—killed my husband. Put . . ." She swallowed, grimacing, and the big cop looked at her benignly, seeming almost to smile encouragement: *Get this out, Mary, sick it up, you'll feel better when you do.* "Put his arm around him like he did me just now, and shot him four times."

"He killed our little girl," Ellen Carver told her, and something in her tone struck David with a moment of utter dreamlike unreality. It was as if the two of them were playing Can You Top This. Next the woman named Mary would say, Well, he killed our *dog* and then his *mother* would say—

"We don't *know* that," David's father said. He looked horrible, face swollen and bloody, like a heavyweight boxer who has taken twelve full rounds of punishment. "Not for *sure*." He looked at the cop, a terrible expression of hope on his swollen face, but the cop ignored him. It was Mary he was interested in.

"That's enough chit-chat," he said. He sounded like the world's kindliest grandpa. "Hop into your room, Mary-mine. Into your gilded cage, my little blue-eyed parakeet."

"Or what? You'll kill me?"

"I already told you I won't," he said in that same Kind Old Gramps voice, "but you don't want to forget the world-renowned fate worse than death." His voice hadn't changed, but she was now looking up at him raptly, like a staked goat at an approaching boa constrictor. "I can hurt you, Mary," he said. "I can hurt you so badly you'll wish I *had* killed you. Now, you believe that, don't you?"

She looked at him a moment longer, then tore her eyes away—and that was just what it felt like to David from his place twenty feet away, her *pulling* free, the way you'd pull a piece of tape off the flap of a letter or a package—and walked into the cell. Her face shivered as she went, then broke apart as the cop slammed the cell's barred door behind her. She threw herself onto one of the four bunks at the rear, put her face into her arms, and began to sob. The cop stood watching her for a moment, head lowered. David had time to look down at the shotgun shell again and think about grabbing it. Then the big cop jerked and kind of shook himself, like someone waking from a doze, and turned away from the cell with the sobbing woman in it. He walked across to where David was standing.

The white-haired man retreated rapidly from the bars as the cop came, until the backs of his knees struck the edge of the bunk and he folded down to a sitting position. Then he put his hands over his eyes again. Before, that had seemed like a gesture of despair to David, but now it seemed to echo the horror he himself had felt when the cop's stare had fallen upon him— not despair but the instinctive hiding gesture of someone who will not look at a thing unless absolutely *forced* to look.

"How's it going, Tom?" the cop asked the man on the bunk. "How they hanging, oldtimer?"

Mr. White Hair shrank away from the sound of the voice without taking his hands away from his eyes. The cop looked at him a moment longer, then turned his gray gaze on David again. David found he couldn't look away—now it was *his* eyes that had been taped. And there was something else, wasn't there. A sense of being *called.*

"Having fun, David?" the big blond cop asked. His eyes seemed to be expanding, turning into bright gray ponds filled with light. "Are you filling this interlude, measure for measure?"

"I—" It came out a dusty croak. He licked his lips and tried again. "I don't know what you're talking about."

"Don't you? I wonder about that. Because I see . . ." He raised one hand to the corner of his mouth, touched it, then dropped it again. The expression on his face seemed to be one of genuine puzzlement. "I don't know *what* I see. It's a question, yes sir, it is. Who *are* you, boy?"

David glanced quickly at his mother and father and could not look for long at what he saw on their faces. They thought the cop was going to kill him, as he had killed Pie and Mary's husband.

He turned his eyes back at the cop. "I'm David Carver," he said. "I live at 248 Poplar Street, in Wentworth, Ohio."

"Yes, I'm sure that's true, but little Dave, who made thee? Canst thou say who made thee? *Tak!*"

He's not reading my mind, David thought, *but I think maybe he could. If he wanted to.*

An adult would likely have admonished himself for such a thought, told himself not to be silly, not to succumb to fear-driven paranoia. *That's just what he wants you to believe, that he's a mind-reader,* the adult would think. But David wasn't a man, he was a boy of eleven. Not just *any* boy of eleven, either; not since last November. There had been some big changes since then. He could only hope they would help him deal with what he was seeing and experiencing now.

The cop, meanwhile, was looking at him with narrowed, considering eyes.

"I guess my mother and father made me," David said. "Isn't that the way it works?"

"A boy who understands the birds and bees! Wonderful! And what about my other question, Trooper—are you having any fun?"

"You killed my sister, so don't ask stupid questions."

"Son, don't provoke him!" his father called in a high, scared voice. It didn't really sound like his father at all.

"Oh, I'm not *stupid*," the cop said, bending that horrid gray gaze even more closely on David. The irises actually seemed to be in motion, turning and turning like pin-wheels. Looking at them made David feel nauseated, close to vomiting, but he couldn't look away. "I may be a lot of things, but stupid isn't one of them. I know a lot, Trooper. I do. I know a *lot*."

"Leave him *alone*!" David's mother screamed. David couldn't see her; the cop's bulk blocked her out entirely. "Haven't you done enough to our family? If you touch him, I'll kill you!"

The cop paid no notice. He raised his index fingers to his lower lids and pulled them down, making the eyeballs themselves bulge out grotesquely. "I've got eagle eyes, David, and those are eyes that see the truth from afar. You just want to believe that. Eagle eyes, yes sir." The cop continued to stare through the bars, and now it was almost as if eleven-year-old David Carver had hypnotized *him*.

"You're quite a one, aren't you?" the cop breathed. "You're quite a one indeed. Yes, I think so."

Think whatever you want, just don't think about me thinking about the shotgun shell.

The cop's eyes widened slightly, and for a hideous moment David thought that was *exactly* what the cop was thinking about, that he had tuned into David's mind as if it were a radio signal. Then a coyote howled outside, a long, lonely sound, and the cop glanced in that direction. The thread between them—maybe telepathy, maybe just a combination of fear and fascination—snapped.

The cop bent to pick up the shotgun. David held his breath, fully expecting him to see the shell lying on the floor off to his right, but the cop did not glance in that direction. He stood up, flipping a lever on the side of the shotgun as he did so. It broke open, the barrels lying over his arm like an obedient animal. "Don't go away, David," he said in a confidential, just-us-guys voice. "We've got a lot to talk about. That's a conversation I'm looking forward to, believe me, but just now I'm a little busy."

He walked back toward the center of the room, head down, picking up shells as he went. The first two he loaded into the gun; the rest he stuffed absently into his pockets. David dared wait no longer. He bent, snaked his hand between the two bars on the left side of the cell, and grabbed the fat green tube. He slipped it into the pocket of his jeans. The woman named Mary didn't see; she was still lying on the bunk with her face buried in her arms, sobbing. His parents didn't see; they were standing at the bars of their cell, arms around each other's waist, watching the man in the khaki uniform with horrified fascination. David turned around and saw that old Mr. White Hair—Tom—still had his hands to his face, so maybe *that* was okay, too. Except old Tom's watery eyes were open behind his fingers, David could see them, so maybe it *wasn't* okay. Either way, it was too late now to take it back. Still facing the man the cop had called Tom, David raised the side of one hand to his mouth in a brief shushing gesture. Old Tom gave no sign that he saw; his eyes, in their own prison, only continued to stare out from between the bars of his fingers.

The cop who had killed Pie picked up the last shell on the floor, took a brief look under the desk, then straightened and snapped the shotgun closed with a single flick of his wrist. David had watched him closely through the picking-up process, trying to get a sense of whether or not the cop was counting the shells. He hadn't thought so . . . until now. Now the cop was just standing there, back-to, head down. Then he turned and strode back to David's cell, and the boy felt his stomach turn to lead.

For a moment the cop just stood there looking at him,

seeming to *pry* at him, and David thought: *He's trying to pick my brains the way a burglar tries to pick a lock.*

"Are you thinking about God?" the cop asked. "Don't bother. Out here, God's country stops at Indian Springs and even Lord Satan don't step his cloven feet much north of Tonopah. There's no God in Desperation, baby boy. Out here there's only *can de lach.*"

That seemed to be it. The cop walked out of the room with the shotgun now riding under his arm. There were perhaps five seconds of silence in the holding area, broken only by the muffled sobs of the woman named Mary. David looked at his parents, and they looked back at him. Standing that way, with their arms around each other, he could see how they must have looked as small children, long before they met each other at Ohio Wesleyan, and this frightened him out of all measure. He would rather have come upon them naked and fucking. He wanted to break the silence, couldn't think how.

Then the cop suddenly sprang back into the room. He had to duck his head to keep from bumping it on the top of the doorway. He was grinning in a mad way that made David think of Garfield, the comic-strip cat, when Garfield did his impromptu backfence vaudeville routines. Which this was, it seemed. There was an old telephone hung on the wall, its beige plastic casing cracked and filthy. The cop snatched it off its hook, held it to his ear, and cried: "Room service! Send me up a room!" He slammed the phone back down and turned his mad Garfield grin on his prisoners. "Old Jerry Lewis bit," he said. "American critics don't understand Jerry Lewis, but he's *huge* in France. I mean he's a *stud.*"

He looked at David.

"No God in France, either, Trooper. Take it from *moi.* Just Cinzano and escargots and women who don't shave their arm-pits."

He flashed the others with his regard, the grin fading as he did so.

"You people *have* to stay put," he said. "I know that you're scared of me, and maybe you're *right* to be scared, but you're locked up for a reason, believe it. This is the only safe place for miles around. There are forces out there you don't want to even think about. And when tonight comes—" He only looked at them and shook his head somberly, as if the rest was too awful to be spoken aloud.

You lie, you liar, David thought . . . but then another howl drifted through the open window in the stairwell, and he wondered.

"In any case," the cop said, "these are good locks and good cells. They were built by hardasses for roughneck miners, and escape's not an option. If that's been in your mind, send it home to its momma. You mind me, now. That's the best thing to do. Believe me, it is." Then he was gone, this time for real—David could hear his booted feet thudding down the stairs, shaking the whole building.

The boy stood where he was for a moment, knowing what he had to do now—absolutely *had* to do—but reluctant to do it in front of his parents. Still, there was no choice, was there? And he had been right about the cop. The big man hadn't exactly been reading his mind like it was a newspaper, but he'd been getting some of it—he'd been getting the God stuff. But maybe that was good. Better the cop should see God than the shotgun shell, maybe.

He turned and took two slow steps to the foot of the bunk. He could feel the weight of the shell in his pocket as he went. That weight was very clear, very distinct. It was as if he had a lump of gold hidden in there.

No, more dangerous than gold. A chunk of something radioactive, maybe.

He stood where he was for a moment, back to the room, and then, very slowly, sank down on his knees. He took a deep breath, pulling in air until his lungs would absolutely hold no more, then let it out again in a long silent whoosh. He folded his hands on the rough woolen blanket, dropped his forehead softly onto them.

"David, what's wrong with you?" his mother called. *"David!"*

"There isn't anything wrong with him," his father said, and David smiled a little as he closed his eyes.

"What do you mean, nothing wrong?" Ellie screamed. "Look at him, he fell down, he's fainting! *David!*"

Their voices were distant now, fading, but before they went out entirely, he heard his dad say, "Not fainting. *Praying.*"

No God in Desperation? Well, let's just see about that.

Then he was gone, no longer concerned about what his parents might be thinking, no longer worried that old Mr. White Hair might have seen him filch the shotgun shell and might tell the monster cop what he had seen, no longer grieving for sweet little Pie, who had never hurt anyone in her life and hadn't deserved to die as she had. He was not, in fact, precisely even inside his own head anymore. He was in the black now, blind but not deaf, in the black and listening for his God.

2

Like most spiritual conversions, David Carver's was dramatic only on the outside; on the inside it was quiet, almost mundane. Not rational, perhaps—matters of the spirit may never be strictly rational—but possessed of its own clarity and logic. And to David, at least, its genuineness was beyond question. He had found God, that was all. And (this he considered probably more important) God had found him.

In November of the previous year, David's best friend had

been struck by a car while riding his bike to school. Brian Ross was thrown twenty feet, into the side of a house. On any other morning David would have been with him, but on that particular day he had stayed home sick, nursing a not-too-serious virus. The phone had rung at eight-thirty and his mother had come into the living room ten minutes later, pale and trembling. "David, something's happened to Brian. Please try not to be too upset." After that he didn't remember much of the conversation, only the words *not expected to live.*

It had been his idea to go and see Brian in the hospital the next day, after calling the hospital all on his own that evening and ascertaining that his friend was still alive.

"Honey, I understand how you feel, but that's a really bad idea," his father had said. His use of "honey," a term of endearment long since retired along with David's stuffed toys, indicated how upset Ralph Carver was. He had looked at Ellen, but she only stood by the sink, wringing a dishcloth nervously back and forth in her hands. Obviously no help there. Not that Ralph had felt very helpful himself, God knew, but who had ever expected such a conversation? My God, the boy was only eleven, Ralph hadn't even gotten around to telling him the facts of *life*, let alone those of death. Thank God Kirstie was in the other room, watching cartoons on TV.

"No," David had said. "It's a *good* idea. In fact, it's the *only* idea." He thought of adding something heroically modest like *Besides, Brian'd do it for me,* and decided not to. He didn't think Brian *would* do it for him, actually. That didn't change anything, though. Because he had vaguely understood, even then, before what had happened in Bear Street Woods, that he'd be going not for Brian but for himself.

His mother had advanced a few hesitant steps from her bastion by the sink. "David, you've got the dearest heart in the world . . . the *kindest* heart in the world . . . but Brian . . . he was . . . well . . . *thrown* . . ."

"What she's trying to say is that he hit a brick wall head-first," his father said. He had reached across the table and taken one of his son's hands. "There was extensive brain-damage. He's in a coma, and there are no good vital signals. Do you know what that means?"

"That they think his brain turned into a cabbage."

Ralph had winced, then nodded. "He's in a situation where the best thing that could happen would be for it to end fast. If you went to see him, you wouldn't be seeing the friend you know, the one you used to have sleepovers with . . ."

His mother had gone into the living room at that point, had swept the bewildered Pie into her lap and begun to cry again.

David's father glanced after her as if he'd like to join her, then turned back to David again. "It's best if you remember Bri the way he was when you saw him the last time. Understand?"

"Yes, but I can't do that. I have to go see him. If you don't want to take me, that's okay, though. I'll take the bus after school."

Ralph had sighed heavily. "Shit, kid, I'll take you. You won't have to wait until after school, either. Just don't for God's sake say anything about this to—" He lifted his chin toward the living room.

"To Pie? Gosh, no." He didn't add that Pie had already been into his room to ask him what had happened to Brian, and had it hurt, and what did David think it was like to die, did you go somewhere, and about a hundred other questions. Her face had been so solemn, so attentive. She had been . . . well, she had been absolutely Pie-eyed. But it was often best if you didn't tell your parents everything. They were old, and stuff got on their nerves.

"Brian's parents won't let you in," Ellie had said, coming back into the room. "I've known Mark and Debbie for years. They're grief-stricken—sure they are, if it had been you I'd be *insane*—but they'll know better than to let a little boy look at . . . at another little boy who's dying."

"I called them after I called the hospital and asked if I could come see him," David said quietly. "Mrs. Ross said okay." His dad was still holding his hand. That was okay. He loved his mom and dad very much, and had been sorry this was distressing for them, but there was no question in his mind about what he was supposed to do. It had been as if some other power, one from outside, were guiding him even then. The way an older, smarter person might guide a little kid's hand, to help him make a picture of a dog or a chicken or a snowman.

"What's the matter with her?" Ellen Carver asked in a distraught voice. "Just what in hell is the *matter* with her, that's what I'd like to know."

"She said she was glad I could come say goodbye. She said they're going to turn off the life-support stuff this weekend, after his grandparents come to say goodbye, and she was glad I could come first."

The following day, Ralph took the afternoon off from work and picked his son up at school. David had been standing at the curb with his blue EXCUSED EARLY pass sticking out of his shirt pocket. When they got to the hospital, they rode up to the fifth floor, ICU, in the world's slowest elevator. On the way, David tried to prepare himself for what he was going to see. *Don't be shocked, David,* Mrs. Ross had said on the phone. *He doesn't look very nice. We're sure he doesn't feel any pain—he's down much too deep for that—but he doesn't look very nice.*

"Want me to come in with you?" his father had asked outside the door of the room Brian was in. David had shaken his head. He was still powerfully in the grip of the feeling which had more or less swallowed him since his pallid mother had given him the news about the accident: that feeling of being guided by someone more experienced than he was, someone who would be brave for him if his own courage faltered.

He had gone into the room. Mr. and Mrs. Ross were there, sitting in red vinyl chairs. They had books in their hands that they weren't reading. Brian was in the bed by the window, surrounded by equipment that beeped and sent green lines rolling across video screens. A light blanket was pulled up to his waist. Above it, a thin white hospital shirt lay open like cheesy school-play angel's wings on either side of his chest. There were all sorts of rubber suckers on him down there, and more attached to his head, below a vast white cap of bandage. From beneath this cap, one long cut descended Brian's left cheek to the corner of his mouth, where it curved up like a fishhook. The cut had been sutured with black thread. To David it had looked like something out of a Frankenstein movie, one of the old ones with Boris Karloff they showed on Saturday nights. Sometimes, when he slept over at Brian's, the two of them stayed up and ate popcorn and watched those movies. They loved the old black-and-white monsters. Once, during *The Mummy*, Brian had turned to David and said, "Oh shit, the mummy's after us, let's all walk a little faster." Stupid, but at quarter to one in the morning, *anything* can strike eleven-year-olds funny, and the two of them had laughed like fiends.

Brian's eyes had looked up at him from the hospital bed. And through him. They were open and as empty as school classrooms in August.

Feeling more than ever as if he were not moving but being moved, David had walked into the magic circle of the machines. He observed the suction cups on Brian's chest and temples. He observed the wires coming out of the suction cups. He observed the oddly misshapen look of the helmet-sized bandage on the left side of Brian's head, as if the shape beneath it had been radically changed. David supposed it had been. When you hit the side of a brick house, something had to give. There was a tube in Brian's right arm and another coming out of his chest. The tubes went to bags of liquid hanging off poles. There was a plastic doodad in Brian's nose and a band on his wrist.

David thought, *These are the machines that are keeping him alive. And when they turn them off, when they pull out the needles—* Disbelief filled him at the idea, buds of wonder which were only grief rolled tight. He and Brian squirted each other at the waterfountain outside their home room at school whenever they thought they could get away with it. They rode their bikes in the fabled Bear Street Woods, pretending they were commandos. They swapped books and comics and baseball cards and sometimes just sat on David's back porch, playing with Brian's Gameboy or reading and drinking David's mom's lemonade. They slapped each other high fives and called each other "bad boy." (Sometimes, when it was just the two of them, they called each other "fuckhead" or "dickweed.") In the second grade they'd pricked their fingers with pins and smooshed them together and sworn themselves blood-brothers. In August of this year they had made, with Mark Ross's help, a bottlecap Parthenon from a picture in a book. It turned out so well that Mark kept it in the downstairs hall and showed it to company. At the first of the year the bottlecap Parthenon was slated to travel the block and a half to the Carver house.

It was the Parthenon that David's mind had fixed upon most firmly as he stood by his comatose friend's bed. They had built it—him, Brian, Brian's dad—out in the Ross garage while the tape player endlessly recycled *Rattle and Hum* on the shelf behind them. A silly thing because it was just bottlecaps, a cool thing because it looked like what it was supposed to look like, you could tell what it was. Also a cool thing because they had made it with their own hands. And soon Brian's hands would be picked up and scrubbed by an undertaker who would use a special brush and pay particular attention to the fingernails. No one would want to look at a corpse with dirty nails, David supposed. And after Bri's hands were clean and he was in the coffin his folks would pick out for him, the undertaker would lace his fingers together like they were a pair of sneakers. And that was how they'd stay, down in the ground. Neatly folded, the way they had been supposed to fold their hands on their desks back in the second grade. No more bottlecap buildings for those hands. No more waterfountain nozzles for those fingers. Down into the dark with them.

It was not terror this thought had called up in his mind and heart but despair, as if the image of Brian's fingers laced together in his coffin proved that nothing was worth anything, that doing never once in the world stopped dying, that not even kids were exempted from the horror-show that roared on and on behind the peppermint sitcom facade your parents believed in and wanted you to believe in.

Neither Mr. nor Mrs. Ross spoke to him as he stood by the bed, meditating on these things in the shorthand of children. And their silence was all right with David; he liked them just fine, especially Mr. Ross, who had a sort of interesting crazy streak, but he hadn't come here to see them. They weren't the ones with the food-tubes and breathing machinery that were going to be taken away after the grandparents got a chance to say goodbye.

He had come to see Brian.

David had taken his friend's hand. It was astoundingly cool and lax in his own, but still alive. You could feel the life in it, running like a motor. He squeezed it gently and whispered, "How you doin, bad boy?"

No response but the sound of the machine that was doing Brian's breathing for him now that his brain had blown most of its fuses. This machine was at the head of the bed, and it was the biggest. It had a clear plastic tube mounted on one side of it. Inside the tube was something that looked like a white accordion. The sound this machine made was quiet—*all* the machines were quiet—but the accordion-thing was unsettling, just the same. It made a low, emphatic noise each time it went up. A *gasping* noise. It was as if part of Brian *wasn't* down too deep to feel pain, but that part had been taken out of his body and penned up in the plastic tube, where it was now being hurt even worse. Where it was being pressed to death by the white accordion-thing.

And then there were the eyes.

David felt *his* eyes drawn back to them again and again. Nobody had told him Brian's eyes would be open; until just now he hadn't known your eyes *could* be open when you were unconscious. Debbie Ross had told him not to be shocked, that Brian didn't look very nice, but she hadn't told him about that stuffed-moose stare. Maybe that was all right, though; maybe you could never be prepared about the really awful things, not at any age.

One of Brian's eyes was bloodshot, with a huge black pupil that ate up all but the thinnest ring of brown. The other was clear and the pupil appeared to be normal, but nothing else was normal because there was no sign of his friend in those eyes, *none.* The boy who had cracked him up by saying *Oh shit, the mummy's after us, let's all walk a little faster* wasn't here at all . . . unless he was in the plastic tube, at the mercy of the white accordion.

David would look away—at the stitched fishhook cut, at the bandage, at the one waxy ear he could see below the bandage—and then his gaze would wander back to Brian's open, staring eyes with their mismatched pupils. It was the *nothing* that drew him, the *absence,* the *goneness* in those eyes. It was more than wrong. It was . . . was . . .

Evil, a voice deep in his head whispered. It was like no voice he had ever heard in his thoughts before, a total stranger, and when Debbie Ross's hand dropped on his shoulder, he'd had to clamp his lips together against a scream.

"The man who did it was drunk," she said in a husky, tear-clotted voice. Fresh tears were rolling down her cheeks. "He says he doesn't remember any of it, that he was in a blackout, and do you know the horrible thing, Davey? I believe him."

"Deb—" Mr. Ross began, but Brian's mom took no notice of him.

"How could God let that man *not remember* hitting my son with his car?" Her voice had begun to rise. Ralph Carver had poked his head around the edge of the open door, startled, and a nurse rolling a cart up the hall stopped dead in her tracks. She looked into room 508 with a pair of big blue oh-goodness eyes. "How could God be so merciful to someone who deserves to wake up screaming with memories of the blood coming out of my son's poor hurt head *every night for the rest of his life?*"

Mr. Ross put his arm around her shoulders. Outside the door, Ralph Carver pulled his head back like a turtle withdrawing into its shell. David saw this and might have hated his dad a little for it. He couldn't remember for sure, one way or the other. What he remembered was looking down at Brian's pale, still face with the misshapen bandage seeming to bear down on it—the waxy ear, the cut with its red lips drawn together in a smooch by the black thread, and the eyes. Most of all what he remembered was the eyes. Brian's mother was right there, crying and screaming, and those eyes didn't change a bit.

But he is *in there,* David thought suddenly, and that thought, like so much that had happened to him since his mother had told him about Brian's accident, did not feel like something that was coming from him but only something going *through* him . . . as if his mind and body had turned into some sort of pipe.

He is *in there, I know he is. Still in there, like someone caught in a landslide . . . or a cave-in . . .*

Debbie Ross's control had given way entirely. She was almost howling, shaking in her husband's grip, trying to pull free. Mr.

Ross got her headed back toward the red chairs, but it looked like a job. The nurse hurried in and slipped an arm around her waist. "Mrs. Ross, sit down. You'll feel better if you do."

"What sort of God lets a man forget killing a little boy?" Brian's mom had screamed. *"The kind that wants that man to get loaded and do it again, that's who! A God who loves drunks and hates little boys!"*

Brian, looking up with his absent eyes. Harking to his mother's sermon with a waxy ear. Not noticing. Not here. But . . .

Yes, something whispered. *Yes, he is. He is. Somewhere.*

"Nurse, can you give my wife a shot?" Mr. Ross had asked. By then he was having a hard time keeping her from leaping back across the room and grabbing David, her son, maybe both of them. Something in her head had broken free. It was something that had a lot to say.

"I'll get Dr. Burgoyne, he's just up the hall." She hurried out.

Brian's dad gave David a strained smile. There was sweat trickling down his cheeks and standing out on his forehead in a galaxy of fine dots. His eyes were red, and to David he looked like he had already lost weight. David didn't think such a thing was possible, but that was how he had looked. Mr. Ross now had one arm around his wife's waist and his other hand clamped on her shoulder.

"You have to go now, David," Mr. Ross said. He was trying not to pant, and panting a little anyway. "We're . . . we're not doing so good."

But I didn't say goodbye to him, David wanted to say, and then realized it wasn't sweat trickling down Mr. Ross's cheeks but tears. That got him moving. It wasn't until he got to the door and turned back and saw Mr. and Mrs. Ross had blurred into a whole crowd of parents that he realized he was shortly going to be crying himself.

"May I come back, Mr. Ross?" he asked in a cracked, shivery voice he barely recognized. "Tomorrow, maybe?"

Mrs. Ross had stopped struggling now. Mr. Ross's hands had ended up locked together just below her breasts, and her head was bent so her hair hung in her face. The way they looked made David think of the World Federation Wrestling matches he and Bri had also sometimes watched, and how sometimes one guy would hug another guy like that. *Oh shit, the mummy's after us,* David thought for no good reason at all.

Mr. Ross was shaking his head. "I don't think so, Davey."

"But—"

"No, I don't think so. You see, the doctors say there's no chance at all for Brian to . . . t-to-to . . ." His face began to change as David had never seen an adult's face change—it seemed to be tearing itself apart from the inside. It was only later, out in the Bear Street Woods, that he got a handle on it . . . sort of. He'd been seeing what happened when someone who hadn't cried in a long time—years, maybe—finally couldn't hold back any longer. This was what it was like when the dam burst.

"Oh, my boy!" Mr. Ross screamed. *"Oh, my boy!"* He let go of his wife and fell back against the wall between the two red vinyl chairs. He stood there for a moment, kind of leaning, then folded at the knees. He slid down the wall until he was sitting, hands held out toward the bed, cheeks wet, snot hanging from his nostrils, hair sticking up in the back, shirttail out, pants pulled up so you could see the tops of his socks. He sat there like that and wailed. His wife knelt by him and took him in her arms as best she could, and that was when the doctor came in with the nurse right behind him, and when David slipped out, crying hard but trying not to sob. They were in a hospital, after all, and some people were trying to get well.

His father was as pale as his mother had been when she told

him about Brian, and when he took David's hand, his skin was much colder than Brian's had been.

"I'm sorry you had to see that," his father said as they waited for the world's slowest elevator. David had an idea it was all he could *think* of to say. On the ride home, Ralph Carver started to speak twice, then stopped. He turned on the radio, found an oldies station, then turned it down to ask David if he wanted an ice-cream soda, or anything. David shook his head, and his father turned the music up again, louder than ever.

When they got home, David told his father he thought he'd shoot some baskets in the driveway. His father said that was fine, then hurried inside. As David stood behind the crack in the hottop that he used as a foul line, he heard his parents in the kitchen, their voices drifting out of the open window over the sink. She wanted to know what had happened, how David had taken it. "Well, there was a scene," his father said, as though Brian's coma and approaching death were part of some play.

David tuned out. That sense of otherness had come on him again, that feeling of being small, a part instead of a whole, someone else's business. He suddenly felt very strongly that he wanted to go down to the Bear Street Woods, down to the little clearing. A path—narrow, but you could ride bikes along it if you went single-file—led into this clearing. It was here, up in the Viet Cong Lookout, that the boys had tried one of Debbie Ross's cigarettes the year before and found it awful, here that they had looked through their first copy of *Penthouse* (Brian had seen it lying on top of the Dumpster behind the E-Z Stop 24 down the hill from his house), here that they had hung their feet down and had their long conversations and dreamed their dreams . . . mostly about how they were going to be the kings of West Wentworth Middle School when they were ninth-graders. It was here, in the clearing you got to by way of the Ho Chi Minh Trail, that the boys had most enjoyed their friendship, and it was here that David suddenly felt he had to go.

He had bounced the ball, with which he and Brian had played about a billion games of Horse, one final time, bent his knees, and shot. Swish—nothing but net. When the ball returned to him, he tossed it into the grass. His folks were still in the kitchen, their voices still droning out the open window, but David didn't even think about poking his head in and telling them where he was going. They might have forbidden him.

Taking his bike never occurred to him. He walked, head down, the bright blue EXCUSED EARLY pass still sticking out of his shirt pocket, although school was over for the day by then. The big yellow buses were rolling their homeward routes; yelling flocks of little kids pounded past, waving their papers and lunchboxes. David took no notice. His mind was elsewhere. Later, Reverend Martin would tell him about "the still, small voice" of God, and David would feel a tug of recognition, but it hadn't seemed like a voice then, or a thought, or even an intuition. The idea his mind kept returning to was how, when you were thirsty, your whole body cried for water, and how you would eventually lie down and drink from a mudpuddle, if that was all you could get.

He came to Bear Street, then to the Ho Chi Minh Trail. He walked slowly down it, his head still lowered, so that he looked like a scholar with his mind on some immense problem. The Ho Chi Minh hadn't been his and Brian's exclusive property, lots of kids ordinarily used it on their way to and from school, but no one had been on it that warm fall afternoon; it seemed to have been cleared especially for him. Halfway to the clearing he spotted a 3 Musketeers candybar wrapper and picked it up. It was the only kind of candybar Brian would eat—he called them 3 Muskies—and David had no doubt that Brian had dropped this one beside the path a day or two before the accident. Not that Brian was ordinarily a litterbug sort of guy; he'd stuff the wrapper in his pocket, under ordinary circumstances. But—

But maybe something made him drop it. Something that knew I'd come along after that car hit him and threw him and broke his head on the bricks, something that knew I'd find it and remember him.

He told himself that was crazy, absolutely nutzoid, but maybe the nuttiest thing of all was that he didn't really think it was. Perhaps it would sound nutty if spoken aloud, but inside his head, it seemed perfectly logical.

With no thought of what he was doing, David stuck the red-and-silver wrapper into his mouth and sucked the little bits of sweet chocolate off the inside. He did this with his eyes closed and fresh tears squeezing out from under the lids. When the chocolate was all gone and there was nothing left but the taste of wet paper, he spat the wrapper out and went on his way.

At the east edge of the clearing was an oak with two thick branches spreading out in a V about twenty feet up. The boys hadn't quite dared to go whole hog and build a treehouse in this beckoning fork—someone might notice and make them tear it down again—but they had brought boards, hammers, and nails down here one summer day a year ago and made a platform that still remained. David and Brian knew that the high school kids sometimes used it (they had found cigarette butts and beer-cans on the weather-darkened old boards from time to time, and once a pair of pantyhose), but never until after dark, it seemed, and the idea of big kids using something they had made was actually sort of flattering. Also, the first handholds you had to grab in order to make the climb were high enough to discourage the little kids.

David went up, cheeks wet, eyes swollen, still tasting chocolate and wet paper in his mouth, still hearing the gasp of the accordion-thing in his ears. He felt he would find some other sign of Brian on the platform, like the 3 Muskies wrapper on the path, but there was nothing. Just the sign nailed to the tree, the one that said VIET CONG LOOKOUT, which they had put up a couple of weeks after completing the platform. The inspiration for that (and for the name they'd given the path) was some old movie with Arnold Schwarzenegger in it, David didn't remember the name. He kept expecting to come up here someday and find that the big kids had pulled the sign down or spray-painted something like SUCK MY DICK on it, but none ever had. He guessed they must like it, too.

A breeze soughed through the trees, cooling his hot skin. Any other day and Brian would have been sharing that breeze with him. They would have been dangling their feet, talking, laughing. David started to cry again.

Why am I here?

No answer.

Why did I come? Did something make me come?

No answer.

If anyone's there, please answer!

No answer for a long time . . . and then one *did* come, and he didn't think he was just talking to himself inside his own head, then fooling himself about what he was doing in order to gain a little comfort. As when he had stood over Brian, the thought which came seemed in no way his own.

Yes, this voice had said. *I'm here.*

Who are you?

Who I am, the voice said, and then fell silent, as if that actually explained something.

David crossed his legs, sitting tailor-fashion in the middle of the platform, and closed his eyes. He cupped his knees in his palms and opened his mind as best he could. He had no idea what else to do. In this fashion he waited for an unknown length of time, hearing the distant voices of the home-going children, aware of shifting red and black shapes on the insides of his eyelids as the breeze moved the branches above him and dapples of sunlight slipped back and forth on his face.

Tell me what you want, he asked the voice.

No answer. The voice didn't seem to want anything.

Tell me what to do, then.

No answer from the voice.

Distant, distant, he heard the sound of the firehouse whistle over on Columbus Broad. It was five o'clock. He had been sitting up on the platform with his eyes closed for at least an hour, probably more like two. His mom and dad would have noticed he was no longer in the driveway, would have seen the ball lying in the grass, would be worried. He loved them and didn't want to worry them—on some level he understood that Brian's impending death had struck at them as hard as it had struck at him—but he couldn't go home yet. Because he wasn't *done* yet.

Do you want me to pray? he asked the voice. *I'll try if you want me to, but I don't know how—we don't go to church, and—*

The voice overrode his, not angry, not amused, not impatient, not *anything* he could read. *You're praying already,* it said.

What should I pray for?

Oh shit, the mummy's after us, the voice said. *Let's all walk a little faster.*

I don't know what that means.

Yes you do.

No I don't!

"Yes I do," he said, almost moaned. "Yes I do, it means ask for what none of them dare to ask for, pray for what none of them dare to pray for. Is that it?"

No answer from the voice.

David opened his eyes and the afternoon bombed him with late light, the red-gold glow of November. His legs were numb from the knees down, and he felt as if he had just awakened from a deep sleep. The day's simple unzipped loveliness stunned him, and for a moment he was very aware of himself as a part of something whole—a cell on the living skin of the world. He lifted his hands from his knees, turned them over, and held them out.

"Make him better," he said. "God, make him better. If you do, I'll do something for you. I'll listen for what you want, and then I'll do it. I promise."

He didn't close his eyes but listened carefully, waiting to see if the voice had anything more to say. At first it seemed it did not. He lowered his hands, started to stand up, then winced at the burst of pins and needles that went whooshing up his legs from the balls of his feet. He even laughed a little. He grabbed a branch to steady himself, and as he was doing this, the voice *did* speak again.

David listened, head cocked, still holding the branch, still feeling his muscles tingle crazily as the blood worked its way back into them. Then he nodded. They had put three nails into the trunk of the tree to hold the VIET CONG LOOKOUT sign. The wood had shrunk and warped since then, and the rusty heads of the nails stuck out. David took the blue pass with EXCUSED EARLY printed on it from his shirt pocket and poked it onto one of the nailheads. That done, he marched in place until the tingling in his legs began to subside and he trusted himself to climb back down the tree.

He went home. He hadn't even gotten to the driveway before his parents were out the kitchen door. Ellen Carver stood on the stoop, hand raised to her forehead to shade her eyes, while Ralph almost ran down to the sidewalk to meet him and grab him by the shoulders.

"Where were you? Where in hell *were* you, David?"

"I went for a walk. Into the Bear Street Woods. I was thinking about Brian."

"Well, you scared the devil out of us," his mom said. Kirsten joined her on the stoop. She was eating a bowl of Jell-O and had her favorite doll, Melissa Sweetheart, tucked under her arm. "Even Kirstie was worried, weren't you?"

"Nope," Pie said, and went on eating her Jell-O.

"Are you all right?" his father had asked.

"Yes."

"Are you sure?"

"Yes."

He went into the house, yanking on one of Pie's braids as he went past her. Pie wrinkled her nose at him, then smiled.

"Supper's almost ready, go wash up," Ellen said.

The telephone started to ring. She went to answer it, then called sharply to David as he headed for the downstairs bathroom to wash his hands, which *had* been pretty dirty—sticky, sappy, treeclimbing dirty. He turned and saw his mom holding out the telephone in one fist while she twisted the other restlessly in her apron. She tried to talk, but at first no sound came out when her lips moved. She swallowed and tried again. "It's Debbie Ross, for you. She's crying. I think it must be over. For God's sake be kind to her."

David crossed the room and took the phone. That feeling of otherness had swept over him again. He had been sure his mom was at least half-right: *something* was over.

"Hello?" he said. "Mrs. Ross?"

She was crying so hard that at first she couldn't talk. She tried, but what came through her sobs was just *wahh-wahh-wahh.* From a little distance he heard Mr. Ross say, "Let me do it," and Mrs. Ross said, "No, I'm okay." There was a mighty honk in David's ear—it sounded like a hungry goose—and then she said: "Brian's awake."

"Is he?" David said. What she had just said made him feel happier than he had ever been in his life . . . and yet it had not surprised him at all.

Is he dead? Ellen was mouthing at him. One hand was still plunged deep in her apron, twisting and turning.

"No," David said, putting his hand over the mouthpiece to talk to his mother and father. It was all right, he could do that; Debbie Ross was sobbing again. He thought she'd do that every time she told anyone, at least for awhile. She wouldn't be able to help it, because her heart had given him up.

Is he dead? Ellen mouthed again.

"No!" he told her, a little irritated—it was like she was deaf. "Not dead, alive. She says he's awake."

His mother and father gaped like fish in an aquarium. Pie went past them, still eating Jell-O, her face turned down to the face of her doll, which was sticking stiffly out from the crook of her arm. "Told you this would happen," she said to Melissa Sweetheart in a forbidding this-closes-the-discussion tone of voice. "Didn't I say so?"

"Awake," David's mother had said in a stunned, musing voice. *"Alive."*

"David, are you there?" Mrs. Ross asked.

"Yes," he said. "Right here."

"About twenty minutes after you left, the EEG monitor started to show waves. I saw them first—Mark was down in the caff, getting sodas—and I went to the nurses' station. They didn't believe me." She laughed through her tears. "Well, of course, who would? And when I finally got someone to come look, they called maintenance instead of a doctor, that's how sure they were that it couldn't be happening. They actually *replaced the monitor,* isn't that the most amazing thing you ever heard?"

"Yes," David said. "Wild."

Both parents were mouthing at him now, and his dad was also making big hand-gestures. To David he looked like an insane-asylum inmate who thought he was a gameshow host. That made him want to laugh. He didn't want to do that while he was on the phone, Mrs. Ross wouldn't understand, so he turned and faced the wall.

"It wasn't until they saw the same high waves on the new

monitor—only even stronger—that one of the nurses called Dr. Waslewski. He's the neurologist. Before he got here, Brian opened his eyes and looked around at us. He asked me if I'd fed the goldfish today. I said yes, the goldfish were fine. I didn't cry or anything. I was too *stunned* to cry. Then he said his head ached and closed his eyes again. When Dr. Waslewski came in, Brian looked like he was still in the coma, and I saw him give the nurse a look, like 'Why do you bother me with this?' You know?"

"Sure," David said.

"But when the doctor clapped his hands beside Brian's ear, he opened his eyes again right away. You should have seen that old Polack's face, Davey!" She laughed—the cracked, cackling laugh of a madwoman. "Then . . . then Brian suh-suh-said he was thirsty, and asked if h-he could have a drink of wuh-wuh-*water*."

She broke down entirely then, her sobs so loud in his ear that they almost hurt. Then they faded and Bri's dad said, "David? You still there?" He sounded none too steady himself, but he wasn't outright bawling, which was a relief.

"Sure."

"Brian doesn't remember the accident, doesn't remember *anything* after doing his homework in his room the night before it happened, but he remembers his name, and his address, and *our* names. He knows who the President is, and he can do simple math problems. Dr. Waslewski says he's heard of cases like this, but never actually seen one. He called it 'a clinical miracle.' I don't know if that actually means anything or if it's just something he's always wanted to say, and I don't care. I just want to thank you, David. So does Debbie. From the bottom of our hearts."

"*Me?*" David asked. A hand was tugging his shoulder, trying to get him to turn around. He resisted it. "What are you thanking *me* for?"

"For bringing Brian back to us. You were talking to him; the waves started showing up just after you left. He heard you, Davey. He heard you and came back."

"It wasn't me," David said. He turned around. His folks were all but looming over him, their faces frantic with hope, amazement, confusion. His mother was crying. What a day for tears it had been! Only Pie, who usually bawled at least six hours out of every twenty-four, seemed to have her shit together.

"I know what I know," Mr. Ross said. "I know what I know, David."

He had to talk to his parents before they stared at him so hard they set his shirt on fire . . . but before he did, there was one other thing he had to know. "What time did he wake up and ask about his goldfish? How long after you started seeing his brainwaves?"

"Well, they changed the monitor . . . she told you that . . . and then . . . I don't know . . ." He trailed off for a moment, then said: "Yes I do. I remember hearing the Columbus Broad fire-whistle just before everything happened. So it must've been a few minutes past five."

David had nodded, unsurprised. Right around the time the voice in his head had told him *You're praying already.* "Can I come and see him tomorrow?"

Mr. Ross had laughed then. "David, you can come see him at *midnight,* if that's what you want. Why not? Dr. Waslewski says we have to keep waking him up, anyway, and asking him stupid questions. I know what he's afraid of—that Brian will slip back into the coma—but I don't think that's going to happen, do you?"

"Nope," David said. "Bye, Mr. Ross."

He'd hung up the telephone then, and his parents all but pounced on him. *How did it happen?* they wanted to know. *How did it happen, and what do they think* you *had to do with it?*

David felt an urge then—an amazingly strong one—to cast his eyes down modestly and say, *Well, he woke up, that's really all I know. Except . . . well . . .* He would pause with seeming reluctance, then add: *Mr. and Mrs. Ross think he might have heard my voice and responded to it, but you know how upset they've been.* That's all it would take to start a legend; part of him knew it. And he wanted to do it.

Part of him really, really wanted to do it.

It wasn't the strange inside-out voice that stopped him but a thought of his own, one that was more intuited than articulated: *If you take the credit, it stops here.*

What stops?

Everything that matters, the voice of intuition responded. *Everything that matters.*

"David, come *on,*" his father said, giving his shoulders a little shake. "We're *dying* here."

"Brian's awake," he said, choosing his words carefully. "He can talk, he can remember. The brain-guy says it's a miracle. Mr. and Mrs. Ross think I had something to do with it, that he heard me talking to him and came back, but nothing like that happened. I was holding his hand, and he wasn't there. He was the most gone person I ever saw in my life. That's why I cried—not because his folks were having a fit but because he was gone. I don't know what happened, and I don't care. He's awake, that's all I care about."

"That's all you *need* to care about, darling," his mother said, and gave him a brief, hard hug.

"I'm hungry," he said. "What's for supper?"

3

Now he hung in the black, blind but not deaf, listening for the voice, the one Reverend Gene Martin called the still, small voice of God. Reverend Martin had listened carefully to David's story not once but many times over the last seven months, and he seemed especially pleased by David's recounting of how he had felt during the conversation with his parents after he had finished talking with Mr. Ross.

"You were completely correct," Reverend Martin had said. "It *wasn't* another voice you heard at the end, especially not the voice of God . . . except in the sense that God always speaks to us through our consciences. Secular people, David, believe that the conscience is only a kind of censor, a place where social sanctions are stored, but in fact it is itself a kind of outsider, often guiding us to good solutions even in situations far beyond our understanding. Do you follow me?"

"I think so."

"You didn't know *why* it was wrong to take the credit for your friend's recovery, but you didn't need to. Satan tempted you as he tempted Moses, but in this case you did what Moses didn't, or couldn't: first *under*stood, then *with*stood."

"What about Moses? What did he do?"

Reverend Martin told him the story of how, when the Israelites he'd led out of Egypt were thirsty, Moses had struck a stone with Aaron's staff and brought water gushing out of it. And when the Israelites asked to whom their thanks should be directed, Moses said they could thank him. Reverend Martin sipped from a teacup with HAPPY, JOYOUS, AND FREE printed on the side as he told this story, but what was in the cup didn't exactly smell like tea to David. It smelled more like the whiskey his dad sometimes drank while watching the late news.

"Just one little misstep in a long, hardworking life in the service of the Lord," Reverend Martin said cheerfully, "but God kept him out of the Promised Land for it. Joshua led em across the river—nasty, ungrateful bunch that they were."

This conversation had taken place on a Sunday afternoon in June. By then the two of them had known each other for quite awhile, and grown comfortable with each other. David had fallen into the habit of going to church in the morning, then walking over to the Methodist parsonage on Sunday afternoon and talking with Reverend Martin for an hour or so in his study. David looked forward to these meetings, and Gene Martin did, too. He was immensely taken with the child, who seemed at one moment an ordinary boy and at the next someone much older than his years. And there was something else: he believed that David Carver had been touched by God, and that God's touch might not yet have departed.

He was fascinated with the story of Brian Ross, and by how what had happened to Brian had caused David, a perfect late-twentieth-century religious illiterate, to seek answers . . . to seek God. He told his wife that David was the only honest convert he had ever seen, and that what had happened to David's friend was the only modern miracle he'd ever heard of that he could actually believe in. Brian had turned out fine and dandy except for a slight limp, and the doctors said even that might be gone in a year or so.

"Marvellous," Stella Martin replied. "That will be a comfort to me and the baby if your young friend says the wrong thing about his religious instruction and you wind up in court, facing child-abuse charges. You have to be careful, Gene—and you're *crazy* to be drinking around him."

"I'm *not* drinking around him," Reverend Martin had replied, suddenly finding something interesting to look at out the window. At last he had returned his eyes to his wife. "As to the other, the Lord is my shepherd."

He went on seeing David on Sunday afternoons. He was not quite thirty himself, and discovering for the first time the pleasures of writing on a perfectly blank slate. He didn't quit mixing Seagram's with his tea, a Sunday-afternoon tradition of long standing, but he left the study door open whenever he and David were together. The TV was always on during their conversations, always punched to Mute and tuned to the various Sunday-afternoon athletic contests—soundless football when David first came to Reverend Martin, then soundless basketball, then soundless baseball.

It was during a soundless baseball game between the Indians and the A's that David sat mulling over the story of Moses and the water from the rock. After awhile he looked up from the TV screen and said: "God isn't very forgiving, is he?"

"Yes, indeed he *is*," Reverend Martin said, sounding a little surprised. "He *has* to be, because he is so demanding."

"But he's cruel, too—isn't he?"

Gene Martin hadn't hesitated. "Yes," he said. "God is cruel. I have popcorn, David—would you like me to make some?"

Now he floated in the black, listening for Reverend Martin's cruel God, the one who had refused Moses entry into Canaan because Moses had one single time claimed God's work as his own, the one who had used him in some fashion to save Brian Ross, the one who had then killed his sweet little sister and put the rest of them in the hands of a giant lunatic who had the empty eyes of a coma patient.

There were other voices in the dark place where he went when he prayed; he heard them frequently while he was there—usually distant, like the dim voices you sometimes heard in the background when you made a long-distance call, sometimes more clearly. Today one of them was very clear, indeed.

If you want to pray, pray to me, it said. *Why would you pray to a God who kills baby sisters? You'll never laugh at how funny she is again, or tickle her until she squeals, or pull her braids. She's dead and you and your folks are in jail. When he comes back, the crazy cop, he'll probably kill all three of you. The others as well. This is what your God did, and really, what else would you expect from a God who kills baby sisters? He's as crazy as the cop, when you get right down to cases. Yet you kneel before him. Come on, Davey, get a life. Get a* grip. *Pray to me. At least I'm not* crazy.

He wasn't rocked by this voice—not very, anyway. He'd heard it before, perhaps first wrapped inside that strong impulse to give his folks the impression that he had called Brian back from the deep reaches of his coma. He heard it more clearly, more *personally*, during his daily prayers, and this had troubled him, but when he told Reverend Martin about how that voice would sometimes cut in as if it were on a telephone extension, Reverend Martin had only laughed. "Like God, Satan tends to speak to us most clearly in our prayers and meditations," he said. "It's when we're most open, most in touch with our *pneuma*."

"*Pneuma?* What's that?"

"Spirit. The part of you that yearns to fulfill its God-made potential and be eternal. The part that God and Satan are squabbling over even now."

He had taught David a little mantra to use at such times, and he used it now. *See in me, be in me,* he thought, over and over again. He was waiting for the voice of the other to fade, but he also needed to get above the pain again. It kept coming back like cramps. Thinking about what had happened to Pie hurt so *deep*. And yes, he *did* resent God for letting the insane cop push her down those stairs. Resented, hell, *hated*.

See in me, God. Be in me, God. See in me, be in me.

The voice of Satan (if it was indeed him; David didn't know for sure) faded away, and for awhile there was only the dark.

Tell me what to do, God. Tell me what you want. And if it's your will that we should die here, help me not to waste time being mad or being scared or yelling for an explanation.

Distant, the howl of a coyote. Then, nothing.

He waited, trying to stay open, and still there was nothing. At last he gave up and spoke the prayer-ending words that Reverend Martin had taught him, muttering them into his clasped hands: "Lord, make me be useful to myself and help me to remember that until I am, I can't be useful to others.

Help me to remember that you are my creator. I am what you made—sometimes the thumb on your hand, sometimes the tongue in your mouth. Make me a vessel which is whole to your service. Thanks. Amen."

He opened his eyes. As always, he first stared into the darkness in the center of his clasped hands, and as always, the first thing it reminded him of was an eye—a hole like an eye. Whose, though? God's? The devil's? Perhaps just his own?

He stood up, turned slowly around, looked at his parents. They were looking back at him, Ellie amazed, Ralph grave.

"Well thank *heaven*," his mother said. She gave him a chance to reply, and when he didn't she asked: "*Were* you praying? You were down on your knees almost half an hour, I thought you must have gone to sleep, *were* you praying?"

"Yes."

"Do you do it all the time, or is this a special case?"

"I do it three times a day. In the morning, at night, and once somewhere in the middle. The middle one I use to say thanks for the good things in my life and ask for help with the stuff I don't understand." He laughed—a small, nervous sound. "There's always plenty of that."

"Is this a recent development, or have you been doing it since you started going to that church?" She was still looking at him with a perplexity that made David feel self-conscious. Part of it was the black eye—she was developing a hell of shiner from where the cop had hit her—but that wasn't all of it, or even most of it. She was looking at him as if she had never seen him before.

"He's been doing it since Brian's accident," Ralph said. He touched the swollen place over his left eye, winced, and dropped his hand again. He stared at David through two sets of bars, looking as self-conscious as David felt. "I came upstairs to kiss you goodnight this one time—it was a few days after they let Brian go home—and I saw you down on your knees at the foot of your bed. At first I thought you might be . . . well, I don't know, doing something else . . . then I heard some of what you were saying, and understood."

David smiled, feeling a blush heat his cheeks. That was pretty absurd, under the circumstances, but there it was. "I do it in my head now. I don't even move my lips. A couple of kids heard me mumbling to myself one day in study-hall and thought I was going feeble."

"Maybe your father understands, but I don't," Ellen said.

"I talk to God," he said. This was embarrassing, but maybe if it was said once, and right out straight, it wouldn't have to be said again. "That's what praying is, talking to God. At first it feels like talking to yourself, but then it changes."

"Is that something you know for yourself, David, or is it something your new Sunday pal told you?"

"Something I know for myself."

"And does God answer?"

"Sometimes I think I hear him," David said. He reached into his pocket and touched the shotgun shell with the tips of his fingers. "And once I know I did. I asked him to let Brian be all right. After Dad took me to the hospital, I went to the Bear Street Woods and climbed to the platform me and Bri made in a tree there and asked God to let him be all right. I said that if he did that, I'd kind of give him an IOU. Do you know what I mean?"

"Yes, David, I know what an IOU is. And has he collected on it? This God of yours?"

"Not yet. But when I got up to climb back down the tree, God told me to put my EXCUSED EARLY pass on a nail that was sticking out of the bark up there. It was like he wanted me to turn it in, only to him instead of Mrs. Hardy in the office. And something else. He wanted me to find out as much as I could about him—what he is, what he wants, what he does, and what he won't do. I didn't exactly hear that in words, but I heard the name of the man he wanted me to go to—Reverend Martin. That's why I go to the Methodist church. I don't think the brand name matters much to God, though. He just said to do church for my heart and spirit, and Reverend Martin for my mind. I didn't even know who Reverend Martin was at first."

"But you *did*," Ellie Carver said. She spoke in the soft, soothing voice of a person who suddenly understands that the person she's talking with is having mental problems. "Gene Martin has come to the house two or three years in a row to collect for African Relief."

"Really? I didn't see him. I guess I must have been in school when he came."

"Nonsense," his mother said, now in tones of absolute finality. "He would have come around near Christmas, so you wouldn't have been in school. Now listen to me, David. Very carefully. When the stuff with Brian happened, you must have . . . well, I don't know . . . thought you needed outside help. And your subconscious dredged up the only name it knew. The God you heard in your moment of bereavement was your subconscious mind, looking for answers." She turned to Ralph and spread her hands. "The obsessive Bible-reading was bad enough, but *this* . . . why didn't you tell me about this praying business?"

"Because it looked private." He shrugged, not meeting her eyes. "And it wasn't hurting anybody."

"Oh no, praying is great, without it the thumbscrews and the Iron Maiden probably never would have been invented." This was a voice David had heard before, a nervous, hectoring voice that his mother adopted when she was trying to keep from breaking down completely. It was the way she'd spoken to him and his dad when Brian had been in the hospital; she had gone on in that vein for a week or so even after Brian came around.

David's father turned away from her, stuffing his hands in

his pockets and looking nervously down at the floor. That seemed to make her more furious than ever. She swung back to David, mouth working, eyes shiny with new tears.

"What kind of deal did he make with you, this wonderful God? Was it like one of the baseball-card trades you do with your buds? Did he say 'Hey, I'll trade you this neat Brian Ross '84 for this Kirstie Carver '88?' Was it like that? Or more like—"

"Lady, he's your boy and I don't mean to interfere, but why don't you give it a rest? I guess you lost your little girl; I lost my husband. We've all had a tough day."

It was the woman who had shot at the cop. She was sitting on the end of the bunk. Her black hair hung against her cheeks like limp wings but did not obscure her face; she looked shocked and stricken and tired. Most of all tired. David couldn't remember ever having seen such a weary pair of eyes.

He thought for a moment that his mother would turn her rage on the dark-haired woman. It wouldn't have surprised him; she sometimes went nuclear with total strangers. He remembered once, when he'd been about six, she'd flamed a political candidate trolling for votes outside their neighborhood supermarket. The guy had made the tactical mistake of trying to hand her a leaflet when she had an armload of groceries and was late for an appointment. She had turned on him like some small, biting animal, asking him who he thought he was, what he thought he stood for, what his position was on the trade deficit, had he ever smoked pot, had he ever in his life converted the six-ten split, did he support a woman's right to choose. On that last one the guy had been emphatic—he *did* support a woman's right to choose, he told Ellen Carver proudly. "Good, great, because I choose right now to tell you to GET THE HOLY HELL OUT OF MY FACE!" she had screamed, and that was when the guy had simply turned tail and fled. David hadn't blamed him, either. But something in the dark-haired woman's face (*Mary,* he thought, *her name is Mary)* changed his mother's mind, if blowing up had indeed been on it.

She focused on David again instead.

"So—any word from the big G on how we're supposed to get out of this? You were on your knees long enough, there must have been *some* sort of message."

Ralph turned back to her. "Quit *riding* him!" he growled. "Just quit it! Do you think you're the only one who's hurting?"

She gave him a look which was perilously close to contempt, then looked back at David again. "Well?"

"No," he said. "No message."

"Someone's coming," Mary said sharply. There was a window behind her bunk. She stood on the bunk and tried to look out. "Shit! Bars and frosted glass with goddam chicken-wire in it! But I hear it, I do!"

David heard it, too—an approaching motor. Suddenly it revved up, blatting at full power. The sound was accompanied by a scream of tires. He looked around at the old man. The old man shrugged and raised his hands, palms up.

David heard what might have been a yell of pain, and then another scream. Human, this time. It would be better to think it had been a scream of wind caught in a gutter or a downspout, but he thought it had almost certainly been human.

"What the hell?" Ralph said. "Jesus! Someone's screaming his head off! Is it the cop, do you think?"

"God I hope so!" Mary cried fiercely, still standing on the bunk and peering at the useless window. "I hope someone's pulling the son of a bitch's lungs right out of his chest!" She looked around at them. Her eyes were still tired, but now they looked wild, as well. "It could be help. Have you thought of that? It could be help!"

The engine—not too close but by no means distant—revved. The tires screamed again, screamed the way they did in the movies and on TV but hardly ever in real life. Then there was a crunching sound. Wood, metal, maybe both. A brief honk, as if someone had inadvertently struck the car's horn. A coyote howl rose, wavering and glassy. It was joined by another and another and another. They seemed to be mocking the dark-haired woman's idea of help. Now the motor was approaching, rumbling at a sedate level just above an idle.

The man with the white hair was sitting at the foot of the cell's bunk, his hands pressed together finger-to-finger between his thighs. He talked without raising his eyes from his hands. "Don't get your hopes up." His voice sounded as cracked and dusty as the salt flats west and north of here. "Ain't nobody but him. I reckernize the sound of the motor."

"I refuse to believe that," Ellie Carver said flatly.

"Refuse all you want," the old man said. "It don't matter. I was on the committee that approved the money for a new town cruiser. Just before I finished my term and retired from poli-tics, that was. I went over to Carson City last November with Collie and Dick and we bought it at a DEA auction. That very car. I had my head under the hood before we bid on her and drove her halfway home at speeds varying from sixty-five to a hunnert n ten. I reckernize her, all right. It's our'n."

And, as David turned to look at the old man, the still, small voice—the one he had first heard in Brian's hospital room—spoke to him. As usual, its arrival came pretty much as a surprise, and the two words it spoke made no immediate sense.

The soap.

He heard the words as clearly as he had heard *You're praying already* while he'd been sitting in the Viet Cong Lookout with his eyes closed.

The soap.

He looked into the left rear corner of the cell he was shar-ing with old Mr. White Hair. There was a toilet with no seat. Beside it was an ancient rust-stained porcelain sink. Sitting beside the righthand spigot was a green bar of what could only be Irish Spring soap.

Outside, the engine-sound of the Desperation police-cruiser grew fatter and closer. A little farther off, the coyotes howled. To David that howling had begun to sound like the laughter of lunatics after the keepers have decamped the asylum.

4

The Carver family had been too distraught and too focused on their captor to notice the dead dog hung from the welcome-to-town sign, but John Marinville was a trained noticer. And in truth, the dog was now hard to miss. Since the Carvers had passed this way, the buzzards had found it. They sat on the ground below the carcass, the ugliest birds Johnny had ever seen, one pulling on Old Shep's tail, the other gnawing at one of his dangling feet. The body swung back and forth on the rope twisted around its neck. Johnny made a sound of disgust.

"Buzzards!" the cop said. "Gosh, aren't they something?" His voice had thickened a great deal. He had sneezed twice more on the ride in from town, and the second time there had been teeth in the blood he sprayed out of his mouth. Johnny didn't know what was happening to him and didn't care; he only wished it would hurry up. "I'll tell you something about buzzards," the cop continued. "They wake to sleep and take their waking slow. They learn by going where they have to go. Wouldn't you agree, *mon capitaine?*"

A lunatic cop who quoted poetry. How Sartre.

"Whatever you say, Officer." He had no intention of antago-nizing the cop again, if he could help it; the guy seemed to be self-destructing, and Johnny wanted to be around when the process was over.

They rolled past the dead dog and the grisly skinned-looking things dining on it.

What about the coyotes, Johnny? What was up with them?

But he wouldn't let himself think about the coyotes, lined up along both sides of the road at neat intervals like an honor guard, or of how they had peeled off like the Blue Angels as soon as the cruiser passed, running back into the desert as if their heads were on fire and their asses were catching—

"They fart, you know," the cop said in his bloodsoaked voice. "Buzzards fart."

"No, I didn't know that."

"Yessir, only birds that do. I tell you so you can put it in your book. Chapter 16 of *Travels with Harley.*"

Johnny thought the putative title of his book had never sounded so quintessentially stupid.

They were now passing a trailer park. Johnny saw a sign in front of one rusty, roof-sagging doublewide which read:

I'M A GUN-TOTIN' SNAPPLE-DRINKIN'
BIBLE-READIN' CLINTON-BASHIN' SON OF A BITCH!
NEVER MIND THE DOG, BEWARE OF THE *OWNER*!

Welcome to country music hell, Johnny thought.

The cruiser rolled past a mining-company building. There were quite a few cars and pickups in the parking lot, which struck Johnny as peculiar. It was past quitting time now, and not by a little. Why weren't these cars in their own driveways, or down in front of the local watering hole?

"Yep, yep," the cop said. He lifted one hand, as if to frame a picture. "I can see it now. Chapter 16: The Farting Buzzards of Desperation. Sounds like a goddam Edgar Rice Burroughs novel, doesn't it? Burroughs was a better writer than you, though, and do you know why? Because he was a hack without pretensions. One with *priorities.* Tell the story, do the work, give people something they can enjoy without feeling too stupid, and stay out of the gossip columns."

"Where are you taking me?" Johnny asked, striving for a neutral tone.

"Jail," the big cop said in his stuffy, liquid voice. "Where anything you bray will be abused against you in a sort of caw."

He leaned forward, wincing at the pain in his back where the cop had kicked him. "You need help," he said. He tried to keep his voice non-accusatory, even gentle. "Do you know that, Officer?"

"*You're* the one who needs help," the cop replied. "Spiritual, physical, and editorial. *Tak!* But no help is going to come, Big John. You've eaten your last literary lunch and fucked your last culture cunt. You're on your own in the wilderness, and this is going to be the longest forty days and forty nights of your entire useless life."

The words rang in his head like the peal of some sickly bell. Johnny closed his eyes for a moment, then opened them again. They were in the town proper now, passing Gail's Beauty Bar on one side and True Value Hardware on the other. There was nobody on the sidewalks—absolutely nobody. He'd never seen a small Western town that was actually *bustling*, but this was ridiculous. No one at *all*? As they passed the Conoco station he saw a guy in the office, rocked back in his chair with his feet up on the desk, but that was it. Except . . . up ahead . . .

A pair of animals went trotting lazily across what appeared to be the town's only intersection, moving on a diagonal beneath the blinker-light. Johnny tried to tell himself they were dogs, but they weren't dogs. They were coyotes.

It's not all the cop, Johnny, don't you think it is. Something not normal is going on here. Something very much not normal.

As they reached the intersection, the cop slammed on the brakes. Johnny, not expecting it, was thrown forward into the mesh between the front and back seats. He hit his nose and bellowed with surprised pain.

The cop took no notice of him. "Billy Rancourt!" he cried, delighted. "Damn, that's Billy Rancourt! I *wondered* where he got off to! Drunk in the basement of The Broken Drum, I bet you that's where he was! Dollars to doughnuts! Big-Balls Billy, damn if it's not!"

"My *dose*!" Johnny cried. It had started bleeding again, and he once more sounded like a human foghorn. "Oh Christ, it *hurts*!"

"Shut up, you baby," the cop said. "Gosh, aren't you spleeny?"

He backed up a little, then turned the cruiser so it was facing west on the cross-street. He cranked his window down and poked his head out. The nape of his neck was now the color of age-darkened bricks, badly blistered, crisscrossed with cracks. Bright lines of blood filled some of these. *"Billy!"* the cop yelled. "Yo, you Billy Rancourt! *Hey,* you old cuss!"

The western end of Desperation appeared to be a residential section—dusty and dispirited, but maybe a cut or two above the trailer park. Through his watering eyes, Johnny saw a man in bluejeans and a cowboy hat standing in the center of the street. He had been looking at two bicycles which sat there upside down, with their wheels sticking up. There had been three, but the smallest—a candy-pink little girl's bike—had fallen over in the strengthening wind. The wheels of the other two spun madly. Now this fellow looked up, saw the cruiser, waved hesitantly, then started toward them.

The cop pulled his large square head back in. He turned to look at Johnny, who understood at once that the guy out there couldn't have gotten a good look at this particular officer of the law; if he had, he would be running in the other direction right now. The cop's mouth had the sunken, infirm look of lips with no teeth to back them up, and blood ran from the corners in little streams. One of his eyes was a cauldron of gore—except for an occasional gray flash from its swimming depths, it could have been a plucked socket. A shiny mat of blood covered the top half of his khaki shirt.

"That's Billy Rancourt," he confided happily. "He cuts my hair. I been *looking* for him." He lowered his voice to that register at which confidences are imparted and added, "He drinks a bit." Then he faced front, dropped the transmission into Drive, and floored the accelerator. The rumbling engine howled; the tires squalled; Johnny was thrown backward, yelling with surprise. The cruiser shot forward.

Johnny reached out, hooked his fingers through the mesh, and hauled himself back to a sitting position. He saw the man in the jeans and cowboy hat—Big-Balls Billy Rancourt—just standing there in the street ten feet or so in front of the bikes, frozen, watching them come. He seemed to swell in the windshield as the cruiser ran at him; it was like watching some crazy camera trick.

"*No!*" Johnny shrieked, beating his left hand at the mesh behind the cop's head. "*No, don't! Don't! MISTER, LOOK OUT!*"

At the last minute, Billy Rancourt understood and tried to run. He broke to his right, toward a ramshackle house squatting tiredly behind a picket fence, but it was too little and too late. He yelled, then there was a crump as the cruiser struck him hard enough to make the frame shudder. Blood spattered the picket fence, there was a double thud from beneath the car as the wheels ran over the fallen man, and then the cruiser hit the fence and knocked it down. The big cop jammed on the brakes, bringing the cruiser to a stop in the bald dirt dooryard of the ramshackle house. Johnny was thrown forward into the mesh again, but this time he managed to get his arm up and his head down, protecting his nose.

"Billy, you *bugger*!" the cop cried happily. "*Tak an lah!*"

Billy Rancourt screamed. Johnny turned in the back seat of the cruiser and saw him crawling as fast as he could toward the north side of the street. That wasn't very fast; he was trailing a broken leg. There were tread-marks running across the back of his shirt and the set of his jeans. His cowboy hat was sitting on the pavement, now turned upside down like the bicycles. Billy Rancourt bumped it with one knee, knocking it aslant, and blood poured out over the brim like water. More blood was gushing from his split skull and broken face. He was badly hurt, but although he had been struck amidships and then run over, he didn't appear even close to dead. That didn't surprise Johnny much. Most times it took a lot to kill a man—he had seen it again and again in Vietnam. Guys alive with half their heads blown off, guys alive with their guts piled in their laps and drawing flies, guys alive with their jugulars spouting through their dirty fingers. People usually died hard. That was the horror of it.

"YeeHAW!" the cop yelled, and dropped the cruiser's transmission into Reverse. The tires screamed and smoked across the sidewalk, bounced back into the street, and ran over Billy Rancourt's cowboy hat. The cruiser's back deck hit one of the bikes (it made a hell of a bang, cracked the rear window, then flew out of sight for a moment before coming down in front). Johnny had time to see that Billy Rancourt had stopped crawling, that he was looking back over his shoulder at them, that his blood-streaked broken-nosed face wore an expression of unspeakable resignation. *He can't even be thirty,* Johnny thought, and then the man was borne under the reversing car. It lurched over the body and came to a stop, idling, against the far curb. The cop hit the horn with the point of his elbow, making it blip briefly, as he turned to face forward again. Ahead of the cruiser's nose, Billy Rancourt lay face-down in a huge splat of blood. One of his feet twitched, then stopped.

"Whoa," the cop said. "What a damn mess, huh?"

"Yeah, you killed him," Johnny said. Suddenly he didn't care anymore about playing this guy up, outlasting him. He didn't care about the book, or his Harley, or where Steve Ames might be. Maybe later—if there *was* a later—he would care about some of those things, but not now. Now, in his shock and dismay, an earlier draft of himself had come out from someplace inside; a pre-edited version of Johnny Marinville who didn't give a shit about the Pulitzer Prize or the National Book Award or fucking actresses, with or without emeralds. "Ran him over in the street like a damn rabbit. Brave boy!"

The cop turned, gave him a considering look with his one good eye, then turned back to face the windshield again. "'I have taught thee in the way of wisdom,'" he said, "'I have led thee in right paths. When thou goest, thy steps shall not be straitened; and when thou runnest, thou shalt not stumble.' That's from the Book of Adverbs, John. But I think old Billy stumbled. Yes, I do. He was always a gluefoot. I think that was his basic problem."

Johnny opened his mouth. For one of the few times in his entire life, nothing came out. Maybe that was just as well.

"'Take fast hold of instruction; let her not go: keep her; for she is thy life.' That's a little advice you could afford to take, Mr. Marinville, sir. Excuse me a minute."

He got out and walked to the dead man in the street, his boots seeming to shimmer as the strengthening wind blew sand across them. There was a large bloody patch on the seat of his uniform pants now, and when he bent to pick up the late Billy Rancourt, Johnny saw more blood oozing out through the ripped seams under the cop's arms. It was as if he were literally sweating blood.

Maybe so. Probably *so. I think he's on the verge of crashing and bleeding out, the way hemophiliacs sometimes do. If he wasn't so Christing big, he'd probably be dead already. You know what you have to do, don't you?*

Yes, of course he did. He had a bad temper, a *horrible* temper, and it seemed that not even getting the shit kicked out of him by a homicidal maniac had changed that. What he had to do now was keep that temper of his under control. No more cracks, like calling the cop a brave boy just now. That had earned him a look Johnny hadn't liked at all. A *dangerous* look.

The cop carried Billy Rancourt's body across the street, stepping between the two fallen bikes and past the one with its wheels still whirring and its spokes shining in the evening light. He tromped over the knocked-down piece of picket fence, climbed the steps of the house behind it, and shifted his burden so he could try the door. It opened with no trouble. Johnny wasn't surprised. He supposed that people out here did not, as a rule, bother locking their doors.

He'll have to kill the people inside, he thought. *That's pretty much automatic.*

But the cop only bent, offloaded his burden, then backed out onto the porch's little stoop again. He closed the door and then wiped his hands above it, leaving smears of blood on the lintel. He was so tall he didn't even have to reach to do this. The gesture gave Johnny a deep chill—it was like something out of the Book of Exodus, instructions for the Angel of Death to pass on by . . . except this man *was* the Angel of Death. The destroyer.

The cop walked back to the cruiser, got in, and drove sedately back toward the intersection.

"Why'd you take him into there?" Johnny asked.

"What did you *want* me to do?" the cop asked. His voice was thicker than ever; now he seemed almost to be gargling his words. "Leave him for the buzzards? I'm ashamed of you, *mon capitaine.* You've been living so long with so-called civilized folk that you're starting to think like them."

"The dog—"

"A man is not a dog," the cop said in a prim, lecturely voice.

He turned right at the intersection, then almost immediately hung a left, turning into a parking lot next to the town's Municipal Building. He killed the engine, got out, and opened the right-hand rear door. That at least spared Johnny the pain and effort of sliding his banged-up body out past the sagging driver's seat. "A chicken is not a chicken dinner and a man is not a dog, Johnny. Not even a man like you. Come on. Get out. Alley-zoop."

Johnny got out. He was very aware of the silence; the sounds he could hear—wind, the spick-spack of alkali hitting the brick side of the Municipal Building, a monotonous squeaking sound from somewhere nearby—only emphasized that silence, turned it into something like a dome. He stretched, wincing at the pain in his back and leg but needing to do something for the rest of his muscles, which were badly cramped. Then he forced himself to look up into the ruin of the cop's face. The man's height was intimidating, somehow disorienting. It wasn't just that at six-three Johnny was used to looking down into people's faces instead of up; it was the *amount* of the height differential, not an inch or two but at least four. Then there was the breadth of the man. The sheer breadth. He didn't just stand; he *loomed.*

"Why didn't you kill me like you did that guy back there? Billy? Or does it even make any sense to ask? Are you beyond why?"

"Oh shit, we're all beyond why, *you* know that," the cop said, exposing bloody teeth in a smile Johnny could have done without. "The *important* thing is . . . listen closely . . . *I could let you go.* Would you like that? You must have at least two more stupid, pointless books left in your head, maybe as many as half a dozen. You could write a few before that thunderclap coronary that's waiting for you up the road finally takes you off. And I'm sure that, given time, you could put this interlude behind you and once more convince yourself that what you are doing somehow justifies your existence. Would you like that, Johnny? Would you like me to let you go free?"

Erin go bragh, Johnny thought for no reason at all, and for one nightmarish moment felt he would laugh. Then the urge was gone and he nodded. "Yes, I'd like that very much."

"Free! Like a bird out of a cage." The cop flapped his arms to demonstrate, and Johnny saw that the bloody patches under his arms had spread. His uniform shirt was now stained crimson along the torn side-seams almost all the way down to his beltline.

"Yes." Not that he believed his new playmate had the slightest intention in the world of letting him free; oh no. But said playmate was shortly going to be nothing but blood-sausage held together by the casing of his uniform, and if he could just remain whole and functional himself until that happened . . .

"All right. Here's the deal, bigshot: suck my cock. Do that and I'll let you go. Straight trade."

He unzipped his fly and pulled down the elastic front of his shorts. Something that looked like a dead whitesnake fell out. Johnny observed the thin stream of blood drizzling from it without surprise. The cop was bleeding from every other orifice, wasn't he?

"Speaking in the lit'ry sense," the cop said, grinning, "this particular blowjob is going to be a little more Anne Rice than Armistead Maupin. I suggest you follow Queen Victoria's advice—close your eyes and think of strawberry shortcake."

Johnny Marinville looked at the maniac's prick, then up at the maniac's grinning face, then back at his prick again. He didn't know what the cop expected—screams, revulsion, tears, melodramatic pleading—but he had a clear sense that he wasn't feeling what the cop wanted him to feel, what the cop probably thought he *was* feeling.

You don't seem to understand that I've seen a few worse things in my time than a cock dripping blood. Not just in Vietnam, either.

He realized that the anger was creeping up on him again, threatening to take him over. Oh shit, of course it was. Anger had always been his primary addiction, not whiskey or coke or 'ludes. Plain old rage. It didn't have anything to do with what the cop had taken out of his pants, and that might be what the guy didn't understand. It wasn't a sex issue. The thing was, Johnny Marinville had never liked *anything* stuck in his face.

"I'll get down on my knees in front of you if you want," he said, and although his voice was mild, something in the cop's face changed—really changed for the first time. It *blanked out* somehow, except for the good eye, which narrowed suspiciously.

"Why are you looking at me that way? What in the hell gives you the *right* to look at me that way? *Tak!*"

"Never mind how I'm looking at you. Just hear me out, motherfucker: three seconds after I put that trouser-rat of yours into my mouth, it's going to be lying on the pavement. You got that? *Tak!*"

He *spat* this last word up into the cop's face, standing on tiptoe to do it, and for a moment the big man looked more than surprised—he looked shocked. Then the expression tightened into a cramp of rage, and he shoved Johnny away from him so hard that for a moment he felt as if he were flying. He hit the side of the building, saw stars as the back of his head connected with rough brick, bounced back, then went sprawling when his feet tangled together. New places hurt and old places howled, but the expression he had seen on the cop's face made it all worthwhile. He looked up to see if it was still there, wanting to sample it again like a bee sampling the sweet heart of a flower, and his heart staggered in his chest.

The cop's face had tautened. The skin on it now looked like makeup, or a thin coat of paint—unreal. Even the blood-filled eye looked unreal. It was as if there was another face beneath the one Johnny could see, pushing at the overlying flesh, trying to get out.

The cop's good eye fixed on him for a moment, and then his head lifted. He pointed at the sky with all five fingers of his left hand. *"Tak ah lah,"* he said in his guttural, gargling voice. *"Timoh. Can de lach! On! On!"*

There was a flapping sound, like clothes on a line, and a shadow fell over Johnny's face. There was a harsh cry, not quite a caw, and then something with scabrous, flapping wings dropped on him, its crooked claws gripping his shoulders and folding themselves into the fabric of his shirt, its beak digging into his scalp as it uttered its inhuman cry again.

It was the smell that told Johnny what it was—a smell like meat gone feverish with rot. Its huge, unkempt wings flapped against the sides of his face as it solidified its position, driving that stench into his mouth and nose, *jamming* it in, making him gag. He saw the Shepherd on its rope, swinging as the peeled-looking bald things pulled at its tail and feet with their beaks. Now one of them was roosting on *him*—one which had apparently never heard that buzzards were fundamental cowards that only attacked dead things—and its beak was plowing his scalp in furrows, bringing blood.

"Get it off!" he screamed, completely unnerved. He tried to grab the wide, beating wings, but got only two fistfuls of feathers. Nor could he see; he was afraid that if he opened his eyes, the buzzard would shift its position and peck them out. *"Jesus, please, please get it off me!"*

"Are you going to look at me properly if I do?" the cop asked. "No more insolence? No more disrespect?"

"No! No more!" He would have promised anything. Whatever had leaped out of him and spoken against the cop was gone now; the bird had plucked it out like a worm from an ear of corn.

"You promise?"

The bird, flapping and squalling and pulling. Smelling like green meat and exploded guts. On him. Eating him. Eating him *alive.*

"Yes! Yes! I promise!"

"Fuck you," the cop said calmly. "Fuck you, *os pa,* and fuck your promise. Take care of it yourself. Or die."

Eyes squeezed to slits, kneeling, head lowered, Johnny gripped blindly for the bird, caught its wings where they joined its body, and tore it off his head. It spasmed wildly in the air above him, shitting white streams that the wind pulled away in banners, uttering its rough cry (only there was pain in it now), its head whipping from side to side. Sobbing—mostly what he felt was revulsion—Johnny ripped one of its wings off and threw the buzzard against the wall. It stared at him with eyes as black as tar, its bloodstained beak popping open and then snapping closed with liquid little clicks.

That's my *blood, you bastard,* Johnny thought. He dropped the wing he'd torn off the bird and got to his feet. The buzzard tried to lurch away from him, flapping its one good wing like an oar, stirring up dust and feathers. It went in the direction of the Desperation police-cruiser, but before it managed more than five feet, Johnny brought one motorcycle boot down on it, snapping its back. The bird's scaly legs splayed out to either side, as if it were trying to do the split. Johnny put his hands over his eyes, convinced for one moment that his mind was going to snap just as the bird's back had snapped.

"Not bad," the cop said. "You got him, pard. Now turn around."

"No." He stood, trembling all over, hands to his face.

"Turn around."

There was no denying the voice. He turned and saw the cop pointing up, once again with all five splayed fingers. Johnny raised his head and saw more buzzards—two dozen at least—sitting in a line along the north side of the parking lot, looking down at them.

"Want me to call them?" the cop asked in a deceptively

gentle tone of voice. "I can, you know. Birds are a hobby of mine. They'll eat you alive, if that's what I want."

"N-N-No." He looked back at the cop and was relieved to see his fly was zipped again. There was a bloodstain spreading across the front of his pants, though. "No, d-don't."

"What's the magic word, Johnny?"

For a moment—a *horrible* moment—he had no idea what the cop wanted him to say. Then it came to him. *"Please."*

"Are you ready to be reasonable?"

"Y-Yes."

"I wonder about that," the cop said. He seemed to be speaking to himself. "I just wonder."

Johnny stood looking at him, saying nothing. The anger was gone. *Everything* felt gone, replaced by a kind of deep numbness.

"That boy," the cop said, looking up toward the second floor of the Municipal Building, where there were a number of opaque windows with bars outside them. "That boy troubles my mind. I wonder if I shouldn't talk to you about him. Perhaps you could counsel me."

The cop folded his arms against his body, raised his hands, and began to tap his fingers lightly against his collarbones, much as he'd tapped them against the steering wheel earlier. He stared at Johnny as he did this.

"Or maybe I should just kill you, Johnny. Maybe it would be the best thing—once you're dead they might award you that Nobel you've always lusted after. What do you think?"

The cop raised his head to the buzzard-lined roofline of the Municipal Building and began to laugh. They cried harsh cawing sounds back down at him, and Johnny was not able to stifle the thought which came to him then. It was horrible because it was so convincing.

They are laughing with him. Because it's not his *joke; it's* their *joke.*

A gust of air snapped across the parking lot, making Johnny stagger on his feet, blowing the torn-off buzzard wing across the pavement like a featherduster. The light was fading out of the day—fading too fast. He looked to the west and saw that rising dust had blurred the mountains in that direction and might soon erase them completely. The sun was still above the dust, but wouldn't be for long. It was a windstorm, and headed their way.

5

The five people in the holding cells—the Carvers, Mary Jackson, and old Mr. White Hair—listened to the man screaming and to the sounds that accompanied the screams—harsh bird-cries and flapping wings. At last they stopped. David hoped no one else was dead down there, but when you got right to it, what were the chances?

"What did you say his name was?" Mary asked.

"Collie Entragian," the old man said. He sounded as if listening to the screams had pretty much tired him out. "Collie's short for Collier. He come here from one of those mining towns in Wyoming, oh, fifteen-sixteen years ago. Little more than a teenager then, he was. Wanted police work, couldn't get it, went to work for the Diablo Company up to the pit instead. That was around the time Diablo was gettin ready to pack up and go home. Collie was part of the close-down crew, as I remember."

"He told Peter and me the mine was open," Mary said.

The old man shook his head in what might have been weariness or exasperation. "There's some thinks old China ain't played out, but they're wrong. It's true they been bustling around up there again, but they won't take doodley-squat out of it—just lose their investors' money and then shut her down.

Won't be nobody any happier about it than Jim Reed, either. He's tired of barroom fights. All of us'll be glad when they leave old China alone again. It's haunted, that's what the ignorant folks round these parts think." He paused. "I'm one of em."

"Who's Jim Reed?" Ralph asked.

"Town Safety Officer. What you'd call Chief of Police in a bigger burg, but there's only two hundred or so people in Desperation these days. Jim had two full-time deputies—Dave Pearson and Collie. Nobody expected Collie to stay around after Diablo folded, but he did. He wasn't married, and he had workman's comp. He floated along for awhile, odd-jobbin, and eventually Jim started to throw work his way. He was good enough so that the town officers took Jim's recommendation and hired him on full-time in '91."

"Three guys seems like a lot of law for a town this small," Ralph said.

"I reckon. But we got some money from Washin'un, Rural Law Enforcement Act, plus we landed a contract with Sedalia County to keep school on the unincorporated lands round here—pop the speeders, jug the drunks, all such as that."

More coyote wails from outside; they sounded shimmery in the rising wind.

Mary asked, "What did he get workman's comp for? Some kind of mental problem?"

"No'm. Pickup he was ridin in turned turtle on its way down into the pit yonder—the China. Just before the Diablo people gave it up as a bad job, this was. Blew out his knee. Boy was fit enough after, but he had a limp, no question about that."

"Then it's not him," Mary said flatly.

The old man looked at her, shaggy eyebrows raised.

"The man who killed my husband does not limp."

"No," the old man agreed. He spoke with a weird kind of serenity. "No, he don't. But it's Collie, all right. I been seein him most every day for fifteen years, have bought him drinks in The Broken Drum and had him buy me a few in return over at Bud's Suds. He was the one came to the clinic, took pictures, and dusted for prints the time those fellows broke in. Probably looking for drugs, they were, but I don't know. They never caught em."

"Are you a doctor, mister?" David asked.

"Vet," the old man said. "Tom Billingsley is my name." He held out a big, worn hand that shook a little. David took it gingerly.

Downstairs, a door smashed open. "Here we are, Big John!" the cop said. His voice rolled jovially up the stairs. "Your room awaits! Room? Hell, a regular efficiency apartment! Up you go! We forgot the word processor, but we left you some *great* walls and a few little Hallmark sentiments like SUCK MY COCK and I FUCKED YOUR SISTER to get you started!"

Tom Billingsley glanced toward the door which gave upon the stairs, then looked back at David. He spoke loud enough for the others to hear but it *was* David he looked at, David he seemed to want to tell. "Tell you something else," he said. "He's bigger."

"What do you mean?" But David thought he knew.

"What I said. Collie was never a midget—stood about six-four, I'd judge, and probably weighed about two hundred and thirty. But now . . ."

He glanced toward the doorway to the stairs again—toward the sound of approaching, clumping footsteps. Two sets. Then he looked back at David.

"Now I'd say he's at least three inches more'n that, wouldn't you? And maybe sixty pounds heavier."

"That's crazy!" Ellen cried. "Absolutely nuts!"

"Yessum," the white-haired vet agreed. "But it's true."

The door to the stairs flew all the way open and a man with a bloody face and shoulder-length gray hair—it was also streaked and clumped with blood—flew into the room. He didn't cross it with Mary Jackson's balletic grace but stumbled at the halfway point and fell to his knees, holding his hands out in front of him to keep from crashing into the desk. The man who followed him through the door was the man who had brought them all to this place, and yet he wasn't—he was a kind of blood-gorgon, a creature who appeared to be disintegrating before their very eyes.

He surveyed them from the melting ramparts of his face, and his mouth spread in a wide, lip-splitting grin. "Look at us," he said in a thick, sentimental voice. "Look at us, would you? Gosh! Just one big happy family!"

PART II

DESPERATION: IN THESE SILENCES SOMETHING MAY RISE

CHAPTER 1

1

"Steve?"

"What?"

"Is that what I think it is?"

She was pointing out her window, pointing west.

"What do you *think* it is?"

"Sand," she said. "Sand and wind."

"Yep. I'd say that's what it is."

"Pull over a minute, would you?"

He looked at her, questioning.

"Just for a minute."

Steve Ames pulled the Ryder van over to the side of the road which led south from Highway 50 to the town of Desperation. They had found it with no trouble at all. Now he sat behind the wheel and looked at Cynthia Smith, who had tickled him even in his unease by calling him her nice new friend. She wasn't looking at her nice new friend now; she was looking down at the bottom of her funky Peter Tosh shirt and plucking at it nervously.

"I'm a hard-headed babe," she said without looking up. "A little psychic, but hard-headed just the same. Do you believe that?"

"I guess."

"And practical. Do you believe *that*?"

"Sure."

"That's why I made fun of your intuition, or whatever. But you thought we'd find something out there by the road, and we did."

"Yes. We did."

"So it was a good intuition."

"Would you get to the point? My boss—"

"Right. Your boss, your boss, your boss. I know that's what you're thinking about and practically *all* you're thinking about, and that's what's got me worried. Because I have a bad feeling about this, Steve. A bad *intuition*."

He looked at her. Slowly, reluctantly, she raised her head and looked back at him. What he saw in her eyes startled him badly—it was the flat shine of fear.

"What is it? What are you afraid of?"

"I don't know."

"Look, Cynthia . . . all we're going to do is find a cop—lacking that, a phonebooth—and report Johnny missing. Also a bunch of people named Carver."

"Just the same—"

"Don't worry, I'll be careful. Promise."

"Would you try 911 on your cellular again?" She asked this in a small, meek voice that was not much like her usual one.

He did, to please her, expecting nothing, and nothing was what he got. Not even a recording this time. He didn't know for sure, but he thought the oncoming windstorm, or duststorm, or whatever they called them out here, might be screwing things up even worse.

"Sorry, no go," he said. "Want to give it a try yourself? You might have better luck. The woman's touch, and all that."

She shook her head. "Do *you* feel anything? Anything at all?"

He sighed. Yes, he felt something. It reminded him of the way he had sometimes felt in early puberty, back in Texas. The summer he turned thirteen had been the longest, sweetest, strangest summer of his life. Toward the end of August, evening thunderstorms had often moved through the area—brief but hellacious convulsions the old cowboys called "benders." And in that year (a year when it seemed that every other pop song on the radio was by The Bee Gees), the hushed minutes before these storms—black sky, still air, sharpening thunder, lightning jabbing at the prairie like forks into tough meat—had somehow turned him on in a way he had never experienced since. His eyes felt like globes of electricity in chrome sockets, his stomach rolled, his penis filled with blood and stood up hard as a skillet-handle. A feeling of terrified ecstasy came in those hushes, a sense that the world was about to give up some great secret, to play it like a special card. In the end, of course, there had never been a revelation (unless his discovery of how to masturbate a year or so later had been it), only rain. That was how he felt now, only there was no hardon, no tingling armhairs, no ecstasy, and no sense of terror, not really. What he had been feeling ever since she had uncovered the boss's motorcycle helmet was a sense of low foreboding, a sense that things had gone wrong and would soon go wronger. Until she had spoken up just now, he'd pretty much written that feeling off. As a kid, he'd probably just been responding to changes in the air-pressure as the storm approached, or electricity in the air, or some other damned thing. And a storm was coming now, wasn't it? Yes. So it was probably the same thing, déjà vu all over again, as they said, perfectly understandable. Yet—

"Yeah, okay, I *do* feel something. But what in the hell can I do about it? You don't want me to turn back, do you?"

"No. We can't do that. Just be careful. 'Kay?"

A gust of wind shook the Ryder truck. A cloud of tawny sand blew across the road, turning it into a momentary mirage.

"Okay, but you've got to help."

He got the truck moving again. The setting sun had touched

the rising membrane of sand in the west now, and its bottom arc had gone as red as blood.

"Oh yeah," she said, grimacing as a fresh blast of wind hit the truck. "You can count on that."

2

The bloodsoaked cop locked the newcomer into the cell next to David Carver and Tom Billingsley. That done, he turned slowly on his heels in a complete circle, his half-peeled, bleeding face solemn and contemplative. Then he reached into his pocket and brought out the keyring again. He selected the same one as before, David noticed—square, with a black mag-strip on it—so it was probably a master.

"Eeenie-meenie-miney-moe," he said. "Catch a tourist by the toe." He walked toward the cell which held David's mother and father. As he approached they drew back, arms around each other again.

"You leave them alone!" David cried, alarmed. Billingsley took his arm above the elbow, but David shook it off. "Do you hear me? *Leave them alone!*"

"In your dreams, brat," Collie Entragian said. He poked the key into the cell's lock and there was a little thump as the tumblers turned. He pulled the door open. "Good news. Ellie—your parole came through. Pop on out here."

Ellen shook her head. Shadows had begun to gather in the holding area now and her face swam in them, pale as paper. Ralph put his other arm around her waist and drew her back even farther. "Haven't you done enough to our family?" he asked.

"In a word, no." Entragian drew his cannon-sized gun, pointed it at Ralph, and cocked it. "You come out of here right now, little lady, or I'll shoot this no-chin pecker-checker spang between the eyes. You want his brains in his head or drying on the wall? It's all the same to me either way."

God, make him quit it, David prayed. *Please make him quit it. If you could bring Brian back from wherever he was, you can do that. You can make him quit it. Dear God, please don't let him take my mother.*

Ellen was pushing Ralph's hands down, pushing them off her.

"Ellie, no!"

"*I have* to. Don't you see that?"

Ralph let his hands fall to his sides. Entragian dropped the hammer on his gun and slid it back into his holster. He held one hand out to Ellen, as if inviting her to take a spin on the dance floor. And she went to him. When she spoke, her voice was very low. David knew she was saying something she didn't want him to hear, but his ears were good.

"If you want . . . that, take me where my son won't have to see."

"Don't worry," Entragian said in that same low, conspirator's voice. "I don't want . . . that. Especially not from . . . you. Now come on."

He slammed the cell door shut, giving it a little shake to make sure it was locked, while he held onto David's mother with the other hand. Then he led her toward the door.

"*Mom!*" David screamed. He seized the bars and shook them. The cell door rattled a little, but that was all. "*Mom, no! Leave her alone, you bastard! LEAVE MY MOTHER ALONE!*"

"Don't worry, David, I'll be back," she said, but the soft, almost uninflected quality of her voice scared him badly—it was as if she were already gone. Or as if the cop had hynotized her just by touching her. "Don't worry about me."

"*No!*" David screamed. "*Daddy, make him stop! Make him stop!*" In his heart was a growing certainty: if the huge, bloody cop took his mother out of this room, they would never see her again.

"David . . ." Ralph took two blundering steps backward, sat on the bunk, put his hands over his face, and began to cry.

"I'll take care of her, Dave, don't worry," Entragian said. He was standing by the door to the stairs and holding Ellen Carver's arm above the elbow. He wore a grin that would have been resplendent if not for his blood-streaked teeth. "I'm sensitive—a real *Bridges of Madison County* kind of guy, only without the cameras."

"If you hurt her, you'll be sorry," David said.

The cop's smile faded. He looked both angry and a little hurt. "Perhaps I will . . . but I doubt it. I really do. You're a little prayboy, aren't you?"

David looked at him steadily, saying nothing.

"Yes, yes you are. You've just got that prayboy look about you, great-gosh-a'mighty eyes and a real jeepers-creepers mouth. A little prayboy in a baseball shirt! Gosh!" He put his head close to Ellen's and looked slyly at the boy through the gauze of her hair. "Do all the praying you want, David, but don't expect it to do you any help. Your God isn't here, any more than he was with Jesus when Jesus hung dying on the cross with flies in his eyes. *Tak!*"

Ellen saw it coming up the stairs. She screamed and tried to pull back, but Entragian held her where she was. The coyote oiled through the doorway. It didn't even look at the screaming woman with her arm pinched in the cop's fist but crossed calmly to the center of the room. Then it stopped, turned its head over one shoulder, and fixed its yellow stuffed-animal stare on Entragian.

"*Ah lah,*" he said, and let go of Ellen's arm long enough to spank his right hand across the back of his left hand in a quick gesture that reminded David of a flat stone skipping across the surface of a pond. "*Him en tow.*"

The coyote sat down.

"This guy is fast," Entragian said. He was apparently speaking to all of them, but it was David he was looking at. "I mean the guy is *fast*. Faster than most dogs. You stick a hand or foot out of your cell, he'll have it off before you know it's gone. I guarantee that."

"You leave my mother alone," David said.

"Son," Entragian said regretfully, "I'll put a stick up your mother's twat and spin her until she catches fire, if I so decide, and you'll not stop me. And I'll be back for *you*."

He went out the door, pulling David's mother with him.

3

There was silence in the room, broken only by Ralph Carver's choked sobs and the coyote, which sat panting and regarding David with its unpleasantly intelligent eyes. Little drops of spittle fell from the end of its tongue like drops from a leaky pipe.

"Take heart, son," the man with the shoulder-length gray hair said. He sounded like a guy more used to taking comfort than giving it. "You saw him—he's got internal bleeding, he's losing his teeth, one eye's ruptured right out of his head. He can't last much longer."

"It won't take him long to kill my mom, if he decides to," David said. "He already killed my little sister. He pushed her down the stairs and broke . . . broke her n-n-neck." His eyes abruptly blurred with tears and he willed them back. This was no time to get bawling.

"Yes, but . . ." The gray-haired man trailed off.

David found himself remembering an exchange with the cop when they had been on their way to this town—when they had still thought the cop was sane and normal and only helping them out. He had asked the cop how he knew their name, and the cop had said he'd read it on the plaque over the table.

It was a good answer, there *was* a plaque with their name on it over the table . . . but Entragian never would have been able to see it from where he was standing at the foot of their RV's stairs. *I've got eagle eyes, David,* he'd said, *and those are eyes that see the truth from afar.*

Ralph Carver came slowly forward to the front of his cell again, almost shuffling. His eyes were bloodshot, the lids puffy, his face ravaged. For a moment David felt almost blinded with rage, shaken by a desire to scream: *This is all your fault! Your fault that Pie's dead! Your fault that he's taken Mom off to kill her or rape her! You and your gambling! You and your stupid vacation ideas! He should have taken you, Dad, he should have taken* you!

Stop it, David. His thought, Gene Martin's voice. *That's just the way it wants you to think.*

It? The cop, Entragian, was that who the voice meant by *it?* And what way did he . . . or it . . . *want* him to think? For that matter, why would it care what way he thought at all?

"Look at that thing," Ralph said, staring at the coyote. "How could he call it in here like that? And why does it stay?"

The coyote turned toward Ralph's voice, then glanced at Mary, then looked back at David. It panted. More saliva fell to the hardwood floor, where a little puddle was forming.

"He's got them trained, somehow," the gray-haired man said. "Like the birds. He's got some trained buzzards out there. I killed one of the scraggy bastards. I stomped it—"

"No," Mary said.

"No," Billingsley echoed. "I'm sure that coyotes can be trained, but this is not training."

"Of course it is," the gray-haired man snapped.

"That cop?" David said. "Mr. Billingsley says he's taller than he used to be. Three inches, at least."

"That's insane." The gray-haired man was wearing a motorcycle jacket. Now he unzipped one of the pockets, took out a battered roll of Life Savers, and put one in his mouth.

"Sir, what's your name?" Ralph asked the gray-haired man.

"Marinville. Johnny Marinville. I'm a—"

"What you are is blind if you can't see that something very terrible and very out of the ordinary is going on here."

"I didn't say it wasn't terrible, and I certainly didn't say it was ordinary," the gray-haired man replied. He went on, but then the voice came again, the outside voice, and David lost track of their conversation.

The soap. David, the soap.

He looked at it—a green bar of Irish Spring sitting beside the spigot—and thought of Entragian saying *I'll be back for you.*

The soap.

Suddenly he understood . . . or thought he did. *Hoped* he did.

I better be right. I better be right, or—

He was wearing a Cleveland Indians tee-shirt. He pulled it off, dropped it by the cell door. He looked up and saw the coyote staring at him. Its ragged ears were all the way up again, and David thought he could hear it growling, low and far back in its throat.

"Son?" his father asked. "What do you think you're doing?"

Without answering, he sat down on the end of the bunk, took off his sneakers, and tossed them over to where his shirt lay. Now there was no question that the coyote was growling. As if it knew what he was planning to do. As if it meant to stop him if he actually tried it.

Don't be a dope, of course it means to stop you if you try it, why else did the cop leave it there? You just have to trust. Trust and have faith.

"Have faith that God will protect me," he murmured.

He stood up, unbuckled his belt, then paused with his fingers on the snap of his jeans. "Ma'am?" he said. "Ma'am?" She looked at him, and David felt himself blush. "I wonder if you'd mind turning around," he said, "I have to take off my pants, and I guess I better take off my underwear, too."

"What in God's name are you thinking about?" his father asked. There was panic in his voice now. "Whatever it is, I forbid it! Absolutely!"

David didn't reply, only looked at Mary. Looked at her as steadily as the coyote was looking at him. She returned his look for a moment, then, without saying a word, turned her back. The man in the motorcycle jacket sat on his bunk, crunching his Life Saver and watching him. David was as body-shy as most eleven-year-olds, and that steady gaze made him uncomfortable . . . but as he had already pointed out to himself, this was no time to be a dope. He took another glance at the bar of Irish Spring, then thumbed down his pants and undershorts.

4

"Nice," Cynthia said. "I mean, that's class."

"What?" Steve asked. He was sitting forward, watching the road carefully. More sand and tumbleweeds were blowing across it now, and the driving had gotten tricky.

"The sign. See it?"

He looked. The sign, which had originally read DESPERATION'S CHURCH & CIVIC ORGANIZATIONS WELCOME YOU! had been changed by some wit with a spraycan; it now read DESPERATION'S DEAD DOGS WELCOME YOU! A rope, frayed at one end, flapped back and forth in the wind. Old Shep himself was gone, however. The buzzards had gotten their licks in first; then the coyotes had come. Hungry and not a bit shy about eating a first cousin, they had snapped the rope and dragged the Shepherd's carcass away, pausing only to squabble and fight with one another. What remained (mostly bones and toenails) lay over the next rise. The blowing sand would cover it soon enough.

"Boy, folks around here must love a good laugh," Steve said.

"They must." She pointed. "Stop there."

It was a rusty Quonset hut. The sign in front read DESPERA-
TION MINING CORP. There was a parking lot beside it with ten
or twelve cars and trucks in it.

He pulled over but didn't turn in to the lot, at least not yet.
The wind was blowing more steadily now, the gusts gradually
merging into one steady blast. To the west, the sun was a surreal red-orange disc hanging over the Desatoya Mountains, as
flat and bloated as a photo of the planet Jupiter. Steve could
hear a fast and steady *tink-tink-tink-tink* coming from somewhere nearby, possibly the sound of a steel lanyard-clip banging against a flagpole.

"What's on your mind?" he asked her.

"Let's call the cops from here. There's people; see the lights?"

He glanced toward the Quonset and saw five or six golden
squares of brightness toward the rear of the building. In the
dusty gloom they looked like lighted windows in a train-car.
He looked back at Cynthia and shrugged. "Why from here,
when we could just drive to the local cop-shop? The middle of
town—such as it is—can't be far."

She rubbed one hand across her forehead as if she were tired,
or getting a headache. "You said you'd be careful. I said I'd *help*
you be careful. That's what I'm trying to do now. I sort of want
to see how things are hanging before someone in a uniform
sits me down in a chair and starts shooting questions. And
don't ask me why, because I don't really know. If we call the
cops and they sound cool, that's fine. They're cool, we're cool.
But . . . where the fuck *were* they? Never mind your boss, he
disappeared almost clean, but an RV parked beside the road,
the tires flat, door unlocked, valuables inside? I mean, gimme
a break. Where were the cops?"

"It goes back to that, doesn't it?"

"Yeah, back to that." The cops could have been at the
scene of a road-accident or a ranch-fire or a convenience-store

stickup, even a murder, and she knew it—*all* of them, because there just weren't that many cops out in this part of the world. But still, yeah, it came back to that. Because it felt more than funny. It felt *wrong.*

"Okay," Steve said mildly, and turned into the parking lot. "Might not be anybody at what passes for the Desperation P.D., anyhow. It's getting late. I'm surprised there's anyone still here, tell you the truth. Must be money in minerals, huh?"

He parked next to a pickup, opened the door, and the wind snatched it out of his hand. It banged the side of the truck. Steve winced, half-expecting a Slim Pickens type to come running toward him, holding his hat on with one hand and yelling *Hey thar, boy!* No owner did. A tumbleweed zoomed by, apparently headed for Salt Lake City, but that was all. And the alkali dust was flying—plenty of it. He had a red bandanna in his back pocket. He took it out, knotted it around his neck, and pulled it up over his mouth.

"Hold it, hold it," he said, tugging her arm to keep her from opening her door just yet. He leaned over so he could open the glove compartment. He rummaged and found another bandanna, this one blue, and handed it to her. "Put that on first."

She held it up, examined it gravely, then turned her wide little-girl eyes on him again. "No cootiebugs?"

He snorted and grinned behind the red bandanna. "Airy a one, ma'am, as we say back in Lubbock. Put it on."

She knotted it, then pulled it up. "Butch and Sundance," she said, her voice a little muffled.

"Yeah, Bonnie and Clyde."

"Omar and Sharif," she said, and giggled.

"Be careful getting out. The wind's really getting cranked up."

He stepped out and the wind slapped him in the face, making him stagger as he reached the front of the van. Flying grit stung his forehead. Cynthia was holding onto her doorhandle, head down, the Peter Tosh shirt flapping out behind her skinny midriff like a sail. There was still some daylight left, and the sky overhead was still blue, but the landscape had taken on a strange shadowless quality. It was stormlight if Steve had ever seen it.

"Come on!" he yelled, and put an arm around Cynthia's waist. "Let's get out of this!"

They hurried across the cracked asphalt to the long building. There was a door at one end of it. The sign bolted to the corrugated metal beside it read DESPERATION MINING CORP., like the one out front, but Steve saw that this one had been painted over something else, some other name that was starting to show through the white paint like a red ghost. He was pretty sure that one of the painted-over words was DIABLO, with the *I* modified into a devil's pitchfork.

Cynthia was tapping the door with one bitten fingernail. A sign had been hung on the inside from one of those little transparent suction cups. Steve thought there was something perfectly, irritatingly, showily Western about the message on the sign.

IF WE'RE OPEN, WE'RE OPEN
IF WE'RE CLOSED, Y'ALL COME BACK

"They forgot *son*," he said.

"Huh?"

"It should say 'Y'all come back, *son*.' Then it would be perfect." He glanced at his watch and saw that it was twenty past seven. Which meant they *were* closed, of course. Except if they were closed, what were those cars and trucks doing in the parking lot?

He tried the door. It pushed open. From inside came the sound of country music, broken by heavy static. *"I built it one piece at a time,"* Johnny Cash sang, *"And it didn't cost me a dime."*

They stepped in. The door closed on a pneumatic arm. Outside, the wind played rattle and hum along the ridged metal sides of the building. They were in a reception area. To the right were four chairs with patched vinyl seats. They looked like they were mostly used by beefy men wearing dirty jeans and workboots. There was a long coffee-table in front of the chairs, piled with magazines you didn't find in the doctor's office: *Guns and Ammo, Road and Track, MacLean's Mining Report, Metallurgy Newsletter, Arizona Highways.* There was also a very old *Penthouse* with Tonya Harding on the cover.

Straight ahead of them was a field-gray receptionist's desk, so dented that it might have been kicked here all the way from Highway 50. It was loaded down with papers, a crazily stacked set of volumes marked *MSHA Guidelines* (an overloaded ashtray sat on top of these), and three wire baskets full of rocks. A manual typewriter perched on one end of the desk; no computer that Steve could see, and a chair in the kneehole, the kind that runs on casters, but nobody sitting in it. The air conditioner was running, and the room was uncomfortably cool.

Steve walked around the desk, saw a cushion sitting on the chair, and picked it up so Cynthia could see it. PARK YER ASS had been crocheted across the front in old-fashioned Western-style lettering.

"Oh, tasteful," she said. "Operators are standing by, use Tootie."

On the desk, flanked by a joke sign (LEAD ME NOT INTO TEMPTATION, FOR I SHALL FIND IT MYSELF) and a name-plaque (BRAD JOSEPHSON), was a stiff studio photo of an overweight but pretty black woman flanked by two cute kids. A male receptionist, then, and not exactly Mr. Neat. The radio, an old cracked Philco, sat on a nearby shelf, along with the phone. *"Right about then my wife walked out,"* Johnny Cash bawled through wild cannonades of static, *"And I could see right away that she had her doubts, But she opened the door and said 'Honey, take me for a—'"*

Steve turned off the radio. The hardest gust of wind yet hit the building, making it creak like a submarine under pressure. Cynthia, still with the bandanna he'd given her pulled up over her nose, looked around uneasily. The radio was off, but—very faintly—Steve could still hear Johnny Cash singing about how he'd smuggled his car out of the GM plant in his lunchbucket, one piece at a time. Same station, different radio, way back. Where the lights were, he guessed.

Cynthia pointed to the phone. Steve picked it up, listened, dropped it back into its cradle again. "Dead. Must be a line down somewhere."

"Aren't they underground these days?" she asked, and Steve noticed an interesting thing: they were both talking in low tones, really not more than a step or two above a whisper.

"I think maybe they haven't gotten around to that in Desperation just yet."

There was a door behind the desk. He reached for the handle, and she grabbed his arm.

"What?" Steve asked.

"I don't know." She let go of him, reached up, pulled her bandanna down. Then she laughed nervously. "I don't know, man, this is just so . . . wacky."

"Got to be someone back there," he said. "The door's unlocked, lights on, cars in the parking lot."

"You're scared, too. Aren't you?"

He thought it over and nodded. Yes. It was like before the thunderstorms—the benders—when he'd been a kid, only with all the strange joy squeezed out of it. "But we still ought to . . ."

"Yeah, I know. Go on." She swallowed, and he heard something go click in her throat. "Hey, tell me we're gonna be laughin at each other and feelin stupid in a few seconds. Can you do that, Lubbock?"

"In a few seconds we're gonna be laughing at each other and feeling stupid."

"Thanks."

"No problem," he said, and opened the door. A narrow hall-way ran down it, thirty feet or so. There was a double run of flu-orescent bars overhead and all-weather carpet on the floor. There were two doors on one side, both open, and three on the other, two open and one shut. At the end of the corridor, bright yel-low light filled up what looked to Steve like a work area of some kind—a shop, maybe, or a lab. That was where the lighted win-dows they'd seen from the outside were, and where the music was coming from. Johnny Cash had given way to The Tractors, who claimed that baby liked to rock it like a boogie-woogie choo-choo train. Sounded like typical brag and bluster to Steve.

This is fucked. You know that, don't you?

He knew. There was a radio. There was the wind, loaded with sour alkali grit, now hitting the building's metal sides hard enough to sound like a Montana blizzard. But where were the *voices?* Men talking, joking, shooting the shit? The men who went with the vehicles parked out front?

He started slowly down the corridor, thinking that he should call out something like *Hey! Anybody home?* and not quite dar-ing to. The place felt simultaneously empty and somehow *not* empty, although how it could be both things at the same time was—

Cynthia yanked on the back of his shirt. The tug was so hard and so sudden that he almost screamed.

"What?" he asked—exasperated, heart pounding—and re-alized that now he *was* whispering.

"Do you hear that?" she asked. "Sounds like . . . I dunno . . . a kid bubbling Kool-Aid through a straw."

At first he could only hear The Tractors—*"She said her name was Emergency and asked to see my gun, She said her telephone number was 911"*—and then he *did* hear it, a fast liquid sound. Mechan-ical, not human. A sound he almost knew. "Yeah, I hear it."

"Steve, I want to get out of here."

"Go back to the truck, then."

"No."

"Cynthia, for Christ's sake—"

He looked at her, at her big eyes looking back up at him, her pursed, anxious mouth, and quit it. No, she didn't want to go back to the Ryder van by herself, and he didn't blame her. She'd called herself a hard-headed babe, and maybe she was, but right now she was also an almost-scared-to-death babe. He took her by her thin shoulders, pulled her toward him, and planted a loud smackeroo on her forehead, right between the eyes. "Do not worry, little Nell," he said in a very passable Dudley Do-Right imitation, "for I will protect you."

She grinned in spite of herself. "Fuckin dork."

"Come on. Stay close. And if we *do* have to run, run *fast*. Or else I might trample you."

"You don't need to worry about that," Cynthia said. "I'll be out the door and gone before you even get it in gear."

The first door on the right was an office. Empty. There was a cork-board on the wall covered with Polaroid shots of an open-pit mine. That was the big wall of earth they'd seen looming behind the town, Steve assumed.

The first door on the left, also an office. Also empty. The bubbling sound was louder now, and Steve knew what it was even before he looked into the next door on the right. He felt a measure of relief. "It's an aquarium," he said, "that's all it is."

This was a much nicer office than the first two they'd peeped into, with a real rug on the floor. The aquarium was on a stand to the left of the desk, under a photograph of two men in boots, hats, and Western-style business suits shaking hands by a flagpole—the one out back, most likely. It was a well-populated aquarium; he saw tigers, angelfish, goldfish, and a couple of black beauties. There was also some strange geegaw lying on the sand at the bottom, one of the things people put into their aquariums to decorate them, he assumed, except this one wasn't a sunken ship or a pirate chest or King Neptune's castle. This one was something else, something that looked like—

"Hey Steve," Cynthia whispered in a strengthless little voice. "That's a hand."

"What?" he asked, honestly not understanding, although later he would think he must have known what it was, lying there at the bottom of the aquarium, what else could it have been?

"A *hand*," she almost moaned. "A fuckin *hand*."

And, as one of the tigers swam between the second and third fingers (the third had a slim gold wedding ring on it), he saw that she was right. There were fingernails on it. There was a thin white thread of scar on the thumb. It was a hand.

He stepped forward, ignoring her grab at his shoulder, and bent down for a better look. His hope that the hand was fake despite the wedding ring and the realistic thread of scar glimmered away. There were shreds of flesh and sinew rising from the wrist. They wavered like plankton in the currents generated by the tank's regulator. And he could see the bones.

He straightened up and saw Cynthia standing at the desk. The top of this one was much neater. There was a PowerBook on it, closed. Next to it was a telephone. Next to the phone was an answering machine with the red message-light blinking. Cynthia picked up the telephone, listened, then put it back. He was startled by the whiteness of her face. *With that little blood in her head, she should be lying on the floor dead-fainted away,* he thought. Instead of fainting, she reached a finger toward the PLAY MESSAGES button on the answering machine.

"Don't do that!" he hissed. God knew why, and it was too late, anyway.

There was a beep. A click. Then a strange voice—it seemed to be neither male nor female, and it scared the hell out of Steve—began to speak. *"Pneuma,"* it said in a contemplative voice. *"Soma. Sarx. Pneuma. Soma. Sarx. Pneuma. Soma. Sarx."*

It went on slowly enunciating these words, seeming to grow louder as it spoke. Was that possible? He stared at the machine, fascinated, the words hitting into his brain

(*soma sarx pneuma*)

like tiny sharp carpet-tacks. He might have gone on staring at it for God knew how long if Cynthia hadn't reached past him and banged the STOP button hard enough to make the machine jump on the desk.

"Sorry, nope, too creepy." She sounded both apologetic and defiant.

They left the office. Farther down the corridor, in the workroom or lab or whatever it was, The Tractors were still singing about the boogie-woogie girl who had it stacked up to the ceiling and sticking in your face.

How long is *that fucking song?* Steve wondered. *It's been playing fifteen minutes already, got to've been.*

"Can we go now?" Cynthia asked. *"Please?"*

He pointed down the hall toward the bright yellow lights.

"Oh Jesus, you're nuts," she said, but when he started in that direction, she followed him.

5

"Where are you taking me?" Ellen Carver asked for the third time. She leaned forward, hooking her fingers through the mesh between the cruiser's front and back seats. "Please, can't you tell me?"

At first she'd just been thankful not to be raped or killed . . . and relieved that, when they got to the foot of the lethal stairs, poor sweet little Kirstie's body was gone. There had been a huge bloodstain on the steps outside the doors, however, still not entirely dry and only partially covered by the blowing sand which had stuck to it. She guessed it had belonged to Mary's husband. She tried to step over it, but the cop, Entragian, had her arm in a pincers grip and simply pulled her through it, so that her sneakers left three ugly red tracks behind as they went around the corner to the parking lot. Bad. All of it. *Horrible.* But she was still alive.

Yes, relief at first, but that had been replaced by a growing sense of dread. For one thing, whatever was happening to this awful man was now speeding up. She could hear little liquid pops as his skin let go in various places, and trickling noises as blood flowed and dripped. The back of his uniform shirt, formerly khaki, was now a muddy red.

And she didn't like the direction he had taken—south. There was nothing in that direction but the vast bulwark of the open-pit mine.

The cruiser rolled slowly along Main Street (she *assumed* it was Main Street, weren't they always?), passing a final pair of businesses: another bar and Harvey's Small Engine Repair. The last shop on the street was a somehow sinister little shack with BODEGA written above the door and a sign out front which the wind had blown off its stand. Ellen could read it anyway: MEXI-CAN FOOD'S.

The sun was a declining ball of dusty furnace-fire, and the landscape had a kind of clear daylight darkness about it that struck her as apocalyptic. It wasn't so much a question of where she was, she realized, as *who* she was. She couldn't be-lieve she was the same Ellen Carver who was on the PTA and had been considering a run for school board this fall, the same Ellen Carver who sometimes went out to lunch with friends at China Happiness, where they would all get silly over mai-tais and talk about clothes and kids and marriages—whose was shaky and whose was not. Was she the Ellen Carver who picked her nicest clothes out of the Boston Proper catalogue and wore Red perfume when she was feeling amorous and had a funny rhinestone tee-shirt that said QUEEN OF THE UNIVERSE?

The Ellen Carver who had raised two lovely children and had kept her man when those all about her were losing theirs? The one who examined her breasts for lumps once every six weeks or so, the one who liked to curl up in the living room on weekend nights with a cup of hot tea and a few chocolates and paperbacks with titles like *Misery in Paradise*? Really? Oh *really*? Well, yes, probably; she was those Ellens and a thousand others: Ellen in silk and Ellen in denim and Ellen sitting on the commode and peeing with a recipe for Brown Betty in one hand; she was, she supposed, both her parts and more than her parts, when summed, could account for . . . but could that possibly mean she was also the Ellen Carver whose well-loved daughter had been murdered and who now sat huddled in the back of a police-car that was beginning to stink unspeakably, a woman being driven past a fallen sign reading MEXICAN FOOD'S, a woman who would never see her home or friends or husband again? Was she the Ellen Carver being driven into a dirty, windy darkness where no one read the Boston Proper catalogue or drank mai-tais with little paper umbrellas poking out of them and only death awaited?

"Oh God, please don't kill me," she said in a boneless, trembly voice she could not recognize as her own. "Please, sir, don't kill me, I don't want to die. I'll do whatever you say, but don't kill me. Please don't."

He didn't answer. There was a thump from beneath them as the tar quit. The cop pulled the knob that turned on the headlights, but they didn't seem to help much; what she saw were two bright cones shining into a world of roiling dust. Every now and then a tumbleweed would fly in front of them, headed east. Gravel rumbled beneath the tires and pinged against the undercarriage.

They passed a long, ramshackle building with rusty metal sides—a factory or some kind of mill, she thought—and then the road tilted up. They started to climb the embankment.

"Please," she whispered. "Please, just tell me what you want."

"Uck," he said, grimacing, and reached into his mouth like a man who's got a hair on his tongue. Instead of a hair he pulled out the tongue itself. He looked at it for a moment, lying limply in his fist like a piece of liver, and then tossed it aside.

They passed two pickup trucks, a dumptruck, and a yellow-ghost backhoe, all parked together inside the first switchback the road made on its way to the top.

"If you're going to kill me, make it quick," she said in her trembly voice. "Please don't hurt me. Do that much, at least, promise you won't hurt me."

But the slumped, bleeding figure behind the wheel of the cruiser promised her nothing. It simply drove through the flying dust, guiding the car to the crest of the bulwark. The cop didn't hesitate at the top but crossed the rim and started down, leaving the wind above them as he did. Ellen looked back, wanting to see some last light, but she was too late. The walls of the pit had already hidden what remained of the sunset. The cruiser was descending into a vast lake of darkness, an abyss that made a joke of the headlights.

Down here, night had already fallen.

CHAPTER 2

1

You've had a conversion, Reverend Martin once told David. This was near the beginning. It was also around the time that David began to realize that by four o'clock on most Sunday afternoons, Reverend Gene Martin was no longer strictly sober. It would still be some months, however, before David realized just how much his new teacher drank. *In fact, yours is the only genuine conversion I've ever seen, perhaps the only genuine one I'll ever see. These are not good times for the God of our fathers, David. Lot of people talking the talk, not many walking the walk.*

David wasn't sure that "conversion" was the right word for what had happened to him, but he hadn't spent much time worrying about it. *Something* had happened, and just coping with it was enough. The something had brought him to Reverend Martin, and Reverend Martin—drunk or not—had told him things he needed to know and set him tasks that he needed to do. When David had asked him, at one of those Sunday-afternoon meetings (soundless basketball on the TV that day), what he should be doing, Reverend Martin had responded promptly. "The job of the new Christian is to meet God, to know God, to trust God, to love God. That's not like taking a list to the supermarket, either, where you can dump stuff into your basket in any order you like. It's a progression, like working your way up the math ladder from counting to calculus. You've met God, and rather spectacularly, too. Now you've got to get to know him."

"Well, I talk to you," David had said.

"Yes, and you talk to God. You do, don't you? Haven't given up on the praying?"

"Nope. Don't often hear back, though."

Reverend Martin had laughed and taken a sip from his teacup. "God's a lousy conversationalist, no question about that, but he left us a user's manual. I suggest you consult it."

"Huh?"

"The Bible," Reverend Martin had said, looking at him over the rim of his cup with bloodshot eyes.

So he had read the Bible, starting in March and finishing Revelation ("The grace of our Lord Jesus Christ be with you all. Amen") just a week or so before they had left Ohio. He had done it like homework, twenty pages a night (weekends off), making notes, memorizing stuff that seemed important, skipping only the parts Reverend Martin told him he could skip, mostly the begats. And what he remembered most clearly now, as he stood shivering at the sink in the jail cell, dousing himself with icy water, was the story of Daniel in the lions' den. King Darius hadn't really wanted to throw Danny in there, but his advisers had mousetrapped him somehow. David had been amazed at how much of the Bible was politics.

"*You STOP THAT!*" his father screamed, startling David out of his thoughts and making him look around. In the growing gloom Ralph Carver's face was long with terror, his eyes red with grief. In his agitation he sounded like an eleven-year-old himself, one having a hell of a tantrum. "*Stop that RIGHT NOW, do you hear me?*"

David turned back to the sink without answering and began to splash water on his face and in his hair. He remembered King Darius's parting advice to Daniel before Daniel was led away: "Thy God whom thou servest in your days and nights will deliver thee." And something else, something Daniel had said the next day about why God had shut the lions' mouths—

"David! DAVID!"

But he wouldn't look again. *Couldn't.* He hated it when his father cried, and he had never seen or heard him cry like this. It was awful, as if someone had cut open a vein in his heart.

"David, you answer me!"

"Put a sock in it, pal," Marinville said.

"*You* put a sock in it," Mary told him.

"But he's getting the coyote riled!"

She ignored him. "David, what are you doing?"

David didn't answer. This wasn't the kind of thing you could discuss rationally, even if there was time, because faith wasn't rational. This was something Reverend Martin had told him over and over again, drilling him with it like some important spelling rule, *i* before *e* except after *c: sane men and women don't believe in God. That was all, that was flat. You can't say it from the pulpit, because the congregation'd run you out of town, but it's the truth. God isn't about reason; God is about faith and belief. God says, "Sure, take away the safety net. And when that's gone, take away the tightrope, too."*

He filled his hands with water once more and splashed it over his face and into his hair. His head. That would be where he succeeded or failed, he knew that already. It was the biggest part of him, and he didn't think there was much give to a person's skull.

David grabbed the bar of Irish Spring and began to lather himself with it. He didn't bother with his legs, there would be no problem there, but worked from the groin on up, rubbing harder and generating more suds as he went. His father was still yelling at him, but now there was no time to listen. The thing was, he had to be quick . . . and not just because he was apt to lose his nerve if he stopped too long to think about the coyote sitting out there. If he let the soap dry, it wouldn't serve to grease him; it would gum him up and hold him back instead.

He gave his neck a fast lube-job, then did his face and hair. Eyes slitted, soap still clutched in one hand, he padded to the cell door. A horizontal bar crossed the vertical ones about three feet off the floor. The gap between the vertical bars was at least four inches and maybe five. The cells in the holding area had been built to hold men—brawny miners, for the most part—not skinny eleven-year-old boys, and he didn't expect much trouble slipping through.

At least until he got to his head.

Quick, hurry, don't think, trust God.

He knelt, shivering and covered with green soap-slime from the hips on up, and began rubbing the cake of soap up and down, first on the inside of one white-painted vertical bar, then on the other.

Out by the desk, the coyote got to its feet. Its growl rose to a snarl. Its yellow eyes were fixed intently on David Carver. Its muzzle wrinkled back in an unpleasantly toothy grin.

"David, no! Don't do it, son! Don't be crazy!"

"He's right, kid." Marinville was standing at the bars of his cell now, hands wrapped around them. So was Mary. That was embarrassing but probably natural enough, considering the way his father was carrying on. And it couldn't be helped. He had to go, and go now. He hadn't been able to draw any hot water from the tap, and he thought the cold would dry the soap on his skin even quicker.

He recalled the story of Daniel and the lions again as he dropped to one knee, gathering himself. Not very surprising, given the circumstances. When King Darius arrived the next day, Daniel had been fine. "My God hath sent his angel, and hath shut the lions' mouths," Daniel told him, "forasmuch as innocency was found in me." That wasn't exactly right, but

David knew the word "innocency" was. It had fascinated him, chimed somewhere deep inside him. Now he spoke it to the being whose voice he sometimes heard—the one he identified as the voice of the other: *Find innocency in me, God. Find innocency in me and shut that fleabag's mouth. Jesus' name I pray, amen.*

He turned sideways, then propped his whole weight on one arm, like Jack Palance doing pushups at the Academy Awards. In this fashion he was able to stick both feet out through the bars at the same time. He wriggled backward, now out to his ankles, now his knees, now his thighs . . . which was where he first felt the painted bars press their soapslick coolness against him.

"*No!*" Mary screamed. "*No, get away from him, you ugly fuck! GET AWAY FROM HIM!*"

There was a clink. It was followed by a thin rolling-marble sound. David turned his head long enough to see Mary with her hands now outside the bars of her cell. The left was cupped. He saw her pick another coin out of it with her right hand and throw it at the coyote. This time it barely paid attention, although the quarter struck it on the flank. The animal started toward David's bare feet and legs instead, head lowered, snarling.

2

Oh Christ almighty, Johnny thought. Goddam kid must have checked his brains at the door.

Then he yanked the belt out of the bottom of his motorcycle jacket, stuck his arm as far out through the bars as he could, and brought the buckle end down on the coyote's scant flank just as it was about to help itself to the kid's right foot.

The coyote yelped in pain as well as surprise this time. It whirled, snatching at the belt. Johnny yanked it away—it was too thin, too apt to give out in the coyote's jaws before the kid could get out . . . if the kid actually *could* get out, which Johnny doubted. He let the belt go flying over his shoulder and yanked off the heavy leather jacket itself, trying to hold the coyote's yellow gaze as he did so, willing it not to look away. The animal's eyes reminded him of the cop's eyes.

The kid shoved his butt through the bars with a gasp, and Johnny had time to wonder how *that* felt on the old family jewels. The coyote started to turn toward the sound and Johnny flung the leather jacket out at it, holding on by the collar. If the animal hadn't taken two steps forward to snatch at the belt, the jacket wouldn't have reached it . . . but the coyote had and the jacket did. When it brushed the animal's shoulder, it whirled and seized the jacket so fiercely that it was almost snapped out of Johnny's hands. As it was he was dragged head-first into the bars. It hurt like a mother and a bright red rocket went off behind his eyes, but he still had time to be grateful that his nose had gone *between* the bars rather than *into* one.

"No, you don't," he grunted, winding his hands into the leather collar and pulling. "Come on, hon . . . come on, you nasty gopher-eating bugger . . . come on over . . . and say *howdy.*"

The coyote snarled bitterly at him, the sound muffled through its mouthful of jacket—twelve hundred bucks at Barneys in New York. Johnny had never quite pictured it like this when he had tried it on.

He bunched his arms—not as powerful as they'd been thirty years ago, but not puny, either—and dragged the coyote foward. Its claws slid on the hardwood floor. It got one front leg braced against the desk and shook the jacket from side to side, trying to yank it out of Johnny's hands. His collection of Life Savers went flying, his maps, his spare set of keys, his pocket pharmacy (aspirin, codeine caps, Sucrets, a tube of Preparation-H), his sunglasses, and his goddam cellular phone. He let the coyote take a step or two backward, trying to keep it interested, to play it like a fish, then yanked it forward again. It bonked its head on the corner of the desk this time, a sound that warmed Johnny's heart. *"Arriba!"* he grunted. "How'd that feel, honey?"

"Hurry up!" Mary screamed. "Hurry up, David!"

Johnny glanced over at the kid's cell. What he saw made his muscles relax with fear—when the coyote yanked on the jacket this time, the animal came very close to pulling it free.

"Hurry UP!" the woman screamed again, but Johnny saw that the kid *couldn't* hurry up. Soaped up, naked as a peeled shrimp, he had gotten as far as his chin, and there he was stuck, with the whole length of his body out in the holding area and his head back inside the cell. Johnny had one overwhelming impression, mostly called to mind by the twist of the neck and the stressed line of the jaw.

The kid was hung.

3

He did okay until he got to his head, and there he stuck fast with his cheek on the boards and the shelf of his jaw pressed against one soapy bar and the back of his head against the other. A panic driven by claustrophobia—the smell of the wood floor, the iron touch of the bars, a nightmare memory of a picture he'd once seen of a Puritan in stocks—dimmed his vision like a dark curtain. He could hear his dad shouting, the woman screaming, and the coyote snarling, but those sounds were all far away. His head was stuck, he'd have to go back, only he wasn't sure he *could* go back because now his arms were out and one was pinned under him and—

God help me, he thought. It didn't seem like a prayer; it was maybe too scared and up against it to be a prayer. *Please help me, don't let me be stuck, please help me.*

Turn your head, the voice he sometimes heard now told him. As always, it spoke in an almost disinterested way, as if the things it was saying should have been self-evident, and as always David recognized it by the way it seemed to pass *through* him rather than to come *from* him.

An image came to him then: hands pressing the front and back of a book, squeezing the pages together a little in spite of the boards and the binding. Could his head do that? David thought—or perhaps only hoped—that it could. But he would have to be in the right position.

Turn your head, the voice had said.

From somewhere behind him came a thick ripping sound, then Marinville's voice, somehow amused, scared, and outraged all at the same time: "Do you know how much that thing *cost?*"

David twisted around so he lay on his back instead of his side. Just having the pressure of the bar off his jaw was an incredible relief. Then he reached up and placed his palms against the bars.

Is this right?

No answer. So often there was no answer. Why was that?

Because God is cruel, the Reverend Martin who kept school inside his head replied. *God is cruel. I have popcorn, David, why don't I make some? Maybe we can find one of those old horror movies on TV, something Universal, maybe even* The Mummy.

He pushed with his hands. At first nothing happened, but then, slowly, slowly, his soapy head began sliding between the bars. There was one terrible moment when he stopped with his ears crushed against the sides of his head and the pressure beating on his temples, a sick throb that was maybe the worst physical hurt he had ever known. In that moment he was sure he was going to stick right where he was and die in agony, like a heretic caught in some Inquisitorial torture device. He shoved harder with his palms, eyes looking up at the dusty ceiling with agonized concentration, and gave a small, relieved moan as he began to move again almost at once. With the narrowest aspect of his skull presented to the bars, he was able to deliver himself into the holding area without too much more trouble. One of his ears was trickling blood, but he was out. He had made it. Naked, covered with foamy greenish curds of Irish Spring soap, David sat up. A monstrous bolt of pain shot through his head from back to front, and for a moment he felt his eyes were literally bugging out, like those of a cartoon Romeo who has just spotted a dishy blonde.

The coyote was the least of his problems, at least for the time being. God had shut its mouth with a motorcycle jacket. Stuff from the pockets was scattered everywhere, and the jacket itself was torn straight down the middle. A limp rag of saliva-coated black leather hung from the side of the coyote's muzzle like a well-chewed cheroot.

"Get out, David!" his father cried. His voice was hoarse with tears and anxiety. "Get out while you still can!"

The gray-haired man, Marinville, flicked his eyes up to David momentarily. "He's right, kid. Get lost." He looked back down at the snarling coyote. "Come on, Rover, you can do better than that! By Jesus, I'd like to be around when you start shitting zippers by the light of the moon!" He yanked the jacket hard. The coyote came skidding along the floor, head down, neck stretched, forelegs stiff, shaking its narrow head from side to side as it tried to pull the jacket away from Marinville.

David turned on his knees and pulled his clothes out through the bars. He squeezed his pants, feeling for the tube of the shotgun shell in the pocket. The shotgun shell was there. He got to his feet, and for a few seconds the world turned into a merry-go-round. He had to reach out for the bars of his erstwhile cell to keep from falling over. Billingsley put a hand over his. It was surprisingly warm. "Go, son," he said. "Time's almost up."

David turned and tottered toward the door. His head was still throbbing, and his balance was badly off; the door seemed to be on a rocker or a spindle or something. He staggered, regained his footing, and opened the door. He turned to look at his father. "I'll be back."

"Don't you *dare*," his father said at once. "Find a phone and call the cops, David. The *State* cops. And be careful. Don't let—"

There was a harsh ripping sound as Johnny's expensive leather jacket finally tore in two. The coyote, not expecting such a sudden victory, went flying backward, rolled over on its side, and saw the naked boy in the doorway. It scrambled to its feet and flew at him with a snarl. Mary screamed.

"Go, kid, GET OUT!" Johnny yelled.

David ducked out and yanked the door shut behind him. A split second later, the coyote hit it with a thud. A howl— terrible because it was so close—rose from the holding area. It was as if it knew it had been fooled, David thought; as if it also knew that, when the man who had summoned it here returned, he would not be pleased.

There was another thud as the coyote threw itself at the door again, a pause, then a third. The animal howled again. Gooseflesh rose on David's soapy arms and chest. Just ahead of him were the stairs down which his kid sister had tumbled to her death; if the crazy cop hadn't moved her, she would still be at the bottom, waiting for him in the gloom, eyes open and accusing, asking him why he hadn't stopped Mr. Big Boogeyman, what good was a big brother if he couldn't stop the boogeyman?

I can't go down there, he thought. *I can't, I absolutely can't.*

No . . . but all the same, he had to.

Outside, the wind gusted hard enough to make the brick building creak like a ship in a working sea. David could hear dust, too, hitting the side of the building and the street doors down there like fine snow. The coyote howled again, separated from him only by an inch or so of wood . . . and knowing it.

David closed his eyes and pressed his fingers together in front of his mouth and chin. "God, this is David Carver again. I'm in such a mess, God, such a mess. Please protect me and help me do what I have to do. Jesus' name I pray, amen."

He opened his eyes, took a deep breath, and groped for the stair railing. Then, naked, holding his clothes against his chest with his free hand, David Carver started down into the shadows.

4

Steve tried to speak and couldn't. Tried again and still couldn't, although this time he *did* manage a single dry squeak. *You sound like a mouse farting behind a baseboard,* he thought.

He was aware that Cynthia was squeezing his hand in a grip powerful enough to be painful, but the pain didn't seem to matter. He didn't know how long they would have stood there in the doorway of the big room at the end of the Quonset hut if the wind hadn't blown something over outside and sent it clattering down the street. Cynthia gasped like someone who has been punched and put the hand not holding Steve's up to one side of her face. She turned to look at him that way, so he could see only one wide, horrified eye. Tears were trickling down from it.

"Why?" she whispered. *"Why?"*

He shook his head. He didn't know why, didn't have a clue. The only two things he was sure of were that the people who had done this were gone, or he and Cynthia would have been dead already, and that he, Steven Ames of Lubbock, Texas, did not want to be here if they decided to come back.

The large space at the end of the Quonset hut looked like a combination workroom, lab, and storage area. It was lit by hanging hi-intensity lamps with metal hoods, a little like the lights which hang over the tables in billiard emporiums.

They cast a bright lemony glow. It looked to Steve as if two crews might have worked here at the same time, one doing assay work on the left side of the room, the other sorting and cataloguing on the right. There were Dandux laundry baskets lined up against the wall on the sorting side, each with chunks of rock in it. These had clearly been sorted; one basket was filled with rocks that were mostly black, another with smaller rocks, almost pebbles, that were shot through with glitters of quartz.

On the assay side (if that was what it was), there was a line of Macintosh computers set up on a long table littered with tools and manuals. The Macs were running screen-saver programs. One featured pretty, multicolored helix shapes above the words GAS CHROMATOGRAPH READY. Another, surely not Disney-sanctioned, showed Goofy pulling down his pants every seven seconds or so, revealing a large boner with the words HYUCK HYUCK HYUCK written on it.

At the far end of the room, inside a closed overhead garage door with the words WELCOME TO HERNANDO'S HIDEAWAY printed on it in blue paint, was an ATV with an open carrier hooked up behind it. This was also full of rock samples. On the wall to its left was a sign reading YOU *MUST* WEAR A HARDHAT MSHA REGULATIONS NO EXCUSES. There was a row of hooks running below the sign, but there were no hardhats hung from them. The hardhats were scattered on the floor, below the dangling feet of the people who *had* been hung from the hooks, hung like roasts in a butcher's walk-in freezer.

"Steve . . . Steve, are they like . . . dummies? Department store mannequins? Is it . . . you know . . . a joke?"

"No." The word was small and felt as dusty as the air outside, but it was a start. "You know they're not. Let up, Cynthia, you're breaking my hand."

"Don't make me let go," she said in a wavery voice. Her hand was still up to her face and she stared one-eyed at the dangling corpses across the room. On the radio, The Tractors had been replaced by David Lee Murphy, and David Lee Murphy had given way to an ad for a place called Whalen's, which the announcer described as "Austin's Anything Store!"

"You don't have to let go, just let up a little," Steve said. He raised an unsteady finger and began to count. One . . . two . . . three . . .

"I think I wet my pants a little," she said.

"Don't blame you." Four . . . five . . . six . . .

"We have to get out of here, Steve, this makes the guy who broke my nose look like Santa Cl—"

"Be quiet and let me count!"

She fell silent, her mouth trembling and her chest hitching as she tried to contain her sobs. Steve was sorry he'd shouted—this one had been through a lot even before today—but he wasn't thinking very well. Christ, he wasn't entirely sure he was thinking at all.

"Thirteen," he said.

"Fourteen," she corrected in a shaky, humble voice. "Do you see? In the corner? One of them fell off. One of them fell off the h-h-h—"

"Hook" was what she was trying to say, but the stutter turned into miserable little cries and she began to weep. Steve took her in his arms and held her, feeling her hot, wet face throb against his chest. *Low* on his chest. She was so goddam small.

Over the fuzz of her extravagantly colored hair he could see the other side of the room, and she was right—there was another body crumpled in the corner. Fourteen dead in all, at least three of them women. With their heads hanging and their chins on their chests, it was hard to tell for sure about some of the others. Nine were wearing lab coats—no, ten, counting the one in the corner—and two were in jeans and open-necked shirts. Two others were wearing suits, string ties, dress boots.

One of these appeared to have no left hand, and Steve had a pretty good idea of where that hand might be, oh yes indeed he did. Most had been shot, and they must have been facing their killers, because Steve could see gaping exit wounds in the backs of most of the dropped heads. At least three, however, had been opened like fish. They hung with their white coats stained maroon and pools of blood beneath them and their guts dangling.

"Now here's Mary Chapin Carpenter to tell us why she feels lucky today," the radio announcer said, emerging gamely from another blast of static. "Maybe she's been to Whalen's in Austin. Let's find out."

Mary Chapin Carpenter began to tell the hanging dead men and women in the lab of the Desperation Mining Corporation about her lucky day, how she'd won the lottery and all, and Steve let go of Cynthia. He took a step into the lab and sniffed the air. No gunsmoke that he could smell, and maybe that didn't mean much—the air conditioners probably turned over the air in here pretty fast—but the blood was dry on the corpses which had been eviscerated, and that probably meant whoever had done this was long gone.

"Let's go!" Cynthia hissed, tugging his arm.

"Okay," he said. "Just—"

He broke off as something caught his eye. It was sitting on the end of the computer table, to the right of the screen with the Goofy-flasher on it. Not a rock, or not *just* a rock, anyway. Some kind of stone artifact. He walked over and looked down at it.

The girl scurried after him and yanked his arm again. "What's the matter with you? This isn't a guided tour! What if—" Then she saw what he was looking at—really *saw* it—and broke off. She reached out a tentative finger and touched it. She gasped and drew her finger back. At the same moment her hips jerked forward as if she'd gotten an electric shock and her pelvis banged into the edge of the table. "Holy shit," she breathed. "I think I just—" And there she stopped.

"Just what?"

"Nothing." But she looked as if she was blushing, so Steve guessed maybe it was something, at that. "There ought to be a picture of that thing next to *ugly* in the dictionary."

It was a rendering of what might have been a wolf or a coyote, and although it was crude, it had enough power to make them both forget, at least for a few seconds, that they were standing sixty feet from the leftovers of a mass murder. The beast's head was twisted at a strange angle (a somehow *hungry* angle), and its eyeballs appeared to be starting out of their sockets in utter fury. Its snout was wildly out of proportion to its body—almost the snout of an alligator—and it was split open to show a jagged array of teeth. The statue, if that was what it was, had been broken off just below the chest. There were stumps of forelegs, but that was all. The stone was pitted and eroded with age. It was glittery in places, too, like the rocks collected in one of the Dandux baskets. Beside it, anchored by a plastic box of pushpins, was a note: *Jim—What the hell is this? Any idea? Barbie.*

"Look at its *tongue*," Cynthia said in a strange, dreaming voice.

"What about it?"

"It's a snake."

Yes, he saw, it was. A rattler, maybe. Something with fangs, anyway.

Cynthia's head snapped up. Her eyes were wide and alarmed. She grabbed his shirt again and pulled it. "What are we *doing*?" she asked. "This isn't art-appreciation class, for Christ's sake— we've got to get out of here!"

Yeah, we do, Steve thought. *The question is, where do we go?*

They'd worry about it when they got to the truck. Not in here. He had an idea it would be impossible to do any productive thinking in here.

"Hey, what happened to the radio?" she asked.

"Huh?" He listened, but the music was gone. "I don't know."

With a strange, set expression on her face, Cynthia reached out to the crumbling fragment on the table again. This time she touched it between the ears. She gasped. The hanging lights flickered—Steve *saw* them flicker—and the radio came back on. *"Hey Dwight, hey Lyle, boys, you don't need to fight,"* Mary Chapin Carpenter sang through the static, *"hot dog, I feel lucky tonight!"*

"Christ," Steve said. "Why'd you do that?"

Cynthia looked at Steve. Her eyes looked oddly hazy. She shrugged, touched her tongue to the middle of her upper lip. "I don't know." Suddenly she put her hand to her forehead and squeezed her temples, hard. When she took it away, her eyes were clear again, but frightened. "What the *hell*?" she said, more to herself than to him.

Steve reached out to touch the thing himself. She grabbed his wrist before he could. "Don't. It feels nasty."

He shook her off and put his finger on the wolf's back (all at once he was sure that was what it was, not a coyote but a wolf). The radio went dead again. At the same time there was a cough of broken glass from somewhere behind them. Cynthia yelped.

Steve had already taken his finger off the rock; he would have done that even if nothing at all had happened, because she was right: it felt nasty. But for a moment, something *did* happen. It felt as if one of the more vital circuits in his head had shorted out, for one thing. Except . . . hadn't he been thinking about the girl? *Doing* something to the girl, with the girl? The kind of thing both of you might like to try but would never talk about to your friends? A kind of experiment?

Even as he was mulling this over, trying to remember what the experiment might have been, he was reaching out for the stone again with his finger. He didn't make a conscious decision to do this, but now that he was, it seemed like a good idea. *Just let that old finger go where it wants,* he thought, bemused. *Let it touch whatever it—*

She grabbed his hand and twisted it away from the piece of stone just as he was about to put his finger on the wolf's back. "Hey, sport, read my lips: *I want to get out of here! Right now!*"

He took a deep breath, let it out. Repeated the process. His head began to feel like familiar territory again, but he was suddenly more frightened than ever. Of exactly what he didn't know. Wasn't sure he *wanted* to know. "Okay. Let's go."

Holding her hand, he led her back into the hallway. He glanced over his shoulder once, at the crumbled gray bit of carving. Twisted, predatory head. Bulging eyes. Too-long snout. Snake tongue. And beyond it, something else. Both the helix and the exhibitionist Goofy were gone. Those screens were dark, as if some power-surge had shorted them out.

Water was pouring through the open door of the office with the aquarium in it. There was a molly stranded on the edge of the hallway carpet, flopping its last. *Well,* Steve thought, *now we know what broke, no need to wonder about that.*

"Don't look when we go by," he said. "Just—"

"Did you hear something just then?" she asked. "Bangs or booms or something like that?"

He listened, heard only the wind . . . then thought he heard a stealthy shuffling from behind him.

He wheeled around quickly. Nothing there. Of course there wasn't, what had he been thinking? That one of the corpses had wriggled down off its hook and was coming after them? Dumb. Even under these stressful circumstances, that was plumb loco, Wild Bill. But there was something else, something he couldn't dismiss, dumb or not: that statue. It was like a physical presence in his head, a thumb poking rudely into the actual tissue of his brain. He wished he hadn't looked at it. Even more, he wished he hadn't touched it.

"Steve? *Did* you hear anything? It could have been gunshots. There! There's another one!"

The wind screamed along the side of the building and something else fell over out there, making them cry out and grab for each other like kids in the dark. The thing that had fallen over went scraping along the ground outside.

"I don't hear anything but the wind. Probably what *you* heard was a door banging shut somewhere. If you heard anything."

"There were at least three of them," she said. "Maybe they weren't gunshots, more like thuds, but—"

"Could have been something flying in the wind, too. Come on, cookie, let's shake some tailfeathers."

"Don't call me cookie and I won't call you cake," she said faintly, not looking when they passed the office with the water still draining out of it.

Steve did. The aquarium was now nothing but a rectangle of wet sand surrounded by jags of glass. The hand lay on the soaked carpet beside the desk. It had landed on its back. There was a dead guppy stranded on its palm. The fingers seemed almost to beckon him—come on in, stranger, pull up a chair, take a load off, *mi casa es su casa.*

No thanks, Steve thought.

He had no more than started to open the door between the littery reception area and the outside when it was snatched prankishly out of his hands. Dust was blowing past in ribbons. The mountains to the west had been completely obliterated by moving membranes of darkening gold—sand and alkali grit flying in the day's last ten minutes or so of light—but he could see the first stars glowing clearly overhead. The wind was at near gale force now. A rusty old barrel with the words ZOOM CHEMTRONICS DISPOSE OF PROPERLY stencilled on it rolled across the parking lot, past the Ryder truck, and across the road. Into the desert it went. The *tink-tink-tink* of the lanyard-clip against the flagpole was feverish now, and something to their left thumped twice, hard, a sound like silencer-muffled pistol shots. Cynthia jerked against him. Steve turned toward the sound and saw a big blue Dumpster. As he looked, the wind half-lifted its lid, then dropped it. There was another muffled thump.

"There's your gunshots," he said, raising his voice to be heard over the wind.

"Well . . . it didn't sound *just* like that."

A concatenation of coyote-howls rose in the night, some from the west, flying to them on the wind and grit, some from the north. The sound reminded Steve of old newsclips he'd seen of Beatlemania, girls screaming their heads off for the moptops from Liverpool. He and Cynthia looked at each other. "Come on," he said. "The truck. Right now."

They hurried to it, arms around each other and the wind at their backs. When they were in the cab again, Cynthia locked her door, bopping the button down decisively with the heel of her hand. Steve did the same, then started the engine. Its steady rumble and the glow from the dashboard when he pulled the headlight knob comforted him. He turned to Cynthia.

"All right, where do we go to report this? Austin's out. It's too far west and in the direction this shit is coming from. We'd end up by the side of the road, hoping we could start the damn engine again once the storm passed. That leaves Ely, which is a two-hour drive—longer, if the storm overtakes us—or downtown Desperation, which is maybe less than a mile."

"Ely," she said at once. "The people who did this could be up there in town, and I doubt if a couple of local cops or even county mounties could match up to guys who could do what we saw in there."

"The people who did it could also be back on Route 50," he said. "Remember the RV, and the boss's bike."

"But we *did* see traffic," she said, then jumped as something else fell over nearby. It sounded big and metallic. "Christ, Steve, can't we *please* just get the fuck out of here?"

He wanted to as badly as she did, but he shook his head. "Not until we figure this out. It's important. Fourteen dead people, and that doesn't count the boss or the people from the RV."

"The Carver family."

"This is gonna be big when it comes out—nationwide. If we go back to Ely and if it turns out there were two cops with phones and radios less than a mile up the road, and if the people who did this get away because we took too long blowing the whistle . . . well, our decision is going to be questioned. *Harshly.*"

The dashlights made her face look green and sick. "Are you saying they'd think *we* had something to do with it?"

"I don't know, but I'll tell you this: You're not the Duchess of Windsor and I'm not the Duke of Earl. We're a couple of road-bums, is what we are. How much ID do you have? A driver's license?"

"I never took the test. Moved around too much."

"Social Security?"

"Well, I lost the *card* someplace, I think I left it behind when I split from the guy who fucked up my ear, but I remember the *number.*"

"What have you got for actual paperwork?"

"My discount card from Tower Records and Video," she snapped. "Two punches left and I get a free CD. I'm shooting for *Out Come the Wolves.* Seems fitting, given the soundtrack in these parts. Satisfied?"

"Yeah," he said, and began to laugh. She stared at him for a moment, cheeks green, shadows rippling across her brow, eyes dark, and he felt sure she was going to launch herself at him and see how much of his skin she could pull off. Then she began to laugh, too, a helpless screamy sound he didn't care for much. "Come here a second," he said, and held out his hand.

"Don't you get funny with me, I'm warning you," she said, but she scooted across the seat and into the circle of his arm with no hesitation. He could feel her shoulder trembling against his. She was going to be cold in that tank-top if they had to get out of the truck. The temperature fell off the table in this part of the world once the sun went down.

"You really want to go into town, Lubbock?"

"What I want is to be in Disneyland eating a Sno-Kone, but I think we ought to go up there and take a look. If things are normal . . . if they *feel* normal . . . okay, we'll try reporting it there. But if we see anything that looks the slightest bit wrong, we head for Ely on the double."

She looked up at him solemnly. "I'm going to hold you to that."

"You can." He put the truck in gear and began to roll slowly toward the road. To the west, the gold glow which had been filtering through the sand was down to an ember. Overhead, more stars were poking through, but they were beginning to shimmy as the flying sand thickened.

"Steve? You don't happen to have a gun, do you?"

He shook his head, thought about going back into the Quonset to look for one, and then put the idea out of his head. He wasn't going back in there, that was all; he just wasn't. "No gun, but I've got a really *big* Swiss Army knife, one with all the bells and whistles. It's even got a magnifying glass."

"That makes me feel a lot better."

He thought of asking her about the statue, or if she'd had any funny ideas—*experimental* ideas—and then didn't. Like the thought of going back into the Quonset building again, it was just too creepy. He turned onto the road, one arm still about her shoulders, and started toward town. The sand blew thickly across the wedge of light thrown by his high beams, twisting into lank shadows that persistently reminded him of hanged men dangling from hooks.

5

The body of his sister was gone from the foot of the stairs, and that was something. David stood looking out through the double doors for a moment. Daylight was fading, and although the sky overhead was still clear—a darkening indigo—the light was dying down here at ground-level in a choke of dust. Across the street, an overhead sign reading DESPERATION COFFEE SHOP AND VIDEO STOP swung back and forth in the wind. Sitting beneath it, and looking attentively across at him, were two more coyotes. Sitting between them, tatty feathers flapping in the wind like the feathers on some old woman's church-and-Bingo hat, was a large bald-looking bird David recognized as a buzzard. Sitting right between the coyotes.

"That's impossible," he whispered, and maybe it was, but he was seeing it, just the same.

He dressed quickly, looking at a door to his left as he did. Printed on the frosted-glass pane were the words DESPERATION TOWN OFFICE, along with the hours—nine to four. He tied his sneakers and then opened the door, ready to turn and run if he sensed anything dangerous . . . if he sensed anything moving, really.

But where would I run? Where is there to run?

The room beyond the door was gloomy and silent. He groped to his left, expecting something or someone to reach out of the darkness and grab his hand, but nothing did. He found a switchplate, then the switch itself. He flipped it, blinked as his eyes adjusted to the old-fashioned hanging globes, then stepped forward. Straight ahead was a long counter with several barred windows like tellers' stations in an old-fashioned bank. One was marked TAX CLERK, another HUNTING PERMITS, another MINES AND ASSAY. The last one, smaller, bore a sign reading MSHA and FEDERAL LAND-USE REGS. Spray-painted on the wall behind the clerks' area in big red letters was this: IN THESE SILENCES SOMETHING MAY RISE.

I guess something did, too, David thought, turning his head to check the other side of the room. *Something not very—*

He never finished the thought. His eyes widened, and his hands went to his mouth to stifle a shriek. For a moment the world went gray, and he believed he might faint. To stop it happening he took his hands away from his mouth and squeezed them against his temples instead, renewing the pain there. Then he let them drop to his sides, looking with wide eyes and a hurt, quivering mouth at what was on the wall to the right of the door. There were coathooks. A Stetson with a snakeskin band hung on the one nearest the windows. Two women hung on the next two, one shot, the other gutted. This second woman had long red hair and a mouth that was open in a silent frozen scream. To her left was a man in khaki, his head down, his holster empty. Pearson, maybe, the other deputy. Next to him was a man in jeans and a blood-spattered workshirt. Last in line was Pie. She had been hung up by the back of her MotoKops shirt. Cassie Styles was on it, standing in front of her Dream Floater van with her arms folded and a big grin on her face. Cassie had always been Pie's favorite MotoKop. Pie's head lolled over her broken neck and her sneakers dangled limply down.

Her hands. He kept looking at her hands. Small and pink, the fingers slightly open.

I can't touch her, I can't go near her!

But he could. He *had* to, unless he planned to leave her there with Entragian's other victims. And after all, what else was a big brother for, especially one who wasn't quite big enough to stop the boogeyman from doing such an unspeakable thing in the first place?

Chest hitching, greenish-white curds of soap drying to scales on his skin, he put his hands together again and raised them in front of his face. He closed his eyes. His voice, when it came out, was trembling so badly he hardly recognized it as his own. "God, I know that my sister is with you, and that this is just what she left behind. Please help me do what I have to for her." He opened his eyes again and looked at her. "I love you, Pie. I'm sorry for all the times I yelled at you or pulled your braids too hard."

That last was too much. He knelt on the floor and put his hands on top of his bowed head and held them there, gasping and trying not to pass out. His tears cut trails in the green goo on his face. What hurt most was the knowledge that the door which had swung shut between them would never be opened, at least not in this world. He would never see Pie go out on a date or shoot a basket from downtown two seconds before the buzzer. She would never again ask him to spot her while she stood on her head or want to know if the light in the refrigerator stayed on even when the door was closed. He understood now why people in the Bible rent their clothes.

When he had control of himself, he dragged one of the chairs which stood against the wall over to where she was. He looked at her hands, her pink palms, and his mind wavered again. He forced it steady—just finding he could do that, if he had to, was a welcome surprise. That wavering toward grief returned more insistently as he stood on the chair and observed the waxy, unnatural pallor of her face and the purplish cast of her lips. Cautiously, he let some of the grief in. He sensed it would be better for him if he did. This was his first dead person, but it was also *Pie*, and he did not want to be scared of her or grossed out by her. So it was better to feel sorry, and he did. He did.

Hurry, David.

He wasn't sure if that was his voice or the other's, but this time it didn't matter. The voice was right. Pie was dead, but his father and the others upstairs weren't. And then there was his mother. That was the worst thing, in a way even worse than what had happened to Pie, because he didn't *know.* The crazy cop had taken his mother somewhere, and he might be doing anything to her. *Anything.*

I won't think about that. I won't let myself.

He thought instead of all the hours Pie had spent in front of the TV with Melissa Sweetheart in her lap, watching *KrayZee Toons.* Professor KrayZee had yielded his place of honor in her heart to the MotoKops (especially Cassie Styles and the handsome Colonel Henry) over the last year or so, but the old Prof still seemed like the right answer to David. He only remembered one of Prof. KrayZee's little songs, and he sang it now as he slipped his arms around the dead girl and lifted her free of the hook: *"This old man . . . he played one . . ."*

Her head fell against his shoulder. It was amazingly heavy—how had she ever held it up all day long, as little as she was?

"He played knick-knack on my thumb . . ."

He turned, stepped clumsily down from the chair, staggered but did not fall, and took Pie over to the windows. He smoothed her shirt down in the back as he went. It had torn, but only a little. He laid her down, one hand under her neck to keep from bumping her head on the floor. It was the way Mom had showed him when Pie had been just a baby and he had asked to hold her. Had he sung to her then? He couldn't remember. He supposed he might have.

"With a knick-knack paddy whack, give a dog a bone . . ."

Ugly dark-green drapes hung at the sides of the windows, which were narrow nine-foot floor-to-ceiling jobs. David tugged one down.

"Krazy Prof goes rolling home . . ."

He laid the drape out beside his sister's body, singing the stupid little song over again. He wished he could give her

Melissa Sweetheart to keep her company, but 'Lissa was back by the Wayfarer. He lifted Pie onto the drape and folded the bottom half over her. It came all the way up to her neck and she looked better to him now, a *lot*. As if she were at home, sleeping in bed.

"With a knick-knack paddy whack, give a dog a bone," he sang again, *"Krazy Prof went rolling home."* He kissed her forehead. "I love you, Pie," he said, and he drew the top of the drape over her.

He remained beside her for a moment with his hands clasped tightly between his thighs, trying to get control of his emotions again. When he felt steadier, he got to his feet. The wind was howling, daylight was almost gone, and the sound of the dust against the windowpanes was like the light tapping of many fingers. He could hear a harsh, monotonous squeaking sound—*reek-reek-reek*—as something turned in the wind, and he jumped when something else out there in the growing darkness fell over with a bang.

He turned from the window and went hesitantly around the counter. There were no more bodies, but papers had been spilled behind the window marked TAX CLERK, and there were spots of dried blood on some of them. The Tax Clerk's high-backed, long-legged chair had been knocked over.

Behind the counter area was an open safe (David saw more stacks of paper but no money, and nothing that looked disturbed). To the right was a small cluster of desks. To the left were two closed doors, both with gold lettering on them. The one marked FIRE CHIEF didn't interest him, but the other one, the office of the Town Safety Officer, did. Jim Reed, that was his name.

"Town Safety Officer. What you'd call Chief of Police in a bigger burg," David murmured, and went over to the door. It was unlocked. He felt along the wall again, located the light-switch, and flicked it. The first thing he saw when the lights came on was the huge caribou's head on the wall to the left of the desk. The second was the man behind the desk. He was tilted back in his office chair. Except for the ballpoint pens sticking out of his eyes and the desk-plaque protruding from his mouth, he might have been sleeping there, that was how relaxed his posture was. His hands had been laced together across his ample belly. He was wearing a khaki shirt and an across-the-chest belt like Entragian's.

Outside, something else fell over and coyotes howled in unison like a doowop group from hell. David jumped, then glanced over his shoulder to make sure Entragian wasn't sneaking up on him. He wasn't. David looked back at the Town Safety Officer. He knew what he had to do, and he thought if he could touch Pie, he could probably touch this stranger.

First, however, he picked up the phone. He expected it to be dead and it was. He hit the cut-off buttons a time or two anyway, saying "Hello? Hello?"

Room service, send me up a room, he thought, and shivered as he put the handset back in the cradle. He went around the desk and stood next to the cop with the pens in his eyes. The dead man's name-plaque—JAMES REED, TOWN SAFETY OFFICER—was still on his desk, so the one in his mouth was something else. OPS HERE was printed on the part sticking out between his teeth.

David could smell something familiar—not aftershave or cologne. He looked at the dead man's folded hands, saw the deep cracks in the skin, and understood. It was hand lotion he smelled, either the same stuff his mother used or something similar. Jim Reed must have finished rubbing some into his hands not long before he was killed.

David tried to look into Reed's lap and couldn't. The man was too fat and pulled in too close to his desk for David to be able to see what he needed to see. There was a small black hole in the center of the chairback—that he could see just fine.

Reed had been shot; the thing with the pens had been done (David hoped) after he was already dead.

Get going. Hurry.

He started to pull the chair back, then shouted with surprise and jumped out of the way when it over-balanced almost at his touch and spilled Jim Reed's dead weight onto the floor. The corpse uttered a great dead belch when it hit. The plaque in its mouth flew out like a missile leaving its silo. It landed upside down, but David could read it with no trouble just the same: THE BUCK STOPS HERE.

Heart pounding harder than ever, he dropped to one knee beside the body. Reed's uniform pants were unbuttoned and unzipped, exposing some decidedly non-reg underdrawers (vast, silk, peach-colored), but David barely noticed these. He was looking for something else, and he sighed with relief when he saw it. On one well-padded hip was Reed's service revolver. On the other was a keychain clipped to a belt-loop. Biting his lower lip, somehow sure that the dead cop was going to reach out

(oh shit the mummy's after us)

and grab him, David struggled to free the keys from the belt-loop. At first the clip wouldn't open for him, but he was finally able to get it loose. He picked through the keys quickly, praying to find what he needed . . . and did. A square one that almost didn't look like a key at all. A black magnetic strip ran down its length. The key to the holding cells upstairs.

He hoped.

David put the keyring in his pocket, glanced curiously at Reed's open pants again, then unsnapped the strap over the cop's gun. He pulled it out, holding it in both hands, feeling its extraordinary weight and sense of inheld violence. A revolver, not an automatic with the bullets buried away in the handle. David turned the muzzle toward himself, careful to keep his fingers outside the trigger-guard, so he could look at the cylinder. There were bullet-heads in every hole he could see, so that was probably all right. The first chamber might be empty—in the movies cops sometimes did that to keep from shooting themselves by accident—but he reckoned that wouldn't matter if he pulled the trigger at least twice, and fast.

He turned the gun around again and inspected it from the butt forward, looking for a safety-catch. He didn't see one, and very gingerly pulled back on the trigger a little. When he saw the hammer start to rise out of its hood, he let off the pressure in a hurry. He didn't want to fire the gun down here. He didn't know how smart coyotes were, but he guessed that if they were smart about anything, it would probably be about guns.

He went back out into the main office. The wind howled, throwing sand against the window. The panes were bruise-purple now. Soon they'd be black. He looked over at the ugly green curtain, and the shape which lay beneath it. *Love you, Pie,* he thought, then went back out into the hall. He stood there a moment, taking deep breaths, eyes closed, gun held at his side with the muzzle pointed at the floor.

"God, I never shot a gun in my life," he said. "Please help me be able to shoot this one. Jesus' sake, amen."

That taken care of, David started up the stairs.

CHAPTER 3

1

Mary Jackson was sitting on her bunk, looking down at her folded hands and thinking arsenic thoughts about her sister-in-law. Deirdre Finney, with her pretty pale face and sweet, stoned smile and pre-Raphaelite curls. Deirdre who didn't eat meat ("It's like, cruel, you know?") but smoked the smoke, oh yes, Deirdre had been going steady with that rascal Panama Red for years now. Deirdre with her Mr. Smiley-Smile stickers. Deirdre who had gotten her brother killed and her sister-in-law slammed into a hicksville jail cell that was really Death Row, and all because she was too fucking fried to remember that she'd left her extra pot under the spare tire.

That's not fair, a more rational part of her mind replied. *It was the license plate, not the pot. That's why Entragian stopped you. In a way it was like the Angel of Death seeing a doorway without the right mark on it. If the dope hadn't been there, he would've found something else. Once you caught his eye, you were cooked, that's all. And you know it.*

But she didn't *want* to know it; thinking of it that way, as some sort of weird natural disaster, was just too awful. It was better to blame it on Peter's idiot sister, to imagine punishing Deirdre in a number of nonlethal but painful ways. Caning—the sort they administered to thieves in Hong Kong—was the most satisfying, but she also saw herself hiking the tip of a pointed high-heeled shoe into Deirdre's flat little fashion-plate ass. Anything to get that room-for-rent look out of her eyes long enough for Mary to scream *"YOU GOT YOUR BROTHER KILLED, YOU STUPID TWAT, ARE YOU READING ME?"* into Deirdre's face and to see the understanding there.

"Violence breeds violence," she told her hands in a calm, teacherly tone. Talking to herself under these circumstances seemed perfectly normal. "I know it, *everybody* knows it, but thinking about it is so *pleasant*, sometimes."

"What?" Ralph Carver asked. He sounded dazed. In fact— gruesome idea—he sounded quite a bit like the walking short-circuit that was her sister-in-law.

"Nothing. Never mind."

She got up. Two steps took her to the front of the cell. She wrapped her hands around the bars and looked out. The coyote was sitting on the floor with the remains of Johnny Marin-ville's leather jacket in front of its forepaws, looking up at the writer as if mesmerized.

"Do you think he got away?" Ralph asked her. "Do you think my boy got away, ma'am?"

"It's not ma'am, it's Mary, and I don't know. I *want* to be-lieve it, I can tell you that. I think there's a pretty good chance that he did, actually." *As long as he didn't run into the cop,* she added to herself.

"Yeah, I guess so. I had no idea he was so serious about the praying stuff," Ralph said. He sounded almost apologetic, which Mary found weird, under the circumstances. "I thought it was probably . . . I don't know . . . a passing fad. Sure didn't look that way, did it?"

"No," Mary agreed. "It didn't."

"Why do you keep staring at me, Bosco?" Marinville asked the coyote. "You got my fucking jacket, what else do you want? As if I didn't have a pretty good idea." He looked up at Mary. "You know, if one of us could get out of here, I think that mangebasket might actually turn tail and—"

"Hush!" Billingsley said. "Someone coming up the stairs!"

The coyote heard it, too. It broke eye-contact with Marinville and turned around, growling. The footfalls neared, reached the landing, stopped. Mary snatched a glance at Ralph Carver, but couldn't look for long; the combination of hope and terror on his face was too awful. She had lost her husband, and that hurt worse than she had ever imagined anything could. What would it be like to see your whole family snatched away in the course of an afternoon?

The wind rose, howling along the eaves. The coyote looked nervously over its shoulder at the sound, then took three slow steps toward the door, ragged ears twitching.

"Son!" Ralph called desperately. "Son, if that's you, don't come in! That thing's standing right in front of the door!"

"How close?" It was him, the boy. It really was. Amazing. And the self-possession in his voice was even more amazing. Mary thought that perhaps she should re-evaluate the power of prayer.

Ralph looked bewildered, as if he didn't understand the question. The writer did, though. "Probably five feet, and looking right at it. Be careful."

"I've got a gun," the boy said. "I think you better all get under your bunks. Mary, get as far over to my dad's side as you can. Are you *sure* he's right in front of the door, Mr. Marinville?"

"Yes. Big as life and twice as ugly is my friend Bosco. Have you ever fired a gun before, David?"

"No."

"Oh, Moses." Marinville rolled his eyes.

"David, no!" Ralph called. Belated alarm was filling his face; he seemed to be just realizing what was happening here. "Run and get help! Open the door and that bastard'll be on you in two jumps!"

"No," the kid said. "I thought about it, Dad, and I'd rather chance the coyote than the cop. Plus I have a key. I think it'll work. It looks just the same as the one the cop used."

"I'm convinced," Marinville said, as if that settled it. "Everybody get down. Count to five, David, then do it."

"You'll get him killed!" Ralph yelled furiously at Marinville. "You'll get my boy killed just to save your own ass!"

Mary said, "I understand your concern, Mr. Carver, but I think if we don't get out of here, we're all dead."

"Count to five, David!" Marinville repeated. He got down on his knees, then slid under his bunk.

Mary looked across at the door, realized that her cell would be directly in the kid's line of fire, and understood why David had told her to get way over to his father's side. He might only be eleven, but he was thinking better than she was.

"One," the boy on the other side of the door said. She could hear how scared he was, and she didn't blame him. Not a bit. "Two."

"Son!" Billingsley called. "Listen to me, son! Get on your knees! Hold the gun in both hands and be ready to shoot up— *up*, son! It won't come on the floor, it'll jump for you! Do you understand?"

"Yeah," the kid said. "Yeah, okay. You under your bunk, Dad?"

Ralph wasn't. He was still standing at the bars of his cell. There was a scared, set look on the swollen face hovering between the white-painted bars. "Don't do it, David! I *forbid* you to do it!"

"Get down, you asshole," Marinville said. He was staring out from under his bunk at David's father with furious eyes.

Mary approved of the sentiment but thought that Marinville's technique sucked—she would have expected better from a writer. Some other writer, anyway; she had this one placed. The guy who'd written *Delight,* perhaps the century's dirtiest book, was cooling his heels in the cell next to hers, surreal but true, and although his nose looked as if it might never recover from what the cop had done to it, Marinville still had the attitude of a guy who expects to get whatever he wants. Probably on a silver tray.

"*Is* my dad out of the way?" The kid sounded unsure as well as scared now, and Mary hated his father for what he was doing—plucking the boy's already overstrained nerves as if they were guitar strings.

"No!" Ralph bawled. "And I'm not going to *get* out of the way! Get out of here! Find a phone! Call the State Cops!"

"I tried the one on Mr. Reed's desk," David called back. "It's dead."

"Then try another one! Goddammit, keep trying until you find one that—"

"Quit being dumb and get under your bunk," Mary said to him in a low voice. "What do you want him to remember about today? That he saw his sister killed and shot his father by mistake, all before suppertime? *Help!* Your son's trying; you try, too."

He looked at her, his cheeks shiny-pale, a vivid contrast to the blood clotted on the left side of his face. "He's all I got left," he said in a low voice. "Do you understand that?"

"Of course I do. Now get under your bunk, Mr. Carver."

Ralph stepped back from the bars of his cell, hesitated, then dropped to his knees and slid under his bunk.

Mary glanced over at the cell David had wriggled out of— God, that had taken guts—and saw that the old veterinarian was under his bunk. His eyes, the only young part of him, gleamed out of the shadows like luminous blue gems.

"David!" Marinville called. "We're clear!"

The voice that returned was tinged with doubt: "My dad, too?"

"I'm under the bunk," Ralph called. "Son, you be careful. If—" His voice trembled, then firmed. "If it gets on you, hold onto the gun and try to shoot up into its belly." He poked his head out from under the bunk, suddenly alarmed. "Is the gun even loaded? Are you sure?"

"Yeah, I'm sure." He paused. "Is it still in front of the door?"

"Yes!" Mary called.

The coyote had taken a step closer, in fact. Its head was down, its growl as steady as the idle of an outboard motor. Every time the boy spoke from his side of the door, its ears twitched attentively.

"Okay, I'm on my knees," the boy said. Mary could hear the nerves in his voice more clearly now. She had an idea he might be approaching the outer edges of his control. "I'm going to start counting again. Make sure you're as far back as you can be when I get to five. I . . . I don't want to hurt anyone by accident."

"Remember to shoot uphill," the vet said. "Not a lot, but a little. Okay?"

"Because it'll jump. Right. I'll remember. One . . . two . . ."

Outside, the wind dropped briefly. In the quiet, Mary could hear two things with great clarity: the rumbling growl of the coyote, and her own heartbeat in her ears. Her life was in the hands of an eleven-year-old with a gun. If David shot and missed or froze up and didn't shoot at all, the coyote would likely kill him. And then, when the psycho cop came back, they would all die.

". . . three . . ." The quiver which had crept into the boy's voice made him sound eerily like his father. ". . . four . . . *five*."

The doorknob turned.

2

For Johnny Marinville it was like being tumbled back into Vietnam again, where mortal things happened at a zany speed that always surprised you. He hadn't held out much hope for the kid, thought he was apt to spray bullets wildly everywhere but into Bosco's hide, but the kid was all they had. Like Mary, he had decided that if they weren't out of here when the cop came back, they were through.

And the kid surprised him.

To begin with, he didn't *throw* the door open, so it would hit the wall and then bounce back, obscuring his line of fire; he seemed to *toss* it open. He was on his knees, and dressed again, but his cheeks were still green with Irish Spring soap and his eyes were very wide. The door was still swinging open when he clamped his right hand over his left on the butt of the gun, which looked to Johnny like a .45. A big gun for a kid. He held it at chest-level, the barrel tilted upward at a slight angle. His face was solemn, even studious.

The coyote, perhaps not expecting the door to open in spite of the voice which had been coming from behind it, took half a step backward, then tensed on its haunches and sprang at the boy with a snarl. It was, Johnny thought, the little backward flinch that sealed its doom; it gave the boy all the time he needed to settle himself. He fired twice, allowing the gun to kick and then return to its original aiming point before pulling the trigger a second time. The reports were deafening in the enclosed space. Then the coyote, which had gone airborne after the first shot and before the second, hit David and knocked him backward.

His father screamed and scrambled out from under his bunk. The kid appeared to be fighting with the animal on the landing beyond the doorway, but Johnny found it almost impossible to believe the coyote could have much fight left in it; he had *heard* the slugs go home, and both the hardwood floor and the desk were painted with the animal's blood.

"David! David! Shoot it in the guts!" his father screamed, dancing up and down in his anxiety.

Instead of shooting, the kid fought free of the coyote, as if it were a coat he had somehow gotten tangled in. He scooted away on his butt, looking bewildered. The front of his shirt was matted with blood and fur. He got the wall against his back and used it to push his way onto his feet. He looked at the gun as he did it, seemingly amazed to see it was still there at the end of his arm.

"I'm okay, Dad, settle down. I got it, it never even nipped me." He ran his hand over his chest and then down the arm holding the gun, as if confirming this to himself, as well. Then he looked at the coyote. It was still alive, panting harshly and rapidly with its head hung over the first stair riser. Where its chest had been there was now a wide bloody dent.

David dropped to one knee beside it and put the barrel of the .45 against the dangling head. He then turned his own head away. Johnny saw the kid's eyes clenched shut, and his heart went out to the boy. He had never enjoyed his own kids much—they had a tiresome way of upsetting you for the first twenty years and trying to upstage you for the second twenty—but one like this wouldn't be so bad to have around, maybe. He had some game, as the basketball players said.

I'd even get down on my knees with him at bedtime, Johnny thought. *Shit, anybody would. Look at the results.*

Still wearing that stressful expression—the look of a child who knows he must eat his liver before he can go out and play—David pulled the trigger a third time. The report was just as loud but not quite as sharp, somehow. The coyote's body jumped. A fan of red droplets as fine as lace appeared below the stairwell's railing. That harsh panting sound quit. The kid opened his eyes and looked down at what he had done. "Thank you, God," he said in a small, dull voice. "It was awful, though. Really awful."

"You did a good job, boy," Billingsley said.

David got up and walked slowly into the holding area. He looked at his father. Ralph held his arms out. David went over to him, starting to cry again, and let his father hold him in a clumsy embrace that had bars running through the middle of it.

"I was afraid for you, guy," Ralph said. "That's why I told you to go away. You know that, don't you?"

"Yes, Daddy." David was crying harder now, and Johnny realized even before the kid went on that these tears weren't about the fleabag, no, not these. "Pie was on a huh-huh-hook downstairs. Other people, t-t-too. I took her down. I couldn't take the other ones down, they were gruh-grownups, but I took Pie down. I s-sang . . . sang to h-h—"

He tried to say more, but the words were swallowed in hysterical, exhausted sobs. He pressed his face between the bars while his father stroked his back and told him to hush, just hush, he was sure David had done everything for Kirsten that he could, that he had done fine.

Johnny let them have a full minute of this by his watch—the kid deserved that much just for opening the goddam door when he knew there was a wild dog on the other side waiting for him to do it—and then spoke the kid's name. David didn't look around, so he said it a second time, louder. The boy *did* look around then. His eyes were red-rimmed and streaming.

"Listen, kiddo, I know you've been through a lot," Johnny said, "and if we get out of this thing alive, I'll be the first one to write you a commendation for the Silver Star. But right now we have to get gone. Entragian could be on his way back. If he was close by, he probably heard the gunshots. If you've got a key, now's the time to try it out."

David pulled a thick ring of keys out of his pocket and found the one which looked like the one Entragian had used. He put it in the lock of his father's cell. Nothing happened. Mary cried out in frustration and slammed the heel of her hand against the bars of her own cell.

"Other way," Johnny said. "Turn it around."

David turned the key over and slid it into the lock-slot

again. This time there was a loud click—almost a thud—and the cell door popped open.

"Yes!" Mary cried. "Oh, *yes!*"

Ralph stepped out and swept his son into his arms, this time with no bars between them. And when David kissed the puffy place on the left side of his father's face, Ralph Carver cried out in pain and laughed at the same time. Johnny thought it one of the most extraordinary sounds he had ever heard in his life, and one you could never convey in a book; the quality of it, like the expression on Ralph Carver's face as he looked into his son's face, would always be just out of reach.

3

Ralph took the mag-key from his son and used it to unlock the other cells. They stepped out and stood in a little cluster in front of the guard's desk—Mary from New York, Ralph and David from Ohio, Johnny from Connecticut, old Tom Billingsley from Nevada. They looked at each other with the eyes of train-wreck survivors.

"Let's get out of here," Johnny said. The boy had given the gun to his father, he saw. "Can you shoot that, Mr. Carver? Can you *see* to shoot that?"

"Yes to both," Ralph said. "Come on."

He led them through the door, holding David's hand as he went. Mary walked behind them, then Billingsley. Johnny brought up the rear. As he stepped over the coyote, he saw that the final shot had pretty much pulverized the animal's head. He wondered if the kid's father could have done that. He wondered if *he* could have done it.

At the foot of the stairs, David told them to hold on. The glass doors were black now; night had come. The wind screamed beyond them like something that was lost and pissed off about it. "You won't want to believe this, but it's true," the boy said, and then told them what he had seen on the other side of the street.

"Behold, the buzzard shall lie down with the coyote," Johnny said, peering out through the glass. "That's in the Bible. Jamaicans, chapter three."

"I don't think that's funny," Ralph said.

"Actually, neither do I," Johnny said. "It's too much like something the cop would say." He could see the shapes of the buildings over there, and the occasional tumbleweed bouncing past, but that was all. And did it matter? Would it matter even if there were a pack of werewolves standing outside the local poolhall, smoking crack and watching for escapees? They couldn't stay here in any case. Entragian would be back, guys like him *always* came back.

There are *no guys like him,* his mind whispered. *There were never in the history of the world any guys like him, and you know it.*

Well, maybe he did, but it didn't change the principle of the thing a bit. They had to get out.

"*I* believe you," Mary told David. She looked at Johnny. "Come on. Let's go into the Police Chief's office, or whatever they call it here."

"For?"

"Lights and guns. Do you want to come, Mr. Billingsley?"

Billingsley shook his head.

"David, may I have the keys?"

David handed them to her. Mary slipped them into the pocket of her jeans. "Keep your eyes open," she said. David nodded. Mary reached out, took Johnny's hand—her fingers were cold as ice—and pulled him through the door which led into the clerks' area.

He saw what was spray-painted on the wall and pointed to it. "'In these silences something may rise.' What do you suppose *that* means?"

"Don't know, don't care. I just want to get to someplace where there are lights and people and phones and we can—"

She was turning to the right as she spoke, her eyes touching on the fold of green drape below the tall windows with no particular interest (the shape beneath it was too slight for her to recognize). Then she saw the bodies hung on the wall. She gasped and doubled over, as if someone had struck her in the belly, then turned to flee. Johnny caught her, but for a moment he was sure she was going to get away from him—there was a lot of strength hidden in that slim body.

"*No!*" he said, shaking her in what was partly exasperation. He was ashamed of that but couldn't entirely suppress it. "No, you have to help me! *Just don't look at them!*"

"But one of them's *Peter*!"

"And he's dead. I'm sorry, but he is. We're not. Yet, anyhow. Don't look at him. Come on."

He led her swiftly toward the door marked TOWN SAFETY OF-FICER, trying to think how they should proceed. And here was another disgusting little facet of this experience: he was becoming aroused by Mary Jackson. She was quivering in the circle of his arm, he could feel the softness of her breast just above his hand, and he wanted her. Her husband was hung up like a fucking overcoat right behind them, but he was still getting a fairly respectable stiffy, especially for a man with possible prostate woes. *Terry was right all along,* he thought. *I am an asshole.*

"Come on," he said, squeezing her in what he hoped was a brotherly way. "If that kid could do what he did, then you can hang in there. I know you can. Get it together, Mary."

She pulled in a deep breath. "I'm *trying.*"

"Good g . . . oh shit. We've got another mess here. I'd tell you not to look, but I think we're a little beyond the niceties."

Mary looked at the sprawled body of the Town Safety Officer and made a thick noise in her throat. "The boy . . . David . . . Jesus Christ . . . how did he *do* it?"

"I don't know," Johnny said. "He's some kid, all right. I think he must have knocked Sheriff Jim there out of his chair trying to get his keys. Can you go next door to the Fire Chief's office? It'll be quicker if we toss both of em at once."

"Yes."

"Be prepared; if Fireman Bob was at home when Entragian went nuclear, he's probably just as dead as the rest of them."

"I'll be okay. Take these."

She handed him the keys, then went to the door marked FIRE CHIEF. Johnny saw her start to glance toward her husband, then look away again. He nodded and tried to send her some mental encouragement—good girl, good idea. She turned the knob of the Fire Chief's door, then pushed it open with tented fingers, as if it might be booby-trapped. She looked in, let out a breath, and gave Johnny a thumbs-up.

"Three things, Mary: lights, guns, any car-keys you spot. Okay?"

"Okay."

He went into the cop's office, running quickly through the keys on the ring David had gotten as he did. There was a set of GM car-keys which Johnny guessed probably belonged to the cruiser Entragian had brought him back in. If it was out there in the parking lot it would help them, but Johnny didn't think it was. He had heard an engine start up shortly after the madman had taken Carver's wife away.

The desk drawers were locked, but the right key in the lock of the wide drawer above the kneehole opened all of them. He found a flashlight in one and a locked box marked RUGER in another. He tried several different little keys on the box. None worked.

Take it anyway? Maybe. If neither of them found other guns somewhere else.

He crossed the room, pausing to look out a window. Flying

dust was all he could see. Probably all there *was* to see. God, why hadn't he taken the interstate?

That struck him funny; he giggled under his breath as he looked at the closed door behind Reed's desk. *Sound like a crazyman,* he thought. *Never mind* Travels with Harley; *if you get out of this alive, you should think about calling the book* Travels with Loony.

That made him laugh even harder. He put one hand over his mouth to stifle it and opened the door. The laughter stopped in a hurry. Sitting amid the boots and shoes, partly obscured by hanging coats and spare uniforms, was a dead woman. She was propped against the closet's side wall and dressed in clothes Johnny thought of as Boot Scootin Secretarial—tapered slacks, not denim, and a silk shirt with entwined roses embroidered over the left breast. The woman appeared to be staring at him with round-eyed wonder, but that was only an illusion.

Because you expect to see eyes, he thought, *and not just big red sockets where they used to be.*

He restrained an urge to slam the closet shut and pushed the hanging garments to either side along the pole instead, so he could see the rear wall. A good idea. There was a gun-rack with half a dozen rifles and a shotgun in it back there. One of the grooves was empty, third from the right, and Johnny guessed that was where another shotgun, the one Entragian had pointed at him, usually went.

"Hot damn, paydirt!" he exclaimed, and stepped into the closet. He planted one foot on either side of the sitting corpse's body, but that made him acutely uncomfortable; he had once gotten head from a woman who had been sitting against a bedroom wall in almost that exact same position. At a party in East Hampton, that had been. Spielberg had been there. Joyce Carol Oates, too.

He stepped back, put one foot on the corpse's shoulder, and

pushed. The woman's body slid slowly and stiffly to the right. Her huge red eyesockets seemed to stare at him with an expression of surprise as she went, as if she were wondering how a cultured fellow such as himself, a National Book Award winner, for goodness' sake, could possibly stoop to pushing over a lady in a closet. Tendrils of her hair slid along the wall, trailing after her.

"Sorry, ma'am," he said, "but it's better for both of us this way, believe me."

The guns were held in place by a length of cable threaded through the trigger-guards. The cable was padlocked to an eyebolt on the side of the case. Johnny hoped he would have better luck finding the key to this lock than he'd have finding the one that opened the box with the Ruger in it.

The third key he tried popped the padlock. He stripped the cable back through the trigger-guards with a jerk so hard that one of them—a Remington .30-.06—came tumbling out. He caught it, turned . . . and the woman, Mary, was standing right there. Johnny gave a strangled little whoop that probably would have been a scream if he hadn't been so scared. His heart stopped beating, and for one very long moment he was positive it wasn't going to restart; he'd be dead of fright even before he fell backward onto the corpse in the silk shirt. Then, thank God, it got going again. He slammed a fist into his chest just above the left nipple (an area which had once been hard and now wasn't very) just to show the pump underneath who was the boss.

"Don't ever do that," he told Mary, trying not to wheeze. "What's wrong with you?"

"I thought you heard me." She didn't look terribly sympathetic. There was a golfbag, of all things, slung over her shoulder. A *tartan* golfbag. She looked at the corpse in the closet. "There's a body in the Fire Chief's closet, too. A man."

"What was his handicap, any idea?" His heart was still galloping, but maybe not so fast now.

"You never quit, do you?"

"Fuck you, Mary, I'm trying to kid myself out of dying, here. Every martini I ever drank just jumped on my heart. *Christ,* you scared me."

"I'm sorry, but we've got to hurry up. He could come back any time."

"A concept that never crossed my poor excuse for a mind. Here, take this. And be careful." He handed her the .30-.06, thinking of an old Tom Waits song. *Black crow shells from a .30-.06,* Waits sang in his stripped and somehow ghoulish voice. *Whittle you into kindlin.*

"How careful? Is it loaded?"

"I don't even remember how to check. I did a tour of Vietnam, but as a journalist. That was a long time ago, in any case. The only guns I've seen fired since then have been on movie screens. We'll figure the guns out later, okay?"

She put it gingerly into the golfbag. "I found two flashlights. They both work. One's a long-barrel job. Very bright."

"Good." He handed her the flashlight he had found.

"The bag was hung on the back of the door," Mary said, dropping the flashlight in. "The Fire Chief . . . if it was him . . . well, one of the clubs was stuck down through the top of his head. *Way* down. He was sort of . . . *skewered* on it."

Johnny took two more rifles and the shotgun from the rack and turned with them in his arms. If the walnut doodad on the floor below the rack contained ammo, as he assumed it did, all would be well; a rifle or shotgun for each of the grownups. The kid could have Sheriff Jim's .45 back. Shit, the kid could have any gun he wanted, as far as Johnny was concerned. So far, at least, David Carver was the only one of them who had demonstrated he could use one if he had to.

"I'm sorry you had to see that," he said, helping Mary ease the guns into the golfbag.

She shook her head impatiently, as if that wasn't the point.

"How much strength would it take to do something like that? To push the handle of a golf-club down through a man's head and neck and right into his chest? To push it down until there was nothing but the head sticking up like a . . . a little hat, or something?"

"I don't know. A lot, I guess. But Entragian's a moose." A moose indeed, but now that she'd put it in this light, it *did* seem strange.

"It's the *level* of violence that scares me the most," she said. "The ferocity. That woman in the closet . . . her eyes are gone, aren't they?"

"Yes."

"The Carvers' little girl . . . what he did to Peter, shooting him point-blank in the stomach over and over . . . the people out there hung up like deer in hunting season . . . do you see what I mean?"

"Of course." *And you're not even* touching *the rest of it, Mary,* he thought. *He's not just a serial killer; he's the Bram Stoker version of Dr. Dolittle.*

She looked around nervously as a particularly strong gust of wind hit the building. "It doesn't matter where we go next, as long as we're out of *here. Come* on. For God's sake!"

"Right, just thirty seconds, okay?"

He knelt by the woman's legs, smelling blood and perfume. He went through the keys again, and this time had almost reached the end of his choices before one popped the lock on what did indeed turn out to be a small but exceedingly well stocked ammo chest. He took eight or nine boxes of shells, ones he hoped would fit the weapons he had already taken, and dumped them into the golfbag.

"I'll never in this life be able to carry all that," Mary said.

"That's okay, I will."

Except he couldn't. He was ashamed to find he couldn't even get the golfbag off the floor, let alone sling it over his shoulder.

If the bitch hadn't scared me so bad—he thought, and then had to laugh at himself. He really did.

"What are you grinning about?" she asked him sharply.

"Nothing." He made the grin disappear. "Here, grab the strap. Help me pull it."

Together they dragged the bag across the floor, Mary keeping her head down and her eyes fixed firmly on the steel bouquet of protruding gunbarrels as they came around the counter and backed toward the door. Johnny took a single look up at the hanging corpses and thought: *The storm, the coyotes sitting along the road like an honor guard, the one in the holding area, the buzzards, the dead.* How comforting it would be to believe this was all an adventure in dreamland. But it wasn't; he had only to sniff the sour aroma of his own sweat through the clogged and painful channels of his nose to be sure of that. Something beyond anything he had ever believed—anything he had ever *considered* believing—was happening here, and it wasn't a dream.

"That's it, don't look," he panted.

"I'm not, don't worry," she replied. Johnny was pleased to hear *her* panting a little, too.

Out in the hall, the wind was louder than ever. Ralph was standing at the doors with his arm curled around his son's shoulders, looking out. The old guy was behind them. They all turned to Johnny and Mary.

"We heard a motor," David said at once.

"We *think* we did," Ralph amended.

"Was it the cruiser?" Mary asked. She pulled one of the rifles out of the golfbag, and when the barrel drifted toward Billingsley, he pushed it away again with the flat of his hand, grimacing.

"I'm not even sure it *was* a motor," Ralph said. "The wind—"

"It wasn't the wind," David said.

"See any headlights?" Johnny asked.

David shook his head. "No, but the sand is flying so *thick*."

Johnny looked from the gun Mary was holding (the barrel was now pointed at the floor, which seemed like a step in the right direction) to the others protruding from the golfbag to Ralph. Ralph shrugged and looked at the old man.

Billingsley caught the look and sighed. "Go on, dump em out," he said. "Let's see what you got."

"Can't this *wait?*" Mary asked. "If that psycho comes back—"

"My boy says he saw more coyotes out there," Ralph Carver said. "We shouldn't take a chance on getting savaged, ma'am."

"For the last time, it's *Mary*, not ma'am," she said crossly. "Okay, all right. But hurry!"

Johnny and Ralph held the golfbag while Billingsley pulled the rifles out and handed them to David. "Put em a-row," he said, and David did, lining them up neatly at the foot of the stairs, where the light from the clerks' area would fall on them.

Ralph picked the bag up and tipped it. Johnny and Mary caught the flashlights and shells as they slid out. The old man handed the ammunition to David a box at a time, telling him which guns to put them by. They finished with three boxes stacked by the .30-.06 and none by the gun on the end. "You didn't get nothing that'll fit that Mossberg," he said. "It's a damned fine gun, but it's chambered for .22s. You want to go back n see if you can find some .22s?"

"No," Mary said immediately.

Johnny looked at her, irritated—he didn't like women answering questions that had been aimed at him—and then let it go. She was right. "There's no time," he told Billingsley. "We'll carry it anyway, though. *Somebody* in town'll have .22s. You take it, Mary."

"No thanks," she said coolly, and selected the shotgun, which the veterinarian had identified as a Rossi twelve-gauge. "If it's to be used as a club instead of a firearm, it ought to be a man who swings it. Don't you agree?"

Johnny realized he had been mousetrapped. Quite neatly, too. *You bitch,* he thought, and might have said it aloud, husband hung on a coathook or not, except that David Carver cried out *"Truck!"* at that moment, and tore open one of the municipal building's glass doors.

They had been hearing the wind for some time now, and had felt it shake the brick building they were in, but none of them was quite prepared for the ferocity of the gust that ripped the door out of David's hand and slammed it against the wall hard enough to crack the glass. The posters thumbtacked to the hallway bulletin board rattled. Some tore free and went swirling up the stairwell. Sand sheeted in, stinging Johnny's face. He put a hand up to shield his eyes and accidentally bumped his nose instead. He yelled with pain.

"David!" Ralph cried, and grabbed for his son's shirt. Too late. The boy darted out into the howling dark, unmindful of anything that might be waiting. And now Johnny understood what had galvanized David: headlights. *Turning* headlights that swept across the street from right to left, as if mounted on a gimbal. Sand danced wildly in the moving beams.

"Hey!" David screamed waving his arms. *"Hey, you! You in the truck!"*

The headlights began to ebb. Johnny snatched up one of the flashlights from the floor and ran out after the Carvers. The wind assaulted him, making him stagger on his feet and grab at the doorjamb so he wouldn't go tumbling off the steps. David had run into the middle of the street, dropping one shoulder to dodge a dark, speeding object which Johnny at first thought was a buzzard. He clicked on the flashlight and saw a tumbleweed instead.

He turned the flashlight toward the departing taillights and swung it back and forth in an arc, slitting his eyes against the sand. The light appeared puny in the sand-thickened dark.

"HEY!" David screamed. His father was behind him, the

revolver in his hand. He was trying to look in all directions at once, like a presidential bodyguard who senses danger. *"HEY, COME BACK!"*

The taillights were receding, heading north along the road which led back to Highway 50. The blinker was dancing in the wind, and Johnny caught just a glimpse of the departing truck in its stuttery glow. A panel-job with something printed on the back. He couldn't read it—there was too much flying sand.

"Get back inside, you guys!" he shouted. "It's gone!"

The boy stood in the street a moment longer, looking toward where the taillights had disappeared. His shoulders were slumped. His father touched one of his hands. "Come on, David. We don't need that truck. We're in town. We'll just find someone who can help us, and . . ."

He trailed off, looking around and seeing what Johnny had seen already. The town was dark. That might only mean that people were hunkered down, that they knew what had been happening and were hiding from the crazyman until the cavalry arrived. That made a certain degree of sense, but it wasn't how it felt to Johnny's heart.

To his heart, the town felt like a graveyard.

David and his father started back toward the steps, the boy head-down dejected, the man still looking everywhere for trouble. Mary stood in the doorway, watching them come, and Johnny thought she looked extraordinarily beautiful, with her hair flying around her head.

The truck, Johnny. Was there something about the truck? There was, wasn't there? Terry's voice.

Howls rose in the windy dark. They sounded mocking, like laughter, and seemed to come from everywhere. Johnny hardly heard them. Yes, something about the truck. Definitely. About the *size* of it, and the *lettering,* and just the *look* of it, even in the dark and the blowing sand. Something—

"Oh, *shit*!" he cried, and clutched his chest again. Not at his heart, not this time, but for a pocket that was no longer there. In his mind's eye he saw the coyote shaking his expensive motorcycle jacket back and forth, ripping the lining, spilling shit to the four points of the compass. Including—

"What?" Mary asked, alarmed at the look on his face. *"What?"*

"You-all better get back in here till these guns're loaded," Billingsley told them, "'less you want some varmint down on you."

Johnny barely heard that, either. The letters on the back of the truck receding into the windy dark could have spelled Ryder. It made sense, didn't it? Steve Ames was looking for him. He had poked his head into Desperation, seen nothing, and was now driving out of town again to look somewhere else.

Johnny leaped past the astonished Billingsley, down on one knee loading guns, and pelted upstairs toward the holding area, praying to David Carver's God that his cellular telephone was still intact.

4

If things are normal, feel normal, Steve Ames had said, *we'll try reporting it there. But if we see anything that looks the slightest bit wrong, we head for Ely on the double.*

And, as the Ryder truck sat idling beneath the dancing blinker-light which marked Desperation's only intersection, Cynthia reached out and twitched Steve's shirt. "Time to head for Ely," she said, and pointed out her window, west along the cross-street. "Bikes in the street down there, see them? My old grammy used to say bikes in the street are one of those bigtime whammies, like breaking a mirror or leaving a hat on the bed. Time to boogie."

"Your grammy said that, huh?"

"Actually, I never had a grammy, not one that I knew, anyway, but get real—what are they doing there? Why hasn't anybody taken them out of the storm? Don't you see how *wrong* all this is?"

He looked at the bikes, which were lying on their sides as if they had fallen over in the wind, then farther down the east-west cross-street. "Yeah, but people're home. There are lights." He pointed.

Yes, she saw there were lights in some of the houses, but she thought the pattern they made looked *random,* somehow. And—

"There were lights on at that mining place, too," she said. "Besides, take a good look—most of the houses are dark. Now why is that, do you think?" She heard the little sarcastic edge rising in her voice, didn't like it, couldn't stop it. "Do you think maybe most of the local yokels chartered a bus to go watch the Desperation Dorks play a doubleheader with the Austin Assholes? Big desert rivalry? Something they look forward to all y . . . hey, what are you doing?"

Not that she needed to ask. He was turning west along the cross-street. A tumbleweed flew at the truck like something jumping out of the screen at you in a 3-D movie. Cynthia cried out and raised an arm over her face. The tumbleweed hit the windshield, bounced, scraped briefly on the roof of the cab, and was gone.

"This is stupid," she said. "And dangerous."

He glanced over at her briefly, smiled, and nodded. She should have been pissed at him, smiling at a time like this, but she wasn't. It was hard to be pissed at a man who could light up that way, and she knew that was half her damned problem. As Gert Kinshaw back at D & S had been fond of saying, those who do not learn from the past are condemned to get beat up by it. She didn't think Steve Ames was the sort of man who would use his fists on a woman, but that wasn't the only way that men hurt women. They also hurt them by smiling pretty, so pretty, and getting them to follow along into the lion's jaws. Usually with a covered-dish casserole in their hands.

"If you know it's dangerous, why're you doing it, Lubbock?"

"Because we need to find a phone that works, and because I don't trust the way I feel. It's almost dark and I've got the worst case of the jimjams in history. I don't want to let them control me. Look, just let me check a couple of places. You can stay in the truck."

"The fuck I . . . hey, check it out. Over there." She pointed at a length of picket fence that had been knocked over and was lying on the lawn of a small frame house. In the glare of the headlights it was all but impossible to tell what color the house was, but she had no trouble seeing the tire-tracks printed on the length of downed fence; they were too clear to miss.

"A drunk driver could have done that," he said. "I saw two bars already, and I haven't even been looking." A stupid idea, in her opinion, but she was getting to like his Texas accent more and more. Another bad sign.

"Come on, Steve, get real." Coyote-howls rose in the night, counterpointing the wind. She slid next to him again. "Jesus, I hate that. What's *with* them?"

"I don't know."

He was creeping along at no more than ten miles an hour, wanting to be able to stop before he was on top of anything the headlights might reveal. Probably smart. What would have been even smarter, in her humble opinion, was a quick turn-around and an even quicker get-the-hell-out-of-Dodge.

"Steve, I can't wait to get somewhere with billboards and bank signs and sleazy used-car lots that stay open all night."

"I hear you," he said, and she thought: *You don't, though. When people say "I hear you," they almost never do.*

"Just let me check here—this one house—and then this burg is history," he said, and turned into the driveway of a small ranch-style home on the left side of the street. They had come perhaps a quarter of a mile west from the intersection; Cynthia could still see the blinker through the flying sand.

There were lights on in the house Steve had picked, bright ones that fell through the sheers across the living-room window, dimmer, yellowy ones shining through the trio of oblongs set into the front door in a rising diagonal line.

He pulled his bandanna up over his mouth and nose and then opened the truck door, holding on as the wind tried to rip it out of his hand. "Stay here."

"Yeah, right, eat me." She opened her own door and the wind *did* pull it away from her. She slid out before he could say anything else.

A hot gust pushed her backward, making her stagger and grab the edge of the door for balance. The sand stung her lips and cheeks, making her wince as she pulled her own bandanna up. And the worst thing of all was that this storm might just be warming up.

She looked around for coyotes—they sounded close—and saw none. Yet, anyway. Steve was already climbing the steps to the porch, so much for the protective male. She went after him, wincing as another strong gust rocked her back on her heels.

We're behaving like characters in a cheap horror movie, she thought dismally, *staying when we know we should go, poking where we have no business poking.*

True enough, she supposed . . . except wasn't that what people did? Wasn't that why, when Richie Judkins had come home in a really badass ear-ripping mood, Little Miss Cynthia had still been there? Wasn't that what most of the bad stuff in the world was about, staying when you knew damned well you should go, pushing on when you knew you should cut and run? Wasn't that, in the last analysis, why so many people liked cheap horror movies? Because they recognized the scared kids who refused to leave the haunted house even after the murders started as themselves?

Steve was standing on the top step in the howling wind and dust, head hunched down, bandanna flapping . . . and ringing the doorbell. Actually *ringing the bell,* like he was going to ask the lady of the house if he could come in and explain the advantages of Sprint over AT&T. It was too much for Cynthia. She pushed rudely past, almost knocking him into the bushes beside the stoop, grabbed the doorknob, and turned it. The door opened. She couldn't see the bottom half of Steve's face because of the bandanna, but the look of amazement in his eyes as she followed the opening door into the house was very satisfactory.

"Hey!" she shouted. "Hey, anybody home? Fucking Avon calling, you guys!"

No answer—but there was a strange noise coming from an open doorway ahead to the right. A kind of hissing.

She turned to Steve. "Nobody home, see? Now let's go."

Instead, he started up the hall toward the sound.

"No!" she whispered fiercely, and grabbed his arm. *"No, en-oh, that spells no, enough is enough!"*

He shook free without even looking at her—men, goddam men, such parfit knightly assholes they were—and went on up the hall. "Hello?" he asked as he went . . . just so that anyone intent on killing him would know *exactly* where to look. Cynthia had every intention of going back outside and getting into the truck. She would wait three minutes by her watch, and if he wasn't out by then she'd put the truck in gear and drive away, damned if she wouldn't.

Instead, she followed him up the hall.

"Hello?" He stopped just short of the open doorway—maybe he had some sense left, a little, anyway—and then cautiously poked one eye around the jamb. "Hell—" He stopped.

That funny hissing was louder than ever now, a *shaky* sort of sound, loose, almost like—

She looked over his shoulder, not wanting to but not able to help herself. Steven had gone white above his bandanna, and that wasn't a good sign.

No, not a hissing, not really. A *rattling*.

It was the dining room. The family had been about to eat what looked like the evening meal—although not *this* evening's meal, she saw that right away. There were flies buzzing over the pot roast, and some of the slices were already supporting colonies of maggots. The creamed corn had congealed in its bowl. The gravy was a greasy clot in its boat.

Three people were seated at the table: a woman, a man, and a baby in a high chair. The woman was still wearing the full-length apron in which she had cooked the meal. The baby wore a bib which read I'M A BIG BOY NOW. He was slumped sideways behind his tray, on which were several stiff-looking orange slices. He regarded Cynthia with a frozen grin. His face was purple. His eyes bulged from puffy sockets like glass marbles. His parents were equally puffed. She could see several pairs of holes on the man's face, small ones, almost hypodermic-sized, one set in the side of his nose.

Several large rattlesnakes were on the table, crawling restlessly among the dishes, shaking their tails. As she looked, the bodice of the woman's apron bulged. For one moment Cynthia thought the woman was still alive in spite of her purple face and glazed eyes, that she was breathing, and then a triangular snake's head pushed up through the ruffles, and tiny black buckshot eyes looked across at her.

The snake opened its mouth and hissed. Its tongue danced.

And more of them. Snakes on the floor under the table, crawling over the dead man's shoes. Snakes beyond them, in the kitchen—she could see a huge one, a diamond-back, slithering along the Formica counter beneath the microwave.

The ones on the floor were coming for them, and coming fast.

Run! she shrieked at herself, and found she couldn't move— it was as if her shoes had been glued to the floor. She hated snakes above all creatures; they revolted her in some fundamental sense far below her ability to articulate or understand. And this house was *full* of them, there could be more behind them, between them and the door—

Steve grabbed her and yanked her backward. When he saw she was unable to run, he picked her up and ran with her in his arms, pelting down the hallway and out into the night, carrying her over the threshold and into the dark like a bridegroom in reverse.

5

"Steve, did you see—"

The door on her side of the truck was still open. He threw her inside, slammed her door, then ran around to his side and got in. He looked through the windshield at the rectangle of light falling through the open door of the ranch-house, then at her. His eyes were huge above the bandanna.

"Sure I saw," he said. "Every snake in the mother-fucking universe, and all of them coming at us."

"I couldn't run . . . snakes, they scare me so bad . . . I'm sorry."

"My fault for getting us in there in the first place." He put the truck in reverse and backed jerkily out of the driveway, swinging around so the truck's nose was pointed east, toward the fallen bikes, the flattened piece of fence, and the dancing blinker-light. "We're getting the fuck back to Highway 50 so fast it'll make your head spin." He stared at her with horrified perplexity. "They were *there*, weren't they? I mean, I didn't just hallucinate em—they were *there*."

"Yes. Now just go, Steve, *drive.*"

He did, going faster now but still not fast enough to be dangerous. She admired his control, especially since he was so obviously rocked back on his heels. At the blinker he turned left and headed north, back the way they had come.

"Try the radio," he said as the hideous little town at last began to fall behind them. "Find some tunes. Just no achy-breaky heart. I draw the line at that."

"Okay."

She bent forward toward the dash, glancing into the rear-view mirror mounted outside her window as she did. For just a moment she thought she saw a wink of light back there, swinging in an arc. It could have been a flashlight, it could have been some peculiar reflection kicked across the glass by the dancing blinker, or it could have been just her imagination. She preferred to believe that last one. In any case it was gone now, smothered in flying dust. She thought briefly about mentioning it to Steve and decided not to. She didn't *think* he'd want to go back and investigate, she thought he was every bit as freaked out as she was at this point, but it was wise never to underestimate a man's capacity to play John Wayne.

But if there are people *back there—*

She gave her head a small, decisive shake. No. She wasn't falling for that. Maybe there *were* people alive back there, doctors and lawyers and Indian chiefs, but there was also something very bad back there. The best thing they could do for any survivors who might remain in Desperation was to get help.

Besides, I didn't really see anything. I'm almost sure I didn't.

She turned on the radio, got a barrage of static all the way across the dial when she pushed the SEEK button, turned it off again.

"Forget it, Steve. Even the local shitkicking station is—"

"What the *fuck?*" he asked in a high, screamy voice that was completely unlike his usual one. "What the blue *fuck?*"

"I don't see—" she began, and then she did. Something ahead of them, some huge shape looming in the flying dust. It had big yellow eyes. She put her hands to her mouth, but they weren't quite in time to catch her scream. Steve hit the brakes with both feet. Cynthia, who hadn't fastened her seatbelt, was thrown against the dashboard, just managing to get her forearms up in time to spare her head a bump.

"Christ almighty," Steve said. His voice sounded a little more normal. "How the hell did *that* get in the road?"

"What is it?" she asked, and knew even before the question was out of her mouth. No *Jurassic Park* monstrosity (her first thought, God help her), and no oversized piece of mining equipment. No big yellow eyes, either. What she'd mistaken for eyes had been the reflection of their own headlights in a sheet of window-glass. A picture-window, to be exact. It was a trailer. In the road. *Blocking* the road.

Cynthia looked to her left and saw that the stake fence between the road and the trailer park had been knocked over. Three of the trailers—the biggest ones—were gone; she could tell where they had been by the cement-block foundations upon which they had sat. Those trailers were now drawn across the road, the biggest in front, the others behind it like a secondary wall put up in case the main line of defense is breached. One of these latter two was the rusty Airstream on which the Rattlesnake Trailer Park's satellite dish had been mounted. The dish itself now lay upended at the edge of the park like a vast black hubcap. It had taken down some lady's clothesline when it fell. Pants and shirts flapped from it.

"Go around," she said.

"I can't on this side of the road—the dropoff's too steep. The trailer park side's pretty steep, too, but—"

"You can do it," she said, fighting back the quiver in her voice. "And you *owe* me. I went in that house with you—"

"Okay, okay." He reached for the transmission lever, probably meaning to drop it into the lowest gear, and then his hand froze in midair. He cocked his head. She heard it a second later and her first panicky thought was

(*they're here oh Jesus they got in the truck somehow*)

of snakes. But this wasn't the same. This was a harsh whirring sound, almost like a piece of paper caught in a fan, or—

Something came falling out of the dancing air above them, something that looked like a big black stone. It hit the windshield hard enough to make a bullet-snarl of opacity at the point of impact and send long, silvery cracks shooting out in either direction. Blood—it looked black in this light—splatted across the glass like an inkblot. There was a nasty *crack-crunch* as the kamikaze accordioned in on itself, and for a moment she saw one of its merciless, dying eyes peering in at her. She screamed again, this time making no attempt to muffle it with her hands.

There was another hard thud, this one from over their heads. She looked up and saw the roof of the cab was dented down. *"Steve, get us out of here!"* she cried.

He turned on the wipers, and one of them pushed the squashed buzzard down onto the outside air vents. It lay there in a lump like some bizarre tumor with a beak. The other wiper smeared blood and feathers across the glass in a fan. Sand immediately started to stick in this mess. Steve goosed the washer-fluid switch. The windshield cleared a little near the top, but the bottom part was hopeless; the hulk of the dead bird made it impossible for the wiper-blades to do their job.

"Steve," she said. She heard his name coming out of her mouth but couldn't feel it; her lips were numb. And her midsection felt entirely gone. No liver, no lights, just an empty place filled with its own whistling windstorm. "Under the trailer. Coming out from under that trailer. See them?"

She pointed. He saw. The sand had drifted crosswise along the tar in east-west lines that looked like clutching fingers.

Later, if the wind kept up at this pitch, those dunelets would fatten to arms, but now they were just fingers. Emerging from beneath the trailer, strutting like the vanguard of an advancing army, was a battalion of scorpions. She couldn't tell how many—how could she, when she was still finding it difficult to believe she was seeing them at all? Less than a hundred, probably, but still dozens of them. Dozens.

There were snakes crawling among and behind them, wriggling along in rapid *s*-shapes, sliding over the ridges of sand with the ease of water moccasins speeding across a pond.

They can't get in here, she told herself, *take it easy, they can't get in!*

No, and maybe they didn't want to. Maybe they weren't *supposed* to. Maybe they were supposed to—

Came another of those harsh whickering sounds, this time on her side of the truck, and she leaned toward Steve, *cringed* toward Steve with her right arm held up to protect the side of her face. The buzzard hit the passenger window of the truck like a bomb filled with blood instead of explosive. The glass turned milky and sagged in toward her, holding for the time being. One of the buzzard's wings flapped weakly at the windshield. The wiper on her side tore a chunk of it off.

"It's all right!" he cried, almost laughing and putting an arm around her as he echoed her thought. *"It's okay, they can't get in!"*

"Yes, they *can*!" she shouted back. "The *birds* can, if we stay here! If we give them time! And the snakes . . . the scorpions . . ."

"What? What are you saying?"

"Could they make holes in the tires?" It was the RV she was seeing in her mind's eye, all its tires flat . . . the RV, and the purplefaced man back there in the ranch-house, his face tattooed with holes in pairs, holes so small they looked almost like flecks of red pepper. "They could, couldn't they? Enough of them, all stinging and biting at once, they *could*."

"No," he said, and gave a strange little yawp of laughter. "Little bitty desert scorpions, four inches long, stingers no bigger than thorns, are you kidding?" But then the wind dropped momentarily, and from beneath them—already from beneath them—they heard scurrying, jostling sounds, and she saw something she could have skipped: he didn't believe what he was saying. He *wanted* to, but he didn't.

CHAPTER 4

1

The cellular phone was lying all the way across the holding area, at the foot of a file-cabinet with a PAT BUCHANAN FOR PRESIDENT sticker on it. The gadget didn't look broken, but—

Johnny pulled up the antenna and flipped it open. The phone beeped and the *S* appeared, good, but there were no transmission-bars, bad. *Very* bad. Still, he had to try. He pushed the NAME/MENU button until STEVE appeared, then squeezed the SEND button.

"Mr. Marinville." It was Mary, standing in the doorway. "We have to go. The cop—"

"I know, I know, just a second."

Nothing. No ring, no robot, no reception. Just a very faint hollow roaring sound, the sort of thing you heard in a conch shell.

"Fucked," he said, and closed the phone's speaker-pad. "But that *was* Steve, I know it was. If we'd only gotten outside thirty seconds sooner . . . thirty cocksucking little *seconds* . . ."

"Johnny, *please.*"

"Coming." He followed her back downstairs.

Mary had the Rossi shotgun in her hand, and when they were back outside, Johnny saw that David Carver had taken back the pistol and was holding it beside his leg. Ralph now held one of the rifles. He had it in the crook of his arm, like he thought he was Dan'l Boone. *Oh, Johnny,* a mocking voice spoke up from inside his head—it was Terry, the never-say-die bitch who had gotten him into this fuckarow in the first place. *Don't tell me you're jealous of Mr. Suburban Ohio*—you?

Well, maybe. Just a little. Mostly because Mr. Suburban Ohio's rifle was loaded, unlike the Mossberg shotgun which Johnny now picked up.

"That's a Ruger .44," the old man was telling Ralph. "Four rounds. I left the chamber empty. If you have to shoot, remember that."

"I will," Ralph said.

"She'll kick you hard. Remember that, too."

Billingsley lifted the last gun, the .30–.06. For a moment Johnny thought the old fart was going to offer to trade him, but he didn't. "All right," he said, "I guess we're ready. Don't shoot at any varmints unless they come at us. You'd just miss, use up ammunition, and probably draw more. Do you understand that, Carver?"

"Yes," Ralph said.

"Son?"

"Yes."

"Ma'am?"

"Yes," Mary said. She sounded resigned to being a ma'am, at least until she got back to civilization.

"And I won't swing unless they get close, I promise," Johnny said. It was supposed to be a joke, a little mood-brightener, but all it earned him from Billingsley was a look of cool contempt. It wasn't a look Johnny thought he deserved.

"Do you have a problem with me, Mr. Billingsley?" he asked.

"I don't care for your looks much," Billingsley shot back. "We don't have much respect out in these parts for older folks who wear their hair long. As to whether or not I have a *problem* with you, that I couldn't say just yet."

"So far as I can see, what you do to folks out in these parts is gutshoot them and then hang them on hooks like deer, so maybe you'll pardon me if I don't take your opinions too deeply to heart."

"Now listen here—"

"And if that hair's laying across your ass because you missed your daily quart of sour mash, don't take it out on me." He was ashamed at the way the old man's eyes flickered when he said that, and at the same time he was bitterly gratified. You knew your own, by God. There were a lot of know-it-all butt-heads in Alcoholics Anonymous, but they were right about that. You knew your own even when you couldn't smell the booze on their breath or wafting out of their pores. You could almost *hear* them, pinging in your head like sonar.

"Stop it!" Mary snapped at him. "If you want to be an asshole, do it on your own time!"

Johnny looked at her, wounded by her tone of voice, wanting to say something childish like *Hey, he started it!*

"Where should we go?" David asked. He shone his light across the street, at the Desperation Coffee Shop and Video Stop. "Over there? The coyotes and the buzzard I saw are gone."

"Too close, I think," Ralph said. "What about we get out of here completely? Did you find any car-keys?"

Johnny rummaged and came up with the keyring David had taken from the dead cop. "Only one set on here. I imagine they go to the cruiser Entragian was driving."

"*Is* driving," David said. "It's gone. It's what he took my mom away in." His face as he said this was unreadable. His father put a hand on the back of the boy's neck.

"It might be safer not to be driving just now, anyway," Ralph said. "A car's pretty conspicuous when it's the only one on the road."

"Anyplace will do, at least to start with," Mary said.

"Anyplace, yeah, but the farther from the cop's home base, the better," Johnny said. "That's the asshole's opinion, anyhow."

Mary gave him an angry look. Johnny bore it, not looking away. After a moment she did, flustered.

Ralph said, "We might do well to hide up, at least for a little while."

"Where?" Mary asked.

"Where do you think, Mr. Billingsley?" David asked.

"The American West," he said after a moment's thought. "Reckon that'd do to start with."

"What is it?" Johnny asked. "A bar?"

"Movie theater," Mary said. "I saw it when he drove us into town. It looked closed up."

Billingsley nodded. "Is. Would have been torn down ten year ago, if there was anything to put up in its place. It's locked, but I know a way in. Come on. And remember what I said about the varmints. Don't shoot unless you have to."

"And stay close together," Ralph added. "Lead the way, Mr. Billingsley."

Once again Johnny brought up the rear as they set off north along Main Street, their shoulders hunched against the scouring drive of the west wind. Johnny looked ahead at Billingsley, who just happened to know a way into the town's old deserted movie theater. Billingsley, who turned out to have all sorts of opinions on all sorts of issues, once you got him wound up a little. *You're a late-stage alcoholic, aren't you, my friend?* Johnny thought. *You've got all the bells and whistles.*

If so, the man was operating well for one who hadn't had a shot in awhile. Johnny wanted something to reduce the throb in his nose, and he suspected that getting a drink into old Tommy at the same time might be an investment in their future.

They were passing beneath the battered awning of Desperation's Owl's Club. "Hold it," Johnny said. "Going in here for a minute."

"Are you *nuts?*" Mary asked. "We have to get off the street!"

"There's nobody *on* the street but us," Johnny said, "didn't you notice?" He moderated his voice, tried to sound reasonable. "Look, I just want to get some aspirin. My nose is killing me. Thirty seconds—a minute, max."

He tried the door before she could answer. It was locked. He hit the glass with the rifle butt, actually looking forward to the bray of the burglar alarm, but the only sound was the tinkle of glass falling onto the floor inside and the relentless howl of the wind. Johnny knocked out the few jagged bits of glass sticking up from the side of the doorframe, then reached through and felt for the lock.

"Look," Ralph murmured. He pointed across the street.

Four coyotes stood on the sidewalk in front of a squat brick building with the word UTILITY printed on one window and WATER on the other. They didn't move, but their eyes were trained on the little cluster of people across the street. A fifth came trotting down the sidewalk from the south and joined them.

Mary raised the Rossi and pointed it toward the coyotes. David Carver pushed it down again. His face was distant, abstracted. "No, it's all right," he said. "They're just watching."

Johnny found the lock, turned it, and opened the door. The light-switches were to the left. They turned on a bank of old-fashioned fluorescents, the kind that look like inverted ice-cube trays. These illuminated a little restaurant area (deserted), a cluster of slot machines (dark), and a pair of blackjack tables. Hanging from one of the light-fixtures was a parrot. Johnny at first thought it must be stuffed, but when he got a little closer, he observed the bulging eyes and the splatter of mixed blood and guano on the wood below it. It was real enough. Someone had strung it up.

Entragian must not have liked the way it said "Polly want a cracker," Johnny thought.

The Owl's smelled of old hamburgers and beer. At the far end of the room was a little shopping area. Johnny took a large bottle of generic aspirin, then went behind the bar.

"Hurry *up*!" Mary cried at him. "Hurry *up*, can't you?"

"Right there," he said. A man in dark pants and a shirt that had once been white was lying on the dirty linoleum floor, staring up at Johnny with eyes as glassy as those of the hanged parrot. The bartender, from the look of his clothes. His throat had been cut. Johnny pulled a quart of Jim Beam off the shelf.

He held it up to the light for a moment, checking the level, then hurried out. A thought—not a nice one—tried to surface and he shoved it back down. Hard. He wanted to lubricate the old horse-doctor, that was all, keep him loose. When you got right down to it, it was an act of Christian charity.

You're more than a sweetheart, Terry said inside his head. *You're really a saint, aren't you? St. John the Lubricator.* And then her cynical laughter.

Shut up, bitch, he thought . . . but as always, Terry was reluctant to go.

2

Be cool, Steven, he told himself. *It's the only way you'll get out of this. If you panic, I think there's a good chance both of you are going to die in this goddam rented truck.*

He put the transmission in reverse, and, steering by the outside mirror (he didn't dare open his door and lean out; it would be too easy for a dive-bombing buzzard to break his neck), began to move backward. The wind had picked up again, but he could still hear the crunching from under the truck as they rolled over the scorpions. It reminded him of how cereal sounded when you were chewing it.

Don't drive off the side, for Christ's sake don't do that.

"They're not following," Cynthia said. The relief in her voice was unmistakable.

He took a look, saw that she was right, and stopped. He had backed up about fifty feet, far enough so that the lead trailer across the road was just a vague shape in the blowing sand again. He could see brown blotches against the whitish-gray sand in the road. Squashed scorpions. From here they looked like pats of cowdung. And the others were retreating. In another moment he would find it hard to believe they had been there at all.

Oh, they were, he thought. *If you start doubting that, old buddy, all you have to do is take a look at the dead bird currently blocking the air-vents at the bottom of the windshield.*

"What do we do now?" she asked.

"I don't know." He looked out his window and saw the Desert Rose Cafe. Half of its pink awning had come down in the wind. He looked out the other window, past Cynthia, and saw a vacant lot with three boards nailed across the entrance. KEEP OUT OF HERE had been painted across the center board in sloppy white capitals, presumably by someone who didn't believe in Western hospitality.

"Something wants to keep us in town," she said. "You know that, don't you?"

He backed the Ryder truck into the parking lot of the Desert Rose, trying to think of a plan. What came instead was a series of disjointed images and words. The doll lying face-down at the bottom of the RV's steps. The Tractors, saying her name was Emergency and her telephone number was 911. Johnny Cash, saying he built it one piece at a time. Bodies on hooks, a tigerfish swimming between the fingers of the hand at the bottom of the aquarium, the baby's bib, the snake on the kitchen counter under the microwave.

He realized he was on the edge of panic, maybe on the edge of doing something really stupid, and groped for anything that would pull him back from the edge, get him thinking straight again. What came to his mind, unbidden, was something he never would have expected. It was an image—clearer than any of the preceding ones—of the piece of stone sculpture they had seen on the computer table in the mining corporation's Quonset. The coyote with the strange, twisted head and the starting eyeballs, the coyote whose tongue had been a snake.

There ought to be a picture of that thing next to ugly *in the dictionary,* Cynthia had said, and she was right about that, oh yes, no question, but Steve was suddenly overwhelmed by the idea that anything that ugly also had to be powerful.

Are you kidding? he thought distractedly. *The radio turned on and off when you touched it, the lights flickered, the aquarium fucking exploded. Of course it's powerful.*

"What was that little piece of statuary we found back there?" he asked. "What was up with that?"

"I don't know. I only know that when I touched it . . ."

"What? When you touched it, what?"

"It seemed like I remembered every rotten thing that ever happened to me in my life," she said. "Sylvia Marcucci spitting on me in the eighth grade, out in the playground—she said I stole her boyfriend, and I didn't even know who the hell she was talking about. The time my dad got drunk at my Aunt Wanda's second wedding and felt my ass while we were dancing and pretended it was a mistake. Like his hardon was a mistake, too." Her hand crept to the side of her head. "Gettin yelled at. Gettin dumped on. Richie Judkins, almost ripping my fuckin ear off. I thought of all those things."

"Yeah, but what did you *really* think of?"

She looked for a moment as if she were going to tell him not to be a wise-ass, then didn't. "Sex," she said, and let out a shaky sigh. "Not just fucking, either. All of it. The dirtier the better."

Yes, he thought, *the dirtier the better. Things you might like to try but would never talk about. Experimental stuff.*

"What are you thinking about?" Her voice was oddly sharp, at the same time oddly pungent, like a smell. Steve looked over at her and suddenly wondered if her pussy was tight. An insane thought to be having at a time like this, but it was what came into his head.

"Steve?" Sharper than ever. "What are you thinking?"

"Nothing," he said. His voice was thick, the voice of a man struggling out of a deep sleep. "Nothing, never mind."

"Does it start with *C* and end with *E?*"

Actually, my dear, "cunt" ends with a T, *but you're in the ball-park.*

What was wrong with him? What in God's name? It was as if that funny piece of rock had turned on another radio, this one in his head, and it was broadcasting a voice that was almost his own.

"What are you talking about?" he asked her.

"Coyote, coyote," she said, lilting the words like a child. No, she wasn't accusing him of anything, although he supposed that briefly thinking so had been a natural enough mistake; she was just falling all over herself with excitement. "The thing we saw back in the lab! If we had it, we could get out of here! I *know* we could, Steve! And don't waste my time—*our* time— by telling me I'm crazy!"

Considering the stuff they had seen and the stuff that had happened to them in the last ninety minutes or so, he had no intention of doing that. If she was crazy, they both were. But—

"You told me not to touch it." He was still struggling to talk; it was as if there were mud packed into his thinking equipment. "You said it felt . . ." Felt *what?* What *had* she said?

Nice. That was it. "Touch it, Steve. It feels nice."

No. Wrong.

"You said it felt nasty."

She smiled at him. In the green glow of the dashlights, the smile looked cruel. "You want to feel something nasty? Feel this."

She took his hand, put it between her legs, and twitched her hips upward twice. Steve closed his hand on her down there—hard enough to hurt, maybe—but her smile stayed on. Widened, even.

What are we doing? And why in God's name are we doing it now?

He heard the voice, but it was almost lost—like a voice screaming fire in a ballroom full of yelling people and jagged music. The cleft between her legs was closer, more urgent. He could feel it right through her jeans, and it was burning. Burning.

She said her name was Emergency and asked to see my gun, Steve thought. *You're going to see it, all right, honey, thirty-eight pistol on a forty-five frame, shoots tombstone bullets with a ball and chain.*

He made a tremendous effort to catch hold of himself, grabbing for anything that would shut the pile down before the containment rods melted. What he got hold of was an image—the curious, wary expression on her face as she looked at him through the truck's open passenger door, not getting in right away, wide blue eyes checking him out first, trying to decide if he was the kind of guy who might bite or maybe try to yank something off her. An ear, for instance. *Are you a nice person?* she'd asked him, and he had said *Yeah, I guess so,* and then, nice person that he was, he had brought her to this town of the dead, and his hand was in her crotch, and he was thinking he'd like to fuck her and hurt her at the same time, kind of an experiment, you could say, one having to do with pleasure and pain, the sweet and the salty. Because that was the way it was done in the place of the wolf, that was how it was done in the house of the scorpion, it was what passed for love in Desperation.

Are you a nice person? Not a crazy serial killer or anything? Are
you nice, are you nice, are you a nice person?

He pulled his hand away from her, shuddering. He turned
to the window and looked out into the blowing blackness
where sand danced like snow. He could feel sweat on his chest
and arms and in his armpits, and although it was a little better
now, he still felt like a sick man between fits of delirium. Now
that he had thought of the stone wolf, he couldn't unthink it,
it seemed; he kept seeing its crazy corkscrewed head and bulging eyes. It hung in his head like an unsatisfied habit.

"What's wrong?" she moaned from beside him. "Oh, Jesus,
Steve, I didn't mean to do that, what's *wrong* with us?"

"I don't know," he said hoarsely, "but I'll tell you something
I *do* know—we just got us a little taste of what happened in
this town, and I don't like it much. I can't get that fucking
stone thing out of my mind."

He finally found enough courage to look at her. She was all
the way over against the passenger door, like a scared teenager
on a first date that had gone too far, and although she looked
calm enough, her cheeks were fiery red and she was wiping
away tears with the side of her hand.

"Me, either," she said. "I remember once I got a little piece
of glass in my eye. That's what this feels like. I keep thinking
I'd like to take that stone and rub it against my . . . you know.
Except it's not much like *thinking.* It's not like *thinking* at all."

"I know," he said, wishing savagely that she hadn't said
that. Because now the idea was in *his* mind, too. He saw himself rubbing that ugly damned thing—ugly but powerful—
against his erect penis. And from there he saw the two of them
fucking on the floor beneath that row of hooks, beneath those
dangling corpses, with that crumbling gray piece of stone held
between them, in their teeth.

Steve swept the images away . . . although how long he

would be able to keep them away he didn't know. He looked at her again and managed a smile. "Don't call me cookie," he said. "Don't call me cookie and I won't call you cake."

She let out a long, trembling, half-vocalized breath that fell just a little short of laughter. "Yeah. Somethin like that, anyway. I think it might be getting a little better."

He nodded cautiously. Yes. He still had a world-class hard-on, and he could badly use a reprieve from that, but now his thoughts seemed a little more his own. If he could keep them diverted from that piece of stone a little while longer, he thought he'd be okay. But for a few seconds there it had been bad, maybe the worst thing that had ever happened to him. In those seconds he had known how guys like Ted Bundy must feel. He could have killed her. Maybe *would* have killed her, if he hadn't broken his physical contact with her when he had. Or, he supposed, she might have killed him. It was as if sex and murder had somehow changed places in this horrible little town. Except even sex wasn't what it was about, not really. He remembered how, when she had touched the wolf, the lights had flickered and the radio had come back on.

"Not sex," he said. "Not murder, either. *Power.*"

"Huh?"

"Nothing. I'm going to drive us right back through the middle of town. Out toward the mine."

"That big wall off to the south?"

He nodded. "It's an open-pit. There'll have to be at least one equipment road out there that cuts back to 50. We're going to find it and take it. I'm actually glad this one is blocked off. I don't want to go anywhere near that Quonset, or that—"

She reached out and grabbed his arm. Steve followed her gaze and saw something come slinking into the arc of the truck's headlights. The dust was now so thick that at first the animal looked like a ghost, some Indian-conjured spirit from a hundred years ago. It was a timberwolf, easily the length and height of a German Shepherd, but leaner. Its eyes were sockets of crimson in the headlights. Following it like attendants in some malign fairy-tale were two files of desert scorpions with their stingers furled over their backs. Flanking the scorpions were coyotes, two on each side. They appeared to be grinning nervously.

The wind gusted. The truck rocked on its springs. To their left, the fallen piece of awning flapped like a torn sail.

"The wolf's carrying something," she said hoarsely.

"You're nuts," he said, but as it drew closer, he saw that she *wasn't* nuts. The wolf stopped about twenty feet from the truck, as bald and real as something in a high-resolution crime-scene photograph. Then it lowered its head and dropped the thing it had been holding in its mouth. It looked at it attentively for a moment, then backed off three steps. It sat down and began to pant.

It was the statue-fragment, lying there on its side at the entrance to the cafe parking lot, lying there in the blowing dust, mouth snarling, head twisted, eyes starting from their sockets. Fury, rage, sex, power—it seemed to broadcast these things at the truck in a tight cone, like some sort of magnetic field.

The image of fucking Cynthia recurred, of being buried in her like a sword jammed hilt-deep in hot, packed mud, the two of them face-to-face, lips drawn back in identical snarls as they gripped the snarling stone coyote between them like a thong.

"Should I get it?" she asked, and now she was the one who sounded as if she were sleeping.

"Are you kidding?" he asked. His voice, his Texas accent, but not his words, not now. These words were coming from the radio in his head, the one the piece of stone statue had turned on.

Its eyes, glaring at him from where it lay in the dust.

"What, then?"

He looked at her and grinned. The expression felt ghastly on his face. It also felt wonderful. "We'll get it together, of course. Okay by you?"

His *mind* was the storm now, filled with roaring wind from side to side and top to bottom, driving before it the images of what he would do to her, what she would do to him, and what they would do to anyone who got in their way.

She grinned back, her thin cheeks stretching upward until it was like looking at a skull grin. Greenish-white light from the dashboard painted her brow and lips, filled in her eyesockets. She stuck her tongue out through that grin and flicked it at him, like the snake-tongue of the statue. He stuck his own tongue out and wriggled it back at her. Then he groped for the doorhandle. He would race her to the fragment, and they would make love among the scorpions with it held in their mouths between them, and whatever happened after that wouldn't matter.

Because in a very real sense, they would be gone.

3

Johnny came back out onto the sidewalk and handed the bottle of Jim Beam to Billingsley, who looked at it with the unbelieving eyes of a man who has just been told he's won the Powerball lottery. "There you go, Tom," he said. "Have yourself a tonk—just the one, mind you—and then pass it on. None for me, I've taken the pledge." He looked across the street, expecting to see more coyotes, but there were still just the five of them. I'll take the fifth, Johnny thought, watching as the veterinarian spun the cap off the bottle of whiskey. You'd go along with that, wouldn't you, Tom? Of course you would.

"What is wrong with you?" Mary asked him. "Just what in the hell is *wrong* with you?"

"Nothing," Johnny said. "Well, a broken nose, but I guess that isn't what you meant, is it?"

Billingsley tilted the bottle back with a short, sharp flick of the wrist that looked as practiced as a nurse's injection technique, and then coughed. Tears welled in his eyes. He put the mouth of the bottle to his lips again, and Johnny snatched it away. "Nope, I don't think so, oldtimer."

He offered the bottle to Ralph, who took it, looked at it, then bit off a quick swallow. Ralph then offered it to Mary.

"No."

"Go on," Ralph said. His voice was quiet, almost humble. "Better if you do."

She looked at Johnny with hateful, perplexed eyes, then took a nip from the bottle. She coughed, holding it away from her and looking at it as if it were toxic. Ralph took it back, plucked the cap from Billingsley's left hand, and put it back on. During this, Johnny opened the bottle of aspirin, shook out half a dozen, bounced them in his hand for a moment, then tossed them into his mouth.

"Come on, Doc," he said to Billingsley. "Lead the way."

They started down the street, Johnny telling them as they went why he had all but broken his neck to get his cellular phone back. The coyotes on the other side of the street got up and paced them. Johnny didn't care for that much, but what were they supposed to do about it? Try shooting at them? Pretty noisy. At least there was no sign of the cop. And if they saw him before they made it down to the movie theater, they could always duck into one of these other places. Any old port in a storm.

He swallowed, grimacing at the burn as the half-liquefied aspirin slid down his throat, and tried to put the bottle into his breast pocket. It bumped the top of the phone. He took it out, put the bottle of pills in its place, started to shove the cellular into his pants pocket, then decided it couldn't hurt to try again. He pulled the antenna and flipped the phone open. Still no transmission-bars. Zilch.

"You really think that was your friend?" David asked.

"I think so, yes."

David held out his hand. "Could I try it?"

Something in his voice. His father heard it, too. Johnny could see it in the way the man was looking at him.

"David? Son? Is something wr—"

"Could I try it *please*?"

"Sure, if you want." He held the useless phone out to the boy, and as David took it, Johnny saw three transmission-bars appear beside the *S*. Not one or two but *three*.

"Son of a *bitch*!" he breathed, and grabbed the phone back. David, who had been studying the keypad functions, saw him reaching a moment too late to stop him.

The moment the cellular phone was back in Johnny's hand, the transmission-bars disappeared again, leaving only the *S*.

They were never there in the first place, you know that, don't you? You hallucinated them. You—

"Give it *back*!" David shouted. Johnny was stunned by the anger in his voice. The phone was snatched away again, but not too fast for him to see the transmission-bars reappear, glowing gold in the dark.

"This is so damned dumb," Mary said, looking first back over her shoulder, then at the coyotes across the street. They had stopped when the people had. "But if it's the way you want to play it, why don't we just drag a table out and get drunk in the middle of the fucking street?"

No one paid any attention. Billingsley was still looking at the bottle of Beam. Johnny and Ralph were staring at the kid, who was stuttering his finger on the NAME/MENU button with the speed of a veteran video-game player, hurrying past Johnny's agent and ex-wife and editor, finally getting to STEVE.

"David, what is it?" Ralph asked.

David ignored him and turned urgently to Johnny. "Is this him, Mr. Marinville? Is the guy with the truck Steve?"

"Yes."

David pushed SEND.

4

Steve had heard of being saved by the bell, but this was ridiculous.

Just as his fingers found the doorhandle—and he could hear Cynthia grabbing for hers on the other end of the seat—the cellular telephone gave out its nasal, demanding cry: *Hmeep! Hmeep!*

Steve froze. Looked at the phone. Looked across the seat at Cynthia, whose door was actually open a little. She was staring back at him, the grin on her lips fading.

Hmeep! Hmeep!

"Well?" she asked. "Aren't you going to answer that?" And there was something in her tone, something so *wifely,* that he laughed.

Outside, the wolf pointed its nose into the darkness and howled, as if it had heard Steve's laughter and disapproved. The coyotes seemed to take that howl as a signal. They got up and disappeared back the way they had come, walking into the blowing dust with their heads lowered. The scorpions were already gone. If, that was, they had been there at all. They might not have been; his head felt like a haunted house, one filled with hallucinations and false memories instead of ghosts.

Hmeep! Hmeep!

He grabbed the phone off the dashboard, pushed the SEND button, and put it to his ear. He stared out at the wolf as he did it. And the wolf stared back. "Boss? Boss, that you?"

Of course it was, who else would be calling him? Only it wasn't. It was a kid.

"Is your name Steve?" the kid asked.

"Yes. How'd you get the boss's phone? Where—"

"Never mind that," the kid said. "Are you in trouble? You are, aren't you?"

Steve opened his mouth. "I don't—" Closed it again. Outside, the wind screamed around the cab of the Ryder truck. He held the little phone to the side of his face and looked over an oozing lump of buzzard at the wolf. He saw the chunk of statue lying in front of it as well. The crude images of intermingled sex and violence which had filled his mind were fading, but he could remember the power they had exercised over him the way he could remember certain vivid nightmares.

"Yeah," he said. "I guess you could say that."

"Are you in the truck we saw?"

"If you saw a truck, likely that was us, yeah. *Is* my boss with you?"

"Mr. Marinville's here. He's okay. Are *you* all right?"

"I don't know," Steve said. "There's a wolf, and he brought this thing . . . it's like a statue, only—"

Cynthia's hand darted into the lower part of his vision and honked the horn. Steve jumped. At the entrance to the cafe parking lot, the wolf jumped, too. Steve could see its muzzle draw back in a snarl. Its ears flattened against its skull.

Doesn't like the horn, he thought. Then another thought came, one of those simple ones that made you want to slam your hand against your own forehead, as if to punish your laggard brains. *If it won't get out of the way, I can run the fucker over, can't I?*

Yes. Yes, he could. After all, he was the one with the truck.

"What was that?" the kid asked sharply. Then, as if realizing that was the wrong question: "Why are you doing that?"

"We've got company. We're trying to get rid of it."

Cynthia honked the horn again. The wolf got to its feet. Its ears were still laid back. It looked pissed, but it also looked confused. When Cynthia honked the horn a third time, Steve put both of his hands over hers and helped. The wolf looked at them a moment longer, its head cocked and its eyes a nasty yellow-green in the glare of the headlights. Then it bent, seized the piece of statuary in its teeth, and disappeared back the way it had come.

Steve looked at Cynthia, and she looked back at him. She still looked scared, but she was smiling a little just the same.

"Steve?" The voice was faint, dodging in and out of static-bursts. "Steve, are you there?"

"Yes."

"Your company?"

"Gone. For the time being, at least. The question is, what do we do next? Any suggestions?"

"I might have." Damned if it didn't sound as if maybe *he* was smiling, too.

"What's your name, kid?" Steve asked.

5

Behind them, back in the direction of the Municipal Building, something gave in to the wind and fell over with a huge loose crash. The sound made Mary wheel around in that direction, but she saw nothing. She was grateful for the mouthful of whiskey Carver had talked her into taking. Without it, that sound—she guessed it might have been some building's false front tumbling into the street—would have had her halfway out of her skin.

The boy was still on the phone. The three men were gathered around him. Mary could see how badly Marinville wanted to take the phone back again; she could also see he didn't quite dare. *It'll do you good not to be able to have what you want, Johnny,* she thought. *Do you a* world *of good.*

"I might have," David said, smiling a little. He listened, gave his first name, then turned around so he was facing the Owl's Club. He ducked his head, and when he spoke again, Mary could hardly hear him. A kind of dark wonder passed over her like a dizzy spell.

He doesn't want the coyotes across the street to hear what he's saying. I know how crazy that sounds, but it's what he's doing. And you know something even crazier? I think he's right.

"There's an old movie theater," David said in a low voice. "It's called The American West." He glanced at Billingsley for confirmation.

Billingsley nodded. "Tell him to go around to the back," he said, and Mary decided that if she was crazy, at least she wasn't the only one; Billingsley also spoke in a low voice, and glanced over his shoulder, once, quickly, as if to make sure the coyotes weren't creeping closer, trying to eavesdrop. After he had made sure they were still on the sidewalk in front of the Water and Utility Building, he turned back to David. "Tell him there's an alley."

David did. As he finished, something apparently occurred to Marinville. He started to grab for the phone, then restrained himself. "Tell him to park the truck away from the theater," he said. The great American novelist also spoke in low tones, and he had one hand up to his mouth, as if he thought there might be a lipreader or two among the coyotes. "If he leaves it in front and Entragian comes back . . ."

David nodded and passed this on, as well. Listened as Steve said something else, nodding, the smile resurfacing. Mary's eyes drifted, to the coyotes. As she looked at them, she realized an exceedingly perverse thing: if they managed to hide from Entragian long enough to regroup and get out of town, part of her would be sorry. Because once this was over, she would have to confront the fact of Peter's death; she would have to grieve for him and for the destruction of the life they had made together. And that was maybe not the worst of it. She would also have to *think* about all this, try and make some sense of it, and she wasn't sure she could do it. She wasn't sure *any* of them would be able to do it. Except maybe for David.

"Come as fast as you can," he said. There was a faint bleep as he pushed the END button. He collapsed the antenna and handed the phone back to Marinville, who immediately pulled the antenna out again, studied the LED readout, shook his head, and closed the phone up.

"How'd you do it, David? Magic?"

The kid looked at him as if Marinville were crazy. "God," he said.

"*God,* you dope," Mary said, smiling in a way that did not feel familiar to her at all. This wasn't the time to be pulling Marinville's chain, but she simply couldn't resist.

"Maybe you should have just told Mr. Marinville's friend to come and pick us up," Ralph said dubiously. "That probably would have been the simplest, David."

"It's *not* simple," David replied. "Steve'll tell you that when they get here."

"*They?*" Marinville asked.

David ignored him. He was looking at his father. "Also, there's Mom," he said. "We're not leaving without her."

"What are we going to do about *them?*" Mary asked, and pointed across the street at the coyotes. She could have sworn that they not only saw the gesture but understood it.

Marinville stepped off the sidewalk and into the street, his long gray hair blowing out and making him look like an Old Testament prophet. The coyotes got to their feet, and the wind brought her the sound of their growls. Marinville had to be hearing them, too, but he went on another step or two nevertheless. He half-closed his eyes for a moment, not as if the sand was bothering them but as if he was trying to remember something. Then he clapped his hands together once, sharply. *"Tak!"* One of the coyotes lifted its snout and howled. The sound made Mary shudder. *"Tak, ah lah! Tak!"*

The coyotes appeared to move a little closer together, but that was all.

Marinville clapped his hands again. *"Tak! . . . Ah lah . . . Tak! . . .* oh, shit on this, I was never any good at foreign languages, anyhow." He stood looking disgusted and uncertain. That they might attack him—him and his unloaded Mossberg .22—seemed the furthest thing from his mind.

David stepped down from the sidewalk. His father grabbed at his collar. "It's okay, Dad," David said.

Ralph let go, but followed as David went to Marinville. And then the boy said something Mary thought she might remember even if her mind succeeded in blocking the rest of this out—it was the sort of thing that came back to you in dreams, if nowhere else.

"Don't speak to them in the language of the dead, Mr. Marinville."

David took another step forward. Now he was alone in the middle of the street, with Ralph and Marinville standing behind him. Mary and Billingsley were behind them, up on the sidewalk. The wind had reached a single high shriek. Mary could feel the dust stinging her cheeks and forehead, but for the time being, that seemed far away, unimportant.

David put his hands together in front of his mouth, finger to finger, in that child's gesture of prayer. Then he held them out again, palms up, in the direction of the coyotes. "May the Lord bless you and keep you, may the Lord make his face to shine upon you, and lift you up, and give you peace," he said. "Now get out of here. Take a hike."

It was as if a swarm of bees had settled on them. They whirled in a clumsy, jostling mass of snouts and ears and teeth and tails, nipping at one another's flanks and at their own. Then they raced off, yapping and yowling in what sounded like some painful argument. She could hear them, even with the contending shriek of the wind, for a long time.

David turned back, surveyed their dumbfounded faces— expressions too large to miss, even in the gloom—and smiled a little. He shrugged, as if to say *Well, what are you gonna do?* Mary observed that his face was still tinted Irish Spring green. He looked like the victim of an inept Halloween makeup job.

"Come on," David said. "Let's go."

They clustered in the street. "And a little child shall lead them," Marinville said. "So come on, child—lead."

The five of them began trudging north along Main Street toward The American West.

CHAPTER 5

1

"I think that's it." Cynthia pointed out her window. "See it?"

Steve, hunched over the wheel and squinting through the bloodsmeared windshield (although it was the sand sticking in the blood that was the real problem), nodded. Yes, he could see the old-fashioned marquee, held by rusty chains to the side of a weathered brick building. There was only one letter left on the marquee, a crooked *R*.

He turned left, onto the tarmac of the Conoco station. A sign reading BEST CIG PRICES IN TOWN had fallen over. Sand had piled against the concrete base of the single pump-island like a snowdrift.

"Where you going? I thought the kid told you the movie theater!"

"He also told me not to park the truck near it. He's right, too. That wouldn't . . . hey, there's a *guy* in there!"

Steve brought the truck to a hard stop. There was indeed a guy in the Conoco station's office, rocked back in his chair with his feet on his desk. Except for something in his posture—mostly the awkward way his head was lying over on his neck—he could have been sleeping.

"Dead," Cynthia said, and put a hand on Steve's shoulder as he opened his door. "Don't bother. I can tell from here."

"We still need a place to hide the truck. If there's room in the garage, I'll open the door. You drive in." There was no need to ask if she could do it; he hadn't forgotten the spiffy way she'd handled the truck out on Highway 50.

"Okay. But do it fast."

"Believe me," he said. He started to get out, then hesitated. "You *are* all right, aren't you?"

She smiled. It clearly took some effort, but it was a working smile, all the same. "For the time being. You?"

"Smokin."

He got out, slammed the door behind him, and hurried across the tarmac to the gas station's office door. He was amazed at how much sand had accumulated already. It was as if the west wind were intent on burying the town. Judging from what he had seen of it so far, that wasn't such a bad idea.

There was a tumbleweed caught in the recessed doorway, its skeletal branches rattling. Steve booted it and it flew away into the night. He turned, saw that Cynthia was now behind the wheel of the truck, and gave her a little salute. She held her fists up in front of her, her face serious and intent, then popped the thumbs. *Mission Control, we are A-OK.* Steve grinned, nodded, and went inside. God, she could be funny. He didn't know if she knew it or not, but she could be.

The guy in the office chair needed a spot of burying. Inside the shadow thrown by the bill of his cap, his face was purple, the skin stretched and shiny. It had been stencilled with maybe two dozen black marks. Not snakebites, and too small even to be scorpion stings—

There was a skin magazine on the desk. Steve could read the title—*Lesbo Sweethearts*—upside down. Now something crawled over the edge of the desk and across the naked women on the cover. It was followed by two friends. The three of them reached the edge of the desk and stopped there in a neat line, like soldiers at parade rest.

Three more came out from under the desk and scurried

across the dirty linoleum floor toward him. Steve took a step backward, set himself, then brought a workboot down, hard. He got two of the three. The other zigged to the right and raced off toward what was probably the bathroom. When Steve looked back at the desk, he saw there were now eight fellows lined up along the edge, like movie Indians on a ridge.

They were brown recluse spiders, also known as fiddle-back spiders, because the shape on their backs looked vaguely like a country fiddle. Steve had seen plenty in Texas, had even been stung by one while rooting in his Aunt Betty's woodpile as a boy. Over in Arnette, that had been, and it had hurt like a bastard. Like an ant-bite, only *hot*. Now he understood why the dead man smelled so spoiled in spite of the dry climate. Aunt Betty had insisted on disinfecting the bite with alcohol immediately, telling him that if you ignored a fiddleback's bite, the flesh around it was apt to start rotting away. It was something in their spit. And if enough of them were to attack a person all at once . . .

Another pair of fiddlebacks appeared, these two crawling out of the dark crease at the center of the gas-jockey's stroke-book. They joined their pals. Ten, now. Looking at him. He knew they were. Another one crawled out of the pump-jockey's hair, journeyed down his forehead and nose, over his puffed lips, across his cheek. It was probably on its way to the convention at the edge of the desk, but Steve didn't wait to see. He headed for the garage, turning up his collar as he went. For all he knew, the goddam garage could be full of them. Recluse spiders liked dark places.

So be quick. Right?

There was a light-switch to the left of the door. He turned it. Half a dozen dirty fluorescents buzzed to life above the garage area. There were actually two bays, he saw. In one was a pickup which had been raised on oversized tires and customized into an all-terrain vehicle—silky blue metal-flake paint,

THE DESERT ROVER written in red on the driver's side of the cab. The other bay would do for the Ryder truck, though, if he moved a pile of tires and the recapping machine.

He waved to Cynthia, not knowing if she could actually see him or not, and crossed to the tires. He was bending over them when a rat leaped out of the dark hole in the center of the stack and sank its teeth into his shirt. Steve cried out in surprise and revulsion and hit himself in the chest with his right fist, breaking its back. The rat began to wriggle and pedal its back legs in the air, squealing through its clenched teeth, trying to bite him.

"*Ah, fuck!*" Steve screamed. "*Ah, fuck, you fuck, let go, you little fuck!*"

Not so little, though—it was almost the size of a full-grown cat. Steve leaned forward, bowing so his shirt would bell out (he did this without thinking, any more than he was aware he was screaming and cursing), then grabbed the rat's hairless tail and yanked. There was a harsh ripping sound as his shirt tore open, and then the rat was doubling over on the lumpy knuckles of its broken spine, trying to bite his hand.

Steve swung it by its tail like a lunatic Tom Sawyer, then let it fly. It zoomed across the garage, a ratsteroid, and smacked into the wall beyond THE DESERT ROVER. It lay still with its clawed feet sticking up. Steve stood watching it, making sure it wasn't going to get up and come at him again. He was shuddering all over, and the noise that came out of his mouth made him sound cold—*Brr-rrrr-ruhhh.*

There was a long, tool-littered table to the right of the door. He snatched up a tire iron, holding it by the pry-bar end, and kicked over the stack of tires. They rolled like tiddlywinks. Two more rats, smaller ones, ran out, but they wanted no part of him; they sprinted, squeaking, toward the shadowy nether regions of the garage.

He couldn't stand the sick ratblood heat against his skin another second. He tore his shirt the rest of the way open and then pulled it off. He did it one-handed. There was no way he was going to drop the tire iron. *You'll take my tire iron when you pry it from my cold dead fingers*, he thought, and laughed. He was still shuddering. He examined his chest carefully, obsessively, for any break in the skin. There was none. "Lucky," he muttered to himself as he pulled the recapper over to the wall and then hurried to the garage door. "Lucky, goddam lucky, fucking goddam rat-in-the-box."

He pushed the button by the door and it began trundling up. He stepped to one side, giving Cynthia room, looking everywhere for rats and spiders and God knew what other nasty surprises. Next to the worktable was a gray mechanic's coverall hanging from a nail, and as Cynthia drove the Ryder truck into the garage, engine roaring and lights glaring, Steve began to beat this coverall with the tire iron, working from the legs up like a woman beating a rug, watching to see what might run out of the legs or armholes.

Cynthia killed the truck's engine and slid down from the driver's seat. "Whatcha doin? Why'd you take your shirt off? You'll catch your death of cold, the temperature's already started to—"

"Rats." He had reached the top of the coverall without spooking any wildlife; now he started working his way back down again. Better safe than sorry. He kept hearing the sound the rat's spine had made when it broke, kept feeling the rat's tail in his fist. Hot, it had been. *Hot.*

"Rats?" She looked around, eyes darting.

"And spiders. The spiders are what got the guy in th—"

He was suddenly alone, Cynthia out the open garage door and on the tarmac, standing in the wind and blowing sand with her arms wrapped around her thin shoulders. "Spiders, ouug, I hate spiders! Worse'n snakes!" She sounded pissed, as if the spiders were *his* fault. "Get out of there!"

He decided the coverall was safe. He pulled it off the hook, started to toss the tire iron away, then changed his mind. Holding the coverall draped over one arm, he pushed the button beside the door and then went over to Cynthia. She was right, it was getting cold. The alkali dust stung his bare shoulders and stomach. He began to wriggle his way into the coverall. It was going to be a little baggy in the gut, but better too big than too small, he supposed.

"I'm sorry," she said, wincing and holding a hand to the side of her face as the wind gusted, driving a sheet of sand at them. "It's just, spiders, ouug, so bad, I can't . . . what kind?"

"You don't want to know." He zipped the coverall up the front, then put an arm around her. "Did you leave anything in the truck?"

"My backpack, but I guess I can do without a change of underwear tonight," she said, and smiled wanly. "What about your phone?"

He patted his left front jeans pocket through the coverall. "Don't leave home without it," he said. Something tickled across the back of his neck and he slapped at it madly, thinking of the brown recluses lined up so neatly along the edge of the desk, soldiers in some unknown cause out here in nowhere.

"What's wrong?"

"I'm just a little freaked. Come on. Let's go to the movies."

"Oh," she said in that prim little no-nonsense voice that just cracked him up. "A date. Yes, thanks."

2

As Tom Billingsley led Mary, the Carvers, and America's greatest living novelist (at least in the novelist's opinion) down the alley between The American West and the Desperation Feed and Grain, the wind hooted above them like air blown across the mouth of a pop bottle.

"Don't use the flashlights," Ralph said.

"Right," Billingsley said. "And watch out here. Garbage cans, and a pile of old crap. Lumber, tin cans."

They skirted around the huddle of cans and the pile of scrap lumber. Mary gasped as Marinville took her arm, at first not sure who it was. When she saw the long, somehow theatrical hair, she attempted to pull free. "Spare me the chivalry. I'm doing fine."

"*I'm* not," he said, holding on. "I don't see for shit at night anymore. It's like being blind." He sounded different. Not humble, exactly—she had an idea that John Marinville could no more be humble than some people could sing middle C off a pitch-pipe—but at least *human*. She let him hold on.

"Do you see any coyotes?" Ralph asked her in a low voice.

She restrained an urge to make a smart come-back—at least he hadn't called her "ma'am." "No. But I can barely see my own hand in front of my face."

"They're gone," David said. He sounded completely sure of himself. "At least for now."

"How do you know?" Marinville asked.

David shrugged in the gloom. "Just do."

And Mary thought they could probably trust him on it. That was how crazy things had gotten.

Billingsley led them around the corner. A rickety board fence ran along the backside of the movie theater, leaving a gap of about four feet. The old man walked slowly along this path with his hands held out. The others followed in single file; there was no room to double up. Mary was just starting to think Billingsley had gotten them down here on some sort of wild-goose chase when he stopped.

"Here we are."

He bent, and Mary saw him pick something up—a crate, it looked like. He put it on top of another one, then stepped up onto the makeshift platform with a wince. He was standing in front of a dirty frosted-glass window. He put his hands on this, the fingers spread like starfish, and pushed. The window slid up.

"It's the ladies'," he said. "Watch out. There's a little drop."

He turned around and slid through, looking like a large, wrinkled boy entering the Over-the-Hill Gang's clubhouse. David followed, then his father. Johnny Marinville went next, first almost falling off the crate platform as he turned around. He really *was* close to blind in the dark, she thought, and reminded herself never to ride in a car this man was driving. And a motorcycle? Had he really crossed the country on a *motorcycle*? If so, God must love him a lot more than she ever would.

She grabbed him by the back of the belt and steadied him. "Thanks," he said, and this time he did sound humble. Then he was wriggling through the window, puffing and grunting, his long hair hanging in his face.

Mary took one quick look around, and for a moment she heard ghost-voices in the wind.

Didn't you see it?

See what?

On that sign. That speed-limit sign.

What about it?

There was a dead cat on it.

Now, standing on the crate, she thought: *The people who said those things really are ghosts, because they're dead. Me as much as him—certainly the Mary Jackson who left on this trip is gone. The person back here behind this old movie house, she's someone new.*

She passed her gun and flashlight through the window to the hands held up to take them, then turned around and slid easily over the sill and into the ladies'.

Ralph caught her around the hips and eased her down. David was shining his flashlight around, holding one hand over the top of the lens in a kind of hood. The place had a smell that made her wrinkle her nose—damp, mildew, booze. There was a carton filled with empty liquor bottles in one corner. In one of the toilet-stalls there were two large plastic bins filled with beer-cans. These had been placed over a hole where, once upon a time, she supposed, there had been an actual toilet. *Around the time James Dean died, from the look of the place,* she thought. She realized she could use a toilet herself, and that no matter how the place smelled, she was hungry, as well. Why not? She hadn't had anything to eat for almost eight hours. She felt guilty about being hungry when Peter would never eat again, but she supposed the feeling would pass. That was the hell of it, when you thought it over. That was the exact hell of it.

"Holy shit," Marinville said, pulling his own flashlight out of his shirt and shining it into the beer-can repository. "You and your friends must party hearty, Thomas."

"We clean the whole place out once a month," Billingsley said, sounding defensive. "Not like the kids that used to run wild upstairs until the old fire escape finally fell down last winter. We don't pee in the corners, and we don't use drugs, either."

Marinville considered the carton of liquor empties. "On top of all that J. W. Dant, a few drugs and you'd probably explode."

"Where *do* you pee, if you don't mind me asking?" Mary said. "Because I could use a little relief in that direction."

"There's a Port-A-Potty across the hall in the men's. The kind they have in sickrooms. We keep that clean, too." He gave Marinville a complex look, equal parts truculence and timidity. Mary supposed that Marinville was preparing to tee off on Billingsley. She had an idea Billingsley felt it coming, too. And why? Because guys like Marinville needed to establish a pecking order, and the veterinarian was clearly the most peckable person in attendance.

"Excuse me," she said. "Might I borrow your flashlight, Johnny?"

She held out her hand. He looked at it dubiously, then handed it over. She thanked him and headed for the door.

"Whoa—neat!" David said softly, and that stopped her.

The boy had focused his flashlight on one of the few sections of wall where the tiles were still mostly intact. On it someone had drawn a gloriously rococo fish in various Magic Marker colors. It was the sort of flippy-tailed, half-mythological beast that one sometimes found disporting atop the wavelets of very old sea-maps. Yet there was nothing fearsome or sea-monsterish about the fellow swimming on the wall above the broken Towl-Master dispenser; with its blue Betty Boop eyes and red gills and yellow dorsal fin, there was something sweet and exuberant about it—here in the fetid, booze-smelling dark, the fish was almost miraculous. Only one tile had fallen out of the drawing, eradicating the lower half of the tail.

"Mr. Billingsley, did you—"

"Yes, son, yes," he said, sounding both defiant and embarrassed. "I drew it." He looked at Marinville. "I was probably drunk at the time."

Mary paused in the doorway, bracing for Marinville's reply. He surprised her. "I've been known to draw a few drunkfish myself," he said. "With words rather than coloring pens, but I imagine the principle is the same. Not bad, Billingsley. But why here? Of all places, why here?"

"Because I like this place," he said with considerable dignity. "Especially since the kids cleared out. Not that they ever bothered us much back here; they liked the balcony, mostly. I suppose that sounds crazy to you, but I don't much care. It's where I come to be with my friends since I retired and quit the Town Committee. I look forward to the nights I spend with them. It's just an old movie theater, there's rats and the seats are full of mildew, but so what? It's our business, ain't it?

Our own business. Only now I suppose they're all dead. Dick Onslo, Tom Kincaid, Cash Lancaster. My old pals." He uttered a harsh, startling cry, like the caw of a raven. It made her jump.

"Mr. Billingsley?" It was David. The old man looked at him. "Do you think he killed *everyone* in town?"

"That's crazy!" Marinville said.

Ralph yanked his arm as if it were the stop-cord on a bus. "Quiet."

Billingsley was still looking at David and rubbing at the flesh beneath his eyes with his long, crooked fingers. "I think he may have," he said, and glanced at Marinville again for a moment. "I think he may have at least tried."

"How many people are we talking about?" Ralph asked.

"In Desperation? Hundred and ninety, maybe two hundred. With the new mine people starting to trickle in, maybe fifty or sixty more. Although it's hard to tell how many of em would've been here and how many up to the pit."

"The pit?" Mary asked.

"China Pit. The one they're reopening. For the copper."

"Don't tell me one man, even a moose like that, went around town and killed *two hundred people*," Marinville said, "because, excuse me very much, I don't believe it. I mean, I believe in American enterprise as much as anyone, but that's just nuts."

"Well, he might have missed a few on the first pass," Mary said. "Didn't you say he ran over a guy when he was bringing you in? Ran him over and killed him?"

Marinville turned and favored her with a weighty frown. "I thought you had to take a leak."

"I've got good kidneys. He did, didn't he? He ran someone down in the street. You said so."

"All right, yeah. Rancourt, he called him. Billy Rancourt."

"Oh Jesus." Billingsley closed his eyes.

"You knew him?" Ralph asked.

"Mister, in a town the size of this one, everybody knows

everybody. Billy worked at the feed store, cut some hair in his spare time."

"All right, yeah, Entragian ran this Rancourt down in the street—ran him down like a dog." Marinville sounded upset, querulous. "I'm willing to accept the idea that Entragian may have killed a *lot* of people. I know what he's capable of."

"Do you?" David asked softly, and they all looked at him. David looked away, at the colorful fish floating on the wall.

"For one guy to kill hundreds of people . . ." Marinville said, and then quit for a moment, as if he'd temporarily lost his train of thought. "Even if he did it at night . . . I mean, *guys* . . ."

"Maybe it wasn't just him," Mary said. "Maybe the buzzards and the coyotes helped."

Marinville tried to push this away—even in the gloom she could see him trying—and then gave up. He sighed and rubbed at one temple, as if it hurt. "Okay, maybe they did. The ugliest bird in the universe tried to scalp me when he told it to, that I *know* happened. But still—"

"It's like the story of the Angel of Death in Exodus," David said. "The Israelites were supposed to put blood on their door-tops to show they were the good guys, you know? Only here, *he's* the Angel of Death. So why did he pass over *us*? He could have killed us all just as easy as he killed Pie, or your husband, Mary." He turned to the old man. "Why didn't he kill you, Mr. Billingsley? If he killed everyone else in town, why didn't he kill *you*?"

Billingsley shrugged. "Dunno. I was laying home drunk. He came in the new cruiser—same one I helped pick out, by God—and got me. Stuck me in the back and hauled me off to the *calabozo*. I asked him why, what I'd done, but he wouldn't tell me. I *begged* him. I cried. I didn't know he was crazy, not then, how could I? He was quiet, but he didn't give any signs that he was *crazy*. I started to get that idea later, but at first I was just convinced I'd done something bad in a blackout. That

I'd been out driving, maybe, and hurt someone. I . . . I did something like that once before."

"When did he come for you?" Mary asked.

Billingsley had to think about it in order to be sure. "Day before yesterday. Just before sundown. I was in bed, my head hurting, thinking about getting something for my hangover. An aspirin, and a little hair of the dog that bit me. He came and got me right out of bed. I didn't have anything on but my underwear shorts. He let me dress. *Helped* me. But he wouldn't let me take a drink even though I was shaking all over, and he wouldn't tell me why he was taking me in." He paused, still rubbing the flesh beneath his eyes. Mary wished he would stop doing that, it was making her nervous. "Later on, after he had me in a cell, he brought me a hot dinner. He sat at the desk for a little while and said some stuff. That's when I started to think he must be crazy, because none of it made sense."

" 'I see holes like eyes,' " Mary said.

Billingsley nodded. "Yeah, like that. 'My head is full of black-birds,' that's another one I remember. And a lot more I don't. They were like Thoughts for the Day out of a book written by a crazy person."

"Except for being in town to start with, you're just like us," David said. "And you don't know why he let you live any more than we do."

"I guess that's right."

"What happened to you, Mr. Marinville?"

Marinville told them about how the cop had pulled up behind his bike while he had been whizzing and contemplating the scenery north of the road, and how he had seemed nice at first. "We talked about my books," he said. "I thought he was a fan. I was going to give him a fuckin autograph. Pardon my French, David."

"Sure. Did cars go by while you were talking? I bet they did."

"A few, I guess, and a couple of semis. I didn't really notice."

"But he didn't bother any of them."

"No."

"Just you."

Marinville looked at the boy thoughtfully.

"He picked you out," David persisted.

"Well . . . maybe. I can't say for sure. Everything seemed jake until he found the dope."

Mary held her hands up. "Whoa, whoa, time out."

Marinville looked at her.

"This dope you had—"

"It wasn't *mine,* don't go getting that idea. You think I'd try driving cross-country on a Harley with half a pound of grass in my saddlebag? My brains may be fried, but not *that* fried."

Mary began to giggle. It made her need to pee worse, but she couldn't help it. It was all just too perfect, too wonderfully round. "Did it have a smile-sticker on it?" she asked, giggling harder than ever. She didn't really need an answer to this question, but she wanted it, just the same. "Mr. Smiley-Smile?"

"How did you know that?" Marinville looked astounded. He also looked remarkably like Arlo Guthrie, at least in the glow of the flashlights, and Mary's giggles became little screams of laughter. She realized that if she didn't get to the bathroom soon, she was going to wet her pants.

"B-Because it came from our t-t-*trunk,*" she said, holding her stomach. "It b-belonged to my sih-sih-*sister*-in-law. She's a total ding dong. Entragian may be c-c-crazy, but at least he r-r-recycles . . . excuse me, I'm about to h-have an accident."

She hurried across the hall. What she saw when she opened the men's-room door made her laugh even harder. Set up like some comic-opera throne in the center of the floor was a porta-ble toilet with a canvas bag suspended below the seat in a steel frame. On the wall across from it was another Magic Marker drawing, obviously from the same hand which had created the fish. This one was a horse at full gallop. There was orange smoke jetting from its nostrils and a baleful rose-madder glint in its eyes. It appeared to be headed out into an expanse of prairie somewhere east of the sun and west of the washbasins. None of the tiles had fallen out of this wall, but most had buckled, giving the stallion a warped and dreamish look.

Outside, the wind howled. As Mary unsnapped her pants and sat down on the cold toilet seat, she suddenly thought of how Peter sometimes put his hand up to his mouth when *he* laughed—his thumb touching one corner, his first finger touching the other, as if laughter somehow made him vulnerable—and all at once, with no break at all, at least none she could detect, she was crying. How stupid all this was, to be a widow at thirty-five, to be a fugitive in a town full of dead people, to be sitting in the men's room of an abandoned movie theater on a canvas Port-A-Potty, peeing and crying at the same time, pissing and moaning, you might say, and looking at a dim beast on a wall so warped that it seemed to be running underwater, how stupid to be so frightened, and to have grief all but stolen away by her mind's brute determination to survive at any cost . . . as if Peter had never meant anything anyway, as if he had just been a footnote.

How stupid to still feel so hungry . . . but she was.

"Why is this happening? Why does it have to be me?" she whispered, and put her face into her hands.

3

If either Steve or Cynthia had had a gun, they probably would have shot her.

They were passing Bud's Suds (the neon sign in the window read ENJOY OUR SLOTSPITALITY) when the door of the next business up—the laundrymat—opened and a woman sprang out. Steve, seeing only a dark shape, drew back the tire iron to hit her.

"No!" Cynthia said, grabbing at his wrist and holding it. "Don't do that!"

The woman—she had a lot of dark hair and very white skin, but that was all Cynthia could tell at first—grabbed Steve by the shoulders and shoved her face up into his. Cynthia didn't think the laundrymat woman ever saw the upraised tire iron at all. *She's gonna ask him if he's found Jeeeesus,* Cynthia thought. *It's never Jesus when they grab you like that, it's always Jeeeesus.*

But of course that was not what she said.

"We have to get out." Her voice was low, hoarse. "Right now." She snatched a glance over her shoulder, flicked a look at Cynthia, then seemed to dismiss her entirely as she focused on Steve again. Cynthia had seen this before and wasn't offended by it. When it got to be crunch-time, a certain kind of woman could only see the guy. Sometimes it was the way they had been raised; more often it seemed actually hard-wired into their cunning little Barbie Doll circuits.

Cynthia was getting a better look at her now, in spite of the dark and the blowing dust. An older woman (thirty, at least), intelligent-looking, not unsexy. Long legs poking out of a short dress that looked somehow gawky, as if the chick inside it wasn't accustomed to wearing dresses. Yet she was far from clumsy, judging from the way she moved with Steve when he moved, as if they were dancing. "Do you have a car?" she rapped.

"That's no good," Steve said. "The road out of town is blocked."

"Blocked? Blocked how?"

"A couple of house trailers," he said.

"Where?"

"Near the mining company," Cynthia said, "but that's not the only problem. There are a lot of dead people—"

"Tell me about it," she said, and laughed shrilly. "Collie's gone nuts. I saw him kill half a dozen myself. He drove after them in his cruiser and shot them down in the street. Like they were cattle and Main Street was the killing-floor." She was still holding onto Steve, shaking him as she spoke, as if scolding him, but her eyes were everywhere. "We have to get off the street. If he catches us . . . come in here. It's safe. I've been in here since yesterday forenoon. He came in once. I hid under the desk in the office. I thought he'd follow the smell of my perfume and find me . . . come around the desk and find me . . . but he didn't. Maybe he had a stuffy nose!"

She began to laugh hysterically, then abruptly slapped her own face to make herself stop. It was funny, in a shocking way; the sort of thing the characters in old Warner Brothers cartoons sometimes did.

Cynthia shook her head. "Not the laundrymat. The movie theater. There are other people there."

"I saw his shadow," the woman said. She was still holding Steve by the shoulders and her face was still turned confidentially up to his, as if she thought he was Humphrey Bogart and she was Ingrid Bergman and there was a soft filter on the camera. "I saw his shadow, it fell across the desk and I was sure . . . but he didn't, and I think we'll be safe in the office while we think about what to do next—"

Cynthia reached out, took the woman's chin in her hand, and turned it toward her.

"What are you *doing*?" the dark-haired woman asked angrily. "Just what in the hell do you think you're *doing*?"

"Getting your attention, I hope."

Cynthia let go of the woman's face, and be damned if she didn't immediately turn back to Steve, every bit as brainless as a flower turning on its stalk to follow the sun, and resume her speed-rap.

"I was under the desk . . . and . . . and . . . we have to . . . listen, we have to . . . ."

Cynthia reached out again, grasped the woman's lower face again, turned it back in her direction again.

"Hon, read my lips. *The theater. There are other people there.*"

The woman looked at her, frowning as if she were trying to get the sense of this. Then she looked past Cynthia's shoulder at the chain-hung marquee of The American West.

"The old movieshow?"

"Yes."

"Are you sure? I tried the door last night, after it got dark. It's locked."

"We're supposed to go around to the back," Steve said. "I have a friend, that's where he told me to go."

"How'd he do that?" the dark-haired woman asked suspiciously, but when Steve started walking in that direction, she went along. Cynthia fell in next to her, walking on the outside. "How *could* he do that?"

"Cellular phone," Steve said.

"They don't work very well around here as a rule," the dark-haired woman said. "Too many mineral deposits."

They walked under the theater's marquee (a tumbleweed caught in an angle between the glassed-in ticket-booth and the lefthand door rattled like a maraca) and stopped on the far side. "There's the alley," Cynthia said. She started forward but the woman stayed where she was, frowning from Steve to Cynthia and then back to Steve again.

"What friend, what other people?" she asked. "How did they get here? How come that fuck Collie didn't kill them?"

"Let's save all that for later." Steve took her arm.

She resisted his tug, and when she spoke this time, there was a catch in her voice. "You're taking me to him, aren't you?"

"Lady, we don't even know who you're talking about," Cynthia said. "Just for Christ's sake will you come *on*!"

"I hear a motor," Steve said. His head was cocked to one side. "Coming from the south, I think. Coming in this direction for sure."

The woman's eyes widened. "Him," she whispered. *"Him."*

She looked over her shoulder, as if longing for the safety of the laundrymat, and then made her decision and bolted down the alley. By the time they got to the board fence running along the back of the theater, Cynthia and Steve were hurrying just to keep up.

4

"Are you *sure* . . ." the woman began, and then a flashlight flicked, once, from farther down the building. They were in single-file, Steve between the women, the one from the laundry-mat ahead of him. He took her hand (very cold) in his right and reached back to Cynthia's (marginally warmer) with his left. The dark-haired woman led them slowly down the path. The flash-light blinked on again, this time pointed down at two stacked crates.

"Climb up and get on in here," a voice whispered. It was one Steve was delighted to hear.

"Boss?"

"You bet." Marinville sounded as if he might be smiling. "Love the coverall look—it's so *masculine.* Get on in here, Steve."

"There are three of us."

"The more the merrier."

The dark-haired woman hiked her skirt in order to get up on the crates, and Steve could see the boss helping himself to an eyeful. Even the apocalypse couldn't change some things, apparently.

Steve helped Cynthia up next, then followed. He turned around, slid partway in, then reached down and pushed the top crate off the one underneath. He didn't know if it would be enough to fool the guy the dark-haired woman was so afraid of if he came back here sniffing around, but it was better than nothing.

He slid into the room, a wino-hideout if he had ever seen one, then grabbed the boss and hugged him. Marinville laughed, sounding both surprised and pleased. "Just no tongue, Steve, I insist."

Steve held him by the shoulders, grinning. "I thought you were dead. We found your scoot buried in the sand."

"You found it?" Now Marinville sounded delighted. "Son of a bitch!"

"What happened to your face?"

Marinville held the lens of the flashlight under his chin, turning his lumpy, discolored face into something out of a horror movie. His nose looked like roadkill. His grin, although cheerful, made matters even worse. "If I made a speech to PEN America looking like this, do you think the assholes would finally listen?"

"Man," Cynthia said, awed, "someone put a real hurt on you."

"Entragian," Marinville said gravely. "Have you met him?"

"No," Steve said. "And judging from what I've heard and seen so far, I don't want to."

The bathroom door swung open, squalling on its hinges, and a kid stood there—short hair, pale face, blood-smeared Cleveland Indians tee-shirt. He had a flashlight in one hand, and he moved it quickly, picking out the newcomers' faces one at a time. Things came together in Steve's mind as neatly as jigsaw-puzzle pieces. He supposed the kid's shirt was the key connection.

"Are you Steve?" the boy asked.

Steve nodded. "That's me. Steve Ames. This is Cynthia Smith. And you're my phone-pal."

The boy smiled wanly at that.

"That was good timing, David. You'll probably never know *how* good. It's nice to meet you. David Carver, isn't it?"

He stepped forward and shook the boy's free hand, enjoying

the look of surprise on his face. God knew the kid had surprised him, coming through on the phone that way.

"How do you know my last name?"

Cynthia took David's hand when Steve let it go. She shook it once, firmly. "We found your Humvee or Winnebago or whatever it is. Steve there checked out your baseball cards."

"Be honest," Steve said to David. "Do you think Cleveland's *ever* gonna win the World Series?"

"I don't care, just as long as I'm around to see them play another game," David said with a trace of a smile.

Cynthia turned toward the woman from the laundrymat, the one they might have shot if they'd had guns. "And this is—"

"Audrey Wyler," the dark-haired woman said. "I'm a consulting geologist for Diablo Mining. At least, I was." She scanned the ladies' room with large dazed eyes, taking in the carton of liquor bottles, the bins of beer-cans, the fabulous fish swimming on one dirty tiled wall. "Right now I don't know what I am. What I feel like is meatloaf three days left over."

She turned, little by little, toward Marinville as she spoke, much as she had turned toward Steve outside the laundrymat, and took up her original scripture.

"We have to get out of town. Your pal here says the road out is blocked, but I know another one. It's goes from the staging area down at the bottom of the embankment out to Highway 50. It's a mess, but there are ATVs in the motor-pool, half a dozen of them—"

"I'm sure your knowledge will come in very handy, but I think we ought to pass that part by, for the time being," Marinville said. He spoke in a professionally soothing voice, one Steve recognized right away. It was how the boss talked to the women (it was invariably women, usually in their fifties or early sixties) who set up his literary lectures—what he called his cultural bombing runs. "We had better talk things over a little, first.

Come on into the theater. There's quite a setup there. I think you'll be amazed."

"What are you, stupid?" she asked. "We don't need to talk things over, we need to *get out of here*." She looked around at them. "You don't seem to grasp what has happened here. This man, Collie Entragian—"

Marinville raised his flashlight and shone it full into his face for a moment, letting her get a good look. "I've met the man, as you can see, and I grasp plenty. Come on out front, Ms. Wyler, and we'll talk. I see you're impatient with that idea, but it's for the best. The carpenters have a saying—measure twice, cut once. It's a good saying. All right?"

She gave him a reluctant look, but when he started toward the door, she followed. So did Steve and Cynthia. Outside, the wind screamed around the theater, making it groan in its deepest joints.

5

The dark shape of a car, one with lightbars on the roof, rolled slowly north through the windscreaming dark, away from the rampart that marked China Pit at the south end of Desperation. It rolled with its lights off; the thing behind the wheel saw quite well in the dark, even when that darkness was stuffed with flying grit.

The car passed the bodega at the town's south end. The fallen sign reading MEXICAN FOOD'S was now mostly covered by blowing sand; all that still showed in the weak glow of the porch bulb was CAN FOO. The cruiser drove slowly on up the street to the Municipal Building, turned into the lot, and parked where it had before. Behind the wheel, the large, slumped figure wearing the Sam Browne belt with the badge on the cross-strap was singing an old song in a tuneless, droning voice: *"And we'll go dancin, baby, then you'll see . . . How the magic's in the music and the music's in me . . ."*

The creature in the driver's seat killed the Caprice's engine and then just sat there, head down, fingers tapping at the wheel. A buzzard flapped out of the flying dirt, made a last-minute course adjustment as the wind gusted, then landed on the hood of the cruiser. A second followed, and a third. This latest arrival squalled at his mates, then squirted a thick stream of guano onto the car's hood.

They lined up, looking in through the dirty windshield.

"Jews," the driver said, "must die. And Catholics. Mormons, too. *Tak.*"

The door opened. One foot swung out, then another. The figure in the Sam Browne belt stood up, slammed the door shut. It held its new hat under its arm for the time being. In its other hand it held the shotgun the woman, Mary, had grabbed off the desk. It walked around to the front door. Here, flanking the steps, were two coyotes. They whined uneasily and shrank down on their haunches, grinning sycophantic doggy grins at the approaching figure, which passed them with no acknowledgment at all.

It reached for the door, and then its hand froze. The door was ajar. A vagary of the wind had sucked it most of the way shut . . . but not *completely.*

"What the fuck?" it muttered, and opened the door. It went upstairs fast, first putting the hat on (jamming it down hard; it didn't fit so well now) and then shifting the shotgun to both hands.

A coyote lay dead at the top of the stairs. The door which led into the holding area was also standing open. The thing with the shotgun in its hands stepped in, knowing already what it would see, but the knowing did not stop the angry roar which came out of its chest. Outside, at the foot of the steps, the coyotes whined and cringed and squirted urine. On the police-cruiser, the buzzards also heard the cry of the thing upstairs and fluttered their wings uneasily, almost lifting off and then settling back, darting their heads restlessly at each other, as if to peck.

In the holding area, all the cells which had been occupied were now standing open and empty.

"That boy," the figure in the doorway whispered. Its hands were white on the stock of the shotgun. "That nasty little drug user."

It stood there a moment longer, then stepped slowly into the room. Its eyes shifted back and forth in its expressionless face. Its hat—a Smokey-style with a flat brim—was slowly rising again as the thing's hair pushed it up. It had a great deal more hair than the hat's previous owner. The woman Collie Entragian had taken from the detention area and down the stairs had been five-six, a hundred and thirty pounds. This thing looked like that woman's very big sister: six-three, broad-shouldered, probably two hundred pounds. It was wearing a coverall it had taken from the supply shed before driving back out of what the mining company called Rattlesnake Number Two and the townspeople had for over a hundred years called the China Pit. The coverall was a bit tight in the breast and the hip, but still better than this body's old clothes; they were as useless to it now as Ellen Carver's old concerns and desires. As for Entragian, it had his belt, badge, and hat; it wore his pistol on her hip.

Of course it did. After all, Ellen Carver was the only law west of the Pecos now. It was her job, and God help anyone who tried to keep her from doing a good one.

Her former son, for instance.

From the breast pocket of the coverall it took a small piece of sculpture. A spider carved from gray stone. It canted drunkenly to the left on Ellen's palm (one of its legs on that side was broken off), but that in no way dissipated its ugliness or its malevolence. Pitted stone eyes, purple with iron that had been volcano-cooked millennia ago, bulged from above its mandible, which gaped to show a tongue that was not a tongue but the grinning head of a tiny coyote. On the spider's back was a shape which vaguely resembled a country fiddle.

"*Tak!*" the creature standing by the desk said. Its face was slack and doughy, a cruel parody of the face of the woman who, ten hours before, had been reading her daughter a *Curious George* book and sharing a cup of cocoa with her. Yet the eyes in that face were alive and aware and venomous, hideously like the eyes of the thing resting on her palm. Now she took it in her other hand and raised it over her head, into the light of the hanging glass globe over the desk. "*Tak ah wan! Tak ah lah! Mi him, en tow! En tow!*"

Recluse spiders came hurrying toward it from the darkness of the stairwell, from cracks in the baseboard, from the dark corners of the empty cells. They gathered around it in a circle. Slowly, it lowered the stone spider to the desk.

"*Tak!*" it cried softly. "*Mi him, en tow.*"

A ripple went through the attentive circle of spiders. There were maybe fifty in all, most no bigger than plump raisins. Then the circle broke up, streaming toward the door in two lines. The thing that had been Ellen Carver before Collie Entragian took her down into the China Pit stood watching them go. Then it put the carving back into its pocket.

"Jews must die," it told the empty room. "Catholics must die. Mormons must die. Grateful Dead fans must die." It paused. "Little prayboys must also die."

It raised Ellen Carver's hands and began tapping Ellen Carver's fingers meditatively against Ellen Carver's collarbones.

PART III

THE AMERICAN WEST: LEGENDARY SHADOWS

CHAPTER 1

1

"Holy shit!" Steve said. "This is amazing."

"Fucking weird is what it is," Cynthia replied, then looked around to see if she had offended the old man. Billingsley was nowhere in sight.

"Young lady," Johnny said. "Weird is the mosh pit, the only invention for which your generation can so far take credit. This is not weird. This is rather nice, in fact."

"Weird," Cynthia repeated, but she was smiling.

Johnny guessed that The American West had been built in the decade following World War II, when movie theaters were no longer the overblown Xanadus they had been in the twenties and thirties, but long before malling and multiplexing turned them into Dolby-equipped shoe-boxes. Billingsley had turned on the pinspots above the screen and those in what once would have been called the orchestra-pit, and Johnny had no trouble seeing the place. The auditorium was big but bland. There were vaguely art-deco electric wall-sconces, but no other grace-notes. Most of the seats were still in place, but the red plush was faded and threadbare and smelled powerfully of mildew. The screen was a huge white rectangle upon which Rock Hudson had once clinched with Doris Day, across which Charlton Heston had once matched chariots with Stephen Boyd. It had to be at least forty feet long and twenty feet high; from where Johnny stood, it looked the size of a drive-in screen.

There was a stage area in front of the screen—a kind of architectural holdover, Johnny assumed, since vaudeville must have been dead by the time this place was built. Had it *ever* been used? He supposed so; for political speeches, or high school graduations, maybe for the final round of the Cowshit County Spelling Bee. Whatever purposes it had served in the past, surely none of the people who had attended those quaint country ceremonies could have predicted this stage's final function.

He glanced around, a little worried about Billingsley now, and saw the old man coming down the short, narrow corridor which led from the bathrooms to the backstage area, where the rest of them were clustered. *Old fella's got a bottle stashed, he went back for a quick snort, that's all,* Johnny thought, but he couldn't smell fresh booze on the old guy when he brushed past, and that was a smell he never missed now that he had quit drinking himself.

They followed Billingsley out onto the stage, the group of people Johnny was coming to think of (and not entirely without affection) as The Collie Entragian Survival Society, their feet clumping and echoing, their shadows long and pallid in the orchestra sidelights. Billingsley had turned these on from a box in the electrical closet by the stage-left entrance. Above the tatty red plush seats, the weak light petered out in a hurry and there was only darkness ascending to some unseen height. Above that—and on all sides as well—the desert wind howled. It was a sound that cooled Johnny's blood . . . but he could not deny the fact that there was also something strangely attractive about it . . . although what that attraction might be, he didn't know.

Oh, don't lie. You know. Billingsley and his friends knew as well, that's why they came here. God made you to hear that sound, and a room like this is a natural amplifier for it. You can hear it even better when you sit in the front of the screen with your old pals, throwing legendary shadows and drinking to the past. That sound says quitting is okay, that quitting is in fact the only choice that makes any sense. That sound is about the lure of emptiness and the pleasures of zero.

In the middle of the dusty stage and in front of the curtainless screen was a living room—easy chairs, sofas, standing lamps, a coffee-table, even a TV. The furniture stood on a big piece of carpet. It was a little like a display in the Home Living section of a department store, but what Johnny kept coming back to was the idea that if Eugène Ionesco had ever written an episode of *The Twilight Zone*, the set would probably have looked a lot like this. Dominating the decor was a fumed-oak bar. Johnny ran a hand over it as Billingsley snapped on the standing lamps, one after the other. The electrical cords, Johnny saw, ran through small slits in the lower part of the screen. The edges of these rips had then been mended with electrical tape to keep them from widening.

Billingsley nodded at the bar. "That come from the old Circle Ranch. Part of the Clayton Loving auction, it was. Buzz Hansen n me teamed together and knocked it down for seventeen bucks. Can you b'lieve it?"

"Frankly, no," Johnny said, trying to imagine what an item like this might go for in one of those precious little shops down in SoHo. He opened the double doors and saw the bar was fully stocked. Good stuff, too. Not primo, but good. He closed the doors again in a hurry. The bottles inside called to him in a way the bottle of Beam he'd taken out of the Owl's had not.

Ralph Carver sat down in a wing-chair and looked out over the empty seats with the dazed hopefulness of a man who dares to think he may be dreaming after all. David went over to the television. "Do you get anything on this—oh, I see." He had spotted the VCR underneath. He squatted down to look at the cassettes stacked on top of it.

"Son—" Billingsley began, then gave up.

David shuffled through the boxes quickly—*Sex-Starved Co-eds, Dirty Debutantes, Cockpit Honeys, Part 3*—and then put them back. "You guys watch these?"

Billingsley shrugged. He looked both tired and embarrassed. "We're too old to rodeo, son. Someday maybe you'll understand."

"Hey, it's your business," David said, standing up. "I was just asking."

"Steve, look at this," Cynthia said. She stepped back, raised her arms over her head, crossed them at the wrists, and wiggled them. A huge dark shape flapped lazily on the screen, which was dingy with several decades' worth of accumulated dust. "A crow. Not bad, huh?"

He grinned, stepped next to her, and placed his hands together out in front of him with one finger jutting down.

"An elephant!" Cynthia laughed. "Too cool!"

David laughed with her. It was an easy sound, cheerful and free. His father turned his head toward it and smiled himself.

"Not bad for a kid from Lubbock!" Cynthia said.

"Better watch that, unless you want me to start in calling you cookie again."

She stuck her tongue out, eyes closed, fingers twiddling in her ears, reminding Johnny so strongly of Terry that he laughed out loud. The sound startled, almost frightened him. He supposed that, somewhere between Entragian and sundown, he had pretty much decided that he would never laugh again . . . not at the funny stuff, anyway.

Mary Jackson, who had been walking around the onstage living room and looking at everything, now glanced up at Steve's elephant. "I can make the New York City skyline," she announced.

"My ass!" Cynthia said, although she looked intrigued by the concept.

"Let's see!" David said. He was looking up at the screen as expectantly as a kid waiting for the start of the newest *Ace Ventura* movie.

"Okay," Mary said, and raised her hands with the fingers pointing up. "Now, let's see . . . give me a second . . . I learned this in summer camp, and that was a long time ago—"

"What the *fuck* are you people *doing*?"

The strident voice startled Johnny badly, and he wasn't the only one. Mary gave a little scream. The city skyline which had begun to form on the old movie screen went out of focus and disappeared.

Audrey Wyler was standing halfway between the stage-left entrance and the living-room grouping, her face pale, her eyes wide and hot. Her shadow loomed on the screen behind her, making its own image, all unknown to its creator: Batman's cloak.

"You guys're as insane as he is, you must be. He's out there somewhere, looking for us. *Right now.* Don't you remember the car you heard, Steve? That was him, coming back! But you stand here . . . *with the lights on* . . . playing party-games!"

"The lights wouldn't show from the outside even if we had all of them on," Billingsley said. He was looking at Audrey in a way that was both thoughtful and intense . . . as if, Johnny thought, he had the idea he'd seen her somewhere before. Possibly in *Dirty Debutantes.* "It's a movie theater, remember. Pretty much soundproof and light-proof. That's what we liked about it, my gang."

"But he'll come looking. And if he looks long enough and hard enough, he'll find us. When you're in Desperation, there aren't that many places to hide."

"Let him," Ralph Carver said hollowly, and raised the Ruger .44. "He killed my little girl and took my wife away. I saw what he's like as much as you did, lady. So let him come. I got some Express Mail for him."

Audrey looked at him uncertainly for a moment. He looked back at her with dead eyes. She glanced at Mary, found nothing there to interest her, and looked at Billingsley again. "He could sneak up. A place like this must have half a dozen ways in. Maybe more."

"Yup, and every one locked except for the ladies'-room window," Billingsley said. "I went back there just now and set up a line of beer-bottles on the windowledge inside. If he opens the window, it'll swing in, hit the bottles, knock em over, smash em on the floor. We'll hear him, ma'am, and when he walks out here we'll fill him so full of lead you could cut im up and use im for sinkers." He was looking at her closely as he uttered this grandiosity, eyes alternating between her face, which was okay, and her legs, which were, in John Edward Marinville's 'umble opinion, pretty fooking spectacular.

She continued to look at Billingsley as if she had never seen a bigger fool. "Ever heard of keys, oldtimer? The cops have keys to *all* the businesses in these little towns."

"To the *open* ones, that's so," Billingsley replied quietly. "But The American West hasn't been open for a long time. The doors ain't just locked, they're boarded shut. The kids used the fire escape to get in up front, but that ended last March, when it fell down. Nope, I reckon we're as safe here as anywhere."

"Probably safer than out on the street," Johnny said.

Audrey turned to him, hands on her hips. "Well, what do you intend to do? Stay here and amuse yourselves by making shadow-animals on the goddam movie screen?"

"Take it easy," Steve said.

"*You* take it easy!" she almost snarled. "*I want to get out of here!*"

"We all do, but this isn't the time," Johnny said. He looked around at the others. "Does anyone disagree?"

"It'd be insanity to go out there in the dark," Mary said. "The wind's got to be blowing fifty miles an hour, and with the sand flying the way it is, he'd be apt to pick us off one by one."

"What do you think's going to change tomorrow, when the storm ends and the sun comes out?" Audrey asked. It was Johnny she was asking, not Mary.

"I think that friend Entragian may be dead by the time the storm ends," he said. "If he's not already."

Ralph looked over and nodded. David hunkered by the TV, hands loosely clasped between his knees, looking at Johnny with deep concentration.

"Why?" Audrey asked. "How?"

"You haven't seen him?" Mary asked her.

"Of course I have. Just not today. Today I only heard him driving around . . . walking around . . . and *talking* to himself. I haven't actually *seen* him since yesterday."

"Is there anything radioactive around here, ma'am?" Ralph asked Audrey. "Was it ever, like, some sort of dumping ground for nuclear waste, or maybe old weapons? Missile warheads, or something? Because the cop looked like he was falling apart."

"I don't think it was radiation sickness," Mary said. "I've seen pictures of that, and—"

"Whoa," Johnny said, raising his hands. "I want to make a suggestion. I think we should sit down and talk this out. Okay? It'll pass the time, if nothing else, and an idea of what we should do next may come out of it." He looked at Audrey, gave her his most winning smile, and was delighted to see her relax a little, if not exactly melt. Maybe not all of the old charm had departed after all. "At the very least, it will be more constructive than making shadows on the movie screen."

His smile faded a little and he turned to look at them: Audrey, standing on the edge of the rug in her gawky-sexy dress; David, squatting by the TV; Steve and Cynthia, now sitting on the arms of an overstuffed easy chair that looked like it might also have come from the old Circle Ranch; Mary, standing by the screen and looking schoolteacherly with her arms folded under her breasts; Tom Billingsley, now inspecting the open upper cabinet of the bar, with his hands tightly clasped behind his back; Ralph in the wing-chair at the edge of the light, with his left eye now puffed almost completely shut. The Collie Entragian Survival Society, all present and accounted for.

What a crew, Johnny thought. Manhattan Transfer *in the desert.*

"There's another reason we have to talk," he said. He glanced at their shadows bobbing on the curtainless movie screen. For a moment they all looked to him like the shadows of giant birds. He thought of Entragian, telling him buzzards farted, they were the only birds that did. Of Entragian saying *Oh shit, we're all beyond why,* you *know that.* Johnny thought that might well be the scariest thing anyone had said to him in his whole life. Mostly because it rang true.

Johnny nodded slowly, as if in agreement with some interior speaker, then went on.

"I've seen some extraordinary things in my life, but I've never had what I could in any way characterize as a supernatural experience. Until—maybe—today. And what scares me the most about it is that the experience may be ongoing. I don't know. All I can say for sure is that things have happened to me in the last few hours that I can't explain."

"What are you *talking* about?" Audrey sounded close to tears. "Isn't what's happening bad enough without turning it into some kind of a . . . a campfire story?"

"Yes," Johnny said, speaking in a low, compassionate voice that he hardly recognized. "But that doesn't change things."

"I listen and talk better when I'm not starving to death," Mary remarked. "I don't suppose there's anything to eat in this place, is there?"

Tom Billingsley shuffled his feet and looked embarrassed.

"Well, no, not a whole lot, ma'am. Mostly we came here in the evenings to drink and talk over the old days."

She sighed. "That's what I thought."

He pointed vaguely across toward the stage-right entrance. "Marty Ives brought in a little bag of somethin a couple of nights ago. Probably sardines. Marty loves sardines and crackers."

"Yuck," Mary said, but she looked interested almost in spite of herself. Johnny supposed that in another two or three hours even anchovies would look good to her.

"I'll take a peek, maybe he brought in something else," Billingsley said. He didn't sound hopeful.

David got up. "I'll do it, if you want."

Billingsley shrugged. He was looking at Audrey again and seemed to have lost interest in Marty Ives's sardines. "There's a light-switch to the left just as you get offstage. Straight ahead you'll see some shelves. Anything people brought to eat, they most generally put it on those. You might find some Oreos, too."

"You guys might've drunk a tad too much, but at least you kept the minimum nutrition needs in mind," Johnny said. "I like that." The vet gave him a glance, shrugged, and went back to Audrey Wyler's legs. She seemed not to notice his interest in them. Or to care.

David started across the stage, then went back and picked up the .45. He glanced at his father, but Ralph was staring vacantly out into the house again, at red plush seats which faded back into the gloom. The boy put the gun carefully into the pocket of his jeans so that only the handle stuck out, then started offstage. As he passed Billingsley he said, "Is there running water?"

"This is the desert, son. When a building goes vacant, they turn the water off."

"Crud. I've still got soap all over me. It itches."

He left them, crossed the stage, and leaned into the opening over there. A moment later the light came on. Johnny relaxed slightly—only realizing as he did that part of his mind had expected something to jump the boy—and realized Billingsley was looking at him.

"What that kid did back there—the way he got out of that cell—that was impossible," Billingsley said.

"Then we must still be back there, locked up," Johnny said. He thought he sounded all right—pretty much like himself—but what the old veterinarian was saying had already occurred to him. Even a phrase to describe it had occurred to him—*unobtrusive miracles.* He would have written it down in his notebook, if he hadn't dropped it beside Highway 50. "Is that what you think?"

"No, we're here, and we saw him do what he did," Billingsley said. "Greased himself up with soap and squeezed out through the bars like a watermelon seed. Looked like it made sense, didn't it? But I tell you, friend, not even Houdini could have done it that way. Because of the head. He shoulda stuck at the head, but he didn't." He looked them over, one by one, finishing with Ralph. Ralph was looking at Billingsley now instead of at the seats, but Johnny wasn't sure he understood what the old guy was saying. And maybe that was for the best.

"What are you driving at?" Mary asked.

"I'm not sure," Billingsley replied. "But I think we'd do well to kind of gather 'round young Master Carver." He hesitated, then added: "The oldtimers say that any campfire does on a cold night."

2

It picked the dead coyote up and examined it. "*Soma* dies; *pneuma* departs; only *sarx* remains," it said in a voice that was a paradox: both sonorous and entirely without tone. "So it has always been; so shall it always be; life sucks, then you die."

It carried the animal downstairs, paws and shattered head dangling, body swaying like a bloody fur stole. The creature holding it stood for a moment inside the main doors of the Municipal Building, looking out into the blowy dark, listening to the wind.

"So cah set!" it exclaimed, then turned away and took the animal into the Town Office. It looked at the coathooks to the right of the door and saw immediately that the girl— Pie, to her brother—had been taken down and wrapped in a drape.

Its pale face twisted in anger as it looked at the child's covered form.

"Took her down!" it told the dead coyote in its arms. "Rotten boy took her down! Stupid, troublemaking boy!"

Yes. Feckless boy. Rude boy. *Foolish* boy. In some ways that last was the best, wasn't it? The truest. Foolish prayboy trying to make at least some part of it come right, as if any part of a thing like this ever *could* be, as if death were an obscenity that could be scrubbed off life's wall by a strong arm. As if the closed book could be reopened and read again, with a different ending.

Yet its anger was twisted through with fear, like a yellow stitch through red cloth, because the boy was not giving up, and so the rest of them were not giving up. They should not have dared to run from

(Entragian her it them)

even if their cell doors had been standing wide open. Yet they had. Because of the boy, the wretched overblown prideful praying boy, who had had the insolence to take down his little cunt of a sister and try to give her something approximating a decent burial—

A kind of dull warmth on its fingers and palms. It looked

down and saw that it had plunged Ellen's hands into the coyote's belly all the way to the wrists.

It had intended to hang the coyote on one of the hooks, simply because that was what it had done with some of the others, but now another idea occurred. It carried the coyote across to the green bundle on the floor, knelt, and pulled the drape open. It looked down with a silent snarling mouth at the dead girl who had grown inside this present body.

That he should have covered her!

It pulled Ellen's hands, now dressed in lukewarm blood-gloves, out of the coyote and laid the animal down on top of Kirsten. It opened the coyote's jaws and placed them around the child's neck. There was something both grisly and fantastic about this *tableau de la mort*; it was like a woodcut illustration from a black fairy-tale.

"Tak," it whispered, and grinned. Ellen Carver's lower lip split open when it did. Blood ran down her chin in an unnoticed rill. The rotten, presumptuous little boy would probably never view this revision of his revision, but how nice it was to imagine his reaction to it if he did! If he saw how little his efforts had come to, how easily respect could be snatched back, how naturally zero reasserted itself in the artificially concocted integers of men.

It pulled the drape up to the coyote's neck. Now the child and the beast almost seemed to be lovers. How it wished the boy were here! The father, too, but especially the boy. Because it was the boy who so badly needed instruction.

It was the boy who was the dangerous one.

There was scuttering from behind it, a sound too low to be heard . . . but it heard it anyway. It pivoted on Ellen's knees and saw the recluse spiders returning. They came through the Town Office door, turned left, then streamed up the wall, over posters announcing forthcoming town business and soliciting volunteers for this fall's Pioneer Days extravaganza. Above the one announcing an informational meeting at which Desperation Mining Corporation officials would discuss the resumption of copper mining at the so-called China Pit, the spiders re-formed their circle.

The tall woman in the coverall and the Sam Browne belt got up and approached them. The circle on the wall trembled, as if expressing fear or ecstasy or perhaps both. The woman put bloody hands together, then opened them to the wall, palms out. *"Ah lah?"*

The circle dissolved. The spiders scurried into a new shape, moving with the precision of a drill-team putting on a half-time show. T, they made, then broke up, scurried, and made an H. An E followed, an A, another T, another E—

It waved them off while they were still scrambling around up there, deciding how to fall in and make an R.

"En tow," it said. *"Ras."*

The spiders gave up on their R and resumed their faintly trembling circle.

"Ten ah?" it asked after a moment, and the spiders formed a new figure. It was a circle, the shape of the *ini*. The woman with Ellen Carver's fingerprints looked at it for several moments, tapping Ellen's fingers against Ellen's collarbones, then waved Ellen's hand at the wall. The figure broke up. The spiders began to stream down to the floor.

It walked back out into the hall, not looking at the spiders streaming about its feet. The spiders would be available if it needed them, and that was all that mattered.

It stood at the double doors, once more looking out into the night. It couldn't see the old movie house, but that was all right; it knew where The American West was, about an eighth of a mile north of here, just past the town's only intersection. And, thanks to the fiddlebacks, she now knew where *they* were, as well.

Where *he* was. The shitting little prayboy.

3

Johnny Marinville told his story again—all of it, this time. For the first time in a good many years he tried to keep it short— there were critics all over America who would have applauded, partly in disbelief. He told them about stopping to take a leak, and how Entragian had planted the pot in his saddlebag while he was doing it. He told them about the coyotes—the one Entragian had seemed to talk to and the others, posted along the road at intervals like a weird honor guard—and about how the big cop had beaten him up. He recounted the murder of Billy Rancourt, and then, with no appreciable change in his voice, about how the buzzard had attacked him, seemingly at Collie Entragian's command.

There was an expression of frank disbelief on Audrey Wyler's face at this, but Johnny saw Steve and the skinny little girl he'd picked up somewhere along the way exchange a look of sick understanding. Johnny didn't glance around to see how the others were taking it, but instead looked down at his hands on his knees, concentrating as he did when he was trying to work through a tough patch of composition.

"He wanted me to suck his cock. I think that was supposed to start me gibbering and begging for mercy, but I didn't find the idea as shocking as Entragian maybe expected. Cocksucking's a pretty standard sexual demand in situations where authority's exceeded its normal bounds and restrictions, but it's not what it looks like. On the surface, rape is about dominance and aggression. Underneath, though, it's about fear-driven anger."

"Thank you, Dr. Ruth," Audrey said. "Next ve vill be discussink ze imberdence."

Johnny looked at her without rancor. "I did a novel on the subject of homosexual rape. *Tiburon.* Not a big critical success, but I talked to a lot of people and got the basics down pretty well, I think. The point is, he made me mad instead of scaring me. By then I'd decided I didn't have a lot to lose, anyway. I told him that I'd take his cock, all right, but once it was in my mouth I'd bite it off. Then . . . then . . ."

He thought harder than he had in at least ten years, nodding to himself as he did.

"Then I threw one of his own nonsense-words back at him. At least it *seemed* like nonsense to me, or something in a made-up language. It had a guttural quality . . ."

"Was it *tak*?" Mary asked.

Johnny nodded. "And it didn't seem to be nonsense to the coyotes, or to Entragian, either. When I said it he kind of recoiled . . . and that's when he called the buzzard bombing-strike down on me."

"I don't believe that happened," Audrey said. "I guess you're a famous writer or something, and you've got the look of a guy who isn't used to having doubt cast, so to speak, but I just don't believe it."

"It's what happened, though," he said. "You didn't see anything like that? Strange, aggressive animal behavior?"

"I was hiding in the *town laundrymat*," she said. "I mean, hello? Are we talking the same language here?"

"But—"

"Listen, you want to talk about strange and aggressive animal behavior?" Audrey asked. She leaned forward, eyes bright and fixed on Marinville's. "That's *Collie* you're talking about. Collie as he is now. He killed everyone he saw, everyone who crossed his path. Isn't that enough for you? Do we have to have trained buzzards, as well?"

"What about spiders?" Steve asked. He and the skinny girl were in the chair instead of sitting on the arms now, and Steve had his arm around her shoulders.

"What about them?"

"Did you see any spiders kind of . . . well . . . flocking together?"

"Like birds of a feather?" She was favoring him with a gaze that said CAUTION, LUNATIC AT WORK.

"Well, no. Wrong word. *Travelling* together. In packs. Like wolves. Or coyotes."

She shook her head.

"What about snakes?"

"Haven't seen any of them, either. Or coyotes in town. Not even a dog riding a bike and wearing a party hat. This is all news to me."

David came back onto the stage with a brown bag in his hands, the kind that convenience-store clerks put small purchases in—Twinkies and Slim Jims, cartons of milk, single cans of beer. He also had a box of Ritz crackers under his arm. "Found some stuff," he said.

"Uh-huh," Steve said, eyeing the box and the little bag. "That should certainly take care of hunger in America. What does it come to, Davey? One sardine and two crackers apiece, do you think?"

"Actually, there's quite a lot," David said. "More than you'd think. Um . . ." He paused, looking at them thoughtfully, and a little anxiously. "Would anybody mind if I said a prayer before I hand this stuff around?"

"Like grace?" Cynthia asked.

"Grace, yeah."

"It works for me," Johnny said. "I think we can use all the grace we can lay our hands on."

"Amen," Steve said.

David put the bag and the box of crackers down between his sneakers. Then he closed his eyes and put his hands together again before his face, finger to finger. Johnny was struck by the kid's lack of pretension. There was a simplicity about the gesture that had been honed by use into beauty.

"God, please bless this food we are about to eat," David began.

"Yeah, what there is of it," Cynthia said, and immediately looked sorry that she had spoken. David didn't seem to mind, though; might not have even heard her.

"Bless our fellowship, take care of us, and deliver us from evil. Please take care of my mom, too, if it's your will." He paused, then said in a lower voice: "It's probably not, but *please*, if it's your will. Jesus' sake, amen." He opened his eyes again.

Johnny was moved. The kid's little prayer had touched him in the very place Entragian had tried and failed to reach.

Sure it did. Because he believes it. In his own humble way, this kid makes Pope John Paul in his fancy clothes and Las Vegas hat look like an Easter-and-Christmas Christian.

David bent over and picked up the stuff he'd found, seeming as cheerful as a soup-kitchen tycoon presiding over Thanksgiving dinner as he rummaged in the bag.

"Here, Mary." He took out a can of Blue Fjord Fancy Sardines, and handed it to her. "Key's on the bottom."

"Thank you, David."

He grinned. "Thank Mr. Billingsley's friend. It's his food, not mine." He handed her the crackers. "Pass em on."

"Take what you need and leave the rest," Johnny said expansively. "That's what us Friends of the Circle say . . . right, Tom?"

The veterinarian gave him a watery gaze and didn't reply.

David gave a can of sardines to Steve and another to Cynthia.

"Oh, no, honey, that's okay," Cynthia said, trying to give hers back. "Me'n Steve can share."

"No need to," David said, "there's plenty. Honest."

He gave a can to Audrey, a can to Tom, and a can to Johnny. Johnny turned his over twice in his hand, as if trying to make sure it was real, before pulling off the wrapper, taking the key off the back, and inserting it in the tab of metal at the end of the can. He opened it. As soon as he smelled the fish, he was savagely hungry. If anyone had told him he would ever have such a reaction to a lousy can of sardines, he would have laughed.

Something tapped him on the shoulder. It was Mary, holding out the box of crackers. She looked almost ecstatic. Fish-oil ran down from the corner of her mouth to her chin in a shiny little runnel. "Go on," she said. "They're wonderful on crackers. Really!"

"Yep," Cynthia said cheerfully, "everything tastes better when it shits on a Ritz, that's what I always say."

Johnny accepted the box, looked in, and saw there was only a single cylinder of waxed paper left, half-full. He took three of the round dark orange crackers. His growling stomach protested this forbearance, and he found himself unable to keep from taking three more before passing the box to Billingsley. Their eyes met for a moment, and he heard the old man saying not even Houdini could have done it that way. Because of the head. And of course there was the phone—three transmission-bars showing when it had been in the kid's hands, none at all when he had held it in his own.

"This settles it once and for all," Cynthia said, her mouth full. She sounded the way Mary looked. "Food is *way* better than sex."

Johnny looked at David. He was sitting on one arm of his father's chair, eating. Ralph's can of sardines sat in his lap, unopened, as the man continued to look out over the rows of empty seats. David took a couple of sardines from his own can, laid them carefully on a cracker, and gave them to his dad, who began to chew mechanically, doing it as if his only goal was to clear his mouth again. Seeing the boy's expression of attentive love made Johnny uncomfortable, as if he were violating David's privacy. He looked away and saw the box of crackers on the floor. Everyone was busy eating, and no one paid Johnny any particular attention when he picked up the box and looked into it.

It had gone all the way around the group, everyone had at least half a dozen crackers (Billingsley might have taken even more; the old goat was really cramming them in), but that cylinder of waxed paper was still in there, and Johnny could have sworn that it was still half-full; that the number of crackers in it had not changed at all.

4

Ralph recounted the crash of the Carver family as clearly as he could, eating sardines between bursts of talk. He was trying to clear his head, trying to come back—for David's sake more than his own—but it was hard. He kept seeing Kirstie lying motionless at the foot of the stairs, kept seeing Entragian pulling Ellie across the holding area by the arm. *Don't worry, David, I'll be back,* she had said, but to Ralph, who believed he had heard every turn and lift of Ellie's voice in their fourteen years of marriage, she had sounded already gone. Still, he owed it to David to try and be here. To come back himself, from wherever it was his shocked, over-stressed—and guilty, yes, there was that, too—mind wanted to take him.

But it was hard.

When he had finished, Audrey said: "Okay, no revolt from the animal kingdom, at least. But I'm very sorry about your wife and your little girl, Mr. Carver. You too, David."

"Thanks," Ralph said, and when David added, "My mom could still be okay," he ruffled the boy's hair and told him yes, that was right.

Mary went next, telling about the Baggie under the spare

tire, the way Entragian had mixed "I'm going to kill you" into the Miranda warning, and the way he had shot her husband on the steps, completely without warning or provocation.

"Still no wildlife," Audrey said. This now seemed to be her central concern. She tilted her sardine-can up to her mouth and drank the last of the fish oil without so much as a flicker of embarrassment.

"You either didn't hear the part about the coyote he brought upstairs to guard us or you don't *want* to hear it," Mary said.

Audrey dismissed this with a wave of her hand. She was sitting down now, providing Billingsley with at least another four inches of leg to look at. Ralph was looking, too, but he felt absolutely nothing about what he was seeing. He had an idea there was more juice in some old car batteries than there was in his emotional wiring right now.

"You *can* domesticate them, you know," she said. "Feed them Gaines-burgers and train them like dogs, in fact."

"Did you ever see Entragian walking around town with a coyote on a leash?" Marinville asked politely.

She gave him a look and set her jaw. "No. I knew him to speak to, like anyone else in town, but that was all. I spend most of my time in the pit or the lab or out riding. I'm not much for town life."

"What about you, Steve?" Marinville asked. "What's your tale?"

Ralph saw the rangy fellow with the Texas accent exchange a glance with his girlfriend—if that was what she was—and then look back at the writer. "Well, first off, if you tell your agent I picked up a hitchhiker, I guess I'll lose my bonus."

"I think you can consider him the least of your worries at this point. Go on. Tell it."

They both told it, alternating segments, both clearly aware that the things they had seen and experienced upped the ante of belief considerably. They both expressed frustration at their

inability to articulate how awful the stone fragment in the lab/
storage area had been, how powerfully it had affected them,
and neither seemed to want to come out and say what had happened when the wolf (they agreed that that was what it had
been, not a coyote) brought the fragment out of the lab and
laid it before them. Ralph had an idea it was something sexual,
although what could be so bad about that he didn't know.

"Still a doubting Thomas?" Marinville asked Audrey when
Steve and Cynthia had finished. He spoke mildly, as if he did
not want her to feel threatened. *Of course he doesn't want her to feel
threatened,* Ralph thought. *There's only seven of us, he wants us all
on the same team. And he's really not too bad at it.*

"I don't know what I am." She sounded dazed. "I don't
want to believe any of this shit—just *considering* it freaks me
severely—but I can't imagine why you'd lie." She paused,
then said thoughtfully: "Unless seeing those people hung up
in Hernando's Hideaway . . . I don't know, scared you so badly
that . . ."

"That we started seeing things?" Steve asked.

She nodded. "The snakes you saw in the house—that at least
makes sense of a sort. They feel this kind of weather coming
as much as three days in advance sometimes, and go for any
sheltered place. As for the rest . . . I don't know. I'm a scientist,
and I can't see how—"

"Come on, lady, you're like a kid pretending her mouth is
stitched shut so she won't have to eat the broccoli," Cynthia
said. "Everything we saw dovetails with what Mr. Marinville
there saw before *us*, and Mary saw before *him*, and the Carvers
saw before *them*. Right down to the knocked-over piece of picket
fence where Entragian greased the barber, or whoever he was.
So quit the I'm-a-scientist crap for awhile. *We're* all on the same
page; you're the one that's on a different one."

"But I didn't see any of these things!" Audrey almost
wailed.

"What *did* you see?" Ralph asked. "Tell us."

Audrey crossed her legs, tugged at the hem of her dress. "I was camping. I had four days off, so I packed up Sally and headed north, into the Copper Range. It's my favorite place in Nevada." Ralph thought she looked defensive, as if she had taken a ribbing for this sort of behavior in the past.

Billingsley looked as if he had just wakened from a dream . . . one of having Audrey's long legs wrapped around his scrawny old butt, perhaps. "Sally," he said. "How *is* Sally?"

Audrey gave him an uncomprehending look for a moment, then grinned like a girl. "She's fine."

"Strain all better?"

"Yes, thanks. It was good liniment."

"Glad to hear it."

"What're you talking about?" Marinville asked.

"I doctored her horse a year or so back," Billingsley said. "That's all."

Ralph wasn't sure he would let Billingsley work on *his* horse, if he had one; he wasn't sure he would let Billingsley work on a stray cat. But he supposed the vet might have been different a year ago. When you made drinking a career, twelve months could make a lot of changes. Few of them for the better.

"Getting Rattlesnake back on its feet has been pretty stressful," she said. "Lately it's been the switch-over from rainbirds to emitters. A few eagles died—"

"A *few?*" Billingsley said. "Come now. I'm no tree-hugger, but you can do better than that."

"All right, about forty, in all. No big deal in terms of the species; there's no shortage of eagles in Nevada. As you know, Doc. The greens know it, too, but they treat each dead eagle as if it were a boiled baby, just the same. What it's really about—and *all* it's about—is trying to stop us from mining the copper.

God, they make me so *tired* sometimes. They come out here in their perky little foreign cars, fifty pounds of American copper in each one, and tell us we're earth-raping monsters. They—"

"Ma'am?" Steve said softly. "Pardon, but ain't a one of us folks from Greenpeace."

"Of course not. What I'm saying is that we *all* felt bad about the eagles—the hawks and the ravens too, for that matter—in spite of what the treehuggers say." She looked around at them, as if to evaluate their impression of her honesty, then went on. "We leach copper out of the ground with sulfuric acid. The easiest way to apply it is with rainbirds—they look like big lawn-sprinklers. But rainbirds can leave pools. The birds see them, come down to bathe and drink, then die. It's not a nice death, either."

"No," Billingsley agreed, blinking at her with his watery eyes. "When it was gold they were taking out of China Pit and Desatoya Pit—back in the fifties—it was cyanide in the pools. Just as nasty. No greenie-treehuggers back then, though. Must have been nice for the company, eh, Miss Wyler?" He got up, went to the bar, poured himself a finger of whiskey, and swallowed it like medicine.

"Could I have one about the same?" Ralph asked.

"Yessir, I b'lieve you could," Billingsley said. He handed Ralph his drink, then set out more glasses. He offered warm soft drinks, but the others opted for spring-water, which he poured out of a plastic jug.

"We pulled the rainbirds and replaced them with distribution heads and emitters," Audrey said. "It's a drip-system, more expensive than rainbirds—a *lot*—but the birds don't get into the chemicals."

"No," Billingsley agreed. He poured himself another tot. This he drank more slowly, looking at Audrey's legs again over the rim of his glass.

5

A problem?

Maybe not yet . . . but there *could* be, if steps weren't taken.

The thing that looked like Ellen Carver sat behind the desk in the now-empty holding area, head up, eyes gleaming lustrously. Outside, the wind rose and fell, rose and fell. From closer by came the pad-click of paws ascending the stairs. They stopped outside the door. There came a coughing growl. Then the door swung open, pushed by the snout of a cougar. She was big for a female—perhaps six feet from snout to haunches, with a thick, switching tail that added another three feet to her overall length.

As the cougar came through the door and into the holding area, slinking low to the board floor, her ears laid back against her wedgeshaped skull, the thing cored into her head a little further, wanting to experience a bit of what the cougar was feeling as well as to draw her. The animal was frightened, sorting through the smells of the place and finding no comfort in any of them. It was a human den-place; but that was only part of her problem.

The cougar smelled a lot of trouble here. Gunpowder, for one thing; to the cougar, the smell of the fired guns was still sharp and acrid. Then there was the smell of fear, like a mixture of sweat and burned grass. There was the smell of blood, too—coyote blood and human blood, mixed together. And there was the thing in the chair, looking down at her as she slunk toward it, not wanting to go but not able to stop. It looked like a human being but didn't smell like one. It didn't smell like anything the cougar had ever scented before. She crouched by its feet and voiced a low whining, mewing sound.

The thing in the coverall got out of the chair, dropped to Ellen Carver's knees, lifted the cougar's snout, and looked into the cougar's eyes. It began to speak rapidly in that other language, the tongue of the unformed, telling the cougar where she must go, how she must wait, and what she must do when the time came. They were armed and would likely kill the animal, but she would do her job first.

As it spoke, Ellen's nose began to trickle blood. It felt the blood, wiped it away. Blisters had begun to rise on Ellen's cheeks and neck. Fucking yeast infection! Nothing more than that, at least to start with! Why was it some women simply could not take care of themselves?

"All right," it told the cougar. "Go on, now. Wait until it's time. I'll listen with you."

The cougar made its whining, mewing sound again, licked with its rough tongue at the hand of the thing wearing Ellen Carver's body, then turned and padded out of the room.

It resumed the chair and leaned back in it. It closed Ellen's eyes and listened to the ceaseless rattle of sand against the windows, and let part of itself go with the animal.

CHAPTER 2

1

"You had some downtime coming, you saddled up, and you went camping," Steve said. "What then?"

"I spent four days in the Coppers. Fishing, taking pictures—photography's what I do for fun. Great days. Then, three nights ago, I came back. Went right to my house, which is north of town."

"What brought you back?" Steve asked. "It wasn't bad weather on the way, was it?"

"No. I had my little radio with me, and all I heard was fair and hot."

"All I heard, too," Steve said. "This shit's a total mystery."

"I had a meeting scheduled with Allen Symes, the company comptroller, to summarize the switchover from rainbirds to heads and emitters. He was flying in from Arizona. I was supposed to meet him at Hernando's Hideaway at nine o'clock, the morning before last. That's what we'd taken to calling the lab and the offices out there on the edge of town. Anyway, that's why I'm wearing this damned dress, because of the meeting and because Frank Geller told me that Symes doesn't—didn't—like women in jeans. I know everything was okay when I got back from my camping trip, because that's when Frank called me and told me to wear a dress to the meeting. That night, around seven."

"Who's Frank Geller?" Steve asked.

"Chief mining engineer," Billingsley said. "In charge of reopening the China Pit. At least he was." He gave Audrey a questioning look.

She nodded. "Yes. He's dead."

"Three nights ago," Marinville mused. "Everything in Desperation was peachy three nights ago, at least as far as you know."

"That's right. But the next time I saw Frank, he was hung up on a hook. And one of his hands was gone."

"We saw him," Cynthia said, and shivered. "We saw his hand, too. At the bottom of an aquarium."

"Before all that, during the night, I woke up at least twice. The first time I thought it was thunder, but the second time it sounded like gunshots. I decided I'd been dreaming and went back to sleep, but that must be around the time he . . . got started. Then, when I got to the mining office . . ."

At first, she said, she hadn't sensed anything wrong—certainly not from the fact that Brad Josephson wasn't at his desk. Brad never was, if he could help it. So she had gone out back to Hernando's Hideaway, and there she had seen what Steve and Cynthia would come along and see themselves not long after—bodies on hooks. Apparently everyone who had come in that morning. One of them, dressed in a string tie and dress boots that would have tickled a country-and-western singer, had been Allen Symes. He had come all the way from Phoenix to die in Desperation.

"If what you say is right," she said to Steve, "Entragian must've gotten more of the mining people later on. I didn't count—I was too scared to even *think* of counting them—but there couldn't have been more than seven when I was there. I froze. I might even have blacked out for a little while, I can't say for sure. Then I heard gunshots. No question what they were that time. And someone screaming. Then there were more gunshots and the screaming stopped."

She went back to her car, not running—she said she was afraid that panic would take her over if she started running—and then drove into town. She intended to report what she'd found to Jim Reed. Or, if Jim was out on county business, as he often was, to one of his deputies, Entragian or Pearson.

"I didn't run to the car and I didn't go speeding into town, but I was in shock, just the same. I remember feeling around in the glove compartment for my cigarettes, even though I haven't smoked in five years. Then I saw two people go running through the intersection. You know, under the blinker-light?"

They nodded.

"The town's new police-car came roaring through right after them. Entragian was driving it, but I didn't know that then. There were three or four gunshots, and the people he was chasing were thrown onto the sidewalk, one right by the grocery store, the other just past it. There was blood. A lot. He never slowed, just went on through the intersection, heading west, and pretty soon I heard more shots. I'm pretty sure I heard him yelling 'Yee-haw,' too.

"I wanted to help the people he'd shot if I could. I drove up a little way, parked, and got out of my car. That's probably what saved my life, getting out of my car. Because everything that moved, Entragian killed it. Anyone. Anything. Everything. There were cars and trucks sitting dead in the street like toys, all zigzagged here and there, at least a dozen of them. There was an El Camino truck turned on its side up by the hardware store. Tommy Ortega's, I think. That truck was almost his girlfriend."

"I didn't see *anything* like that," Johnny said. "The street was clear when he brought me in."

"Yeah—the son of a bitch keeps his room picked up, you have to give him that. He didn't want anyone wandering into town and wondering what had happened, that's what I think.

He hasn't done much more than sweep the mess under the rug, but it'll hold for awhile. Especially with this goddam storm."

"Which wasn't forecast," Steve said thoughtfully.

"Right, which wasn't forecast."

"What happened then?" David asked.

"I ran up to the people he shot. One of them was Evelyn Shoenstack, the lady who runs the Cut n Curl and works part-time in the library. She was dead with her brains all over the sidewalk."

Mary winced. Audrey saw it and turned toward her.

"That's something else you need to remember. If he can see you and he decides to shoot you, you're gone." She passed her eyes over the rest of them, apparently wanting to be sure they didn't think she was joking. Or exaggerating. "He's a dead shot. Accent on the *dead*."

"We'll keep it in mind," Steve said.

"The other one was a delivery guy. He was wearing a Tastykake uniform. Entragian got him in the head, too, but he was still alive." She spoke with a calm Johnny recognized. He had seen it in Vietnam, in the aftermath of half a dozen firefights. He'd seen it as a noncombatant, of course, notebook in one hand, pen in the other, Uher tape-recorder slung over his shoulder on a strap with a peace sign pinned to it. Watching and listening and taking notes and feeling like an outsider. Feeling *jealous*. The bitter thoughts which had crossed his mind then—eunuch in the harem, piano-player in the whorehouse—now struck him as insane.

"The year I was twelve, my old man gave me a .22," Audrey Wyler said. "The first thing I did was to go outside our house in Sedalia and shoot a jay. When I went over to it, it was still alive, too. It was trembling all over, staring straight ahead, and its beak was opening and closing, very slowly. I've never in my whole life wanted so badly to take something back. I got down on my knees beside it and waited for it to be finished. It seemed that I owed it that much. It just went on trembling all over until it died. The Tastykake man was trembling like that. He was looking down the street past me, although there wasn't anybody there, and his forehead was covered with tiny beads of sweat. His head was all pushed out of shape, and there was white stuff on his shoulder. I had this crazy idea at first that it was Styrofoam poppers—you know, the packing stuff people put in the box when they mail something fragile?—and then I saw it was bone chips. From his, you know, his skull."

"I don't want to hear any more of this," Ralph said abruptly.

"I don't blame you," Johnny said, "but I think we need to know. Why don't you and your boy take a little walk around backstage? See what you can find."

Ralph nodded, stood up, and took a step toward David.

"No," David said. "We have to stay."

Ralph looked at him uncertainly.

David nodded. "I'm sorry, but we do," he said.

Ralph stood where he was a moment longer, then sat down again.

During this exchange, Johnny happened to look over at Audrey. She was staring at the boy with an expression that could have been fear or awe or both. As if she had never seen a creature quite like him. Then he thought of the crackers coming out of that bag like clowns out of the little car at the circus, and he wondered if *any* of them had ever seen a creature quite like David Carver. He thought of the transmission-bars, and Billingsley saying not even Houdini could have done it. Because of the head. They were concentrating on the buzzards and the spiders and the coyotes, on rats that jumped out of stacks of tires and houses that might be full of rattlesnakes; most of all they were concentrating on Entragian, who spoke in tongues and shot like Buffalo Bill. But what about David? Just what, exactly, was he?

"Go on, Audrey," Cynthia said. "Only maybe you could,

you know, drop back from R to PG-13." She lifted her chin in David's direction.

Audrey looked at her vaguely for a moment, not seeming to understand. Then she gathered herself and continued.

2

"I was kneeling there by the delivery guy, trying to think what I should do next—stay with him or run and call someone—when there were more screams and gunshots up on Cotton Street. Glass broke. There was a splintering sound—wood—and then a big clanging, banging sound—metal. The cruiser started to rev again. It seems like that's all I've heard for two days, that cruiser revving. He peeled out, and then I could hear him coming my way. I only had a second to think, but I don't guess I would have done anything different even if I'd had longer. I ran.

"I wanted to get back to my car and drive away, but I didn't think there was time. I didn't think there was even time to get back around the corner and out of sight. So I went into the grocery store. Worrell's. Wendy Worrell was lying dead by the cash register. Her dad—he's the butcher as well as the owner—was sitting in the little office area, shot in the head. His shirt was off. He must have been just changing into his whites when it happened."

"Hugh starts work early," Billingsley said. "Lots earlier than the rest of his family."

"Oh, but Entragian keeps coming back and *checking*," Audrey said. Her voice was light, conversational, hysterical. "That's what makes him so dangerous. *He keeps coming back and checking.* He's crazy and he has no mercy, but he's also *methodical.*"

"He's one sick puppy, though," Johnny said. "When he

brought me into town, he was on the verge of bleeding out, and that was six hours ago. If whatever's happening to him hasn't slowed down . . ." He shrugged.

"Don't let him trick you," she almost whispered.

Johnny understood what she was suggesting, knew from what he had seen with his own eyes that it was impossible, knew also that telling her so would be a waste of breath.

"Go on," Steve said. "What then?"

"I tried to use the phone in Mr. Worrell's office. It was dead. I stayed in the back of the store for about a half an hour. The cruiser went by twice during that time, once on Main Street, then around the back, probably on Mesquite, or Cotton again. There were more gunshots. I went upstairs to where the Worrells live, thinking maybe the phone up there would still be live. It wasn't. Neither was Mrs. Worrell or the boy. Mert, I think his name was. She was in the kitchen with her head in the sink and her throat cut. He was still in bed. The blood was everywhere. I stood in his doorway, looking in at his posters of rock musicians and basketball players, and outside I could hear the cruiser going by again, fast, accelerating.

"I went down the back way, but I didn't dare open the back door once I got there. I kept imagining him crouched down below the porch, waiting for me. I mean, I'd just heard him go by, but I still kept imagining him waiting for me.

"I decided the best thing I could do was wait for dark. Then I could drive away. Maybe. You couldn't be sure. Because he was just so *unpredictable.* He wasn't *always* on Main Street and you couldn't *always* hear him and you'd start thinking well, maybe he's gone, headed for the hills, and then he'd be back, like a damn rabbit coming out of a magician's hat.

"But I couldn't stay in the store. The sound of the flies was driving me crazy, for one thing, and it was hot. I don't usually mind the heat, you can't mind it if you live in central Nevada, but I kept thinking I *smelled* them. So I waited until I heard him

shooting somewhere over by the town garage—that's on Du-
mont Street, about as far east as you can go before you run out
of town—and then I left. Stepping out of the market and back
onto the sidewalk was one of the hardest things I've ever done
in my life. Like being a soldier and stepping out into no-man's-
land. At first I couldn't move at all; I just froze right where I
was. I remember thinking that I *had* to walk, I couldn't run
because I'd panic if I did, but I had to walk. Except I couldn't.
Couldn't. It was like being paralyzed. Then I heard him coming
back. It was weird. As if he sensed me. Sensed *someone,* anyway,
moving around while his back was turned. Like he was playing
a new kind of kid's game, one where you got to murder the losers instead of just sending them back to the Prisoner's Base, or
something. The engine . . . it's so loud when it starts to rev. So
powerful. So *loud.* Even when I'm not hearing it, I'm *imagining*
I hear it. You know? It sounds kind of like a catamount getting f . . . like a wildcat in heat. That's what I heard coming
toward me, and still I couldn't move. I could only stand there
and listen to it getting closer. I thought about the Tastykake
man, how he was shivering like the jay I shot when I was a kid,
and that finally got me going. I went into the laundrymat and
threw myself down on the floor just as he went by. I heard more
screaming north of town, but I don't know what that was about,
because I couldn't look up. I couldn't *get* up. I must have lain
there on that floor for almost twenty minutes, that's how bad I
was. I can say I was way beyond scared by then, but I can't make
you understand how weird it gets in your head when you're that
way. I lay there on the floor, looking at dust-balls and mashed-
up cigarette butts and thinking how you could tell this was a
laundrymat even down at the level I was, because of the smell
and because all of the butts had lipstick on them. I lay there
and I couldn't have moved even if I'd heard him coming up the
sidewalk. I would have lain there until he put the barrel of his
gun on the side of my head and—"

"Don't," Mary said, wincing. "Don't talk about it."

"*But I can't stop thinking about it!*" she shouted, and something about that jagged on Johnny Marinville's ear as nothing else she'd said had. She made a visible effort to get herself under control, then went on. "What got me past that was the sound of people outside. I got up on my knees and crawled over to the door. I saw four people across the street, by the Owl's. Two were Mexican—the Escolla boy who works on the crusher up at the mine, and his girlfriend. I don't know her name, but she's got a blonde streak in her hair—natural, I'm almost sure—and she's awfully pretty. *Was* awfully pretty. There was another woman, quite heavy, I'd never seen her before. The man with her I've seen playing pool with you in Bud's, Tom. Flip somebody."

"Flip Moran? You saw the Flipper?"

She nodded. "They were working their way up the other side of the street, trying cars, looking for keys. I thought about mine, and how we could all go together. I started to get up. They were passing that little alley over there, the one between the storefront where the Italian restaurant used to be and The Broken Drum, and Entragian came roaring right out of the alley in his cruiser. Like he'd been waiting for them. Probably he *was* waiting for them. He hit them all, but I think your friend Flip was the only one killed outright. The others just went skidding off to one side, like bowling-pins when you miss a good hit. They kind of grabbed each other to keep from falling down. Then they ran. The Escolla boy had his arm around his girlfriend. She was crying and holding her arm against her breasts. It was broken. You could see it was, it looked like it had an extra joint in it above the elbow. The other woman had blood pouring down her face. When she heard Entragian coming after them—that big, powerful engine—she spun around and held her hands up like she was a crossing guard or something. He was driving with his right hand and leaning out the window like a locomotive engineer. He shot her twice before he hit her with the car and ran her under. That was the first really good look I got at him, the first time I knew for sure who I was dealing with."

She looked at them one by one, as if trying to measure the effect her words were having.

"He was grinning. Grinning and laughing like a kid on his first visit to Disney World. Happy, you know? Happy."

3

Audrey had crouched there at the laundrymat door, watching Entragian chase the Escolla boy and his girl north on Main Street with the cruiser. He caught them and ran them down as he had the older woman—it was easy to get them both at once, she said, because the boy was trying to help the girl, the two of them were running together. When they were down, Entragian had stopped, backed up, backed slowly *over* them (there had been no wind then, Audrey told them, and she had heard the sound of their bones snapping very clearly), got out, walked over to them, knelt between them, put a bullet in the back of the girl's head, then took off the Escolla boy's hat, which had stayed on through everything, and put a bullet in the back of *his* head.

"Then he put the hat back on him again," Audrey said. "If I live through this, that's one thing I'll never forget, no matter how long I live—how he took the boy's hat off to shoot him, then put it back on again. It was as if he was saying he understood how hard this was on them, and he wanted to be as considerate as possible."

Entragian stood up, turned in a circle (reloading as he did), seeming to look everywhere at once. Audrey said he was wearing a big, goony smile. Johnny knew the kind she meant. He had seen it. In a crazy way it seemed to him he had seen *all* of this—in a dream, or another life.

It's just dem old kozmic Vietnam blues again, he told himself. The way she described the cop reminded him of certain stoned troopers he had run with, and certain stories he had been told late at night—whispered tales from grunts who had seen guys, *their own guys,* do terrible, unspeakable things with that same look of immaculate good cheer on their faces. *It's Vietnam, that's all, coming at you like an acid flashback. All you need now to complete the circle is a transistor radio sticking out of someone's pocket, playing "People Are Strange" or "Pictures of Matchstick Men."*

But *was* that all? A deeper part of him seemed to doubt the idea. That part thought something else was going on here, something which had little or nothing to do with the paltry memories of a novelist who had fed on war like a buzzard on carrion . . . and had subsequently produced exactly the sort of bad book such behavior probably warranted.

All right, then—if it's not you, what is it?

"What did you do then?" Steve asked her.

"Went back to the laundrymat office. I crawled. And when I got there, I crawled into the kneehole under the desk and curled up in there and went to sleep. I was very tired. Seeing all those things . . . all that death . . . it made me very tired.

"It was thin sleep. I kept hearing things. Gunshots, explosions, breaking glass, screams. I have no idea how much of it was real and how much was just in my mind. When I woke up, it was late afternoon. I was sore all over, at first I thought it had all been a dream, that I might even still be camping. Then I opened my eyes and saw where I was, curled up under a desk, and I smelled bleach and laundry soap, and realized I had to pee worse than ever in my life. Also, both my legs were asleep.

"I started wiggling out from under the desk, telling myself not to panic if I got a little stuck, and that was when I heard somebody come into the front of the store, and I yanked myself back under the desk again. It was him. I knew it just by the way he walked. It was the sound of a man in boots.

"He goes, 'Is anyone here?' and came up the aisle between the washers and dryers. Like he was following my tracks. In a way he was. It was my perfume. I hardly ever wear it, but putting on a dress made me think of it, made me think it might make things go a little smoother at my meeting with Mr. Symes." She shrugged, maybe a little embarrassed. "You know what they say about using the tools."

Cynthia looked blank at this, but Mary nodded.

"'It smells like Opium,' he says. '*Is* it, miss? Is that what you're wearing?' I didn't say anything, just curled up there in the kneehole with my arms wrapped around my head. He goes, 'Why don't you come out? If you come out, I'll make it quick. If I have to find you, I'll make it slow.' And I *wanted* to come out, that's how much he'd gotten to me. How much he'd scared me. I believed he knew for sure that I was still in there somewhere, and that he was going to follow the smell of my perfume to me like a bloodhound, and I wanted to get out from under the desk and go to him so he'd kill me quick. I wanted to go to him the way the people at Jonestown must have wanted to stand in line to get the Kool-Aid. Only I couldn't. I froze up again and all I could do was lie there and think that I was going to die needing to pee. I saw the office chair—I'd pulled it out so I could get into the knee-hole of the desk—and I thought, 'When he sees where the *chair* is, he'll know where *I* am.' That was when he came into the office, while I was thinking that. 'Is someone in here?' he goes. 'Come on out. I won't hurt you. I just want to question you about what's going on. We've got a big problem.'"

Audrey began to tremble, as Johnny supposed she had trembled while she had been hedgehogged in the kneehole of the desk, waiting for Entragian to come the rest of the way into the room, find her, and kill her. Except she was smiling, too, the kind of smile you could hardly bring yourself to look at.

"That's how crazy he was." She clasped her shaking hands together in her lap. "In one breath he says that if you come out he'll reward you by killing you quick; in the next he says he just wants to ask you a few questions. Crazy. But I believed both things at once. So who's the craziest one? Huh? Who's the craziest one?

"He came a couple of steps into the room. I think it was a couple. Far enough for his shadow to fall over the desk and onto the other side, where I was. I remember thinking that if his shadow had eyes, they'd be able to see me. He stood there a long time. I could hear him breathing. Then he said 'Fuck it' and left. A minute or so later, I heard the street door open and close. At first I was sure it was a trick. In my mind's eye I could see him just as clearly as I can see you guys now, opening the door and then closing it again, but still standing there on the inside, next to the machine with the little packets of soap in it. Standing there with his gun out, waiting for me to move. And you know what? I went on thinking that even after he started roaring around the streets in his car again, looking for other people to murder. I think I'd be under there still, except I knew that if I didn't go to the bathroom I was going to wet my pants, and I didn't want to do that. Huh-uh, no way. If he was able to smell my perfume, he'd smell fresh urine even quicker. So I crawled out and went to the bathroom—I hobbled like an old lady because my legs were still asleep, but I got there."

And although she spoke for another ten minutes or so, Johnny thought that was where Audrey Wyler's story essentially ended, with her hobbling into the office bathroom to take a leak. Her car was close by and she had the keys in her dress pocket, but it might as well have been on the moon instead of Main Street for all the good it was to her. She'd gone back and forth several times between the office and the laundrymat proper (Johnny didn't doubt for a moment the courage it must have taken to move around even that much), but she had gone no farther. Her nerve wasn't just shot, it was shattered. When the gunshots and the maddening, ceaselessly revving engine stopped for awhile, she would think about making a break for it, she said, but then she would imagine Entragian catching up to her, running her off the road, pulling her out of her car, and shooting her in the head. Also, she told them, she had been convinced that help would arrive. *Had* to. Desperation was off the main road, yes, sure, but not *that* far off, and with the mine getting ready to reopen, people were always coming and going.

Some people *had* come into town, she said. She had seen a Federal Express panel truck around five that afternoon and a Wickoff County Light and Power pickup around noon of the next day, yesterday. Both went by on Main Street. She had heard music coming from the pickup. She didn't hear Entragian's cruiser that time, but five minutes or so after the pickup passed the laundrymat, there were more gunshots, and a man screaming "Oh, don't! Oh, don't!" in a voice so high it could have been a girl's.

After that, another endless night, not wanting to stay, not quite daring to try and make a break for it, eating snacks from the machine that stood at the end of the dryers, drinking water from the basin in the bathroom. Then a new day, with Entragian still circling like a vulture.

She hadn't been aware, she said, that he was bringing people into town and jugging them. By then all she'd been able to think about were plans for getting away, none of them seeming quite good enough. And, in a way, the laundrymat had begun to feel like home . . . to feel *safe*. Entragian had been in here once, had left, and hadn't returned. He might *never* return.

"I hung onto the idea that he couldn't have gotten *everyone*, that there had to be others like me, who saw what was going on in time to get their heads down. Some would get out. They'd call the State Police. I kept telling myself it was wiser, at least for the time being, to wait. Then the storm came, and I decided to try to use it for cover. I'd sneak back to the mining office. There's an ATV in the garage of the Hideaway—"

Steve nodded. "We saw it. Got a little cart filled with rock samples behind it."

"My idea was to unhook the gondola and drive northwest back to Highway 50. I could grab a compass out of a supply cabinet, so even in the blow I'd be okay. Of course I knew I might go falling into a crevasse or something, but that didn't seem like much of a risk, not after what I'd seen. And I had to get out. Two nights in a laundrymat . . . hey, *you* try it. I was getting ready to do it when you two came along."

"I damn near brained you," Steve said. "Sorry about that."

She smiled wanly, then looked around once more. "And the rest you know," she said.

I don't agree, Johnny Marinville thought. The throb in his nose was increasing again. He wanted a drink, and badly. Since that would be madness—for him, anyway—he pulled the bottle of aspirin out of his pocket and took two with a sip of spring-water. *I don't think we know anything. Not yet, anyway.*

4

Mary Jackson said: "What do we do now? How do we get out of this mess? Do we even try, or do we wait to be rescued?"

For a long time no one replied. Then Steve shifted in the chair he was sharing with Cynthia and said, "We *can't* wait. Not for long, anyway."

"Why do you say that?" Johnny asked. His voice was curiously gentle, as if he already knew the answer to this question.

"Because *somebody* should've gotten away, gotten to a phone outside of town and pulled the plug on the murder-machine.

No one did, though. Even before the storm started, no one did. Something very powerful's happening here, and I think that counting on help from the outside may only get us killed. We have to count on each other, and we have to get out as soon as possible. That's what I believe."

"I'm not going without finding out what happened to my mom," David said.

"You can't think that way, son," Johnny said.

"Yes I can. I *am*."

"No," Billingsley said. Something in his voice made David raise his head. "Not with other lives at stake. Not when you're . . . special, the way you are. We need you, son."

"That's not fair," David almost whispered.

"No," Billingsley agreed. His lined face was stony. "It ain't."

Cynthia said, "It won't do your mother any good if you—and the rest of us—die trying to find her, kiddo. On the other hand, if we can get out of town, we could come back with help."

"Right," Ralph said, but he said it in a hollow, sick way.

"No, it's *not* right," David said. "It's a crock of *shit*, that's what it is."

"*David!*"

The boy surveyed them, his face fierce with anger and sick with fright. "None of you care about my mother, not one of you. Even you don't, Dad."

"That's untrue," Ralph said. "And it's a cruel thing to say."

"Yeah," David said, "but I think it's true, just the same. I know you love her, but I think you'd leave her because you believe she's already dead." He fixed his father with his gaze, and when Ralph looked down at his hands, tears oozing out of his swollen eye, David switched to the veterinarian. "And I'll tell *you* something, Mr. Billingsley. Just because I pray doesn't mean I'm a comic-book wizard or something. Praying's not magic. The only magic I know is a couple of card tricks that I usually mess up on anyway."

"David—" Steve began.

"If we go away and come back, it'll be too late to save her! I know it will be! I *know* that!" His words rang from the stage like an actor's speech, then died away. Outside, the indifferent wind gusted.

"David, it's probably already too late," Johnny said. His voice was steady enough, but he couldn't quite look at the kid as he said it.

Ralph sighed harshly. His son went to him, sat beside him, took his hand. Ralph's face was drawn with weariness and confusion. He looked older now.

Steve turned to Audrey. "You said you knew another way out."

"Yes. The big earthwork you see as you come into town is the north face of the pit we've reopened. There's a road that goes up the side of it, over the top, and into the pit. There's another one that goes back to Highway 50 west of here. It runs along Desperation Creek, which is just a dry-wash now. You know where I mean, Tom?"

He nodded.

"That road—Desperation Creek Road—starts at the motorpool. There are more ATVs there. The biggest only seats four safely, but we could hook up an empty gondola and the other three could ride in it."

Steve, a ten-year veteran of load-ins, load-outs, snap decisions, and rapid getaways (often necessitated by the combination of four-star hotels and rock-band assholes), had been following her carefully. "Okay, what I suggest is this. We wait until morning. Get some rest, maybe even a little sleep. The storm might blow itself out by then—"

"I think the wind *has* let up a little," Mary said. "Maybe that's wishful thinking, but I really think it has."

"Even if it's still going, we can get up to the motorpool, can't we, Audrey?"

"I'm sure we can."

"How far is it?"

"Two miles from the mining office, probably a mile and a half from here."

He nodded. "And in daylight, we'll be able to see Entragian. If we try to go at night, in the storm, we can't count on that."

"We can't count on being able to see the . . . the wildlife, either," Cynthia said.

"I'm talking about moving fast and armed," Steve said. "If the storm plays out, we can head up to the embankment in my truck—three up front in the cab with me, four back in the box. If the weather is still bad—and I actually hope it will be—I think we should go on foot. We'll attract less attention that way. He might never even know we're gone."

"I imagine the Escolla boy and his friends were thinking about the same way when Collie ran em down," Billingsley said.

"They were headed north on Main Street," Johnny said. "Exactly what Entragian would have been looking for. We'll be going *south,* toward the mine, at least initially, and leaving the area on a feeder road."

"Yeah," Steve said. "And then bang, we're gone." He went over to David—the boy had left his father and was sitting on the edge of the stage, staring out over the tacky old theater seats—and squatted beside him. "But we'll come back. You hear me, David? We'll come back for your mom, and for anyone else he's left alive. That's a rock-solid promise, from me to you."

David went on staring out over the seats. "I don't know what to do," he said. "I know I need to ask God to help me straighten out my head, but right now I'm so mad at him that I can't. Every time I try to compose my mind, that gets in the way. He let the cop take my mother! Why? Jesus, *why?*"

Do you know you did a miracle just a little while ago? Steve thought. He didn't say it; it might only make David's confusion and misery worse. After a moment Steve got up and stood looking down at the boy, hands shoved deep into his pockets, eyes troubled.

5

The cougar walked slowly down the alley, head lowered, ears flattened. She avoided the garbage cans and the pile of scrap lumber much more easily than the humans had done; she saw far better in the dark. Still, she paused at the end of the alley, a low, squalling growl rising from her throat. She didn't like this. One of them was strong—very strong. She could sense that one's force even through the brick flank of the building, pulsing like a glow. Still, there was no question of disobedience. The outsider, the one from the earth, was in the cougar's head, its will caught in her mind like a fishhook. That one spoke in the language of the unformed, from the time before, when all animals except for men and the outsider were one.

But she didn't like that sense of force. That glow.

She growled again, a rasp that rose and fell, coming more from her nostrils than her closed mouth. She slipped her head around the corner, wincing at a blast of wind that ruffled her fur and charged her nose with smells of brome grass and Indian paintbrush and old booze and older brick. Even from here she could smell the bitterness from the pit south of town, the smell that had been there since they had charged the last half-dozen blast-holes and reopened the bad place, the one the animals knew about and the men had tried to forget.

The wind died, and the cougar padded slowly down the path between the board fence and the rear of the theater. She stopped to sniff at the crates, spending more time on the one which had been overturned than on the one which still stood against the wall. There were many intermingled scents here. The last person who had stood on the overturned crate had then pushed it off the one still against the wall. The cougar could smell his hands, a different, sharper smell than the others. A skin smell, *undressed* somehow, tangy with sweat and oils. It belonged to a male in the prime of his life.

She could also smell guns. Under other circumstances that smell would have sent her running, but now it didn't matter. She would go where the old one sent her; she had no choice. The cougar sniffed the wall, then looked up at the window. It was unlocked; she could see it moving back and forth in the wind. Not much, because it was recessed, but enough for her to be sure it was open. She could get inside. It would be easy. The window would push in before her, giving way as man-things sometimes did.

No, the voice of the unformed said. *You can't.*

An image flickered briefly in her mind: shiny things. Man-drinkers, sometimes smashed to bright fragments on the rocks when the men were done with them. She understood (in the way that a layperson may vaguely understand a complicated geometry proof, if it is carefully explained) that she would knock a number of these man-drinkers onto the floor if she tried to jump through the window. She didn't know how that could be, but the voice in her head said it was, and that the others would hear them break.

The cougar passed beneath the unlatched window like a dark eddy, paused to sniff at the firedoor, which had been boarded shut, then came to a second window. This one was at the same height as the one with the man-drinkers inside of it, and made of the same white glass, but it wasn't unlatched.

It's the one you'll use, though, the voice in the cougar's head whispered. *When I tell you it's time, that's the one you'll use.*

Yes. She might cut herself on the glass in the window, as she had once cut the pads of her feet on the pieces of man-drinkers up in the hills, but when the voice in her head told her that the time had come, she would jump at the window. Once inside, she would continue to do what the voice told her. It wasn't the way things were supposed to be . . . but for now, it was the way things were.

The cougar lay below the bolted men's-room window, curled her tail around her, and waited for the voice of the thing from the pit. The voice of the outsider. The voice of Tak. When it came, she would move. Until it did, she would lie here and listen to the voice of the wind, and smell the bitterness it brought with it, like bad news from another world.

CHAPTER 3

1

Mary watched the old veterinarian take a bottle of whiskey out of the liquor cabinet, almost drop it, then pour himself a drink. She took a step toward Johnny and spoke to him in a low voice. "Make him stop. That's the one with the drunk in it."

He looked at her with raised eyebrows. "Who elected *you* Temperance Queen?"

"You shithead," she hissed. "Don't you think I know who got him started? Don't you think I *saw*?"

She started toward Tom, but Johnny pulled her back and went himself. He heard her little gasp of pain and supposed he might have squeezed her wrist a little harder than was exactly gentlemanly. Well, he wasn't used to being called a shithead. He had won a National Book Award, after all. He had been on the cover of *Time*. He had also fucked America's sweetheart (well, maybe that was sort of retroactive, or something, she hadn't really been America's sweetheart since 1965 or so, but he *had* still fucked her), and he wasn't used to being called a shithead. Yet, Mary had a point. He, a man not unacquainted with the highways and byways of Alcoholics Anonymous, had nevertheless given that kiddy favorite, Mr. Drunken Doggy Doctor, his first shot of the evening. He'd thought it would pull Billingsley together, get him focused (and they had *needed* him focused, it was his town, after all) . . . but hadn't he also been a teeny-tiny bit pissed off at the tosspot vet awarding himself a loaded gun while The National Book Award Kid had to be contented with an unloaded .22?

No. No, dammit, the gun wasn't the issue. Keeping the old man wired together enough to be of some help, that was the issue.

Well, maybe. Maybe. It felt a little bogus, but you had to give yourself the benefit of the doubt in some situations—especially the crazy ones, which this certainly was. Either way, it maybe hadn't been such a good idea. He had had a large number of not-such-good-ideas in his life, and if anyone was qualified to recognize one when he saw it, John Edward Marinville was probably that fellow.

"Why don't we save that for later, Tom?" he said, and smoothly plucked the glass of whiskey out of the vet's hand just as he was bringing it to his lips.

"Hey!" Billingsley cawed, making a swipe at it. His eyes were more watery than ever, and now threaded with bright red stitches that looked like tiny cuts. "Gimme that!"

Johnny held it away from him, up by his own mouth, and felt a sudden, appallingly strong urge to take care of the problem in the quickest, simplest way. Instead, he put the glass on top of the bar, where ole Tommy wouldn't be able to reach it unless he jumped around to one side or the other. Not that he didn't think Tommy was capable of jumping for a drink; ole Tommy had gotten to a point where he would probably try to fart "The Marine Hymn" if someone promised him a double. Meantime, the others were watching, Mary rubbing her wrist (which *was* red, he observed—but just a little, really no big deal).

"*Gimme!*" Billingsley bawled, and stretched out one hand toward the glass on top of the bar, opening and closing his fingers like an angry baby that wants its sucker back. Johnny suddenly remembered how the actress—the one with the emeralds, the one who had been America's number one honeybunny in days of yore, so sweet sugar wouldn't melt in her snatch—had once pushed him into the pool at the Bel-Air, how everyone had laughed, how he himself had laughed as he came out dripping, with his bottle of beer still in his hand, too drunk to know what was happening, that the flushing sound he heard was the remainder of his reputation going down the shitter. Yes sir and yes ma'am, there he had been on that hot day in Los Angeles, laughing like mad in his wet Pierre Cardin suit, bottle of Bud upraised in one hand like a trophy, everyone else laughing right along with him; they were all having a great old time, he had been pushed into the pool just like in a movie and they were having a great old time, hardy-har and hidey-ho, welcome to the wonderful world of too drunk to know better, let's see you write your way out of this one, Marinville.

He felt a burst of shame that was more for himself than for Tom, although he knew it was Tom they were looking at (except for Mary, who was still making a big deal of her wrist), Tom who was still saying "Gimme that *baack*!" while he clenched and unclenched his hand like Baby Fucking Huey, Tom who was already shot on only three drinks. Johnny had seen this before, too; after a certain number of years spent swimming around in the bottle, drinking everything in sight and yet seeming to remain almost stone-sober, your booze-gills had this weird tendency to suddenly seal themselves shut at almost the first taste. Crazy but true. See the amazing Late-Stage Alcoholic, folks, step right up, you won't believe your eyes.

He put an arm around Tom, leaned into the brown aroma of Dant that hung around the man's head like a fumey halo, and murmured, "Be a good boy now and you can have that shot later."

Tom looked at him with his red-laced eyes. His chapped, cracked lips were wet with spit. "Do you promise?" he whispered back, a conspirator's whisper, breathing out more fumes and running it all together, so it became *Deryapromiz?*

"Yes," Johnny said. "I may have been wrong to get you started, but now that I have, I'm going to maintain you. That's *all* I'll do, though. So have a little dignity, all right?"

Billingsley looked at him. Wide eyes full of water. Red lids. Lips shining. "I can't," he whispered.

Johnny sighed and closed his eyes for a moment. When he opened them again, Billingsley was staring across the stage at Audrey Wyler.

"Why does she have to wear her damned skirt so *short?*" he muttered. The smell of his breath was strong enough for Johnny to decide that maybe this wasn't just a case of three drinks and you're out; Old Snoop Doggy Doc had chipped himself an extra two or three somewhere along the line.

"I don't know," he said, smiling what felt like a big false gameshow host's smile and leading Billingsley back toward the others, getting him turned away from the bar and the drink sitting on top of it. "Are you complaining?"

"No," Billingsley said. "No, I . . . I just . . ." He looked nakedly up at Johnny with his wet drunk's eyes. "What was I talking about?"

"It doesn't matter." A gameshow host's voice was now coming out of the gameshow host's grin: big, hearty, as sincere as a producer's promise to call you next week. "Tell me something—why do they call that hole in the ground China Pit? I've been wondering about that."

"I imagine Miss Wyler knows more about it than I do," Billingsley said, but Audrey was no longer on the stage; as David and his father joined them, looking concerned, Audrey had exited stage-right, perhaps looking for something else to eat.

"Oh, come on," Ralph said, unexpectedly conversational. Johnny looked at him and saw that, despite all his own problems, Ralph Carver understood exactly how the land lay with old Tommy. "I bet you've forgotten more local history than that young lady over there ever learned. And it *is* local history, isn't it?"

"Well . . . yes. History and geology."

"Come on, Tom," Mary said. "Tell us a story. Help pass the time."

"All right," he said. "But it ain't purty, as we say around here."

Steve and Cynthia wandered over. Steve had his arm around the girl's waist; she had hers around his, with her fingers curled in one of his belt-loops.

"Tell it, oldtimer," Cynthia said softly. "Go on."

So he did.

2

"Long before anyone ever thought of mining for copper here, it was gold and silver," Billingsley said. He eased himself down into the wing-chair and shook his head when David offered him a glass of spring-water. "That was long before open-pit mining was thought of, either. In 1858, an outfit called Diablo Mining opened Rattlesnake Number One where the China Pit is now. There was gold, and a good bit of it.

"It was a shaft-mine—back then they all were—and they kept chasing the vein deeper and deeper, although the company had to know how dangerous it was. The surface up there on the south side of where the pit is now ain't bad—it's limestone, skarn, and a kind of Nevada marble. You find wollastonite in it lots of times. Not valuable, but pretty to look at.

"Underneath, on the north side of where the pit is now, that's where they sank the Rattlesnake Shaft. The ground over there is bad. Bad for mining, bad for farming, bad for everything. Sour ground is what the Shoshone called it. They had a word for it, a good one, most Shoshone words are good ones, but I disremember it now. All of this is igneous leavings, you know, stuff that was injected into the crust of the earth by volcanic eruptions that never quite made it to the surface. There's a word for that kind of leavings, but I disremember that one, too."

"Porphyry," Audrey called over to him. She was standing on the right side of the stage, holding a bag of pretzels. "Anyone want some of these? They smell a little funny but they taste all right."

"No, thanks," Mary said. The others shook their heads.

"Porphyry's the word," Billingsley agreed. "It's full of valuable stuff, everything from garnets to uranium, but a lot of it's unstable. The ground where they sank Rattlesnake Number One had a good vein of gold, but mostly it was hornfels—cooked shale. Shale's a sedimentary rock, not strong. You can snap a piece of it in your hands, and when that mine got down seventy feet and the men could hear the walls groaning and squeaking around them, they decided enough was enough. They just walked out. It wasn't a strike for better pay; they just didn't want to die. So what the owners did was hire Chinese. Had them shipped on flatback wagons from Frisco, chained together like convicts. Seventy men and twenty women, all dressed in quilted pajama coats and little round hats. I imagine the owners kicked themselves for not thinking of using them sooner, because they had all sorts of advantages over white men. They didn't get drunk and hooraw through town, they didn't trade liquor to the Shoshone or Paiute, they didn't want whores. They didn't even spit tobacco on the sidewalks. Those were just the bonuses, though. The main thing was they'd go as deep as they were told to go, and never mind the sound of the hornfels squeaking and rubbing in the ground all around them. And the shaft could go deeper faster, because it didn't have to be so big—they were a lot smaller than the white miners, and could be made to work on their knees. Also, any Chinese miner caught with gold-bearing rock on his person could be shot on the spot. And a few were."

"Christ," Johnny said.

"Not much like the old John Wayne movies," Billingsley agreed. "Anyway, they were a hundred and fifty feet down— almost twice as deep as when the white miners threw down their picks—when the cave-in happened. There are all kinds of stories about it. One is that they dug up a *waisin,* a kind of ancient earth-spirit, and it tore the mine down. Another is that they made the tommyknockers mad."

"What're tommyknockers?" David asked.

"Troublemakers," Johnny said. "The underground version of gremlins."

"Three things," Audrey said from her place at stage-right. She was nibbling a pretzel. "First, you call that sort of mine-work a drift, not a shaft. Second, you *drive* a driftway, you don't sink it. Third, it was a cave-in, pure and simple. No tommy-knockers, no earth-spirits."

"Rationalism speaks," Johnny said. "The spirit of the century. Hurrah!"

"I wouldn't go ten feet into that kind of ground," Audrey said, "no sane person would, and there they were, a hundred and fifty feet deep, forty miners, a couple of bossmen, at least five ponies, all of them chipping and tromping and yelling, doing everything but setting off dynamite. What's amazing is how long the tommyknockers *protected* them from their own idiocy!"

"When the cave-in finally *did* happen, it happened in what should have been a good place," Billingsley resumed. "The roof fell in about sixty feet from the adit." He glanced at David. "That's what you call the entrance to a mine, son. The miners got up that far from below, and there they were stopped by twenty feet of fallen hornfels, skarn, and Devonian shale. The whistle went off, and the folks from town came up the hill to see what had happened. Even the whores and the gamblers came up. They could hear the Chinamen inside screaming, begging to be dug out before the rest of it came down. Some said they sounded like they were fighting with each other. But no one wanted to go in and start digging. That squealing sound hornfels makes when the ground's uneasy was louder than ever, and the roof was bowed down in a couple of places between the adit and the first rockfall."

"Could those places have been shored up?" Steve asked.

"Sure, but nobody wanted to take the responsibility for doing it. Two days later, the president and vice president of Diablo Mines showed up with a couple of mining engineers from Reno. They had a picnic lunch outside the adit while they talked over what to do, my dad told me. Ate it spread out on linen while inside that shaft—pardon me, the *drift*—not ninety feet from where they were, forty human souls were screaming in the dark.

"There had been cave-ins deeper in, folks said they sounded like something was farting or burping deep down in the earth, but the Chinese were still okay—still alive, anyway—behind the first rockfall, begging to be dug out. They were eating the mine-ponies by then, I imagine, and they'd had no water or light for two days. The mining engineers went in—poked their heads in, anyway—and said it was too dangerous for any sort of rescue operation."

"So what did they do?" Mary asked.

Billingsley shrugged. "Set dynamite charges at the front of the mine and brought that down, too. Shut her up."

"Are you saying they deliberately buried forty people alive?" Cynthia asked.

"Forty-two counting the line-boss and the foreman," Billingsley said. "The line-boss was white, but a drunk and a man known to speak foul language to decent women. No one spoke up for him. The foreman either, far as that goes."

"How could they do it?"

"Most were Chinese, ma'am," Billingsley said, "so it was easy."

The wind gusted. The building trembled beneath its rough caress like something alive. They could hear the faint sound of the window in the ladies' room banging back and forth. Johnny kept waiting for it to yawn wide enough to knock over Billingsley's bottle booby-trap.

"But that's not quite the end of the story," Billingsley said. "You know how stuff like this grows in folks' minds over the years." He put his hands together and wiggled the gnarled fingers. On the movie screen a gigantic bird, a legendary death-kite, seemed to soar. "It grows like shadows."

"Well, what's the end of it?" Johnny asked. Even after all these years he was a sucker for a good story when he heard one, and this one wasn't bad.

"Three days later, two young Chinese fellows showed up at the Lady Day, a saloon which stood about where The Broken Drum is now. Shot seven men before they were subdued. Killed two. One of the ones they killed was the mining engineer from Reno who recommended that the shaft be brought down."

"Drift," Audrey said.

"Quiet," Johnny said, and motioned for Billingsley to go on.

"One of the 'coolie-boys'—that's what they were called—was killed himself in the fracas. A knife in the back, most likely, although the story most people like is that a professional gambler named Harold Brophy flicked a playing-card from where he was sitting and cut the man's throat with it.

"The one still alive was shot in five or six places. That didn't stop em from taking him out and hanging him the next day, though, after a little sawhorse trial in front of a kangaroo court. I bet he was a disappointment to them; according to the story, he was too crazy to have any idea what was happening.

They had chains on his legs and cuffs on his wrists and still he fought them like a catamount, raving in his own language all the while."

Billingsley leaned forward a little, seeming to stare at David in particular. The boy looked back at him, eyes wide and fascinated.

"All of what he said was in the heathen Chinee, but one idea everyone got was that *he and his friend had gotten out of the mine* and come to take revenge on those who first put them there and then left them there."

Billingsley shrugged.

"Most likely they were just two young men from the so-called Chinese Encampment south of Ely, men not quite so passive or resigned as the others. By then the story of the cave-in had travelled, and folks in the Encampment would have known about it. Some probably had relatives in Desperation. And you have to remember that the one who actually survived the shootout didn't have any English other than cuss-words. Most of what they got from him must have come from his gestures. And you know how people love that last twist of the knife in a tall tale. Why, it wasn't a year before folks were saying the Chinese miners were *still* alive in there, that they could hear em talking and laughing and pleading to be let out, moaning and promising revenge."

"Would it have been possible for a couple of men to have gotten out?" Steve asked.

"No," Audrey said from the doorway.

Billingsley glanced her way, then turned his puffy, red-rimmed eyes on Steve. "I reckon," he said. "The two of them might've started back down the shaft together, while the rest clustered behind the rockfall. One of em might have remembered a vent or a chimney—"

"Bullshit," Audrey said.

"It *ain't*," Billingsley said, "and you know it. This is an old volcano-field. There's even extrusive porphyry east of town—looks like black glass with chips of ruby in it: garnets, they are. And wherever there's volcanic rock, there's shafts and chimneys."

"The chances of two men ever—"

"It's just a hypothetical case," Mary said soothingly. "A way of passing the time, that's all."

"Hypothetical bullshit," Audrey grumbled, and ate another dubious pretzel.

"Anyway, that's the story," Billingsley said, "miners buried alive, two get out, both insane by then, and they try to take their revenge. Later on, ghosts in the ground. If that ain't a tale for a stormy night, I don't know what is." He looked across at Audrey, and on his face was a sly drunk's smile. "You been diggin up there, miss. You new folks. Haven't come across any short bones, have you?"

"You're drunk, Mr. Billingsley," she said coldly.

"No," he said. "I wish I was, but I ain't. Excuse me, ladies and gents. I get yarning and I get the whizzies. It never damn fails."

He crossed the stage, head down, shoulders slumped, weaving slightly. The shadow which followed him was ironic both in its size and its heroic aspect. His bootheels clumped. They watched him go.

There was a sudden flat smacking sound that made them all jump. Cynthia smiled guiltily and raised her sneaker. "Sorry," she said. "A spider. I think it was one of those fiddle-heads."

"Fiddle*backs,*" Steve said.

Johnny bent down to look, hands planted on his legs just above the knees. "Nope."

"Nope, what?" Steve asked. "Not a fiddleback?"

"Not a singleton," Johnny said. "A pair." He looked up, not quite smiling. "Maybe," he said, "they're *Chinese* fiddlebacks."

3

Tak! Can ah wan me. Ah lah.

The cougar's eyes opened. She got up. Her tail began switching restlessly from side to side. It was almost time. Her ears cocked forward, twitching, at the sound of someone entering the room behind the white glass. She looked up at it, all rapt attention, a net of measurement and focus. Her leap would have to be perfect to carry her through, and perfection was exactly what the voice in her head demanded.

She waited, that small, squalling growl once more rising up from her throat . . . but now it came out of her mouth as well as from her nostrils, because her muzzle was wrinkled back to show her teeth. Little by little, she began to tense down on her haunches.

Almost time.

Almost time.

Tak ah ten.

4

Billingsley poked his head into the ladies' first, and shone his light at the window. The bottles were still in place. He had been afraid that a strong gust of wind might open the window wide enough to knock some of them off the ledge, causing a false alarm, but that hadn't happened and now he thought it very unlikely that it would. The wind was dying. The storm, a summer freak the likes of which he had never seen, was winding down.

Meantime, he had this problem. This thirst to quench.

Except, in the last five years or so, it had come to seem less and less like a thirst than an *itch,* as if he had contracted some awful form of poison ivy—a kind that affected one's brain instead of one's skin. Well, it didn't matter, did it? He knew how to take care of his problem, and that was the important thing. And it kept his mind off the rest, as well. The madness of the rest. If it had just been danger, someone out of control waving a gun around, that he thought he could have faced, old or not, drunk or not. But this was nothing so cut and dried. The geologist woman kept insisting that it *was,* that it was all Entragian, but Billingsley knew better. Because Entragian was different now. He'd told the others that, and Ellen Carver had called him crazy. But . . .

But *how* was Entragian different? And why did he, Billingsley, somehow feel that the change in the deputy was important, perhaps vital, to them right now? He didn't know. He *should* know, it should be as clear as the nose on his face, but these days when he drank everything got swimmy, like he was going senile. He couldn't even remember the name of the geologist woman's horse, the mare with the strained leg—

"Yes I can," he murmured. "Yes I can, it was . . ."

Was what, *you old rummy? You don't know, do you?*

"Yes I do, it was Sally!" he cried triumphantly, then walked past the boarded-up firedoor and pushed his way into the men's room. He shone his flashlight briefly on the potty. "Sally, that's what it was!" He shifted his light to the wall and the smoke-breathing horse which galloped there. He couldn't remember drawing it—he'd been in a blackout, he supposed—but it was indubitably his work, and not bad of its kind. He liked the way the horse looked both mad and free, as if it had come from some other world where goddesses still rode bareback, sometimes leaping whole leagues as they went their wild courses.

His memories suddenly clarified a little, as if the picture on the wall had somehow opened his mind. Sally, yes. A year ago, give or take. The rumors that the mine was going to be reopened were just beginning to solidify into acknowledged fact. Cars and trucks had started to show up in the parking lot of the Quonset hut that served as mining headquarters, planes had started to fly into the airstrip south of town, and he had been told one night—right here in The American West, as a matter of fact, drinking with the boys—that there was a lady geologist living out at the old Rieper place. Young. Single. Supposedly pretty.

Billingsley needed to pee, he hadn't lied, but that wasn't his strongest need right now. There was a filthy blue rag in one of the washbasins, the sort of thing you wouldn't handle without tongs unless you absolutely needed to. The old veterinarian now plucked it up, exposing a bottle of Satin Smooth, rotgut whiskey if ever rotgut whiskey had been bottled . . . but any port in a storm.

He unscrewed the cap and then, holding the bottle in both hands because of the way they were shaking, took a long, deep drink. Napalm slid down his throat and exploded in his gut. It burned, all right, but what was that Patty Loveless song that used to play all the time on the radio? Hurt me, baby, in a real good way.

He chased the first gulp with a smaller sip (holding the bottle easier, now; the shakes were gone), then replaced the cap and put the bottle back in the sink.

"She called me," he muttered. Outside the window, the cougar's ears flicked at the sound of his voice. She tensed down a little more on her haunches, waiting for him to move closer to where she was, closer to where her leap would bring her. "Woman called me on the phone. Said her horse was a three-year-old mare named Sally. Yessir."

He put the rag back over the bottle, not thinking about it, hiding by habit, his mind on that day last summer. He had gone out to the Rieper place, a nice adobe up in the hills, and a fellow from the mine—the black guy who later became the office receptionist, in fact—had taken him to the horse. He

said Audrey had just gotten an urgent call and was going to
have to fly off to company headquarters in Phoenix. Then, as
they walked to the stable, the black fellow had looked over
Billingsley's shoulder and had said . . .

"He said, 'There she goes now,'" Billingsley murmured.
He had again focused the light on the horse galloping across
the warped tiles and was staring at it with wide, remembering eyes, his bladder temporarily forgotten. "And he called to
her."

Yessir. *Hi, Aud!* he'd called, and waved. She had waved
back. Billingsley had also waved, thinking the stories were
right: she *was* young, and she *was* goodlooking. Not moviestar-
knockout goodlooking, but mighty fine for a part of the world
where *no* single woman had to pay for her own drinks if she
didn't want to. He had tended her horse, had given the black
man a liniment sample to put on, and later she'd come in
herself to buy more. Marsha had told him that; he'd been over
near Washoe, looking after some sick sheep. He'd seen her
around town plenty since, though. Not to talk to, nosir, not
hardly, they ran with different crowds, but he'd seen her eating
dinner in the Antlers Hotel or the Owl's, once at The Jailhouse
in Ely; he'd seen her drinking in Bud's Suds or the Drum with
some of the other mining folk, rolling dice out of a cup to see
who'd pay; in Worrell's Market, buying groceries, at the Conoco, buying gas, in the hardware store one day, buying a can of
paint and a brush, yessir, he had seen her around, in a town this
small and this isolated you saw *everybody* around, had to.

Why are you running all this through your dumb head? he asked
himself, at last starting toward the potty. His boots gritted in
dirt and dust, in grout that had crumbled out from between
decaying tiles. He stopped still a little bit beyond aiming-and-
shooting distance, flashlight beam shining on the scuffed tip of
one boot while he pulled down his fly. What did Audrey Wyler
have to do with Collie? What *could* she have to do with Collie?

He didn't recall ever seeing them together, or hearing that they were an item, it wasn't that. So what *was* it? And why did his mind keep insisting it had something to do with the day he'd gone out to look at her mare? He hadn't even *seen* her that day. Well . . . for a minute . . . from a distance . . .

He lined himself up with the potty and pulled out the old hogleg. Boy, he had to go. Drink a pint and piss a quart, wasn't that what they said?

Her waving . . . hurrying for her car . . . headed for the air-strip . . . headed for Phoenix. Wearing a business-suity kind of rig, sure, because she wasn't going to any Quonset hut mining headquarters out in the desert, she was going someplace where there was a carpet on the floor and the view was from more than three stories up. Going to see the big boys. Nice legs she had . . . I'm getting on but I ain't too old to appreciate a pretty knee . . . nice, yessir, but—

And suddenly it all came together in his mind, not with a click but with a big loud *ka-pow*, and for a moment, before the cougar uttered her coughing, rising growl, he thought the sound of breaking glass was in his mind, that it was the sound of understanding.

Then the growl began, quickly rising to a howl that started him urinating in pure fear. For a moment it was impossible to associate that sound with anything which had ever walked on the earth. He wheeled, spraying a pin-wheel of piss, and saw a dark, green-eyed shape splayed out on the tiles. Bits of broken glass gleamed in the fur on its back. He knew what it was im-mediately, his mind quickly putting the shape together with the sound in spite of his startlement and terror.

The mountain lion—the flashlight showed it to be an ex-tremely large female—raised her face to his and spat at him, revealing two rows of long white teeth. And the .30-.06 was back on the stage, leaned up against the movie screen.

"Oh my God *no*," Billingsley whispered, and threw the flashlight past the cougar's right shoulder, missing it intentionally. When the snarling animal snapped its head around to see what had been thrown at it, Billingsley broke for the door.

He ran with his head down, tucking himself back into his pants with the hand that had been holding the flashlight. The cougar loosed another of its screaming, distraught cries—the shriek of a woman being burned or stabbed, deafening in the closed bathroom—and then launched herself at Billingsley, front paws splayed, long claws out. These sank through his shirt and into his back as he groped for the doorhandle, slicing through scant muscle, flaying him in bloodlines that came together like a V. Her big paws snagged in the waistband of his pants and held for a moment, pulling the old man—who was screaming himself now—back into the room. Then his belt broke and he went tumbling backward, actually landing on top of the cougar. He rolled, hit the glass-littered floor on his side, got to one knee, and then the cougar was on him. She knocked him onto his back and went for his throat. Billingsley got his hand up and she bit off the side of it. Blood beaded on her whiskers like skarn-garnets. Billingsley screamed again and shoved his other hand under the shelf of her chin, trying to push her back, trying to make her let go. He felt her breath on his cheek, pushing like hot fingers. He looked past her shoulder and saw the horse on the wall, *his* horse, prancing wild and free. Then the cougar lunged forward again, shaking his hand in her jaws, and there was only pain. It filled the world.

5

Cynthia was pouring herself a fresh glass of spring-water when the cougar let go its first cry. The sound of it unwound all her nerves and muscles. The plastic bottle slipped from her relaxing fingers, hit the floor between her sneakers, and exploded like a balloon waterbomb. She knew the sound for what it was—the yowl of a wildcat—immediately, although she had never heard such a sound outside of a movie theater. And, of course—weird but true—that was still the case.

Then it was a man screaming. Tom Billingsley screaming.

She turned, saw Steve stare at Marinville, saw Marinville look away, cheeks leaden, lips pressed together but trembling all the same. In that moment the writer looked weak and lost and oddly female with his long gray hair, like an old woman who's lost track not only of where she is but of who she is.

Still, what Cynthia felt most for Johnny Marinville in that moment was contempt.

Steve looked to Ralph, who nodded, grabbed his gun, and ran toward the stage-left opening. Steve caught up with him and they disappeared that way, running abreast. The old man screamed again, but this time the cry had a gruesome liquid quality, as if he were trying to gargle and scream at the same time, and it didn't last long. The cougar yowled again.

Mary went to Steve's boss and held out the shotgun she had up until then barely let go of. "Take it. Go help them."

He looked at her, biting his lip. "Listen," he said. "I have lousy night-vision. I know how that sounds, but—"

The wildcat screamed, the sound so loud it seemed to drill into Cynthia's ears. Gooseflesh danced up her back.

"Yeah, like a gutless blowhard, that's how it sounds," Mary said, and turned away. That got Marinville moving, but slowly, like someone who has been roused from a deep sleep. Cynthia saw Billingsley's rifle leaning against the movie screen and didn't wait for him. She grabbed the gun and sprinted across the stage, going with it held high over her head like a freedom fighter in a poster—not because she wanted to look romantic but because she didn't want to run into something and risk having the gun go off. She might shoot someone up ahead of her.

She ran past a couple of dusty chairs standing by what

looked like a defunct lighting control-panel, then down the
narrow hall they had taken to get to the stage in the first place.
Brick on one side, wood on the other. A smell of old men with
too much time on their hands. And too much jizz, judging
from their video library.

There was another animal scream—much louder now—but
no more noise from the old man. Not a good sign. A door
banged open not far ahead, the sound slightly hollow, the
sound only a public restroom door can make when it's banged
against tile. *So,* she thought. *The men's or the women's, and it must
be the men's, 'cause that's where the toilet is.*

"Look out!" Ralph's voice, raised in a near-scream. *"Jesus
Christ, Steve—"*

From the cat there came a kind of spitting roar. There was
a thud. Steve yelled, although whether in pain or surprise she
couldn't tell. Then there were two deafening explosions. The
muzzle-flashes washed the wall outside the men's room, for a
moment revealing a fire extinguisher on which someone had
hung a ratty old sombrero. She ducked instinctively, then
turned the corner into the bathroom. Ralph Carver was holding the door propped open with his body. The bathroom was
lit only by the old man's flashlight, which lay in the corner
with the lens pointed at the wall, spraying light up the tiles
and kicking back just enough to see by. That faint light and
the rolling smoke from Ralph's discharged rifle gave what she
was looking at a sultry hallucinatory quality that made her
think of her half a dozen experiments with peyote and mesca-
line.

Billingsley was crawling, dazed, toward the urinals, his
head down so far it was dragging on the tiles. His shirt and
undershirt had been torn open down the middle. His back
was pouring blood. He looked as if he had been flogged by a
maniac.

In the middle of the floor, a bizarre waltz was going on. The cougar was up on her hind legs, paws on Steve Ames's shoulders. Blood was pouring down her flanks, but she did not seem to be seriously hurt. One of Ralph's shots must have missed her entirely; Cynthia saw that half of the horse on the wall had been blown to smithereens. Steve had his arms crossed in front of his chest; his elbows and forearms were against the cougar's chest.

"Shoot it!" he screamed. *"For Christ's sake, shoot it again!"*

Ralph, his face a drawn mask of shadows in the faint light, raised the rifle, aimed it, then lowered it again with an anguished expression, afraid of hitting Steve.

The cat shrieked and darted its triangular head forward. Steve snapped his own head back. They tangoed drunkenly that way, the cat's claws digging deeper into Steve's shoulders, and now Cynthia could see blood-blossoms spreading on the coverall he wore, around the places where the cat's claws were dug in. Its tail was lashing madly back and forth.

They did another half-turn, and Steve collided with the potty in the middle of the floor. It crashed over on its side and Steve tottered on the edge of balance, frantically holding off the lunging cougar with his crossed arms. Beyond them, Billingsley had reached the far corner of the men's room yet continued trying to crawl, as if the wildcat's attack had turned him into some sort of windup toy, doomed to go on until he finally ran down.

"Shoot this fucking thing!" Steve yelled. He managed to get one foot between the lower part of the potty's frame and its canvas catchbag without falling, but now he was out of backing room; in a moment or two the cougar would push him over. *"Shoot it, Ralph, SHOOT IT!"*

Ralph raised the rifle again, eyes wide, gnawing at his lower lip, and then Cynthia was slammed aside. She reeled across the room and caught the middle washbasin in a line of three just in time to keep herself from smashing face-first into the wall-length steel mirror. She turned and saw Marinville stride into the room with the stock of Mary's gun laid against the inside of his right forearm. His matted gray hair swung back and forth, brushing his shoulders. Cynthia thought she had never seen anyone in her life who looked so terrified, but now that he was in motion, Marinville didn't hesitate; he socked the shotgun's double muzzle against the side of the animal's head.

"Push!" he bellowed, and Steve pushed. The cat's head rocked up and away from him. Its luminous eyes seemed to be lit from within, as if it were not a living thing at all but some sort of jack-o'-lantern. The writer winced, turned his head slightly away, and pulled both triggers. There was a deafening roar that dwarfed the sound of Carver's rifle. Bright light leaped from the barrel, and then Cynthia smelled frying hair. The cougar fell sideways, its head mostly gone, the fur on the back of its neck smouldering.

Steve waved his arms for balance. Marinville, dazed, made only a token effort to catch him, and Steve—her nice new friend—went sprawling.

"Oh Christ, I think I shit myself," Marinville said, almost conversationally, and then: "No, I guess it was just the wind in the willows. Steve, you okay?"

Cynthia was on her knees beside him. He sat up, looked around dazedly, and winced as she tentatively pressed a finger to one of the blood-blossoms on the shoulder of the coverall.

"I think so." He was trying to get up. Cynthia put an arm around his waist, braced, hauled. "Thanks, boss."

"I don't believe it," Marinville said. He sounded completely natural to Cynthia for the first time since she'd met him, like a man living a life instead of playing a role. "I don't believe I did it. That woman shamed me into it. Steven, *are* you all right?"

"He's got punctures," Cynthia said, "but never mind that now. We have to help the old guy."

Mary came in with Marinville's gun—the one that was

unloaded—held up by one shoulder. Her hands were wrapped around the end of the barrel. To Cynthia her face looked almost eerily composed. She surveyed the scene—even more dreamlike now, not just tinged with gunsmoke but hazed with it—and then hurried across the room toward Billingsley, who made two more tired efforts to crawl into the wall and then collapsed from the knees upward, his face going last, first tilting and then sliding down the tiles.

Ralph reached for Steve's shoulder, saw the blood there, and settled for gripping his arm high on the bicep. "I couldn't," he said. "I wanted to, but I couldn't. After the first two rounds I was afraid of hitting you instead of it. When you finally got turned around so I could make a side-shot, Marinville was there."

"It's okay," Steve said. "All's well that ends well."

"I owed it to him," the writer said with a winning-quarterback expansiveness Cynthia found rather nauseating. "If it hadn't been for me, he wouldn't have been here in the—"

"Get over here!" Mary said, her voice cracking. "Jesus Christ, oh man, he's bleeding so *bad*!"

The four of them gathered around Mary and Billingsley. She had gotten him onto his back, and Cynthia winced at what she saw. One of the old geezer's hands was mostly gone—all the fingers but the pinky chewed to stubs—but that wasn't the worst. His lower neck and shoulder had been flayed open. Blood was spilling out in freshets. Yet he was awake, his eyes bright and aware.

"Skirt," he whispered hoarsely. *"Skirt."*

"Don't try to talk, oldtimer," Marinville said. He bent, scooped up the flashlight, and trained it on Billingsley. It made what had looked bad enough in the shadows even worse. There was a pond of blood beside the old guy's head; Cynthia didn't understand how he could still be alive.

"I need a compress," Mary said. "Don't just stand there, *help* me, he's going to die if we don't stop the bleeding *right now*!"

Too late, babe, Cynthia thought but didn't say.

Steve saw what looked like a rag in one of the sinks and grabbed it. It turned out to be a very old shirt with Joe Camel on it. He folded the shirt twice, then handed it to Mary. She nodded, folded it once more, then pressed it against the side of Billingsley's neck.

"Come on," Cynthia said, taking Steve's arm. "Back on stage. If there's nothing else, I can at least wash those out with water from the bar. There's plenty on the bottom sh—"

"No," the old man whispered. "Stay! Got to . . . hear this."

"You can't talk," Mary said. She pushed harder on the side of his neck with the makeshift compress. The shirt was already darkening. "You'll never stop bleeding if you talk."

He rolled his eyes toward Mary. "Too late . . . f'doctorin." His voice was hoarse. "Dyin."

"No you're not, that's ridiculous."

"Dyin," he repeated, and moved violently beneath her hands. His torn back squelched on the tiles, a sound that made Cynthia feel nauseated. "Get down here . . . all of you, close . . . and listen to me."

Steve glanced at Cynthia. She shrugged, then the two of them knelt beside the old man's leg, Cynthia shoulder to shoulder with Mary Jackson. Marinville and Carver leaned in from the sides.

"He shouldn't talk," Mary said, but she sounded doubtful.

"Let him say what he needs to," Marinville said. "What is it, Tom?"

"Too short for business," Billingsley whispered. He was looking up at them, begging them with his eyes to understand.

Steve shook his head. "I'm not getting you."

Billingsley wet his lips. "Only seen her once before in a dress. That's why it took me too long to figure out . . . what was wrong."

A startled expression had come over Mary's face. "That's right, she said she had a meeting with the comptroller! He comes all the way from Phoenix to hear her report on something important, something that means big bucks, and she puts on a dress so short she'll be flashing her pants at him every time she crosses her legs? I don't think so."

Beads of sweat ran down Billingsley's pale, stubbly cheeks like tears. "Feel so stupid," he wheezed. "Not all my fault, though. Nope. Didn't know her to talk to. Wasn't there the one time she came into the office to pick up more liniment. Always saw her at a distance, and out here women mostly wear jeans. But I had it. I did. Had it and then got drinking and lost track of it again." He looked at Mary. "The dress would have been all right . . . when she put it on. Do you see? Do you understand?"

"What's he talking about?" Ralph asked. "How could it be all right when she put it on and too short for a business meeting later?"

"Taller," the old man whispered.

Marinville looked at Steve. "What was that? It sounded like he said—"

"*Taller,*" Billingsley said. He enunciated the word carefully, then began to cough. The folded shirt Mary held against his neck and shoulder was now soaked. His eyes rolled back and forth among them. He turned his head to one side, spat out a mouthful of blood, and the coughing fit eased.

"Dear God," Ralph said. "She's like *Entragian*? Is that what you're saying, *that she's like the cop*?"

"Yes . . . no," Billingsley whispered. "Don't know for sure. Would have . . . seen that right away . . . but . . ."

"Mr. Billingsley, do you think she might have caught a milder dose of whatever the cop has?" Mary asked.

He looked at her gratefully and squeezed her hand.

Marinville said, "She's sure not bleeding out like the cop."

"Or not where we can see it," Ralph said. "Not yet, anyway."

Billingsley looked past Mary's shoulder. "Where . . . where . . ."

He began coughing again and wasn't able to finish, but he didn't need to. A startled look passed among them, and Cynthia turned around. Audrey wasn't there.

Neither was David Carver.

CHAPTER 4

1

The thing which had been Ellen Carver, taller now, still wearing the badge but not the Sam Browne belt, stood on the steps of the Municipal Building, staring north along the sand-drifted street, past the dancing blinker-light. It couldn't see the movie theater, but knew where it was. More, it knew what was going on *inside* the movie theater. Not all, but enough to anger it. The cougar hadn't been able to shut the drunk up in time, but at least she had drawn the rest of them away from the boy. That would have been fine, except the boy had eluded its other emissary as well, at least temporarily.

Where had he gone? It didn't know, couldn't see, and that was the source of its anger and fear. *He* was the source. David Carver. The goddamned shitting *prayboy*. It should have killed him when it had been inside the cop and had had the chance—should have shot him right on the steps of his own damned motor home and left him for the buzzards. But it hadn't, and it knew *why* it hadn't. There was a blankness about Master Carver, a shielded quality. That was what had saved Little Prayboy earlier.

Its hands clenched at its sides. The wind gusted, blowing Ellen Carver's short, red-gold hair out like a flag. *Why is he even here, someone like him? Is it an accident? Or was he sent?*

Why are you here? Are you an accident? Were you sent?

Such questions were useless. It knew its purpose, *tak ah lah*, and that was enough. It closed its Ellen-eyes, focusing inward at first, but only for a second—it was unpleasant. This body had already begun to fail. It wasn't a matter of decay so much as *intensity*; the force inside it—*can de lach*, heart of the unformed—was literally pounding it to pieces . . . and its replacements had escaped the pantry.

Because of Prayboy.

Shitting Prayboy.

It turned its gaze outward, not wanting to think about the blood trickling down this body's thighs, or the way its throat had begun to throb, or the way that, when it scratched Ellen's head, large clumps of Ellen's red hair had begun to come away under its nails.

It sent its gaze into the theater instead.

What it saw, it perceived in overlapping, sometimes contradictory images, all fragmentary. It was like watching multiple TV screens reflected in a heap of broken glass. Primarily the eyes of the infiltrating spiders were what it was looking through, but there were also flies, cockroaches, rats peering out of holes in the plaster, and bats hanging from the auditorium's high ceiling. These latter were projecting strange cool images that were actually echoes.

It saw the man from the truck, the one who had come into town on his own, and his skinny little girlfriend leading the others back to the stage. The father was shouting for the boy, but the boy wasn't answering. The writer walked to the edge of the stage, cupped his hands around his mouth, and screamed Audrey's name. And Audrey, where was she? No way of telling for sure. It couldn't see through her eyes as it saw through the eyes of the lesser creatures. She'd gone after the boy, certainly. Or had she already found him? It thought not. Not yet, anyway. That it would have sensed.

It pounded one hand against Ellen's thigh in anxiety and

frustration, leaving an instant bruise like a rotten place on the skin of an apple, then shifted focus once more. No, it saw, they were *not* all onstage; the prismatic quality of what it was seeing had misled it.

Mary was still with old Tom. If Ellen could get to her while the others were preoccupied with Audrey and David, it might solve all sorts of problems later on. It didn't need her now, this current body was still serviceable and would continue so for awhile, but it wouldn't do to have it fail at a crucial moment. It would be better, safer, if . . .

The image that came was of a spiderweb with many silk-wrapped flies dangling from it. Flies that were drugged but not dead.

"Emergency rations," the old one whispered in Ellen Carver's voice, in Ellen Carver's language. "Knick-knack paddywhack, give the dog a bone."

And Mary's disappearance would demoralize the rest, take away any confidence they might have gained from escaping, finding shelter, and killing the cougar. It had thought they might manage that last; they were armed, after all, and the cougar was a physical being, *sarx* and *soma* and *pneuma,* not some goblin from the metaphysical wastes. But who could have imagined that pretentious old windbag doing it?

He called the other one on a phone he had. You didn't guess that, either. You didn't know until the yellow truck came.

Yes, and missing the phone had been a lapse, something right in the front of Marinville's mind that it should have picked up easily, but it didn't hold that against itself. At that point its main goals had been to get the old fool jugged and replace Entragian's body before it could fall apart completely. It had been sorry to lose Entragian, too. Entragian had been *strong.*

If it meant to take Mary, there would never be a better time than now. And perhaps while it did that, Audrey would find the boy and kill him. That would be wonderful. No worries then. No sneaking around. It could replace Ellen with Mary and pick the rest off at its leisure.

And later? When its current (and limited) supply of bodies ran out? Snatch more travellers from the highway? Perhaps. And when people, curious people, came to town to see what the hell was going on in Desperation, what then? It would cross that bridge when it got to the river; it had little memory and even less interest in the future. For now, getting Mary up to China Pit would be enough.

Tak went down the steps of the Municipal Building, glanced at the police-car, then crossed the street on foot. No driving, not for this errand. Once it reached the far sidewalk, it began to run in long strides, sand spurting up from beneath sneakers which had been sprung out to the sides by feet which were now too big for them.

2

Onstage, Audrey could hear them still calling David's name . . . and hers. Soon they would spread out and begin to search. They had guns, which made them dangerous. The idea of being killed didn't bother her—not much, anyway, not as it had at first—but the idea that it might happen before she was able to kill the boy did. To the cougar, the voice of the thing from the earth had been like a fishhook; in Audrey Wyler's mind it was like an acid-coated snake, winding its way into her, melting the personality of the woman who had been here before it even as it enfolded her. This melting sensation was extremely pleasant, like eating some sweet soft food. It hadn't been at first, at first it had been dismaying, like being over-whelmed by a fever, but as she collected more of the *can tahs* (like a child participating in a scavenger hunt), that feeling had passed. Now she only cared about finding the boy. Tak, the unformed one, did not dare approach him, so she must do it in Tak's place.

At the top of the stairs, the woman who had been five-feet-seven on the day Tom Billingsley had first glimpsed her stopped, looking around. She should have been able to see nothing—there was only one window, and the only light that fell through its filthy panes came from the blinker and a single weak streetlamp in front of Bud's Suds—but her vision had improved greatly with each *can tah* she had found or been given. Now she had almost the vision of a cat, and the littered hallway was no mystery to her.

The people who had hung out in this part of the building had been far less neatness-minded than Billingsley and his crew. They had smashed their bottles in the corners instead of collecting them, and instead of fantasy fish or smoke-breathing horses, the walls were decorated with broad Magic Marker pictographs. One of these, as primitive as any cave-drawing, showed a horned and misshapen child hanging from a gigantic breast. Beneath it was scrawled a little couplet: LITTLE BITTY BABY SMITTY, I SEEN YOU BITE YOUR MOMMY'S TITTY. Paper trash—fast-food sacks, candy wrappers, potato-chip bags, empty cigarette packs and condom envelopes—had drifted along both sides of the hall. A used rubber hung from the knob of the door marked MANAGER, pasted there in its own long-dried fluids like a dead snail.

The door to the manager's office was on her right. Across from it was one marked JANITOR. Up ahead on the left was another door, this one unmarked, and then an arch with a word written on it in ancient black paint half flaked away. Even her eyes couldn't make out what the word was, at least from this distance, but a step or two closer and it came clear: BALCONY. The archway had been boarded up, but at some point the boards had been pulled away and heaped to either side of it. Hanging from the top of the arch was a mostly deflated sex-doll with blond Arnel hair, a red-ringed hole of a mouth, and a bald rudimentary vagina. There was a noose around its neck, the coils dark with age. Also around its neck, hanging against the doll's sagging plastic bosom, was a hand-lettered sign which looked as if it might have been made by a hardworking first-grader. It was decorated with a red-eyed skull and crossbones at the top. DON'T COME OUT HERE, it said, REDY TO FALL DOWN, IM SERIAS. Across from the balcony was an alcove which had once probably held a snackbar. At the far end of the hall were more steps going up into darkness. To the projectionist's booth, she assumed.

Audrey went to the door marked MANAGER, grasped the knob, and leaned her brow against the wood. Outside, the wind moaned like a dying thing.

"David?" she asked gently. She paused, listened. "David, do you hear me? It's Audrey, David. Audrey Wyler. I want to help you."

No answer. She opened the door and saw an empty room with an ancient poster for *Bonnie and Clyde* on the wall and a torn mattress on the floor. In the same Magic Marker, someone had written I'M A MIDNIGHT CREEPER, ALL-DAY SLEEPER below the poster.

She tried the janitor's cubby next. It wasn't much bigger than a closet and completely empty. The unmarked door gave on a room that had probably once been a supply closet. Her nose (keener now, like her eyesight) picked up the aroma of long-ago popcorn. There were a lot of dead flies and a fair scattering of mouseshit, but nothing else.

She went to the archway, swept aside the dangling dolly with her forearm, and peered out. She couldn't see the stage from back here, just the top half of the screen. The skinny girl was still yelling for David, but the others were silent. That might not mean anything, but she didn't like not knowing where they were.

Audrey decided that the sign around the dolly's neck was probably a true warning. The seats had been taken out, making it easy to see the way the balcony floor heaved and twisted; it made her think of a poem she'd read in college, something about a painted ship on a painted ocean. If the brat wasn't out on the balcony, he was somewhere else. Somewhere close. He couldn't have gone far. And he *wasn't* on the balcony, that much was for sure. With the seats gone, there was nowhere to hide, not so much as a drape or a velvet swag on the wall.

Audrey dropped the arm which had been holding the half-deflated doll aside. It swung back and forth, the noose around its neck making a slow rubbing sound. Its blank eyes stared at Audrey. Its hole of a mouth, a mouth with only one purpose, seemed to leer at her, to laugh at her. *Look at what you're doing,* Frieda Fuckdolly seemed to be saying. *You were going to become the most highly paid woman geologist in the country, own your own consulting firm by the time you were thirty-five, maybe win the Nobel Prize by the time you were fifty . . . weren't those the dreams? The Devonian Era scholar, the* summa cum laude *whose paper on tectonic plates was published in* Geology Review, *is chasing after little boys in crumbling old movie theaters. And no ordinary little boy, either. He's special, the way you always assumed* you *were special. And if you do find him, Aud, what then? He's strong.*

She grabbed the hangman's noose and yanked hard, snapping the old rope and pulling out a pretty country-fair bunch of Arnel hair at the same time. The doll landed face-down at Audrey's feet, and she drop-kicked it onto the balcony. It floated high, then settled. *Not stronger than Tak,* she thought. *I don't care what he is, he's not stronger than Tak. Not stronger than the* can tahs, *either. It's our* town, *now. Never mind the past and the dreams of the past; this is the present, and it's sweet. Sweet to kill, to take, to own. Sweet to rule, even in the desert. The boy is just a boy. The others are only food. Tak is here now, and he speaks with the voice of the older age; with the voice of the unformed.*

She looked up the hall toward the stairs. She nodded, her right hand slipping into the pocket of her dress to touch the things that were there, to fondle them against her thigh. He was in the projection booth. There was a big padlock hanging on the door which led into the basement, so where else *could* he be?

"Him en tow," she whispered, starting forward. Her eyes were wide, the fingers of her right hand moving ceaselessly in the pocket of her dress. From beneath them came small, stony clicking sounds.

3

The kids who partied hearty upstairs in The American West until the fire escape fell down had been slobs, but they had mostly used the hall and the manager's office for their revels; the other rooms were relatively untouched, and the projectionist's little suite—the booth, the office cubicle, the closet-sized toilet-stall—was almost exactly as it had been on the day in 1979 when five cigarette-smoking men from Nevada Sunlite Entertainment had come in, dismantled the carbon-filament projectors, and taken them to Reno, where they still languished, in a warehouse filled with similar equipment, like fallen idols.

David was on his knees, head down, eyes closed, hands pressed together in front of his chin. The dusty linoleum beneath him was lighter than that which surrounded him. Straight ahead was a second lighter rectangle. It was here that the old projectors—clattery, baking-hot dinosaurs that raised the temperature in this room as high as a hundred and twenty on some summer nights—had stood. To his left were the cut-outs through which they had shone their swords of light and projected their larger-than-life shadows: Gregory Peck and

Kirk Douglas, Sophia Loren and Jayne Mansfield, a young
Paul Newman hustling pool, an old but still vital Bette Davis
torturing her wheelchair-bound sister.

Dusty coils of film lay here and there on the floor like dead
snakes. There were old stills and posters on the walls. One
of the latter showed Marilyn Monroe standing on a subway
grating and trying to hold down her flaring skirt. Beneath
a hand-drawn arrow pointing at her panties, some wit had
printed *Carefully insert Shaft A in Slot B, making sure tool is
seated firmly & cannot slip out.* There was an odd, decayed smell
in here, not quite mildew, not quite dry-rot, either. It smelled
curdled, like something that had gone spectacularly bad before finally drying up.

David didn't notice the smell any more than he heard
Audrey softly calling his name from the hall which ran past
the balcony. He had come here when the others had run to
Billingsley—even Audrey had gone as far as stage-left at first,
perhaps to make sure they were all going down the hall—
because he had been nearly overwhelmed by a need to pray.
He had an idea that this time it would just be a matter of getting to someplace quiet and opening the door—this time God
wanted to talk to him, not the other way around. And this was
a good place to do it. Pray in your closet and not in the street,
the Bible said, and David thought that was excellent advice.
Now that he had a closed door between him and the rest of
them, he could open the one inside him.

He wasn't afraid of being observed by spiders or snakes or
rats; if God wanted this to be a private meeting, it would be a
private meeting. The woman Steve and Cynthia had found was
the real problem—she for some reason made him nervous, and
he had a feeling she felt the same about him. He had wanted to
get away from her, so he had slipped over the edge of the stage
and run up the center aisle. He was under the sagging balcony
and into the lobby before Audrey turned back from the stage-

left side of the movie screen, looking for him. From the lobby he had come up to the second floor, and then had simply let some interior compass—or maybe it was Reverend Martin's "still, small voice"—lead him up here.

He had walked across the room, barely seeing the old curls of film and the remaining posters, barely smelling the odor which might or might not have been celluloid fantasies stewed by the desert sun until they fell apart. He had stopped on this patch of linoleum, considering for a moment the large holes at the corners of the lighter rectangle shape, holes where the kingbolts which held the projector firmly in place had once gone. They reminded him

(I see holes like eyes)

of something, something which fluttered briefly in his mind and then was gone. False memory, real memory, intuition? All of the above? None of the above? He hadn't known, hadn't really cared. His priority then had been to get in touch with God, if he could. He had never needed to more than now.

Yes, Reverend Martin said calmly inside his head. *And this is where your work is supposed to pay off. You keep in touch with God when the cupboard's full so you can reach out to him when it's empty. How many times did I tell you that last winter and this spring?*

A lot. He just hoped that Martin, who drank more than he should and maybe couldn't be entirely trusted, had been telling the truth instead of just mouthing what David's dad called "the company line." He hoped that with all his mind and heart.

Because there were other gods in Desperation.

He was sure of it.

He began his prayer as he always did, not aloud but in his mind, sending words out in clear, even pulses of thought: *See in me, God. Be in me. And speak in me, if you mean to, if it's your will.*

As always at these times when he felt really in need of God, the front of his mind was serene, but the deeper part, where faith did constant battle with doubt, was terrified that there would be no answer. The problem was simple enough. Even now, after all his reading and praying and instruction, even after what had happened to his friend, he doubted God's existence. *Had* God used him, David Carver, to save Brian Ross's life? Why would God do a wild and crazy thing like that? Wasn't it more likely that what Dr. Waslewski had called a clinical miracle and what David himself had thought of as an answered prayer had actually been nothing more than a clinical coincidence? People could make shadows that looked like animals, but they were still only shadows, minor tricks of light and projection. Wasn't it likely that God was the same kind of thing? Just another legendary shadow?

David closed his eyes tighter, concentrating on the mantra and trying to clear his mind.

See in me. Be in me. Speak in me if it's your will.

And a kind of darkness came down. It was like nothing he had ever known or experienced before. He sagged side-ways against the wall between two of the projection-cutouts, eyes rolling up to whites, hands falling into his lap. A low, guttural sound came from his throat. It was followed by sleeptalk which perhaps only David's mother could have understood.

"Shit," he muttered. "The mummy's after us."

Then he fell silent, leaning against the wall, a silver runner of drool almost as fine as a spider's thread slipping from one corner of what was, essentially, still a child's mouth. Outside the door which he had shut in order to be alone with his God (there had once been a bolt on it, but that was long gone), approaching footsteps could now be heard. They stopped outside the door. There was a long, listening pause, and then the knob turned. The door opened. Audrey Wyler stood there. Her eyes widened when they happened on the unconscious boy.

She came into the fuggy little room, closed the door behind

her, and looked for something, anything, to tilt and prop under the knob. A board, a chair. It wouldn't hold them off for long if they came up here, but even a thin margin might mean the difference between success and failure at this stage. But there was nothing.

"Fuck," she whispered. She looked at the boy, realizing without much surprise that she was afraid of him. Afraid even to go near him.

Tak ah wan! The voice in her head.

"Tak ah wan!" This time out of her mouth. Assent. Both helpless and heartfelt.

She went down the two steps into the projection-booth proper and crossed, wincing at each gritting step, to where David leaned on his knees against the wall with the cut-outs in it. She kept expecting his eyes to fly open—eyes that would be filled with an electric-blue power. The right hand in her pocket squeezed the *can tahs* together once more, drawing strength, then—reluctantly—left them.

She dropped to her own knees in front of David, her cold and shaking fingers clasped before her. How ugly he was! And the smell coming from him was even more offensive to her. Of *course* she had stayed away from him; he looked like a gorgon and stank like a stew of spoiled meat and sour milk.

"Prayboy," she said. "Ugly little prayboy." Her voice had changed into something that was neither male nor female. Black shapes had begun to move vaguely beneath the skin of her cheeks and forehead, like the beating, membranous wings of small insects. "Here's what I should have done the first time I saw your toad's face."

Audrey's hands—strong and tanned, chipped here and there with scabs from her work—settled around David Carver's throat. His eyelids fluttered when those hands shut off his windpipe and stopped his breath, but just once.

Just once.

4

"Why'd you stop?" Steve asked.

He stood in the center of the improbable onstage living room, beside the elegant old wetbar from the Circle Ranch. His strongest wish at that moment was for a fresh shirt. All day he had been baking (to call the Ryder van's air conditioning substandard was actually to be charitable), but now he was freezing. The water Cynthia was dabbing onto the punctures in his shoulders ran down his back in chill streams. At least he'd been able to talk her out of using Billingsley's whiskey to clean his wounds, like a dancehall girl fixing up a cowpoke in an old movie.

"I thought I saw something." Cynthia spoke in a low voice.

"Waddit a puddy-tat?"

"Very funny." She raised her voice to a shout. "David? *Dayyyy-vid*!"

They were alone onstage. Steve had wanted to help Marinville and Carver look for the kid, but Cynthia had insisted on washing out what she called "the holes in your hide" first. The two men had disappeared into the lobby. Marinville had a new spring in his step, and the way he carried his gun made Steve think of another kind of old movie—the kind where the grizzled but heroic white hunter slogs through a thousand jungle perils and finally succeeds in plucking an emerald as big as a doorknob from the forehead of an idol watching over a lost city.

"What? What did you see?"

"I don't really know. It was weird. Up on the balcony. For a minute I thought it was—you'll laugh—a floating body."

Suddenly something in him changed. It wasn't like a light going on; it was more as if one had been turned out. He forgot about the stinging of the wounds in his shoulders, but all at once his back was colder than ever. Almost cold enough to start him shivering. For the second time that day he remembered being a teenager in Lubbock, and how the whole world seemed to go still and deadly before the benders arrived from the plains, dragging their sometimes deadly skirts of hail and wind. "I'm not laughing," he said. "Let's go on up there."

"It was probably just a shadow."

"I don't think so."

"Steve? You okay?"

"No. I feel like I did when we came into town."

She looked at him, alarmed. "Okay. But we don't have a gun—"

"Fuck that." He grabbed her arm. His eyes were wide, his mouth pinched. "*Now.* Christ, something is *really wrong.* Can't you feel it?"

"I . . . might feel something. Should I get Mary? She's back with Billingsley—"

"No time. Come or stay here. Suit yourself."

He shrugged up the sides of the coverall, jumped off the stage, stumbled, grabbed a seat in the front row to steady himself, then ran up the center aisle. When he got to its head, Cynthia was right behind him, once again not even out of breath. The chick could motor, you had to give her that.

The boss was just coming out of the box office, Ralph Carver behind him. "We've been looking out at the street," Johnny said. "The storm is definitely . . . Steve? What's wrong?"

Without answering, Steve looked around, spotted the stairs, and pelted up them. Part of him was still amazed at the speed with which this feeling of urgency had grabbed hold. Most of him was just scared.

"*David*! David, answer if you hear me!"

Nothing. A grim, trash-lined hallway leading past what were probably the old balcony and a snackbar alcove. Narrow stairs going farther up at the far end. No one here. Yet he had a clear sense that there *had* been, and only a short time ago.

"*David!*" he shouted.

"Steve? Mr. Ames?" It was Carver. He sounded almost as scared as Steve felt. "What's wrong? Has something happened to my son?"

"I don't know."

Cynthia ducked under Steve's arm and hurried down the hallway to the balcony entrance. Steve went after her. A frayed length of rope was hanging down from the top of the arch, still swaying a little.

"Look!" Cynthia pointed. At first Steve thought the thing lying out there was a corpse, then registered the hair for what it was—some kind of synthetic. A doll. One with a noose around its neck.

"Is that what you saw?" he asked her.

"Yes. Someone could have ripped it down and then maybe drop-kicked it." The face she turned up to his was drawn and tense. In a voice almost too low to hear, she whispered, "God, Steve, I don't like this."

Steve took a step back, glanced left (the boss and David's father looked at him anxiously, clutching their weapons against their chests), then looked right. *There*, his heart whispered . . . or perhaps it was his nose, picking up some lingering residue of Opium, that whispered. *Up there. Must be the projection-booth.*

He ran for it, Cynthia once more on his heels. He went up the narrow flight of stairs and was groping for the knob in the dimness when she grabbed the back of his pants to hold him where he was.

"The kid had a pistol. If she's in there with him, she could have it now. Be careful, Steve."

"*David!*" Carver bawled. "*David, are you okay?*"

Steve thought of telling Cynthia there was no time to be careful, that that time had passed when they lost track of David in the first place . . . but there was no time to talk, either.

He turned the knob and shoved the door hard with his shoulder, expecting to encounter either a lock or some other resistance, but there was none. The door flew open; he flew into the room after it.

Across from him, against the wall with the projection-slots cut into it, were David and Audrey. David's eyes were half-open, but only their bulging whites showed. His face was a horrid corpse-color, still greenish from the soap but mostly gray. There were growing lavender patches beneath his eyes and high up on his cheekbones. His hands drummed spastically on the thighs of his jeans. He was making a soft choking sound. Audrey's right hand was clamped around his throat, her thumb buried deep in the soft flesh beneath his jaw on the right, the fingers digging in on the left. Her formerly pretty face was contorted in an expression of hate and rage beyond anything Steve had ever seen in his life—it seemed to have actually darkened her skin, somehow. In her left hand she held the .45 revolver David had used to shoot the coyote. She fired it three times, and then it clicked empty.

The two-step drop into the projection-booth almost certainly saved Steve at least one more hole in his already perforated hide and might have saved his life. He fell forward like a man who has misjudged the number of stairs in a flight, and all three bullets went over his head. One thudded into the doorjamb to Cynthia's right and showered splinters into her exotic hair.

Audrey voiced a ululating scream of frustration. She threw the empty gun at Steve, who simultaneously ducked and raised one hand to bat it away. Then she turned back to the slumping boy and began to throttle him with both hands again, shaking him viciously back and forth like a doll. David's hands abruptly quit thrumming and simply lay on the legs of his jeans, as limp as dead starfish.

5

"Scared," Billingsley croaked. It was, so far as Mary could tell, the last word he ever managed to say. His eyes looked up at her, both frantic and somehow confused. He tried to say something else and produced only a weak gargling noise.

"Don't be scared, Tom. I'm right here."

"Ah. Ah." His eyes shifted from side to side, then came back to her face and seemed to freeze there. He took a deep breath, let it out, took a shallower one, let it out . . . and didn't take another.

"Tom?"

Nothing but a gust of wind and a hard rattle of sand from outside.

"*Tom!*"

She shook him. His head rolled limply from side to side, but his eyes remained fixed on hers in a way that gave her a chill; it was the way the eyes in some painted portraits seemed to stay on you no matter where you were in the room. Somewhere—in this building but sounding very far away, just the same—she could hear Marinville's roadie yelling for David. The hippie-girl was yelling, too. Mary supposed she should join them, help them search for David and Audrey if they were really lost, but she was reluctant to leave Tom until she was positive he was dead. She was *pretty sure* he was, yes, but it surely wasn't like it was on TV, when you *knew*—

"Help?"

The voice, questioning and almost too weak to be heard over the slackening wind, still made Mary jump and cup a hand over her mouth to stifle a cry.

"Help? Is anyone there? Please help me . . . I'm hurt."

A woman's voice. Ellen Carver's voice? Christ, was it? Although she had been in the company of David's mother for only a short time, Mary was sure she was right almost as soon as the idea occurred to her. She got to her feet, sparing another quick glance at poor Tom Billingsley's contorted face and staring eyes. Her legs had stiffened up on her and she staggered for balance.

"Please," the voice outside moaned. It was in the alley which ran behind the theater.

"Ellen?" she asked, suddenly wishing she could throw her voice like a ventriloquist. It seemed she could trust nothing now, not even a hurt, scared woman. "Ellen, is that you?"

"Mary!" Closer now. "Yes, it's me, Ellen. *Is* that Mary?"

Mary opened her mouth, then closed it again. That was Ellen Carver out there, she *knew* it, but . . .

"Is David all right?" the woman out there in the dark asked, then swallowed back a sob. "Please say that he is."

"So far as I know, yes." Mary walked over to the broken window, skirting the pool of the cougar's blood, and looked out. It was Ellen Carver out there, and she didn't look good. She was slumped over her left arm, which she was holding against her breasts with her right. What Mary could see of her face was chalky white. Blood was trickling from her lower lip and from one nostril. She looked up at Mary with eyes so dark and desperate they seemed hardly human.

"How did you get away from Entragian?" Mary asked.

"I didn't. He just . . . died. Bled everywhere and died. He was driving me in his car—taking me up to the mine, I think—when it happened. The car went off the road and turned over. One of the back doors popped open. Lucky for me or I'd still be inside, caught like a bug in a can. I . . . I walked back to town."

"What happened to your arm?"

"It's broken," Ellen said, hunching over it further. There was something unattractive about the pose; Ellen Carver looked like a troll in a fairy story, hunched protectively over a bag of ill-gotten gold. "Can you help me in? I want to see my husband, and I want to see David."

A part of Mary cried out in alarm at the idea, told her that something here did not compute, but when Ellen held up her good arm and Mary saw the dirt and blood smeared on it, and the way it was trembling with exhaustion, her fundamentally kind heart overruled the wary lizard of instinct living far back in her brain. This woman had lost her young daughter to a madman, had been in a car-wreck on the way to what would have most likely been her own murder, had suffered a broken arm, and walked through a howling windstorm back to a town filled mostly with corpses. And the first person she meets suddenly succumbs to a bad case of the jimjams and refuses to let her in?

Uh-uh, Mary thought. *No way.* And, perhaps absurdly: *That's not how I was raised.*

"You can't come in this window. There's a lot of broken glass. Something . . . an animal jumped through it. Go a little farther along the back of the theater. You'll come to the ladies' room. That's better. There are even some boxes to stand on. I'll help you in. Okay?"

"Yes. Thank you, Mary. Thank God I found you." Ellen gave her a horrible, grimacing smile—gratitude, shoe-licking humility, and what might have been terror all mixed together—and then shuffled on, head down, back bent. Twelve hours ago she had been Mrs. Suburban Wifemom, on her way to a nice middle-class vacation in Lake Tahoe, where she had probably planned to wear her new resort clothes from Talbot's over her new underwear from Victoria's Secret. Daytime sun with the kids, nighttime sex with the comfy, known partner, postcards home to the friends—having a great time, the air is so clean, wish you were here. Now she looked and acted like a refugee, a no-age warhag fleeing some ugly desert bloodbath.

And Mary Jackson, that sweet little princess—votes Democratic, gives blood every two months, writes poetry—had actually considered leaving her out there to moan in the dark until she could consult with the men. And what did that mean? That she had been in the same war, Mary supposed. This was how you thought, how you behaved, when it happened to you. Except she wouldn't. Be damned if she would.

Mary crossed the hall, listening for any further shouts from the theater. There were none. Then, just as she pushed open the ladies'-room door, three gunshots rang out. They were muffled by walls and distance, but there was no doubt about what they were. Shouts followed them. Mary froze in place, pulled in two different directions with equal force. What decided her was the soft sound of weeping from beyond the unlatched ladies'-room window.

"Ellen? What is it? What's wrong?"

"I'm stupid, that's all, *stupid*! I bumped my bad arm putting up another crate to stand on!" The woman outside the window—she was just a blur of shadow on the frosted glass—began sobbing harder.

"Hold on, you'll be inside in a jiffy," Mary said, and hurried across the room. She set aside the beer-bottles Billingsley had put up on the windowledge and was lifting the hinged window, trying to think how best to help Ellen into the room without hurting her further, when she remembered what Billingsley had said about the cop: that he was taller. *Dear God,* David's father had said, a look of thunderstruck understanding on his face. *She's like Entragian? Like the cop?*

Maybe she's got a broken arm, Mary thought coldly, *maybe she really does. On the other hand—*

On the other hand, hunching over like that was actually a very good way to disguise one's true height, wasn't it?

The lizard which usually kept its place on the back wall of her brain suddenly leaped forward, chirping in terror. Mary decided to pull back, take a moment or two and think things over . . . but before she could, her arm was seized by a strong hot hand. Another one banged open the window, and all of Mary's strength ran out of her like water as she looked into the grinning face staring up at her. It was Ellen's face, but the badge pinned below it

(*I see you're an organ donor*)

belonged to Entragian.

It *was* Entragian. Collie Entragian somehow living in Ellen Carver's body.

"*No!*" she screamed, yanking backward, heedless of the pain as Ellen's fingernails punched into her arms and brought blood. "*No, let go of me!*"

"Not until I hear you sing 'Leavin' on a Jet Plane,' you cunt," the Ellen-thing said, and as it yanked Mary forward through the window it was still holding open, blood burst from both of Ellen's nostrils in a gush. More blood trickled from Ellen's left eye like gummy tears. "*Oh the dawn is breakin', it's early morn . . .*"

Mary had a confused sensation of flying toward the board fence on the other side of the lane.

"*The taxi-driver is blowin' his horn . . .*"

She managed to get one blocking arm up, but not enough; she took most of the impact with her forehead and went to her knees, head ringing. She could feel warmth spreading over her lips and chin. *Join the nosebleed club, babe,* she thought, and staggered to her feet.

"*Already I'm so lonesome I could cryyyyy . . .*"

Mary took two large, lunging strides, and then the cop (she couldn't stop thinking of it as the cop, only now wearing a wig and falsies) grabbed her by the shoulder, almost tearing one arm off her shirt as it whirled Mary around.

"Let g—" Mary began, and then the Ellen-thing clipped her on the point of the chin, a crisp and elementary blow that put out the lights. It caught Mary under the arms on her way down and pulled her close. When it felt Mary's breath on Ellen's skin, the faint anxiety which had been on Ellen's face cleared.

"Gosh, I love that song," it said, and slung Mary over her shoulder like a sack of grain. "It turns me all gooshy inside. *Tak*!"

She disappeared around the corner with her burden. Five minutes later, Collie Entragian's dusty Caprice was once more on its way out to the China Pit, headlights cutting through the swirls of sand driven by the dying wind. As it drove past Harvey's Small Engine Repair and the bodega beyond it, a thin blue-white sickle of moon appeared in the sky overhead.

CHAPTER 5

1

Even in the boozy, druggy days, Johnny Marinville's recall had been pretty relentless. In 1986, while riding in the back seat of Sean Hutter's so-called Partymobile (Sean had been doing the Friday-night East Hampton rounds with Johnny and three others in the big old '65 Caddy), he had been involved in a fatal accident. Sean, who had been too drunk to *walk*, let alone drive, had rolled the Partymobile over twice, trying to make the turn from Eggamoggin Lane onto Route B without slowing down. The girl sitting next to Hutter had been killed. Sean's spine had been pulverized. The only Partymobile he ran these days was a motorized Cadding wheelchair, the kind you steered with your chin. The others had suffered minor injuries; Johnny had considered himself lucky to get off with a bruised spleen and a broken foot. But the thing was, *he was the only one who remembered what had happened.* Johnny found this so curious that he had questioned the survivors carefully, even Sean, who kept crying and telling him to go away (Johnny hadn't obliged until he'd gotten what he wanted; what the hell, he figured, Sean *owed* him). Patti Nickerson said she had a vague memory of Sean saying *Hold on, we're going for a ride* just before it happened, but that was it. With the others, recall simply stopped short of the accident and then picked up again at some point after it, as if their memories had been squirted with some amnesia-producing ink.

Sean himself claimed to remember nothing after getting out of
the shower that afternoon and wiping the steam off the mirror
so he could see to shave. After that, he said, everything was
black until he'd awakened in the hospital. He might have been
lying about that, but Johnny didn't think so. Yet he himself
remembered everything. Sean hadn't said *Hold on, we're going
for a ride*; he had said *Hang on, we're going wide.* And laughing as he said it. He went on laughing even when the Partymobile had started to roll. Johnny remembered Patti screaming
"My hair! Oh shit, my *hair*!," and how she had landed on his
crotch with a ball-numbing thud when the car went over. He
remembered Bruno Gartner bellowing. And the sound of the
Partymobile's collapsing roof driving Rachel Timorov's head
down into her neck, splitting her skull open like a bone flower.
A tight crunching sound it had been, the sound you hear in
your head when you smash an icecube between your teeth. He
remembered shit. He knew that was part of being a writer, but
he didn't know if it was nature or nurture, cause or effect. He
supposed it didn't matter. The thing was, he remembered shit
even when it was as confusing as the final thirty seconds of a
big fireworks display. Stuff that overlapped seemed to auto-
matically separate and fall into line even as it was happening,
like iron filings lining up under the pull of a magnet. Until
the night Sean Hutter had rolled his Partymobile, Johnny had
never wished for anything different. He had never wished for
anything different since . . . until now. Right now a little ink
squirted into the old memory cells might be just fine.

He saw splinters jump from the jamb of the projection-
booth door and land in Cynthia's hair when Audrey fired the
pistol. He felt one of the slugs drone past his right ear. He saw
Steve, down on one knee but apparently okay, bat away the revolver when the woman hucked it at him. She lifted her upper
lip, snarled at Steve like a cornered dog, then turned back and
clamped her hands around the kid's throat again.

Go on! Johnny shouted at himself. *Go on and help him! Like you did before, when you shot the cat!*

But he couldn't. He could see everything, but he couldn't move.

Things began to overlap then, but his mind insisted on sequencing them, neatening them, giving them a coherent shape, like a narrative. He saw Steve leap at Audrey, telling her to quit it, to let the boy go, cupping her neck with one hand and grabbing her wrists with the other. At this same moment, Johnny was slammed past the skinny girl and into the room with the force of a stuntman shot from a cannon. It was Ralph, of course, hitting him from behind and bawling his son's name at the top of his lungs.

Johnny flew out over the two-step drop, knees bent, convinced he was going to sustain multiple fractures at the very least, convinced that the boy was dying or already dead, convinced that Audrey Wyler's mind had snapped under the strain and she had fallen under the delusion that David Carver was either the cop or a minion of the cop . . . and all the time his eyes went on recording and his brain kept on receiving the images and storing them. He saw the way Audrey's muscular legs were spread, the material of her skirt strained taut between them. He also saw he was going to touch down near her.

He landed on one foot, like a skater who has forgotten his skates. His knee buckled. He let it, throwing himself forward into the woman, grabbing her hair. She pulled her head back and snapped at his fingers. At the same instant (except Johnny's mind insisted it was the *next* instant, even now wanting to reduce this madness to something coherent, a narrative which would flow in train), Steve tore her hands away from the kid's throat. Johnny saw the white marks of her palms and fingers there, and then his momentum was carrying him by. She missed biting him, which was the good news, but he missed his grip on her hair, which was the bad.

She voiced a guttural cry as he collided with the wall. His left arm shot out through one of the projection-slots up to the shoulder, and for one awful moment he was sure that the rest of him was going to follow it—out, down, goodbye. It was impossible, the hole was nowhere near big enough for that, but he thought it anyway.

At this same moment (his mind once more insisting it was the *next* moment, the *next* thing, the *new* sentence) Ralph Carver yelled: *"Get your hands off my boy, bitch!"*

Johnny retrieved his arm and turned around, putting his back to the wall. He saw Steve and Ralph drag the screaming woman off David. He saw the boy collapse against the wall and slide slowly down it, the marks on his throat standing out brutally. He saw Cynthia come down the steps and into the room, trying to look everywhere at once.

"Grab the kid, boss!" Steve panted. He was struggling with Audrey, one hand still clamped on her wrists and the other now around her waist. She bucked under him like a canyon mustang. "Grab him and get him out of h—"

Audrey screamed and pulled free. When Ralph made a clumsy attempt to get his arms around her neck and put her in a headlock, she shoved the heel of one hand under his chin and pushed him back. She retreated a step, saw David, and snarled again, her lips drawing away from her teeth. She made a move to go in his direction and Ralph said, "Touch him again and I'll kill you. Promise."

Ah, fuck this, Johnny thought, and snatched the boy up. He was warm and limp and heavy in his arms. Johnny's back, already outraged by nearly a continent's worth of motorcycling, gave a warning twinge.

Audrey glanced at Ralph, as if daring him to try and make good on his promise, then tensed to leap at Johnny. Before she could, Steve was on her once more. He grabbed her around the waist again, then pivoted on his heels, the two of them face to face. She was uttering a long and continuous caterwauling that made Johnny's fillings ache.

Halfway through his second spin, Steve let her go. Audrey flew backward like a stone cast out of a sling, her feet stuttering on the floor, still caterwauling. Cynthia, who was behind her, dropped to her hands and knees with the speed of a born playground survivor. Audrey collided with her shin-high and went over backward, sprawling on the lighter-colored rectangle where the second projector had rested. She stared up at them through the tumble of her hair, momentarily dazed.

"Get him out of here, boss!" Steve waved his hand at the steps leading up to the projection-booth door. "There's something wrong with her, she's like the animals!"

What do you mean, like *them?* Johnny thought. *She fucking well is one.* He heard what Steve was telling him, but he didn't start toward the door. Once again he seemed incapable of movement.

Audrey scrambled to her feet, sliding up the corner of the room. Her upper lip was still rising and falling in a jagged snarl, eyes moving from Johnny and the unconscious boy cradled in his arms to Ralph, and then to Cynthia, who had now also gotten to her feet and was pressing against Steve's side. Johnny thought briefly and longingly of the Rossi shotgun and the Ruger .44. Both were in the lobby, leaning against the ticket-booth. The booth had offered a good view of the street, but it had been easier to leave the guns outside it, given the limited space. And neither he nor Ralph had thought to bring them up here. He now believed that one of the scariest lessons this nightmare had to offer was how lethally unprepared for survival they all were. Yet they *had* survived. Most of them, anyway. So far.

"*Tak ah lah!*"

The woman spoke in a voice that was both frightening and powerful, nothing like her earlier one, her storytelling voice—

that one had been low and often hesitant. To Johnny, this one seemed only a step or two above a dog's bark. And was she *laughing*? He thought that at least part of her was. And what of that strange, swimming darkness just below the surface of her skin? Was he really seeing that?

"*Min! Min! Min en tow!*"

Cynthia cast a bewildered glance at Steve. "What's she saying?" Steve shook his head. She looked at Johnny.

"It's the cop's language," he said. He cast his peculiarly efficient recollection back to the moment when the cop had apparently sicced a buzzard on him. "*Timoh!*" he snapped at Audrey Wyler. "*Candy-latch!*"

That wasn't quite right, but it must have at least been close; Audrey recoiled, and for a moment there was a very human look of surprise on her face. Then the lip lifted again, and the lunatic smile reappeared in her eyes.

"What did you say to her?" Cynthia asked Johnny.

"I have no idea."

"Boss, you gotta get the kid out. Now."

Johnny took a step backward, meaning to do just that. Audrey reached into the pocket of her dress as he did and brought it out curled around a fistful of something. She stared at him— only at *him*, now, John Edward Marinville, Distinguished Novelist and Extraordinary Thinker—with her snarling beast's eyes. She held her hand out, wrist up. "*Can tah!*" she cried . . . laughed. "*Can tah, can tak!* What you take is what you are! Of course! *Can tah, can tak, mi tow!* Take this! *So tah!*"

When she opened her hand and showed him her offering, the emotional weather inside his head changed at once . . . and yet he still saw everything and sequenced it, just as he had when Sean Hutter's goddamned Partymobile had rolled over. He had kept on recording everything then, when he had been sure he was going to die, and he went on recording everything now, when he was suddenly consumed with hate for the boy in his arms and overwhelmed by a desire to put something—his motorcycle key would do nicely—into the interfering little prayboy's throat and open him like a can of beer.

He thought at first that there were three odd-looking charms lying on her open palm—the sort of thing girls sometimes wore dangling from their bracelets. But they were too big, too heavy. Not charms but carvings, stone carvings, each about two inches long. One was a snake. The second was a buzzard with one wing chipped off. Mad, bulging eyes stared out at him from beneath its bald dome. The third was a rat on its hind legs. They all looked pitted and ancient.

"*Can tah!*" she screamed. "*Can* tah, *can* tak, *kill the* boy, *kill him now, kill him!*"

Steve stepped forward. With her attention and concentration fully fixed on Johnny, she saw him only at the last instant. He slapped the stones from her hand and they flew into the corner of the room. One—it was the snake—broke in two. Audrey screamed with horror and vexation.

The murderous fury which had come over Johnny's mind dissipated but didn't depart completely. He could feel his eyes wanting to turn toward the corner, where the carvings lay. Waiting for him. All he had to do was pick them up.

"*Get him the fuck* out *of here!*" Steve yelled. Audrey lunged for the carvings. Steve seized her arm and yanked her back. Her skin was darkening and sagging. Johnny thought that the process which had changed her was now trying to reverse itself . . . without much success. She was . . . what? Shrinking? Diminishing? He didn't know the right word, but—

"*GET HIM OUT!*" Steve yelled again, and smacked Johnny on the shoulder. That woke him up. He began to turn and then Ralph was there. He had snatched David from Johnny's arms almost before Johnny knew it was happening. Ralph bounded up the stairs, clumsy but powerful, and was gone from the projection-booth without a single look back.

Audrey saw him go. She howled—it was despair Johnny heard in that howl now—and lunged for the stones again. Steve yanked her back. There was a peculiar ripping sound as Audrey's right arm pulled off at the shoulder. Steve was left holding it in his hand like the drumstick of an overcooked chicken.

2

Audrey seemed unaware of what had happened to her. One-armed, the right side of her dress now darkening with blood, she made for the carvings, gibbering in that strange language. Steve was frozen in place, looking at what he held—a lightly freckled human arm with a Casio watch on the wrist. The boss was equally frozen. If it hadn't been for Cynthia, Steve later thought, Audrey would have gotten to the carvings again. God knew what would have happened if she had; even when she had been obviously focusing the power of the stones on the boss, Steve had felt the backwash. There had been nothing sexual about it this time. This time it had been about murder and nothing else.

Before Audrey could fall on her knees in the corner and grab her toys, Cynthia kicked them deftly away, sending them skittering along the wall with the cutouts in it. Audrey howled again, and this time a spray of blood came out of her mouth along with the sound. She turned her head to them, and Steve staggered backward, actually raising a hand, as if to block the sight of her from his vision.

Audrey's formerly pretty face now drooped from the front of her skull in sweating wrinkles. Her staring eyeballs hung from widening sockets. Her skin was blackening and splitting. Yet none of this was the worst; the worst came as Steve dropped the hideously warm thing he was holding and she lurched to her feet.

"I'm very sorry," she said, and in her choked and failing voice Steve heard a real woman, not this decaying monstrosity. "I never meant to hurt anyone. Don't touch the *can tahs*. Whatever else you do, don't touch the *can tahs*!"

Steve looked at Cynthia. She stared back, and he could read her mind in her wide eyes: *I touched one.* Twice. *How lucky was I?*

Very, Steve thought. *I think you were very lucky. I think we both were.*

Audrey staggered toward them and away from the pitted gray stones. Steve could smell a rich odor of blood and decay. He reached out but couldn't bring himself to actually put a restraining hand on her shoulder, even though she was headed for the stairs and the hallway . . . headed in the direction Ralph had taken his boy. He couldn't bring himself to do it because he knew his fingers would sink in.

Now he could hear a plopping, pattering sound as parts of her began to liquefy and fall off in a kind of flesh rain. She mounted the steps and lurched out through the door. Cynthia looked up at Steve for a moment, her faced pinched and white. He put his arm around her waist and followed Johnny up the stairs.

Audrey made it about halfway down the short but steep flight of stairs leading to the second-floor hall, then fell. The sound of her inside her blood-soaked dress was grisly—a *splashing* sound, almost. Yet she was still alive. She began to crawl, her hair hanging in strings, mercifully obscuring most of her dangling face. At the far end, by the stairs leading down to the lobby, Ralph stood with David in his arms, staring at the oncoming creature.

"Shoot her!" Johnny roared. "For God's sake, somebody shoot her!"

"Can't," Steve said. "No guns up here but the kid's, and that one's empty."

"Ralph, get downstairs with David," Johnny said. He started carefully down the hall. "Get down before . . ."

But the thing which had been Audrey Wyler had no further interest in David, it seemed. It reached the arched entrance to the balcony, then crawled through it. Almost at once the support timbers, dried out by the desert climate and dined upon by generations of termites, began to groan. Steve hurried after Johnny, his arm still around Cynthia. Ralph came toward them from the other end of the hall. They met just in time to see the thing in the soaked dress reach the balcony railing. Audrey had crawled over the mostly deflated sex-doll, leaving a broad streak of blood and less identifiable fluids across its plastic midsection. Frieda's pursed mouth might have been expressing outrage at such treatment.

What remained of Audrey Wyler was still clutching the railing, still attempting to pull itself up enough to dive over the side when the supports let go and the balcony tore away from the wall with a large, dusty roar. At first it slipped outward on a level, like a tray or a floating platform, tearing away boards from the edge of the hallway and forcing Steve and the others back as the old carpet first tore open and then gaped like a seismic fault. Laths snapped; nails squealed as they divorced the boards to which they had been wedded. Then, at last, the balcony began to tilt. Audrey tumbled over the side. For just a moment Steve saw her feet sticking out of the dust, and then she was gone. A moment later and the balcony was gone, too, falling like a stone and hitting the seats below with a tremendous crash. Dust boiled up in a miniature mushroom cloud.

"David!" Steve shouted. "What about David? Is he alive?"

"I don't know," Ralph said. He looked at them with dazed and teary eyes. "I'm sure he was when I brought him out of the projection-booth, but now I don't know. I can't feel him breathing at all."

3

All the doors leading into the auditorium had been chocked open, and the lobby was hazed with dust from the fallen balcony. They carried David over to one of the street-doors, where a draft from the outside pushed the worst of the drifting dust away.

"Put him down," Cynthia said. She was trying to think what to do next—hell, what to do *first*—but her thoughts kept junking up on her. "And lay him straight. Let's turn his airways into freeways."

Ralph looked at her hopefully as he and Steve lowered David to the threadbare carpet. "Do you know anything about . . . this?"

"Depends on what you mean," she said. "Some first aid—including artificial respiration—from when I was back at Daughters and Sisters, yeah. But if you're asking if I know anything about ladies who turn into homicidal maniacs and then decay, no."

"He's all I got, miss," Ralph said. "All that's left of my family."

Cynthia closed her eyes and bent toward David. What she felt relieved her enormously—the faint but clear touch of breath on her face. "He's alive. I can feel him breathing." She looked up at Ralph and smiled. "I'm not surprised you couldn't. Your face is swelled up like an inner tube."

"Yeah. Maybe that was it. But mostly I was just so afraid . . ." He tried to smile back at her and failed. He let out a gusty sigh and groped backward to lean against the boarded-over candy counter.

"I'm going to help him now," Cynthia said. She looked down at the boy's pale face and closed eyes. "I'm just going to help you along, David. Speed things up. Let me help you, okay? Let me help you."

She turned his head gently to one side, wincing at the fingermarks on his neck. In the auditorium, a hanging piece of the balcony gave up the ghost and fell with a crash. The others looked that way, but Cynthia's concentration remained on David. She used the fingers of her left hand to open his mouth, leaned forward, and gently pinched his nostrils shut with her right hand. Then she put her mouth on his and exhaled. His chest rose more steeply, then settled as she released his nose and pulled away from him. She bent to one side and spoke into his ear in a low voice. "Come back to us, David. We need you. And you need us."

She breathed deep into his mouth again, and said, "Come back to us, David," as he exhaled a mixture of his air and hers. She looked into his face. His unassisted breathing was a little stronger now, she thought, and she could see his eyeballs moving beneath his blue-tinged lids, but he showed no signs of waking up.

"Come back to us, David. Come back."

Johnny looked around, blinking like someone just back from the further reaches of his thoughts. "Where's Mary? You don't suppose the goddam balcony fell on her, do you?"

"Why would it have?" Steve asked. "She was with the old guy."

"And you think she's *still* with the old guy? After all the yelling? After the goddam *balcony* fell off the goddam *wall*?"

"You've got a point," Steve said.

"Here we go again," Johnny said, "I knew it. Come on, I guess we better go look for her."

Cynthia took no notice. She knelt with her face in front of David's, searching it earnestly with her eyes. "I dunno where you are, kid, but get your ass back here. It's time to saddle up and get out of Dodge."

Johnny picked up the shotgun and the rifle. He handed the

latter to Ralph. "Stay here with your boy and the young lady," he said. "We'll be back."

"Yeah? What if you're not?"

Johnny looked at him uncertainly for a moment, then broke into a sunny grin. "Burn the documents, trash the radio, and swallow your death capsule."

"Huh?"

"How the fuck should *I* know? Use your judgement. I can tell you this much, Ralph: as soon as we've collected Ms. Jackson, we're totally historical. Come on, Steve. Down the far lefthand aisle, unless you've an urge to climb Mount Balcony."

Ralph watched them through the door, then turned back to Cynthia and his son. "What's wrong with David, do you have any idea? Did that bitch choke him into a coma? He had a friend who was in a coma once, David did. He came out of it— it was a miracle, everyone said—but I wouldn't wish that on my worst enemy. Is that what's wrong with him, do you think?"

"I don't think he's unconscious at all, let alone in a coma. Do you see the way his eyelids are moving? It's more like he's asleep and dreaming . . . or in a trance."

She looked up at him. Their eyes met for a moment, and then Ralph knelt down across from her. He brushed his son's hair off his brow and then kissed him gently between the eyes, where the skin was puckered in a faint frown. "Come back, David," he said. "Please come back."

David breathed quietly through pursed lips. Behind his bruised eyelids, his eyes moved and moved.

4

In the men's room they found one dead cougar, its head mostly blown off, and one dead veterinarian with his eyes open. In the ladies' room, they found nothing . . . or so it seemed to Steve.

"Shine your light back over there," Johnny told him. When Steve retrained the flashlight on the window he said, "No, not the window. The floor underneath it."

Steve dropped the beam and ran it along half a dozen beer-bottles standing against the wall just to the right of the window.

"The doc's booby-trap," Johnny said. "Not broken but neatly set aside. Interesting."

"I didn't even notice they were gone from the window-ledge. That's good on you, boss."

"Come on over here." Johnny crossed to the window, held it up, peeked out, then moved aside enough for Steve to join him. "Cast your mind back to your arrival at this bucolic palace of dreams, Steven. What's the last thing you did before sliding all the way into this room? Can you remember?"

Steve nodded. "Sure. We stacked two crates to make it easier to climb in the window. I pushed the top one off, because I figured if the cop came back here and saw them piled up that way, it would be like a pointing arrow."

"Right. But what do you see now?"

Steve used his flashlight, although he didn't really need to; the wind had died almost completely, and all but the most errant skims of dust had dropped. There was even a scantling of moon.

"They're stacked again," he said, and turned to Johnny with an alarmed look. "Oh shit! Entragian came while we were occupied with David. Came and . . ." *took her* was how he meant to finish, but he saw the boss shaking his head and stopped.

"That's not what this says." Johnny took the flashlight and ran it along the row of bottles again. "Not smashed; set neatly aside in a row. Who did that? Audrey? No, she went the other way—after David. Billingsley? Not possible, considering the shape he was in before he died. That leaves Mary, but would she have done it for the cop?"

"I doubt it," Steve said.

"Me too. I think that if the cop had shown up back here, she would have come running to us, screaming bloody murder. And why the stacked crates? I've got some personal experience of Collie Entragian; he's six-six at least, probably more. He wouldn't have needed a step up to get in the window. To me those stacked crates suggest either a shorter person, a ruse to get Mary into a position where she could be grabbed, or maybe both. I could be over-deducing, I suppose, but—"

"So there could be more of them. More like Audrey."

"Maybe, but I don't think you can conclude *that* out of what we see here. I just don't think she would have put those beer-bottles aside for any stranger. Not even a bawling little kid. You know? I think she would have come to get us."

Steve took the flashlight and shone it on Billingsley's tile fish, so joyful and funky here in the dark. He wasn't surprised to find that he no longer liked it much. Now it was like laughter in a haunted house, or a clown at midnight. He snapped the light off.

"What are you thinking, boss?"

"Don't call me that anymore, Steve. I never liked it that much to begin with."

"All right. What are you thinking, Johnny?"

Johnny looked around to make sure they were still alone. His face, dominated by his swelled and leaning nose, looked both tired and intent. As he shook out another three aspirin and dry-swallowed them, Steve realized an amazing thing: Marinville looked younger. In spite of everything he'd been through, he looked younger.

He swallowed again, grimacing at the taste of the old pills, and said: "David's mom."

"*What?*"

"It could have been. Take a second. Think about it. You'll see how pretty it is, in a ghastly kind of way."

Steve did. And saw how completely it made sense of the situation. He didn't know where Audrey Wyler's story had parted company from the truth, but he *did* know that at some point she had been gotten to . . . changed by the stones she had called the *can tahs*. Changed? Afflicted with a kind of horrible, degenerative rabies. What had happened to her could have happened to Ellen Carver, as well.

Steve suddenly found himself hoping Mary Jackson was dead. That was awful, but in a case like this, dead might be better, mightn't it? Better than being under the spell of the *can tahs*. Better than what apparently happened when the *can tahs* were taken away.

"What do we do now?" he asked.

"Get out of this town. By any means possible."

"All right. If David's still unconscious, we'll carry him. Let's do it."

They started back to the lobby.

5

David Carver walked down Anderson Avenue past West Wentworth Middle School. Written on the side of the school-building in yellow spray-paint were the words IN THESE SILENCES SOMETHING MAY RISE. Then he turned an Ohio corner and began walking down Bear Street. That was pretty funny, since Bear Street and the Bear Street Woods were nine big suburban blocks from the junior high, but that's the way things worked in dreams. Soon he would wake up in his own bedroom and the whole thing would fall apart, anyway.

Ahead of him were three bikes in the middle of the street. They had been turned upside down, and their wheels were spinning in the air.

"And Pharaoh said unto Joseph, I have dreamed a dream,"

someone said, "and I have heard say of thee, that thou canst understand a dream to interpret it."

David looked across the street and saw Reverend Martin. He was drunk and he needed a shave. In one hand he held a bottle of Seagram's Seven whiskey. Between his feet was a yellow puddle of puke. David could barely stand to look at him. His eyes were empty and dead.

"And Joseph answered Pharaoh, saying, It is not in me: God shall give Pharaoh an answer of peace." Reverend Martin toasted him with the bottle and then drank. "Go get em," he said. "Now we're going to discover if you know where Moses was when the lights went out."

David walked on. He thought of turning around; then a queer but strangely persuasive idea came to him: if he *did* turn around, he would see the mummy tottering after him in a cloud of ancient wrappings and spices.

He walked a little faster.

As he passed the bikes in the street, he noted that one of the turning wheels made a piercing and unpleasant sound: *Reek-reek-reek.* It made him think of the weathervane on top of Bud's Suds, the leprechaun with the pot of gold under his arm. The one in—

Desperation! I'm in Desperation, and this is *a dream! I fell asleep while I was trying to pray, I'm upstairs in the old movie theater!*

"There shall arise among you a prophet, and a dreamer of dreams," someone said.

David looked across the street and saw a dead cat—a cougar—hanging from a speed-limit sign. The cougar had a human head. Audrey Wyler's head. Her eyes rolled at him tiredly and he thought she was trying to smile. "But if he should say to you, Let us seek other gods, you shalt not hearken unto him."

He looked away, grimacing, and here, on his own side of Bear Street, was sweet Pie standing on the porch of his friend

Brian's house (Brian's house had never been on Bear Street
before, but now the rules had apparently changed). She was
holding Melissa Sweetheart clasped in her arms. "He was Mr.
Big Boogeyman after all," she said. "You know that now, don't
you?"

"Yes. I know, Pie."

"Walk a little faster, David. Mr. Big Boogeyman's after
you."

The desert-smell of wrappings and old spices was stronger
in his nose now, and David walked faster still. Up ahead was
the break in the bushes which marked the entrance to the Ho
Chi Minh Trail. There had never been anything there before
but the occasional hopscotch grid or KATHI LOVES RUSSELL
chalked on the sidewalk, but today the entrance to the path
was guarded by an ancient stone statue, one much too big to be
a *can tah*, little god; this was a *can tak*, big god. It was a jackal
with a cocked head, an open, snarling mouth, and buggy cartoon eyes that were full of fury. One of its ears had been either
chipped away or eroded away. The tongue in its mouth was not
a tongue at all but a human head—Collie Entragian's head,
Smokey Bear hat and all.

"Fear me and turn aside from this path," the cop in the
mouth of the jackal said as David approached. "*Mi tow, can de
lach:* fear the unformed. There are other gods than yours—*can
tah, can tak.* You know I speak the truth."

"Yes, but my God is strong," David said in a conversational
voice. He reached into the jackal's open mouth and seized its
psychotic tongue. He heard Entragian scream—and *felt* it,
a scream that vibrated against his palm like a joy-buzzer. A
moment later, the jackal's entire head exploded in a soundless
shardless flash of light. What remained was a stone hulk that
stopped short at the shoulders.

He walked down the path, aware that he was glimpsing
plants he had never seen anywhere in Ohio before—spiny

cactuses and drum cactuses, winter fat, squaw tea, Russian thistle . . . also known as tumbleweed. From the bushes at the side of the path stepped his mother. Her face was black and wrinkled, an ancient bag of dough. Her eyes drooped. The sight of her in this state filled him with sorrow and horror.

"Yes, yes, your God is strong," she said, "no argument there. But look what he's done to me. Is this strength worth admiring? Is this a God worth having?" She held her hands out to him, displaying her rotting palms.

"*God* didn't do that," David said, and began to cry. "The policeman did it!"

"But God *let* it happen," she countered, and one of her eyeballs dropped out of her head. "The same God who let Entragian push Kirsten downstairs and then hang her body on a hook for you to find. What God is this? Turn aside from him and embrace mine. Mine is at least honest about his cruelty."

But this whole conversation—not just the petitioning but the haughty, threatening tone of it—was so foreign to David's memory of his mother that he began to walk forward again. *Had* to walk forward again. The mummy was behind him, and the mummy was slow, yes, but he reckoned that this was one of the ways in which the mummy caught up with his victims: by using his ancient Egyptian magic to put obstacles in their path.

"Stay away from me!" the rotting mother-thing screamed. "Stay away or I'll turn you to stone in the mouth of a god! You'll be *can tah* in *can tak*!"

"You can't do that," David said patiently, "and you're not my mother. My mother's with my sister, in heaven, with God."

"What a joke!" the rotting thing cried indignantly. Its voice was gargly now, like the cop's voice. It was spitting blood and teeth as it talked. "Heaven's a *joke*, the kind of thing your Reverend Martin would spiel happily on about for hours, if you kept buying him shots and beers—it's no more real than Tom

Billingsley's fishes and horses! You won't tell me you swallowed it, will you? A smart boy like you? *Did* you? Oh Davey! I don't know whether to laugh or cry!" What she did was smile furiously. "There's no heaven, no afterlife at all . . . not for such as us. Only the gods—*can taks, can tahs,* can—"

He suddenly realized what this confused sermon was about: holding him here. Holding him so the mummy could catch up and choke him to death. He stepped forward, seized the raving head, and squeezed it between his hands. He surprised himself by laughing as he did it, because it was so much like the stuff the crazy cable-TV preachers did; they grabbed their victims upside the head and bellowed stuff like *"Sickness come OWWT! Tumors come OWWT! Rheumatiz come OWWWT! In the name of Jeeeesus!"* There was another of those soundless flashes, and this time not even the body was left; he was alone on the path again.

He walked on, sorrow working at his heart and mind, thinking of what the mother-thing had said. *No heaven, no afterlife at all, not for such as us.* That might be true or it might not be; he had no way of knowing. But the thing had also said that God had allowed his mother and sister to be killed, and that *was* true . . . wasn't it?

Well, maybe. How's a kid supposed to know about stuff like that?

Ahead was the oak tree with the Viet Cong Lookout in it. At the base of the tree was a piece of red-and-silver paper—a 3 Muskies wrapper. David bent over, picked it up, and stuck it in his mouth, sucking the smears of sweet chocolate off the inside with his eyes closed. *Take, eat,* he heard Reverend Martin say—this was a memory and not a voice, which was something of a relief. *This is my body, broken for you and for many.* He opened his eyes, fearing he might nevertheless see Reverend Martin's drunken face and dead eyes, but Reverend Martin wasn't there.

David spat the wrapper out and climbed to the Viet Cong Lookout with the sweet taste of chocolate in his mouth. He climbed into the sound of rock-and-roll music.

Someone was sitting cross-legged on the platform and look-ing out at the Bear Street Woods. His posture was so similar to Brian's—legs crossed, chin propped on the palms of his hands—that for a moment David was sure it *was* his old friend, only grown to young adulthood. David thought he could handle that. It wouldn't be any stranger than the rotting effigy of his mother or the cougar with Audrey Wyler's head, and a hell of a lot less distressing.

Slung over the young man's shoulder was a radio on a strap. Not a Walkman or a boombox; it looked older than either. There were two circular decals pasted to its leather case, one a yellow smile-guy, the other the peace sign. The music was coming from a small exterior speaker. The sound was tinny but still way cool, hot drums, killer rhythm guitar, and a somehow perfect rock-and-roll vocal: *"I was feelin' . . . so bad . . . asked my family doctor just what I had . . ."*

"Bri?" he asked, grabbing the bottom of the platform and pulling himself up. "That you?"

The man turned. He was slim, dark-haired under a Yankees baseball cap, wearing jeans, a plain gray tee-shirt, and big re-flector shades—David could see his own face in them. He was the first person David had seen in this . . . whatever-it-was . . . that he didn't know. "Brian's not here, David," he said.

"Who are you, then?" If the guy in the reflector sunglasses started to rot or to bleed out like Entragian, David was va-cating this tree in a hurry, and never mind the mummy that might be lurking somewhere in the woods below. "This is our place. Mine and Bri's."

"Brian *can't* be here," the dark-haired man said pleasantly. "Brian's alive, you see."

"I don't get you." But he was afraid he did.

"What did you tell Marinville when he tried to talk to the coyotes?"

It took David a moment to remember, and that wasn't surprising, because what he'd said hadn't seemed to come *from* him but *through* him. "I said not to speak to them in the language of the dead. Except it wasn't really me who—"

The man in the sunglasses waved this off. "The way Marinville tried to speak to the coyotes is sort of the way we're speaking now: *si em, tow en can de lach.* Do you understand?"

"Yes. 'We speak the language of the unformed.' The language of the dead." David began to shiver. "*I'm* dead, too, then . . . aren't I? I'm dead, too."

"Nope. Wrong. Lose one turn." The man turned up the volume on his radio—"*I said doctor . . . Mr. M.D. . . .*"—and smiled. "The Rascals," he said. "Felix Cavaliere on vocals. Cool?"

"Yes," David said, and meant it. He felt he could listen to the song all day. It made him think of the beach, and cute girls in two-piece bathing suits.

The man in the Yankees cap listened a moment longer, then turned the radio off. When he did, David saw a ragged scar on the underside of his right wrist, as if at some point he had tried to kill himself. Then it occurred to him that the man might have done a lot more than just try; wasn't this a place of the dead?

He suppressed a shiver.

The man took off his Yankees cap, wiped the back of his neck with it, put it back on, and looked at David seriously. "This is the Land of the Dead, but you're an exception. You're special. *Very.*"

"Who are you?"

"It doesn't matter. Just another member of the Young Rascals-Felix Cavaliere Fan Club, if it comes to that," the man said. He looked around, sighed, grimaced a little. "But I'll tell you one thing, young man: it doesn't surprise me at all that the Land of the Dead should turn out to be located in the suburbs of Columbus, Ohio." He looked back at David, his faint smile fading. "I guess it's time we got down to business. Time is short. You're going to have a bit of a sore throat when you wake up, by the way, and you may feel disoriented at first; they're moving you to the back of the truck Steve Ames drove into town. They feel a strong urge to vacate The American West—take it any way you want—and I can't say I blame them."

"Why are you here?"

"To make sure you know why *you're* here, David . . . to begin with, at least. So tell me: why *are* you here?"

"I don't know what you're—"

"Oh please," the man with the radio said. His mirror shades flashed in the sun. "If you don't, you're in deep shit. Why are you on *earth*? Why did God *make* you?"

David looked at him in consternation.

"Come on, come on!" the man said impatiently. "These are easy questions. Why did God make you? Why did God make me? Why did God make anyone?"

"To love and serve him," David said slowly.

"Okay, good. It's a start, anyway. And what is God? What's your experience of the nature of God?"

"I don't want to say." David looked down at his hands, then up at the grave, intent man—the strangely *familiar* man—in the sunglasses. "I'm scared I'll get in dutch." He hesitated, then dragged out what he was really afraid of: "I'm scared *you're* God."

The man uttered a short, rueful laugh. "In a way, that's pretty funny, but never mind. Let's stay focused here. What do you know of the nature of God, David? What is your experience?"

With the greatest reluctance, David said: "God is cruel."

He looked down at his hands again and counted slowly to five. When he had reached it and still hadn't been fried by a lightning-bolt, he looked up again. The man in the jeans and tee-shirt was still grave and intent, but David saw no anger in him.

"That's right, God is cruel. We slow down, the mummy always catches us in the end, and God is cruel. Why is God cruel, David?"

For a moment he didn't answer, and then something Reverend Martin had said came to him—the TV in the corner had been broadcasting a soundless spring-training baseball game that day.

"God's cruelty is refining," he said.

"We're the mine and God is the miner?"

"Well—"

"And all cruelty is good? God is good and cruelty is good?"

"No, hardly any of it's good!" David said. For a single horrified second he saw Pie, dangling from the hook on the wall, Pie who walked around ants on the sidewalk because she didn't want to hurt them.

"What is cruelty done for evil?"

"Malice. Who are you, sir?"

"Never mind. Who is the father of malice?"

"The devil . . . or maybe those other gods my mother talked about."

"Never mind *can tah* and *can tak*, at least for now. We have bigger fish to fry, so pay attention. What is faith?"

That one was easy. "The substance of things hoped for, the evidence of things not seen."

"Yeah. And what is the spiritual state of the faithful?"

"Um . . . love and acceptance. I think."

"And what is the opposite of faith?"

That was tougher—a real hairball, in fact. Like one of those damned reading-achievement tests. Pick *a*, *b*, *c*, or *d*. Except here you didn't even get the choices. "Disbelief?" he ventured.

"No. Not disbelief but *un*belief. The first is natural, the second willful. And when one is in unbelief, David, what is that one's spiritual state?"

He thought about it, then shook his head. "I don't know."

"Yes you do."

He thought about it and realized he did. "The spiritual state of unbelief is desperation."

"Yes. Look down, David!"

He did, and was shocked to see that the Viet Cong Lookout was no longer in the tree. It now floated, like a magic carpet made out of boards, above a vast, blighted countryside. He could see buildings here and there amid rows of gray and listless plants. One was a trailer with a bumper-sticker proclaiming the owner a Snapple-drinkin', Clinton-bashin' son of a bitch; another was the mining Quonset they'd seen on the way into town; another was the Municipal Building; another was Bud's Suds. The grinning leprechaun with the pot of gold under his arm peered out of a dead and strangulated jungle.

"This is the poisoned field," the man in the reflector sunglasses said. "What's gone on here makes Agent Orange look like sugar candy. There will be no sweetening this earth. It must be eradicated—sown with salt and plowed under. Do you know why?"

"Because it will spread?"

"No. It can't. Evil is both fragile and stupid, dying soon after the ecosystem it's poisoned."

"Then why—"

"Because it's an affront to God. There is no other reason. Nothing hidden or held back, no fine print. The poisoned field is a perversity and an affront to God. Now look down again."

He did. The buildings had slipped behind them. Now the Viet Cong Lookout floated above a vast pit. From this perspective, it looked like a sore which has rotted through the skin of the earth and into its underlying flesh. The sides sloped inward and downward in neat zigzags like stairs; in a way, looking into this place was like looking into

(walk a little faster)

a pyramid turned inside out. There were pines in the hills south of the pit, and some growth high up around the edges, but the pit itself was sterile—not even juniper grew here. On the near side—it would be the north face, David supposed, if the poisoned field was the town of Desperation—these neat setbacks had broken through near the bottom. Where they had been there was now a long slope of stony rubble. At the site of the landslide, and not too far from the broad gravel road leading down from the rim of the pit, there was a black and gaping hole. The sight of it made David profoundly uneasy. It was as if a monster buried in the desert ground had opened one eye. The landslide surrounding it made him uneasy, too. Because it looked somehow . . . well . . . *planned.*

At the bottom of the pit, just below the ragged hole, was a parking area filled with ore-freighters, diggers, pickup trucks, and tread-equipped vehicles that looked sort of like World War II tanks. Nearby stood a rusty Quonset hut with a stove-stack sticking crooked out of the roof, WELCOME TO RATTLESNAKE #2, read the sign on the door. PROVIDING JOBS AND TAX-DOLLARS TO CENTRAL NEVADA SINCE 1951. Off to the left of the metal building was a squat concrete cube. The sign on this one was briefer:

POWDER MAGAZINE
AUTHORIZED PERSONNEL ONLY

Parked between the two buildings was Collie Entragian's road-dusty Caprice. The driver's door stood open and the domelight was on, illuminating an interior that looked like an abattoir. On the dash, a plastic bear with a noddy head had been stuck beside the compass.

Then all that was sliding behind them.

"You know this place, don't you, David?"

"Is it the China Pit? It is, isn't it?"

"Yes."

They swooped closer to the side, and David saw that the pit was, in its way, even more desolate than the poisoned field. There were no whole stones or outcrops in the earth, at least not that he could see; everything had been reduced to an awful yellow rubble. Beyond the parking area and the buildings were vast heaps of even more radically crumbled rock, piled on black plastic.

"Those are waste dumps," his guide remarked. "The stuff piled on the plastic is gangue—spoil. But the company's not ready to let it rest, even now. There's more in it, you see . . . gold, silver, molybdenum, platinum. And copper, of course. Mostly it's copper. Deposits so diffuse it's as if they were blown in there like smoke. Mining it used to be uneconomic, but as the world's major deposits of ore and metal are depleted, what used to be uneconomic becomes profitable. The oversized Hefty bags are collection pads—the stuff they want precipitates out onto them, and they just scrape it off. It's a leaching process—spell it either way and it comes to the same. They'll go on working the ground until all of this, which used to be a mountain almost eight thousand feet high, is just dust in the wind."

"What are those big steps coming down the side of the pit?"

"Benches. They serve as ringroads for heavy equipment around the pit, but their major purpose is to minimize earthslides."

"It doesn't look like it worked very well back there." David hooked a thumb over his shoulder. "Up here, either." They were nearing another area where the look of vast stairs descending into the earth was obliterated by a tilted range of crumbled rock.

"That's a slope failure." The Viet Cong Lookout swooped above the slide area. Beyond it, David saw networks of black stuff that at first looked like cobwebs. As they drew nearer, he saw that the strands of what looked like cobwebbing were actually PVC pipe.

"Just lately it's been a switchover from rainbirds to emitters." His guide spoke in the tone of one who recites rather than speaks. David had a moment of *déjà vu*, then realized whiy: the man was repeating what Audrey Wyler had already said. "A few eagles died."

"A few?" David asked, giving Mr. Billingsley's line.

"All right, about forty, in all. No big deal in terms of the species; there's no shortage of eagles in Nevada. Do you see what they replaced the rainbirds with, David? The big pipes are distribution heads—*can taks,* let's say."

"Big gods."

"Yes! And those little hollow cords that stretch between them like mesh, those are emitters. *Can tahs.* They drip weak sulfuric acid. It frees the ore . . . and rots the ground. Hang on, David."

The Viet Cong Lookout banked—also like a flying carpet— with David holding onto the edge of the boards to keep from tumbling off. He didn't want to fall onto that terrible gouged ground where nothing grew and streams of brackish fluid flowed down to the plastic collection pads.

They sank into the pit again and passed above the rusty Quonset with the stove-stack, the powder magazine, and the cluster of machinery where the road ended. Up the slope, above the gaping hole, was a wide area pocked with other, much smaller holes. David thought there had to be fifty of them at least, probably more. From each poked a yellow-tipped stick.

"Looks like the world's biggest gopher colony."

"This is a blast-face, and those are blast-holes," his new acquaintance lectured. "The active mining is going on right here. Each of those holes is three feet in diameter and about thirty feet deep. When you're getting ready to shoot, you lower a stick of dynamite with a blasting cap on it to the bottom of each hole. That's the igniter. Then you pour in a couple of wheelbarrows' worth of ANFO—stands for ammonium nitrate and fuel oil. Those assholes who blew up the Federal Building in Oklahoma City used ANFO. It usually comes in pellets that look like white BBs."

The man in the Yankees cap pointed to the powder magazine.

"Lots of ANFO in there. No dynamite—they used up the last on the day all this started to happen—but plenty of ANFO."

"I don't understand why you're telling me this."

"Never mind, just listen. Do you see the blast-holes?"

"Yes. They look like eyes."

"That's right, holes like eyes. They're sunk into the porphyry, which is crystalline. When the ANFO is detonated, it shatters the rock. The shattered stuff contains the ore. Get it?"

"Yes, I think so."

"That material is trucked away to the leach pads, the distribution heads and emitters—*can tah, can tak*—are laid over it, and the rotting process begins. *Voilà*, there you have it, leach-ore mining at its very finest. But see what the last blast-pattern uncovered, David!"

He pointed at the big hole, and David felt an unpleasant, debilitating coldness begin to creep through him. The hole seemed to stare up at him with a kind of idiot invitation.

"What is it?" he whispered, but he supposed he knew.

"Rattlesnake Number One. Also known as the China Mine or the China Shaft or the China Drift. The last series of shots uncovered it. To say the crew was surprised would be an understatement, because nobody in the Nevada mining business really believes that old story. By the turn of the century, the

Diablo Company was claiming that Number One was simply shut down when the vein played out. But it's been here, David. All along. And now—"

"Is it haunted?" David asked, shivering. "It is, isn't it?"

"Oh yes," the man in the Yankees cap said, turning his silvery no-eyes on David. "Yes indeed."

"Whatever you brought me up here for, I don't want to hear it!" David cried. "I want you to take me back! Back to my dad! I hate this! I hate being in the Land of the—"

He broke off as a horrible thought struck him. The Land of the Dead, that was what the man had said. He'd called David an exception. But that meant—

"Reverend Martin . . . I saw him on my way to the Woods. Is he . . ."

The man looked briefly down at his old-fashioned radio, then looked back up again and nodded. "Two days after you left, David."

"Was he drunk?"

"Toward the end he was always drunk. Like Billingsley."

"Was it suicide?"

"No," the man in the Yankees cap said, and put a kindly hand on the back of David's neck. It was warm, not the hand of a dead person. "At least, not *conscious* suicide. He and his wife went to the beach. They took a picnic. He went in the water too soon after lunch, and swam out too far."

"Take me back," David whispered. "I'm tired of all this death."

"The poisoned field is an affront to God," the man said. "I know it's a bummer, David, but—"

"Then let God clean it up!" David cried. "It's not fair for him to come to me after he killed my mother and my sister—"

"He didn't—"

"I don't care! I don't care! Even if he didn't, he stood aside and let it happen!"

"That's not true, either."

David shut his eyes and clapped his hands to his ears. He didn't want to hear any more. He *refused* to hear any more. Yet the man's voice came through anyway. It was relentless. He would be able to escape it no more than Jonah had been able to escape God. God was as relentless as a bloodhound on a fresh scent. And God was cruel.

"Why are you on earth?" The voice seemed to come from *inside* his head now.

"I don't hear you! I don't hear you!"

"You were put on earth to love God—"

"No!"

"—and serve him."

"No! Fuck God! Fuck his love! Fuck his *service*!"

"God can't make you do anything you don't want to—"

"Stop it! I won't listen, I won't decide! Do you hear? Do you—"

"Shh—listen!"

Not quite against his will, David listened.

PART IV

THE CHINA PIT:
GOD IS
CRUEL

CHAPTER 1

1

Johnny was ready to suggest that they just get going—Cynthia could hold the kid's head in her lap and cushion it from any bumps—when David raised his hands and pressed the heels of his palms to his temples. He took a deeper breath. A moment later his eyes opened and looked up at them: Johnny, Steve, Cynthia, his father. The faces of the two older men were as puffed and discolored as those of journeymen fighters after a bad night in a tank town; all of them looked tired and scared, jumping like spooked horses at the slightest sound. The ragtag remains of The Collie Entragian Survival Society.

"Hi, David," Johnny said. "Great to have you back. You're in—"

"—Steve's truck. Parked near the movie theater. You brought it down from the Conoco station." David struggled to a sitting position, swallowed, winced. "She must've shook me like dice."

"She did," Steve said. He was looking at David cautiously. "You remember Audrey doing that?"

"No," David said, "but I was told."

Johnny shot a glance at Ralph, who shrugged slightly—*Don't ask me.*

"Is there any water? My throat's on fire."

"We got out of the theater in a hurry and didn't bring

anything but the guns," Cynthia said. "But there's this." She pointed to a case of Jolt Cola from which several bottles had already been taken. "Steve keeps it on hand for Mr. Marinville."

"I'm a freak about it since I quit drinking," Johnny said. "Gotta be Jolt, God knows why. It's warm, but—"

David took one and drank deeply, wincing as the carbonation bit into his throat but not slowing down on that account. At last, with the bottle three-quarters empty, he put his head back against the side of the truck, closed his eyes, and burped ringingly.

Johnny grinned. "Sixty points!"

David opened his eyes and grinned back.

Johnny held out the bottle of aspirin he had liberated from the Owl's. "Want a couple? They're old, but they seem to work all right."

David thought it over, then took two and washed them down with the rest of the Jolt.

"We're getting out," Johnny said. "We'll try north first— there are some trailers in the road, but Steve says he thinks we can get around them on the trailer-park side. If we can't, we'll have to go south to the pit-mine and then take the equipment road that runs northwest from there back to Highway 50. You and I'll sit up front with—"

"No."

Johnny raised his eyebrows. "Pardon?"

"We have to go up to the mine, okay, but not to leave town." David's voice sounded hoarse, as if he'd been crying. "We have to go down inside the pit."

Johnny glanced at Steve, who only shrugged and then looked back at the boy. "What are you talking about, David?" Steve asked. "Your mother? Because it would probably be better for her, not to mention the rest of us, if we—"

"No, that's not why . . . Dad?" The boy reached out and

took his father's hand. It was an oddly adult gesture of comfort. "Mom's dead."

Ralph bowed his head. "Well, we don't know that for sure, David, and we mustn't give up hope, but I guess it's likely."

"I *do* know for sure. I'm not just guessing." David's face was haggard in the light of the crisscrossing flashlight beams. His eyes settled on Johnny last. "There's stuff we have to do. You know it, don't you? That's why you waited for me to wake up."

"No, David. Not at all. We just didn't want to risk moving you until we were sure you were okay." Yet this felt like a lie to his heart. He found himself filling up with a vague, fluttery nervousness. It was the way he felt in the last few days before beginning a new book, when he understood that the inevitable could not be put off much longer, that he would soon be out on the wire again, clutching his balance-pole and riding his stupid little unicycle.

But this was worse. By far. He felt an urge to bop the kid over the head with the butt of the Rossi shotgun, knock him out and shut him up before he could say anything else. *Don't you fuck us up, kid,* he thought. *Not when we're starting to see a tiny bit of light at the end of the tunnel.*

David looked back at his father. He was still holding Ralph's hand. "She's dead but not at rest. She can't be as long as Tak inhabits her body."

"Who's Tak, David?" Cynthia asked.

"One of the Wintergreen Twins," Johnny said cheerfully. "The other one is Tik."

David gave him a long, level look, and Johnny dropped his eyes. He hated himself for doing it but couldn't help it.

"Tak is a god," David said. "Or a demon. Or maybe nothing at all, just a name, a nonsense syllable—but a *dangerous* nothing, like a voice in the wind. It doesn't matter. What does is that my mom should be put to rest. Then she can be with my sister in . . . well, in wherever there is for us after we die."

"Son, what matters is that *we have to get out of here*," Johnny said. He was still managing to keep his voice gentle, but now he could hear an undercurrent of impatience and fear in it. "Once we get to Ely, we'll contact the State Police—hell, the FBI. There'll be a hundred cops on the ground and a dozen helicopters in the air by noon tomorrow, that I promise you. But for now—"

"My mom's dead, but Mary's not," David said. "She's still alive. She's in the pit."

Cynthia gasped. "How did you know she was even gone?"

David smiled wanly. "Well, I don't see her, for one thing. The rest I know the same way I know it was Audrey who choked me. I was told."

"By who, David?" Ralph asked.

"I don't know," David said. "I don't even know if it matters. What matters is that he told me stuff. *True* stuff. I know it was."

"Story-hour's over, pal," Johnny said. There was a raggedness in his voice. He heard it, but he couldn't help it. And was it surprising? This wasn't a panel-discussion on magical realism or concrete prose, after all. Story-hour was finished; bug-out time had arrived. He had absolutely no desire to listen to a bunch of shit from this spooky little Jesus Scout.

The Jesus Scout slid out of his cell somehow, killed the coyote Entragian set as a guard, and saved your miserable life, Terry spoke up inside his head. *Maybe you should listen to him, Johnny.*

And that, he thought, was why he had divorced Terry in the first place. In a fucking nutshell. She had been a divine lay, but she had never known when to shut up and listen to her intellectual betters.

But the damage was done; it was now too late to derail this train of thought. He found himself thinking of what Billingsley had said about David's escape from the jail cell. Not even Houdini, hadn't that been it? Because of the head.

And then there was the phone. The way he'd sent the coyotes packing. And the matter of the sardines and crackers. The thought which had gone through his own head had been something about unobtrusive miracles, hadn't it?

He had to quit thinking that way. Because what Jesus Scouts did was get people killed. Look at John the Baptist, or those nuns in South America, or—

Not even Houdini.

Because of the head.

Johnny realized there was no point in gilding the lily, or doing little mental tap-dances, or—this was the oldest trick of all—using different voices to argue the question into incoherence. The simple fact was that he was no longer just afraid of the cop, or the other forces which might be loose in this town.

He was also afraid of David Carver.

"It wasn't *really* the cop who killed my mother and sister and Mary's husband," David said, and gave Johnny a look that reminded him eerily of Terry. That look used to drive him to the edge of insanity. *You know what I'm talking about,* it said. *You know* exactly, *so don't waste my time by being deliberately obtuse.* "And whoever I talked to while I was unconscious, it was really God. Only God can't come to people as himself; he'd scare them to death and never get any business done at all. He comes as other stuff. Birds, pillars of fire, burning bushes, whirlwinds . . ."

"Or people," Cynthia said. "Sure, God's a master of disguise."

The last of Johnny's patience broke at the skinny girl's makes-sense-to-me tone. "This is totally insane!" he shouted. "We have to get *gone*, don't you see that? We're parked on goddam Main Street, shut up in here without a single window to look out of, he could be anywhere—up front behind the fucking *wheel*, for all we know! Or . . . I don't know . . . coyotes . . . buzzards . . ."

"He's gone," David said in his quiet voice. He leaned forward and took another Jolt from the case.

"Who?" Johnny asked. "Entragian?"

"The *can tak*. It doesn't matter who it's in—Entragian or my mother or the one it started with—it's always the same. Always the *can tak*, the big god, the guardian. Gone. Can't you feel it?"

"I don't feel anything."

Don't be a gonzo, Terry said in his mind.

"Don't be a gonzo," David said, looking intently up at him. The bottle of Jolt was clasped loosely in his hands.

Johnny bent toward him. "Are you reading my mind?" he asked, almost pleasantly. "If you are, I'll thank you to get the hell out of my head, sonny."

"*What I'm doing is trying to get you to listen,*" David said. "Everyone else will if *you* will! He doesn't need to send his *can tahs* or *can tak* against us if we're in disagreement with one another—if there's a broken window, he'll get in and tear us apart!"

"Come on," Johnny said, "don't go all guilt-trippy. None of this is my fault."

"I'm not saying it *is*. Just listen, okay?" David sounded almost pleading. "You can do that, there's time, because *he's gone.* The trailers he put in the road are gone, too. Don't you get it? *He wants us to leave.*"

"Great! Let's give him what he wants!"

"Let's listen to what David has to say," Steve said.

Johnny wheeled on him. "I think you must have forgotten who pays you, Steve." He loathed the sound of the words as soon as they were out of his mouth, but made no effort to take them back. The urge to get out of here, to jump behind the wheel of the Ryder truck and just roll some miles—in any direction but south—was now so strong it was nearly panic.

"You told me to stop calling you boss. I'm holding you to that."

"Besides, what about Mary?" Cynthia asked. "He says she's alive!"

Johnny turned toward her—turned *on* her. "You may want to pack your suitcases and travel Trans-God Airways with David, but I think I'll pass."

"We'll listen to him," Ralph said in a low voice.

Johnny stared at him, amazed. If he had expected help from anyone, it had been from the boy's father. *He's all I got,* Ralph had said in the lobby of The American West. *All that's left of my family.*

Johnny looked around at the others, and was dismally astounded to see they were in agreement; only he stood apart. And Steve had the keys to the truck in his pocket. Yet it was him the boy was mostly looking at. Him. As it was him, John Edward Marinville, that people had been mostly looking at ever since he had published his first novel at the impossibly precocious age of twenty-two. He thought he had gotten used to it, and maybe he had, but this time it was different. He had an idea that none of the others—the teachers, the readers, the critics, the editors, the drinking buddies, the women—had ever wanted what this boy seemed to want, which was not just for him to listen; listening, Johnny was afraid, was only where it would start.

The eyes were not just looking, though. The eyes were pleading.

Forget it, kid, he thought. *When people like you drive, the bus always seems to crash.*

If it wasn't for David, I think your personal bus would have crashed already, Terry said from *Der Bitchen Bunker* inside his head. *I think you'd be dead and hung up on a hook somewhere. Listen to him, Johnny. For Christ's sake, listen!*

In a much lower voice, Johnny said: "Entragian's gone. You're sure of that."

"Yes," David said. "The animals, too. The coyotes and wolves—hundreds of them, it must have taken, maybe thousands—moved the trailers off the road. Dumped them over the side and onto the hardpan. Now most of them have drawn away, into *mi him,* the watchman's circle." He drank from the bottle of Jolt. The hand holding it shook slightly. He looked at each of them in turn, but it was Johnny his eyes came back to. Always Johnny. "He wants what *you* want. For us to leave."

"Then why did he bring us here in the first place?"

"He didn't."

"What?"

"He thinks he did, but he didn't."

"I don't have any idea what you're—"

"God brought us," David said. "To stop him."

2

In the silence which followed this, Steve discovered he was listening for the wind outside. There was none. He thought he could hear a plane far away—sane people on their way to some sane destination, sleeping or eating or reading *U.S. News & World Report*—but that was all.

It was Johnny who broke the silence, of course, and although he sounded as confident as ever, there was a look in his eyes (a *slidey* look) that Steve didn't like much. He thought he liked Johnny's crazed look better: the wide eyes and terrified Clyde Barrow grin he'd had on when he put the shotgun up to the cougar's ear and blew its head off. That there was a half-bright outlaw in Johnny was something Steve knew very well—he'd seen flickers of that guy from the start of the tour, and knew it was the outlaw Bill Harris had feared when he laid down the Five Commandments that day in Jack Appleton's office—but Clyde Barrow seemed to have stepped out and left the other Marinville, the one with the satiric eyebrow and the windbag William F. Buckley rhetoric, in his place.

"You speak as if we all had the same God, David," he said. "I don't mean to patronize you, but I hardly think that's the case."

"But it *is* the case," David replied calmly. "Compared to Tak, you and a cannibal king would have the same God. You've seen the *can tahs*, I know you have. And you've felt what they can do."

Johnny's mouth twitched—indicating, Steve thought, that he had taken a hit but didn't want to admit it. "Perhaps that's so," he said, "but the person who brought *me* here was a long way from God. He was a big blond policeman with skin problems. He planted a bag of dope in my saddlebag and then beat the shit out of me."

"Yes. I know. The dope came from Mary's car. He put something like nails in the road to get us. It's funny, when you think about it—funny-weird, not ha-ha. He went through Desperation like a whirlwind—shot people, stabbed them, beat them, pushed them out windows, ran them down with his car—but he still couldn't just come up to us, *any* of us, and take out his gun and say 'You're coming with me.' He had to have a . . . I don't know the word." He looked at Johnny.

"Pretext," Steve's erstwhile boss said.

"Yes, right, a pretext. It's like how, in the old horror movies, a vampire can't just come in on his own. You have to invite him in."

"Why?" Cynthia asked.

"Maybe because Entragian—the *real* Entragian—was still inside his head. Like a shadow. Or a person that's locked out of his house but can still look in the windows and pound on the doors. Now Tak's in my mother—what's left of her—and it would kill us if it could . . . but it could probably still make the best Key lime pie in the world, too. If it wanted to."

David looked down for a moment, his lips trembling, then looked back up at them.

"Him needing a pretext to take us doesn't really matter. Many times what he does or says doesn't matter—it's nonsense, or impulse. Although there are clues. Always clues. He gives himself away, shows his real self, like someone who says what he sees in inkblots."

Steve asked, "If that doesn't matter, what does?"

"*That he took us and let other people go.* He thinks he took us at random, like a little kid in a supermarket, just pulling any can that catches his eye off the shelf and dropping it into his mom's cart, but that's not what happened."

"It's like the Angel of Death in Egypt, isn't it?" Cynthia said in a curiously flat voice. "Only in reverse. We had a mark on us that told *our* Angel of Death—this guy Entragian—to stop and grab instead of just going on by."

David nodded. "Yeah. He didn't know it then, but he does now—*mi him en tow,* he'd say—our God is strong, our God is with us."

"If this is an example of God being with us, I hope I never attract his attention when he's in a snit," Johnny said.

"Now Tak wants us to go," David said, "and he knows that we *can* go. Because of the free-will covenant. That's what Reverend Martin always called it. He . . . he . . ."

"David?" Ralph asked. "What is it? What's wrong?"

David shrugged. "Nothing. It doesn't matter. What matters is that God never *makes* us do what he wants us to do. He tells us, that's all, then steps back to see how it turns out. Reverend Martin's wife came in and listened for awhile while he was talking about the free-will covenant. She said her mother had a motto: 'God says take what you want, and pay for it.' Tak's opened the door back to Highway 50 . . . but that isn't where we're supposed to go. If we *do* go, if we leave Desperation without doing what God sent us here to do, we'll pay the price."

He glanced at the circle of faces around him once again, and once again he finished by looking directly at Johnny Marinville.

"I'll stay no matter what, but to work, it really has to be *all* of us. We have to give our will over to God's will, and we have to be ready to die. Because that's what it might come to."

"You're insane, my boy," Johnny said. "Ordinarily I like that in a person, but this is going a little too far, even for me. I haven't survived this long in order to be shot or pecked to death by buzzards in the desert. As for God, as far as I'm concerned, he died in the DMZ back in 1969. Jimi Hendrix was playing 'Purple Haze' on Armed Services Radio at the time."

"Listen to the rest, okay? Will you do that much?"

"Why should I?"

"Because there's a story." David drank more Jolt, grimacing as he swallowed. "A good one. Will you listen?"

"Story-hour's over. I told you that."

David didn't reply.

There was silence in the back of the truck. Steve was watching Johnny closely. If he showed any sign of moving toward the Ryder's back door and trying to run it up, Steve meant to grab him. He didn't want to—he had spent a lot of years in the savagely hierarchical world of backstage rock, and knew that doing such a thing would make him feel like Fletcher Christian to Johnny's Captain Bligh—but he would if he had to.

So it was a relief when Johnny shrugged, smiled, hunkered down next to the kid, and selected his own bottle of Jolt. "Okay, so story-hour's extended. Just for tonight." He ruffled David's hair. The very self-consciousness of the gesture made it oddly charming. "Stories have been my Achilles' heel practically since I ditched the stroller. I have to tell you, though, this is one I'd like to hear end with 'And they lived happily ever after.'"

"Wouldn't we all," Cynthia said.

"I think the guy I met told me everything," David said, "but there are still some parts I don't know. Parts that are blurry, or just plain black. Maybe because I couldn't understand, or because I didn't want to."

"Do the best you can," Ralph said. "That'll be good enough."

David looked up into the shadows, thinking—*summoning*, Cynthia thought—and then began.

3

"Billingsley told the legend, and like most legends, I guess, most of it was wrong. It wasn't a cave-in that closed the China Shaft, that's the first thing. The mine was brought down on purpose. And it didn't happen in 1858, although that *was* when the first Chinese miners were brought in, but in September of 1859. Not forty Chinese down there when it happened but fifty-seven, not two white men but four. Sixty-one people in all. And the drift wasn't a hundred and fifty feet deep, like Billingsley said, but nearly two hundred. Can you imagine? Two hundred feet deep in hornfels that could have fallen in on them at any moment."

The boy closed his eyes. He looked incredibly fragile, like a child who has just begun to recover from some terrible illness and may relapse at any moment. Some of that look might have been caused by the thin green sheen of soap still on his skin, but Cynthia didn't think that was all of it. Nor did she doubt David's power, or have a problem with the idea that he might have been touched by God. She had been raised in a parsonage, and she had seen this look before . . . although never so strongly.

"At ten minutes past one on the afternoon of September twenty-first, the guys at the face broke through into what they at first thought was a cave. Inside the opening was a pile of those stone things. Thousands of them. Statues of certain animals, *low* animals, the *timoh sen cah.* Wolves, coyotes, snakes, spiders, rats, bats. The miners were amazed by these, and did the most natural thing in the world: bent over and picked them up."

"Bad idea," Cynthia murmured.

David nodded. "Some went crazy at once, turning on their friends—heck, turning on their relatives—and trying to rip their throats out. Others, not just the ones farther back in the shaft who didn't actually handle the *can tahs*, but some who were close and actually did handle them, seemed all right, at least for awhile. Two of these were brothers from Tsingtao—Ch'an Lushan and Shih Lushan. Both saw through the break in the face and into the cave, which was really a kind of underground chamber. It was round, like the bottom of a well. The walls were made of faces, these stone animal faces. The faces of *can taks*, I think, although I'm not sure about that. There was a small kind of building to one side, the *pirin moh*—I don't know what that means, I'm sorry—and in the middle, a round hole twelve feet across. Like a giant eye, or another well. A well in a well. Like the carvings, which are mostly animals with other animals in their mouths for tongues. *Can tak* in *can tah*, *can tah* in *can tak.*"

"Or *camera in camera*," Marinville said. He spoke with an eyebrow raised, his sign that he was making fun, but David took him seriously. He nodded and began to shiver.

"That's Tak's place," he said. "The *ini*, well of the worlds."

"I don't understand you," Steve said gently.

David ignored him; it was still Marinville he seemed to be mostly talking to. "The force of evil from the *ini* filled the *can tahs* the same way the minerals fill the ground itself—blown into every particle of it, like smoke. And it filled the chamber I'm talking about the same way. It's not smoke, but smoke is the best way to think about it, maybe. It affected the miners at different rates, like a disease germ. The ones who went nuts right away turned on the others. Some, their bodies started to change the way Audrey's did at the end. Those were the ones who had touched the *can tahs*, sometimes picked up whole handfuls at once and then put them down so they could . . . you know . . . go at the others.

"Some of them were widening the hole between the shaft and the chamber. Others were wriggling through. Some acted drunk. Others acted as if they were having convulsions. Some ran across to the pit and threw themselves into it, laughing. The Lushan brothers saw a man and a woman fucking each other—I have to use that word, it was the furthest thing in the world from making love—with one of the statues held between them. In their teeth."

Cynthia exchanged a startled look with Steve.

"In the shaft itself, the miners were bashing each other with rocks or pulling each other out of the way, trying to get in through the hole first." He looked around at them somberly. "I saw that part. In a way it was funny, like a Three Stooges show. And that made it worse. That it was funny. Do you get it?"

"Yes," Marinville said. "I get it very well, David. Go on."

"The brothers felt it all around them, the stuff that was coming out of the chamber, but not as anything that was inside them, not then. One of the *can tahs* had fallen at Ch'an's feet. He bent to pick it up, and Shih pulled him away. By then they were about the only ones left who seemed sane. Most of the others who weren't affected right away had been killed, and there was a thing—like a snake made of smoke—coming out of the hole. It made a squealing sound, and the brothers ran from it. One of the white men was coming down the crosscut about sixty feet up, and he had his gun out. 'What's all the commotion about, chinkies?' he asked."

Cynthia felt her skin chill. She reached out for Steve, and

was relieved when his fingers folded over hers. The boy hadn't just imitated a gruff bossman's tone; he seemed actually to be speaking in the voice of someone else.

" 'Come on now, fellows, gettee-backee-workee, if you don't want a bullet in the guts.'

"But he was the one who got shot. Ch'an grabbed him around the neck and Shih took away his gun. He put the barrel here"—David poked his forefinger up under the shelf of his jaw—"and blew the guy's head off."

"David, do you know what they were thinking when they did that?" Marinville asked. "Was your dream-friend able to take you in that far?"

"Mostly I just saw."

"Those *can tah* things must've gotten to them after all," Ralph said. "They wouldn't have shot a white man, otherwise. No matter *what* was going on or how bad they wanted to get away."

"Maybe so," David said. "But God was in them too, I think, the way he's in us now. God could move them to his work, no matter if they were *mi en tak* or not, because—*mi him en tow*—our God is strong. Do you understand?"

"I think I do," Cynthia said. "What happened then, David?"

"The brothers ran up the shaft, pointing the foreman's pistol at anyone who tried to hold them back or slow them down. There weren't many; even the other white guys hardly gave them a glance when they ran by. They all wanted to see what was going on, what the miners had found. It drew them, you see. You *do* see, don't you?"

The others nodded.

"About sixty feet in from the adit, the Lushan brothers stopped and went to work on the hanging wall. They didn't talk about it; they saw picks and shovels and just went to work."

"What's a hanging wall?" Steve asked.

"The roof of a mineshaft and the earth above it," Marinville said.

"They worked like madmen," David went on. "The stuff was so loose that it started falling out of the ceiling right away, but the ceiling didn't give way. The screams and howls and laughter coming up from below . . . I know the words for the sounds I heard, but I can't describe how horrible they were. Some of them were changing from human to something else. There was a movie I saw one time, about this doctor on a tropical island who was changing animals into men—"

Marinville nodded. *"The Island of Dr. Moreau."*

David said, "The sounds I heard from the bottom of the mine—the ones I heard with the Lushan brothers' ears—were like that movie, only in reverse. As if the men were turning into animals. I guess they were. I guess that's sort of what the *can tahs* do. What they're for.

"The brothers . . . I see them, two Chinese men who look almost enough alike to be twins, with pigtails hanging down their sweaty bare backs, standing there and looking up and chopping away at the hanging wall that should have come down after about six licks but didn't, looking back along the shaft every two or three strokes to see who was coming. To see *what* was coming. Pieces of the ceiling fell in front of them in big chunks. Sometimes pieces of it fell *on* them, too, and pretty soon their shoulders were bleeding, and their heads—blood was streaming down their faces and necks and chests, as well. By then there were other sounds from below. Things roaring. Things *squelching.* And still the roof wouldn't come down. Then they started seeing lights farther down—maybe candles, maybe the 'seners the crew-bosses wore."

"What—" Ralph began.

"*Kero*seners. They were like these little lighted boxes of oil you put on your forehead with a strip of rawhide. You'd fold a piece of cloth underneath to keep your skin from getting too hot. And then someone came running out of the darkness, someone they knew. It was Yuan Ti. He was a funny guy, I guess—he made animals out of pieces of cloth and then put on shows with them for the kids. Yuan Ti had gone crazy, but that wasn't all. He was *bigger*, so big he had to bend almost double in order to run up the shaft. He was throwing rocks at them, calling them names in Mandarin, condemning their ancestors, commanding them to stop what they were doing. Shih shot him with the foreman's gun. He had to shoot him a lot before Yuan Ti would lie down and be dead. But the others were coming, screaming for their blood. Tak knew what they were doing, you see."

David looked at them, seemed to consider them. His eyes were dreamy, half in a trance, but Cynthia had no sense that the boy had ceased to see them. In a way, that was the most terrible part of what was happening here. David saw them very well . . . and so did the force inside him, the one she could sometimes hear stepping forward to clarify parts of the story David might not have fully understood.

"Shih and Ch'an went back to work on the hanging wall, digging into it with their picks like madmen—which they'd be before it was over for them. By then the part of the ceiling they were working on was like a dome over their heads"—David made curving gestures with his hands, and Cynthia saw that his fingers were trembling—"and they couldn't reach it very well with their picks anymore. So Shih, the older, got on his younger brother's shoulders and dug into it that way. The stuff fell out in showers, there was a pile almost as high as Ch'an Lushan's knees in front of them, and still the ceiling wouldn't come down."

"Were they possessed of God, David?" Marinville asked. There was no sarcasm in his voice now. "Possessed *by* God? What do you think?"

"I don't think so," David said. "I don't think God *has* to

possess, that's what makes him God. I think they wanted what God wanted—to keep Tak in the earth. To bring the ceiling down between them and it, if they could.

"Anyway, they saw 'seners coming up from the mine. Heard people yelling. A whole mob of them. Shih left off on the hangwall and went to work on one of the crossbar supports instead, hitting it with the butt of his pick. The miners coming up from below threw rocks at them, and quite a few hit Ch'an, but he stood firm with his brother on his shoulders. When the crossbar finally came down, the ceiling came down with it. Ch'an was buried up to his knees, but Shih was thrown clear. He pulled his brother out. Ch'an was badly bruised, but nothing was broken. And they were on the right side of the rockfall—that must have seemed like the important thing. They could hear the miners—their friends, cousins, and in the case of Ch'an Lushan, his intended wife—screaming to be let out. Ch'an actually started to pull some of the rocks away before Shih yanked him back and reasoned with him.

"They still *could* reason then, you see.

"Then, as if the people trapped on Tak's side of the fall knew this had happened, the screams for help changed to yelling and howling. The sounds of . . . well, of people who weren't really people at all anymore. Ch'an and Shih ran. They met folks—some white, some Chinese—coming in as they ran out. No questions were asked except for the most obvious one, what happened, and since the answer was just as obvious, they had no trouble. There'd been a cave-in, men were trapped, and the last thing anyone cared about just then were a couple of scared China-boys who happened to get out in the nick of time."

David drank the last of his soda and set the empty bottle aside.

"Everything Mr. Billingsley told us is like that," he said. "Truth and mistakes and outright lies all mixed up."

"The technical term for it is 'legend-making,'" Marinville said with a thin, strained smile.

"The miners and the folks from town could hear the Chinese screaming behind the fallen hanging wall, but they didn't just stand around; they *did* try to dig them out, and they *did* try to shore up the first sixty feet or so. But then there was another fall, a smaller one, and another couple of crossbars snapped. So they pulled back and waited for the experts to show up from Reno. There was no picnic outside the adit—that's a flat lie. Right around the time the mining engineers were getting off the stage in Desperation, there were two cave-ins—*real* cave-ins, big ones—at the mine. The first was on the adit side of the hanging wall the Lushan brothers had pulled down. It sealed off the last sixty feet of the drift like a cork in a bottle. And the thump it made coming down—tons and tons of skarn and hornfels—set off another one, deeper in. That ended the screams, at least the ones close enough to the surface for people to hear. It was all over before the mining engineers got up from town in an ore-wagon. They looked, they sank some core rods, they listened to the story, and when they heard about the second cave-in, which people said shook the ground like an earthquake and made the horses rear up, they shook their heads and said there was probably nobody left alive to rescue. And even if there was, they'd be risking more lives than they could hope to save if they tried to go back in."

"And they *were* only Chinese," Steve said.

"That's right, little chink-chink China-boys. Mr. Billingsley was right about that. And while all this was going on, the two China-boys who *had* escaped were out in the desert near Rose Rock, going mad. It got to them in the end, you see. It caught up with them. It was almost two weeks before they came back to Desperation, not three days. It *was* the Lady Day they walked into—you see how he got the truth all mixed up with the lies?—but they didn't kill anyone there. Shih flashed the foreman's gun, which was empty, and that was all it took. They were brought down by a whole pack of miners and cowboys. They were naked except for loincloths. They were covered with blood. The men in the Lady Day felt like that blood must have been from all the folks they had murdered, but it wasn't. They'd been out in the desert, calling animals to them . . . just like Tak called the cougar that you shot, Mr. Marinville. Only the Lushan brothers didn't want them for anything like that. They only wanted to eat. They ate whatever came—bats, buzzards, spiders, rattlesnakes."

David raised an unsteady hand to his face and wiped first his left eye and then his right.

"I feel very sorry for the Lushan brothers. And I feel like I know them a little. How they must have felt. How they must have been grateful, in a way, when the madness finally took them over completely and they didn't have to think anymore.

"They could have stayed out there in the Desatoya foothills practically forever, I guess, but they were all Tak had, and Tak is always hungry. It sent them into town, because there was nothing else it could do. One of them, Shih, was killed right there in the Lady Day. Ch'an was hung two days later, right about where those three bikes were turned upside down in the street . . . remember those? He raved in Tak's language, the language of the unformed, right up until the end. He tore the hood right off his head, so they hung him barefaced."

"Boy, that God of yours, what a guy!" Marinville said cheerfully. "Really knows how to repay a favor, doesn't he, David?"

"God is cruel," David said in a voice almost too low to hear.

"What?" Marinville asked. "What did you say?"

"You know. But life is more than just steering a course around pain. That's something you used to know, Mr. Marinville. Didn't you?"

Marinville looked off into the corner of the truck and said nothing.

4

The first thing Mary was aware of was a smell—sweetish, rank, nauseating. *Oh Peter, dammit to hell,* she thought groggily. *It's the freezer, everything's spoiled!*

Except that wasn't right; the freezer had gone off during their trip to Majorca, and that had been a long time ago, before the miscarriage. A lot had happened since then. A lot had happened just recently, in fact. Most of it bad. But what?

Central Nevada's full of intense people.

Who said that? Marielle? In her head it certainly sounded like Marielle.

Doesn't matter, if it's true. And it is, isn't it?

She didn't know. Didn't *want* to know. What she mostly wanted was to go back into the darkness part of her was trying to come out of. Because there were voices

(they're a dastardly bunch)

and sounds

(reek-reek-reek)

that she didn't want to consider. Better to just lie here and—

Something scuttered across her face. It felt both light and hairy. She sat up, pawing her cheeks with both hands. An enormous bolt of pain went through her head, bright dots flashed across her vision in sync with her suddenly elevated heartrate, and she had a similarly bright flash of recall, one even Johnny Marinville would have admired.

I bumped my bad arm putting up another crate to stand on.

Hold on, you'll be inside in a jiffy.

And then she had been grabbed. By Ellen. No; by the thing

(Tak)

that had been *wearing* Ellen. That thing had slugged her and then boom, boom, out go the lights.

And in a very literal sense, they were still out. She had to flutter her lids several times simply to assure herself that her eyes were open.

Oh, they're open, all right. Maybe it's just dark in this place . . . but maybe you're blind. How about that for a lovely thought. Mare? Maybe she hit you hard enough to blind y—

Something was on the back of her hand. It ran halfway across and then paused, seeming to throb on her skin. Mary made a sound of revulsion with her tongue pressed to the roof of her mouth and flapped her hand madly in the air, like a woman waving off some annoying person. The throbbing disappeared; the thing on the back of her hand was gone. Mary got to her feet, provoking another cymbal-crash of pain in her head which she barely noticed. There were *things* in here, and she had no time for a mere headache.

She turned slowly around, breathing that sickish-sweet aroma that was so similar to the stench that had greeted her and Pete when they had returned home from their mini-vacation in the Balearic Islands. Pete's parents had given them the trip as a Christmas present the year after they had been married, and how great it had been . . . until they'd walked back in, bags in hand, and the stench had hit them like a fist. They had lost everything: two chickens, the chops and roasts she'd gotten at the good discount meat-cutter's she'd found in Brooklyn, the venison-steaks Peter's friend Don had given them, the pints of strawberries they'd picked at the Mohonk Mountain House the previous summer. This smell . . . so similar . . .

Something that felt the size of a walnut dropped into her hair.

She screamed, at first beating at it with the flat of her hand. That did no good, so she slid her fingers into her hair and got hold of whatever it was. It squirmed, then burst between her fingers. Thick fluid squirted into her palm. She raked the bristly, deflating body out of her hair and shook it off her palm. She heard it hit something . . . *splat.* Her palm felt hot and itchy, as if she had reached into poison ivy. She rubbed it against her jeans.

Please God don't let me be next, she thought. *Whatever happens don't let me end up like the cop. Like Ellen.*

She fought the urge to simply bolt into the black surrounding her. If she did that she might brain herself, disembowel herself, or impale herself, like an expendable character in a horror movie, on some grotesque piece of mining equipment. But even that wasn't the worst. The worst was that there might be something besides the scuttering things in here with her. Something that was just waiting for her to panic and run.

Waiting with its arms held out.

Now she had a sense—perhaps it was only her imagination, but she didn't think so—of stealthy movement all around her. A rustling sound from the left. A slithering from the right. There was a sudden low squalling from behind her, there and gone before she could scream.

That last one wasn't anything alive, she told herself. *At least I don't think so. I think it was a tumbleweed hitting metal and scraping along it. I think I'm in a little building somewhere. She put me in a little building for safekeeping and the fridge is out, just like the lights, and the stuff inside has spoiled.*

But if Ellen was Entragian in a new body, why hadn't he/she just put her back in the cell where he'd put her to start with? Because he/she was afraid the others would find her there and let her out again? It was as plausible a reason as any other she could think up, and there was a thread of hope in it, as well. Holding onto it, Mary began to shuffle slowly forward with her hands held out.

It seemed she walked that way for a very long time—years. She kept expecting something else to touch her, and at last something did. It ran across her shoe. Mary froze. Finally it went about its business. But what followed it was even worse: a low, dry rattle coming out of the darkness at roughly ten o'clock. So far as she knew, there was only one thing that rattled like that. The sound didn't really stop but seemed to die away, like the whine of a cicada on a hot August afternoon. The low squalling returned. This time she was positive it was a tumbleweed sliding along metal. She was in a mining building, maybe the Quonset where Steve and the girl with the wild hair, Cynthia, had seen the little stone statue that had frightened them so badly.

Get moving.

I can't. There's a rattlesnake in here. Maybe more than one. Probably *more than one.*

That's not all that's in here, though. Better get moving, Mary.

Her palm throbbed angrily where the thing in her hair had burst open. Her heart thudded in her ears. As slowly as she could, she began inching forward again, hands out. Terrible ideas and images went with her. She saw a snake as thick as a powerline dangling from a rafter just ahead of her, fanged jaws hinged wide, forked tongue dancing. She would walk right into it and wouldn't know until it battened on her face, injecting its poison straight into her eyes. She saw the closet-demon of her childhood, a bogey she had for some reason called Apple Jack, slumped in the corner with his brown fruit-face all pulled in on itself, grinning, waiting for her to wander into his deadly embrace; the last thing she'd smell would be his cidery aroma, which was for the time being masked by the stench of spoilage, as he hugged her to death, all the time covering her face with wet avid uncle-kisses. She saw a cougar, like the one that had killed poor old Tom Billingsley, crouched in a corner with its tail switching. She saw Ellen, holding a baling hook in one hand and smiling a thin waiting smile which was like a hook itself, simply marking time until Mary got close enough to skewer.

But mostly what she saw was snakes.

Rattlers.

Her fingers touched something. She gasped and almost recoiled, but that was just nerves; the thing was hard, unliving. A straight-edge at the height of her torso. A table? Covered with an oilcloth? She thought so. She walked her fingers across it, and forced herself to freeze when one of the scuttery things touched her. It crawled over the back of her hand and down to her wrist, almost surely a spider of some sort, and then was gone. She walked her hand on, and here was something else investigating her, more of what Audrey had called "wildlife." Not a spider. This thing, whatever it was, had claws and a hard surface.

Mary forced herself to hold still, but couldn't keep entirely quiet; a low, desperate moan escaped her. Sweat ran down her forehead and cheeks like warm motor-oil, stung in her eyes. Then the thing on her hand gave her an obscene little squeeze and was gone. She could hear it click-dragging its way across the table. She moved her hand again, resisting the clamor of her mind to pull back. If she did, what then? Stand here trembling in the dark until the stealthy sounds around her drove her crazy, sent her running in panicked circles until she bashed herself unconscious again?

Here was a plate—no, a bowl—with something in it. Congealed soup? Her fingers fumbled beside it and felt a spoon. Yes, soup. She felt beyond it, touched what could have been a salt- or pepper-shaker, then something soft and flabby. She suddenly remembered a game they had played at slumber-parties when she was a girl in Mamaroneck. A game made to be played in the dark. You'd pass around spaghetti and intone *These are the dead man's guts,* pass around cold Jell-O and intone *These are the dead man's brains.*

Her hand struck something hard and cylindrical. It fell over with a rattle she recognized at once . . . or hoped she did: batteries in the tube of a flashlight.

Please, God, she thought, groping for it. *Please God let it be what it feels like.*

The squalling from outside came again, but she barely heard it. Her hand touched a cold piece of meat

(*this is the dead man's face*)

but she barely felt it. Her heart was hammering in her chest, her throat, even in her sinuses.

There! There!

Cold, smooth metal, it tried to squitter out of her grip, but she squeezed it tight. Yes, a flashlight; she could feel the switch lying against the web of skin between her thumb and forefinger.

Now let it work, God. Please, okay?

She pressed the switch. Light sprang out in a widening cone, and her yammering heartbeat stopped dead in her ears for a moment. *Everything* stopped dead.

The table was long, covered with lab equipment and rock samples at one end, covered with a checked piece of table-cloth at the other. This end had been set, as for dinner, with a soup-bowl, a plate, silverware, and a water-glass. A large black spider had fallen into the waterglass and couldn't get out; it writhed and scratched fruitlessly. The red hourglass on its belly showed in occasional flickers. Other spiders, most also black widows, preened and strutted on the table. Among them were rock-scorpions, stalking back and forth like parliamentarians, their stingers furled on their backs. Sitting at the end of the table was a large bald man in a Diablo Mining Corporation tee-shirt. He had been shot in the throat at close range. The stuff in the soup-bowl, the stuff she had touched with her fingers, wasn't soup but this man's clotted blood.

Mary's heart re-started itself, sending her own blood crashing up into her head like a piston, and all at once the flashlight's yellow fan of light began to look red and shimmery. She heard a high, sweet singing in her ears.

Don't you faint, don't you dare—

The flashlight beam swung to the left. In the corner, under a poster which read GO AHEAD, BAN MINING, LET THE BASTARDS FREEZE IN THE DARK!, was a roiling nest of rattlesnakes. She slid the beam along the metal wall, past congregations of spiders (some of the black widows she saw were as big as her hand), and in the other corner were more snakes. Their daytime torpor was gone, and they writhed together, flowing through sheetbends and clove hitches and double diamonds, occasionally shaking their tails.

Don't faint, don't faint, don't faint—

She turned around with the light, and when it happened upon the other three bodies that were in here with her, she understood several things at once. The fact that she had discovered the source of the bad smell was only the least of them.

The bodies at the foot of the wall were in an advanced state of decay, delirious with maggots, but they hadn't been simply dumped. They were lined up . . . perhaps even laid out. Their puffy, blackening hands had been laced together on their chests. The man in the middle really *was* black, she thought, although it was impossible to tell for sure. She didn't know him or the one on his right, but the one on the black guy's left she *did* know, in spite of the toiling maggots and the decomposition. In her mind she heard him mixing *I'm going to kill you* into the Miranda warning.

As she watched, a spider ran out of Collie Entragian's mouth.

The beam of the light shook as she ran it along the line of corpses again. Three men. Three *big* men, not a one of the three under six-feet-five.

I know why I'm here instead of in jail, she thought. *And I know why I wasn't killed. I'm next. When it's through with Ellen . . . I'm next.*

Mary began to scream.

5

The *an tak* chamber glowed with a faint red light that seemed to come from the air itself. Something which still looked a bit like Ellen Carver walked across it, accompanied by a retinue of scorpions and fiddlebacks. Above it, around it, the stone faces of the *can taks* peered down. Across from it was the *pirin moh*, a jutting facade that looked a bit like the front of a Mexican *hacienda*. In front of it was the pit—the *ini*, well of the worlds. The light could have been coming from here, but it was impossible to tell for sure. Sitting in a circle around the mouth of the ini were coyotes and buzzards. Every now and then one of the birds would rustle its feathers or one of the coyotes would flick an ear; if not for these moves, they might have been stones themselves.

Ellen's body walked slowly; Ellen's head sagged. Pain pulsed deep in her belly. Blood ran down her legs in thin, steady streams. It had stuffed a torn cotton tee-shirt into Ellen's panties and that had helped for awhile, but now the shirt was soaked through. Bad luck it had had, and not just once. The first one had had prostate cancer—undiagnosed—and the rot had started there, spreading through his body with such unexpected speed that it had been lucky to get to Josephson in time. Josephson had lasted a little longer, Entragian—a nearly perfect specimen—longer still. And Ellen? Ellen had been suffering from a yeast infection. Just a yeast infection, nothing at all in the ordinary scheme of things, but it had been enough to start the dominoes falling, and now . . .

Well, there was Mary. It didn't quite dare take her yet, not until it knew what the others were going to do. If the writer won out and took them back to the highway, it would jump to Mary and take one of the ATVs (loaded down with as many *can tahs* as it could transport) up into the hills. It already knew where to go: Alphaville, a vegan commune in the Desatoyas.

They wouldn't be vegans for long after Tak arrived.

If the wretched little prayboy prevailed and they came south, Mary might serve as bait. Or as a hostage. She would serve as neither, however, if the prayboy sensed she was no longer human.

It sat down on the edge of the *ini* and stared into it. The *ini* was shaped like a funnel, its rough walls sliding in toward each other until, twenty-five or thirty-feet down, nothing was left of the mouth's twelve-foot diameter but a hole less than an inch across. Baleful scarlet light, almost too bright to look at, stormed out of this hole in pulses. It was a hole like an eye.

One of the buzzards tried to lay its head in Ellen's blood-stinking lap; it pushed the bird away. Tak had hoped looking into the *ini* would be calming, would help it decide what to do next (for the *ini* was where it really lived; Ellen Carver was just an outpost), but it only seemed to increase its disquiet.

Things were on the verge of going badly wrong. Looking back, it saw clearly that some other force had perhaps been working against it from the start.

It was afraid of the boy, especially in its current weakness. Most of all it was terrified of being completely shut up beyond the narrow throat of the *ini* again, like a genie in a bottle. But that didn't have to be. Even if the boy brought them, it didn't have to be. The others would be weakened by their doubts, the boy would be weakened by his human concerns—especially his concern for his mother—and if the boy died, it could close the door to the outside again, close it with a bang, and then take the others. The writer and the boy's father would have to die, but the two younger ones it would try to sedate and save. Later, it might very well want to use their bodies.

It rocked forward, oblivious to the blood squelching between Ellen's thighs, as it had been oblivious of the teeth falling out of Ellen's head or the three knuckles that had exploded like pine-knots in a fireplace when it had clipped Mary on the chin. It looked into the funnel of the well, and the constricted red eye at the bottom.

The eye of Tak.

The boy *could* die.

He was, after all, *only* a boy . . . not a demon, a god, or a savior.

Tak leaned farther over the funnel with its jagged crystal sides and murky reddish light. Now it could hear a sound, very faint—a kind of low, atonal humming. It was an idiot sound . . . but it was also wonderful, compelling. It closed its stolen eyes and breathed deeply, sucking at the force it felt, trying to get as much inside as it could, wanting to slow—at least temporarily—this body's degeneration. It would need Ellen awhile longer. And besides, now it felt the *ini*'s peace. At last.

"Tak," it whispered into the darkness. *"Tak en tow ini, tak ah lah, tak ah wan."*

Then it was silent. From below, deep in the humming red silence of the *ini*, came the wet-tongue sound of something slithering.

CHAPTER 2

1

David said, "The man who showed me these things—the man who guided me—told me to tell you that none of this is destiny." His arms were clasped around his knees and his head was bent; he seemed to be speaking to his sneakers. "In a way, that's the scariest part. Pie's dead, and Mr. Billingsley, and everyone else in Desperation, because one man hated the Mining Safety and Health Administration and another was too curious and hated being tied to his desk. That's all."

"And God told you all this?" Johnny asked.

The boy nodded, still without looking up.

"So we're really talking miniseries here," Johnny said. "Night One is the Lushan Brothers, Night Two is Josephson, the Footloose Receptionist. They'll love it at ABC."

"Why don't you shut up?" Cynthia said softly.

"Another county heard from!" Johnny exclaimed. "This young woman, this roadbabe with attitude, this flashing female flame of commitment, will now explain, complete with pictures and taped accompaniment by the noted rock ensemble Pearl Jam—"

"Just shut the fuck up," Steve said.

Johnny looked at him, shocked to silence.

Steve shrugged, embarrassed but not backing down. "The

time for whistling past the graveyard's over. You need to cut the crap." He looked back at David.

"I know more about this part," David said. "More than I want to, actually. I got inside this one. I got inside his head." He paused. "Ripton. That was his name. He was the first."

And still looking down between his cocked knees at his sneakers, David began to talk.

2

The man who hates MSHA is Cary Ripton, pit-foreman of the new Rattlesnake operation. He is forty-eight, balding, sunken-eyed, cynical, in pain more often than not these days, a man who desperately wanted to be a mining engineer but wasn't up to the math and wound up here instead, running an open-pit. Stuffing blast-holes full of ANFO and trying not to choke the prancing little faggot from MSHA when he comes out on Tuesday afternoons.

When Kirk Turner runs into the field office this afternoon, face blazing with excitement, to tell him that the last blast-pattern has uncovered an old drift-mine and that there are bones inside, they can see them, Ripton's first impulse is to tell him to organize a party of volunteers, they're going in. All sorts of possibilities dance in his head. He is too old a hand for childish fantasies about lost goldmines and troves of Indian artifacts, much too old, but as he and Turner rush out, part of him is thinking about those things just the same, oh yes.

The cluster of men standing at the foot of the newly turned blast-field, eyeing the hole their latest explosions have uncovered, is a small one: seven guys in all, counting Turner, the crew boss. There are right now fewer than ninety men working for the Desperation Mining Corporation. Next year, if they're lucky—if the copper-yield and the prices both stay up—there may be four times that number.

Ripton and Turner walk up to the edge of the hole. There is a dank, strange smell coming out of it, one Cary Ripton associates with coalgas in the mines of Kentucky and West Virginia. And yes, there are bones. He can see them scattering back into the canted, downsloping darkness of an old-fashioned square-drift mine, and while it's impossible to tell for sure about all of them, he sees a ribcage which is almost certainly human. Farther back, tantalizingly close but still just a little too far for even a powerful flashlight to show clearly, is something that could be a skull.

"What is this?" Turner asks him. "Any idea?"

Of course he does; it's Rattlesnake Number One, the old China Shaft. He opens his mouth to say so, then closes it again. This is not a matter for a blast-monkey like Kirk Turner, and is certainly not one for his crew, nitro-boys who spend their weekends in Ely gambling, whoring, drinking . . . and talking, of course. Talking about anything and everything. Nor can he take them inside. He thinks they would go, that their curiosity would drive them in spite of the obvious risks involved (a drift-mine this old, running through earth this uneasy, shit, a loud yell might be enough to bring the roof down), but the talk would get back to the prancing little MSHA faggot in no time flat, and when it did, losing his job would be the least of Ripton's worries. The MSHA fag (all hat and no cattle is how Frank Geller, the chief mining engineer, sums him up) likes Ripton no more than Ripton likes him, and the foreman who leads an expedition into the long-buried China Shaft today might find himself in federal court, facing a fifty-thousand-dollar fine and a possible five years in jail, the week after next. There are at least nine red-letter regulations expressly forbidding entry into "unsafe and unimproved structures." Which this of course is.

Yet those bones and old dreams call to him like troubled voices from his childhood, like the ghost of every unfulfilled ambition he has ever held, and he knows even then that he isn't going to turn the China Shaft meekly over to the company and the federal pricks without at least one look inside for himself.

He instructs Turner, who is bitterly disappointed but not really argumentative (he understands about MSHA as well as Ripton . . .

maybe, as a blast-monkey, even better), to have yellow RESTRICTED AREA *tapes placed across the opening. He then turns to the rest of the crew and reminds them that the newly uncovered drift, which might turn out to be a historical and archaeological treasure trove, is on DMC property. "I don't expect you to keep this quiet forever," he tells them, "but as a favor to me I'd like you to keep your mouths shut for the next few days. Even with your wives. Let me notify the brass. That part should be easy, at least—Symes, the comptroller, is coming in from Phoenix next week. Will you do that for me?"*

They say they will. Not all will be able to keep their promise even for twenty-four hours, of course—some men are just no good at keeping secrets—but he thinks he commands enough respect among them to buy twelve hours . . . and four would probably be enough. Four hours after quitting time. Four hours in there by himself, with a flashlight, a camera, and an electric follow-me for any souvenirs he may decide to collect. Four hours with all those childhood fantasies he is too old a hand to think about. And if the roof should pick that moment, after almost a hundred and forty years and untold blasts shaking the ground all around it, to let go? Let it. He's a man with no wife, no kids, no parents, and two brothers who have forgotten he's alive. He has a sneaking suspicion that he wouldn't be losing that many years, in any case. He's been feeling punk for almost six months now, and just lately he had taken to pissing blood. Not a lot, but even a little seems like a lot when it's yours you see in the toilet bowl.

If I get out of this, maybe I'll go to the doctor, *he thinks.* Take it as a sign and go to the damned doctor. How about that?

Turner wants to take some pictures of the exposed drift after he clocks out. Ripton lets him. It seems the quickest way to get rid of him.

"How far in do you think we punched it?" Turner asks, standing about two feet beyond the yellow tape and snapping pictures with his Nikon—pictures that, with no flash, will show nothing but a black hole and a few scattered bones that might belong to a deer.

"No way to tell," Ripton says. In his mind he's inventorying the equipment he'll take in with him.

"You ain't gonna do nothin dumb after I'm gone, are you?" Turner asks.

"Nope," Ripton says. "I have too much damned respect for Mining Safety to even think of such a thing."

"Yeah, right," Turner says, laughing, and early the next morning, around two o'clock, a much larger version of Cary Ripton will enter the bedroom Turner shares with his wife and shoot the man as he sleeps. His wife, too. Tak!

It's a busy night for Cary Ripton. A night of killing (not one of Turner's blast-crew lives to see the morning sun) and a night of placing can tahs; *he has taken a gunny sack filled with them when he leaves the pit, over a hundred in all. Some have broken into pieces, but he knows even the fragments retain some of their queer, unpredictable power. He spends most of the night placing these relics, leaving them in odd corners, mailboxes, glove compartments. Even in pants pockets! Yes! Hardly anyone locks their houses out here, hardly anyone stays up late out here, and the homes belonging to Turner's blast-crew are not the only ones Cary Ripton visits.*

He returns to the pit, feeling as trashed-out as Santa Claus returning to the North Pole after the big night . . . only Santa's work ends once the presents have been distributed. Ripton's is only beginning. It's quarter to five; he has over two hours before the first members of Pascal Martínez's small Saturday day-crew show up. It should be enough, but there is certainly no time to waste. Cary Ripton's body is bleeding so badly he's had to stuff his underwear full of toilet paper to absorb it, and twice on his way out to the mine he has had to stop and yark a gutful of blood out the window of Cary's pickup truck. It's splashed all down the side. In the first tentative and somehow sinister light of the coming day, the drying blood looks like tobacco-juice.

In spite of his need to hurry, he's stopped dead for a moment by what the headlights show when he arrives at the bottom of the pit. He sits behind the wheel of the old truck with his eyes wide.

There are enough desert animals on the north slope of the China Pit to fill an ark: wolves, coyotes, hopping baldheaded buzzards, flapping owls with eyes like great gold wedding-rings; cougars and wildcats and even a few scruffy barncats. There are wild dogs with their ribs arcing against their scant hides in cruel detail—many are escapees from the raggedy-ass commune in the hills, he knows—and running around their feet unmolested are hordes of spiders and platoons of rats with black eyes.

Each of the animals coming out of the China Shaft carries a can tah *in its mouth. They lope, flap, and scurry up the pit-road like a flood of weird refugees escaping some underground world. Below them, sitting patiently like customers in a Green Stamp redemption center two days before Christmas—take a number and wait—are more animals. What they're waiting for is their turn to go into the dark.*

Tak begins to laugh with Cary Ripton's vocal cords. "What a hoot!" he exclaims.

Then he drives on to the field office, unlocks the door with Ripton's key, and kills Joe Prudum, the night watchman. Old Joe isn't much of a night watchman; comes on at dark, doesn't have the slightest idea anything's going on in the pit, and doesn't think there's anything strange about Cary Ripton showing up first thing in the morning. He's using the washer in the corner to do some laundry, he's sitting down to have his topsy-turvy version of dinner, and everything's cozy right up to the moment when Ripton puts a bullet in his throat.

That done, Ripton calls the Owl's Club in town. The Owl's is open twenty-four hours a day (although, like a vampire, it's never really alive). It's where Brad Josephson, he of the gorgeous chocolate skin and long, sloping gut, eats breakfast six days a week . . . and always at this brutally early hour. That will come in handy now. Ripton wants Brad on hand, and quickly, before the black man can be polluted by the can tahs. *The* can tahs *are useful in many ways, but they spoil a man or woman for Tak's greater work. Ripton knows he can take some-one from Martinez's crew if he needs to, perhaps even Pascal himself, but he wants (well, Tak wants, actually) Brad. Brad will be useful in other ways.*

How long do the bodies last if they're healthy? *he asks him-*

self as he approaches the phone. How long if the one you push into overdrive hasn't been incubating a juicy case of cancer to start with?

He doesn't know, but thinks he will probably soon have a chance to find out.

"Owl's," *says a woman's voice in his ear—the sun's not even up and she sounds tired already.*

"Howdy, Denise," *he says.* "How they hangin?"

"Who's this?" *Deeply suspicious.*

"Cary Ripton, hon. You don't recognize my voice?"

"You must have a bad case of morning mouth, darlin. Or are you coming down with a cold?"

"Cold, I guess," *he says, grinning and wiping blood off his lower lip. It is oozing out from between his teeth. Down below it feels like all of his innards have come loose and are floating in a sea of blood.* "Listen, hon, is Brad in?"

"Right over in the corner where he always is, livin large and eatin nasty—four eggs, home fries, 'bout half a pound of limpfried bacon. I hope when he finally vapor-locks, he does it somewheres else. What you want Brad for at this hour of a Sat'd'y mornin?"

"Company business."

"Well shut my mouth n go to heaven," *she says.* "You want to take care of that cold, Rip—you sound really congested."

"Just with love for you," *he tells her.*

"Huh," *she says, and the phone goes down with a clunk.* "Brad!" *he hears her yell.* "Phone! For you! Mr. Wonderful!" *A pause while Brad is probably asking her what she's talking about.* "Find out for yourself," *she says, and a moment later Brad Josephson is on the line. He says hello like a man who knows perfectly well that Publishers Clearinghouse doesn't call at five in the morning to tell you you won the big one.*

"Brad, it's Cary Ripton," *he says. He knows just how to get Brad out here; he got the idea from the late great Kirk Turner.* "Have you got your camera gear in your car?" *Of course he does. Brad is, among other things, an ardent birdwatcher. Fancies himself an amateur ornithologist, in fact. But Cary Ripton can do better than birds this morning. A lot better.*

"Yes, sure, what's the deal?"

Ripton leans back against the poster taped up in the corner, the one showing a dirty miner pointing like Uncle Sam and saying GO AHEAD, BAN MINING, LET THE BASTARDS FREEZE IN THE DARK! "If you hop in your car and drive out here right now, I'll show you," *Ripton says. "And if you get here before Pascal Martínez and his boys, I'll give you a chance at the most amazing pictures you'll ever take in your life."*

"What are you talking about?" *Josephson sounds excited now.*

"The bones of forty or fifty dead Chinese, to start with, how's that sound?"

"What—"

"We punched into the old China Shaft yesterday afternoon. Less than twenty feet in you'll get the most amazing—"

"I'm on my way. Don't you move. Don't you goddam move."

The phone clicks in his ear and Ripton grins with red lips. "I won't," *he says.* "Don't worry about that. Can de lach! Ah ten! Tak!"

Ten minutes later, Ripton—now bleeding from the navel as well as the rectum and penis—walks across the crumbled bottom of the pit to the China Slope. Here he spreads his arms like an evangelist and speaks to the animals in the language of the unformed. All of them either fly away or withdraw into the mine. It will not do for Brad Josephson to see them. No, that would not do at all.

Five minutes after that Josephson comes down the steep grade of the pit-road, sitting bolt-upright behind the wheel of an old Buick. The sticker on the front reads MINERS GO DEEPER AND STAY LONGER. *Ripton watches him from the door of the field office. It wouldn't do for Brad to get a good look at* him, *either, not until he gets a little closer.*

No problem there. Brad parks with a scrunch of tires, gets out, grabs three different cameras, and trots toward the field office, pausing only to gape at the open hole twenty feet or so up the slope.

"Holy shit, it's the China, all right," he says. "Got to be. Come on, Cary! For Christ's sake, Martínez be here any time!"

"Nah, they start a little later on Saturday," he says, grinning. "Cool your jets."

"Yeah, but what about old Joe? He could be a prob—"

"Cool your jets, I said! Joe's in Reno. Granddaughter popped a kid."

"Good! Great! Have a cigar, huh?" Brad laughs a little wildly.

"Come in here," Ripton says. "Got something to show you."

"Something you brought out?"

"That's right," Ripton says, and in a way it's true, in a way he does want to show Brad something he brought out. Josephson is still frowning down at his swinging cameras, trying to sort out the straps, when Ripton grabs him and throws him to the back of the room. Josephson squawks indignantly. Later he will be scared, and still later he'll be terrified, but right now he hasn't noticed Joe Prudum's body and is only indignant.

"For the last time, cool your jets!" Ripton says as he steps outside and locks the door. "Gosh! Relax!"

Laughing, he goes to the truck and gets in. Like many Westerners, Cary Ripton believes passionately in the right of Americans to bear arms; there's a shotgun in the rack behind the seat and a nasty little hideout gun—a Ruger Speed-Six—in the glovebox. He loads the shotgun and lays it across his lap. The Ruger, which is already loaded, he simply puts on the seat beside him. His first impulse is to tuck it into his belt, but now he's all but swimming in blood down there (Ripton, you idiot, he thinks, don't you know men your age are supposed to get the old prostate tickled every year or so), and soaking Ripton's pistol in it might not be a good idea.

When Josephson's ceaseless hammering at the field-office door begins to annoy him, he turns on the radio, juices the volume, and sings along with Johnny Paycheck, who is telling whoever wants to listen that he was the only hell his mama ever raised.

Pretty soon Pascal Martínez shows up for some of that good old

Saturday-morning time and a half. He's got Miguel Rivera, his amigo, with him. Ripton waves. Pascal waves back. He parks on the other side of the field office, and then he and Mig walk around to see what Ripton's doing here on Saturday morning, and at this ungodly hour. Ripton sticks the shotgun out the window, still smiling, and shoots both of them. It's easy. Neither tries to run. They die with puzzled looks on their faces. Ripton looks at them, thinking of his granddaddy telling about the passenger pigeons, birds so dumb you could club them on the ground. The men out here all have guns but few of them think, way down deep, that they will ever have to use one. They are all show and no go. Or all hat and no cattle, if you like that better.

The rest of the crew arrives by ones and twos—no one worries much about the timeclock on Saturdays. Ripton shoots them as they come and drags their bodies around to the back of the field office, where they soon begin to stack up beneath the clothes dryer's exhaust-pipe like cordwood. When he runs out of shotgun shells (there's plenty of ammo for the Ruger, but the pistol is useless as a primary weapon, not accurate at a distance greater than a dozen feet), he finds Martínez's keys, opens the back of his Cherokee, and discovers a beautiful (and completely illegal) Iver Johnson auto under a blanket. Next to it are two dozen thirty-round clips in a Nike shoebox. The arriving miners hear the shots as they ascend the north side of the pit, but they think it's target-shooting, which is how a good many Saturdays start in the China Pit. It's a beautiful thing.

By seven forty-five, Ripton has killed everyone on Pascal Martínez's A-crew. As a bonus, he gets the one-legged guy from Bud's Suds who has come out to service the coffee-machine. Twenty-five bodies behind the field office.

The animals start moving in and out of the China Shaft again, streaming toward town with can tahs in their mouths. Soon they will quit for the day, waiting for the cover of night to start again.

In the meantime, the pit is his . . . and it is time to make the jump. He wants out of this unpleasantly decaying body, and if he doesn't make the switch soon, he never will.

When he opens the door, Brad Josephson rushes him. He has heard the gunfire, he has heard the screams when Ripton's first shot hasn't put his victim down cleanly, and he knows that rushing is the only option he has. He expects to be shot, but of course Cary can't do that. Instead he grabs Josephson's arms, calling on the last of this body's strength to do it, and shoves the black man against the wall so hard that the entire prefab building shakes. And it's not just Ripton now, of course; it's Tak's strength. As if to confirm this, Josephson asks how in God's name he got so tall.

"Wheaties!" it exclaims. "Tak!"

"What are you doing?" Josephson asks, trying to squirm away as Ripton's face bears down on his and Ripton's mouth comes open. "What are you d—"

"Kiss me, beautiful!" Ripton exclaims, and slams his mouth down on Josephson's. He makes a blood-seal through which he exhales. Josephson goes rigid in Ripton's arms and begins to tremble wildly. Ripton exhales and exhales, going out and out and out, feeling it happen, feeling the transfer. For one terrible moment the essence of Tak is naked, caught between Ripton, who is collapsing, and Josephson, who has begun to swell like a float on the morning of the Thanksgiving Day Parade. And then, instead of looking out of Ripton's eyes, it is looking out of Josephson's eyes.

It feels a wonderful, intoxicating sense of rebirth. It is filled not only with the strength and purpose of Tak, but with the greasefired energy of a man who eats four eggs and half a pound of limp bacon for breakfast. It feels . . . feels . . .

"I feel GRRRREAT!" Brad Josephson exclaims in a boisterous Tony the Tiger voice. It can hear a tenebrous creaking that is Brad's backbone growing, the taut silk-across-satin sound that is his muscles stretching, the thawing-ice sound of his skull expanding. He breaks wind repeatedly, the sound like the reports of a track-starter's gun.

It drops Ripton's body—the body feels as light as a burst seedpod—and strides toward the door, listening to the seams of Josephson's khaki *shirt tear open as his shoulders widen and his arms lengthen. His feet don't grow as much, but enough to burst the laces of his tennis shoes.*

Tak stands outside, grinning hugely. It has never felt better. Everything is in its eye. The world roars like a waterfall. A recordsetting erection, a pantsbuster if ever there was one, has turned the front of his jeans into a tent.

Tak is here, liberated from the well of the worlds. Tak is great, Tak will feed, and Tak will rule as it has always ruled, in the desert of wastes, where the plants are migrants and the ground is magnetic.

*It gets into the Buick, splitting the seam running up the back of Brad Josephson's pants all the way to the beltloops. Then, grinning at the thought of the bumper-sticker on the front of the car—*MINERS GO DEEPER AND STAY LONGER*—it swings around the field office and heads back toward Desperation, stretching out a rooster-tail of dust behind the fastmoving car.*

3

David stopped. He still sat with his back against the wall of the Ryder truck, looking down at his sneakers. His voice had grown husky with talking. The others stood around him in a semicircle, pretty much as Johnny supposed the wise old wallahs had once stood around the boy Jesus while he gave them the scoop, the lowdown, the latest buzz, the true gen. Johnny's clearest view was of the little punk-chick, Steve Ames's catch of the day, and she looked pretty much the way he himself felt: mesmerized, amazed, but not disbelieving. And that, of course, was the root of his disquiet. He was going to get out of this town, nothing was going to stop him from doing that, but it would be a lot easier on the old ego if he could simply believe the boy was deluded, rapping tall tales straight out of his own imagination. But he didn't think that was the case.

You know *it's not*, Terry said from her cozy little place in Der Bitchen Bunker.

Johnny squatted to get a fresh bottle of Jolt, not feeling his wallet (genuine crocodile, Barneys, three hundred and ninety-five dollars), which had worked most of the way out of his back pocket, slip all the way out and drop to the floor. He tapped David's hand with the neck of the bottle. The boy looked up, smiling, and Johnny was shocked at how tired he looked. He thought about David's explanation of Tak—trapped in the earth like an ogre in a fairytale, using human beings like paper cups because it wore their bodies out so rapidly—and wondered if David's God was much different.

"Anyway, that's how he does it," David said in his husky voice. "He goes across on their breath, like a seed on a gust of wind."

"The kiss of death instead of the kiss of life," Ralph said.

David nodded.

"But what kissed Ripton?" Cynthia asked. "When he went into the mine the night before, *what kissed him*?"

"I don't know," David said. "Either I wasn't shown or I don't understand. All I know is that it happened at the well I told you about. He went into the room . . . the chamber . . . the *can tahs* drew him, but he wasn't allowed to actually touch any of them."

"Because the *can tahs* spoil people as a vessel for Tak," Steve half-said, half-asked.

"Yes."

"But Tak has a physical body? I mean, he—it—we're not just talking about an idea, are we? Or a spirit?"

David was shaking his head. "No, Tak's real, it has a being. It had to get Ripton into the mine because it can't get through the *ini*—the well. It *has* a physical body, and the well is too small for it. All it can do is catch people, inhabit them, make them into *can tak*. And trade them in when they wear out."

"What happened to Josephson, David?" Ralph asked. He sounded quiet, almost drained. Johnny found it increasingly difficult to look at Carver looking at his son.

"He had a leaky heart valve," David said. "It wasn't a big deal. He could have gone on without any problem for years, maybe, but Tak got hold of him, and just . . ." David shrugged. "Just wore him out. It took two and a half days. Then he switched to Entragian. Entragian was strong, he lasted most of a whole week . . . but he had very fair skin. People used to kid him about all the sunburn creams he had."

"Your guide told you all this," Johnny said.

"Yes. I guess that's what he was."

"But you don't know *who* he was."

"I almost know. I feel like I *should* know."

"Are you sure he didn't come from this Tak? Because there's an old saying: 'The devil can wear a pleasing aspect.'"

"He wasn't from Tak, Johnny."

"Let him talk," Steve said. "All right?"

Johnny shrugged and sat down. One of his hands almost touched his fallen wallet as he did so. Almost, but not quite.

"The back part of the hardware store here in town is a clothes store," David resumed. "Work clothes, mostly. Levi's, khakis, Red Wing boots, stuff like that. They order special for this one guy, Curt Yeoman, who works—*worked*—for the telephone company. Six-foot-seven, the tallest man in Desperation. That's why Entragian's clothes weren't ripped when he took us, Dad. Saturday night, Josephson broke into the True Value and grabbed a set of khakis in Curt Yeoman's size. Shoes, too. He took them to the Municipal Building and actually put them in Collie Entragian's locker. Even then he knew who he was going to use next, you see."

"Was that when he killed the Police Chief?" Ralph asked.

"Mr. Reed? No. Not then. He did that Sunday night. By then Mr. Reed didn't matter much, anyway. Ripton left him one of the *can tahs*, you see, and it messed Mr. Reed up. *Bad.* The *can tahs* do different things to different people. When Mr. Josephson killed him, Mr. Reed was sitting at his desk and—"

Looking away, clearly embarrassed, David made his right hand into a tube and moved it rapidly up and down in the air.

"Okay," Steve said. "We get the picture. What about Entragian? Where was he all weekend?"

"Out of town, like Audrey. The Desperation cops have—*had*—a law-enforcement contract with the county. It means a lot of travelling. Friday night, the night Ripton killed the blast-crew, Entragian was in Austin. Saturday night he slept at the Davis Ranch. Sunday night—the last night he was *really* Collie Entragian—he spent on Shoshone tribal land. He had a friend up there. A woman, I think."

Johnny walked toward the back of the Ryder truck, then wheeled around. "What did he do, David? What did *it* do? How did we get to where we are now? How did it happen without anyone finding out? How *could* it happen?" He paused. "And another question. What does Tak want? To get out of its hole in the ground and stretch its legs? Eat pork rinds? Snort cocaine and drink Tequila Sunrises? Screw some NFL cheerleaders? Ask Bob Dylan what the lyrics to 'Gates of Eden' really mean? Rule the earth? What?"

"It doesn't matter," David said quietly.

"*Huh?*"

"All that matters is what *God* wants. And what he wants is for us to go up to the China Pit. All the rest is just . . . storyhour."

Johnny smiled. It felt tight and a little painful, too small for his mouth. "Tell you what, sport: what your God wants doesn't matter in the least to me." He turned back to the Ryder truck's rear door and ran it up. Outside, the air seemed almost breathlessly still and strangely warm in the wake of the storm. The blinker pulsed rhythmically at the intersection. Crossing the street at regular intervals were rippled sand dunes. Seen in the nebulous light of the westering moon and the yellow pulse of the blinker-light, Desperation looked like an outpost in a science fiction movie.

"I can't stop you if you mean to go," David said. "Maybe Steve and my dad could, but it wouldn't do any good. Because of the free-will covenant."

"That's right," Johnny said. "Good old free will." He jumped down from the back of the truck, wincing at another twinge of pain in his back. His nose was hurting again, too. Bigtime. He looked around, checking for coyotes or buzzards or snakes, and saw nothing. Not so much as a bug. "Frankly, David, I trust God about as far as I can sling a piano." He looked back in at the boy, smiling. "You trust him all you want. I guess it's a luxury you can still afford. Your sister's dead and your mother's turned into Christ-knows-what, but there's still your father to get through before Tak goes to work on you personally."

David jerked. His mouth trembled. His face crumpled and he began to cry.

"You *bitch*!" Cynthia shouted at Johnny. "You *cunt*!" She rushed to the back of the truck and kicked at him. Johnny dodged back, the toe of her small foot missing his chin by only an inch or two. He felt the wind of it. Cynthia stood on the edge of the truck, waving her arms for balance. She probably would have fallen into the street if Steve hadn't caught her by the shoulders and steadied her.

"Lady, I never pretended to be a saint," Johnny said, and it came out the way he wanted—easy and ironic and amused—but inside he was horrified. The wince on the kid's face . . . as if he'd been slugged by someone he'd counted on as a friend. And he'd never been called a bitch in his life. A cunt, either, for that matter.

"Get *out*!" Cynthia screamed. Behind her, Ralph was down

on one knee, clumsily holding his son and staring out at Johnny in a kind of stunned disbelief. "We don't need you, we'll do it without you!"

"Why do it at all?" Johnny asked, taking care to stay out of range of her foot. "That's my point. For God? What did he ever do for you, Cynthia, that you should spend your life waiting for him to buzz you on the old intercom or send you a fax? Did God protect you from the guy who jobbed your ear and broke your nose?"

"I'm here, ain't I?" she asked truculently.

"Sorry, that's not enough for me. I'm not going to be the punchline of a joke in God's little comedy club. Not if I can help it. I can't believe *any* of you are seriously contemplating going up there. The idea is insane."

"What about Mary?" Steve asked. "Do you want to leave her? *Can* you leave her?"

"Why not?" Johnny asked, and actually laughed. It was just a short bark of sound . . . but it was not without amusement, and he saw Steve shy away from it, disgusted. Johnny glanced around for animals, but the coast was still clear. So maybe the kid was right—Tak wanted them to go, had opened the door for them. "I don't know her any more than I know the sand-hogs he—*it*, if you like that better—killed in this town. Most of whom were probably so brain-dead they didn't even know they were gone. I mean, don't you see how *pointless* all this is? If you *should* succeed, Steve, what's your reward going to be? A lifetime membership at the Owl's Club?"

"What happened to you?" Steve asked. "You walked up to that cougar big as life and blew her head off. You were like the fucking Wolverine. So I know you've got guts. *Had* em, any-way. Who stole em?"

"You don't understand. That was hot blood. You know what my trouble is? If you give me a chance to think, I'll take it." He took another step backward. No God stopped him. "Good

luck, you guys. David, for whatever it's worth, you're an extraordinary young man."

"If you go, it's over," David said. His face was still against
his father's chest. His words were muffled but audible. "The
chain breaks. Tak wins."

"Yeah, but when playoff-time comes, he's ours," Johnny said,
and laughed again. The sound reminded him of cocktail parties
where you laughed that same meaningless laugh at meaningless
witticisms while, in the background, a meaningless little jazz
combo played meaningless renditions of meaningless old standards like "Do You Know the Way to San Jose" and "Papa Loves
Mambo." It was the way he had been laughing when he climbed
out of the pool at the Bel-Air, still holding his beer in one hand.
But so what. He could laugh any fucking way he wanted to. He
had once won the National Book Award, after all.

"I'm going to take a car from the mining-office lot. I'm
going to drive like hell until I get to Austin, and then I'm
going to make an anonymous call to the State Police, tell them
some bad shit's happened in Desperation. Then I'll take some
rooms in the local Best Western and hope you guys show up to
use them. If you do, drinks are on me. One way or another, I'm
stepping off the wagon tonight. I think Desperation's cured me
of sobriety forever." He smiled at Steve and Cynthia, standing
side by side in the back of the truck with their arms around each
other. "You two are crazy not to come with me now, you know.
Somewhere else you could be good together. I can see that. All
you can do here is be *can tahs* for David's cannibal God."

He turned and began to walk away, head down, heart
pounding. He expected to be followed by anger, invective,
maybe pleas. He was ready for any of them, and perhaps the
only thing that could have stopped him was the thing Steve
Ames *did* say, in the low, almost toneless voice of a man who is
only conveying a fact.

"I don't respect you for this."

Johnny turned around, more hurt by this simple declaration than he would have believed possible. "Dear me," he said. "I've lost the respect of a man once in charge of throwing out Steven Tyler's barf-bags. Ratfuck."

"I never read any of your books, but I read that story you gave me, and I read the book about you," Steve said. "The one by the professor in Oklahoma. I guess you were a hellraiser, and a shit to your women, but you went to Vietnam without a rifle, for God's sake . . . and tonight . . . the cougar . . . what happened to all that?"

"Ran out like piss down a drunk's leg," Johnny said. "I suppose you don't think that happens, but it does. The last of mine ran out in a swimming pool. How's that for absurd?"

David joined Steve and Cynthia at the back of the truck. He still looked pale and worn, but he was calm. "Its mark is on you," he said. "It will let you go, but you'll wish you stayed when you start smelling Tak on your skin."

Johnny looked at the boy for a long time, fighting an urge to walk back to the truck—fighting it with all the considerable force of will at his disposal. "So I'll wear lots of aftershave," he said. "Bye, boys and girls. Live right."

He walked away, and as fast as he could. Any faster and he would have been running.

4

There was silence in the truck; they watched until Johnny was out of sight, and still no one said anything. David stood with his father's arm around him, thinking he had never felt so hollow, so empty, so utterly done in. It was over. They had lost. He kicked one of the empty Jolt bottles, his eye following its skitter to the wall of the truck, where it bounced and came to rest next to—

David stepped forward. "Look, Johnny's wallet. It must have fallen out of his pocket."

"Poor baby," Cynthia said.

"Surprised he didn't lose it sooner," Steve said. He spoke in the dull, preoccupied tone of a man whose real thoughts are somewhere else entirely. "I kept telling him a guy on a motorcycle trip ought to have a wallet with a chain on it." A ghost of a grin touched his lips. "Getting those motel rooms in Austin may not be as easy as he thinks."

"I hope he sleeps in the damn parking lot," Ralph said. "Or beside the road."

David barely heard them. He felt the way he had that day in the Bear Street Woods—not when God was speaking to him, but when he had become aware that God was going to. He bent forward and picked up Johnny's wallet. When he touched it, something that felt like a wallop of electricity exploded in his head. A small, plosive grunt escaped him. He fell against the wall of the truck, clutching the wallet.

"David?" Ralph asked. His voice was distant, his concern echoing over a thousand miles.

Ignoring him, David opened the wallet. There was currency in one compartment and a squash of papers—memoranda, business cards, and such—in another. He ignored both and thumbed a snap on the wallet's left interior side, releasing an accordion of sleeved photographs. He was faintly aware of the others moving in around him as he looked through the pictures, using one finger to spool back through the years: here was a bearded Johnny and a beautiful dark-haired woman with high cheekbones and thrusting breasts, here a gray-mustached Johnny at the railing of a yacht, here a ponytailed Johnny in a tie-dyed *jabbho*, standing beside an actor who looked like Paul Newman before Newman ever thought of selling red-sauce and salad dressing. Each Johnny was a little younger, the head-hair and facial hair darker, the lines in the face less carven, until—

"Here," David whispered. "Oh God, here." He tried to take the photo out of its transparent pocket and couldn't; his hands were shaking too badly. Steve took the wallet, removed the picture, and handed it to the boy. David held it in front of his eyes with the awe of an astronomer who has discovered a brand-new planet.

"What?" Cynthia asked, leaning closer.

"It's the boss," Steve said. "He was over there—'in country,' he usually calls it—almost a year, researching a book. He wrote a few magazine pieces about the war, too, I think." He looked at David. "Did you know that picture was there?"

"I knew *something* was there," David said, almost too faintly for the others to hear. "As soon as I saw his wallet on the floor. But . . . it was him." He paused, then repeated it, wonderingly. "It was *him.*"

"Who was who?" Ralph asked.

David didn't answer, only stared at the picture. It showed three men standing in front of a ramshackle cinderblock building—a bar, judging from the Budweiser sign in the window. The sidewalks were crowded with Asians. Passing in the street at camera left, frozen forever into a half-blur by this old snapshot, was a girl on a motorscooter.

The men on the left and right of the trio were wearing polo shirts and slacks. One was very tall and held a notebook. The other was festooned with cameras. The man in the middle was wearing jeans and a gray tee-shirt. A Yankees baseball cap was pushed far back on his head. A strap crossed his chest; something cased and bulky hung against his hip.

"His radio," David whispered, touching the cased object.

"Nope," Steve said after taking a closer look. "That's a tape-recorder, 1968-style."

"When I met him in the Land of the Dead, it was a radio." David could not take his eyes from the picture. His mouth was dry; his tongue felt large and unwieldy. The man in the middle was grinning, he was holding his reflector sunglasses in one hand, and there was no question about who he was.

Over his head, over the door of the bar from which they had apparently just emerged, was a handpainted sign. The name of the place was The Viet Cong Lookout.

5

She didn't actually faint, but Mary screamed until something in her head gave way and the strength deserted her muscles. She staggered forward, grabbing the table with one hand, not wanting to, there were black widows and scorpions crawling all over it, not to mention a corpse with a nice tasty bowl of blood in front of him, but she wanted to go tumbling face-first onto the floor even less.

The floor was the domain of the snakes.

She settled for dropping to her knees, holding onto the edge of the table with the hand that wasn't holding the flashlight. There was something strangely comforting about this posture. Calming. After a moment's thought she knew what it was: David, of course. Being on her knees reminded her of the simple, trusting way the boy had knelt in the cell he'd shared with Billingsley. In her mind she heard him saying in a slightly apologetic tone, *I wonder if you'd mind turning around . . . I have to take off my pants.* She smiled, and the idea that she was smiling in this nightmare place—that she *could* smile in this nightmare place—calmed her even more. And without thinking about it, she slipped into prayer herself for the first time since she was eleven years old. She'd been at summer camp, lying in a stupid little bunk in a stupid mosquito-infested cabin with a bunch of stupid girls who would probably turn out to be mean and of a pinchy nature. She had been overwhelmed with homesickness, and had prayed for God to send her mother to take her home. God had declined, and from then until now, Mary had considered herself to be pretty much on her own.

"God," she said, "I need help. I'm in a room filled with creepy-crawlies, mostly poisonous, and I'm scared to death. If you're there, anything you can do would be appreciated. A—"

Amen, it was supposed to be, but she broke off before she could finish saying it, her eyes wide. A clear voice spoke in her head—and not her own voice, either, she was sure of it. It was as if someone had just been waiting, and not very patiently, for her to speak first.

There's nothing here that can hurt you, it said.

On the other side of the room, the beam of her flashlight illuminated an old Maytag washer-dryer set. A sign over them read: NO PERSONAL LAUNDRY! THIS MEANS U! Spiders moved back and forth across the sign on long, strutting legs. There were more on top of the washing machine. Closer by, on the table, a small scorpion appeared to be investigating the crushed remains of the spider she had torn out of her hair. Her hand still throbbed from that encounter; the thing must have been *full* of poison, maybe enough to kill her if it had injected her instead of just splashing her. No, she didn't know who that voice belonged to, but if that was the way God answered prayers, she supposed it was no wonder the world was in such deep shit. Because there was plenty here that could hurt her, *plenty.*

No, the voice said patiently, even as she turned the flashlight past the decomposing bodies lined up on the floor and discovered another writhing tangle of snakes. *No, they can't. And you know why.*

"I don't know *anything*," she moaned, and focused the flashlight's beam on her hand. Red and throbby, but not swelling. Because it *hadn't* bitten her.

Hmmmm. *That* was sort of interesting.

Mary put the light back on the bodies, running it from

the first one to Josephson to Entragian. The virus which had haunted these bodies was now in Ellen. And if she, Mary Jackson, was supposed to be its next home, then the things in here really *couldn't* hurt her. Couldn't damage the goods.

"Spider should have bitten me," she murmured, "but it didn't. It let me kill it instead. *Nothing* in here has hurt me." She giggled, a high-pitched, hysterical sound. "We're pals!"

You have to get out of here, the voice told her. *Before it comes back. And it will. Soon, now.*

"Protect me!" Mary said, getting to her feet. "You will, won't you? If you're God, or *from* God, you will!"

No answer from the voice. Maybe its owner didn't want to protect her. Maybe it couldn't.

Shivering, Mary reached out toward the table. The black widows and the smaller spiders—brown recluses—scuttered away from her in all directions. The scorpions did the same. One actually fell off the side of the table. Panic in the streets.

Good. Very good. But not enough. She had to get *out* of here.

Mary stabbed the black with the flashlight until she found the door. She crossed it on legs that felt numb and distant, trying not to tread on the spiders that were scurrying everywhere. The doorknob turned, but the door would only go back and forth an inch or so. When she yanked it hard, she could hear what sounded like a padlock rattling outside. She wasn't very surprised, actually.

She shone the light around again, running it over the poster—LET THE BASTARDS FREEZE IN THE DARK—and the rusty sink, the counter with the coffeemaker and the little microwave, the washer-dryer set. Then the office area with a desk and a few old file cabinets and a time-clock on the wall, a rack of timecards, the potbellied stove, a toolchest, a few picks and shovels in a rusty tangle, a calendar showing a blonde in a bikini. Then she was back to the door again. No windows; not a single one. She shone the light down at the floor, thinking briefly of the shovels, but the boards were flush with the corrugated metal walls, and she doubted very much if the thing in Ellen Carver's body would give her time enough to dig her way out.

Try the dryer, Mare.

That was she herself, *had* to be, but she was damned if it *sounded* like her . . . and it didn't feel exactly like a thought, either.

Not that this was the time to worry about such things. She hurried over to the dryer, taking less care about where she put her feet this time and stepping on several of the spiders. The smell of decay seemed stronger over here, *riper*, which was strange, since the bodies were on the other side of the room, but—

A diamondback rattler poked up the dryer's lid and began slithering out. It was like coming face to face with the world's ugliest jack-in-the-box. Its head swayed back and forth. Its black preacher's eyes were fixed solemnly on her. Mary took a step backward, then forced herself forward again, reaching out to it. She could be wrong about the spiders and snakes, she knew that. But what if this big fellow *did* bite her? Would dying of snakebite be worse than ending up like Entragian, killing everything that crossed her path until her body exploded like a bomb?

The snake's jaws yawned, revealing curved fangs like whalebone needles. It hissed at her.

"Fuck you, bro," Mary said. She seized it, pulled it out of the dryer—it was easily four feet long—and flung it across the room. Then she banged down the lid with the base of the flashlight, not wanting to see what else might be inside, and pulled the dryer away from the wall. There was a pop as the pleated plastic exhaust-hose pulled out of the hole in the wall. Spiders, dozens of them, scattered from beneath the dryer in all directions.

Mary bent down to look at the hole. It was about two feet across, too small to crawl through, but the edges were badly corroded, and she thought . . .

She went back across the room, stepping on one of the scorpions—*crrunch*—and kicking impatiently at a rat which had been hiding behind the bodies . . . and, most likely, gorging on them. She seized one of the picks, went back to the exhaust-hole, and pushed the dryer a little farther aside to give herself room. The smell of putrefaction was stronger now, but she hardly noticed. She worked the short end of the pick through the hole, pulled upward, and gave a little crow of delight when the tool yanked a furrow nearly eighteen inches long through the rotted, rusted metal.

Hurry, Mary—hurry!

She wiped sweat off her forehead, inserted the pick at the end of the furrow, and yanked upward again. The pick lengthened the slit at the top of the hole even more, then came loose so suddenly that she fell over backward, the pick jarring loose from her hand. She could feel more spiders bursting under her back, and the rat she'd kicked earlier—or maybe one of his relatives—crawled over her neck, squeaking. Its whiskers tickled the underside of her jaw.

"Fuck *off*!" she cried, and batted it away. She got to her feet, took the flashlight off the top of the dryer, clasped it between her upper left arm and her left breast. Then she leaned forward and folded back the two sides of the slit she'd made like wings.

She thought it was big enough. Just.

"God, thank you," she said. "Stay with me a little more, please. And if you get me through this, I promise I'll stay in touch."

She got on her knees and peered out through the hole. The stench was now so strong it made her feel like gagging. She shone the light out and down.

"*God!*" she screamed in a high, strengthless voice. "*Oh Jesus, NO!*"

Her first shocked impression was that there were hundreds of bodies stacked behind the building she was in—the whole world seemed to be white, slack faces, glazed eyes, and torn flesh. As she watched, a buzzard that had been roosting on the chest of one man and pulling meat from the face of another took to the air, its wings flapping like sheets on a clothesline.

Not that many, she told herself. *Not that many, Mary old kid, and even if there were a thousand, it wouldn't change your situation.*

Still, she couldn't go forward for a moment. The hole was big enough to crawl out of, she was sure it was, but she would . . . .

"I'll land on them," she whispered. The light in her hand was jittering uncontrollably, picking out cheeks and brows and tufted ears, making her think of that scene at the end of *Psycho* where the cobwebby bulb in the basement starts swinging back and forth, sliding across the wrinkled mummy-face of Norman's dead mother.

You have to go, Mary, the voice told her patiently. *You have to go* now, *or it will be too late.*

All right . . . but she didn't have to *see* her landing zone. No way. Not if she didn't want to.

She turned off the flashlight and tossed it out through the hole. She heard a soft *thunk* as it landed on . . . well, on something. She took a deep breath, closed her eyes, and slipped out. Rust-ragged metal pulled her shirt out of her jeans and scraped her belly. She tilted forward, and then she was falling, still with her eyes squeezed shut. She put her hands out in front of her. One landed on someone's face—she felt the cold, unbreathing prow of the nose in her palm and the eyebrows (bushy ones, by the feel) under her fingers. The other hand squashed into some cold jelly and skidded.

She pressed her lips together, sealing whatever wanted to

come out of her—a scream or a cry of revulsion—behind them. If she screamed, she'd have to breathe. And if she breathed, she'd have to smell these corpses, which had been lying out here in the summer sun for God knew how long. She landed on things that shifted and belched dead breath. Telling herself not to panic, to just hold on, Mary rolled away from them, already rubbing the hand which had skidded in the jelly-stuff on her pants.

Now there was sand beneath her, and the sharp points of small, broken rocks. She rolled once more, onto her belly, got her knees under her, and plunged both hands into this rough, broken scree, rubbing them back and forth, dry-washing them as best she could. She opened her eyes and saw the flashlight lying by an outstretched, waxy hand. She looked up, wanting—needing—the cleanliness and calm disconnection of the sky. A brilliant white crescent of moon rode low in it, seeming almost to be impaled on a sharp devil's prong of rock jutting from the east side of the China Pit.

I'm out, she thought, taking the flashlight. *At least there's that. Dear God, thank you for that.*

She backed away from the deadpile on her knees, the flashlight once more clamped between her arm and breast, still dragging her tingling hands through the broken ground, scouring them.

There was light to her left. She looked that way, and felt a burst of terror as she saw Entragian's cruiser. *Would you step out of the car, please, Mr. Jackson?* he'd said, and that was when it had happened, she decided, when everything she'd once be-lieved solid had blown away like dust in the wind.

It's empty, the car's empty, you can see that, can't you?

Yes, she could, but the residue of the terror remained. It was a taste in her mouth, as if she had been sucking pennies.

The cruiser—road-dusty, even the flasher bars on the roof now crusted with the storm's residue—was standing next to a small concrete building that looked like a pillbox emplacement. The driver's door had been left open (she could see the hideous little plastic bear next to the dashboard compass), and that was why the domelight was on. Ellen had brought her out here in the cruiser, then gone somewhere else. Ellen had other fish to fry, other hooks to bait, other joints to roll. If only she'd left the keys—

Mary got to her feet and hurried to the car, jogging bent over at the waist like a soldier crossing no-man's-land. The cruiser reeked of blood and piss and pain and fear. The dashboard, the wheel, and the front seat were splashed with gore. The instruments were unreadable. Lying in the footwell on the passenger's side was a small stone spider. It was an old thing, and pitted, but just looking at it made Mary feel cold and weak.

Not that she would have to worry about it much; the cruiser's ignition slot was empty.

"Shit!" Mary whispered fiercely. "Shit on toast!" She turned and shone her light first on a cluster of mining equipment and then over to the base of the road leading up the pit's north slope. Packed dirt surfaced with gravel, at least four lanes wide to accommodate the heavy equipment she had just been looking at, probably smoother than the highway she and Peter had been on when the goddam cop stopped them . . . and she couldn't drive the police-cruiser up and out of here because she didn't have the fucking key.

If I can't, I have to make sure he can't either. Or she. Or whatever in hell it is.

She bent into the car again, wincing at the sour smell (and keeping an eye on the nasty statuette in the footwell, as if it might come to life and leap at her). She yanked the hood release, then walked around to the front of the car. She felt along the top of the grille for the catch, found it, and raised the Caprice's hood. The engine inside was huge, but she had no trouble spotting the air-cleaner. She leaned over it, grasped the butterfly nut in the center, and applied pressure. Nothing happened.

She hissed with frustration and blinked more sweat out of her eyes. It stung. A little over a year ago, she had read poems as part of a cultural event called "Women Poets Celebrate Their Sense and Sexuality." She had worn a suit from Donna Karan, and a silk blouse underneath. Her hair had been freshly done, feathered in bangs across her brow. Her long poem, "My Vase," had been quite the hit of the evening. Of course all that had been before her visit to the historic and beautiful China Pit, home of the unique and fascinating Rattlesnake Number Two mine. She doubted if any of the people who had heard her read "My Vase"—

smooth

sided

fragrance of stems

brimmed with shadows

curved   like   the

line of a shoulder

the line of a thigh

—at that event would recognize her now. She no longer recognized herself.

Her right hand, the one she was using on the air-cleaner, itched and throbbed. The fingers slipped. A nail tore painfully, and she gasped. "Please God, help me do this, I wouldn't know the distributor cap from the camshaft, so it has to be the carburetor. Please help me be strong enough to—"

This time when she applied pressure, the butterfly nut turned.

"Thanks," she panted. "Oh yeah, thanks very much. You stay

close. And take care of David and the others, will you? Don't let them leave this shithole without me."

She spun the butterfly nut off and let it fall into the engine. She pulled the air-cleaner off its post and tossed it aside, revealing a carburetor almost as big as . . . well, almost as big as a vase. Laughing, Mary squatted, got a fistful of China Pit, pushed down a metal flap-thingie over one of the carb's chambers, and stuffed the sand and rock in. She added two more handfuls, filling the throat of the carburetor, strangling it, then stepped back.

"Let's see you drive *that*, you bitch," she panted.

Hurry. Mary, you have to hurry.

She shone the flashlight over the parked equipment. There were two pickup trucks among the bigger, bulkier stuff. She walked across to them and shone the light into the cabs. No keys here, either. But there was a hatchet in with the litter of equipment in the back of the Ford F-150, and she used it to flatten two tires on both trucks. She started to throw the hatchet away, then reconsidered. She shone the light around once more, and this time she saw the gaping vaguely square hole twenty yards or so up from the bottom of the pit.

There. The source of all this trouble.

She didn't know how she knew that, if it was the voice or God or just some intuition of her own, and she didn't care. Right now she only cared about one thing: getting the bloody hell out of here.

She snapped off the flash—the moon would give her all the light she needed, at least for awhile—and began to trudge up the road which led out of China Pit.

CHAPTER 3

1

The literary lion stood by the computers set up at one end of the long table, looking across the lab toward the far wall, where over a dozen people had been hung on hooks like experimental subjects in a Nazi deathcamp. All pretty much the way Steve and Cynthia had described it, except for one thing: the woman hanging just beneath the words YOU MUST WEAR A HARDHAT, the one whose head was cocked so far over to the right that her cheek lay on her shoulder, looked weirdly like Terry.

You know that's just your imagination, don't you?

Did he? Well, maybe. But, God! . . . the same red-gold hair . . . the high forehead and slightly crooked nose . . .

"Never mind her nose," he said. "You got a crooked nose of your own to worry about. So just get out of here, okay?"

But at first he couldn't move. He knew what he had to do—cross the room and start going through their pockets, pulling the car-keys—but knowing wasn't the same as doing. To reach in, to feel the stiff dead skin of their legs under his hand with only the thin pocket-material between him and it . . . to handle their stuff . . . not just car-keys but pocket-knives and nail-clippers and maybe aspirin-tins—

Everything people keep in their pockets is hyphenated, he thought. *How fascinating.*

—ticket-stubs, money-clips, change-purses—

"Stop," he whispered. "Just go on and do it."

The radio blurted static like gunfire. He jumped. No music. It was past midnight, and the local shitkickers had signed off. They would be back with another load of Travis Tritt and Tanya Tucker come sunrise, but with any luck, John Edward Marinville, the man *Harper's* had once called the only white male writer in America who *matters*, would be gone.

If you go, it's over.

Brushing at his face as though the thought were an annoying fly he could shoo away, Johnny started across the room. He supposed he *was* deserting them, in a manner of speaking, but be real—they had the means to leave themselves if they wanted to, didn't they? As for him, he was heading back to a life where folks didn't spout nonsense languages and rot before your eyes. A life where you could count on people's last growth-spurts to have taken place by the time they were eighteen. His leather chaps brushed against each other as he approached the corpses. Yes, all right, so for the moment he felt less like a literary lion than one of the ARVN looters he had seen in Quang Tri, looking for gold religious medallions on the corpses, sometimes even separating the buttocks of the dead in hopes of finding a diamond or pearl, but that was a specious comparison . . . and would turn out to be a transitory feeling, he was quite sure. Looting corpses wasn't what he was here for at all. *Keys*—a set that matched one of the cars in the parking lot—was what he was here for and *all* he was here for. Furthermore—

Furthermore the dead girl under YOU MUST WEAR A HARD-HAT really *did* look like Terry. A strawberry-blonde with a bullet-hole in her lab coat. Of course, Terry's strawberry-blond days were long gone, she was mostly gray now, but—

You'll wish you stayed when you start smelling Tak on your skin.

"Oh, please," he said. "Let's not be puerile."

He looked to the left, wanting to get his eyes off the dead

blonde who looked so much like Terry—Terry back in the days when she had been able to drive him wild just by crossing her legs or flipping her hip at him—and what he saw made him grin hopefully. There was an ATV over there. Parked inside the garage door like it was, he thought there was a better than even chance that the keys would be in the ignition. If they were, he would at least be spared the indignity of going through the pockets of Entragian's victims—or maybe he had been Joseph-son when he'd done this, not that it mattered. All he'd have to do would be unhook the ore-carrier, run up the garage door, and ride away.

. . . when you start smelling Tak on your skin.

Maybe he *would* smell it to start with, but he wouldn't smell it for long. David Carver might be a prophet, but he was a *young* prophet, and there were a few things he didn't seem to realize, direct line to God or no. One was the simple fact that stink washed off. Yes indeed it did. That was one of the few things in life Johnny was entirely sure of.

And the key to the ATV was, praise God, in the ignition.

He leaned in, turned the key to Accessory, and observed there was also more than three-quarters of a tank of gas. "All sevens, baby," he said, and laughed. "Rolling all sevens now."

He went to the back of the little Jeep-like vehicle and ex-amined the ore-cart coupling. No problem there, either. Just a glorified cotter pin was all it was. He'd find a hammer . . . knock it out . . .

Not even Houdini could have done it, Marinville. It was the old rumdum's voice this time. *Because of the head. And what about the phone? What about the sardines?*

"What about them? There were just a few more cans in the bag than we thought, that's all."

He was sweating, though. Sweating the way he had in 'Nam, sometimes. It wasn't the heat, although it *had* been hot, and it hadn't been the fear, although you *were* afraid, even when you were sleeping. Mostly it had been the sick sweat that came with knowing you were in the wrong place at the wrong time with fundamentally good people who were spoiling themselves, maybe forever, by doing the wrong thing.

Unobtrusive miracles, he thought, only once again he heard the words in the old rumdum's voice. He was, by God, chattier dead than alive. *Why, if it wasn't for the boy, you'd still be in a jail cell now, wouldn't you? Or dead. Or worse. And you deserted him.*

"If I hadn't distracted that coyote with my jacket, *David'd* be dead now," Johnny said. "Leave me alone, you old fool."

He spotted a hammer lying on a worktable against the wall. He headed in that direction.

"Tell me something, Johnny," Terry said, and he froze in his tracks. "When exactly was it that you decided to deal with your fear of dying by giving up real life completely?"

That voice wasn't in his head, he was all but sure of it. Hell, he *was* sure of it. It was Terry, hanging on the wall. Not a look-alike, not a mirage or a hallucination, but Terry. If he turned around now he would see her with her head raised, her cheek no longer on her shoulder, looking at him as she had always looked at him when he fucked up—patient because Johnny Marinville fucking up was the usual course of things, disillusioned because she was the only one who kept expecting him to do better. Which was dumb, like betting on the Tampa Bay Bucs to win the Super Bowl. Except sometimes, with her—*for* her—he *had* done better, had risen above what he had come to think of as his nature. But when he did, when he excelled, when he fucking *flew over the landscape*, did she ever say anything then? Well, maybe "Change the channel, let's see what's on PBS," but that was about the extent of it.

"You didn't even give up living for writing," she said. "That would at least have been understandable, if contemptible. You gave up living for *talking* about writing. I mean *Jesus*, Johnny!"

He stalked to the table on trembling legs, meaning to

throw the hammer at the bitch, see if that would shut her up. And that was when he heard the low growling from his left.

He turned his head in that direction and saw a timberwolf—very likely the same one that had approached Steve and Cynthia with the *can tah* in its mouth—standing in the doorway leading back to the offices. Its eyes glowed at him. For a moment it hesitated, and Johnny allowed himself to hope—maybe it was afraid, maybe it would back off. Then it was running at him full-tilt, its muzzle wrinkling back to expose its teeth.

2

The thing which had been Ellen had been concentrating on the wolf—using the wolf to finish with the writer—so deeply that it was in a state akin to hypnosis. Now something, some disruption in the expected flow of things, interrupted Tak's concentration. It pulled back for a moment, holding the wolf where it was, but turning toward the Ryder truck with the rest of its terrible curiosity and dark regard. Something had happened at the truck, but Tak was unable to tell what it was. There was a feeling of disorientation, a sense of waking in a room where the positions of all the furniture had been subtly altered.

Perhaps, if it wasn't trying to be in two places at the same time—

"*Mi him, en tow!*" it growled, and sent the wolf at the writer. So much for the man who would be Steinbeck; the thing on four legs was fast and strong, the thing on two, slow and weak. Tak pulled its mind out of the wolf, its vision of Johnny Marinville first dimming, then fading out as the writer turned, groping for something on the worktable with one hand while his eyes went wide with fright.

It turned its full mind toward the truck and the others—although the only one of the others who mattered, who had *ever* mattered (would that it had understood earlier), was the shitting prayboy.

The bright yellow rental truck was still parked on the street—through the overlapping eyes of the spiders and with the low-to-the-ground heat-vision of the snakes Tak saw it clearly—but when it tried to go inside, it was unable. No eyes in there? Not even one tiny scuttering spider? No? Or was it Prayboy again, blocking its vision?

No matter. It didn't have time to *let* it matter. They *were* in there, all of them, they had to be, and Tak would have to leave it at that, because something else was wrong, as well. Something even closer to home.

Something wrong with Mary.

Feeling strangely and uncomfortably harried, feeling *driven*, it let the Ryder truck fade and now centered on the field office, looking through the uneasily shifting eyes of the creatures which filled it. It registered the out-of-place dryer first, then the fact that Mary was gone. She'd gotten out somehow.

"You *bitch*!" it screamed, and blood flew out of Ellen's mouth in a fine spray. The word wasn't good enough to express its feelings, and so it lapsed into the old language, spitting invective as it got to its feet . . . and staggered for balance on the edge of the *ini*. The weakness of this body had advanced in a way that was appalling. What made it worse was that it didn't have a body to which it could immediately go, if necessary; for the time being, it was stuck with this one. It thought briefly of the animals, but there were none here capable of serving Tak in that way. Tak's presence drubbed even the strongest of its human vessels to death in a matter of days. A snake, coyote, rat, or buzzard would simply explode immediately upon or moments after Tak's entry, like a tin can into which someone drops a lit stick of dynamite. The timberwolf might serve for an hour or two, but the wolf was the only one of its kind left in these parts, and currently three miles away, dealing with (and by now probably dining on) the writer.

It had to be the woman.

It had to be Mary.

The thing that looked like Ellen slipped out through the rift in the wall of the *an tak* and limped toward the faint purple square that marked the place where the old shaft now opened into the outside world. Rats squeaked eagerly around Ellen's feet as it went, smelling the blood flowing out of Ellen's stupid, sickly cunt. Tak kicked them aside, cursing them in the old language.

At the entrance to the China Shaft it paused, looking down. The moon had passed behind the far side of the pit, but it still shed some light, and the domelight inside the police-cruiser shed a little more. Enough for Ellen's eyes to see that the cruiser's hood was up and for the creature now inhabiting Ellen's brain to understand that the sly *os pa* had fucked the motor up somehow. How had she gotten out of the field office? And how had she dared do this? How had she *dared*?

For the first time, Tak was afraid.

It looked left and saw that both pickups were standing on flats. It was like the Carvers' RV all over again, only this time *it* was on the receiving end, and it didn't like the feeling one bit. That left the heavy equipment, and although it knew where the keys were—sets for everything in one of the field office file cabinets—they would do it no good; there was nothing down there it could drive. Cary Ripton had known how to run the heavy stuff, but Tak had lost Ripton's physical skills the moment it left him for Josephson. As Ellen Carver, it had some of Ripton's, Josephson's, and Entragian's memories (although even these were now fading like overexposed photographs) but none of their abilities.

Oh, the bitch! *Os pa! Can fin!*

Clenching and unclenching Ellen's fists nervously, aware of her sodden panties and the soaked shirt inside them, aware that Ellen's thighs were painted with blood, Tak closed Ellen's eyes and looked for Mary.

"Mi him, en tow! En tow! En TOW!"

At first there was nothing, just blackness and the slow flux of cramps deep down in Ellen's stomach. And terror. Terror that the *os pa* bitch was gone already. Then it saw what it was looking for, not with Ellen's eyes but with ears inside of Ellen's ears: a sudden alien echo of sound that made the shape of a woman.

It was a circling bat that had seen Mary as she struggled up the road toward the northern rim of the pit, and Mary was a long way from fresh, gasping for breath and turning around every dozen steps or so. Checking for pursuit. The bat "saw" the smells coming off her quite clearly, and what Tak picked up was encouraging. It was the smell of fear, mostly. The sort which might tilt into panic with one hard push.

Still, Mary was only four hundred yards or so from the top, and after that the going would be downhill. And while Mary was tired and breathing hard, the bat did not sense the bitter metallic aroma of exhaustion in the sweat which surrounded her. Not yet, at least. There was also the fact that Mary was not bleeding like a stuck pig. This next-to-useless Ellen Carver body *was*. The bleeding wasn't out of control—not yet—but would be before much longer. Perhaps taking time to collect itself, to rest in the comforting glow of the *ini*, had been a mistake, but who would have believed this could happen?

What about sending the *can toi* to stop her? Those that were not on the perimeter as part of the *mi him*?

It *could*, but what fucking *good* would it do? It could surround Mary with snakes and spiders, with hissing wildcats and laughing coyotes, and the bitch would very likely walk right through them, parting them the way Moses had supposedly parted the Red Sea. She must know that "Ellen" couldn't damage her body, not with the *can toi*, not with any other weapon. If she *didn't* know it, she'd still be in the field office, probably crouched in the corner, all but catatonic with fear, unable to make a sound after screaming herself hoarse.

How had she known? Had it been the prayboy? Or had it been a message from the prayboy's God, David Carver's *can tak*? No matter. The fact that Ellen's body was starting to come apart and Mary had a half-mile head start, those things didn't matter, either.

"I'm coming just the same, sweetheart," it whispered, and began making its way along one of the benches, moving away from the mineshaft and toward the road.

Yes. Coming just the same. It might have to beat this body to flinders in order to catch up with the *os pa*, but it *would* catch up.

Ellen turned her head, spat blood, grinned. She no longer looked much like the woman who had been considering a run for the school board, the woman who had enjoyed lunch with her friends at China Happiness, the woman whose deepest, darkest sexual fantasies involved making love to the hunk in the Diet Coke commercials.

"It doesn't matter how fast you hurry, *os pa*. You're not getting away."

3

The dark shape dive-bombed her again, and Mary swatted it away. "Fuck *off*!" she panted at it.

The bat veered, cheeping, but didn't go far. It circled her like some sort of spotter-plane, and Mary had an unpleasant idea that that was just what it was. She looked up and saw the rim of the pit ahead and above her. Closer now—maybe only two hundred yards—but it still looked mockingly far off. It felt as if she were tearing each breath out of the air, and it hurt going down. Her heart was hammering, and there was a deep stitch in her left side. She had actually thought she was in pretty good shape for a woman who was thirtysomething, as if using the NordicTrack and the StairMaster three times a week at Gold's Gym could get you ready for something like this.

Suddenly the fine gravel surface of the road slid out from under her sneakers, and her trembling legs weren't able to correct her balance in time. She was able to avoid going flat on her face by dropping to one knee, but her jeans tore, she felt the sting of the gravel biting through her skin, and then warm blood was flowing down her lower leg.

The bat was on her at once, cheeping and battering its wings in her hair.

"Get out, you cocksucker!" she cried, and boxed a closed fist at it. It was a lucky punch. She felt the fine-grained surface of one wing give way under the blow and then the bat was fluttering on the road ahead of her, mouth opening and closing, staring at her—or seeming to—with its useless little eyes. Mary struggled to her feet and stamped on it, voicing a sharp, almost birdlike cry of satisfaction as it crunched beneath her sneaker.

She started to turn again, then glimpsed something down below. A shadow moving among shadows.

"Mary?" It was Ellen Carver's voice that came floating up, but at the same time it wasn't. It was gargly, full. If you hadn't been through the hell of the last six or eight hours, you might have thought it was Ellen with a bad cold. "Wait, Mare! I want to go with you! I want to see David! We'll go see him together!"

"Go to hell," Mary whispered. She turned and began to walk again, tearing breath out of the air and rubbing at the pain in her side. She would have run if she could.

"Mary-Mary-quite-contrary!" Not quite laughing, but almost. "You can't get away, dear—don't you know that?"

The rim looked so far away that Mary forced herself to quit looking at it and lowered her head to her sneakers. The next time the voice behind her called her name, it sounded closer. Mary made herself walk a little faster. She fell twice more before she got to the rim, the second time hard enough to knock the wind out of her, and it took her precious, precious seconds of first kneeling and then standing with her head down and her hands on her thighs to get it back. She wished Ellen would call again, but she didn't. And now Mary didn't want to look back. She was too afraid of what she might see.

Five yards from the top, however, she finally did. Ellen was less than twenty yards below her, panting soundlessly through a mouth dropped so wide open that it looked like an airscoop. Blood misted out with each exhalation; her blouse was drenched with it. She saw Mary looking at her, grimaced, reached out with clawed hands, tried to sprint forward and grab her. She couldn't.

Mary, however, found that she *could* sprint. It was mostly the look in Ellen Carver's eyes. Nothing human in them. Nothing at all.

She reached the top of the pit, the air now screaming thinly in and out of her throat. The road ran flat across thirty yards of rim, then tilted down. She could see a tiny yellow spark in the blackness of the desert floor, winking on and off: the blinker in the center of town.

Mary set her eyes on this and ran a little faster.

4

"What are you doing, David?" Ralph asked tightly. After a short period of concentration which was probably silent prayer, David had begun walking toward the back door of the Ryder truck. Ralph had moved instinctively, putting his body between his son and the handle that ran the door up. Steve saw this and sympathized with the feeling behind it, but didn't guess it would do much good. If David decided he was going to leave, David would leave.

The boy held up the wallet. "Taking this back."

"No you don't," Ralph said, shaking his head rapidly. "No way. For God's sake, David, you don't even know where that man is—out of town by now, is my guess. And good riddance to bad rubbish."

"I know where he is," David said calmly. "I can find him. He's close." He hesitated, then added: "I'm *supposed* to find him."

"David?" To his own ears, Steve's voice sounded tentative, oddly young. "You said the chain was broken."

"That was before I saw the picture in his wallet. I have to go to him. I have to go now. It's the only chance we have."

"I don't understand," Ralph said, but he stepped away from the door. "What does that picture *mean*?"

"There's no time, Dad. I'm not sure I could explain even if there was."

"Are we coming with you?" Cynthia asked. "We're not, are we?"

David shook his head. "I'll come back if I can. With Johnny, if I can."

"This's nuts," his father said, but he spoke hollowly, with no strength. "If you go wandering around out there, you'll be eaten alive."

"No more than the coyote ate me alive when I got out of the cell," David said. "The danger isn't if I go out there; it's if we all stay in here."

He looked at Steve, then at the rear door of the Ryder truck. Steve nodded and ran the door up on its tracks. The desert night slipped in, pressed against his face like a cold kiss.

David went to his father and began to hug him. As Ralph's

arms went around the boy in response, David felt that enormous force grab at him again. It ran through him like hard rain. He jerked convulsively in his father's arms, gasping, then took a blind step backward. His hands, shaking wildly, were held out before him.

"David!" Ralph cried. "David, what—"

And it was over. As quickly as that. The force left. But he could still see the China Pit as he had seen it for a moment in the circle of his father's arms; it had been like looking down from a low-flying plane. It glimmered in the last of the moonlight, a wretched alabaster sinkhole. He could hear the ruffle of the wind in his ears and a voice

(*mi him, en tow! mi him, en tow!*)

calling. A voice that wasn't human.

He made an effort to clear his mind and look around at them—so few left now, so few of The Collie Entragian Survival Society. Steve and Cynthia standing together, his father bending down toward him; behind them, the moondrenched night.

"What is it?" Ralph asked unsteadily. "Christ Almighty, what now?"

He saw he had dropped the wallet, and bent to pick it up. Wouldn't do to leave it here, gosh no. He thought of putting it into his own back pocket, then thought of how it had fallen out of Johnny's and dumped it down the front of his shirt instead.

"You have to go to the pit," he told his father. "Daddy, you and Steve and Cynthia have to go out to the China Pit right now. Mary needs help. Do you understand? *Mary needs help!*"

"What are you talk—"

"She got out, she's running down the road toward town, and Tak is chasing her. You have to go now. *Right now!*"

Ralph reached for him again, but this time in a tentative, strengthless way. David ducked easily beneath his arm and jumped from the Ryder truck's tailgate into the street.

"David!" Cynthia cried. "Splitting up like this . . . are you sure it's right?"

"*No!*" he shouted back. He felt desperate and confused and more than a little stunned. "I know how wrong it feels, it feels wrong to me, too, but there's nothing else! I swear to you! There's just nothing else!"

"*You get back in here!*" Ralph bawled.

David turned, dark eyes meeting his father's frantic gaze. "Go, Dad. All three of you. Now. You have to. Help her! For God's sake, *help Mary!*"

And before anyone could ask another question, David Carver turned on his heel and went pelting off into the dark. With one hand he pumped the air; the other he held against the front of his shirt, cupping John Edward Marinville's genuine crocodile wallet, three hundred and ninety-five dollars, Barneys of New York.

5

Ralph tried to jump out after his son. Steve grabbed him by the shoulders, and Cynthia grabbed him around the waist.

"*Let me go!*" Ralph shouted, struggling . . . but not struggling too hard, at that. Steve felt marginally encouraged. "*Let me go after my son!*"

"No," Cynthia said. "We have to believe he knows what he's doing, Ralph."

"I can't lose him, too," Ralph whispered, but he relaxed, quit trying to pull away from them. "I *can't.*"

"Maybe the best way to make sure that doesn't happen is to go along with what he wants," Cynthia said.

Ralph drew a deep breath, then exhaled it. "My son went after that asshole," he said. He sounded as if he were talking to himself. *Explaining* to himself. "He went after that conceited asshole *to give him back his wallet*, and if we asked him why, he'd say because it's God's will. Am I right?"

"Yeah, probably," Cynthia said. She reached out and touched Ralph's shoulder. He opened his eyes and she smiled at him. "And you know the bitch of it? It's probably the truth."

Ralph looked at Steve. "You wouldn't leave him, would you? Pick up Mary, take that equipment-road back to the highway, and leave my boy behind?"

Steve shook his head.

Ralph put his hands to his face, seemed to gather himself, dropped his hands, and stared at them. There was a stony cast to his features now, a look of resolves taken and bridges burned. A queer thought came to Steve: for the first time since he'd met the Carvers, he could see the son in the father.

"All right," Ralph said. "We'll leave God to protect my kid until we get back." He jumped off the back of the truck and looked grimly down the street. "It'll *have* to be God. That bastard Marinville sure won't do it."

CHAPTER 4

1

The thought which flashed across Johnny's mind as the wolf charged him was the kid saying that the creature running this show wanted them to leave town, would be happy to let them go. Maybe it was a little glitch in the kid's second sight . . . or maybe Tak had just seen a chance to pick one of them off and was taking it. Never look a gift-horse in the mouth, and all that.

In either case, he thought, *I am royally fucked.*

You deserve to be, sweetheart, Terry said from behind him— yeah, that was Terry, all right, helpful to the end.

He brandished the hammer at the oncoming wolf and yelled *"Get outta here!"* in a shrill voice he barely recognized as his own.

The wolf broke left and turned in a tight circle, growling as it went, hindquarters low to the ground, tail tucked. One of its powerful shoulders struck a cabinet as it completed its turn, and a teacup balanced on top of it fell off and shattered on the floor. The radio coughed out a long, loud bray of static.

Johnny took one step toward the door, visualizing how he would pelt down the hall and out into the parking lot—fuck the ATV, he'd find wheels elsewhere—and then the wolf was in the aisle again, head down and hackles up, eyes (horribly intelligent, horribly *aware* eyes) glowing. Johnny retreated, holding the hammer up in front of him like a knight saluting the king with his sword, waggling it slightly. He could feel his palm sweating against the hammer's perforated rubber sleeve. The wolf looked huge, the size of a full-grown German Shepherd at least. By comparison, the hammer looked ridiculously small, the kind of pantry-cabinet accessory one kept around for repairing shelves or installing picture-hooks.

"God help me," Johnny said . . . but he felt no presence here; God was just something you said, a word you used when you could see the shit once more getting ready to obey the law of gravity and fall into the fan. No God, no God, he wasn't a suburban kid from Ohio still three years away from his first encounter with a razor, prayer was just a manifestation of what psychologists called "magical thinking," and there was no God.

If there was, why would he come see about me, anyhow? Why would he come see about me after I left the others back in that truck?

The wolf suddenly barked at him. It was an absurd sound, high-pitched, the kind of bark Johnny would have expected from a poodle or a cocker spaniel. There was nothing absurd about its teeth, though. Thick curds of spit flew out from between them with each high-pitched bark.

"Get out!" Johnny yelled at it in his shrill, wavering voice. "Get out right now!"

Instead of getting out, the wolf screwed its hindquarters down toward the floor. For a moment Johnny thought it was going to take a crap, that it was every damn bit as scared as he was, and it was going to take a crap on the laboratory floor. Then, a split second before it happened, he realized the wolf was preparing not to crap but to leap. At him.

"No, God no, please!" he screamed, and turned to run—back toward the ATV and the bodies hanging stiffly on their hooks.

In his head he did this; his body moved in the opposite direction, *forward*, as if directed by hands he could not see. There was no sense of being possessed, but a clear and unmistakable feeling of being *no longer alone.* His terror fell away. His first powerful instinct—to turn and run—also fell away. He took a step forward instead, pushing off from the table with his free hand. He cocked the hammer back to beyond his right shoulder and hurled it just as the wolf launched itself at him.

He expected the hammer to spin and was sure it would sail over the animal's head—he had pitched at Lincoln Park High School about a thousand years ago and still knew the feeling of one that was going to be wild-high—but it didn't. It was no Excalibur, just a plain old Craftsman hammer with a perforated rubber sleeve on it to improve the grip, but it didn't turn over and it didn't go high.

What it did was strike the wolf dead center between the eyes.

There was a sound like a brick dropped on an oak plank. The green glare whiffed out of the wolf's eyes; they turned into old marbles even as the blood began to pour out of the animal's center-split skull. Then it hit him in the chest, driving him back against the table again, setting off a brilliant burst of pain in the small of his back. For a moment Johnny could smell the wolf—a dry smell, almost cinnamony, like the spices the Egyptians had used to preserve the dead. For that moment the animal's bloody face was turned up to his, the teeth which should by all rights have torn out his throat leering impotently. Johnny could see its tongue, and an old crescent-shaped scar on its muzzle. Then it dropped on his feet, like something loose and heavy wrapped in a ratty old steamer blanket.

Gasping, Johnny staggered away from it. He bent to pick up the hammer, then whirled around so clumsily he almost fell, sure that the wolf would be on its feet and coming for him again; there was no way he could have gotten it with the hammer like that, absolutely no *way*, that baby had been going *high*, your muscles remembered what it felt like when you'd uncorked one that was going all the way to the backstop, they remembered it very well.

But the wolf lay where it had fallen.

Is it time to reconsider David Carver's God? Terry asked quietly. Stereo Terry now; she had a place in his head, and she also had a place on the wall under YOU MUST WEAR A HARDHAT.

"No," he said. "It was a lucky shot, that's all. Like the one-in-a-thousand at the carny when you actually *do* win your girl-friend the big stuffed panda-bear."

Thought you said it was going high.

"Well, I was wrong, wasn't I? Just like you used to tell me six or a dozen times every fucking day, you great bitch." He was shocked by the hoarse, almost teary quality of his voice. "Wasn't that pretty much your refrain throughout the course of our charming union? You're wrong, Johnny, you're wrong, Johnny, you're totally fucking wrong, Johnny?"

You left them, Terry's voice said, and what stopped him was not the contempt he heard in that voice (which was, after all, only his own voice, his own mind up to its old bicameral tricks) but the despair. *You left them to die. Worse, you continue to deny God even after you called on him . . . and he answered. What kind of man are you?*

"A man who knows the difference between God and a free-throw," he told the woman with the strawberry-blond hair and the bullet-hole in her lab coat. "A man who also knows enough to get while the getting's good."

He waited for Terry to respond. Terry didn't. He consid-ered what had just happened a final time, scanning it with his nearly perfect recall, and found nothing but his own arm, which apparently hadn't forgotten everything it had learned about throwing a fastball, and an ordinary Craftsman hammer. No blue light. No Cecil B. DeMille special effects. No London Philharmonic swelling with a hundred violins' worth of phony awe in the background. The terror and emptiness and despair he felt were transitory emotions; they would pass. What he was going to do right now was divorce the ATV from the ore-cart behind it, using the hammer to knock loose the cotter-pin coupling. What he was going to do next was get the ATV running and get the hell out of this creepy little—

"Not bad, ace," said a voice from the doorway.

Johnny wheeled around. The boy was standing there. David. Looking at the wolf. Then he raised his unsmiling face to Johnny.

"A lucky shot," Johnny said.

"Think that was it?"

"Does your father know you're out, David?"

"He knows."

"If you came here to try and persuade me to stay, you're shit out of luck," Johnny said. He bent over the coupling between the ore-cart and the ATV and took a swing at the cotter pin. He missed it completely and smashed his hand painfully against an angle of metal. He cried out and stuck his scraped knuckles into his mouth. Yet he had hit the leaping wolf dead between the eyes with the hammer, he—

Johnny blocked the rest. He pulled his hand out of his mouth, tightened his grip on the hammer's rubber sleeve, and bent over the coupling again. This time he hit it pretty well—not dead center, but close enough to pop the cotter pin free and send it rolling across the floor. It stopped beneath the dangling feet of the woman who looked like Terry.

And I'm not going to read anything into that, *either.*

"If you came to talk theology, you're similarly out of luck," Johnny said. "If, however, you'd like to accompany me west to Austin—"

He broke off. The boy now had something in his hand, was holding it out to him. Between them, the dead wolf lay on the lab floor.

"What's that?" Johnny asked, but he knew. His eyes weren't that bad yet. Suddenly his mouth felt very dry. *Why are you chasing me?* he thought suddenly—to what he did not precisely know, only that it wasn't the kid. *Why can't you lose my scent? Just leave me alone?*

"Your wallet," David said. His eyes on him, so steady. "It fell out of your pocket, in the truck. I brought it to you. It's got all your ID in it, in case you forget who you are."

"Very funny."

"I wasn't joking."

"So what do you want?" Johnny asked harshly. "A reward? Okay. Write down your address, I'll send you either twenty bucks or an autographed book. Want a baseball signed by Albert Belle? I can do that. Whatever you want. Whatever strikes your fancy."

David looked down at the wolf for a moment. "Pretty good shot for a man who can't even hit a coupling dead on from four inches away."

"Shut up, wiseguy," Johnny said. "Bring me the wallet if you're coming. Toss it over if you're not. Or just keep the goddam thing."

"There's a picture in it. You and two other guys standing in front of a place called The Viet Cong Lookout. A bar, I think."

"Yeah, a bar," Johnny agreed. He flexed his hand uneasily on the shaft of the hammer, barely feeling the sting run across his scraped knuckles. "The tall guy in that picture's David Halberstam. Very famous writer. Historian. Baseball fan."

"I was more interested in the ordinary-sized guy in the middle," David said, and all at once a part of Johnny—a deep, deep part—knew what the child was driving at, what the child was going to say, and that part moaned in protest. "The guy in the gray shirt and the Yankees hat. The guy that showed me the China Pit from *my* Viet Cong Lookout. That guy was you."

"What crap," Johnny said. "The same kind of crazed crap you've been spouting ever since—"

Softly, perfectly on key, and still holding the wallet out to him on one hand, David Carver sang: *"Well I said doctor . . . Mr. M.D. . . ."*

It was like being slugged square in the middle of the chest. The hammer spilled out of Johnny's hand. "Stop it," he whispered.

". . . can you tell me . . . what's ailin' me . . . And he said yeah-yeah-yeah—"

"Stop it!" Johnny screamed, and the radio burped up another burst of static. He could feel stuff starting to move inside him. Terrible stuff. Sliding. Like an avalanche beginning under a surface that only looks solid. Why did the boy have to come? Because he was sent, of course. It wasn't David's fault. The real question was why couldn't the boy's terrible master let either of them go?

"The Rascals," David said. "Only back then they were still the Young Rascals. Felix Cavaliere on vocals. Very cool. That's the song that was playing when you died, wasn't it, Johnny?"

Images beginning to slide downhill through his mind while Felix Cavaliere sang, *I was feelin' so bad*: ARVN soldiers, many no bigger than American sixth-graders, pulling dead buttocks apart, looking for hidden treasure, a nasty scavenger hunt in a nasty war, *can tah* in *can tak*; coming back to Terry with a dose in his crotch and a monkey on his back, wanting to score so bad he was half out of his mind, slapping her in an airport concourse when she said something smart about the war (his war, she had called it, as if he had invented the fucking thing), slapping her so hard that her mouth and nose bled, and although the marriage had limped along for another year or so, it had really ended right there in Concourse B of the United terminal at LaGuardia, with the sound of that slap; Entragian kicking him as he lay writhing on Highway 50, not kicking a literary lion or a National Book Award winner or the only white male writer in America who *mattered*, but just some potbellied geezer in an overpriced motorcycle jacket, one who owed God a death like anyone else; Entragian saying that the proposed title of Johnny's book made him furious, made him sick with rage.

"I won't go back there," Johnny said hoarsely. "Not for you, not for Steve Ames or your father, not for Mary, not for the world. I won't." He picked up the hammer again and slammed it against the ore-cart, punctuating his refusal. "Do you hear me, David? You're wasting your time. I *won't* go back. *Won't! Won't! Won't!*"

"At first I didn't understand how it *could* have been you," David said, as if he hadn't heard. "It was the Land of the Dead—you even said so, Johnny. But you were alive. That's what I thought, at least. Even when I saw the scar." He pointed at Johnny's wrist. "You died . . . when? 1966? 1968? I guess it doesn't matter. When a person stops changing, stops *feeling*, they die. The times you've tried to kill yourself since, you were just playing catch-up. Weren't you?" And the child smiled at him with a sympathy that was unspeakable in its innocence and kindness and lack of judgement.

"Johnny," David Carver said, "God can raise the dead."

"Oh Jesus, don't tell me that," he whispered. "I don't want to be raised." But his voice seemed to reach him from far away, and curiously *doubled*, as if he were coming apart in some strange but fundamental way. Fracturing like hornfels.

"It's too late," David said. "It's already happened."

"Fuck you, little hero, I'm going to Austin. Do you hear me? *Fucking AUSTIN!*"

"Tak will be there ahead of you," David said. He was still holding out the wallet, the one with the picture of Johnny and David Halberstam and Duffy Pinette standing outside that sleazy little bar, The Viet Cong Lookout. A dive, but it had the best jukebox in the 'Nam. A Wurlitzer. In his head Johnny could taste Kirin beer and hear the Rascals, the drive of the drums, the organ like a dagger, and how hot it had been, how green and how hot, the sun like thunder, the earth smelling like pussy every time it rained, and that song had seemed to come from everywhere, every club, every radio, every shithole juke; in a way, that song *was* Vietnam: *I was feelin' so bad, I asked my family doctor just what I had.*

That's the song that was playing when you died, wasn't it, Johnny?

"Austin," he whispered in a feeble, failing voice. And still there was that sense of twinning, that sense of *twoness.*

"If you leave now, Tak will be waiting for you in a lot of places," David said, his implacable would-be jailer, still holding out his wallet, the one in which that hateful picture was entombed. "Not just Austin. Hotel rooms. Speaking halls. Fancy lunches where people talk about books and things. When you're with a woman, it'll be you who undresses her and Tak who has sex with her. And the worst thing is that you may live like that for a long time. *Can de lach* is what you'll be, heart of the unformed. *Mi him can ini.* The empty well of the eye."

I won't! he tried to scream again, but this time no voice came out, and when he struck at the ore-cart again, the hammer dropped free of his fingers. The strength left his hand. His thighs turned watery and his knees began to unhinge. He slipped onto them with a choked and drowning cry. That sense of doubling, of *twinning*, was even stronger now, and he understood with both dismay and resignation that it was a true sensation. He was literally dividing himself in two. There was John Edward Marinville, who didn't believe in God and didn't want God to believe in him; that creature wanted to go, and understood that Austin would only be the first stop. And there was Johnny, who wanted to stay. More, who wanted to fight. Who had progressed far enough into this mad supernaturalism to want to die in David's God, to burn his brain in it and go out like a moth in the chimney of a kerosene lamp.

Suicide! his heart cried out. *Suicide, suicide!*

ARVN soldiers, war's deadeyed optimists, looking for diamonds in assholes. A drunk with a bottle of beer in his hand and his wet hair in his eyes, climbing out of a hotel swimming pool, laughing as the cameras flashed. Terry's nose bleeding below her hurt, incredulous eyes while a voice from the sky announced that United's flight 507 to Jacksonville was boarding at Gate B-7. The cop kicking him as he writhed on the centerline of a desert highway. *It makes me furious,* the cop had said. *It makes me sick with rage.*

Johnny felt himself leave his own body, felt himself grasped by hands that were not his own and turned out of his flesh like change from a pocket. He stood ghostlike beside the kneeling man and saw the kneeling man holding his hands out.

"I'll take it," the kneeling man said. He was weeping. "I'll take my wallet, what the fuck, give it back."

He saw the boy come to the kneeling man and kneel beside him. He saw the kneeling man take the wallet and then put it in the front pocket of the jeans beneath the chaps so he could press his hands together finger-to-finger, as David had done.

"What do I say?" the kneeling man asked, weeping. "Oh David, how do I start, what do I say?"

"What's in your heart," the kneeling boy said, and that was when the ghost gave up and rejoined the man. Clarity streaked into the world, lighting it up—lighting *him* up—like napalm, and he heard Felix Cavaliere singing *I said baby, it's for sure, I got the fever, you got the cure.*

"Help me, God," Johnny said, raising his hands to a place where they were even with his eyes and he could see them well. "Oh God, please help me. Help me do what I was sent here to do, help me to be whole, help me to live. God, help me to live again."

2

I'm going to catch you, bitch! it thought triumphantly.

At first, chances of that had seemed slim. It had gotten within twenty yards of the *os pa* near the top of the pit—sixty short feet—but the bitch had been able to find a little extra and beat it to the top. Once she started down the other side, Mary had been able to extend her lead in a hurry, from twenty yards to sixty to a hundred and fifty. Because *she* could breathe deeply, *she* could cope with her body's oxygen debt. Ellen Carver's body, on the other hand, was rapidly losing the ability to do either. The vaginal bleeding had become a flood, something that would kill the Ellen-body in the next twenty minutes or so anyway . . . but if Tak was able to catch Mary, it wouldn't matter how much the remains of Ellen Carver bled; it would have a place to go. But as it came over the rim of the pit, something had ruptured in Ellen's left lung, as well. Now with every exhale it was not just spraying a fine mist of red but shooting out liquid jets of blood and tissue from both Ellen's mouth and nose. And it couldn't get enough fresh oxygen to keep up the chase. Not with just one working lung.

Then, a miracle. Running too fast for the grade and trying to look back over her shoulder at the same time, the bitch's feet tangled together and she took a spectacular tumble, hitting the gravel surface of the road in a kind of swandive and ploughing downhill for almost ten feet before she came to a stop, leaving a dark drag-mark behind her. She lay face-down with her arms extended, trembling all over. In the starlight her splayed hands looked like pale creatures fished out of a tide-pool. Tak saw her try to get a knee under her. It came partway up, then relaxed and slid back again.

Now! Now! Tak ah wan!

Tak forced the Ellen-body into a semblance of a run, gambling on the last of that body's energy, gambling on its own agility to keep from tripping and falling as the bitch had done. The back-and-forth of its respiration had become a kind of wet chugging in Ellen's throat, like a piston running in thick grease. Ellen's sensory equipment was graying out at the edges, getting ready to shut down. But she would last a little longer. Just a little. And a little was all it would take.

A hundred and forty yards.

A hundred and twenty.

Tak ran at the woman lying in the road, screaming in soundless, hungry triumph as it closed the gap.

3

Mary could hear something coming, something that was yelling nonsense words in a thick, gargly voice. Could hear the thud of shoes on the gravel. Closing in. But it all seemed unimportant. Like things heard in a dream. And surely this *had* to be a dream . . . didn't it?

Get up, Mary! You have to get up!

She looked around and saw something awful but not in the least dreamlike bearing down on her. Its hair flew out behind it. One of its eyes had ruptured. Blood exploded from its mouth with each breath. And on its face was the look of a starving animal abandoning the stalk and staking everything on one last charge.

GET UP, MARY! GET UP!

I can't, I'm scraped all over and it's too late anyway, she moaned to the voice, but even as she was moaning she was struggling with her knee again, trying to cock it under her. This time she managed the trick and struggled upward with the knee as her center, trying to pull herself out of gravity's well this one last time.

The Ellen-thing was in full sprint now. It seemed to be exploding out of its clothes as it came. And it was screaming: a drawn-out howl of rage and hunger packed in blood.

Mary got on her feet, screaming herself now as the thing swooped down, reaching out, grasping for her with its fingers. She threw herself into a full downhill run, eyes bulging, mouth sprung open in a full-jawed but silent scream.

A hand, sickeningly hot, slapped down between her shoulderblades and tried to twist itself into her shirt. Mary hunched forward and almost fell as her upper body swayed out beyond the point of balance, but the hand slipped away.

"Bitch!" An inhuman, guttural growl—from *right behind her*—and this time the hand closed in her hair. It might have held if the hair had been dry, but it was slick—almost slimy—with sweat. For a moment she felt the thing's fingers on the back of her neck and then they were gone. She ran down the slope in lengthening leaps, her fear now mingling with a kind of crazy exhilaration.

There was a thud from behind her. She risked a look back and saw that the Ellen-thing had gone down. It lay curled in on itself like a crushed snail. Its hands opened and closed on thin air, as if still searching for the woman who had barely managed to elude it.

Mary turned and focused on the blinker-light. It was closer now . . . and there were other lights, as well, she was sure of it. Headlights, and coming this way. She focused on them, ran toward them.

She never even registered the large shape which passed silently above her.

4

All over.

It had come so close—had actually touched the bitch's hair—

but at the last second Mary had eluded it. And even as she began to draw away again, Ellen's feet had crossed and Tak went down, listening to the rupturing sounds from inside the Ellen-body as it rolled onto its side, grasping at the air as if it might find handholds in it.

It rolled over onto Ellen's back, staring up at the star-filled sky, moaning with pain and hate. To have come so close!

That was when it saw the dark shape up there, blotting out the stars in a kind of gliding crucifix, and felt a sudden fresh burst of hope.

It had thought of the wolf and then dismissed the idea because the wolf was too far away, but it had been wrong to believe the wolf was the only *can toi* vessel which might hold Tak for a little while.

There was this.

"Mi him," it whispered in its dying, blood-thick voice. *"Can de lach, mi him, min en tow. Tak!"*

Come to me. Come to Tak, come to the old one, come to the heart of the unformed.

Come to me, vessel.

It held up Ellen's dying arms, and the golden eagle fluttered down into them, staring into Tak's dying face with rapt eyes.

5

"Don't look at the bodies," Johnny said. He was rolling the ore-cart away from the ATV. David was helping.

"I'm not, believe me," David said. "I've seen enough bodies to last me a lifetime."

"I think that's good enough." Johnny started toward the driver's side of the ATV and tripped over something. David grabbed his arm, although he, Johnny, hadn't come especially close to falling. "Watch it, Gramps."

"You got a mouth on you, kid."

It was the hammer he'd tripped on. He picked it up, turned to toss it back onto the worktable, then reconsidered and stuck the rubber-sleeved handle into the belt of his chaps. The chaps now had enough blood and dirt grimed into them to look almost like the real thing, and the hammer felt right there, somehow.

There was a control-box set to the right of the metal door. Johnny pushed the blue button marked UP, mentally prepared for more problems, but the door rattled smoothly along its track. The air that came in, smelling faintly of Indian paint-brush and sage, was fresh and sweet—like heaven. David filled his chest with it, turned to Johnny, and smiled. "Nice."

"Yeah. Come on, hop in this beauty. Take you for a spin."

David climbed into the front passenger seat of the vehicle, which looked like a high-slung, oversized golf-cart. Johnny turned the key and the engine caught at once. As he ran it out through the open door, it occurred to him that none of this was happening. It was all just part of an idea he'd had for a new novel. A fantasy tale, perhaps even an outright horror novel. Something of a departure for John Edward Marinville, either way. Not the sort of stuff of which serious literature was made, but so what? He was getting on, and if he wanted to take him-self a little less seriously, surely he had that right. There was no need to shoulder each book like a backpack filled with rocks and then sprint uphill with it. That might be okay for the kids, the bootcamp recruits, but those days were behind him now. And it was sort of a relief that they were.

Not real, none of this, nah, no way. In reality he was just out for a ride in the old convertible, out for a ride with his son, the child of his middle years. They were going to Milly's on the Square. They'd park around the side of the ice-cream stand, eat their cones, and maybe he'd tell the kid a few war stories about his own boyhood, not enough to bore him, kids had a low tolerance for tales that started "When *I* was a boy," he knew that, he guessed every dad who didn't have his head too far up his own ass did, so maybe just one or two about how he'd tried out for baseball more or less as a lark, and god-damned if the coach hadn't—

"Johnny? Are you all right?"

He realized he had backed all the way to the edge of the street and was now just sitting here with the clutch in and the engine idling.

"Huh? Yeah. Fine."

"What were you thinking about?"

"Kids. You're the first one I've been around in . . . Christ, since my youngest went off to Duke. You're okay, David. A little God-obsessed, but otherwise quite severely cool."

David smiled. "Thanks."

Johnny backed out a little farther, then swung around and shifted into first. As the ATV's high-set headlights swept Main Street, he saw two things: the leprechaun weathervane which had topped Bud's Suds was now lying in the street, and Steve's truck was gone.

"If they did what you wanted, I guess they're on their way up there," Johnny said.

"When they find Mary they'll wait for us."

"*Will* they find her, do you think?"

"I'm almost positive they will. And I think she's okay. It was close, though." He glanced over at Johnny and this time he smiled more fully. Johnny thought it was a beautiful smile. "You're going to come out of this all right, too, I think. Maybe you'll write about it."

"I usually write about the stuff that happens to me. Dress it up a little and it does fine. But this . . . I don't know."

They were passing The American West. Johnny thought of Audrey Wyler, lying in there under the ruins of the balcony. What was left of her.

"David, how much of Audrey's story was true? Do you know?"

"Most of it." David was looking at the theater, too, craning his neck to keep it in view a moment or two longer as they passed. Then he turned back to Johnny. His face was thoughtful . . . and, Johnny thought, sad. "She wasn't a bad person, you know. What happened to her was like being caught in a landslide or a flood, something like that."

"An act of God."

"Right."

"*Our* God. Yours and mine."

"Right."

"And God is cruel."

"Right again."

"You've got some damned tough ideas for a kid, you know it?"

Passing the Municipal Building now. The place where the boy's sister had been killed and his mother snatched away into some final darkness. David looked at it with eyes Johnny couldn't read, then raised his hands and scrubbed at his face with them. The gesture made him look his age again, and Johnny was shocked to see how young that was.

"More of them than I ever wanted to have," David said. "You know what God finally told Job when he got tired of listening to all Job's complaints?"

"Pretty much told him to fuck off, didn't he?"

"Yeah. You want to hear something really bad?"

"Can't wait."

The ATV was riding over ridges of sand in a series of tooth-rattling jounces. Johnny could see the edge of town up ahead. He wanted to go faster, but anything beyond second gear seemed imprudent, given the short reach of the headlights. It might be true that they were in God's hands, but God reputedly helped those who helped themselves. Maybe that was why he had kept the hammer.

"I have a friend. Brian Ross, his name is. He's my *best* friend. Once we made a Parthenon entirely out of bottlecaps."

"Did you?"

"Uh-huh. Brian's dad helped us a little, but mostly we did it ourselves. We'd stay up Saturday nights and watch old horror movies. The black-and-white ones? Boris Karloff was our favorite monster. *Frankenstein* was good, but we liked *The Mummy* even better. We were always going to each other, 'Oh shit, the mummy's after us, we better walk a little faster.' Goofy stuff like that, but fun. You know?"

Johnny smiled and nodded.

"Anyway, Brian was in an accident. A drunk hit him while he was riding to school. I mean, quarter of eight in the morning, and this guy is drunk on his ass. Do you believe that?"

"Sure," Johnny said, "you bet."

David gave him a considering look, nodded, then went on. "Brian hit his head. *Bad.* Fractured his skull and hurt his brain. He was in a coma, and he wasn't supposed to live. But—"

"Let me guess the rest. You prayed to God that your friend would be all right, and two days later, bingo, that boy be walkin n talkin, praise Jesus my lord n savior."

"You don't believe it?"

Johnny laughed. "Actually, I do. After what's happened to me since this afternoon, a little thing like that seems perfectly sane and reasonable."

"I went to a place that was special to me and Brian to pray. A platform we built in a tree. We called it the Viet Cong Lookout."

Johnny looked at him gravely. "You're not kidding about that?"

David shook his head. "I can't remember which one of us named it that now, not for sure, but that's what we called it. We thought it was from some old movie, but if it was, I can't remember which one. We had a sign and everything. That was our place, that's where I went, and what I said was—" He closed his eyes, thinking. "What I said was, 'God, make him better. If you do, I'll do something for you. I promise.'" David opened his eyes again. "He got better almost right away."

"And now it's payback time. That's the bad part, right?"

"No! I don't mind paying back. Last year I bet my dad five bucks that the Pacers would win the NBA championship, and when they didn't, he tried to let me off because he said I was just a kid, I bet my heart instead of my head. Maybe he was right—"

"*Probably* he was right."

"—but I paid up just the same. Because it's bush not to pay what you owe, and it's bush not to do what you promise." David leaned toward him and lowered his voice . . . as if he was afraid God might overhear. "The really bad part is that God knew I'd be coming out here, and he already knew what he wanted me to do. And he knew what I'd have to *know* to do it. My folks aren't religious—Christmas and Easter, mostly—and until Brian's accident, I wasn't, either. All the Bible I knew was John three-sixteen, on account of it's always on the signs the zellies hold up at the ballpark. For God so loved the world."

They were passing the bodega with its fallen sign now. The LP tanks had torn off the side of the building and lay in the desert sixty or seventy yards away. China Pit loomed ahead. In the starlight it looked like a whited sepulchre.

"What are zellies?"

"Zealots. That's my friend Reverend Martin's word. I think he's . . . I think something may have happened to him." David fell silent for a moment, staring at the road. Its edges had been blurred by the sandstorm, and out here there were drifts as well as ridges spilled across their path. The ATV took them easily. "Anyway, I didn't know anything about Jacob and Esau or Joseph's coat of many colors or Potiphar's wife until Brian's accident. Mostly what I was interested in back in those days"—he spoke, Johnny thought, like a nonagenarian war

veteran describing ancient battles and forgotten campaigns—
"was whether or not Albert Belle would ever win the American
League MVP."

He turned toward Johnny, his face grave.

"The bad thing isn't that God would put me in a position
where I'd owe him a favor, but that he'd hurt Brian to do it."

"God is cruel."

David nodded, and Johnny saw the boy was on the verge of
tears. "He sure is. Better than Tak, maybe, but pretty mean,
just the same."

"But God's cruelty is refining . . . that's the rumor, anyway.
Yeah?"

"Well . . . maybe."

"In any case, he's alive, your friend."

"Yes—"

"And maybe it wasn't all about you, anyway. Maybe someday your pal is going to cure AIDS or cancer. Maybe he'll hit in
sixty straight games."

"Maybe."

"David, this thing that's out there—Tak—what is it? Do
you have any idea? An Indian spirit? Something like a mani-
tou, or a wendigo?"

"I don't think so. I think it's more like a disease than a
spirit, or even a demon. The Indians may not have even known
it was here, and it was here before they were. *Long* before. Tak
is the ancient one, the unformed heart. And the place where it
really is, on the other side of the throat at the bottom of the
well . . . I'm not sure that place is on earth at all, or even in
normal space. Tak is a complete outsider, so different from us
that we can't even get our minds around him."

The boy was shivering a little, and his face looked even
paler. Maybe that was just the starlight, but Johnny didn't like
it. "We don't need to talk about it anymore, if you don't want
to. All right?"

David nodded, then pointed up ahead. "Look, there's the Ryder van. It's stopped. They must have found Mary. Isn't that great?"

"It sure is," Johnny said. The truck's headlights were half a mile or so farther on, shining out in a fan toward the base of the embankment. They drove on toward it mostly in silence, each lost in his own thoughts. For Johnny, those questions were mostly concerned with identity; he wasn't entirely sure who he was any longer. He turned to David, meaning to ask if David knew where there might be a few more sardines hiding—hungry as he was, he wouldn't even turn his nose up at a plate of cold lima beans—when his head suddenly turned into a soundless, brilliant airburst. He jerked backward in the driver's seat, shoulders twisting. A strangled cry escaped him. His mouth was drawn down so radically at the corners that it looked like a clown's mask. The ATV swerved toward the left side of the road.

David leaned over, grabbed the wheel, and corrected their course just before the vehicle could nose over the edge and tumble into the desert. By then Johnny's eyes were open again. He braked instinctively, throwing the boy forward. Then they were stopped, the ATV idling in the middle of the road not two hundred feet from the Ryder van's taillights. They could see people standing back there, red-stained silhouettes, watching them.

"Holy shit," David breathed. "For a second or two there—"

Johnny looked at him, dazed and amazed, as if seeing him for the first time in his life. Then his eyes cleared and he laughed shakily.

"Holy shit is right," he said. His voice was low, almost strengthless—the voice of a man who has just received a walloping shock. "Thanks, David."

"Was it a God-bomb?"

"*What?*"

"A big one. Like Saul in Damascus, when the cataracts or whatever they were fell out of his eyes and he could see again. Reverend Martin calls those God-bombs. You just had one, didn't you?"

All at once he didn't want to look at David, was afraid of what David might see in his eyes. He looked at the Ryder's taillights instead.

Steve hadn't used the extraordinary width of the road to turn around, Johnny noticed; the rental truck was still pointed south, toward the embankment. Of course. Steve Ames was a clever old Texas boy, and he must have suspected this wasn't finished yet. He was right. David was right, too—they had to go up to the China Pit—but the kid had some other ideas that were maybe not so right.

Fix your eyes, Johnny, Terry said. *Fix your eyes so you can look at him without a single blink. You know how to do that, don't you?*

Yes, he certainly did. He remembered something an old literature prof of his had said, back when dinosaurs still walked the earth and Ralph Houk still managed the New York Yankees. Lying is fiction, this crusty old reptile had proclaimed with a dry and cynical grin, fiction is art, and therefore all art is a lie.

And now, ladies and gentlemen, stand back as I prepare to practice art on this unsuspecting young prophet.

He turned to David and met David's concerned gaze with a rueful little smile. "No God-bombs, David. Sorry to disappoint you."

"Then what just happened?"

"I had a seizure. Everything just came down on me at once and I had a seizure. As a young man, I used to have one every three or four months. *Petit mal.* Took medication and they went away. When I started drinking heavily around the age of forty—well, thirty-five, and there was a little more involved than just booze, I guess—they came back. Not so *petit* by then, either. The seizures are the main reason I keep trying to go on the wagon. What you just saw was the first one in almost"—he paused, pretending to count back—"eleven months. No booze or cocaine involved this time, either. Just plain old stress."

He got rolling again. He didn't want to look around now; if he did he would be looking to see how much of it David was buying, and the kid might pick up on *that*. It sounded crazy, paranoid, but Johnny knew it wasn't. The kid was amazing and spooky . . . like an Old Testament prophet who has just come striding out of an Old Testament desert, skinburned by the sun and brainburned by God's inside information.

Better to tuck his gaze away, keep it to himself, at least for the time being.

From the corner of his right eye he could see David studying him uncertainly. "Is that really the truth, Johnny?" he asked finally. "No bullshit?"

"Really the truth," Johnny said, still not looking directly at him. "Zero bullshit."

David asked no more questions . . . but he kept glancing over at him. Johnny discovered he could actually feel that glance, like soft, skilled fingers patting their way along the top of a window, feeling for the catch that would unlock it.

CHAPTER 5

1

Tak sat on the north side of the rim, talons digging into the rotted hide of an old fallen tree. Now literally eagle-eyed, it had no trouble picking out the vehicles below. It could even see the two people in the ATV: the writer behind the wheel, and, next to him, the boy.

The shitting prayboy.

Here after all.

Both of them here after all.

Tak had met the boy briefly in the boy's vision and had tried to divert him, frighten him, send him away before he could find the one that had summoned him. It hadn't been able to do it. *My God is strong,* the boy had said, and that was clearly true.

It remained to be seen, however, if the boy's God was strong *enough.*

The ATV stopped short of the yellow truck. The writer and the boy appeared to be talking. The boy's *dama* started walking toward them, a rifle in one hand, then stopped as the open vehicle began moving forward again. Then they were together once more, all those who remained, joined again in spite of its efforts.

Yet all was not lost. The eagle's body wouldn't last long—an hour, two at the most—but right now it was strong and hot and eager, a honed weapon which Tak grasped in the most intimate way. It ruffled the bird's wings and rose into the air as the *dama* embraced his *damane*. (It was losing its human language rapidly now, the eagle's small *can toi* brain incapable of holding it, and reverting back to the simple but powerful tongue of the unformed.)

It turned, glided out over the well of darkness which was the China Pit, turned again, and spiraled down toward the black square of the drift. It landed, uttering a single loud *quowwwk!* as its talons sorted the scree for a good grip. Thirty yards down the drift, pallid reddish-pink light glowed. Tak looked at this for a moment, letting the light of the *an tak* fill and soothe the bird's primitive marble of a brain, then hopped a short distance into the tunnel. Here was a little niche on the left side. The eagle worked its way into it and then stood quiet, wings tightly folded, waiting.

Waiting for all of them, but mostly for Prayboy. It would rip Prayboy's throat out with one of the golden eagle's powerful talons, his eyes with the other; Prayboy would be dead before any of them knew what had happened. Before the *os dam* himself knew what had happened, or even realized he was dying blind.

2

Steve had brought a blanket—an old faded plaid thing—along to cover the boss's scoot with in the event that he *did* end up having to transport the Harley to the West Coast in the back of the truck. When Johnny and David pulled up in the ATV, Mary Jackson had this blanket wrapped around her shoulders like a tartan shawl. The truck's rear door had been run up and she was sitting there with her feet on the bumper, holding the blanket together in front of her. In her other hand was one of the few remaining bottles of Jolt. She thought she had never tasted anything sweeter in her whole life. Her hair was plastered flat against her head in a sweaty helmet. Her eyes were huge. She was shivering in spite of the blanket, and felt like a refugee in a TV newsclip. Something about a fire or an earthquake. She watched Ralph give his son a fierce one-armed hug, the Ruger .44 in his other hand, actually lifting David up off his feet and then setting him down again.

Mary slid to the ground, and staggered a little. The muscles of her legs were still trembling from her run. *I ran for my life,* she thought, *and that's something I'll never be able to explain, not by talking, probably not even in a poem—how it is to run not for a meal or a medal or a prize or to catch a train but for your very fucking* life.

Cynthia put a hand on her arm. "You okay?"

"I'll be fine," she said. "Give me five years and I'll be in the goddam pink."

Steve joined them. "No sign of her," he said—meaning Ellen, Mary supposed. Then he went over to David and Marinville. "David? All right?"

"Yes," David said. "So's Johnny."

Steve looked at the man he had been hired to shepherd, his face noncommittal. "That so?"

"I think so," Marinville said. "I had . . ." He glanced at David. "You tell him, cabbage. You got the head on you."

David smiled wanly at that. "He had a change of heart. And if it was my mother you were looking for . . . the thing that was inside my mother . . . you can stop. She's dead."

"You're sure?"

David pointed. "We'll find her body about halfway up the embankment." Then, in a voice which struggled to be matter-of-fact and failed, he added: "I don't want to look at her. When you move her out of the way, I mean. Dad, I don't think you should, either."

Mary walked over to them, rubbing the backs of her thighs, where the ache was the worst. "The Ellen-body is finished, and it couldn't quite catch me. So it's stuck in its hole again, isn't it?"

"Ye-es . . ."

Mary didn't like the doubtful sound of David's voice. There was more guessing than knowing in it.

"Did it have anyone else it *could* get into?" Steve asked. "*Is* there anyone else up here? A hermit? An old prospector?"

"No," David said. More certain now.

"It's fallen and it can't get up," Cynthia said, and pumped her fist at the star-littered sky. "*Yesss!*"

"David?" Mary asked.

He turned to her.

"We're not done, even if it *is* stuck in there. Are we? We're supposed to close the drift."

"First the *an tak*," David said, nodding, "then the drift, yeah. Seal it in, like it was before." He glanced at his father.

Ralph put an arm around him. "If you say so, David."

"I'm up for it," Steve said. "I can't wait to see where this guy takes his shoes off and puts his feet up on the hassock."

"I was in no particular hurry to get to Bakersfield, anyway," Cynthia said.

David looked at Mary.

"Of course. It was God that showed me how to get out, you know. And there's Peter to think about. It killed my husband. I think I owe it a little something for Peter."

David looked at Johnny.

"Two questions," Johnny said. "First, what happens when this is over? What happens here? If the Desperation Mining Corporation comes back in and starts working the China Pit again, they'll most likely reopen the China Shaft. Won't they? So what good is it?"

David actually grinned. To Mary he looked relieved, as if he had expected a much tougher question. "That's not our problem—that's *God's* problem. Ours is to close the *an tak* and the tunnel from there to the outside. Then we ride away and never look back. What's your other question?"

"Could I take you out for an ice cream when this is over? Tell you some high school war stories?"

"Sure. As long as I can tell you to stop when they get, you know, boring."

"Boring stories are not in my repertoire," Johnny said loftily.

The boy walked back to the truck with Mary, slipping his arm around her waist and leaning his head against her arm as if she were his mother. Mary guessed she could be that for awhile, if he needed her to be. Steve and Cynthia took the cab; Ralph and Johnny Marinville sat on the floor of the box a across from Mary and David.

When the truck stopped halfway up the grade, Mary felt David's grip on her waist tighten and put an arm around his shoulders. They had come to the place where his mother—her shell, anyway—had finished up. He knew it as well as she did. He was breathing rapidly and shallowly through his mouth. Mary put a hand on the side of his head and urged him wordlessly with it. He came willingly enough, putting his face against her breast. The light, rapid mouth-breathing went on, and then she felt the first of his tears wetting her shirt. Across from her, David's father was sitting with his knees pulled up to his chest and his hands over his face.

"That's all right, David," she murmured, and began stroking his hair. "That's all right."

Doors slammed. Feet crunched on the gravel. Then, faintly, Cynthia Smith's voice, full of horror: "Oh jeez, *look* at her!"

Steve: "Be quiet, stupid, they'll hear you."

Cynthia: "Oh sugar. Sorry."

Steve: "Come on. Help me."

Ralph took his hands away from his face, wiped a sleeve across his eyes, then came across to Mary's side of the truck and put his arm around David. David groped for his father's hand

and took it. Ralph's stricken, streaming eyes met Mary's, and she began to cry herself.

She could now hear shuffling steps from outside as Steve and Cynthia carried Ellen out of the road. There was a pause, a little grunt of effort from the girl, and then the footsteps came back to the truck. Mary was suddenly sure that Steve would walk around to the back and tell the boy and his father some outrageous lie—foolishness about how Ellen looked peaceful, like she was maybe just taking a nap out here in the middle of nowhere. She tried to send him a message: *Don't do it, don't come back here and tell well-meaning lies, you can only make things worse. They've been in Desperation, they've seen what's there, don't try to kid them about what's out here.*

The steps paused. Cynthia murmured. Steve said something in return. Then they got back into the truck, the doors slammed, the engine revved, and they started off again. David kept his face pressed against her a moment or two longer, then raised his head. "Thanks."

She smiled, but the truck's rear door was still up and she supposed enough light was getting in for David to see that she had also wept. "Any time," she said. She kissed his cheek. "Really."

She clasped her arms around her knees and looked out the back of the truck, watching the dust spume up. She could still see the blinker-light, a yellow spark in the wide sweep of the dark, but now it was going in the wrong direction, drawing away from them. The world—the one she had always thought to be the *only* world—also seemed to be drawing away from her now. Malls, restaurants, MTV, Gold's Gym workouts, and occasional hot sex in the afternoon, all drawing away.

And it's all so easy, she thought. *As easy as a penny slipping through a hole in your pocket.*

"David?" Johnny asked. "Do you know how Tak got into Ripton in the first place?"

David shook his head.

Johnny nodded as if that was what he had expected and sat back, resting his head against the side of the truck. Mary realized that, as exasperating as Marinville could be, she sort of liked him. And not just because he had come back with David; she had sort of liked him ever since . . . well, since they were looking for guns, she guessed. She'd scared him, but he had bounced back. She guessed he was the kind of guy who had made a second career out of bouncing back from stuff. And when he wasn't concentrating on being an asshole, he could be amusing.

The .30-.06 was lying beside him. Johnny felt around for it without raising his head, picked it up, and laid it across his knees. "I suspect I may miss a lecture tomorrow evening," he said to the ceiling. "It was to be on the subject 'Punks and Post-literates: American Writing in the Twenty-first Century.' I shall have to return the advance. 'Sad, sad, sad, George and Martha.' That's from—"

"*Who's Afraid of Virginia Woolf?*," Mary said. "Edward Albee. We're not *all* bozos on this bus."

"Sorry," Johnny said, sounding startled.

"Just be sure to put the apology in your journal," she said, without the slightest idea of what she was talking about. He lowered his head to look at her, frowned for a moment, then started laughing. After a moment, Mary joined him. Then David was also laughing, and Ralph joined in. His was surprisingly high-pitched for a big man, a kind of cartoon tee-hee, and thinking that made Mary laugh even harder. It hurt her scraped stomach, but the hurt didn't stop her.

Steve pounded on the back of the cab. It was impossible to tell if his muffled voice was amused or alarmed. "What's going on?"

In his best lion's voice, Johnny Marinville roared back: "Be quiet, you Texas longhorn! We're discussing *literature* back here!"

Mary screamed with laughter, one hand pressed to the base of her throat, the other curled against her throbbing belly. She wasn't able to stop until the truck reached the crest of the embankment, crossed the rim, and started down the far side. Then all the humor went out of her at once. The others stopped at about the same time.

"Do you feel it?" David asked his father.

"I feel *something.*"

Mary started shivering. She tried to remember if she had been shivering before, while she was laughing, and couldn't. They felt something, yes, she had no doubt that they did. They might have felt even more if they had been out here earlier, if they'd had to get up this same road before the bleeding thing just behind could—

Push it out of your head, Mare. Push it out and lock the door.

"Mary?" David asked.

She looked at him.

"It won't be much longer."

"Good."

Five minutes later—very long minutes—the truck stopped and the cab doors opened. Steve and Cynthia came around to the back. "Hop out, you guys," Steve said. "Last stop."

Mary worked herself out of the truck, wincing at every move. She hurt all over, but her legs were the worst. If she had sat in the back of the truck much longer, she reckoned she probably wouldn't have been able to walk at all.

"Johnny, do you still have those aspirin?"

He handed them over. She took three, washing them down with the last of her Jolt. Then she walked around to the front of the truck.

They were at the bottom of the China Pit, first time for the others, second for her. The field office was near; looking at it, thinking of what was inside and of how close she had probably come to ending her existence in there, made her feel like screaming. Then her eyes fixed on the cruiser, the driver's door still open, the hood still raised, the air-cleaner still lying by the left front tire.

"Put your arm around me," she told Johnny.

He did, looking down at her with a raised eyebrow.

"Now walk me over to that car."

"Why?"

"There's something I have to do."

"Mary, the sooner we start, the sooner we finish," David said.

"This'll only take a second. Come on, Shakespeare. Let's go."

He walked her over to the car, his arm around her waist, the .30-.06 in his free hand. She supposed he could feel her trembling, but that was all right. She nerved herself, gnawing at her lower lip, remembering the ride into town in the back of this car. Sitting with Peter behind the mesh. Smelling Old Spice and the metallic scent of her own fear. No doorhandles. No window-cranks. And nothing to look at but the back of Entragian's sunburned neck and that stupid blank-eyed bear stuck to the dashboard.

She leaned into Entragian's stink—except it was really *Tak's* stink, she knew that now—and ripped the bear off the dashboard. Now its blank *can toi* eyes stared directly up at hers, as if asking her what all this foolishness could possibly be about, what good it could possibly accomplish, what evil it could possibly change.

"Well," she told it, "*you're* gone, motherfucker, and that's step one." She dropped it to the rough surface of the pit and then stamped down on it. Hard. She felt it crunch under her sneaker. It was, in some fundamental way, the most satisfying moment of the whole miserable nightmare.

"Don't tell me," Johnny said. "It's some new variation of est therapy. A symbolic affirmation expressly designed for stressful life-passages, sort of an 'I'm okay, you're stomped to shit' kind of thing. Or—"

"Shut up," she said, not unkindly. "And you can let loose of me now."

"Do I have to?" His hand moved on her waist. "I was just getting familiar with the topography."

"Too bad I'm not a map."

Johnny dropped his hand and they walked back to the others.

"David?" Steve asked. "Is that the place?"

He pointed past the cluster of heavy machinery and to the left of the rusty Quonset with the stove-stack. About twenty yards up the slope was the squarish hole she had seen earlier. Then she hadn't given it much consideration, as she'd had other fish to fry—staying alive, chiefly—but now looking at it gave her a bad feeling. A weak-in-the-knees feeling. *Well,* she thought, *I did the bear, anyway. It'll never stare at anyone else cooped up in the back of that police-cruiser. There's that much.*

"That's it," David said. "China Shaft."

"*Can tak* in *can tah,*" his father said, as if in a dream.

"Yes."

"And we have to blow it up?" Steve asked. "Just how do we go about that?"

David pointed to the concrete cube near the field office. "First we have to get inside there."

They walked over to the powder magazine. Ralph yanked at the padlock on the door, as if to get the feel of it, then racked the Ruger. The metallic *clack-clack* sound it made was very loud in the stillness of the pit. "The rest of you stand back," he said. "This always works great in the movies, but in real life, who knows."

"Wait a sec, wait a sec," Johnny said, and ran back to the Ryder truck. They heard him rummaging through the cartons of stuff just behind the cab, then: "Oh! There you are, you ugly thing."

He came back carrying a black Bell motorcycle helmet with a full face-shield. He handed it to Ralph. "Brainbucket deluxe.

I hardly ever wear this one, because there's too much of it. I get it over my head and my claustrophobia kicks in. Put it on."

Ralph did. The helmet made him look like a futuristic welder. Johnny stepped back from him as he turned to the lock again. So did the others. Mary had her hands on David's shoulders.

"Why don't you guys turn around?" Ralph said. His voice was muffled by the helmet.

Mary kept expecting David to protest—concern for his father, perhaps even exaggerated concern, wouldn't be unusual, given the fact that he had lost the other two members of his family in the last twelve hours—but David said nothing. His face was only a pale blur in the dark, impossible to read, but she sensed no agitation in him. Certainly the shoulders under her hands were calm enough, at least for now.

Maybe he saw it was going to be all right, she thought. *In that vision he had . . . or whatever it was. Or maybe—*

She didn't want to finish that thought, but was slow closing it off.

—maybe he just knows there's no other choice.

There was a long moment of silence—*very* long, it seemed to Mary—and then a high whipcrack rifle report that should have echoed and didn't. It was just there and then gone, absorbed by the walls and benches and valleys of the open pit. In its aftermath she heard one startled bird-cry—*Quowwwk!*—and then nothing more. She wondered why Tak hadn't sent the animals against them as it had sent them against so many of the people in town. Because the six of them together were something special? Maybe. If so, it was David who had *made* them special, the way a single great player can elevate a whole team.

They turned and saw Ralph bent over the padlock (to Mary he looked like the Pieman bent over Simple Simon on the Howard Johnson's signs), peering at it through the helmet's faceplate. The lock was now warped and twisted, with a large black bullet-hole through the center of it, but when he yanked on it, it continued to hold fast.

"One more time," he said, and twirled his finger at them, telling them to turn around.

They did and there was another whipcrack. No bird-cry followed his one. Mary supposed whatever had called was far away by now, although she had heard no flapping wings. Not that she would have, probably, with two gunshots ringing in her ears.

This time when Ralph yanked, the lock's arm popped free of its ruined innards. Ralph pulled it off the hasp and threw it aside. When he took Johnny's helmet off, he was grinning.

David ran to him and gave him a high-five. "Good going, Dad!"

Steve pulled the door open and peered in. "Man! Darker than a carload of assholes."

"Is there a light-switch?" Cynthia asked. "No windows, there must be."

He felt around, first on the right, then the left. "Watch for spiders," Mary said nervously. "There could be spiders."

"Here it is, I got it," Steve said. There was a *click-click, click-click*, but no light.

"Who's still got a flashlight?" Cynthia asked. "I must've left mine back in the damned movie theater. I don't have it, anyway."

There was no answer. Mary had also had a flashlight—the one she'd found in the field office—and she thought she had tucked it into the waistband of her jeans after disabling the pickup trucks. If so, it was gone now. The hatchet, too. She must have lost both items in her flight from the pit.

"Crap," Johnny said. "Boy Scouts we ain't."

"There's one in the truck, behind the seat," Steve said. "Under the maps."

"Why don't you go get it?" Johnny said, but for a moment

or two, Steve didn't move. He was looking at Johnny with a strange expression, one Mary couldn't quite read, on his face. Johnny saw it, too. "What? Something wrong?"

"Nope," Steve said. "Nothing wrong, boss."

"Then step on it."

3

Steve Ames marked the exact moment when control over their little expeditionary force passed from David to Johnny; the moment when the boss became the boss again. *Why don't you go get it,* he'd said, a question that wasn't a question at all but the first real order Marinville had given him since they'd started out in Connecticut, Johnny on his motorcycle, Steve rolling leisurely along behind in the truck, puffing the occasional cheap cigar. He had called him boss (until Johnny told him to stop) because it was a tradition in the entertainment business: in the theater, sceneshifters called the stage manager boss; on a movie set, key grips called the director boss; out on tour, roadies called the tour-manager or the guys in the band boss. He had simply carried that part of his old life over into this job, but he hadn't *thought* of Johnny as the boss, in spite of his booming stage-voice and his chin-thrust-forward, I-know-exactly-what-I'm-doing manner, until now. And this time, when Steve had called him boss, Johnny hadn't objected.

Why don't you go get it?

A nominal question, just six words, and everything had changed.

What's changed? What, exactly?

"I don't know," he muttered, opening the driver's-side door of the Ryder truck and starting to rummage through the crap behind the seat. "That's the hell of it, I don't really know."

The flashlight—a long-barrelled, six-battery job—was under

a crushed litter of maps, along with the first-aid kit and a cardboard box with a few road-flares in it. He tried the light, saw that it worked, and jogged back to the others.

"Look for spiders first," Cynthia said. Her voice was just a little too high for normal conversation. "Spiders and snakes, just like in that old song. God, I hate em."

Steve stepped into the powder magazine and shone his light around, first running it over the floor, then the cinderblock walls, then the ceiling. "No spiders," he reported. "No snakes."

"David, stand right outside the door," Johnny said. "We shouldn't all cram in there together, I think. And if you see anyone or anything—"

"Give a yell," David finished. "Don't worry."

Steve centered the beam of the flashlight on a sign in the middle of the floor—it was on a stand, like the one in restaurants that said PLEASE WAIT FOR HOSTESS TO SEAT YOU. Only what this one said—in big red letters—was:

WARNING WARNING WARNING
BLASTING AGENTS AND BOOSTERS MUST BE KEPT SEPARATE!
THIS IS A FEDERAL REGULATION
CARELESSNESS WITH EXPLOSIVES
WILL NOT BE TOLERATED!

The rear wall was studded with spikes driven into the cinderblock. Hung on these were coils of wire and fat white cord. Det-cord, Steve assumed. Against the right and left walls, facing each other like bookends with no books between them, were two heavy wooden chests. The one marked DYNAMITE and BLASTING CAPS and USE EXTREME CAUTION was open, the lid up like the lid of a child's toybox. The other, marked simply BLASTING AGENT in black letters against an orange background, was padlocked shut.

"That's the ANFO," Johnny said, pointing at the padlocked cabinet. "Acronym stands for ammonium nitrate and fuel oil."

"How do you know that?" Mary asked.

"Picked it up somewhere," he said absently. "Just picked it up somewhere."

"Well, if you think I'm gonna blow the padlock off *that* one, you're nuts," Ralph said. "You guys have any ideas that don't involve shooting?"

"Not just this second," Johnny said, but he didn't sound very concerned.

Steve walked toward the dynamite chest.

"No dyno in there," Johnny said, still sounding weirdly serene.

He was right about the dynamite, but the chest was far from empty. The body of a man in jeans and a Georgetown Hoyas tee-shirt was crammed into it. He had been shot in the head. His glazed eyes stared up at Steve from below what might once have been blond hair. It was hard to tell.

Steeling himself against the smell, Steve leaned over and worked at the keyring hanging on the man's belt.

"What is it?" Cynthia asked, starting toward him.

A beetle came out of the corpse's open mouth and trundled down his chin. Now Steve could hear a faint rustling. More insects under the dead guy. Or maybe one of his nice new friend's beloved rattlers.

"Nothing," he said. "Stay where you are."

The keyring was stubborn. After several fruitless efforts to depress the clef-shaped clip holding it to the belt-loop, Steve simply tore the whole thing off, loop and all. He closed the lid and crossed the room with the keyring. Johnny, he noticed, was standing about three paces inside the door, gazing raptly down at his motorcycle helmet. "Alas, poor Urine," he said. "I knew him well."

"Johnny? You okay?"

"Fine." Johnny tucked the motorcycle helmet under his arm and smiled winningly at Steve . . . but his eyes looked haunted.

Steve gave the keys to Ralph. "One of these, maybe?"

It didn't take long. The third key Ralph tried slid into the padlock on the chest marked BLASTING AGENT. A moment later the five of them were looking inside. The chest had been partitioned into three bins. Those on the ends were empty. The one in the middle was half full of what looked like long cheesecloth bags. Littered among them were a few escapees: round pellets that looked to Steve like whitewashed birdshot. The bags had drawstring tops. He lifted one out. It looked like a bratwurst and he guessed it weighed about ten pounds. Written on the side in black were the letters ANFO. Below them, in red: CAUTION: FLAMMABLE, EXPLOSIVE.

"Okay," Steve said, "but how are we going to set it off with no booster? You were right, boss—no dynamite, no blasting caps. Just a guy with a .30-.30 haircut. The demolitions foreman, I assume."

Johnny looked at Steve, then at the others. "I wonder if the rest of you would step out with David for a moment. I'd like to speak to Steve alone."

"Why?" Cynthia asked instantly.

"Because I need to," Johnny said in an oddly gentle voice. "It's a little unfinished business, that's all. An apology. I don't apologize well under any circumstances, but I'm not sure I could do it at all with an audience."

Mary said, "I hardly think this is the time—"

The boss had been signalling him—signalling *urgently*—with his eyes. "It's okay," Steve said. "It'll be quick."

"And don't go empty-handed," Johnny said. "Each of you take a bag of this instant Fourth of July."

"My understanding is that without something explosive to boost it, it's more like Instant Campfire," Ralph said.

"I want to know what's going on here," Cynthia said. She sounded worried.

"Nothing," Johnny told her, his voice soothing. "Really."

"The fuck there *ain't*," Cynthia said morosely, but she went with the others, each of them carrying a bag of ANFO.

Before Johnny could say anything, David slipped back inside. There were still traces of dried soap on his cheeks, and his lids were tinged purple. Steve had once dated a girl who'd worn eyeshadow that exact same color. On David it looked like shock instead of glamour.

"Is everything okay?" David asked. He glanced briefly at Steve, but it was Johnny he was talking to.

"Yes. Steve, give David a bag of ANFO."

David stood a moment longer, holding the bag Steve handed him, looking down at it, lost in thought. Abruptly he looked up at Johnny and said, "Turn out your pockets. All of them."

"What—" Steve began.

Johnny shushed him, smiling oddly. It was the smile of someone who has bitten into something which tastes both bitter and compelling. "David knows what he's doing."

He unbuckled the chaps, turned out the pockets of his jeans underneath, handing Steve his goods—the famous wallet, his keys, the hammer which had been stuck in his belt—to hold as he did. He bowed forward so David could look into his shirt pocket. Then he unbuckled his pants and pushed them down. Underneath he was wearing blue bikini briefs. His not inconsiderable gut hung over them. He looked to Steve like one of those rich older guys you saw strolling along the beach sometimes. You knew they were rich not just because they always wore Rolexes and Oakley sunglasses, but because they dared walk along in those tiny spandex ballhuggers in the first place. As if, once your income passed a certain figure, your gut became another asset.

The boss wasn't wearing spandex, at least. Plain old cotton.

He did a three-sixty, arms slightly raised, giving David all the angles and bruises, then pulled up his jeans again. The chaps followed. "Satisfied? I'll take off my boots, if you're not."

"No," David said, but he poked a hand into the pockets of the chaps before stepping back. His face was troubled, but not exactly worried. "Go on and have your talk. But hurry it up."

And he was gone, leaving Steve and Johnny alone.

The boss moved to the rear of the powder magazine, as far from the door as possible. Steve followed. Now he could smell the corpse in the dynamite chest under the stronger fuel-oil aroma of the place, and he wanted to get out of here as soon as possible.

"He wanted to make sure you didn't have a few of those *can tabs* on you, didn't he? Like Audrey."

Johnny nodded. "He's a wise child."

"I guess he is." Steve shuffled his feet, looked at them, then back up at the boss. "Look, you don't need to apologize for buzzing off. The important thing is that you came back. Why don't we just—"

"I owe a *lot* of apologies," Johnny said. He began taking his stuff back, rapidly returning the items to the pockets from which they had come. He took the hammer last, once more tucking it into the belt of his chaps. "It's really amazing how much fuckery a person can get up to in the course of one lifetime. But you're really the least of my worries in that respect, Steve, especially now. Just shut up and listen, all right?"

"All right."

"And this really *does* have to be speedy. David already suspects I'm up to something; that's another reason why he wanted me to turn out my pockets. There'll come a moment— very soon now—when you're going to have to grab David. When you do, make sure you get a good grip, because he's going to fight like hell. And make sure you don't let go."

"*Why?*"

"Will your pal with the creative hairdo help if you ask her to?"

"Probably, but—"

"Steve, you have to trust me."

"Why should I?"

"Because I had a moment of revelation on the way up here. Except that's way too stiff; I like David's phrase better. He asked me if I got hit by a God-bomb. I told him no, but that was another lie. Do you suppose that's why God picked me in the end? Because I'm an accomplished liar? That's sort of funny, but also sort of awful, you know it?"

"What's going to happen? Do you even know?"

"No, not completely." Johnny picked up the .30-.06 in one hand and the black-visored helmet in the other. He looked back and forth between them, as if comparing their relative worth.

"I can't do what you want," Steve said flatly. "I don't *trust* you enough to do what you want."

"You have to," Johnny said, and handed him the rifle. "I'm all you have now."

"But—"

Johnny came a step closer. To Steve he no longer looked like the same man who had gotten on the Harley-Davidson back in Connecticut, his absurd new leathers creaking, showing every tooth in his head as the photographers from *Life* and *People* and the *Daily News* circled him and clicked away. The change was a lot more than a few bruises and a broken nose. He looked younger, stronger. The pomposity had gone out of his face, and the somehow frantic vagueness as well. It was only now, observing its absence, that Steve realized how much of the time that look had been there—as if, no matter what he was saying or doing, most of Marinville's attention was taken up by something that *wasn't*. Something like a misplaced item or a forgotten chore.

"David thinks God means him to die in order to close Tak up in his bolthole again. The final sacrifice, so to speak. But David's wrong." Johnny's voice cracked on the last word, and Steve was astonished to see that the boss was almost crying. "It's not going to be that easy for him."

"What—"

Johnny grabbed his arm. His grip so tight it was painful. "Shut up, Steve. Just grab him when the time comes. It's up to you. Come on now." He bent into the chest, grabbed a bag of ANFO by its drawstring, and tossed it to Steve. He got another for himself.

"Do you know how to set this shit off without any dyno or blasting caps?" Steve asked. "You think you do, don't you? What's going to happen? Is God going to send down a lightning-bolt?"

"That's what *David* thinks," Johnny said, "and after the sardines and crackers, I'm not surprised. I don't think it'll come to anything that extreme, though. Come on. The hour groweth late."

They walked out into what was left of the night and joined the others.

4

At the bottom of the slope, twenty yards below the ragged yawn that was China Shaft, Johnny stopped them and told them to tie the drawstrings of the bags together in pairs. He slipped one of these pairs around his own neck, the sacks hanging down on either side of his chest like the counterweights of a cuckoo clock. Steve took another pair, and Johnny made no objection when David took the last set from his father and slipped the joined drawstrings around his own neck. Ralph, troubled, looked at Johnny. Johnny glanced at David, saw

David was staring up at the drift opening, then looked back at the boy's father, shook his head, and tapped a finger against his lips. *Quiet, Dad.*

Ralph looked doubtful but said nothing.

"Everybody all right?" Johnny asked.

"What's going to happen?" Mary asked. "I mean, what's the plan?"

"We do what God tells us," David said. "That's the plan. Come on."

It was David who led, going up the slope sidesaddle to keep from falling. There was no wide gravel road here, not even a path, and the ground was evil. Johnny could feel it trying to crumble out from under his boots at every upward lurch. Soon his heart was pounding and his battered nose was throbbing in sync. He had been a good boy over the last few months, but a lot of chickens (not to mention some roast ducks and a few caviar-stuffed quail) were now coming home to roost nevertheless.

Yet he felt good. Everything was simple now. That was sort of wonderful.

David was in the lead, his father behind him. Steve and Cynthia next. Johnny and Mary Jackson brought up the rear.

"Why have you still got that motorcycle helmet?" she asked.

Johnny grinned. She reminded him of Terry, in an odd way. Terry as she had been back in the old days. He held the helmet up, stuck on his hand like a puppet. "Ask not for whom the Bell tolls," he said. "It tolls for thee, thou storied honeydew."

She gave a small, breathless laugh. "You're nuts."

If it had been forty yards uphill instead of twenty, Johnny wasn't sure he could have made it. As it was, the pounding of his heart had become so rapid it seemed like one steady thrum in his chest by the time David reached the ragged tunnel opening. And his thighs felt like spaghetti.

Don't weaken now, he told himself. *You're into the final straightaway.*

He made himself move a little faster, suddenly afraid that David might simply turn and go into the shaft before he could get there. It was possible, too. Steve thought the boss knew what was going on, but in fact the boss knew precious little. He was being handed the script a page ahead of the rest of them, that was all.

But David waited, and soon they were all clustered on the slope in front of the opening. A dank smell issued from it, chilly and charred at the same time. And there was a sound Johnny associated with elevator shafts: a faint, windy whisper.

"We ought to pray," David said, sounding timid. He held his hands out to either side of him.

His father took one of his hands. Steve put down the .30-.06 and took the other. Mary took Ralph's, Cynthia took Steve's. Johnny stepped between the two women, dropped the helmet between his boots, and the circle was complete.

They stood in the darkness of China Pit, smelling the dank exhaled breath of the earth, listening to that faint roar, looking at David Carver, who had brought them here.

"Whose father?" David asked them.

"Our father," Johnny said, stepping easily onto the road of the old prayer, as if he had never been away. "Who art in heaven, hallowed be thy name. Thy kingdom come—"

The others joined in, Cynthia, the minister's daughter, first, Mary last.

"—thy will be done, on earth as it is in heaven. Give us this day our daily bread, and forgive us our trespasses as we forgive those who trespass against us. And lead us not into temptation, but deliver us from evil. Amen."

Through the amen, Cynthia continued on: "For thine is the kingdom, and the power, and the glory, forever and ever, amen." She looked up with the little twinkle Johnny had come to like quite a lot. "That's the way I learned it—kind of a Protestant dance-mix, y'know?"

David was looking at Johnny now.

"Help me do my best," Johnny said. "If you're there, God— and I now have reason to believe you are—help me to do my best and not weaken again. I want you to take that request very seriously, because I have a long history of weakening. David, what about you? Anything to say?"

David shrugged and shook his head. "Said it already." He let go of the hands holding his, and the circle broke.

Johnny nodded. "Okay, let's do it."

"Do *what*?" Mary asked. "Do *what*? Will you please tell me?"

"I'm supposed to go in," David said. "Alone."

Johnny shook his head. "Nope. And don't start in with your God-told-me-to stuff, because right now he's not telling you *anything*. Your TV screen has got a PLEASE STAND BY sign on it, am I right?"

David looked at him uncertainly and wet his lips.

Johnny lifted a hand toward the waiting darkness of the drift and spoke in the tone of a man conveying a large favor. "You *can* go first, though. How's that?"

"My dad—"

"Right behind you. He'll catch you if you fall."

"No," David said. He suddenly looked scared—terrified. "I don't want that. I don't want him in there at *all*. The roof might cave in, or—"

"David! What you want doesn't matter."

Cynthia grabbed Johnny's arm. She would have been digging into him if she hadn't nibbled her nails to the quick. "Leave him alone! Christ, he saved your fucking *life*! Can't you quit badgering him?"

"I'm not," Johnny said. "At this point he's badgering himself. If he'll just let go, remember who's in charge . . ."

He looked at David. The boy muttered something under his breath, far too low to hear, but Johnny didn't have to hear it to know what he had said.

"That's right, he's cruel. But you knew that. And you have no control over the nature of God anyway. None of us do. So why won't you relax?"

David made no reply. His head was bowed, but not in prayer this time. Johnny thought it was resignation. In some way, the boy knew what was coming, and that was the worst part. The *cruelest* part, if you liked. *It's not going to be that easy for him,* he had told Steve in the powder magazine, but back there he hadn't really understood how hard hard could be. First his sis, then his mother; now—

"Right," he said in a voice that sounded as dry as the ground they were standing on. "First David, then Ralph, then you, Steve. I'll be behind you. Tonight—sorry, this morning—it's a case of ladies last."

"If we have to go in, I want to go in with Steve," Cynthia said.

"Okay, fine," Johnny said at once—it was as if he had been expecting this. "You and I can switch places."

"Who put you in charge, anyway?" Mary asked.

Johnny turned on her like a snake, startling her into a pre-carious step backward. "Do *you* want to have a go?" he asked with a kind of dangerous good cheer. "Because if you do, lass, I'd be happy to turn it over to you. I asked for this no more than David did. So what do you think? Want to put-um on Big Chief's headdress?"

She shook her head, confused.

"Easy, boss," Steve murmured.

"I'm easy," Johnny said, but he wasn't. He looked at David and his father, standing side by side, heads down, hands en-twined, and wasn't easy. He could barely believe the enormity of what he was allowing. Could *barely* believe? Couldn't be-lieve at all, was more like it. How else could he go on, except with merciful incomprehension held before him like a shield? How could anyone?

"Want me to take those bags, Johnny?" Cynthia asked timidly. "You still sound pretty out of breath, and you look all in, if you don't mind me saying."

"I'll be fine. It's not far now. Is it, David?"

"No," David said in a small, trembling voice. He appeared not to be just holding his father's hand now but caressing it as a lover might do. He looked at Johnny with hopeless, pleading eyes. The eyes of someone who *almost* knows.

Johnny looked away, sick in his stomach, feeling simultaneously hot and cold. He met Steve's bewildered, concerned eyes and tried to send him another message: *Just hold him. When the time comes.* Out loud he said: "Give David the flashlight, Steve."

For a moment he didn't think Steve would do it. Then he pulled the flashlight out of his back pocket and handed it over.

Johnny lifted his hand to the blackness of the shaft again. Toward the dead cold smell of old fire and the faint roaring sound from deep in the middle of the murdered mountain. He listened for some comforting word from Terry, but Terry had split the scene. Maybe just as well.

"David?" His voice, trembling. "Will you light us on our way?"

"I don't want to," David whispered. Then, pulling in a deep breath, he looked up at a sky in which the stars were just beginning to pale and screamed: *"I don't want to! Haven't I done enough? Everything you asked? This isn't fair!* THIS ISN'T FAIR AND I DON'T WANT TO!*"*

The last four words came out in a desperate, throat-tearing shriek. Mary started forward. Johnny grabbed her arm.

"Take your hand off me," she said, and started forward again.

Johnny yanked her back again. "Be still."

She subsided.

Johnny looked at David and silently raised his hand to the drift again.

David looked up at his father with tears running down his cheeks. "Go away, Dad. Go back to the truck."

Ralph shook his head. "If you go in, I go in."

"Don't. I'm telling you. It won't be good for you."

Ralph simply stood his ground and looked patiently at his son.

David looked back up at him, then at Johnny's outstretched hand (a hand which now did not simply invite but demanded), and then turned and walked into the drift. He clicked on the light as he went, and Johnny saw motes dancing in its bright beam . . . motes and something else. Something that might have caused the heart of an old prospector to beat faster. A glint of gold, there and then gone.

Ralph followed David. Steve came next. The light moved in the boy's hand, tracing first along a rock wall, then an ancient support with a trio of symbols carved into it—some long-dead Chinese miner's name, perhaps, or the name of his sweetheart, left far behind in the marsh-side huts of Po Yang—and then to the floor, where it picked out a litter of bones: cracked skulls and ribcages that curved like ghastly Cheshire cat grins. It shifted upward again and to the left. The gold-gleam came again, this time brighter and more defined.

"Hey, look out!" Cynthia cried. "Something's in here with us!"

There was a fluttering explosion in the dark. It was a sound Johnny associated with his Connecticut childhood, pheasant exploding out of the underbrush and into the air as twilight drew down toward dark. For a moment the smell of the mine was stronger, as unseen wings drove the ancient air against his face in pulses.

Mary screamed. The flashlight beam jagged upward at an angle, and for just one moment it pinpointed a nightmarish midair apparition, something with wings and glaring golden eyes and outstretched talons. It was David the eyes were glaring at, David it wanted.

"Look out!" Ralph yelled, and threw himself over David's back, driving him down to the bone-littered floor of the shaft.

The flashlight fell from the boy's hand as he went down, kicking up just enough light to be confusing. Unclear shapes strove together in its reflected glow: David under his father, and the shadow of the eagle flexing and swelling above them both.

"Shoot it!" Cynthia screamed. *"Steve, shoot it, it's gonna tear his head off!"*

Johnny grabbed the barrel of the .30-.06 as Steve brought it up. "No. A gunshot'll bring the whole works down on top of us."

The eagle screeched, wings battering Carver's head. Ralph tried to fend the bird off with his left hand. It seized one of his fingers in the hook of its beak and tore it off. And then its talons plunged into Ralph Carver's face like strong fingers into dough.

"DADDY, NO!" David shrieked.

Steve shoved into the tangle of shadows, and when the side of his foot kicked the downed flashlight, Johnny was treated to a better view than he wanted of the bird with Ralph's head in its grip. Its wings sent furious skirls of dust in motion from the floor and the old shaft walls. Ralph's head wagged wildly from side to side, but his body covered David almost completely.

Steve drew the rifle back, meaning to swing it, and the butt cracked against the wall. There wasn't room. He jabbed it forward instead, like a lance. The eagle turned its gimlet gaze on him, talons shifting their grip on Ralph. Its wings were soft thunder in the closed space. Johnny saw Ralph's finger jutting from the side of its beak. Steve jabbed forward again, this time catching the eagle squarely and knocking the finger out of the beak. Its head was driven back against the wall. Its talons flexed. One drove deeper into Ralph's face. The other lifted, plunged into his neck, and ripped it open. The bird screamed, perhaps in rage, perhaps in triumph. Mary screamed with it.

"GOD, NO!" David howled, his voice cracking. *"OH GOD, PLEASE MAKE IT STOP HURTING MY DADDY!"*

This is hell, Johnny thought calmly, stepping forward and then kneeling. He seized the talon buried in Ralph's throat. It was like grabbing some exotically ugly curio which had been upholstered in alligator-hide. He twisted it as hard as he could and heard a brittle tearing sound. Above him, Steve drove forward with the stock of the .30-.06 again, slamming the eagle's head against the rock side of the shaft. There was a crunch.

A wing battered down on Johnny's head. It was like the buzzard in the parking lot all over again. *Back to the future,* he thought, let go of the talon in favor of the wing, and yanked. The bird came toward him, squalling its ugly, ear-splitting cry, and Ralph came with it, pulled by the talon still buried in his cheek, temple, and orbit of his left eye. Johnny thought Ralph was either unconscious or already dead. He *hoped* he was already dead.

David crawled out from under, face dazed, his shirt soaked with his father's blood. In a moment he would seize the flashlight and plunge deeper into the mine, if they weren't quick.

"Steve!" Johnny shouted, reaching blindly over his head and encircling the eagle's back. It plunged and twisted in his hold like the spine of a bucking bronco. "Steve, finish it! *Finish it!*"

Steve drove the stock of the rifle into the bird's gullet, tilting its shadowy head toward the ceiling. At that moment Mary darted forward. She seized the eagle's neck and wrung it with bitter efficiency. There was a muffled crack, and suddenly the talon buried in Ralph's face relaxed. David's father fell to the floor of the mine, his forehead striking a ribcage and powdering it to dust.

David turned, saw his father lying motionless and facedown. His eyes cleared. He even nodded, as if to say *Pretty much what I expected,* then bent to pick up the flashlight. It was only when

Johnny grabbed him around the waist that his calm broke and he began to struggle.

"Let go!" he screamed. *"It's my job! MINE!"*

"No, David," Johnny said, holding on for dear life. "It's not." He tightened his grip across David's chest with his left hand, wincing as the boy's heels printed fresh pain on his shins, and let his right hand slide down to the boy's hip. From there it moved with a good pickpocket's unobtrusive speed. Johnny took from David what he had been instructed to take . . . and left something, too.

"He can't take them all and then not let me finish! He can't do that! He can't!"

Johnny winced as one of David's feet connected with his left kneecap. "Steve!"

Steve was staring with horrified fascination at the eagle, which was still twitching and slowly fanning one wing. Its talons were red.

"Steve, goddammit!"

He looked up, as if startled out of a dream. Cynthia was kneeling beside Ralph, feeling for a pulse and crying loudly.

"Steve, come here!" Johnny shouted. *"Help me!"*

Steve came over and grabbed David, who began to struggle even harder.

"No!" David whipped his head from side to side in a frenzy. *"No, it's my job! It's mine! He can't take them all and leave me! Do you hear? HE CAN'T TAKE THEM ALL AND—"*

"David! Quit it!"

David stopped struggling and merely hung in Steve's arms like a puppet with its strings cut. His eyes were red and raw. Johnny thought he had never seen such desolation and loss in a human face.

The motorcycle helmet was lying where Johnny had dropped it when the eagle attacked. He bent, picked it up, and looked at the boy in Steve's arms. Steve looked the way Johnny felt—sick, lost, bewildered.

"David—" he began.

"Is God in you?" David asked. "Can you feel him in there, Johnny? Like a hand? Or a fire?"

"Yes," Johnny said.

"Then you won't take this wrong." David spit into his face. It was warm on the skin below Johnny's eyes, like tears.

Johnny made no effort to wipe away the boy's spittle. "Listen to me, David. I'm going to tell you something you didn't learn from your minister or your Bible. For all I know it's a message from God himself. Are you listening?"

David only looked at him, saying nothing.

"You said 'God is cruel' the way a person who's lived his whole life on Tahiti might say 'Snow is cold.' You knew, but you didn't understand." He stepped close to David and put his palms on the boy's cold cheeks. "Do you know how cruel your God can be, David. How fantastically cruel?"

David waited, saying nothing. Maybe listening, maybe not. Johnny couldn't tell.

"Sometimes he makes us live."

Johnny turned, scooped up the flashlight, started down the drift, then turned back once again. "Go to your friend Brian, David. Go to your friend and make him your brother. Then start telling yourself there was an accident out on the highway, a bad one, a no-brain drunk crossed the centerline, the RV you were in rolled over and only you survived. It happens all the time. Just read the paper."

"But that's not the *truth*!"

"It might as well be. And when you get back to Ohio or Indiana or wherever it is you hang your hat, pray for God to get you over this. To make you well again. As for now, you're excused."

"I'll never say another . . . what? What did you say?"

"I said you're excused." Johnny was looking at him fixedly. "Excused early." He turned his head. "Get him out of here, Steven. Get them all out of here."

"Boss, what—"

"The tour's over, Tex. Get them into the truck and up the road. If you want to be safe, I'd get going right now."

Johnny turned and went jogging down into China Shaft, the light bobbing ahead of him into the black. Soon that was gone, too.

5

He tripped over something in spite of the flashlight, almost went sprawling, and slowed to a walk. The Chinese miners had dropped what stuff they had in their frantic, useless rush to escape, and in the end they had dropped themselves, as well. He walked over a littered landscape of bones, powdering them to dust, and moved the light in a steady triangle—left to right, down to the floor, up to the left again—to keep the landscape clear and current in his mind. He saw that the walls fairly jostled with Chinese characters, as if the survivors of the cave-in had succumbed to a sort of writing mania as death first approached and then overtook them.

In addition to the bones, he saw tin cups, ancient picks with rusty heads and funny short handles, small rusty boxes on straps (what David had called 'seners, he imagined), rotted clothes, deerskin slippers (they were tiny, slippers for infants, one might have thought), and at least three pairs of wooden shoes. One of these held the stub of a candle that might have been dipped the year before Abe Lincoln was elected president.

And everywhere, *everywhere* scattered among the remains, were *can tahs*: coyotes with spider-tongues, spiders with weird albino ratlings poking from their mouths, spread-winged bats with obscene baby-tongues (the babies were leering, gnomish). Some depicted nightmarish creatures that had never existed on earth, halfling freaks that made Johnny's eyes hurt. He could feel the *can tahs* calling to him, pulling him as the moon pulls at salt water. He had sometimes been pulled in that same way by a sudden craving to take a drink or to gobble a sweet dessert or to lick along the smooth velvet lining of a woman's mouth with his tongue. The *can tahs* spoke in tones of madness which he recognized from his own past life: sweetly reasonable voices proposing unspeakable acts. But the *can tahs* would have no power over him unless he stopped and bent and touched them. If he could avoid that—avoid despair that would come disguised as curiosity—he reckoned he would be all right.

Had Steve gotten them out yet? He'd have to hope so, and hope that Steve could manage to get them a good distance away in his trusty truck before the end came. A hell of a bang was coming. He only had the two bags of ANFO hung around his neck on the knotted drawstrings, but that would be plenty, all they had ever needed. It had seemed wiser not to tell the others that, though. Safer.

Now he could hear the soft groaning sound of which David had spoken: the squall and shift of hornfels, as if the very earth were speaking. Protesting his intrusion. And now he could see a dim zigzag of red light up ahead. Hard to tell how far away in the dark. The smell was stronger, too, and clearer: cold ashes. To his left, a skeleton—probably not Chinese, judging by its size—knelt against the wall as if it had died praying. Abruptly it turned its head and favored Johnny Marinville with its dead, toothy grin.

—*Get out while there's still time.* Tak ah wan. Tak ah lah.

Johnny punted the skull as if it were a football. It disintegrated (almost vaporized) into bone-fragments and he hurried on toward the red light, which was coming through a rift in the wall. The hole looked just big enough for him to squeeze through.

He stood outside it, looking into the light, not able to see much from the drift side, hearing David's voice in his head almost as a trance-subject must hear the voice of the hypnotist who has put him under: *At ten minutes past one on the afternoon of September twenty-first, the guys at the face broke through into what they at first thought was a cave . . .*

Johnny tossed the flashlight aside—he wouldn't need it anymore—and squeezed through the gap. As he passed into the *an tak*, that murmuring elevator-sound they had heard at the entrance to the drift seemed to fill his head with whispering voices . . . enticing, cajoling, forbidding. All around him, turning the *an tak* chamber into a fantastic hollow column lit in dim scarlet tones, were carved stone faces: wolf and coyote, hawk and eagle, rat and scorpion. From the mouth of each protruded not another animal but an amorphous, reptilian shape Johnny could barely bring himself to look at . . . and could not really *see*, in any case. Was it Tak? The Tak at the bottom of the *ini*? Did it matter?

How *had* it gotten Ripton?

If it was stuck down there, exactly how *had* it gotten Ripton?

He suddenly realized he was crossing the *an tak*, walking toward the *ini*. He tried to stop his legs and discovered he couldn't. He tried to imagine Cary Ripton making the same discovery and found it was easy.

Easy.

The long bags of ANFO swung back and forth against his chest. Images danced crazily in his mind: Terry grabbing his belt-loops and yanking him tight to her belly as he began to come, the best orgasm of his life and it had gone nowhere but into his pants, tell *that* one to Ernest Hemingway; coming out of the pool at the Bel-Air, laughing, hair plastered to his forehead, holding up the beer-bottle as the cameras flashed; Bill Harris telling him that going across country on his motorcycle might change his life and his whole career . . . if he was really up to it, that was. Last of all he saw the cop's empty gray eyes staring at him in the rearview mirror, the cop saying he thought Johnny would shortly come to understand a great deal more about *pneuma*, *soma*, and *sarx* than he had previously.

About that he had been right.

"God, protect me long enough to get this done," he said, and allowed himself to be drawn toward the *ini*. Could he stop even if he tried? Best not to know, maybe.

There were dead animals lying in a rotting ring around the hole in the floor—David Carver's well of the worlds. Coyotes and buzzards, mostly, but he also saw spiders and a few scorpions. He had an idea that these last protectors had died when the eagle had died. Some withdrawing force had hammered the life out of them just as the life had been hammered from Audrey Wyler almost as soon as Steve had slapped the *can tahs* out of her hand.

Now smoke began to rise out of the *ini* . . . except it wasn't smoke at all, not really. It was some sort of greasy brown-black muck, and as it began to curl toward him, Johnny saw it was alive. It looked like clutching three-fingered hands on the ends of scrawny arms. They were not ectoplasmic, those arms, but neither were they strictly physical. Like the carved shapes looming above and all around him, looking at them made Johnny's head hurt, the way a kid's head hurt when he staggered off some viciously swerving amusement park ride. It was the stuff that had crazed the miners, of course. The stuff that had changed Ripton. The glassless windows of the *pirin moh* leered at him, telling him . . . what, exactly? He could almost hear—

(cay de mun)
Open your mouth.

And yes, his mouth *was* open, *wide* open, like when you go to the dentist. Please open wide, Mr. Marinville, open wide, you lousy contemptible excuse for a writer, you make me *furious*, you make me *sick with rage*, but go on, open wide, *cay de mun*, you fucking grayhaired pretentious motherfucker, we'll fix you up, make you good as new, *better* than new, open wide open wide *cay de mun* OPEN WIDE—

The smoke. Muck. Whatever it was. Those were no longer hands on the ends of the arms but tubes. No . . . not tubes . . .

Holes.

Yes, that was it. Holes like eyes. Three of them. Maybe more, but three he could see clearly. A triangle of holes, two on top and one underneath, holes like whispering eyes, like blast-holes—

That's right, David said. *That's right, Johnny. To blast Tak right into you, the way it blasted itself into Cary Ripton, the only way it has to get out of the hole it's in down there, the hole that's too small for anything but this stuff, this jizz, two for your nose and one for your mouth.*

The brownish-black muck twisted toward him, both horrible and enticing, holes that were mouths, mouths that were eyes. Eyes that whispered. Promised. He realized he had an erection. Not exactly a great time for one, but when had that ever stopped him?

Now . . . *sucking* . . . he could feel them sucking the air out of his mouth . . . his throat . . .

He snapped his mouth shut and yanked the motorcycle helmet down over his head. He was just in time. A moment later the brownish ribbons encountered the plexi face-shield and spread over it with an unpleasant wet smooching sound. For a moment he could see spreading suckers like kissing lips, and then they were gone, lost in filthy smears of brown particulate matter.

Johnny reached out, seized the brown stuff floating before

him, and twisted it in opposite directions, as if he were wringing out a facecloth. There was a needling sensation in his palms and fingers, and the flesh went numb . . . but the brown stuff tore away, some of it drawing back toward the *ini*, some dripping to the chamber's floor.

He reached the edge of the hole, standing between a heap of feathers that had been a buzzard and a coyote lying dead on its side. He looked down, reaching up to touch the hanging bags of ANFO as he did, caressing them with tingling, half-numb hands.

Do you know how to set this shit off without dyno or blasting caps? Steve had asked. *You do, don't you? Or you think you do.*

"I *hope* I do," Johnny said. His voice was flat and strange inside the helmet. "I *hope* I—"

"THEN COME ON!" a mad voice cried out from below him. Johnny recoiled in terror and surprise. It was the voice of the cop. Of Collie Entragian. *"COME ON! TAK AH LAH, PIRIN MOH! COME ON, YOU ROTTEN COCKSUCKER! LET'S SEE HOW BRAVE YOU ARE! TAK!"*

He tried to take a step backward, maybe think this over, but tendrils of muck curled around his ankles like hands and jerked his feet out from under him. He went into the well in a graceless feet-first dive, hammering the back of his head against the edge as he fell. If not for the helmet, his skull would likely have been crushed in. He curled the bags of ANFO protectively against his chest, making breasts of them.

Then the pain came, first biting, then searing, then seeming to eat him alive. The *ini* was funnel-shaped, but the descending, narrowing circle was lined with crystal outcrops of quartz and cracked hornfels. Johnny slid down this like a kid down a slide that has grown crooked glass thorns. His legs were protected to some degree by the leather chaps and his head was protected by the motorcycle helmet, but his back and buttocks were shredded in moments. He put down his forearms in an effort to brake his slide. Needles of stone tore through them. He saw his shirt-sleeves turn red; an instant later they were in ribbons.

"*YOU LIKE THAT?*" the voice from the bottom of the *ini* gibed, and now it was Ellen Carver's voice. "*TAK AH LAH, YOU INTERFERING BASTARD! EN TOW! TEN AH LAK!*" Raving. Cursing him in two languages.

Insane in any dimension, Johnny thought, and laughed in his agony. He lurched forward, meaning to somersault or die trying. *Time to tenderize the other side,* he thought, and laughed harder than ever. He could feel blood pouring into his boots like warm water.

The brown-black vapor was all around him, whispering and smearing gaping sucker-mouths across the helmet's faceplate. They appeared, disappeared, then appeared again, rubbing and making those low, suggestive smooching sounds. He couldn't get off his back the way he wanted to, couldn't somersault. The angle of descent was too steep. He turned over on his side instead, clutching at the crystal outcrops that were tearing him open, slashing his hands and not caring, needing to stop himself before he was literally cut to ribbons.

Then, suddenly, it was over.

He lay folded at the bottom of the funnel, bleeding everywhere, it felt like, his slit nerves trying to drown out all rational thought with their mindless screaming. He looked up and saw a wide swath of blood marking his path down the inclined, curving wall. Strips of cloth and leather—his shirt, his Levi's, his chaps—hung from some of the jutting crystals.

Smoke curling up between his legs, coming from the hole at the bottom of the funnel and trying to seize his crotch.

"Let go," he said. "My God commands it."

The brownish-black smoke fell back, curling around his thighs in filthy banners.

"I can let you live," a voice said. It was no wonder, Johnny thought, that Tak was caught on the other side of the funnel. The hole to which it narrowed was stringent, no more than an inch across. Red light pulsed in it like a wink. "I can heal you, make you well, let you live."

"Yeah, but can you win me a goddam Nobel Prize for Literature?"

Johnny slipped the bags of ANFO off his neck, then yanked the hammer from his belt. He'd have to work fast. He was cut in what felt like a billion places, and already he could feel the grayness of blood-loss crowding in on his mind. It made him think of Connecticut again, and the way the fogs came in after dark during the last weeks of March and the first weeks of April. The oldtimers called it strawberry spring, God knew why.

"Yes! Yes, I can do that!" The voice from the narrow red throat sounded eager. It also sounded frightened. "*Anything*! Success . . . money . . . women . . . and I can heal you, don't forget that! I can heal you!"

"Can you bring David's father back?"

Silence from the *ini*. Now the brownish-black mist coming out of the hole found the long confusion of slashes along his back and legs, and suddenly he felt as if he had been attacked by moray eels . . . or piranhas. He screamed.

"I can make the pain stop!" Tak said from its tiny hole. "All you have to do is ask—and stop yourself, of course."

With sweat stinging his eyes, Johnny used the claw end of the hammer to tear open one of the ANFO bags. He tilted the slit over the tiny hole, spread the cloth, and poured through one cupped, bloody hand. The red light was obliterated at once, as if the thing down there feared it might inadvertently set off the charge itself.

"*You can't!*" it screamed, its voice muffled now—but Johnny heard it clearly enough in his head, just the same. "*You can't, damn you! An lah! An lah! Os dam! You bastard!*"

An lah *yourself,* Johnny thought. *And a big fat* can de lach *in the bargain.*

The first bag was empty. Johnny could see dim whiteness in the hole where there had been only black and pulsing red before. The gullet leading back to Tak's world . . . or plane . . . or dimension . . . wasn't that long, then. Not in physical terms of measurement. And was the pain in his back and legs less?

Maybe I've just gone numb, he thought. *Not a new state for me, actually.*

He grabbed the second bag of ANFO and saw one entire side of it was sopped through with his blood. He felt a growing weakness to go along with the fog in his head. Had to be quick now. Had to go like the wind.

He tore open the second bag with the hammer's claw, trying to steel himself against the shrieks in his head; Tak had lapsed entirely into that other language now.

He turned the bag over the hole and watched ANFO pellets pour out. The whiteness grew brighter as the gullet filled. By the time the bag was empty, the top layer of pellets was only three inches or so down.

Just room enough, Johnny thought.

He became aware that a stillness had fallen here in the well, and in the *an tak* above; there was only that faint whispering, which could have been the calling of ghosts that had been penned up in here ever since the twenty-first of September, 1859.

If so, he intended to give them their parole.

He fumbled in the pocket of his chaps for what seemed an age, fighting the fog that wanted to blur his thoughts, fighting his own growing weakness. At last his fingers touched something, slipped away, came back, touched it again, grasped it, brought it out.

A fat green shotgun shell.

Johnny slipped it into the eyehole at the bottom of the *ini,* and wasn't surprised to find it was a perfect fit, its blunt circular top seated firmly against the ANFO pellets.

"You're primed, you bastard," he croaked.

No, a voice whispered in his head. *No, you dare not.*

Johnny looked at the brass circlet plugging the hole at the bottom of the *ini.* He gripped the handle of the hammer, his strength flagging badly now, and thought of what the cop had told him just before he stuck him in the back of the cruiser. *You're a sorry excuse for a writer,* the cop had said. *You're a sorry excuse for a man, too.*

Johnny shoved the helmet off with the heel of his free left hand. He was laughing again as he raised the hammer high above his head, and laughing as he brought it down squarely on the base of the shell.

"GOD FORGIVE ME, I HATE CRITICS!"

He had one fraction of a moment to wonder if he had succeeded, and then the question was answered in a bloom of brilliant, soundless red. It was like swooning into a rose.

Johnny Marinville let himself fall, and his last thoughts were of David—had David gotten out, had David gotten clear, was he all right now, would he be all right later.

Excused early, Johnny thought, and then that was gone, too.

PART V

HIGHWAY 50:
EXCUSED
EARLY

1

There were dead animals lying in a rough ring around the truck—buzzards and coyotes, mostly—but Steve barely noticed them. He was all but eaten alive with a need to get out of here. The steep sides of the China Pit seemed to loom over him like the sides of an open grave. He reached the truck a little ahead of the others (Cynthia and Mary were flanking David, each of them holding one of the boy's arms, although he did not seem to be staggering) and tore open the passenger door.

"Steve, what—" Cynthia began.

"Get in! Ask questions later!" He butt-boosted her up into the seat. "Push over! Make room!"

She did. Steve turned to David. "Are you going to be a problem?"

David shook his head. His eyes were dull and apathetic, but that didn't completely convince Steve. The boy was nothing if not resourceful; he had proved that before he and Cynthia ever met him.

He boosted David into the truck, then looked at Mary. "Get in. We'll have to bundle a little, but if we're not friends by now—"

She scrambled into the cab and closed the door as Steve hurried around the front of the truck, stepping on a buzzard as he went. It was like stepping on a pillowcase stuffed with bones.

How long had the boss been gone? A minute? Two? He had no idea. Any sense of time he might once have had was completely shot. He swung into the driver's seat, and allowed himself just one moment to wonder what they'd do if the engine wouldn't start. The answer, nothing, came at once. He nodded at it, turned the key, and the engine roared to life. No suspense there, thank God. A second later they were rolling.

He turned the Ryder truck in a big circle, skirting the heavy machinery, the powder magazine, and the field office. Between these latter two buildings was the dusty police-cruiser, driver's door open, front-seat area plastered with Collie Entragian's blood. Looking at it—*into* it—made Steve feel cold and a little dizzy, the way he felt when he looked down from a tall building.

"Fuck you," Mary said softly, turning to look back at the car. "Fuck you. And I hope you hear me."

They hit a bump and the truck rattled terrifically. Steve flew up and off the seat, his thighs biting into the bottom arc of the steering wheel, his head bumping the ceiling. He heard a muffled clatter as the stuff in the back flew around. The boss's stuff, mostly.

"Hey," Cynthia said nervously. "Don't you think you got the hammer a little too far down for rocktop, big boy?"

"No," Steve said. He looked into the mirror outside his window as they began tearing up the gravel road which led to the rim of the pit. It was the drift opening he was looking for, but he couldn't see it—it was on the other side of the truck.

About halfway to the rim they hit another bump, a bigger one, and the truck actually seemed to leave the road for an instant or two. The headlights corkscrewed, then dipped as the truck dove deep on its springs. Both Mary and Cynthia screamed. David did not; he sat crooked between them, a life-sized doll half on the seat and half on Mary's lap.

"*Slow down!*" Mary screamed. "*If you go off the road we'll go all the way to the bottom! SLOW DOWN, YOU ASSHOLE!*"

"No," he repeated, not bothering to add that going off *this* road, which was as wide as a California freeway, was the least of his worries. He could see the pit-rim ahead. The sky above it was now a dark, brightening violet instead of black.

He looked past the others and into the mirror outside the passenger window, searching for the dark mouth of the tunnel in the darker well of the China Pit, *can tak* in *can tah,* and then didn't have to bother. A square of white light too brilliant to look at suddenly lit up the pit-floor. It lashed out of the China Shaft like a burning fist and filled the cab of the truck with savage brilliance.

"*Jesus, what's that?*" Mary screamed, throwing a hand up to shield her eyes.

"The boss," Steve said softly.

A heavy thud seemed to run directly beneath them, a muf-fled battering-ram of sound. The truck began to shiver like a frightened dog. Steve heard broken rock and gravel begin to slide. He looked out his window and saw, in the dying glare of the blast, black nets of PVC pipe—emitters and distribution heads—sliding down the pit-face. The porphyry was in mo-tion. China Pit was falling in on itself.

"Oh my God, we're gonna be buried alive," Cynthia moaned.

"Well, let's see," Steve said. "Hang on."

He jammed the gas-pedal to the floor—it didn't have far to go, either—and the truck's engine responded with an angry scream. *Almost there, honey,* he thought at it. *Almost there, come on, work with me, beautiful, be there for me—*

That battering-ram rumble went on and on beneath them, seeming at one moment to fade, then coming back like a wave-form. As they reached the rim of the pit, Steve saw a boulder the size of a gas station go bouncing down the slope on their right. And, more ominous than the rumble from below them, he heard a growing whisper from directly beneath them. It was, Steve knew, the gravel surface of the road. The truck was northbound; the road was headed south. In only a few moments it would collapse down into the pit like a dropped carpet-runner.

"Run, you bitch!" he screamed, pounding on the wheel with his left fist. *"Run for me! Now! Now!"*

The Ryder truck surged over the rim of the pit like a clumsy yellownosed dinosaur. For a moment the issue was still in doubt, as the crumbled earth under the rear wheels ran out and the truck wallowed first sideways and then backward.

"Go!" Cynthia screamed. She sat forward, clutching the dashboard. *"Oh please go! For God's sake get us out of h—"*

She was thrown back in the seat as the wheels found purchase again. Just enough. For a moment the headlights went on stabbing at the lightening sky, and then they were rushing across the rim, headed north. From behind them, out of the pit, rose an endless flume of dust, as if the earlier freak storm had started up all over again, only confined to this one location. It rose in the sky like a pyre.

2

The trip down the north side of the embankment was less adventurous. By the time they were running across the two miles of desert between the pit and the town, the sky in the east was a bright salmon-pink. And, as they passed the bodega with the fallen sign, the sun's upper arc broke over the horizon.

Steve jammed on the brakes just past the bodega, at the south end of Desperation's Main Street.

"Holy shit," Cynthia murmured in a low voice.

"Mother Machree," Mary said, and put a hand to her temple, as if her head hurt.

Steve could say nothing at all.

Until now he and Cynthia had only seen Desperation in the dark, or through veils of blowing sand, and what they *had* seen had been glimpsed in frantic little snatches, their perceptions honed to a narrow focus by the mortal simplicities of survival.

When you were trying to stay alive, you just saw what you had to see; the rest went by the board.

Now, however, he was seeing it all.

The wide street was empty except for one lazily blowing tumbleweed. The sidewalks were drifted deep with sand—drifted completely under in places. Broken windowglass twinkled here and there. Trash had blown everywhere. Signs had fallen down. Powerlines lay snarled in the street like broken distributor heads. And The American West's marquee now lay in the street like a grand old yacht that has finally gone on the rocks. The one remaining letter—a large black *R*—had finally fallen off.

And everywhere there were dead animals, as if some lethal chemical spill had taken place. He saw scores of coyotes, and from the doorway of Bud's Suds there ran a long, curving pigtail of dead rats, some half-covered with the sand skirling about in a light morning breeze. Dead scorpions lay on the fallen leprechaun weathervane. They looked to Steve like shipwreck survivors who had died badly on a barren island. Buzzards lay in the street and on the roofs like dropped heaps of soot.

"And thou shalt set bounds unto the people round about," David said. His voice was dead, expressionless. "And you shall say, 'Take heed to yourselves that you go not up into the mount.'"

Steve looked into his rearview mirror, saw the embankment of the China Pit looming against the brightening sky, saw the dust still pouring out of its sterile caldera, and shuddered.

"'Go not up into the mount, or touch the border of it: whosoever toucheth the mount shall be surely put to death: There shall not be a hand touch it, but he shall surely be stoned or shot through. Whether it be beast or man, it shall not live.'" The boy looked up at Mary, and his face began to shiver apart and become human. His eyes filled with tears.

"David—" she began.

"I'm alone. Do you get it? We came upon the mountain and God slaughtered them all. My family. Now I'm alone."

She put her arms around him and pressed his face against her.

"Say, Chief," Cynthia said, and put a hand on Steve's arm. "Let's blow this shithole of a town and find us a cold beer, what do you say?"

3

Highway 50 again.

"Down this way," Mary said. "We're close now."

They had passed the Carvers' RV. David had turned his face against Mary's breasts again as they approached it, and she put her arms around his head and held him. For almost five minutes he didn't move, didn't even seem to breathe. The only way she could tell for sure that he was alive was by the feel of his tears, slow and hot, wetting her shirt. In a way she was glad to feel them, thought them a good sign.

The storm had also struck the highway, she saw; sand covered it completely in places, and Steve had to wallow the Ryder truck through several drifts in low gear.

"Would they have closed it?" Cynthia asked Steve once. "The cops? Nevada Public Works? Whatever?"

He shook his head. "Probably not. But you can bet there wasn't much of anyone out last night—lots of interstate truckers holed up in Ely and Austin."

"There it is!" Mary cried, and pointed at a sunstar twinkling about a mile ahead of them. Three minutes later they were pulling up to Deirdre's Acura. "Do you want to come in the car with me, David?" she asked. "Assuming the damned thing will even start, that is?"

David shrugged.

"The cop let you keep your keys?" Cynthia asked.

"No, but if I'm lucky . . ."

She hopped out of the truck, landed in a loose dune of sand, and made her way to the car. Looking at it brought Peter back in a rush—Peter, who had been so goddamned, absurdly proud of his James Dickey monograph, never guessing that the planned follow-up wasn't going to happen . . .

The car doubled in her sight, then blurred into prisms.

Chest hitching, she wiped an arm across her eyes, then knelt and felt around under the front bumper. At first she couldn't find what she was looking for and it all seemed like too much. Why did she want to follow the Ryder truck to Austin in this car, anyway? Surrounded by memories? By Peter?

She laid her cheek against the bumper—soon it would be too hot to touch, but for now it was still night-cool—and let herself cry.

She felt a hand touch hers, tentatively, and looked around. David was standing there, his gaunt, too-old face hanging over a slim boy's chest in a bloodstained baseball tee-shirt. He looked at her solemnly, not quite holding her hand but touching her fingers with his, as if he would like to hold it.

"What's wrong, Mary?"

"I can't find the little box," she said, and pulled in a large, watery sniff. "The little magnetic box with the spare key in it. It was under the front bumper, but I guess it must have fallen off. Or maybe the boys who took our license plate took that, too." Her mouth twisted and she began to cry again.

He dropped to his knees beside her, wincing as something pulled in his back. She saw, even through her tears, the bruises on his throat where Audrey had tried to choke him—ugly black-purple blotches like thunderheads.

"Shhh, Mary," he said, and felt along the inside of the bumper with his own hand. She could hear his fingers fluttering in that darkness, and suddenly wanted to cry out: *Be careful! There might be spiders! Spiders!*

Then he showed her a small gray box. "Give it a shot, why don't you? If it doesn't start . . ." He shrugged to show it didn't matter much, one way or the other—there was always the truck.

Yes, always the truck. Except Peter had never ridden in the truck, and maybe she *did* want the smell of him a little longer. The feel of him. *That's a nice set of cantaloupes, ma'am,* he'd said, and then touched her breast.

The memory of his smell, his touch, his voice. The glasses he wore when he drove. Those things would hurt, but—

"Yeah, I'll come with you," David said. They were kneeling in front of Deirdre Finney's car, facing each other that way. "If it starts, that is. And if you want."

"Yes," she said. "I *do* want."

4

Steve and Cynthia joined them, helped them to their feet.

"I feel like I'm a hundred and eight," Mary said.

"Don't worry, you don't look a day over eighty-nine," Steve said, and smiled when she made as if to pop him one. "Do you really want to try making Austin in that little car? What if it gets stuck in the sand?"

"One thing at a time. We're not even sure it'll start, are we, David?"

"No," David said in a kind of sigh. He was going away from her again, Mary could feel it, but she didn't know what to do about it. He stood with his head bent, looking at the Acura's grille as if all the secrets of life and death were there, the emotion draining out of his face again, leaving it distant and thoughtful. One hand was wrapped loosely around the gray metal Magna-Cube with the spare key in it.

"If it *does* start, we'll caravan," she told Steve. "Me behind you. If I get stuck, we'll hop into the truck. I don't think we will, though. It isn't such a bad car, actually. If my goddamned sister-in-law just hadn't used it as a dope-stash . . ." Her voice trembled and she closed her lips tightly.

"I don't think we'll have to go far to get in the clear," David said without looking up from the Acura's grille. "Thirty miles? Forty? Then open road."

Mary smiled at him. "I hope you're right."

"There's a slightly more important question," Cynthia said. "What are we going to tell the police about all this? The *real* police, I mean."

No one said anything for a moment. Then David, still looking at the grille of the Acura, said: "The front part. Let them figure out the rest for themselves."

"I don't get you," Mary said. She actually thought she did, but wanted to keep him talking. Wanted him out here with the rest of them mentally as well as physically.

"I'll tell about how we had flat tires and the bad cop took us back to town. How he got us to go with him by saying there was a guy out in the desert with a rifle. Mary, you tell about how he stopped you and Peter. Steve, you tell about how you were looking for Johnny and Johnny phoned you. I'll say how we escaped after he took my mother away. How we went to the theater. How we called you on the phone, Steve. Then you can tell how you came to the theater, too. And that's where we were all night. In the theater."

"We never went up to the pit at all," Steve mused. Testing it. *Tasting* it.

David nodded. The bruises on his throat glared in the strengthening sun. Already the day was beginning to grow hot. "Right," he said.

"And—sorry, David, I have to—your dad? What about him?"

"Went looking for my mom. He wanted me to stay with you guys in the theater, so I did."

"We never saw anything," Cynthia said.

"No. Not really." He opened the Magna-Cube, took out the key inside, gave it to Mary. "Why don't you try the engine?"

"In a sec. What are the authorities going to think about what they *do* find? All the dead people and dead animals? And what will they say? What will they give out?"

Steve said: "There are people who believe a flying saucer crashed not too far from here, back in the forties. Did you know that?"

She shook her head.

"In Roswell, New Mexico. According to the story, there were even survivors. Astronauts from another world. I don't know if any of it's true, but it might be. The evidence suggests that *something* pretty outrageous happened in Roswell. The government covered it up, whatever it was. The same way they'll cover this up."

Cynthia punched his arm. "Pretty paranoid, cookie."

He shrugged. "As to what they'll *think* . . . poison gas, maybe. Some weird shit that belched out of a pocket in the earth and made people crazy. And that's not so far wrong, is it? Really?"

"No," Mary said. "I think the most important thing is that we all tell the same story, just the way that David outlined it."

Cynthia shrugged, and a ghost of her old pert who-gives-a-shit look came over her face. "Like if we break down and tell them what *really* happened they're going to believe us, right?"

"Maybe they wouldn't," Steve said, "but if it's all the same to you, I'd rather not spend the next six weeks taking polygraph tests and looking at inkblots when I could spend them looking at your exotic and mysterious face."

She punched his arm again. A little harder this time. She caught David watching this byplay and nodded to him. "You think I got a mysterious and exotic face?"

David turned away, studied the mountains to the north.

Mary went around to the driver's door of the Acura and opened it, reminding herself she'd have to pull the seat up before she could drive—Peter had been a foot taller than she. The glovebox was open from when she'd been pawing around in it for the registration, but surely a bulb as small as the one in there couldn't draw more than a trickle of juice, could it? Well, it wasn't exactly life and death in any—

"Oh my Lord," Steve said in a soft, strengthless voice. "Oh my dear Lord, look."

She turned. On the horizon, looking small at this distance, was the north face of the China Pit embankment. Above it was a gigantic cloud of dark gray dust. It hung in the sky, still connected to the pit by a hazy umbilicus of rising dust and powdered earth: the remains of a mountain rising into the sky like poisoned ground after a nuclear blast. It made the shape of a wolf, its tail pointing toward the newly risen sun, its grotesquely elongated snout pointed west, where the night was still draining sullenly from the sky.

The snout hung open. Protruding from it was a strange shape, amorphous but somehow reptilian. There was something of the scorpion in that shape, and of the lizard as well.

Can tak, can tah.

Mary screamed through raised hands. Looked up at the shape in the sky, eyes bulging over her dirty fingers, head shaking from side to side in a useless gesture of negation.

"Stop," David said, and put his arm around her waist. "Stop, Mary. It can't hurt us. And it's going away already. See?"

It was true. The hide of the skywolf was tearing open in some places, appearing to melt in others, letting the sun shine through in long, golden rays that were both beautiful and somehow comical—the sort of shot you expected to see at the end of a Bible epic.

"I think we ought to go," Steve said at last.

"I think we never should have come in the first place," Mary said faintly, and got into the car. Already she could smell the aroma of her dead husband's aftershave.

5

David stood watching as she pulled the seat forward and slipped the key into the ignition. He felt distant from himself, a creature floating in space somewhere between a dark star and a light one. He thought of sitting at the kitchen table back home, sitting there and playing slap-jacks with Pie. He thought he would see Steve and Mary and Cynthia, nice as they were, dead and in hell for just one more game of Slap-jacks in the kitchen with her—Pie with a glass of Cranapple juice, him with a Pepsi, both of them giggling like mad. He would see himself in hell, for that matter. How far could it be, after all, from Desperation?

Mary turned the key in the ignition. The engine cranked briskly and started almost at once. She grinned and clapped her hands.

"David? Ready to go?"

"Sure. I guess."

"Hey?" Cynthia put a hand on the back of his neck. "You all right, my man?"

He nodded, not looking up.

Cynthia bent over and kissed his cheek. "You have to fight it," she whispered in his ear. "You have to *fight* it, you know?"

"I'll try," he said, but the days and weeks and months ahead looked impossible to him. *Go to your friend Brian,* Johnny had said. *Go to your friend and make him your brother.* And that might be a place to start, yes, but after that?

There were holes in him that cried out in pain, and would go on crying out for so much of the future. One for his mother, one for his father, one for his sister. Holes like faces. Holes like eyes.

In the sky, the wolf had gone except for a paw and what might have been—perhaps—the tip of a tail. Of the reptilian thing in its mouth there was no sign.

"We beat you," David whispered, starting around to the passenger side of the car. "We beat you, you son of a bitch, there's that."

Tak, whispered a smiling, patient voice far back in his mind. *Tak ah lah. Tak ah wan.*

He turned his mind and heart from it with an effort.

Go to your friend and make him your brother.

Maybe. But Austin first. With Mary and Steve and Cynthia. He intended to stay with them as long as possible. They, at least, could understand . . . and in a way no one else would ever be able to. They had been in the pit together.

As he reached the passenger-side door, he closed the small metal box and slipped it absently into his pocket. He stopped suddenly, free hand frozen in midair as it reached for the door-handle.

Something was gone; the shotgun shell.

Something had been put in its place: a piece of stiff paper.

"David?" Steve called from the open window of the truck. "Something wrong?"

He shook his head, opening the car door with one hand and taking the folded paper from his pocket with the other. It was blue. And there was something familiar about it, although he couldn't remember having a paper like this in his pocket yesterday. There was a ragged hole in it, as if it had been punched onto something. As if—

Leave your pass.

It was the last thing the voice had said on that day last fall when he had prayed for God to make Brian better. He hadn't understood, but he had obeyed, had hung the blue pass on a nailhead. The next time he'd shown up at the Viet Cong Lookout—a week later? two?—it had been gone. Taken by some kid who wanted to write down a girl's telephone number, maybe, or blown off by the wind. Except . . . here it was.

All I want is lovin', all I need is lovin'.

Felix Cavaliere on vocal, most severely cool.

No, he thought. *This can't be.*

"David?" Mary. Far away. "David, what is it?"

Can't be, he thought again, but when he unfolded it, the words printed at the top were completely familiar:

WEST WENTWORTH MIDDLE SCHOOL
100 Viland Avenue

Then, in big black tabloid type:

EXCUSED EARLY

And, last of all:

Parent of excused student must sign this pass.
Pass must be returned to attendance office.

Except now there was more. A brief scrawled message below the last line of printing.

Something moved inside him. Some huge thing. His throat closed up, then opened to let out a long, wailing cry that was only grief at the top. He swayed, clutching at the Acura's roof, lowered his forehead to his arm, and began to sob. From some great distance he heard the truck doors opening, heard Steve and Cynthia racing toward him. He wept. He thought of Pie, holding her doll and smiling up at him. He thought of his mother, dancing to the radio in the laundry room with the iron in one hand, laughing at her own foolishness. He thought of his father, sitting on the porch with his feet cocked up on the rail, a book in one hand and a beer in the other, waving to him as he came home from Brian's, pushing his bike up the driveway toward the garage in the thick twilight. He thought of how much he had loved them, how much he would always love them.

And Johnny. Johnny standing on the dark edge of the China Shaft, saying *Sometimes he makes us live.*

David wept with his head down and the EXCUSED EARLY pass now crumpled in his closed fist, that huge thing still moving inside him, something like a landslide . . . but maybe not so bad.

Maybe, in the end, not so bad.

"David?" It was Steve, shaking him. *"David!"*

"I'm all right," he said, raising his head and wiping his eyes with a shaking hand.

"What happened?"

"Nothing. I'm okay. Go on. We'll follow you."

Cynthia was looking at him doubtfully. "Sure?"

He nodded.

They went back, looking over their shoulders at him. David was able to wave. Then he got into the Acura and closed the door.

"What was it?" Mary asked. "What did you find?"

She reached for the folded piece of stiff blue paper, but David held it in his own hand for the time being. "Do you remember when the cop threw you into the holding area where we were?" he asked. "How you went for the gun?"

"I'll never forget it."

"While you were fighting with him, a shotgun shell fell off

the desk and rolled over to me. When I had a chance, I picked it up. Johnny must have stolen it out of my pocket when he was hanging onto me. In the mineshaft. After my dad was killed. Johnny used the shell to set off the ANFO. And when he took it out of my pocket, he put this in."

"Put what in? What is it?"

"It's an EXCUSED EARLY pass from my school back in Ohio. Last fall I poked it on a nail in a tree and left it there."

"A tree back in Ohio. Last fall." She was looking at him thoughtfully, her eyes very large and still. "Last *fall*!"

"Yes. So I don't know where he got it . . . and I don't know where he *had* it. When he was in the powder magazine, I made him empty out all his pockets. I was afraid he might have picked up one of the *can tahs*. He didn't have it then. He stripped right down to his underwear, and he didn't have it then."

"Oh, David," she said.

He nodded and handed the blue pass over to her. "Steve will know if this is his handwriting," he said. "I bet you a million dollars it is."

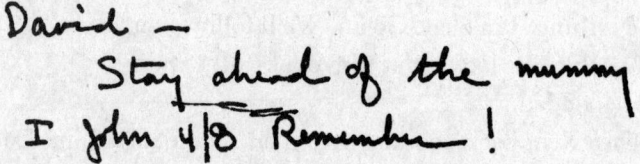

David —
Stay ahead of the mummy
I John 4/8 Remember !

She read the scrawled message, her lips moving. "I'd bet a million of my own that it's his, if I had a million," she said. "Do you understand the reference, David?"

David took the blue pass. "Of course. First John, chapter four, verse eight. 'God is love.'"

She looked at him for a long time. "Is he, David? Is he love?"

"Oh, yes," David said. He folded the pass along its crease. "I guess he's sort of . . . everything."

Cynthia waved. Mary waved back and gave her a thumbs-up. Steve pulled out and Mary followed him, the Acura's wheels rolling reluctantly through the first ridge of sand and then picking up speed.

David put his head back against the seat, closed his eyes, and began to pray.

Bangor, Maine
November 1, 1994–December 5, 1995